E. T. A. Hoffmann
Weird Tales Volume I and II

Translator: J. T. Bealby

Ernst Theodor Wilhelm Hoffmann (1776 – 1822), better known by his pen name E. T. A. Hoffmann (Ernst Theodor Amadeus Hoffmann), was a German Romantic author of fantasy and horror, a jurist, composer, music critic, draftsman and caricaturist.] His stories form the basis of Jacques Offenbach's famous opera The Tales of Hoffmann, in which Hoffman appears (heavily fictionalized) as the hero. He is also the author of the novella The Nutcracker and the Mouse King, on which the famous ballet The Nutcracker is based. The ballet Coppélia is based on two other stories that Hoffmann wrote, while Schumann's Kreisleriana is based on Hoffmann's character Johannes Kreisler.

Index:

Weird Tales. Vol. I 3
THE CREMONA VIOLIN. 3
THE FERMATA. 11
SIGNOR FORMICA 19
    I. 19
    II. 23
    III. 30
    IV. 35
  V. 40
  VI. 46
THE SAND-MAN. 51
  NATHANAEL TO LOTHAIR. 51
  CLARA TO NATHANAEL. 54
  NATHANAEL TO LOTHAIR. 56
THE ENTAIL. 65
ARTHUR'S HALL. 96
Weird Tales, Vol. II. 107
THE DOGE AND DOGESS 107
MASTER MARTIN, THE COOPER, AND HIS JOURNEYMAN. 126
MADEMOISELLE DE SCUDÉRI. A TALE OF THE TIMES OF LOUIS XIV. 149
GAMBLER'S LUCK. 176
MASTER JOHANNES WACHT. 187

Weird Tales. Vol. I

THE CREMONA VIOLIN.

Councillor Krespel was one of the strangest, oddest men I ever met with in my life. When I went to live in H—— for a time the whole town was full of talk about him, as he happened to be just then in the midst of one of the very craziest of his schemes. Krespel had the reputation of being both a clever, learn lawyer and a skilful diplomatist. One of the reigning princes of Germany—not, however, one of the most powerful—had appealed to him for assistance in drawing up a memorial, which he was desirous of presenting at the Imperial Court with the view of furthering his legitimate claims upon a certain strip of territory. The project was crowned with the happiest success; and as Krespel had once complained that he could never find a dwelling sufficiently comfortable to suit him, the prince, to reward him for the memorial, undertook to defray the cost of building a house which Krespel might erect just as he pleased. Moreover, the prince was willing to purchase any site that he should fancy. This offer, however, the Councillor would not accept; he insisted that the house should be built in his garden, situated in a very beautiful neighbourhood outside the town-walls. So he bought all kinds of materials and had them carted out. Then he might have been seen day after day, attired in his curious garments (which he had made himself according to certain fixed rules of his own), slacking the lime, riddling the sand, packing up the bricks and stones in regular heaps, and so on. All this he did without once consulting an architect or thinking about a plan. One fine day, however, he went to an experienced builder of the town and requested him to be in his garden at daybreak the next morning, with all his journeymen and apprentices, and a large body of labourers, &c., to build him his house. Naturally the builder asked for the architect's plan, and was not a little astonished when Krespel replied that none was needed, and that things would turn out all right in the end, just as he wanted them. Next morning, when the builder and his men came to the place, they found a trench drawn out in the shape of an exact square; and Krespel said, "Here's where you must lay the foundations; then carry up the walls until I say they are high enough." "Without windows and doors, and without partition walls?" broke in the builder, as if alarmed at Krespel's mad folly. "Do what I tell you, my dear sir," replied the Councillor quite calmly; "leave the rest to me; it will be all right." It was only the promise of high pay that could induce the builder to proceed with the ridiculous building; but none has ever been erected under merrier circumstances. As there was an abundant supply of food and drink, the workmen never left their work; and amidst their continuous laughter the four walls were run up with incredible quickness, until one day Krespel cried, "Stop!" Then the workmen, laying down trowel and hammer, came down from the scaffoldings and gathered round Krespel in a circle, whilst every laughing face was asking, "Well, and what now?" "Make way!" cried Krespel; and then running to one end of the garden, he strode slowly towards the square of brick-work. When he came close to the wall he shook his head in a dissatisfied manner, ran to the other end of the garden, again strode slowly towards the brick-work square, and proceeded to act as before. These tactics he pursued several times, until at length, running his sharp nose hard against the wall, he cried, "Come here, come here, men! break me a door in here! Here's where I want a door made!" He gave the exact dimensions in feet and inches, and they did as he bid them. Then he stepped inside the structure, and smiled with satisfaction as the builder remarked that the walls were just the height of a good two-storeyed house. Krespel walked thoughtfully backwards and forwards across the space within, the bricklayers behind him with hammers and picks, and wherever he cried, "Make a window here, six feet high by four feet broad!" "There a little window, three feet by two!" a hole was made in a trice.

It was at this stage of the proceedings that I came to H——; and it was highly amusing to see how hundreds of people stood round about the garden and raised a loud shout whenever the stones flew out and a new window appeared where nobody had for a moment expected it. And in the same manner Krespel proceeded with the buildings and fittings of the rest of the house, and with all the work necessary to that end; everything had to be done on the spot in accordance with the instructions which the Councillor gave from time to time. However, the absurdity of the whole business, the growing conviction that things would in the end turn out better than might have been expected, but above all, Krespel's generosity—which indeed cost him nothing—kept them all in good-humour. Thus were the difficulties overcome which necessarily arose out of this eccentric way of building, and in a short time there was a completely finished house, its outside, indeed, presenting a most extraordinary appearance, no two windows, &c., being alike, but on the other hand the interior arrangements suggested a peculiar feeling of comfort. All who entered the house bore witness to the truth of this; and I too experienced it myself when I was taken in by Krespel after I had become more intimate with him. For hitherto I had not exchanged a word with this eccentric man; his building had occupied him so much that he had not even once been to Professor M——'s to dinner, as he was in the habit of going on Tuesdays. Indeed, in reply to a special invitation, he sent word that he should not set foot over the threshold before the house-warming of his new building took place. All his friends and acquaintances, therefore, confidently looked forward to a great banquet; but Krespel invited nobody except the masters, journeymen, apprentices, and labourers who had built the house. He entertained them with the choicest viands: bricklayer's apprentices devoured partridge pies regardless of consequences; young joiners polished off roast pheasants with the greatest success; whilst hungry labourers helped themselves for once to the choicest morsels of *truffes fricassées*. In the evening their wives and daughters came, and there was a great ball. After waltzing a short while with the wives of the masters, Krespel sat down amongst the town-musicians, took a violin in his hand, and directed the orchestra until daylight.

On the Tuesday after this festival, which exhibited Councillor Krespel in the character of a friend of the people, I at length saw him appear, to my no little joy, at Professor M——'s. Anything more strange and fantastic than Krespel's behaviour it would be impossible to find. He was so stiff and awkward in his movements, that he looked every moment as if he would run up against something or do some damage. But he did not; and the lady of the house seemed to be well aware that he would not, for she did not grow a shade paler when he rushed with heavy steps round a table crowded with beautiful cups, or when he manœuvred near a large mirror that reached down to the floor, or even when he seized a flower-pot of beautifully painted porcelain and swung it round in the air as if desirous of making its colours play. Moreover, before dinner he subjected everything in the Professor's room to a most minute examination; he also took down a picture from the wall and hung it up again, standing on one of the cushioned chairs to do so. At the same time he talked a good deal and vehemently; at one time his thoughts kept leaping, as it were, from one subject to another (this was most conspicuous during dinner); at another, he was unable to have done with an idea; seizing upon it again and again, he gave it all sorts of wonderful twists and turns, and couldn't get back into the ordinary track until something else took hold of his fancy. Sometimes his voice was rough and harsh and screeching, and sometimes it was low and drawling and singing; but at no time did it harmonize with what he was talking about. Music was the subject of conversation; the praises of a new composer were being sung, when Krespel, smiling, said in his low singing tones, "I wish the devil with his pitchfork would hurl that atrocious garbler of music millions of fathoms down to the bottomless pit of hell!" Then he burst out passionately and wildly, "She is an angel of heaven, nothing but pure God-given music!—the paragon and queen of song!"—and tears stood in his eyes. To understand this, we had to go back to a celebrated *artiste*, who had been the subject of conversation an hour before.

Just at this time a roast hare was on the table; I noticed that Krespel carefully removed every particle of meat from the bones on his plate, and was most particular in his inquiries after the hare's feet; these the Professor's little five-year-old daughter now brought to him with a very pretty smile. Besides, the children had cast many friendly glances towards Krespel during dinner; now they rose and drew nearer to him, but not without signs of timorous awe. What's the meaning of that? thought I to myself. Dessert was brought in; then the Councillor took a little box from his pocket, in which he had a miniature lathe of steel. This he immediately screwed fast to the table, and turning the bones with incredible skill and rapidity, he made all sorts of little fancy boxes and balls, which the children received with cries of delight. Just as we were rising from table, the Professor's niece asked, "And what is our Antonia doing?" Krespel's face was like that of one who has bitten of a sour orange and wants to look as if it were a sweet one; but this expression soon changed into the likeness of a hideous mask, whilst he laughed behind it with downright bitter, fierce, and as it seemed to me, satanic scorn. "Our Antonia? our dear Antonia?" he asked in his drawling, disagreeable singing way. The Professor hastened to intervene; in the reproving glance which he gave his niece I read that she had touched a point likely to stir up unpleasant memories in Krespel's heart. "How are you getting on with your violins?" interposed the Professor in a jovial manner, taking the Councillor by both hands. Then Krespel's countenance cleared up, and with a firm voice he replied, "Capitally, Professor; you recollect my telling you of the lucky chance which threw that splendid Amati into my hands. Well, I've only cut it open to-day—not before to-day. I hope Antonia has carefully taken the rest of it to pieces." "Antonia is a good child," remarked the Professor. "Yes, indeed, that she is," cried the Councillor, whisking himself round; then, seizing his hat and stick, he hastily rushed out of the room. I saw in the mirror how that tears were standing in his eyes.

As soon as the Councillor was gone, I at once urged the Professor to explain to me what Krespel had to do with violins, and particularly with Antonia. "Well," replied the Professor, "not only is the Councillor a remarkably eccentric fellow altogether, but he practises violin-making in his own crack-brained way." "Violin-making!" I exclaimed, perfectly astonished. "Yes," continued the Professor, "according to the judgment of men who understand the thing, Krespel makes the very best violins that can be found nowadays; formerly he would frequently let other people play on those in which he had been especially successful, but that's been all over and done with now for a long time. As soon as he has finished a violin he plays on it himself for one or two hours, with very remarkable power and with the most exquisite expression, then he hangs it up beside the rest, and never touches it again or suffers anybody else to touch it. If a violin by any of the eminent old masters is hunted up anywhere, the Councillor buys it immediately, no matter what the price put upon it. But he plays it as he does his own violins, only once; then he takes it to pieces in order to examine closely its inner structure, and should he fancy he hasn't found exactly what he sought for, he in a pet throws the pieces into a big chest, which is already full of the remains of broken violins." "But who and what is Antonia?" I inquired, hastily and impetuously. "Well, now, that," continued the Professor, "that is a thing which might very well make me conceive an unconquerable aversion to the Councillor, were I not convinced that there is some peculiar secret behind it, for he is such a good-natured fellow at bottom as to be sometimes guilty of weakness. When he came to H—— several years ago, he led the life of an anchorite, along with an old housekeeper, in —— Street. Soon, by his oddities, he excited the curiosity of his neighbours; and immediately he became aware of this, he sought and made acquaintances. Not only in my house but everywhere we became so accustomed to him that he grew to be indispensable. In spite of his rude exterior, even the children liked him, without ever proving a nuisance to him; for notwithstanding all their friendly passages together, they always retained a certain timorous awe of him, which secured him against all over-familiarity. You have to-day had an example of the way in which he wins their hearts by his ready skill in various things. We all took him at first for a crusty old bachelor, and he never contradicted us. After he had been living here some time, he went away, nobody knew where, and returned at the end of some months. The evening following his return his windows were lit up to an unusual extent! this alone was sufficient to arouse his neighbours' attention, and they soon heard the surpassingly beautiful voice of a female singing to the accompaniment of a piano. Then the music of a violin was heard chiming in and entering upon a keen ardent contest with the voice. They knew at once that the player was the Councillor. I myself mixed in the large crowd which had gathered in front of his house to listen to this extraordinary concert; and I must confess that, beside this voice and the peculiar, deep, soul-stirring impression which the execution made upon me, the singing of the most celebrated *artistes* whom I had ever heard seemed to me feeble and void of expression. Until then I had had no conception of such long-sustained notes, of such nightingale trills, of such undulations of musical sound, of such swelling up to the strength of organ-notes, of such dying away to the faintest whisper. There was not one whom the sweet witchery did not enthral; and when the singer ceased, nothing but soft sighs broke the impressive silence. Somewhere about midnight the Councillor was heard talking violently, and another male voice seemed, to judge from the tones, to be reproaching him, whilst at intervals the broken words of a sobbing girl could be detected. The Councillor continued to shout with increasing violence, until he fell into that drawling, singing way that you know. He was interrupted by a loud scream from the girl, and then all was as still as death. Suddenly a loud racket was heard on the stairs; a young man rushed out sobbing, threw himself into a post-chaise which stood below, and drove rapidly away. The next day the Councillor was very cheerful, and nobody had the courage to question him about the events of the previous night. But on inquiring of the housekeeper, we gathered that the Councillor had brought home with him an extraordinarily pretty young lady whom he called Antonia, and she it was who had sung so beautifully. A young man also had come along with them; he had treated Antonia very tenderly, and must evidently have been her betrothed. But he, since the Councillor peremptorily insisted on it, had had to go away again in a hurry. What the relations between Antonia and the Councillor are has remained until now a secret, but this much is certain, that he tyrannises over the poor girl in the most hateful fashion. He watches her as Doctor Bartholo watches his ward in the *Barber of Seville*; she hardly dare show herself at the window; and if, yielding now and again to her earnest entreaties, he takes her into society, he follows her with Argus' eyes, and will on no account suffer a musical note to be sounded, far less let Antonia sing—indeed, she is not permitted to sing in his own house. Antonia's singing on that memorable night, has, therefore, come to be regarded by the townspeople in the light of a tradition of some marvellous wonder that suffices to stir the heart and the fancy; and even those who did not hear it often exclaim, whenever any other singer attempts to display her powers in the place, 'What sort of a wretched squeaking do you call that? Nobody but Antonia knows how to sing.'"

Having a singular weakness for such like fantastic histories, I found it necessary, as may easily be imagined, to make Antonia's acquaintance. I had myself often enough heard the popular sayings about her singing, but had never imagined that that exquisite *artiste* was living in the place, held a captive in the bonds of this eccentric Krespel like the victim of a tyrannous sorcerer. Naturally enough I heard in my dreams on the following night Antonia's marvellous voice, and as she besought me in the most touching manner in a glorious *adagio* movement (very ridiculously it seemed to me, as if I had composed it myself) to save her, I soon resolved, like a second Astolpho, to penetrate into Krespel's house, as if into another Alcina's magic castle, and deliver the queen of song from her ignominious fetters.

It all came about in a different way from what I had expected; I had seen the Councillor scarcely more than two or three times, and eagerly discussed with him the best method of constructing violins, when he invited me to call and see him. I did so; and he showed me his treasures of violins. There were fully thirty of them hanging up in a closet; one amongst them bore conspicuously all the marks of great antiquity (a carved lion's head, &c.), and, hung up higher than the rest and surmounted by a crown of flowers, it seemed to exercise a queenly supremacy over them. "This violin," said Krespel, on my making some inquiry relative to it, "this violin is a very remarkable and curious specimen of the work of some unknown master, probably of Tartini's age. I am perfectly convinced that there is something especially exceptional in its inner construction, and that, if I took it to pieces, a secret would be revealed to me which I have long been seeking to discover, but—laugh at me if you like—this senseless thing which only gives signs of life and sound as I make it, often speaks to me in a strange way of itself. The first time I played upon it I somehow fancied that I was only the magnetiser who has the power of moving his subject to reveal of his own accord in words the visions of his inner nature. Don't go away with the belief that I am such a fool as to attach even the slightest importance to such fantastic notions, and yet it's certainly strange that I could never prevail upon myself to cut open that dumb lifeless thing there. I am very pleased now that I have not cut it open, for since Antonia has been with me I sometimes play to her upon this violin. For Antonia is fond of it—very fond of it." As the Councillor uttered these words with visible signs of emotion, I felt encouraged to hazard the question, "Will you not play it to me, Councillor." Krespel made a wry face, and falling into his drawling, singing way, said, "No, my good sir!" and that was an end of the matter. Then I had to look at all sorts of rare curiosities, the greater part of them childish trifles; at last thrusting his arm into a chest, he brought out a folded piece of paper, which he pressed into my hand, adding solemnly, "You are a lover of art; take this present as a priceless memento, which you must value at all times above everything else." Therewith he took me by the shoulders and gently pushed me towards the door, embracing me on the threshold. That is to say, I was in a symbolical manner virtually kicked out of doors. Unfolding the paper, I found a piece of a first string of a violin about an eighth of an inch in length, with the words, "A piece of the treble string with which the deceased Staraitz strung his violin for the last concert at which he ever played."

This summary dismissal at mention of Antonia's name led me to infer that I should never see her; but I was mistaken, for on my second visit to the Councillor's I found her in his room, assisting him to put a violin together. At first sight Antonia did not make a strong impression; but soon I found it impossible to tear myself away from her blue eyes, her sweet rosy lips, her uncommonly graceful, lovely form. She was very pale; but a shrewd remark or a merry sally would call up a winning smile on her face and suffuse her cheeks with a deep burning flush, which, however, soon faded away to a faint rosy glow. My conversation with her was quite unconstrained, and yet I saw nothing whatever of the Argus-like watchings on Krespel's part which the Professor had imputed to him; on the contrary, his behaviour moved along the customary lines, nay, he even seemed to approve of my conversation with Antonia. So I often stepped in to see the Councillor; and as we became accustomed to each other's society, a singular feeling of homeliness, taking possession of our little circle of three, filled our hearts with inward happiness. I still continued to derive exquisite enjoyment from the Councillor's strange crotchets and oddities; but it was of course Antonia's irresistible charms alone which attracted me, and led me to put up with a good deal which I should otherwise, in the frame of mind in which I then was, have impatiently shunned. For it only too often happened that in the Councillor's characteristic extravagance there was mingled much that was dull and tiresome; and it was in a special degree irritating to me that, as often as I turned the conversation upon music, and particularly upon singing, he was sure to interrupt me, with that sardonic smile upon his face and those repulsive singing tones of his, by some remark of a quite opposite tendency, very often of a commonplace character. From the great distress which at such times Antonia's glances betrayed, I perceived that he only did it to deprive me of a pretext for calling upon her for a song. But I didn't relinquish my design. The hindrances which the Councillor threw in my way only strengthened my resolution to overcome them; I must hear Antonia sing if I was not to pine away in reveries and dim aspirations for want of hearing her.

One evening Krespel was in an uncommonly good humour; he had been taking an old Cremona violin to pieces, and had discovered that the sound-post was fixed half a line more obliquely than usual—an important discovery! one of incalculable advantage in the practical work of making violins! I succeeded in setting him off at full speed on his hobby of the true art of violin-playing. Mention of the way in which the old masters picked up their dexterity in execution from really great singers (which was what Krespel happened just then to be expatiating upon), naturally paved the way for the remark that now the practice was the exact opposite of this, the vocal score erroneously following the affected and abrupt transitions and rapid scaling of the instrumentalists. "What is more nonsensical," I cried, leaping from my chair, running to the piano, and opening it quickly, "what is more nonsensical than such an execrable style as this, which, far from being music, is much more like the noise of peas rolling across the floor?" At the same time I sang several of the modern *fermatas*, which rush up and down and hum like a well-spun peg-top, striking a few villanous chords by way of accompaniment Krespel laughed outrageously and screamed, "Ha! ha! methinks I hear our German-Italians or our Italian-Germans struggling with an aria from Pucitta, or Portogallo, or some other *Maestro di capella*, or rather *schiavo d'un primo uomo*." Now, thought I, now's the time; so turning to Antonia, I remarked, "Antonia knows nothing of such singing as that, I believe?" At the same time I struck up one of old Leonardo Leo's beautiful soul-stirring songs. Then Antonia's cheeks glowed; heavenly radiance sparkled in her eyes, which grew full of reawakened inspiration; she hastened to the piano; she opened her lips; but at that very moment Krespel pushed her away, grasped me by the shoulders, and with a shriek that rose up to a tenor pitch, cried, "My son—my son—my son!" And then he immediately went on, singing very softly, and grasping my hand with a bow that was the pink of politeness, "In very truth, my esteemed and honourable student-friend, in very truth it would be a violation of the codes of social intercourse, as well as of all good manners, were I to express aloud and in a stirring way my wish that here, on this very spot, the devil from hell would softly break your neck with his burning claws, and so in a sense make short work of you; but, setting that aside, you must acknowledge, my dearest friend, that it is rapidly growing dark, and there are no lamps burning to-night so that, even though I did not kick you downstairs at once, your darling limbs might still run a risk of suffering damage. Go home by all means; and cherish a kind remembrance of your faithful friend, if it should happen that you never,—pray, understand me,—if you should never see him in his own house again." Therewith he embraced me, and, still keeping fast hold of me, turned with me slowly towards the door, so that I could not get another single look at Antonia. Of course it is plain enough that in my position I couldn't thrash the Councillor, though that is what he really deserved. The Professor enjoyed a good laugh at my expense, and assured me that I had ruined for ever all hopes of retaining the Councillor's friendship. Antonia was too dear to me, I might say too holy, for me to go and play the part of the languishing lover and stand gazing up at her window, or to fill the *rôle* of the lovesick adventurer. Completely upset, I went away from H——; but, as is usual in such cases, the brilliant colours of the picture of my fancy faded, and the recollection of Antonia, as well as of Antonia's singing (which I had never heard), often fell upon my heart like a soft faint trembling light, comforting me.

Two years afterwards I received an appointment in B——, and set out on a journey to the south of Germany. The towers of M—— rose before me in the red vaporous glow of the evening; the nearer I came the more was I oppressed by an indescribable feeling of the most agonising distress; it lay upon me like a heavy burden; I could not breathe; I was obliged to get out of my carriage into the open air. But my anguish continued to increase until it became actual physical pain. Soon I seemed to hear the strains of a solemn chorale floating in the air; the sounds continued to grow more distinct; I realised the fact that they were men's voices chanting a church chorale. "What's that? what's that?" I cried, a burning stab darting as it were through my breast "Don't you see?" replied the coachman, who was driving along beside me, "why, don't you see? they're burying somebody up yonder in yon churchyard." And indeed we were near the churchyard; I saw a circle of men clothed in black standing round a grave, which was on the point of being closed. Tears started to my eyes; I somehow fancied they were burying there all the joy and all the happiness of life. Moving on rapidly down the hill, I was no longer able to see into the churchyard; the chorale came to an end, and I perceived not far distant from the gate some of the mourners returning from the funeral. The Professor, with his niece on his arm, both in deep mourning, went close past me without noticing me. The young lady had her handkerchief pressed close to her eyes, and was weeping bitterly. In the frame of mind in which I then was I could not possibly go into the town, so I sent on my servant with the carriage to the hotel where I usually put up, whilst I took a turn in the familiar neighbourhood, to get rid of a mood that was possibly only due to physical causes, such as heating on the journey, &c. On arriving at a well-known avenue, which leads to a pleasure resort, I came upon a most extraordinary spectacle. Councillor Krespel was being conducted by two mourners, from whom he appeared to be endeavouring to make his escape by all sorts of strange twists and turns. As usual, he was dressed in his own curious home-made grey coat; but from his little cocked-hat, which he wore perched over one ear in military fashion, a long narrow ribbon of black crape fluttered backwards and forwards in the wind. Around his waist he had buckled a black sword-belt; but instead of a sword he had stuck a long fiddle-bow into it. A creepy shudder ran through my limbs: "He's insane," thought I, as I slowly followed them. The Councillor's companions led him as far as his house, where he embraced them, laughing loudly. They left him; and then his glance fell upon me, for I now stood near him. He stared at me fixedly for some time; then he cried in a hollow voice, "Welcome, my student-friend! you also understand it!" Therewith he took me by the arm and pulled me into the house, up the steps, into the room where the violins hung. They were all draped in black crape; the violin of the old master was missing; in its place was a cypress wreath. I knew what had happened. "Antonia! Antonia!" I cried in inconsolable grief. The Councillor, with his arms crossed on his breast, stood beside me, as if turned into stone. I pointed to the cypress wreath. "When she died," said he in a very hoarse solemn voice, "when she died, the soundpost of that violin broke into pieces with a ringing crack, and the sound-board was split from end to end. The faithful instrument could only live with her and in her; it lies beside her in the coffin, it has been buried with her." Deeply agitated, I sank down upon a chair, whilst the Councillor began to sing a gay song in a husky voice; it was truly horrible to see him hopping about on one foot, and the crape strings (he still had his hat on) flying about the room and up to the violins hanging on the walls. Indeed, I could not repress a loud cry that rose to my lips when, on the Councillor making an abrupt turn, the crape came all over me; I fancied he wanted to envelop me in it and drag me down into the horrible dark depths of insanity. Suddenly he stood still and addressed me in his singing way, "My son! my son! why do you call out? Have you espied the angel of death? That always precedes the ceremony." Stepping into the middle of the room, he took the violin-bow out of his sword-belt and, holding it over his head with both hands, broke it into a thousand pieces. Then, with a loud laugh, he cried, "Now you imagine my sentence is pronounced, don't you, my son? but it's nothing of the kind—not at all! not at all! Now I'm free—free—free— hurrah! I'm free! Now I shall make no more violins—no more violins—Hurrah! no more violins!" This he sang to a horrible mirthful tune, again spinning round on one foot. Perfectly aghast, I was making the best of my way to the door, when he held me fast, saying quite calmly, "Stay, my student friend, pray don't think from this outbreak of grief, which is torturing me as if with the agonies of death, that I am insane; I only do it because a short time ago I made myself a dressing-gown in which I wanted to look like Fate or like God!" The Councillor then went on with a medley of silly and awful rubbish, until he fell down utterly exhausted; I called up the old housekeeper, and was very pleased to find myself in the open air again.

I never doubted for a moment that Krespel had become insane; the Professor, however, asserted the contrary. "There are men," he remarked, "from whom nature or a special destiny has taken away the cover behind which the mad folly of the rest of us runs its course unobserved. They are like thin-skinned insects, which, as we watch the restless play of their muscles, seem to be misshapen, while nevertheless everything soon comes back into its proper form again. All that with us remains thought, passes over with Krespel into action. That bitter scorn which the spirit that is wrapped up in the doings and dealings of the earth often has at hand, Krespel gives vent to in outrageous gestures and agile caprioles. But these are his lightning conductor. What comes up out of the earth he gives again to the earth, but what is divine, that he keeps; and so I believe that his inner consciousness, in spite of the apparent madness which springs from it to the surface, is as right as a trivet. To be sure, Antonia's sudden death grieves him sore, but I warrant that tomorrow will see him going along in his old jog-trot way as usual." And the Professor's prediction was almost literally filled. Next day the Councillor appeared to be just as he formerly was, only he averred that he would never make another violin, nor yet ever play on another. And, as I learned later, he kept his word.

Hints which the Professor let fall confirmed my own private conviction that the so carefully guarded secret of the Councillor's relations to Antonia, nay, that even her death, was a crime which must weigh heavily upon him, a crime that could not be atoned for. I determined that I would not leave H—— without taxing him with the offence which I conceived him to be guilty of; I determined to shake his heart down to its very roots, and so compel him to make open confession of the terrible deed. The more I reflected upon the matter the clearer it grew in my own mind that Krespel must be a villain, and in the same proportion did my intended reproach, which assumed of itself the form of a real rhetorical masterpiece, wax more fiery and more impressive. Thus equipped and mightily incensed, I hurried to his house. I found him with a calm smiling countenance making playthings. "How can peace," I burst out, "how can peace find lodgment even for a single moment in your breast, so long as the memory of your horrible deed preys like a serpent upon you?" He gazed at me in amazement, and laid his chisel aside. "What do you mean, my dear sir?" he asked; "pray take a seat." But my indignation chafing me more and more, I went on to accuse him directly of having murdered Antonia, and to threaten him with the vengeance of the Eternal.

Further, as a newly full-fledged lawyer, full of my profession, I went so far as to give him to understand that I would leave no stone unturned to get a clue to the business, and so deliver him here in this world into the hands of an earthly judge. I must confess that I was considerably disconcerted when, at the conclusion of my violent and pompous harangue, the Councillor, without answering so much as a single word, calmly fixed his eyes upon me as though expecting me to go on again. And this I did indeed attempt to do, but it sounded so ill-founded and so stupid as well that I soon grew silent again. Krespel gloated over my embarrassment, whilst a malicious ironical smile flitted across his face. Then he grew very grave, and addressed me in solemn tones. "Young man, no doubt you think I am foolish, insane; that I can pardon you, since we are both confined in the same madhouse; and you only blame me for deluding myself with the idea that I am God the Father because you imagine yourself to be God the Son. But how do you dare desire to insinuate yourself into the secrets and lay bare the hidden motives of a life that is strange to you and that must continue so? She has gone and the mystery is solved." He ceased speaking, rose, and traversed the room backwards and forwards several times. I ventured to ask for an explanation; he fixed his eyes upon me, grasped me by the hand, and led me to the window, which he threw wide open. Propping himself upon his arms, he leaned out, and, looking down into the garden, told me the history of his life. When he finished I left him, touched and ashamed.

In a few words, his relations with Antonia rose in the following way. Twenty years before, the Councillor had been led into Italy by his favourite engrossing passion of hunting up and buying the best violins of the old masters. At that time he had not yet begun to make them himself, and so of course he had not begun to take to pieces those which he bought. In Venice he heard the celebrated singer Angela ——i, who at that time was playing with splendid success as *prima donna* at St. Benedict's Theatre. His enthusiasm was awakened, not only in her art—which Signora Angela had indeed brought to a high pitch of perfection—but in her angelic beauty as well. He sought her acquaintance; and in spite of all his rugged manners he succeeded in winning her heart, principally through his bold and yet at the same time masterly violin-playing. Close intimacy led in a few weeks to marriage, which, however, was kept a secret, because Angela was unwilling to sever her connection with the theatre, neither did she wish to part with her professional name, that by which she was celebrated, nor to add to it the cacophonous "Krespel." With the most extravagant irony he described to me what a strange life of worry and torture Angela led him as soon as she became his wife. Krespel was of opinion that more capriciousness and waywardness were concentrated in Angela's little person than in all the rest of the *prima donnas* in the world put together. If he now and again presumed to stand up in his own defence, she let loose a whole army of abbots, musical composers, and students upon him, who, ignorant of his true connection with Angela, soundly rated him as a most intolerable, ungallant lover for not submitting to all the Signora's caprices. It was just after one of these stormy scenes that Krespel fled to Angela's country seat to try and forget in playing fantasias on his Cremona, violin the annoyances of the day. But he had not been there long before the Signora, who had followed hard after him, stepped into the room. She was in an affectionate humour; she embraced her husband, overwhelmed him with sweet and languishing glances, and rested her pretty head on his shoulder. But Krespel, carried away into the world of music, continued to play on until the walls echoed again; thus he chanced to touch the Signora somewhat ungently with his arm and the fiddle-bow. She leapt back full of fury, shrieking that he was a "German brute," snatched the violin from his hands, and dashed it on the marble table into a thousand pieces. Krespel stood like a statue of stone before her; but then, as if awakening out of a dream, he seized her with the strength of a giant and threw her out of the window of her own house, and, without troubling himself about anything more, fled back to Venice—to Germany. It was not, however, until some time had elapsed that he had a clear recollection of what he had done; although he knew that the window was scarcely five feet from the ground, and although he was fully cognisant of the necessity, under the above-mentioned circumstances, of throwing the Signora out of the window, he yet felt troubled by a sense of painful uneasiness, and the more so since she had imparted to him in no ambiguous terms an interesting secret as to her condition. He hardly dared to make inquiries; and he was not a little surprised about eight months afterwards at receiving a tender letter from his beloved wife, in which she made not the slightest allusion to what had taken place in her country house, only adding to the intelligence that she had been safely delivered of a sweet little daughter the heartfelt prayer that her dear husband and now a happy father would come at once to Venice. That however Krespel did not do; rather he appealed to a confidential friend for a more circumstantial account of the details, and learned that the Signora had alighted upon the soft grass as lightly as a bird, and that the sole consequences of the fall or shock had been psychic. That is to say, after Krespel's heroic deed she had become completely altered; she never showed a trace of caprice, of her former freaks, or of her teasing habits; and the composer who wrote for the next carnival was the happiest fellow under the sun, since the Signora was willing to sing his music without the scores and hundreds of changes which she at other times had insisted upon. "To be sure," added his friend, "there was every reason for preserving the secret of Angela's cure, else every day would see lady singers flying through windows." The Councillor was not a little excited at this news; he engaged horses; he took his seat in the carriage. "Stop!" he cried suddenly. "Why, there's not a shadow of doubt," he murmured to himself, "that as soon as Angela sets eyes upon me again the evil spirit will recover his power and once more take possession of her. And since I have already thrown her out of the window, what could I do if a similar case were to occur again? What would there be left for me to do?" He got out of the carriage, and wrote an affectionate letter to his wife, making graceful allusion to her tenderness in especially dwelling upon the fact that his tiny daughter had like him a little mole behind the ear, and—remained in Germany. Now ensued an active correspondence between them. Assurances of unchanged affection—invitations—laments over the absence of the beloved one—thwarted wishes—hopes, &c.—flew backwards and forwards from Venice to H——, from H—— to Venice. At length Angela came to Germany, and, as is well known, sang with brilliant success as *prima donna* at the great theatre in F——. Despite the fact that she was no longer young, she won all hearts by the irresistible charm of her wonderfully splendid singing. At that time she had not lost her voice in the least degree. Meanwhile, Antonia had been growing up; and her mother never tired of writing to tell her father how that a singer of the first rank was developing in her. Krespel's friends in F—— also confirmed this intelligence, and urged him to come for once to F—— to see and admire this uncommon sight of two such glorious singers. They had not the slightest suspicion of the close relations in which Krespel stood to the pair. Willingly would he have seen with his own eyes the daughter who occupied so large a place in his heart, and who moreover often appeared to him in his dreams; but as often as he thought upon his wife he felt very uncomfortable, and so he remained at home amongst his broken violins. There was a certain promising young composer, B—— of F——, who was found to have suddenly disappeared, nobody knew where. This young man fell so deeply in love with Antonia that, as she returned his love, he earnestly besought her mother to consent to an immediate union, sanctified as it would further be by art. Angela had nothing to urge against his suit; and the Councillor the more readily gave his consent that the young composer's productions had found favour before his rigorous critical judgment. Krespel was expecting to hear of the consummation of the marriage, when he received instead a black-sealed envelope addressed in a strange hand. Doctor R—— conveyed to the Councillor the sad intelligence that Angela had fallen seriously ill in consequence of a cold caught at the theatre, and that during the night immediately preceding what was to have been Antonia's wedding-day, she had died. To him, the Doctor, Angela had disclosed the fact that she was Krespel's wife, and that Antonia was his daughter; he, Krespel, had better hasten therefore to take charge of the orphan. Notwithstanding that the Councillor was a good deal upset by this news of Angela's death, he soon began to feel that an antipathetic, disturbing influence had departed out of his life, and that now for the first time he could begin to breathe freely. The very same day he set out for F——. You could not credit how heartrending was the Councillor's description of the moment when he first saw Antonia. Even in the fantastic oddities of his expression there was such a marvellous power of description that I am unable to give even so much as a faint indication of it. Antonia inherited all her mother's amiability and all her mother's charms, but not the repellent reverse of the medal. There was no chronic moral ulcer, which might break out from time to time. Antonia's betrothed put in an appearance, whilst Antonia herself, fathoming with happy instinct the deeper-lying character of her wonderful father, sang one of old Padre Martini's motets, which, she knew, Krespel in the heyday of his courtship had never grown tired of hearing her mother sing. The tears ran in streams down Krespel's cheeks; even Angela he had never heard sing like that. Antonia's voice was of a very remarkable and altogether peculiar timbre, at one time it was like the sighing of an Æolian harp, at another like the warbled gush of the nightingale. It seemed as if there was not room for such notes in the human breast. Antonia, blushing with joy and happiness, sang on and on—all her most beautiful songs, B—— playing between whiles as only enthusiasm that is intoxicated with delight can play. Krespel was at first transported with rapture, then he grew thoughtful—still—absorbed in reflection. At length he leapt to his feet, pressed Antonia to his heart, and begged her in a low husky voice, "Sing no more if you love me—my heart is bursting—I fear—I fear—don't sing again."

"No!" remarked the Councillor next day to Doctor R——, "when, as she sang, her blushes gathered into two dark red spots on her pale cheeks, I knew it had nothing to do with your nonsensical family likenesses, I knew it was what I dreaded." The Doctor, whose countenance had shown signs of deep distress from the very beginning of the conversation, replied, "Whether it arises from a too early taxing of her powers of song, or whether the fault is Nature's—enough, Antonia labours under an organic failure in the chest, while it is from it too that her voice derives its wonderful power and its singular timbre, which I might almost say transcend the limits of human capabilities of song. But it bears the announcement of her early death; for, if she continues to sing, I wouldn't give her at the most more than six months longer to live." Krespel's heart was lacerated as if by the stabs of hundreds of stinging knives. It was as though his life had been for the first time overshadowed by a beautiful tree full of the most magnificent blossoms, and now it was to be sawn to pieces at the roots, so that it could not grow green and blossom any more. His resolution was taken. He told Antonia all; he put the alternatives before her—whether she would follow her betrothed and yield to his and the world's seductions, but with the certainty of dying early, or whether she would spread round her father in his old days that joy and peace which had hitherto been unknown to him, and so secure a long life. She threw herself sobbing into his arms, and he, knowing the heartrending trial that was before her, did not press for a more explicit declaration. He talked the matter over with her betrothed; but, notwithstanding that the latter averred that no note should ever cross Antonia's lips, the Councillor was only too well aware that even B—— could not resist the temptation of hearing her sing, at any rate arias of his own composition. And the world, the musical public, even though acquainted with the nature of the singer's affliction, would certainly not relinquish its claims to hear her, for in cases where pleasure is concerned people of this class are very selfish and cruel. The Councillor disappeared from F—— along with Antonia, and came to H——. B———— was in despair when he learnt that they had gone. He set out on their track, overtook them, and arrived at H———— at the same time that they did. "Let me see him only once, and then die!" entreated Antonia "Die! die!" cried Krespel, wild with anger, an icy shudder running through him. His daughter, the only creature in the wide world who had awakened in him the springs of unknown joy, who alone had reconciled him to life, tore herself away from his heart, and he—he suffered the terrible trial to take place. B—— sat down to the piano; Antonia sang; Krespel fiddled away merrily, until the two red spots showed themselves on Antonia's cheeks. Then he bade her stop; and as B was taking leave of his betrothed, she suddenly fell to the floor with a loud scream. "I thought," continued Krespel in his narration, "I thought that she was, as I had anticipated, really dead; but as I had prepared myself for the worst, my calmness did not leave me, nor my self-command desert me. I grasped B——, who stood like a silly sheep in his dismay, by the shoulders, and said (here the Councillor fell into his singing tone), 'Now that you, my estimable pianoforte-player, have, as you wished and desired, really murdered your betrothed, you may quietly take your departure; at least have the goodness to make yourself scarce before I run my bright hanger through your heart. My daughter, who, as you see, is rather pale, could very well do with some colour from your precious blood. Make haste and run, for I might also hurl a nimble knife or two after you.' I must, I suppose, have looked rather formidable as I uttered these words, for, with a cry of the greatest terror, B—— tore himself loose from my grasp, rushed out of the room, and down the steps." Directly after B—— was gone, when the Councillor tried to lift up his daughter, who lay unconscious on the floor, she opened her eyes with a deep sigh, but soon closed them again as if about to die. Then Krespel's grief found vent aloud, and would not be comforted. The Doctor, whom the old housekeeper had called in, pronounced Antonia's case a somewhat serious but by no means dangerous attack; and she did indeed recover more quickly than her father had dared to hope. She now clung to him with the most confiding childlike affection; she entered into his favourite hobbies—into his mad schemes and whims. She helped him take old violins to pieces and glue new ones together. "I won't sing again any more, but live for you," she often said, sweetly smiling upon him, after she had been asked to sing and had refused. Such appeals however the Councillor was anxious to spare her as much as possible; therefore it was that he was unwilling to take her into society, and solicitously shunned all music. He well understood how painful it must be for her to forego altogether the exercise of that art which she had brought to such a pitch of perfection. When the Councillor bought the wonderful violin that he had buried with Antonia, and was about to take it to pieces, she met him with such sadness in her face and softly breathed the petition, "What! this as well?" By some power, which he could not explain, he felt impelled to leave this particular instrument unbroken, and to play upon it. Scarcely had he drawn the first few notes from it than Antonia cried aloud with joy, "Why, that's me!—now I shall sing again." And, in truth, there was something remarkably striking about the clear, silvery, bell-like tones of the violin; they seemed to have been engendered in the human soul. Krespel's heart was deeply moved; he played, too, better than ever. As he ran up and down the scale, playing bold passages with consummate power and expression, she clapped her hands together and cried with delight, "I did that well! I did that well!"

From this time onwards her life was filled with peace and cheerfulness. She often said to the Councillor, "I should like to sing something, father." Then Krespel would take his violin down from the wall and play her most beautiful songs, and her heart was right glad and happy. Shortly before my arrival in H——, the Councillor fancied one night that he heard somebody playing the piano in the adjoining room, and he soon made out distinctly that B—— was flourishing on the instrument in his usual style. He wished to get up, but felt himself held down as if by a dead weight, and lying as if fettered in iron bonds; he was utterly unable to move an inch. Then Antonia's voice was heard singing low and soft; soon, however, it began to rise and rise in volume until it became an ear-splitting fortissimo; and at length she passed over into a powerfully impressive song which B—— had once composed for her in the devotional style of the old masters. Krespel described his condition as being incomprehensible, for terrible anguish was mingled with a delight he had never experienced before. All at once he was surrounded by a dazzling brightness, in which he beheld B—— and Antonia locked in a close embrace, and gazing at each other in a rapture of ecstasy. The music of the song and of the pianoforte accompanying it went on without any visible signs that Antonia sang or that B—— touched the instrument. Then the Councillor fell into a sort of dead faint, whilst the images vanished away. On awakening he still felt the terrible anguish of his dream. He rushed into Antonia's room. She lay on the sofa, her eyes closed, a sweet angelic smile on her face, her hands devoutly folded, and looking as if asleep and dreaming of the joys and raptures of heaven. But she was—dead.

* * * * * * *

THE FERMATA.

Hummel's amusing, vivacious picture, "Company in an Italian Inn," became known by the Art Exhibition at Berlin in the autumn of 1814, where it appeared, to the delight of all who saw and studied it An arbour almost hidden in foliage—a table covered with wine-flasks and fruits—two Italian ladies sitting at it opposite each other, one singing, the other playing a guitar; between them, more in the background, stands an abbot, acting as music-director. With his baton raised, he is awaiting the moment when the Signora shall end, in a long trill, the cadence which, with her eyes directed heavenwards, she is just in the midst of; then down will come his hand, whilst the guitarist gaily dashes off the dominant chord. The abbot is filled with admiration—with exquisite delight—and at the same time his attention is painfully on the stretch. He wouldn't miss the proper downward beat for the world. He hardly dare breathe. He would like to stop the mouth and wings of every buzzing bee and midge. So much the more therefore is he annoyed at the bustling host who must needs come and bring the wine just at this supreme, delicious moment. An outlook upon an avenue, patterned by brilliant strips of light! There a horseman has pulled up, and a glass of something refreshing to drink is being handed up to him on horseback.

Before this picture stood the two friends Edward and Theodore. "The more I look at this singer," said Edward, "in her gay attire, who, though rather oldish, is yet full of the true inspiration of her art, and the more I am delighted with the grave but genuine Roman profile and lovely form of the guitarist, and the more my estimable friend the abbot amuses me, the more does the whole picture seem to me instinct with free, strong, vital power. It is plainly a caricature in the higher sense of the term, but rich in grace and vivacity. I should just like to step into that arbour and open one of those dainty little flasks which are ogling me from the table. I tell you what, I fancy I can already smell something of the sweet fragrance of the noble wine. Come, it were a sin for this solicitation to be wasted on the cold senseless atmosphere that is about us here. Let us go and drain a flask of Italian wine in honour of this fine picture, of art, and of merry Italy, where life is exhilarating and given for pleasure."

Whilst Edward was running on thus in disconnected sentences, Theodore stood silent and deeply absorbed in reflection. "Ay, that we will, come along," he said, starting up as if awakening out of a dream; but nevertheless he had some difficulty in tearing himself away from the picture, and as he mechanically followed his friend, he had to stop at the door to cast another longing lingering look back upon the singer and guitarist and abbot. Edward's proposal easily admitted of being carried into execution. They crossed the street diagonally, and very soon a flask exactly like those in the picture stood before them in Sala Tarone's little blue room. "It seems to me," said Edward, as Theodore still continued very silent and thoughtful, even after several glasses had been drunk, "it seems to me that the picture has made a deeper impression upon you than upon me, and not such an agreeable impression either." "I assure you," replied Theodore, "that I lost nothing of the brightness and grace of that animated composition; yet it is very singular,—it is a faithful representation of a scene out of my own life, reproducing the portraits of the parties concerned in it in a manner startlingly lifelike. You will, however, agree with me that diverting memories also have the power of strangely moving the mind when they suddenly spring up in this extraordinary and unexpected way, as if awakened by the wave of a magician's wand. That's the case with me just now." "What! a scene out of your own life!" exclaimed Edward, quite astonished. "Do you mean to say the picture represents an episode in your own life? I saw at once that the two ladies and the priest were eminently successful portraits, but I never for a moment dreamed that you had ever come across them in the course of your life. Come now, tell me all about it, how it all came about; we are quite alone, nobody else will come at this time o' day." "Willingly," answered Theodore, "but unfortunately I must go a long way back—to my early youth in fact." "Never mind; fire away," rejoined Edward; "I don't know over much about your early days. If it lasts a good while, nothing worse will happen than that we shall have to empty a bottle more than we at first bargained for; and to that nobody will have any objection, neither we, nor Mr. Tarone."

"That, throwing everything else aside, I at length devoted myself entirely to the noble art of music," began Theodore, "need excite nobody's astonishment, for whilst still a boy I would hardly do anything else but play, and spent hours and hours strumming on my uncle's old creaking, jarring piano. The little town was very badly provided for music; there was nobody who could give me instruction except an old opinionated organist; he, however, was merely a dry arithmetician, and plagued me to death with obscure, unmelodious toccatas and fugues. But I held on bravely, without letting myself be daunted. The old fellow was crabby, and often found a good deal of fault, but he had only to play a good piece in his own powerful style, and I was at once reconciled both with him and with his art. I was then often in a curious state of mind; many pieces particularly of old Sebastian Bach were almost like a fearful ghost-story, and I yielded myself up to that feeling of pleasurable awe to which we are so prone in the days of our fantastic youth. But I entered into a veritable Eden when, as sometimes happened in winter, the bandmaster of the town and his colleagues, supported by a few other moderate dilettante players, gave a concert, and I, owing to the strict time I always kept, was permitted to play the kettledrum in the symphony. It was not until later that I perceived how ridiculous and extravagant these concerts were. My teacher generally played two concertos on the piano by Wolff or Emanuel Bach, a member of the town band struggled with Stamitz, while the receiver of excise duties worked away hard at the flute, and took in such an immense supply of breath that he blew out both lights on his music-stand, and always had to have them relighted again. Singing wasn't thought about; my uncle, a great friend and patron of music, always disparaged the local talent in this line. He still dwelt with exuberant delight upon the days gone by, when the four choristers of the four churches of the town agreed together to give *Lottchen am Hofe*. Above all, he was wont to extol the toleration which united the singers in the production of this work of art, for not only the Catholic and the Evangelical but also the Reformed community was split into two bodies—those speaking German and those speaking French. The French chorister was not daunted by the *Lottchen*, but, as my uncle maintained, sang his part, spectacles on nose, in the finest falsetto that ever proceeded forth from a human breast. Now there was amongst us (I mean in the town) a spinster named Meibel, aged about fifty-five, who subsisted upon the scanty pension which she received as a retired court singer of the metropolis, and my uncle was rightly of opinion that Miss Meibel might still do something for her money in the concert hall. She assumed airs of importance, required a good deal of coaxing, but at last consented, so that we came to have *bravuras* in our concerts. She was a singular creature this Miss Meibel. I still retain a lively recollection of her lean little figure. Dressed in a many-coloured gown, she was wont to step forward with her roll of music in her hand, looking very grave and solemn, and to acknowledge the audience with a slight inclination of the upper part of her body. Her head-dress was a most remarkable head-dress. In front was fastened a nosegay of Italian flowers of porcelain, which kept up a strange trembling and tottering as she sang. At the end, after the audience had greeted her with no stinted measure of applause, she proudly handed the music-roll to my uncle, and permitted him to dip his thumb and finger into a little porcelain snuff-box, fashioned in the shape of a pug dog, out of which she took a pinch herself with evident relish. She had a horrible squeaky voice, indulged in all sorts of ludicrous flourishes and roulades, and so you may imagine what an effect all this, combined with her ridiculous manners and style of dress, could not fail to have upon me. My uncle overflowed with panegyrics; that I could not understand, and so turned the more readily to my organist, who, looking with contempt upon vocal efforts in general, delighted me down to the ground as in his hypochondriac malicious way he parodied the ludicrous old spinster.

"The more decidedly I came to share with my master his contempt for singing, the higher did he rate my musical genius. He took a great and zealous interest in instructing me in counterpoint, so that I soon came to write the most ingenious toccatas and fugues. I was once playing one of these ingenious specimens of my skill to my uncle on my birthday (I was nineteen years old), when the waiter of our first hotel stepped into the room to announce the visit of two foreign ladies who had just arrived in the town. Before my uncle could throw off his dressing-gown—it was of a large flower pattern—and don his coat and vest, his visitors were already in the room. You know what an electric effect every strange event has upon those who are brought up in the narrow seclusion of a small country town; this in particular, which crossed my path so unexpectedly, was pre-eminently fitted to work a complete revolution within me. Picture to yourself two tall, slender Italian ladies, dressed fantastically and in bright colours, quite up to the latest fashion, meeting my uncle with the freedom of professional *artistes*, and yet with considerable charms of manner, and addressing him in firm and sonorous voices. What the deuce of a strange tongue they speak! Only now and then does it sound at all like German. My uncle doesn't understand a word; embarrassed, mute as a maggot, he steps back and points to the sofa. They sit down, talk together—it sounds like music itself. At length they succeed in making my good uncle comprehend that they are singers on a tour; they would like to give a concert in the place, and have come to him, as he is the man to conduct such musical negotiations.

"Whilst they were talking together I picked up their Christian names, and I fancied that I could now more easily and more distinctly distinguish the one from the other, for their both making their appearance together had at first confused me. Lauretta, apparently the elder of the two, looked about her with sparkling eyes, and talked away at my embarrassed old uncle with gushing vivacity and with demonstrative gestures. She was not too tall, and of a voluptuous build, so that my eyes wandered amid many charms that hitherto had been strangers to them. Teresina, taller, more slender, with a long grave face, spoke but seldom, but what she did say was more intelligible. Now and then a peculiar smile flitted across her features; it almost seemed as if she were highly amused at my good uncle, who had withdrawn into his silken dressing-gown like a snail into its shell, and was vainly endeavouring to push out of sight a treacherous yellow string, with which he fastened his night-jacket together, and which would keep tumbling out of his bosom yards and yards long. At length they rose to depart; my uncle promised to arrange everything for the concert for the third day following; then the sisters gave him and me, whom he introduced to them as a young musician, a most polite invitation to take chocolate with them in the afternoon.

"We mounted the steps with a solemn air and awkward gait; we both felt very peculiar, as if we were going to meet some adventure to which we were not equal. In consequence of due previous preparation my uncle had a good many fine things to say about art, which nobody understood, neither he himself nor any of the rest of us. This done, and after I had thrice burned my tongue with the scalding hot chocolate, but with the stoical fortitude of a Scævola had smiled under the fiery infliction, Lauretta at length said that she would sing to us. Teresina took her guitar, tuned it, and struck a few full chords. It was the first time I had heard the instrument, and the characteristic mysterious sounds of the trembling strings made a deep and wonderful impression upon me. Lauretta began very softly and held on, the note rising to *fortissimo*, and then quickly broke into a crisp complicated run through an octave and a half. I can still remember the words of the beginning, '*Sento l'amica speme*.' My heart was oppressed; I had never had an idea of anything of the kind. But as Lauretta continued to soar in bolder and higher flights, and as the musical notes poured upon me like sparkling rays, thicker and thicker, then was the music that had so long lain mute and lifeless within me enkindled, rising up in strong, grand flames. Ah! I had never heard what music was in my life before! Then the sisters sang one of those grand impressive duets of Abbot Steffani which confine themselves to notes of a low register. My soul was stirred at the sound of Teresina's alto, it was so sonorous, and as pure as silver bells. I couldn't for the life of me restrain my emotion; tears started to my eyes. My uncle coughed warningly, and cast angry glances upon me; it was all of no use, I was really quite beside myself. This seemed to please the sisters; they began to inquire into the nature and extent of my musical studies; I was ashamed of my performances in that line, and with the hardihood born of enthusiastic admiration, I bluntly declared that

that day was the first time I had ever heard music. 'The dear good boy!' lisped Lauretta, so sweetly and bewitchingly.

"On reaching home again, I was seized with a sort of fury: I pounced upon all the toccatas and fugues that I had hammered out, as well as a beautiful copy of forty-five variations of a canonical theme that the organist had written and done me the honour of presenting to me,—all these I threw into the fire, and laughed with spiteful glee as the double counterpoint smoked and crackled. Then I sat down at the piano and tried first to imitate the tones of the guitar, then to play the sisters' melodies, and finished by attempting to sing them. At length about midnight my uncle emerged from his bedroom and greeted me with, 'My boy, you'd better just stop that screeching and troop off to bed;' and he put out both candles and went back to his own room. I had no other alternative but to obey. The mysterious power of song came to me in my dreams—at least I thought so—for I sang '*Sento l'amica speme*' in excellent style.

"The next morning my uncle had hunted up everybody who could fiddle and blow for the rehearsal. He was proud to show what good musicians the town possessed; but everything seemed to go perversely wrong. Lauretta set to work at a fine scene; but very soon in the recitative the orchestra was all at sixes and sevens, not one of them had any idea of accompaniment Lauretta screamed—raved—wept with impatience and anger. The organist was presiding at the piano; she attacked him with the bitterest reproaches. He got up and in silent obduracy marched out of the hall. The bandmaster of the town, whom Lauretta had dubbed a 'German ass!' took his violin under his arm, and, banging his hat on his head with an air of defiance, likewise made for the door. The members of his company, sticking their bows under the strings of their violins, and unscrewing the mouthpieces of their brass instruments, followed him. There was nobody but the dilettanti left, and they gazed about them with disconsolate looks, whilst the receiver of excise duties exclaimed, with a tragic air, 'O heaven! how mortified I feel!' All my diffidence was gone,—I threw myself in the bandmaster's way, I begged, I prayed, in my distress I promised him six new minuets with double trios for the annual ball. I succeeded in appeasing him. He went back to his place, his companions followed suit, and soon the orchestra was reconstituted, except that the organist was wanting. He was slowly making his way across the market-place, no shouting or beckoning could make him turn back. Teresina had looked on at the whole scene with smothered laughter, while Lauretta was now as full of glee as before she had been of anger. She was unstinted in her praise of my efforts; she asked me if I played the piano, and ere I knew what I was about, I sat in the organist's place with the music before me. Never before had I accompanied a singer, still less directed an orchestra. Teresina sat down beside me at the piano and gave me every time; Lauretta encouraged me with repeated 'Bravos!' the orchestra proved manageable, and things continued to improve. Everything was worked out successfully at the second rehearsal; and the effect of the sisters' singing at the concert is not to be described.

"The sovereign's return to his capital was to be celebrated there with several festive demonstrations; the sisters were summoned to sing in the theatre and at concerts. Until the time that their presence was required they resolved to remain in our little town, and thus it came to pass that they gave us a few more concerts. The admiration of the public rose to a kind of madness. Old Miss Meibel, however, took with a deliberate air a pinch of snuff out of her porcelain pug and gave her opinion that 'such impudent caterwauling was not singing; singing should be low and melodious.' My friend, the organist, never showed himself again, and, in truth, I did not miss him in the least I was the happiest fellow in the world. The whole day long I spent with the sisters, copying out the vocal scores of what they were to sing in the capital. Lauretta was my ideal; her vile caprices, her terribly passionate violence, the torments she inflicted upon me at the piano—all these I bore with patience. She alone had unsealed for me the springs of true music. I began to study Italian, and try my hand at a few canzonets. In what heavenly rapture was I plunged when Lauretta sang my compositions, or even praised them. Often it seemed to me as if it was not I who had thought out and set what she sang, but that the thought first shone forth in her singing of it. With Teresina I could not somehow get on familiar terms; she sang but seldom, and didn't seem to make much account of all that I was doing, and sometimes I even fancied that she was laughing at me behind my back. At length the time came for them to leave the town. And now I felt for the first time how dear Lauretta had become to me, and how impossible it would be for me to separate from her. Often, when she was in a tender, playful mood, she had caressed me, although always in a perfectly artless fashion; nevertheless, my blood was excited, and it was nothing but the strange coolness with which she was more usually wont to treat me that restrained me from giving reins to my ardour and clasping her in my arms in a delirium of passion. I possessed a tolerably good tenor voice, which, however, I had never practised, but now I began to cultivate it assiduously. I frequently sang with Lauretta one of those tender Italian duets of which there exists such an endless number. We were just singing one of these pieces, the hour of departure was close at hand—'*Senza di te ben mio, vivere non poss' io*' ('Without thee, my own, I cannot live!') Who could resist that? I threw myself at her feet—I was in despair. She raised me up—'But, my friend, need we then part?' I pricked up my ears with amazement. She proposed that I should accompany her and Teresina to the capital, for if I intended to devote myself wholly to music I must leave this wretched little town some time or other. Picture to yourself one struggling in the dark depths of boundless despair, who has given up all hopes of life, and who, in the moment in which he expects to receive the blow that is to crush him for ever, suddenly finds himself sitting in a glorious bright arbour of roses, where hundreds of unseen but loving voices whisper, 'You are still alive, dear,—still alive'—and you will know how I felt then. Along with them to the capital! that had seized upon my heart as an ineradicable resolution. But I won't tire you with the details of how I set to work to convince my uncle that I ought now by all means to go to the capital, which, moreover, was not very far away. He at length gave his consent, and announced his intention of going with me. Here was a tricksy stroke of fortune! I dare not give utterance to my purpose of travelling in company with the sisters. A violent cold, which my uncle caught, proved my saviour.

"I left the town by the stage-coach, but only went as far as the first stopping-station, where I awaited my divinity. A well-lined purse enabled me to make all due and fitting preparations. I was seized with the romantic idea of accompanying the ladies in the character of a protecting paladin—on horseback; I secured a horse, which, though not particularly handsome, was, its owner assured me, quiet, and I rode back at the appointed time to meet the two fair singers. I soon saw the little carriage, which had two seats, coming towards me. Lauretta and Teresina sat on the principal seat, whilst on the other, with her back to the driver, sat their maid, the fat little Gianna, a brown-cheeked Neapolitan. Besides this living freight, the carriage was packed full of boxes, satchels, and baskets of all sizes and shapes, such as invariably accompany ladies when they travel. Two little pug-dogs which Gianna was nursing in her lap began to bark when I gaily saluted the company.

"All was going on very nicely; we were traversing the last stage of the journey, when my steed all at once conceived the idea that it was high time to be returning homewards. Being aware that stern measures were not always blessed with a remarkable degree of success in such cases, I felt advised to have recourse to milder means of persuasion; but the obstinate brute remained insensible to all my well-meant exhortations. I wanted to go forwards, he backwards, and all the advantage that my efforts gave me over him was that instead of taking to his heels for home, he continued to run round in circles. Teresina leaned forward out of the carriage and had a hearty laugh; Lauretta, holding her hands before her face, screamed out as if I were in imminent danger. This gave me the courage of despair, I drove the spurs into the brute's ribs, but that very same moment I was roughly hurled off and found myself sprawling on the ground. The horse stood perfectly still, and, stretching out his long neck, regarded me with what I took to be nothing else than derision. I was not able to rise to my feet; the driver had to come and help me; Lauretta had jumped out and was weeping and lamenting; Teresina did nothing but laugh without ceasing. I had sprained my foot, and couldn't possibly mount again. How was I to get on? My steed was fastened to the carriage, whilst I crept into it. Just picture us all—two rather robust females, a fat servant-girl, two pug-dogs, a dozen boxes, satchels, and baskets, and me as well, all packed into a little carriage. Picture Lauretta's complaints at the uncomfortableness of her seat, the howling of the pups, the chattering of the Neapolitan, Teresina's sulks, the unspeakable pain I felt in my foot, and you will have some idea of my enviable situation! Teresina averred that she could not endure it any longer. We stopped; in a trice she was out of the carriage, had untied my horse, and was up in the saddle, prancing and curvetting around us. I must indeed admit that she cut a fine figure. The dignity and elegance which marked her carriage and bearing were still more prominent on horseback. She asked for her guitar, then dropping the reins on her arm, she began to sing proud Spanish ballads with a full-toned accompaniment. Her light silk dress fluttered in the wind, its folds and creases giving rise to a sheeny play of light, whilst the white feathers of her hat quivered and shook, like the prattling spirits of the air which we heard in her voice. Altogether she made such a romantic figure that I could not keep my eyes off her, notwithstanding that Lauretta reproached her for making herself such a fantastic simpleton, and predicted that she would suffer for her audacity. But no accident happened; either the horse had lost all his stubbornness or he liked the fair singer better than the paladin; at any rate, Teresina did not creep back into the carriage again until we had almost reached the gates of the town.

"If you had seen me then at concerts and operas, if you had seen me revelling in all sorts of music, and as a diligent accompanist studying arias, duets, and I don't know what besides at the piano, you would have perceived, by the complete change in my behaviour, that I was filled with a new and wonderful spirit. I had cast off all my rustic shyness, and sat at the pianoforte with my score before me like an experienced professional, directing the performances of my *prima donna*. All my mind—all my thoughts—were sweet melodies. Utterly regardless of all the rules of counterpoint, I composed all sorts of canzonets and arias, which Lauretta sang, though only in her own room. Why would she never sing any of my pieces at a concert? I could not understand it. Teresina also arose before my imagination curvetting on her proud steed with the lute in her hands, like Art herself disguised in romance. Without thinking of it consciously, I wrote several songs of a high and serious nature. Lauretta, it is true, played with her notes like a capricious fairy queen. There was nothing upon which she ventured in which she had not success. But never did a roulade cross Teresina's lips; nothing more than a simple interpolated note, at most a *mordent*; but her long-sustained tones gleamed like meteors through the darkness of night, awakening strange spirits, who came and gazed with earnest eyes into the depths of my heart. I know not how I remained ignorant of them so long!

"The sisters were granted a benefit concert; I sang with Lauretta a long scena from Anfossi. As usual I presided at the piano. We came to the last *fermata*. Lauretta exerted all her skill and art; she warbled trill after trill like a nightingale, executed sustained notes, then long elaborate roulades—a whole *solfeggio*. In fact, I thought she was almost carrying the thing too far this time; I felt a soft breath on my cheek; Teresina stood behind me. At this moment Lauretta took a good start with the intention of swelling up to a 'harmonic shake,' and so passing back into *a tempo*. The devil entered into me; I jammed down the keys with both hands; the orchestra followed suit; and it was all over with Lauretta's trill, just at the supreme moment when she was to excite everybody's astonishment. Almost annihilating me with a look of fury, she crushed her roll of music together, tore it up, and hurled it at my head, so that the pieces flew all over me. Then she rushed like a madwoman through the orchestra into the adjoining room; as soon as we had concluded the piece, I followed her. She wept; she raved. 'Out of my sight, villain,' she screamed as soon as she saw me. 'You devil, you've completely ruined me—my fame, my honour—and oh! my trill. Out of my sight, you devil's own!' She made a rush at me; I escaped through the door. Whilst some one else was performing, Teresina and the music-director at length succeeded in so far pacifying her rage, that she resolved to appear again; but I was not to be allowed to touch the piano. In the last duet that the sisters sang, Lauretta did contrive to introduce the swelling 'harmonic shake,' was rewarded with a storm of applause, and settled down into the best of humours.

"But I could not get over the vile treatment which I had received at her hands in the presence of so many people, and I was firmly resolved to set off home next morning for my native town. I was actually engaged in packing my things together when Teresina came into my room. Observing what I was about, she exclaimed, astonished, 'Are you going to leave us?' I gave her to understand that after the affront which had been put upon me by Lauretta I could not think of remaining any longer in her society. 'And so,' replied Teresina, 'you're going to let yourself be driven away by the extravagant conduct of a little fool, who is now heartily sorry for what she has done and said. Where else can you better live in your art than with us? Let me tell you, it only depends upon yourself and your own behaviour to keep her from such pranks as this. You are too compliant, too tender, too gentle. Besides, you rate her powers too highly. Her voice is indeed not bad, and it has a wide compass; but what else are all these fantastic warblings and flourishes, these preposterous runs, these never-ending shakes, but delusive artifices of style, which people admire in the same way that they admire the foolhardy agility of a rope-dancer? Do you imagine that such things can make any deep impression upon us and stir the heart? The 'harmonic shake' which you spoilt I cannot tolerate; I always feel anxious and pained when she attempts it. And then this scaling up into the region of the third line above the stave, what is it but a violent straining of the natural voice, which after all is the only thing that really moves the heart? I like the middle notes and the low notes. A sound that penetrates to the heart, a real quiet, easy transition from note to note, are what I love above all things. No useless ornamentation—a firm, clear, strong note—a definite expression, which carries away the mind and soul—that's real true singing, and that's how I sing. If you can't be reconciled to Lauretta again, then think of Teresina, who indeed likes you so much that you shall in your own way be her musical composer. Don't be cross—but all your elegant canzonets and arias can't be matched with this single ——,' she sang in her sonorous way a simple devotional sort of canzona which I had set a few days before. I had never dreamed that it could sound like that I felt the power of the music going through and through me; tears of joy and rapture stood in my eyes; I seized Teresina's hand, and pressing it to my lips a thousand times, swore I would never leave her.

"Lauretta looked upon my intimacy with her sister with envious but suppressed vexation, and she could not do without me, for, in spite of her skill, she was unable to study a new piece without help; she read badly, and was rather uncertain in her time. Teresina, on the contrary, sang everything at sight, and her ear for time was unparalleled. Never did Lauretta give such free rein to her caprice and violence as when her accompaniments were being practised. They were never right for her; she looked upon them as a necessary evil; the piano ought not to be heard at all, it should always be *pianissimo*; so there was nothing but giving way to her again and again, and altering the time just as the whim happened to come into her head at the moment But now I took a firm stand against her; I combated her impertinences; I taught her that an accompaniment devoid of energy was not conceivable, and that there was a marked difference between supporting and carrying along the song and letting it run to riot, without form and without time. Teresina faithfully lent me her assistance. I composed nothing but pieces for the Church, writing all the solos for a voice of low register. Teresina, too, tyrannised over me not a little, to which I submitted with a good grace, since she had more knowledge of, and (so at least I thought) more appreciation for, German seriousness than her sister.

"We were touring in South Germany. In a little town we met an Italian tenor who was making his way from Milan to Berlin. My fair companions went in ecstasies over their countryman; he stuck close to them, cultivating in particular Teresina's acquaintance, so that to my great vexation I soon came to play rather a secondary part.

Once, just as I was about to enter the room with a roll of music under my arm, the voices of my companions and the tenor, engaged in an animated conversation, fell upon my ear. My name was mentioned; I pricked up my ears; I listened. I now understood Italian so well that not a word escaped me. Lauretta was describing the tragical occurrence of the concert when I cut short her trill by prematurely striking down the concluding notes of the bar. 'A German ass!' exclaimed the tenor. I felt as if I must rush in and hurl the flighty hero of the boards out of the window, but I restrained myself. She then went on to say that she had been minded to send me about my business at once, but, moved by my clamorous entreaties, she had so far had compassion upon me as to tolerate me some time longer, since I was studying singing under her. This, to my utter amazement, Teresina confirmed. 'Yes, he's a good child,' she added; 'he's in love with me now and sets everything for the alto. He is not without talent, but he must rub off that stiffness and awkwardness which is so characteristic of the Germans. I hope to make a good composer out of him; then he shall write me some good things—for there's very little written as yet for the alto voice—and afterwards I shall let him go his own way. He's very tiresome with his billing and cooing and love-sick sighing, and he worries me too much with his wearisome compositions, which have been but poor stuff up to the present.' 'I at least have now got rid of him,' interrupted Lauretta; 'and Teresina, how the fellow pestered me with his arias and duets you know very well.' And now she began to sing a duet of my composing, which formerly she had praised very highly. The other sister took up the second voice, and they parodied me both in voice and in execution in the most shameful manner. The tenor laughed till the walls rang again. My limbs froze; at once I formed an irrevocable resolve. I quietly slipped away from the door back into my own room, the windows of which looked upon a side street. Opposite was the post-office; the post-coach for Bamberg had just driven up to take in the mails and passengers. The latter were all standing ready waiting in the gateway, but I had still an hour to spare. Hastily packing up my things, I generously paid the whole of the bill at the hotel, and hurried across to the post-office. As I crossed the broad street I saw the fair sisters and the Italian still standing at the window, and looking out to catch the sound of the post-horn. I leaned back in the corner, and dwelt with a good deal of satisfaction upon the crushing effect of the bitter scathing letter that I had left behind for them in the hotel."

* * * * * * *

With evident gratification Theodore tossed off the rest of the fiery Aleatico that Edward had poured into his glass. The latter, opening a new flask and skilfully shaking off the drops of oil which swam at the top, remarked, "I should not have deemed Teresina capable of such falseness and artfulness. I cannot banish from my mind the recollection of what a charming figure she made as she sat on horseback singing Spanish ballads, whilst the horse pranced along in graceful curvets." "That was her culminating point," interrupted Theodore; "I still remember the strange impression which the scene made upon me. I forgot my pain; she seemed to me like a creature of a higher race. It is indeed very true that such moments are turning-points in one's life, and that in them many images arise which time does not avail to dim. Whenever I have succeeded with any fine *romance*, it has always been when Teresina's image has stepped forth from the treasure-house of my mind in clear bright colours at the moment of writing it."

"But," said Edward, "but let us not forget the artistic Lauretta; and, scattering all rancour to the winds, let us drink to the health of the two sisters." They did so. "Oh," exclaimed Theodore, "how the fragrant breezes of Italy arise out of this wine and fan my cheeks,—my blood rolls with quickened energy in my veins. Oh! why must I so soon leave that glorious land again!" "As yet," interrupted Edward, "as yet in all that you have told me I can see no connection with the beautiful picture, and so I believe that you still have something more to tell me about the sisters. Of course I perceive plainly that the ladies in the picture are none other than Lauretta and Teresina themselves." "You are right, they are," replied Theodore; "and my ejaculations and sighs, and my longings after the glorious land of Italy, will form a fitting introduction to what I still have to say. A short time ago, perhaps about two years since, just before leaving Rome, I made a little excursion on horseback. Before an inn stood a charming girl; the idea struck me how nice it would be to receive a cup of wine at the hands of the pretty child. I pulled up before the door, in a walk so thickly planted on each side with shrubs that the sunlight could only make its way through in patches. In the distance I heard sounds of singing and the tinkling of a guitar. I pricked up my ears and listened, for the two female voices affected me somehow in a singular fashion; strangely enough dim recollections began to stir within my mind, but they refused to take definite shape. I dismounted and slowly drew near to the vine-clad arbour whence the music seemed to proceed, eagerly catching up every sound in the meantime. The second voice had ceased to sing. The first sang a canzonet alone. As I came nearer and nearer that which had at first seemed familiar to me, and which had at first attracted my attention, gradually faded away. The singer was now in the midst of a florid, elaborate *fermata*. Up and down she warbled, up and down; at length she stopped, holding a note on for some time. But all at once a female voice began to let off a torrent of abuse, maledictions, curses, vituperations! A man protested; a second laughed. The other female voice took part in the altercation. The quarrel continued to wax louder and more violent, with true Italian fury. At length I stood immediately in front of the arbour; an abbot rushes out and almost runs over me; he turns his head to look at me; I recognise my good friend Signor Lodovico, my musical news-monger from Rome. 'What in the name of wonder'—I exclaim. 'Oh, sir! sir!' he screams, 'save me, protect me from this mad fury, from this crocodile, this tiger, this hyæna, this devil of a woman. Yes, I did, I did; I was beating time to Anfossi's canzonet, and brought down my baton too soon whilst she was in the midst of the *fermata*; I cut short her trill; but why did I meet her eyes, the devilish divinity! The deuce take all *fermatas*, I say!' In a most curious state of mind I hastened into the arbour along with the priest, and recognised at the first glance the sisters Lauretta and Teresina. The former was still shrieking and raging, and her sister still seriously remonstrating with her. Mine host, his bare arms crossed over his chest, was looking on laughing, whilst a girl was placing fresh flasks on the table. No sooner did the sisters catch sight of me than they threw themselves upon me exclaiming, 'Ah! Signor Teodoro!' and covered me with caresses. The quarrel was forgotten. 'Here you have a composer,' said Lauretta to the abbot, 'as charming as an Italian and as strong as a German.' Both sisters, continually interrupting each other, began to recount the happy days we had spent together, to speak of my musical abilities whilst still a youth, of our practisings together, of the excellence of my compositions; never did they like singing anything else but what I had set. Teresina at length informed me that a manager had engaged her as his first singer in tragic casts for the next carnival; but she would give him to understand that she would only sing on condition that the composition of at least one tragic opera was intrusted to me. The tragic was above all others my special department, and so on, and so on. Lauretta on her part maintained that it would be a pity if I did not follow my bent for the light and the graceful, in a word, for *opera buffa*. She had been engaged as first lady singer for this species of composition; and that nobody but I should write the piece in which she was to appear was simply a matter of course. You may fancy what my feelings were as I stood between the two. In a word, you perceive that the company which I had joined was the same as that which Hummel painted, and that just at the moment when the priest is on the point of cutting short Lauretta's *fermata*."

"But did they not make any allusion," asked Edward, "to your departure from them, or to the scathing letter?" "Not with a single syllable," answered Theodore, "and you may be sure I didn't, for I had long before banished all animosity from my heart, and come to look back upon my adventure with the sisters as a merry prank. I did, however, so far revert to the subject that I related to the priest how that, several years before, exactly the same sort of mischance befell me in one of Anfossi's arias as had just befallen him. I painted the period of my connection with the sisters in tragi-comical colours, and, distributing many a keen side-blow, I let them feel the superiority, which the ripe experiences, both of life and of art, of the years that had elapsed in the interval had given me over them. 'And a good thing it was,' I concluded, 'that I did cut short that *fermata*, for it was evidently meant to last through eternity, and I am firmly of opinion that if I had left the singer alone, I should be sitting at the piano now.' 'But, signor,' replied the priest, 'what director is there who would dare to prescribe laws to the *prima donna*? Your offence was much more heinous than mine, you in the concert hall, and I here in the leafy arbour. Besides, I was only director in imagination; nobody need attach any importance to that, and if the sweet fiery glances of these heavenly eyes had not fascinated me, I should not have made an ass of myself.' The priest's last words proved tranquillising, for, although Lauretta's eyes had begun to flash with anger as the priest spoke, before he had finished she was quite appeased.

"We spent the evening together. Many changes take place in fourteen years, which was the interval that had passed since I had seen my fair friends. Lauretta, although looking somewhat older, was still not devoid of charms. Teresina had worn better, without losing her graceful form. Both were dressed in rather gay colours, and their manners were just the same as before, that is, fourteen years younger than the ladies themselves. At my request Teresina sang some of the serious songs that had once so deeply affected me, but I fancied that they sounded differently from what they did when I first heard them; and Lauretta's singing too, although her voice had not appreciably lost anything, either in power or in compass, seemed to me to be quite different from my recollection of it of former times The sisters' behaviour towards me, their feigned ecstasies, their rude admiration, which, however, took the shape of gracious patronage, had done much to put me in a bad humour, and now the obtrusiveness of this comparison between the images in my mind and the not over and above pleasing reality, tended to put me in a still worse. The droll priest, who in all the sweetest words you can imagine was playing the *amoroso* to both sisters at once, as well as frequent applications to the good wine, at length restored me to good humour, so that we spent a very pleasant evening in perfect concord and gaiety. The sisters were most pressing in their invitations to me to go home with them, that we might at once talk over the parts which I was to set for them and so concert measures accordingly. I left Rome without taking any further steps to find out their place of abode."

"And yet, after all," said Edward, "it is to them that you owe the awakening of your genius for music." "That I admit," replied Theodore, "I owed them that and a host of good melodies besides, and that is just the reason why I did not want to see them again. Every composer can recall certain impressions which time does not obliterate. The spirit of music spake, and his voice was the creative word which suddenly awakened the kindred spirit slumbering in the breast of the artist; then the latter rose like a sun which can nevermore set. Thus it is unquestionably true that all melodies which, stirred up in this way, proceed from the depths of the composer's being, seem to us to belong to the singer alone who fanned the first spark within us. We hear her voice and record only what she has sung. It is, however, the inheritance of us weak mortals that, clinging to the clods, we are only too fain to draw down what is above the earth into the miserable narrowness characteristic of things of the earth. Thus it comes to pass that the singer becomes our lover—or even our wife. The spell is broken, and the melody of her nature, which formerly revealed glorious things, is now prostituted to complaints about broken soup-plates or ink-stains in new linen. Happy is the composer who never again so long as he lives sets eyes upon the woman who by virtue of some mysterious power enkindled in him the flame of music. Even though the young artist's heart may be rent by pain and despair when the moment comes for parting from his lovely enchantress, nevertheless her form will continue to exist as a divinely beautiful strain which lives on and on in the pride of youth and beauty, engendering melodies in which time after time he perceives the lady of his love. But what is she else if not the Highest Ideal which, working its way from within outwards, is at length reflected in the external independent form?"

"A strange theory, but yet plausible," was Edward's comment, as the two friends, arm in arm, passed out from Sala Tarone's into the street.

* * * * * * *

SIGNOR FORMICA.

I.

The celebrated painter Salvator Rosa comes to Rome, and is attacked by a dangerous illness. What befalls him in this illness.

Celebrated people commonly have many ill things said of them, whether well-founded or not And no exception was made in the case of that admirable painter Salvator Rosa, whose living pictures cannot fail to impart a keen and characteristic delight to those who look upon them.

At the time that Salvator's fame was ringing through Naples, Rome, and Tuscany—nay, through all Italy, and painters who were desirous of gaining applause were striving to imitate his peculiar and unique style, his malicious and envious rivals were laboring to spread abroad all sorts of evil reports intended to sully with ugly black stains the glorious splendor of his artistic fame. They affirmed that he had at a former period of his life belonged to a company of banditti, and that it was to his experiences during this lawless time that he owed all the wild, fierce, fantastically-attired figures which he introduced into his pictures, just as the gloomy fearful wildernesses of his landscapes—the *selve selvagge* (savage woods)—to use Dante's expression, were faithful representations of the haunts where they lay hidden. What was worse still, they openly charged him with having been concerned in the atrocious and bloody revolt which had been set on foot by the notorious Masaniello in Naples. They even described the share he had taken in it, down to the minutest details.

The rumor ran that Aniello Falcone, the painter of battle-pieces, one of the best of Salvator's masters, had been stung into fury and filled with bloodthirsty vengeance because the Spanish soldiers had slain one of his relatives in a hand-to-hand encounter. Without delay he leagued together a band of daring spirits, mostly young painters, put arms into their hands, and gave them the name of the "Company of Death." And in truth this band inspired all the fear and consternation suggested by its terrible name. At all hours of the day they traversed the streets of Naples in little companies, and cut down without mercy every Spaniard whom they met. They did more—they forced their way into the holy sanctuaries, and relentlessly murdered their unfortunate foes whom terror had driven to seek refuge there. At night they gathered round their chief, the bloody-minded madman Masaniello, and painted him by torchlight, so that in a short time there were hundreds of these little pictures circulating in Naples and the neighbourhood.

This is the ferocious band of which Salvator Rosa was alleged to have been a member, working hard at butchering his fellow-men by day, and by night working just as hard at painting. The truth about him has however been stated by a celebrated art-critic, Taillasson, I believe. His works are characterised by defiant originality, and by fantastic energy both of conception and of execution. He delighted to study Nature, not in the lovely attractiveness of green meadows, flourishing fields, sweet-smelling groves, murmuring springs, but in the sublime as seen in towering masses of rock, in the wild sea-shore, in savage inhospitable forests; and the voices that he loved to hear were not the whisperings of the evening breeze or the musical rustle of leaves, but the roaring of the hurricane and the thunder of the cataract. To one viewing his desolate landscapes, with the strange savage figures stealthily moving about in them, here singly, there in troops, the uncomfortable thoughts arise unbidden, "Here's where a fearful murder took place, there's where the bloody corpse was hurled into the ravine," etc.

Admitting all this, and even that Taillasson is further right when he maintains that Salvator's "Plato," nay, that even his "Holy St. John proclaiming the Advent of the Saviour in the Wilderness," look just a little like highway robbers—admitting this, I say, it is nevertheless unjust to argue from the character of the works to the character of the artist himself, and to assume that he, who represents with lifelike fidelity what is savage and terrible, must himself have been a savage, terrible man. He who prates most about the sword is often he who wields it the worst; he who feels in the depths of his soul all the horrors of a bloody deed, so that, taking the palette or the pencil or the pen in his hand, he is able to give living form to his feelings, is often the one least capable of practising similar deeds. Enough! I don't believe a single word of all those evil reports, by which men sought to brand the excellent Salvator an abandoned murderer and robber, and I hope that you, kindly reader, will share my opinion. Otherwise, I see grounds for fearing that you might perhaps entertain some doubts respecting what I am about to tell you of this artist; the Salvator I wish to put before you in this tale—that is, according to my conception of him—is a man bubbling over with the exuberance of life and fiery energy, but at the same time a man endowed with the noblest and most loyal character—a character, which, like that of all men who think and feel deeply, is able even to control that bitter irony which arises from a clear view of the significance of life. I need scarcely add that Salvator was no less renowned as a poet and musician than as a painter. His genius was revealed in magnificent refractions. I repeat again, I do not believe that Salvator had any share in Masaniello's bloody deeds; on the contrary, I think it was the horrors of that fearful time which drove him from Naples to Rome, where he arrived a poor poverty-stricken fugitive, just at the time that Masaniello fell.

Not over well dressed, and with a scanty purse containing not more than a few bright sequins in his pocket, he crept through the gate just after nightfall. Somehow or other, he didn't exactly know how, he wandered as far as the Piazza Navona. In better times he had once lived there in a large house near the Pamfili Palace. With an ill-tempered growl, he gazed up at the large plate-glass windows glistening and glimmering in the moonlight "Hm!" he exclaimed peevishly, "it'll cost me dozens of yards of coloured canvas before I can open my studio up there again." But all at once he felt as if paralysed in every limb, and at the same moment more weak and feeble than he had ever felt in his life before. "But shall I," he murmured between his teeth as he sank down upon the stone steps leading up to the house door, "shall I really be able to finish canvas enough in the way the fools want it done? Hm! I have a notion that that will be the end of it!"

A cold cutting night wind blew down the street. Salvator recognised the necessity of seeking a shelter. Rising with difficulty, he staggered on into the Corso, and then turned into the Via Bergognona. At length he stopped before a little house with only a couple of windows, inhabited by a poor widow and her two daughters. This women had taken him in for little pay the first time he came to Rome, an unknown stranger noticed of nobody; and so he hoped again to find a lodging with her, such as would be best suited to the sad condition in which he then was.

He knocked confidently at the door, and several times called out his name aloud. At last he heard the old woman slowly and reluctantly wakening up out of her sleep. She shuffled to the window in her slippers, and began to rain down a shower of abuse upon the knave who was come to worry her in this way in the middle of the night; her house was not a wine-shop, &c., &c. Then there ensued a good deal of cross-questioning before she recognised her former lodger's voice; but on Salvator's complaining that he had fled from Naples and was unable to find a shelter in Rome, the old dame cried, "By all the blessed saints of Heaven! Is that you, Signor Salvator? Well now, your little room up above, that looks on to the court, is still standing empty, and the old fig-tree has pushed its branches right through the window and into the room, so that you can sit and work like as if you was in a beautiful cool arbour. Ay, and how pleased my girls will be that you have come back again, Signor Salvator. But, d'ye know, my Margarita's grown a big girl and fine-looking? You won't give her any more rides on your knee now. And—and your little pussy, just fancy, three months ago she choked herself with a fish-bone. Ah well, we all shall come to the grave at last. But, d'ye know, my fat neighbour, who you so often laughed at and so often painted in such funny ways—d'ye know, she *did* marry that young fellow, Signor Luigi, after all. Ah well! *nozze e magistrati sono da dio destinati* (marriages and magistrates are made in heaven) they say."

"But," cried Salvator, interrupting the old woman, "but, Signora Caterina, I entreat you by the blessed saints, do, pray, let me in, and then tell me all about your fig-tree and your daughters, your cat and your fat neighbour—I am perishing of weariness and cold."

"Bless me, how impatient we are," rejoined the old dame; "*Chi va piano va sano, chi va presto more lesto* (more haste less speed, take things cool and live longer), I tell you. But you are tired, you are cold; where are the keys? quick with the keys!"

But the old woman still had to wake up her daughters and kindle a fire—but oh! she was such a long time about it—such a long, long time. At last she opened the door and let poor Salvator in; but scarcely had he crossed the threshold than, overcome by fatigue and illness, he dropped on the floor as if dead. Happily the widow's son, who generally lived at Tivoli, chanced to be at his mother's that night He was at once turned out of his bed to make room for the sick guest, which he willingly submitted to.

The old woman was very fond of Salvator, putting him, as far as his artistic powers went, above all the painters in the world; and in everything that he did she also took the greatest pleasure. She was therefore quite beside herself to see him in this lamentable condition, and wanted to run off to the neighbouring monastery to fetch her father confessor, that he might come and fight against the adverse power of the disease with consecrated candles or some powerful amulet or other. On the other hand, her son thought it would be almost better to see about getting an experienced physician at once, and off he ran there and then to the Spanish Square, where he knew the distinguished Doctor Splendiano Accoramboni dwelt. No sooner did the doctor learn that the painter Salvator Rosa lay ill in the Via Bergognona than he at once declared himself ready to call early and see the patient.

Salvator lay unconscious, struck down by a most severe attack of fever. The old dame had hung up two or three pictures of saints above his bed, and was praying fervently. The girls, though bathed in tears, exerted themselves from time to time to get the sick man to swallow a few drops of the cooling lemonade which they had made, whilst their brother, who had taken his place at the head of the bed, wiped the cold sweat from his brow. And so morning found them, when with a loud creak the door opened, and the distinguished Doctor Splendiano Accoramboni entered the room.

If Salvator had not been so seriously ill that the two girls' hearts were melted in grief, they would, I think, for they were in general frolicsome and saucy, have enjoyed a hearty laugh at the Doctor's extraordinary appearance, instead of retiring shyly, as they did, into the corner, greatly alarmed. It will indeed be worth while to describe the outward appearance of the little man who presented himself at Dame Caterina's in the Via Bergognona in the grey of the morning. In spite of all his excellent capabilities for growth, Doctor Splendiano Accoramboni had not been able to advance beyond the respectable stature of four feet Moreover, in the days of his youth, he had been distinguished for his elegant figure, so that, before his head, always indeed somewhat ill-shaped, and his big cheeks, and his stately double chin had put on too much fat, before his nose had grown bulky and spread owing to overmuch indulgence in Spanish snuff, and before his little belly had assumed the shape of a wine-tub from too much fattening on macaroni, the priestly cut of garments, which he at that time had affected, had suited him down to the ground. He was then in truth a pretty little man, and accordingly the Roman ladies had styled him their *caro puppazetto* (sweet little pet).

That however was now a thing of the past. A German painter, seeing Doctor Splendiano walking across the Spanish Square, said—and he was perhaps not far wrong—that it looked as if some strapping fellow of six feet or so had walked away from his own head, which had fallen on the shoulders of a little marionette clown, who now had to carry it about as his own. This curious little figure walked about in patchwork—an immense quantity of pieces of Venetian damask of a large flower pattern that had been cut up in making a dressing-gown; high up round his waist he had buckled a broad leather belt, from which an excessively long rapier hung; whilst his snow-white wig was surmounted by a high conical cap, not unlike the obelisk in St. Peter's Square. Since the said wig, like a piece of texture all tumbled and tangled, spread out thick and wide all over his back, it might very well be taken for the cocoon out of which the fine silkworm had crept.

The worthy Splendiano Accoramboni stared through his big, bright spectacles, with his eyes wide open, first at his patient, then at Dame Caterina. Calling her aside, he croaked with bated breath, "There lies our talented painter Salvator Rosa, and he's lost if my skill doesn't save him, Dame Caterina. Pray tell me when he came to lodge with you? Did he bring many beautiful large pictures with him?"

"Ah! my dear Doctor," replied Dame Caterina, "the poor fellow only came last night. And as for pictures—why, I don't know nothing about them; but there's a big box below, and Salvator begged me to take very good care of it, before he became senseless like what he now is. I daresay there's a fine picture packed in it, as he painted in Naples."

What Dame Caterina said was, however, a falsehood; but we shall soon see that she had good reasons for imposing upon the Doctor in this way.

"Good! Very good!" said the Doctor, simpering and stroking his beard; then, with as much solemnity as his long rapier, which kept catching in all the chairs and tables he came near, would allow, he approached the sick man and felt his pulse, snorting and wheezing, so that it had a most curious effect in the midst of the reverential silence which had fallen upon all the rest. Then he ran over in Greek and Latin the names of a hundred and twenty diseases that Salvator had not, then almost as many which he might have had, and concluded by saying that on the spur of the moment he didn't recollect the name of his disease, but that he would within a short time find a suitable one for it, and along therewith, the proper remedies as well. Then he took his departure with the same solemnity with which he had entered, leaving them all full of trouble and anxiety.

At the bottom of the steps the Doctor requested to see Salvator's box; Dame Caterina showed him one—in which were two or three of her deceased husband's cloaks now laid aside, and some old worn-out shoes. The Doctor smilingly tapped the box, on this side and on that, and remarked in a tone of satisfaction "We shall see! we shall see!" Some hours later he returned with a very beautiful name for his patient's disease, and brought with him some big bottles of an evil-smelling potion, which he directed to be given to the patient constantly. This was a work of no little trouble, for Salvator showed the greatest aversion for—utter loathing of the stuff, which looked, and smelt, and tasted, as if it had been concocted from Acheron itself. Whether it was that the disease, since it had now received a name, and in consequence really signified something, had only just begun to put forth its virulence, or whether it was that Splendiano's potion made too much of a disturbance inside the patient—it is at any rate certain that the poor painter grew weaker and weaker from day to day, from hour to hour. And notwithstanding Doctor Splendiano Accoramboni's assurance that, after the vital process had reached a state of perfect equilibrium, he would give it a new start like the pendulum of a clock, they were all very doubtful as to Salvator's recovery, and thought that the Doctor had perhaps already given the pendulum such a violent start that the mechanism was quite impaired.

Now it happened one day that when Salvator seemed scarcely able to move a finger he was suddenly seized with the paroxysm of fever; in a momentary accession of fictitious strength he leapt out of bed, seized the full medicine bottles, and hurled them fiercely out of the window. Just at this moment Doctor Splendiano Accoramboni was entering the house, when two or three bottles came bang upon his head, smashing all to pieces, whilst the brown liquid ran in streams all down his face, and wig, and ruff. Hastily rushing into the house, he screamed like a madman, "Signer Salvator has gone out of his mind, he's become insane; no skill can save him now, he'll be dead in ten minutes. Give me the picture, Dame Caterina, give me the picture—it's mine, the scanty reward of all my trouble. Give me the picture, I say."

But when Dame Caterina opened the box, and Doctor Splendiano saw nothing but the old cloaks and torn shoes, his eyes spun round in his head like a pair of fire-wheels; he gnashed his teeth; he stamped; he consigned poor Salvator, the widow, and all the family to the devil; then he rushed out of the house like an arrow from a bow, or as if he had been shot from a cannon.

After the violence of the paroxysm had spent itself, Salvator again relapsed into a death-like condition. Dame Caterina was fully persuaded that his end was really come, and away she sped as fast as she could to the monastery, to fetch Father Boniface, that he might come and administer the sacrament to the dying man. Father Boniface came and looked at the sick man; he said he was well acquainted with the peculiar signs which approaching death is wont to stamp upon the human countenance, but that for the present there were no indications of them on the face of the insensible Salvator. Something might still be done, and he would procure help at once, only Doctor Splendiano Accoramboni with his Greek names and infernal medicines was not to be allowed to cross the threshold again. The good Father set out at once, and we shall see later that he kept his word about sending the promised help.

Salvator recovered consciousness again; he fancied he was lying in a beautiful flower-scented arbour, for green boughs and leaves were interlacing above his head. He felt a salutary warmth glowing in his veins, but it seemed to him as if somehow his left arm was bound fast "Where am I?" he asked in a faint voice. Then a handsome young man, who had stood at his bedside, but whom he had not noticed until just now, threw himself upon his knees, and grasping Salvator's right hand, kissed it and bathed it with tears, as he cried again and again, "Oh! my dear sir! my noble master! now it's all right; you are saved, you'll get better."

"But do tell me"—began Salvator, when the young man begged him not to exert himself, for he was too weak to talk; he would tell him all that had happened. "You see, my esteemed and excellent sir," began the young man, "you see, you were very ill when you came from Naples, but your condition was not, I warrant, by any means so dangerous but that a few simple remedies would soon have set you, with your strong constitution, on your legs again, had you not through Carlos's well-intentioned blunder in running off for the nearest physician fallen into the hands of the redoubtable Pyramid Doctor, who was making all preparations for bringing you to your grave."

"What do you say?" exclaimed Salvator, laughing heartily, notwithstanding the feeble state he was in. "What do you say?—the Pyramid Doctor? Ay, ay, although I was very ill, I saw that the little knave in damask patchwork, who condemned me to drink his horrid, loathsome devil's brew, wore on his head the obelisk from St. Peter's Square—and so that's why you call him the Pyramid Doctor?"

"Why, good heavens!" said the young man, likewise laughing, "why, Doctor Splendiano Accoramboni must have come to see you in his ominous conical nightcap; and, do you know, you may see it flashing every morning from his window in the Spanish Square like a portentous meteor. But it's not by any means owing to this cap that he's called the Pyramid Doctor; for that there's quite another reason. Doctor Splendiano is a great lover of pictures, and possesses in truth quite a choice collection, which he has gained by a practice of a peculiar nature. With eager cunning he lies in wait for painters and their illnesses. More especially he loves to get foreign artists into his toils; let them but eat an ounce or two of macaroni too much, or drink a glass more Syracuse than is altogether good for them, he will afflict them with first one and then the other disease, designating it by a formidable name, and proceeding at once to cure them of it. He generally bargains for a picture as the price of his attendance; and as it is only specially obstinate constitutions which are able to withstand his powerful remedies, it generally happens that he gets his picture out of the chattels left by the poor foreigner, who meanwhile has been carried to the Pyramid of Cestius, and buried there. It need hardly be said that Signor Splendiano always picks out the best of the pictures the painter has finished, and also does not forget to bid the men take several others along with it. The cemetery near the Pyramid of Cestius is Doctor Splendiano Accoramboni's corn-field, which he diligently cultivates, and for that reason he is called the Pyramid Doctor. Dame Caterina had taken great pains, of course with the best intentions, to make the Doctor believe that you had brought a fine picture with you; you may imagine therefore with what eagerness he concocted his potions for you. It was a fortunate thing that in the paroxysm of fever you threw the Doctor's bottles at his head, it was also a fortunate thing that he left you in anger, and no less fortunate was it that Dame Caterina, who believed you were in the agonies of death, fetched Father Boniface to come and administer to you the sacrament. Father Boniface understands something of the art of healing; he formed a correct diagnosis of your condition and fetched me"——

"Then you also are a doctor?" asked Salvator in a faint whining tone.

"No," replied the young man, a deep blush mantling his cheeks, "no, my estimable and worthy sir, I am not in the least a doctor like Signor Splendiano Accoramboni; I am however a chirurgeon. I felt as if I should sink into the earth with fear—with joy—when Father Boniface came and told me that Salvator Rosa lay sick unto death in the Via Bergognona, and required my help. I hastened here, opened a vein in your left arm, and you were saved. Then we brought you up into this cool airy room that you formerly occupied. Look, there's the easel which you left behind you; yonder are a few sketches which Dame Caterina has treasured up as if they were relics. The virulence of your disease is subdued; simple remedies such as Father Boniface can prepare is all that you want, except good nursing, to bring back your strength again. And now permit me once more to kiss this hand—this creative hand that charms from Nature her deepest secrets and clothes them in living form. Permit poor Antonio Scacciati to pour out all the gratitude and immeasurable joy of his heart that Heaven has granted him to save the life of our great and noble painter, Salvator Rosa." Therewith the young surgeon threw himself on his knees again, and, seizing Salvator's hand, kissed it and bathed it in tears as before.

"I don't understand," said the artist, raising himself up a little, though with considerable difficulty, "I don't understand, my dear Antonio, what it is that is so especially urging you to show me all this respect. You are, you say, a chirurgeon, and we don't in a general way find this trade going hand in hand with art——"

"As soon," replied the young man, casting down his eyes, "as soon as you have picked up your strength again, my dear sir, I have a good deal to tell you that now lies heavy on my heart."

"Do so," said Salvator; "you may have every confidence in me—that you may, for I don't know that any man's face has made a more direct appeal to my heart than yours. The more I look at you the more plainly I seem to trace in your features a resemblance to that incomparable young painter—I mean Sanzio." Antonio's eyes were lit up with a proud, radiant light—he vainly struggled for words with which to express his feelings.

At this moment Dame Caterina appeared, followed by Father Boniface, who brought Salvator a medicine which he had mixed scientifically according to prescription, and which the patient swallowed with more relish and felt to have a more beneficial effect upon him than the Acheronian waters of the Pyramid Doctor Splendiano Accoramboni.

II.

By Salvator Rosa's intervention Antonio Scacciati attains to a high honour. Antonio discloses the cause of his persistent trouble to Salvator, who consoles him and promises to help him.

And Antonio's words proved true. The simple but salutary remedies of Father Boniface, the careful nursing of good Dame Caterina and her daughters, the warmer weather which now came—all co-operated so well together with Salvator's naturally robust constitution that he soon felt sufficiently well to think about work again; first of all he designed a few sketches which he thought of working out afterwards.

Antonio scarcely ever left Salvator's room; he was all eyes when the painter drew out his sketches; whilst his judgment in respect to many points showed that he must have been initiated into the secrets of art.

"See here," said Salvator to him one day, "see here, Antonio, you understand art matters so well that I believe you have not merely cultivated your excellent judgment as a critic, but must have wielded the brush as well."

"You will remember," rejoined Antonio, "how I told you, my dear sir, when you were just about coming to yourself again after your long unconsciousness, that I had several things to tell you which lay heavy on my mind. Now is the time for me to unfold all my heart to you. You must know then, that though I am called Antonio Scacciati, the chirurgeon, who opened the vein in your arm for you, I belong also entirely to art—to the art which, after bidding eternal farewell to my hateful trade, I intend to devote myself for once and for all."

"Ho! ho!" exclaimed Salvator, "Ho! ho! Antonio, weigh well what you are about to do. You are a clever chirurgeon, and perhaps will never be anything more than a bungling painter all your life long; for, with your permission, as young as you are, you are decidedly too old to begin to use the charcoal now. Believe me, a man's whole lifetime is scarce long enough to acquire a knowledge of the True—still less the practical ability to represent it."

"Ah! but, my dear sir," replied Antonio, smiling blandly, "don't imagine that I should now have come to entertain the foolish idea of taking up the difficult art of painting had I not practised it already on every possible occasion from my very childhood. In spite of the fact that my father obstinately kept me away from everything connected with art, yet Heaven was graciously pleased to throw me in the way of some celebrated artists. I must tell you that the great Annibal interested himself in the orphan boy, and also that I may with justice call myself Guido Reni's pupil."

"Well then," said Salvator somewhat sharply, a way of speaking he sometimes had, "well then, my good Antonio, you have indeed had great masters, and so it cannot fail but that, without detriment to your surgical practice, you must have been a great pupil. Only I don't understand how you, a faithful disciple of the gentle, elegant Guido, whom you perhaps outdo in elegance in your own pictures—for pupils do do those sort of things in their enthusiasm—how you can find any pleasure in my productions, and can really regard me as a master in the Art."

At these words, which indeed sounded a good deal like derisive mockery, the hot blood rushed into the young man's face.

"Oh, let me lay aside all the diffidence which generally keeps my lips closed," he said, "and let me frankly lay bare the thoughts I have in my mind. I tell you, Salvator, I have never honoured any master from the depths of my soul as I do you. What I am amazed at in your works is the sublime greatness of conception which is often revealed You grasp the deepest secrets of Nature: you comprehend the mysterious hieroglyphics of her rocks, of her trees, and of her waterfalls, you hear her sacred voice, you understand her language, and possess the power to write down what she has said to you. Verily I can call your bold free style of painting nothing else than writing down. Man alone and his doings does not suffice you; you behold him only in the midst of Nature, and in so far as his essential character is conditioned by natural phenomena; and in these facts I see the reason why you are only truly great in landscapes, Salvator, with their wonderful figures. Historical painting confines you within limits which clog your imagination to the detriment of your genius for reproducing your higher intuitions of Nature."

"That's talk you've picked up from envious historical painters," said Salvator, interrupting his young companion; "like them, Antonio, you throw me the choice bone of landscape-painting that I may gnaw away at it, and so spare their own good flesh. Perhaps I do understand the human figure and all that is dependent upon it. But this senseless repetition of others' words"——

"Don't be angry," continued Antonio, "don't be angry, my good sir; I am not blindly repeating anybody's words, and I should not for a moment think of trusting to the judgment of our painters here in Rome at any rate. Who can help greatly admiring the bold draughtsmanship, the powerful expression, but above all the living movement of your fingers? It's plain to see that you don't work from a stiff, inflexible model, or even from a dead skeleton form; it is evident that you yourself are your own breathing, living model, and that when you sketch or paint, you have the figure you want to put on your canvas reflected in a great mirror opposite to you."

"The devil! Antonio," exclaimed Salvator, laughing, "I believe you must often have had a peep into my studio when I was not aware of it, since you have such an accurate knowledge of what goes on within."

"Perhaps I may," replied Antonio; "but let me go on. I am not by a long way so anxious to classify, the pictures which your powerful mind suggests to you as are those pedantic critics who take such great pains in this line. In fact, I think that the word 'landscape,' as generally employed, has but an indifferent application to your productions; I should prefer to call them historical representations in the highest sense of the word. If we fancy that this or the other rock or this or the other tree is gazing at us like a gigantic being with thoughtful earnest eyes, so again, on the other hand, this or the other group of fantastically attired men resembles some remarkable stone which has been endowed with life; all Nature, breathing and moving in harmonious unity, lends accents to the sublime thought which leapt into existence in your mind. This is the spirit in which I have studied your pictures, and so in this way it is, my grand and noble master, that I owe to you my truer perceptions in matters of art. But pray don't imagine that I have fallen into childish imitation. However much I would like to possess the free bold pencil that you possess, I do not attempt to conceal the fact that Nature's colours appear to me different from what I see them in your pictures. Although it is useful, I think, for the sake of acquiring technique, for the pupil to imitate the style of this or that master, yet, so soon as he comes to stand in any sense on his own feet, he ought to aim at representing Nature as he himself sees her. Nothing but this true method of perception, this unity with oneself, can give rise to character and truth. Guido shared these sentiments; and that fiery man Preti, who, as you are aware, is called *Il Calabrese*—a painter who certainly, more than any other man, has reflected upon his art—also warned me against all imitation. Now you know, Salvator, why I so much respect you, without imitating you."

Whilst the young man had been speaking, Salvator had kept his eyes fixed unchangeably upon him; he now clasped him tumultuously to his heart.

"Antonio," he then said, "what you have just now said are wise and thoughtful words. Young as you are, you are nevertheless, so far as the true perception of art is concerned, a long way ahead of many of our old and much vaunted masters, who have a good deal of stupid foolish twaddle about their painting, but never get at the true root of the matter. Body alive, man! When you were talking about my pictures, I then began to understand myself for the first time, I believe; and because you do not imitate my style,—do not, like a good many others, take a tube of black paint in your hand, or dab on a few glaring colours, or even make two or three crippled figures with repulsive faces look up from the midst of filth and dirt, and then say, 'There's a Salvator for you!'—just for these very reasons I think a good deal of you. I tell you, my lad, you'll not find a more faithful friend than I am—that I can promise you with all my heart and soul."

Antonio was beside himself with joy at the kind way in which the great painter thus testified to his interest in him. Salvator expressed an earnest desire to see his pictures. Antonio took him there and then to his studio.

Salvator had in truth expected to find something fairly good from the young man who spoke so intelligently about art, and who, it appeared, had a good deal in him; but nevertheless he was greatly surprised at the sight of Antonio's fine pictures. Everywhere he found boldness in conception, and correctness in drawing; and the freshness of the colouring, the good taste in the arrangement of the drapery, the uncommon delicacy of the extremities, the exquisite grace of the heads, were all so many evidences that he was no unworthy pupil of the great Reni. But Antonio had avoided this master's besetting sin of an endeavour, only too conspicuous, to sacrifice expression to beauty. It was plain that Antonio was aiming to reach Annibal's strength, without having as yet succeeded.

Salvator spent some considerable time of thoughtful silence in the examination of each of the pictures. Then he said, "Listen, Antonio: it is indeed undeniable that you were born to follow the noble art of painting. For not only has Nature endowed you with the creative spirit from which the finest thoughts pour forth in an inexhaustible stream, but she has also granted you the rare ability to surmount in a short space of time the difficulties of technique. It would only be false flattery if I were to tell you that you had yet advanced to the level of your masters, that you are yet equal to Guido's exquisite grace or to Annibal's strength; but certain I am that you excel by a long way all the painters who hold up their heads so proudly in the Academy of St. Luke here—Tiarini, Gessi, Sementa, and all the rest of them, not even excepting Lanfranco himself, for he only understands fresco-painting. And yet, Antonio, and yet, if I were in your place, I should deliberate awhile before throwing away the lancet altogether, and confining myself entirely to the pencil That sounds rather strange, but listen to me. Art seems to be having a bad time of it just now, or rather the devil seems to be very busy amongst our painters now-a-days, bravely setting them together by the ears. If you cannot make up your mind to put up with all sorts of annoyances, to endure more and more scorn and contumely in proportion as you advance in art, and as your fame spreads to meet with malicious scoundrels everywhere, who with a friendly face will force themselves upon you in order to ruin you the more surely afterwards,—if you cannot, I say, make up your mind to endure all this—let painting alone. Think of the fate of your teacher, the great Annibal, whom a rascally band of rivals malignantly persecuted in Naples, so that he did not receive one single commission for a great work, being everywhere rejected with contempt; and this is said to have been instrumental in bringing about his early death. Think of what happened to Domenichino when he was painting the dome of the chapel of St. Januarius. Didn't the villains of painters—I won't mention a single name, not even the rascals Belisario and Ribera—didn't they bribe Domenichino's servant to strew ashes in the lime? So the plaster wouldn't stick fast on the walls, and the painting had no stability. Think of all that, and examine yourself well whether your spirit is strong enough to endure things like that, for if not, your artistic power will be broken, and along with the resolute courage for work you will also lose your ability."

"But, Salvator," replied Antonio, "it would hardly be possible for me to have more scorn and contumely to endure, supposing I took up painting entirely and exclusively, then I have already endured whilst merely a chirurgeon. You have been pleased with my pictures, you have indeed! and at the same time declared from inner conviction that I am capable of doing better things than several of our painters of the Academy. But these are just the men who turn up their noses at all that I have industriously produced, and say contemptuously, 'Do look, here's our chirurgeon wants to be a painter!' And for this very reason my resolve is only the more unshaken; I will sever myself from a trade that grows with every day more hateful. Upon you, my honoured master, I now stake all my hopes. Your word is powerful; if you would speak a good word for me, you might overthrow my envious persecutors at a single blow, and put me in the place where I ought to be."

"You repose great confidence in me," rejoined Salvator. "But now that we thoroughly understand each other's views on painting, and I have seen your works, I don't really know that there is anybody for whom I would rather take up the cudgels than for you."

Salvator once more inspected Antonio's pictures, and stopped before one representing a "Magdalene at the Saviour's feet," which he especially praised.

"In this Magdalene," he said, "you have deviated from the usual mode of representation. Your Magdalene is not a thoughtful virgin, but a lovely artless child rather, and yet she is such a marvellous child that hardly anybody else but Guido could have painted her. There is a unique charm in her dainty figure; you must have painted with inspiration; and, if I mistake not, the original of this Magdalene is alive and to be found in Rome. Come, confess, Antonio, you are in love!"

Antonio's eyes sought the ground, whilst he said in a low shy voice, "Nothing escapes your penetration, my dear sir; perhaps it is as you say, but do not blame me for it. That picture I set the highest store by, and hitherto I have guarded it as a holy secret from all men's eyes."

"What do you say?" interrupted Salvator. "None of the painters here have seen your picture?"

"No, not one," was Antonio's reply.

"All right then, Antonio," continued Salvator, his eyes sparkling with delight "Very well then, you may rely upon it, I will overwhelm your envious overweening persecutors, and get you the honour you deserve. Intrust your picture to me; bring it to my studio secretly by night, and then leave all the rest to me. Will you do so?"

"Gladly, with all my heart," replied Antonio. "And now I should very much like to talk to you about my love-troubles as well; but I feel as if I ought not to do so to-day, after we have opened our minds to each other on the subject of art. I also entreat you to grant me your assistance both in word and deed later on in this matter of my love."

"I am at your service," said Salvator, "for both, both when and where you require me." Then as he was going away, he once more turned round and said, smiling, "See here, Antonio, when you disclosed to me the fact that you were a painter, I was very sorry that I had spoken about your resemblance to Sanzio. I took it for granted that you were as silly as most of our young folk, who, if they bear but the slightest resemblance in the face to any great master, at once trim their beard or hair as he does, and from this cause fancy it is their business to imitate the style of the master in their art achievements, even though it is a manifest violation of their natural talents to do so. Neither of us has mentioned Raphael's name, but I assure you that I have discerned in your pictures clear indications that you have grasped the full significance of the inimitable thoughts which are reflected in the works of this the greatest of the painters of the age. You understand Raphael, and would give me a different answer from what Velasquez did when I asked him not long ago what he thought of Sanzio. 'Titian,' he replied, 'is the greatest painter; Raphael knows nothing about carnation.' This Spaniard, methinks, understands flesh but not criticism; and yet these men in St. Luke elevate him to the clouds because he once painted cherries which the sparrows picked at."

It happened not many days afterwards that the Academicians of St. Luke met together in their church to prove the works which had been announced for exhibition. There too Salvator had sent Scacciati's fine picture. In spite of themselves the painters were greatly struck with its grace and power; and from all lips there was heard nothing but the most extravagant praise when Salvator informed them that he had brought the picture with him from Naples, as the legacy of a young painter who had been cut off in the pride of his days.

It was not long before all Rome was crowding to see and admire the picture of the young unknown painter who had died so young; it was unanimously agreed that no such work had been done since Guido Reni's time; some even went so far in their just enthusiasm as to place this exquisitely lovely Magdalene before Guido's creations of a similar kind. Amongst the crowd of people who were always gathered round Scacciati's picture, Salvator one day observed a man who, besides presenting a most extraordinary appearance, behaved as if he were crazy. Well advanced in years, he was tall, thin as a spindle, with a pale face, a long sharp nose, a chin equally as long, ending moreover in a little pointed beard, and with grey, gleaming eyes. On the top of his light sand-coloured wig he had set a high hat with a magnificent feather; he wore a short dark red mantle or cape with many bright buttons, a sky-blue doublet slashed in the Spanish style, immense leather gauntlets with silver fringes, a long rapier at his side, light grey stockings drawn up above his bony knees and gartered with yellow ribbons, whilst he had bows of the same sort of yellow ribbon on his shoes.

This remarkable figure was standing before the picture like one enraptured: he raised himself on tiptoe; he stooped down till he became quite small; then he jumped up with both feet at once, heaved deep sighs, groaned, nipped his eyes so close together that the tears began to trickle down his cheeks, opened them wide again, fixed his gaze immovably upon the charming Magdalene, sighed again, lisped in a thin, querulous, mutilated voice, "*Ah! carissima—benedettissima! Ah! Marianna—Mariannina—bellissima*," &c. ("Oh! dearest—most adored! Ah! Marianna—sweet Marianna! my most beautiful!") Salvator, who had a mad fancy for such oddities, drew near to the old fellow, intending to engage him in conversation about Scacciati's work, which seemed to afford him so much exquisite delight Without paying any particular heed to Salvator, the old gentleman stood cursing his poverty, because he could not give a million sequins for the picture, and place it under lock and key where nobody could set their infernal eyes upon it. Then, hopping up and down again, he blessed the Virgin and all the holy saints that the reprobate artist who had painted the heavenly picture which was driving him to despair and madness was dead.

Salvator concluded that the man either was out of his mind, or was an Academician of St. Luke with whom he was unacquainted.

All Rome was full of Scacciati's wonderful picture; people could scarcely talk about anything else, and this of course was convincing proof of the excellence of the work. And when the painters were again assembled in the church of St. Luke, to decide about the admission of certain other pictures which had been announced for exhibition, Salvator Rosa all at once asked, whether the painter of the "Magdalene at the Saviour's Feet" was not worthy of being admitted a member of the Academy. They all with one accord, including even that hairsplitter in criticism, Baron Josépin, declared that such a great artist would have been an ornament to the Academy, and expressed their sorrow at his death in the choicest phrases, although, like the crazy old man, they were praising Heaven in their hearts that he was dead. Still more, they were so far carried away by their enthusiasm that they passed a resolution to the effect that the admirable young painter whom death had snatched away from art so early should be nominated a member of the Academy in his grave, and that masses should be read for the benefit of his soul in the church of St. Luke. They therefore begged Salvator to inform them what was the full name of the deceased, the date of his birth, the place where he was born, &c.

Then Salvator rose and said in a loud voice, "Signors, the honour you are anxious to render to a dead man you can more easily bestow upon a living man who walks in your midst. Learn that the 'Magdalene at the Saviour's Feet'—the picture which you so justly exalt above all other artistic productions that the last few years have given us, is not the work of a dead Neapolitan painter as I pretended (this I did simply to get an unbiassed judgment from you); that painting, that masterpiece, which all Rome is admiring, is from the hand of Signor Antonio Scacciati, the chirurgeon."

The painters sat staring at Salvator as if suddenly thunderstruck, incapable of either moving or uttering a single sound. He, however, after quietly exulting over their embarrassment for some minutes, continued, "Well now, signors, you would not tolerate the worthy Antonio amongst you because he is a chirurgeon; but I think that the illustrious Academy of St. Luke has great need of a surgeon to set the limbs of the many crippled figures which emerge from the studios of a good many amongst your number. But of course you will no longer scruple to do what you ought to have done long ago, namely, elect that excellent painter Antonio Scacciati a member of the Academy."

The Academicians, swallowing Salvator's bitter pill, feigned to be highly delighted that Antonio had in this way given such incontestable proofs of his talent, and with all due ceremony nominated him a member of the Academy.

As soon as it became known in Rome that Antonio was the author of the wonderful picture he was overwhelmed with congratulations, and even with commissions for great works, which poured in upon him from all sides. Thus by Salvator's shrewd and cunning stratagem the young man emerged all at once out of his obscurity, and with the first real step he took on his artistic career rose to great honour.

Antonio revelled in ecstasies of delight. So much the more therefore did Salvator wonder to see him, some days later, appear with his face pale and distorted, utterly miserable and woebegone. "Ah! Salvator!" said Antonio, "what advantage has it been to me that you have helped me to rise to a level far beyond my expectations, that I am now overwhelmed with praise and honour, that the prospect of a most successful artistic career is opening out before me? Oh! I am utterly miserable, for the picture to which, next to you, my dear sir, I owe my great triumph, has proved the source of my lasting misfortune."

"Stop!" replied Salvator, "don't sin against either your art or your picture. I don't believe a word about the terrible misfortune which, you say, has befallen you. You are in love, and I presume you can't get all your wishes gratified at once, on the spur of the moment; that's all it is. Lovers are like children; they scream and cry if anybody only just touches their doll. Have done, I pray you, with that lamentation, for I tell you I can't do with it. Come now, sit yourself down there and quietly tell me all about your fair Magdalene, and give me the history of your love affair, and let me know what are the stones of offence that we have to remove, for I promise you my help beforehand. The more adventurous the schemes are which we shall have to undertake, the more I shall like them. In fact, my blood is coursing hotly in my veins again, and my regimen requires that I engage in a few wild pranks. But go on with your story, Antonio, and as I said, let's have it quietly without any sighs and lamentations, without any Ohs! and Ahs!"

Antonio took his seat on the stool which Salvator had pushed up to the easel at which he was working, and began as follows:—

"There is a high house in the Via Ripetta, with a balcony which projects far over the street so as at once to strike the eye of any one entering through the Porta del Popolo, and there dwells perhaps the most whimsical oddity in all Rome,—an old bachelor with every fault that belongs to that class of persons—avaricious, vain, anxious to appear young, amorous, foppish. He is tall, as thin as a switch, wears a gay Spanish costume, a sandy wig, a conical hat, leather gauntlets, a rapier at his side"——

"Stop, stop!" cried Salvator, interrupting him, "excuse me a minute or two, Antonio." Then, turning about the picture at which he was painting, he seized his charcoal and in a few free bold strokes sketched on the back side of the canvas the eccentric old gentleman whom he had seen behaving like a crazed man in front of Antonio's picture.

"By all the saints!" cried Antonio, as he leapt to his feet, and, forgetful of his unhappiness, burst out into a loud laugh, "by all the saints! that's he! That's Signor Pasquale Capuzzi, whom I was just describing, that's he to the very T."

"So you see," said Salvator calmly, "that I am already acquainted with the worthy gentleman who most probably is your bitter enemy. But go on."

"Signor Pasquale Capuzzi," continued Antonio, "is as rich as Crœsus, but at the same time, as I just told you, a sordid miser and an incurable coxcomb. The best thing about him is that he loves art, particularly music and painting; but he mixes up so much folly with it all that even in these things there's no getting on with him. He considers himself the greatest musical composer in the world, and that there's not a singer in the Papal choir who can at all approach him. Accordingly he looks down upon our old Frescobaldi with contempt; and when the Romans talk about the wonderful charm of Ceccarelli's voice, he informs them that Ceccarelli knows as much about singing as a pair of top-boots, and that he, Capuzzi, knows which is the right way to fascinate the public. But as the first singer of the Pope bears the proud name of Signor Odoardo Ceccarelli di Merania, so our Capuzzi is greatly delighted when anybody calls him Signor Pasquale Capuzzi di Senigaglia; for it was in Senigaglia that he was born, and the popular rumour goes that his mother, being startled at sight of a sea-dog (seal) suddenly rising to the surface, gave birth to him in a fisherman's boat, and that accounts, it is said, for a good deal of the sea-cur in his nature. Several years ago he brought out an opera on the stage, which was fearfully hissed; but that hasn't cured him of his mania for writing execrable music. Indeed, when he heard Francesco Cavalli's opera *Le Nozze di Feti e di Peleo*, he swore that the composer had filched the sublimest of the thoughts from his own immortal works, for which he was near being thrashed and even stabbed. He still has a craze for singing arias, and accompanies his hideous squalling on a wretched jarring, jangling guitar, all out of tune. His faithful Pylades is an ill-bred dwarfish eunuch, whom the Romans call Pitichinaccio. There is a third member of the company—guess who it is?—Why, none other than the Pyramid Doctor, who kicks up a noise like a melancholy ass and yet fancies he's singing an excellent bass, quite as good as Martinelli of the Papal choir. Now these three estimable people are in the habit of meeting in the evening on the balcony of Capuzzi's house, where they sing Carissimi's motets, until all the dogs and cats in the neighbourhood round break out into dirges of miawing and howling, and all their neighbours heartily wish the devil would run away with all the blessed three.

"With this whimsical old fellow, Signor Pasquale Capuzzi, of whom my description will have enabled you to form a tolerably adequate idea, my father lived on terms of intimacy, since he trimmed his wig and beard. When my father died, I undertook this business; and Capuzzi was in the highest degree satisfied with me, because, as he once affirmed, I knew better than anybody else how to give his moustaches a bold upward twirl; but the real reason was because I was satisfied with the few pence with which he rewarded me for my pains. But he firmly believed that he more than richly indemnified me, since, whilst I was trimming his beard, he always closed his eyes and croaked through an aria from his own compositions, which, however, almost split my ears; and yet the old fellow's crazy gestures afforded me a good deal of amusement, so that I continued to attend him. One day when I went, I quietly ascended the stairs, knocked at the door, and opened it, when lo, there was a girl—an angel of light, who came to meet me. You know my Magdalene; it was she. I stood stock still, rooted to the spot. No, Salvator, you shall have no Ohs! and Ahs! Well, the first sight of this, the most lovely maiden of her sex, enkindled in me the most ardent passionate love. The old man informed me with a smirk that the young lady was the daughter of his brother Pietro, who had died at Senigaglia, that her name was Marianna, and that she was quite an orphan; being her uncle and guardian, he had taken her into his house. You can easily imagine that henceforward Capuzzi's house was my Paradise. But no matter what devices I had recourse to, I could never succeed in getting a *téte-à-téte* with Marianna, even for a single moment. Her glances, however, and many a stolen sigh, and many a soft pressure of the hand, resolved all doubts as to my good fortune. The old man divined what I was after,—which was not a very difficult thing for him to do. He informed me that my behaviour towards his niece was not such as to please him altogether, and he asked me what was the real purport of my attentions. Then I frankly confessed that I loved Marianna with all my heart, and that the greatest earthly happiness I could conceive was a union with her. Whereupon Capuzzi, after measuring me from top to toe, burst out in a guffaw of contempt, and declared that he never had any idea that such lofty thoughts could haunt the brain of a paltry barber. I was almost boiling with rage; I said he knew very well that I was no paltry barber but rather a good surgeon, and, moreover, in so far as concerned the noble art of painting, a faithful pupil of the great Annibal Caracci and of the unrivalled Guido Reni. But the infamous Capuzzi only replied by a still louder guffaw of laughter, and in his horrible falsetto squeaked, 'See here, my sweet Signor barber, my excellent Signor surgeon, my honoured Annibal Caracci, my beloved Guido Reni, be off to the devil, and don't ever show yourself here again, if you don't want your legs broken.' Therewith the cranky, knock-kneed old fool laid hold of me with no less an intention than to kick me out of the room, and hurl me down the stairs. But that, you know, was past everything. With ungovernable fury I seized the old fellow and tripped him up, so that his legs stuck uppermost in the air; and there I left him screaming aloud, whilst I ran down the stairs and out of the house-door; which, I need hardly say, has been closed to me ever since.

"And that's how matters stood when you came to Rome and when Heaven inspired Father Boniface with the happy idea of bringing me to you. Then so soon as your clever trick had brought me the success for which I had so long been vainly striving, that is, when I was accepted by the Academy of St. Luke, and all Rome was heaping up praise and honour upon me to a lavish extent, I went straightway to the old gentleman and suddenly presented myself before him in his own room, like a threatening apparition. Such at least he must have thought me, for he grew as pale as a corpse, and retreated behind a great table, trembling in every limb. And in a firm and earnest way I represented to him that it was not now a paltry barber or a surgeon, but a celebrated painter and Academician of St. Luke, Antonio Scacciati, to whom he would not, T hoped, refuse the hand of his niece Marianna. You should have seen into what a passion the old fellow flew. He screamed; he flourished his arms about like one possessed of devils; he yelled that I, a ruffianly murderer, was seeking his life, that I had stolen his Marianna from him since I had portrayed her in my picture, and it was driving him mad, driving him to despair, for all the world, all the world, were fixing their covetous, lustful eyes upon his Marianna, his life, his hope, his all; but I had better take care, he would burn my house over my head, and me and my picture in it. And therewith he kicked up such a din, shouting, 'Fire! Murder! Thieves! Help!' that I was perfectly confounded, and only thought of making the best of my way out of the house.

"The crackbrained old fool is over head and ears in love with his niece; he keeps her under lock and key; and as soon as he succeeds in getting dispensation from the Pope, he will compel her to a shameful alliance with himself. All hope for me is lost!"

"Nay, nay, not quite," said Salvator, laughing, "I am of opinion that things could not be in a better form for you, Marianna loves you, of that you are convinced; and all we have to do is to get her out of the power of that fantastic old gentleman, Signor Pasquale Capuzzi. I should like to know what there is to hinder a couple of stout enterprising fellows like you and me from accomplishing this. Pluck up your courage, Antonio. Instead of bewailing, and sighing, and fainting like a lovesick swain, it would be better to set to work to think out some plan for rescuing your Marianna. You just wait and see, Antonio, how finely we'll circumvent the old dotard; in such like emprises, the wildest extravagance hardly seems to me wild enough. I'll set about it at once, and learn what I can about the old man, and about his usual habits of life. But you must not be seen in this affair, Antonio. Go away quietly home, and come back to me early to-morrow morning, then we'll consider our first plan of attack."

Herewith Salvator shook the paint out of his brush, threw on his mantle, and hurried to the Corso, whilst Antonio betook himself home as Salvator had bidden him—his heart comforted and full of lusty hope again.

* * * * * *

III.

Signor Pasquale Capuzzi turns up at Salvator Rosa's studio. What takes place there. The cunning scheme which Rosa and Scacciati carry out, and the consequences of the same.

Next morning Salvator, having in the meantime inquired into Capuzzi's habits of life, very greatly surprised Antonio by a description of them, even down to the minutest details.

"Poor Marianna," said Salvator, "leads a sad life of it with the crazy old fellow. There he sits sighing and ogling the whole day long, and, what is worse still, in order to soften her heart towards him, he sings her all and sundry love ditties that he has ever composed or intends to compose. At the same time he is so monstrously jealous that he will not even permit the poor young girl to have the usual female attendance, for fear of intrigues and amours, which the maid might be induced to engage in. Instead, a hideous little apparition with hollow eyes and pale flabby cheeks appears every morning and evening to perform for sweet Marianna the services of a tiring-maid. And this little apparition is nobody else but that tiny Tomb Thumb of a Pitichinaccio, who has to don female attire. Capuzzi, whenever he leaves home, carefully locks and bolts every door; besides which there is always a confounded fellow keeping watch below, who was formerly a bravo, and then a gendarme, and now lives under Capuzzi's rooms. It seems, therefore, a matter almost impossible to effect an entrance into his house, but nevertheless I promise you, Antonio, that this very night you shall be in Capuzzi's own room and shall see your Marianna, though this time it will only be in Capuzzi's presence."

"What do you say?" cried Antonio, quite excited; "what do you say? We shall manage it to-night? I thought it was impossible."

"There, there," continued Salvator, "keep still, Antonio, and let us quietly consider how we may with safety carry out the plan which I have conceived. But in the first place I must tell you that I have already scraped an acquaintance with Signor Pasquale Capuzzi without knowing it. That wretched spinet, which stands in the corner there, belongs to the old fellow, and he wants me to pay him the preposterous sum of ten ducats for it. When I was convalescent I longed for some music, which always comforts me and does me a deal of good, so I begged my landlady to get me some such an instrument as that Dame Caterina soon ascertained that there was an old gentleman living in the Via Ripetta who had a fine spinet to sell I got the instrument brought here. I did not trouble myself either about the price or about the owner. It was only yesterday evening that I learned quite by chance that the gentleman who intended to cheat me with this rickety old thing was Signor Pasquale Capuzzi. Dame Caterina had enlisted the services of an acquaintance living in the same house, and indeed on the same floor as Capuzzi,—and now you can easily guess whence I have got all my budget of news."

"Yes," replied Antonio, "then the way to get in is found; your landlady"——

"I know very well, Antonio," said Salvator, cutting him short, "I know what you're going to say. You think you can find a way to your Marianna through Dame Caterina. But you'll find that we can't do anything of that sort; the good dame is far too talkative; she can't keep the least secret, and so we can't for a single moment think of employing her in this business. Now just quietly listen to me. Every evening when it's dark Signor Pasquale, although it's very hard work for him owing to his being knock-kneed, carries his little friend the eunuch home in his arms, as soon as he has finished his duties as maid. Nothing in the world could induce the timid Pitichinaccio to set foot on the pavement at that time of night. So that when"——

At this moment somebody knocked at Salvator's door, and to the consternation of both, Signor Pasquale stepped in in all the splendour of his gala attire. On catching sight of Scacciati he stood stock still as if paralysed, and then, opening his eyes wide, he gasped for air as though he had some difficulty in breathing. But Salvator hastily ran to meet him, and took him by both hands, saying, "My dear Signor Pasquale, your presence in my humble dwelling is, I feel, a very great honour. May I presume that it is your love for art which brings you to me? You wish to see the newest things I have done, perchance to give me a commission for some work. Pray in what, my dear Signor Pasquale, can I serve you?"

"I have a word or two to say to you, my dear Signor Salvator," stammered Capuzzi painfully, "but—alone—when you are alone. With your leave I will withdraw and come again at a more seasonable time."

"By no means," said Salvator, holding the old gentleman fast, "by no means, my dear sir. You need not stir a step; you could not have come at a more seasonable time, for, since you are a great admirer of the noble art of painting, and the patron of all good painters, I am sure you will be greatly pleased for me to introduce to you Antonio Scacciati here, the first painter of our time, whose glorious work—the wonderful 'Magdalene at the Saviour's Feet'—has excited throughout all Rome the most enthusiastic admiration. *You* too, I need hardly say, have also formed a high opinion of the work, and must be very anxious to know the great artist himself."

The old man was seized with a violent trembling; he shook as if he had a shivering fit of the ague, and shot fiery wrathful looks at poor Antonio. He however approached the old gentleman, and, bowing with polished courtesy, assured him that he esteemed himself happy at meeting in such an unexpected way with Signor Pasquale Capuzzi, whose great learning in music as well as in painting was a theme for wonder not only in Rome but throughout all Italy, and he concluded by requesting the honour of his patronage.

This behaviour of Antonio, in pretending to meet the old gentleman for the first time in his life, and in addressing him in such flattering phrases, soon brought him round again. He forced his features into a simpering smile, and, as Salvator now let his hands loose, gave his moustache an elegant upward curl, at the same time stammering out a few unintelligible words. Then, turning to Salvator, he requested payment of the ten ducats for the spinet he had sold him.

"Oh! that trifling little matter we can settle afterwards, my good sir," was Salvator's answer. "First have the goodness to look at this sketch of a picture which I have drawn, and drink a glass of good Syracuse whilst you do so." Salvator meanwhile placed his sketch on the easel and moved up a chair for the old gentleman, and then, when he had taken his seat, he presented him with a large and handsome wine-cup full of good Syracuse—the little pearl-like bubbles rising gaily to the top.

Signor Pasquale was very fond of a glass of good wine—when he had nothing to pay for it; and now he ought to have been in an especially happy frame of mind, for, besides nourishing his heart with the hope of getting ten ducats for a rotten, worn-out spinet, he was sitting before a splendid, boldly-designed picture, the rare beauty of which he was quite capable of estimating at its full worth. And that he was in this happy frame of mind he evidenced in divers way; he simpered most charmingly; he half closed his little eyes; he assiduously stroked his chin and moustache; and lisped time after time, "Splendid! delicious!" but they did not know to which he was referring, the picture or the wine.

When he had thus worked himself round into a quiet cheerful humour, Salvator suddenly began—"They tell me, my dear sir, that you have a most beautiful and amiable niece, named Marianna—is it so? All the young men of the city are so smitten with love that they stupidly do nothing but run up and down the Via Ripetta, almost dislocating their necks in their efforts to look up at your balcony for a sight of your sweet Marianna, to snatch a single glance from her heavenly eyes."

Suddenly all the charming simpers, all the good humour which had been called up into the old gentleman's face by the good wine, were gone. Looking gloomily before him, he said sharply, "Ah! that's an instance of the corruption of our abandoned young men. They fix their infernal eyes, there probate seducers, upon mere children. For I tell you, my good sir, that my niece Marianna is quite a child, quite a child, only just outgrown her nurse's care."

Salvator turned the conversation upon something else; the old gentleman recovered himself. But just as he, his face again radiant with sunshine, was on the point of putting the full wine-cup to his lips, Salvator began anew. "But pray tell me, my dear sir, if it is indeed true that your niece, with her sixteen summers, really has such beautiful auburn hair, and eyes so full of heaven's own loveliness and joy, as has Antonio's 'Magdalene?' It is generally maintained that she has."

"I don't know," replied the old gentleman, still more sharply than before, "I don't know. But let us leave my niece in peace; rather let us exchange a few instructive words on the noble subject of art, as your fine picture here of itself invites me to do."

Always when Capuzzi raised the wine-cup to his lips to take a good draught, Salvator began anew to talk about the beautiful Marianna, so that at last the old gentleman leapt from his chair in a perfect passion, banged the cup down upon the table and almost broke it, screaming in a high shrill voice, "By the infernal pit of Pluto! by all the furies! you will turn my wine into poison—into poison I tell you. But I see through you, you and your fine friend Signor Antonio, you think to make sport of me. But you'll find yourselves deceived Pay me the ten ducats you owe me immediately, and then I will leave you and your associate, that barber-fellow Antonio, to make your way to the devil."

Salvator shouted, as if mastered by the most violent rage, "What! you have the audacity to treat me in this way in my own house! Do you think I'm going to pay you ten ducats for that rotten box; the woodworms have long ago eaten all the goodness and all the music out of it? Not ten—not five—not three—not one ducat shall you have for it, it's scarcely worth a farthing. Away with the tumbledown thing!" and he kicked over the little instrument again and again, till the strings were all jarring and jangling together.

"Ha!" screeched Capuzzi, "justice is still to be had in Rome; I will have you arrested, sir,—arrested and cast into the deepest dungeon there is," and off he was rushing out of the room, blustering like a hailstorm. But Salvator took fast hold of him with both hands, and drew him down into the chair again, softly murmuring in his ear, "My dear Signor Pasquale, don't you perceive that I was only jesting with you? You shall have for your spinet, not ten, but *thirty* ducats cash down." And he went on repeating, "thirty bright ducats in ready money," until Capuzzi said in a faint and feeble voice, "What do you say, my dear sir? Thirty ducats for the spinet without its being repaired?"

Then Salvator released his hold of the old gentleman, and asserted on his honour that within an hour the instrument should be worth thirty—nay, forty ducats, and that Signor Pasquale should receive as much for it.

Taking in a fresh supply of breath, and sighing deeply, the old gentleman murmured, "Thirty—forty ducats!" Then he began, "But you have greatly offended me, Signor Salvator"—— "Thirty ducats," repeated Salvator. Capuzzi simpered, but then began again, "But you have grossly wounded my feelings, Signor Salvator"—— "Thirty ducats," exclaimed Salvator, cutting him short; and he continued to repeat, "Thirty ducats! thirty ducats!" as long as the old gentleman continued to sulk—till at length Capuzzi said, radiant with delight, "If you will give me thirty,—I mean forty ducats for the spinet, all shall be forgiven and forgotten, my dear sir."

"But," began Salvator, "before I can fulfil my promise, I still have one little condition to make, which you, my honoured Signor Pasquale Capuzzi di Senigaglia, can easily grant. You are the first musical composer in all Italy, besides being the foremost singer of the day. When I heard in the opera *Le Nozze di Teti e Peleo* the great scene which that shameless Francesco Cavalli has thievishly taken from your works, I was enraptured. If you would only sing me that aria whilst I put the spinet to rights you would confer upon me a pleasure than which I can conceive of none more enjoyable."

Puckering up his mouth into the most winning of smiles, and blinking his little grey eyes, the old gentleman replied, "I perceive, my good sir, that you are yourself a clever musician, for you possess taste and know how to value the deserving better than these ungrateful Romans. Listen—listen—to the aria of all arias."

Therewith he rose to his feet, and, stretching himself up to his full height, spread out his arms and closed both eyes, so that he looked like a cock preparing to crow; and he at once began to screech in such a way that the walls rang again, and Dame Caterina and her two daughters soon came running in, fully under the impression that such lamentable sounds must betoken some accident or other. At sight of the crowing old gentleman they stopped on the threshold utterly astonished; and thus they formed the audience of the incomparable musician Capuzzi.

Meanwhile Salvator, having picked up the spinet and thrown back the lid, had taken his palette in hand, and in bold firm strokes had begun on the lid of the instrument the most remarkable piece of painting that ever was seen. The central idea was a scene from Cavalli's opera *Le Nozze di Teti*, but there was a multitude of other personages mixed up with it in the most fantastic way. Amongst them were the recognisable features of Capuzzi, Antonio, Marianna (faithfully reproduced from Antonio's picture), Salvator himself, Dame Caterina and her two daughters,—and even the Pyramid Doctor was not wanting,—and all grouped so intelligently, judiciously, and ingeniously, that Antonio could not conceal his astonishment, both at the artist's intellectual power as well as at his technique.

Meanwhile old Capuzzi had not been content with the aria which Salvator had requested him to give, but, carried away by his musical madness, he went on singing or rather screeching without intermission, working his way through the most awful recitatives from one execrable scene to another. He must have been going on for nearly two hours when he sank back in his chair, breathless, and with his face as red as a cherry. And just at this same time also Salvator had so far worked out his sketch that the figures began to wear a look of vitality, and the whole, viewed at a little distance, had the appearance of a finished work.

"I have kept my word with respect to the spinet, my dear Signer Pasquale," breathed Salvator in the old man's ear. He started up as if awakening out of a deep sleep. Immediately his glance fell upon the painted instrument, which stood directly opposite him. Then, opening his eyes wide as if he saw a miracle, and jauntily throwing his conical hat on the top of his wig, he took his crutch-stick under his arm, made one bound to the spinet, tore the lid off the hinges, and holding it above his head, ran like a madman out of the room, down the stairs, and away, away out of the house altogether, followed by the hearty laughter of Dame Caterina and both her daughters.

"The old miser," said Salvator, "knows very well that he has only to take yon painted lid to Count Colonna or to my friend Rossi and he will at once get forty ducats for it, or even more."

Salvator and Antonio then both deliberated how they should carry out the plan of attack which was to be made when night came. We shall soon see what the two adventurers resolved upon, and what success they had in their adventure.

As soon as it was dark, Signer Pasquale, after locking and bolting the door of his house, carried the little monster of an eunuch home as usual. The whole way the little wretch was whining and growling, complaining that not only did he sing Capuzzi's arias till he got catarrh in the throat and burn his fingers cooking the macaroni, but he had now to lend himself to duties which brought him nothing but sharp boxes of the ear and rough kicks, which Marianna lavishly distributed to him as soon as ever he came near her. Old Capuzzi consoled him as well as he could, promising to provide him an ampler supply of sweetmeats than he had hitherto done; indeed, as the little man would nohow cease his growling and querulous complaining, Pasquale even laid himself under the obligation to get a natty abbot's coat made for the little torment out of an old black plush waistcoat which he (the dwarf) had often set covetous eyes upon. He demanded a wig and a sword as well. Parleying upon these points they arrived at the Via Bergognona, for that was where Pitichinaccio dwelt, only four doors from Salvator.

The old man set the dwarf cautiously down and opened the street door; and then, the dwarf on in front, they both began to climb up the narrow stairs, which were more like a rickety ladder for hens and chickens than steps for respectable people. But they had hardly mounted half way up when a terrible racket began up above, and the coarse voice of some wild drunken fellow was heard cursing and swearing, and demanding to be shown the way out of the damned house. Pitichinaccio squeezed himself close to the wall, and entreated Capuzzi, in the name of all the saints, to go on first. But before Capuzzi had ascended two steps, the fellow who was up above came tumbling headlong downstairs, caught hold of the old man, and whisked him away like a whirlwind out through the open door below into the middle of the street. There they both lay,—Capuzzi at bottom and the drunken brute like a heavy sack on top of him. The old gentleman screamed piteously for help; two men came up at once and with considerable difficulty freed him from the heavy weight lying upon him; the other fellow, as soon as he was lifted up, reeled away cursing.

"Good God! what's happened to you, Signor Pasquale? What are you doing here at this time of night? What big quarrel have you been getting mixed up in in that house there?" thus asked Salvator and Antonio, for that is who the two men were.

"Oh, I shall die!" groaned Capuzzi; "that son of the devil has crushed all my limbs; I can't move."

"Let me look," said Antonio, feeling all over the old gentleman's body, and suddenly he pinched his right leg so sharply that Capuzzi screamed out aloud.

"By all the saints!" cried Antonio in consternation, "by all the saints! my dear Signer Pasquale, you've broken your right leg in the most dangerous place. If you don't get speedy help you will within a short time be a dead man, or at any rate be lame all your life long."

A terrible scream escaped the old man's breast. "Calm yourself, my dear sir," continued Antonio, "although I'm now a painter, I haven't altogether forgotten my surgical practice. We will carry you to Salvator's house and I will at once bind up"——

"My dear Signor Antonio," whined Capuzzi, "you nourish hostile feelings towards me, I know." "But," broke in Salvator, "this is now no longer the time to talk about enmity; you are in danger, and that is enough for honest Antonio to exert all his skill on your behalf. Lay hold, friend Antonio."

Gently and cautiously they lifted up the old man between them, him screaming with the unspeakable pain caused by his broken leg, and carried him to Salvator's dwelling.

Dame Caterina said that she had had a foreboding that something was going to happen, and so she had not gone to bed. As soon as she caught sight of the old gentleman and heard what had befallen him, she began to heap reproaches upon him for his bad conduct. "I know," she said, "I know very well, Signor Pasquale, who you've been taking home again. Now that you've got your beautiful niece Marianna in the house with you, you think you've no further call to have women-folk about you, and you treat that poor Pitichinaccio most shameful and infamous, putting him in petticoats. But look to it. *Ogni carne ha il suo osso* (Every house has its skeleton). Why if you have a girl about you, don't you need women-folk? *Fate il passo secondo la gamba* (Cut your clothes according to your cloth), and don't you require anything either more or less from your Marianna than what is right. Don't lock her up as if she were a prisoner, nor make your house a dungeon. *Asino punto convien che trotti*(If you are in the stream, you had better swim with it); you have a beautiful niece and you must alter your ways to suit her, that is, you must only do what she wants you to do. But you are an ungallant and hard-hearted man, ay, and even in love, and jealous as well, they say, which I hope at your years is not true. Your pardon for telling you it all straight out, but *chi ha nel petto fiele non puo sputar miele* (when there's bile in the heart there can't be honey in the mouth). So now, if you don't die of your broken leg, which at your great age is not at all unlikely, let this be a warning to you; and leave your niece free to do what she likes, and let her marry the fine young gentleman as I know very well."

And so the stream went on uninterruptedly, whilst Salvator and Antonio cautiously undressed the old gentleman and put him to bed. Dame Caterina's words were like knives cutting deeply into his breast; but whenever he attempted to intervene, Antonio signed to him that all speaking was dangerous, and so he had to swallow his bitter gall. At length Salvator sent Dame Caterina away, to fetch some ice-cold water that Antonio wanted.

Salvator and Antonio satisfied themselves that the fellow who had been sent to Pitichinaccio's house had done his duty well. Notwithstanding the apparently terrible fall, Capuzzi had not received the slightest damage beyond a slight bruise or two. Antonio put the old gentleman's right foot in splints and bandaged it up so tight that he could not move. Then they wrapped him up in cloths that had been soaked in ice-cold water, as a precaution, they alleged, against inflammation, so that the old gentleman shook as if with the ague.

"My good Signor Antonio," he groaned feebly, "tell me if it is all over with me. Must I die?"

"Compose yourself," replied Antonio. "If you will only compose yourself, Signor Pasquale! As you have come through the first dressing with so much nerve and without fainting, I think we may say that the danger is past; but you will require the most attentive nursing. At present we mustn't let you out of the doctor's sight."

"Oh! Antonio," whined the old gentleman, "you know how I like you, how highly I esteem your talents. Don't leave me. Give me your dear hand—so! You won't leave me, will you, my dear good Antonio?"

"Although I am now no longer a surgeon," said Antonio, "although I've quite given up that hated trade, yet I will in your case, Signor Pasquale, make an exception, and will undertake to attend you, for which I shall ask nothing except that you give me your friendship, your confidence again. You were a little hard upon me"——

"Say no more," lisped the old gentleman, "not another word, my dear Antonio"——

"Your niece will be half dead with anxiety," said Antonio again, "at your not returning home. You are, considering your condition, brisk and strong enough, and so as soon as day dawns we'll carry you home to your own house. There I will again look at your bandage, and arrange your bed as it ought to be, and give your niece her instructions, so that you may soon get well again."

The old gentleman heaved a deep sigh and closed his eyes, remaining some minutes without speaking. Then, stretching out his hand towards Antonio, he drew him down close beside him, and whispered, "It was only a jest that you had with Marianna, was it not, my dear sir?—one of those merry conceits that young folks have"——

"Think no more about that, Signor Pasquale," replied Antonio. "Your niece did, it is true, strike my fancy; but I have now quite different things in my head, and—to confess honestly to it—I am very pleased that you did return a sharp answer to my foolish suit. I thought I was in love with your Marianna, but what I really saw in her was only a fine model for my 'Magdalene.' And this probably explains how it is that, now that my picture is finished, I feel quite indifferent towards her."

"Antonio," cried the old man, in a strong voice, "Antonio, you glorious fellow! What comfort you give me—what help—what consolation! Now that you don't love Marianna I feel as if all my pain had gone."

"Why, I declare, Signor Pasquale," said Salvator, "if we didn't know you to be a grave and sensible man, with a true perception of what is becoming to your years, we might easily believe that you were yourself by some infatuation in love with your niece of sixteen summers."

Again the old gentleman closed his eyes, and groaned and moaned at the horrible pain, which now returned with redoubled violence.

The first red streaks of morning came shining in through the window. Antonio announced to the old gentleman that it was now time to take him to his own house in the Via Ripetta. Signor Pasquale's reply was a deep and piteous sigh. Salvator and Antonio lifted him out of bed and wrapped him in a wide mantle which had belonged to Dame Caterina's husband, and which she lent them for this purpose. The old gentleman implored them by all the saints to take off the villainous cold bandages in which his bald head was swathed, and to give him his wig and plumed hat. And also, if it were possible, Antonio was to put his moustache a little in order, that Marianna might not be too much frightened at sight of him.

Two porters with a litter were standing all ready before the door. Dame Caterina, still storming at the old man, and mixing a great many proverbs in her abuse, carried down the bed, in which they then carefully packed him; and so, accompanied by Salvator and Antonio, he was taken home to his own house.

No sooner did Marianna see her uncle in this wretched plight than she began to scream, whilst a torrent of tears gushed from her eyes; without noticing her lover, who had come along with him, she grasped the old man's hands and pressed them to her lips, bewailing the terrible accident that had befallen him—so much pity had the good child for the old man who plagued and tormented her with his amorous folly. Yet at this same moment the inherent nature of woman asserted itself in her; for it only required a few significant glances from Salvator to put her in full possession of all the facts of the case. Now, for the first time, she stole a glance at the happy Antonio, blushing hotly as she did so; and a pretty sight it was to see how a roguish smile gradually routed and broke through her tears. Salvator, at any rate, despite the "Magdalene," had not expected to find the little maiden half so charming, or so sweetly pretty as he now really discovered her to be; and, whilst almost feeling inclined to envy Antonio his good fortune, he felt that it was all the more necessary to get poor Marianna away from her hateful uncle, let the cost be what it might.

Signor Pasquale forgot his trouble in being received so affectionately by his lovely niece, which was indeed more than he deserved. He simpered and pursed up his lips so that his moustache was all of a totter, and groaned and whined, not with pain, but simply and solely with amorous longing.

Antonio arranged his bed professionally, and, after Capuzzi had been laid on it, tightened the bandage still more, at the same time so muffling up his left leg as well that he had to lay there motionless like a log of wood. Salvator withdrew and left the lovers alone with their happiness.

The old gentleman lay buried in cushions; moreover, as an extra precaution, Antonio had bound a thick piece of cloth well steeped in water round his head, so that he might not hear the lovers whispering together. This was the first time they unburdened all their hearts to each other, swearing eternal fidelity in the midst of tears and rapturous kisses. The old gentleman could have no idea of what was going on, for Marianna ceased not, frequently from time to time, to ask him how he felt, and even permitted him to press her little white hand to his lips.

When the morning began to be well advanced, Antonio hastened away to procure, as he said, all the things that the old gentleman required, but in reality to invent some means for putting him, at any rate for some hours, in a still more helpless condition, as well as to consult with Salvator what further steps were then to be taken.

IV.

Of the new attack made by Salvator Rosa and Antonio Scacciati upon Signer Pasquale Capuzzi and upon his company, and of what further happens in consequence.

Next morning Antonio came to Salvator, melancholy and dejected.

"Well, what's the matter?" cried Salvator when he saw him coming, "what are you hanging your head about? What's happened to you now, you happy dog? can you not see your mistress every day, and kiss her and press her to your heart?"

"Oh! Salvator, it's all over with my happiness, it's gone for ever," cried Antonio. "The devil is making sport of me. Our stratagem has failed, and we now stand on a footing of open enmity with that cursed Capuzzi."

"So much the better," said Salvator; "so much the better. But come, Antonio, tell me what's happened."

"Just imagine, Salvator," began Antonio, "yesterday when I went back to the Via Ripetta after an absence of at the most two hours, with all sorts of medicines, whom should I see but the old gentleman standing in his own doorway fully dressed. Behind him was the Pyramid Doctor and the deuced ex-gendarme, whilst a confused something was bobbing about round their legs. It was, I believe, that little monster Pitichinaccio. No sooner did the old man get sight of me than he shook his fist at me, and began to heap the most fearful curses and imprecations upon me, swearing that if I did but approach his door he would have all my bones broken. 'Be off to the devil, you infamous barber-fellow,' he shrieked; 'you think to outwit me with your lying and knavery. Like the very devil himself, you lie in wait for my poor innocent Marianna, and fancy you are going to get her into your toils—but stop a moment! I will spend my last ducat to have the vital spark stamped out of you, ere you're aware of it. And your fine patron, Signor Salvator, the murderer—bandit—who's escaped the halter—he shall be sent to join his captain Masaniello in hell—I'll have him out of Rome; that won't cost me much trouble.'

"Thus the old fellow raged, and as the damned ex-gendarme, incited by the Pyramid Doctor, was making preparations to bear down upon me, and a crowd of curious onlookers began to assemble, what could I do but quit the field with all speed? I didn't like to come to you in my great trouble, for I know you would only have laughed at me and my inconsolable complaints. Why, you can hardly keep back your laughter now."

As Antonio ceased speaking, Salvator did indeed burst out laughing heartily.

"Now," he cried, "now the thing is beginning to be rather interesting. And now, my worthy Antonio, I will tell you in detail all that took place at Capuzzi's after you had gone. You had hardly left the house when Signor Splendiano Accoramboni, who had learned—God knows in what way—that his bosom-friend, Capuzzi, had broken his right leg in the night, drew near in all solemnity, with a surgeon. Your bandage and the entire method of treatment you have adopted with Signor Pasquale could not fail to excite suspicion. The surgeon removed the splints and bandages, and they discovered, what we both very well know, that there was not even so much as an ossicle of the worthy Capuzzi's right foot dislocated, still less broken. It didn't require any uncommon sagacity to understand all the rest."

"But," said Antonio, utterly astonished, "but my dear, good sir, do tell me how you have learned all that; tell me how you get into Capuzzi's house and know everything that takes place there."

"I have already told you," replied Salvator, "that an acquaintance of Dame Caterina lives in the same house, and moreover, on the same floor as Capuzzi. This acquaintance, the widow of a wine-dealer, has a daughter whom my little Margaret often goes to see. Now girls have a special instinct for finding out their fellows, and so it came about that Rose—that's the name of the wine-dealer's daughter—and Margaret soon discovered in the living-room a small vent-hole, leading into a dark closet that adjoins Marianna's apartment. Marianna had been by no means inattentive to the whispering and murmuring of the two girls, nor had she failed to notice the vent-hole, and so the way to a mutual exchange of communications was soon opened and made use of. Whenever old Capuzzi takes his afternoon nap the girls gossip away to their heart's content. You will have observed that little Margaret, Dame Caterina's and my favourite, is not so serious and reserved as her elder sister, Anna, but is an arch, frolicsome, droll little thing. Without expressly making mention of your love-affair I have instructed her to get Marianna to tell her everything that takes place in Capuzzi's house. She has proved a very apt pupil in the matter; and if I laughed at your pain and despondency just now it was because I knew what would comfort you, knew I could prove to you that the affair has now taken a most favourable turn. I have quite a big budget full of excellent news for you."

"Salvator!" cried Antonio, his eyes sparkling with joy, "how you cause my hopes to rise! Heaven be praised for the vent-hole. I will write to Marianna; Margaret shall take the letter with her"——

"Nay, nay, we can have none of that, Antonio," replied Salvator. "Margaret can be useful to us without being your love-messenger exactly. Besides, accident, which often plays many fine tricks, might carry your amorous confessions into old Capuzzi's hands, and so bring an endless amount of fresh trouble upon Marianna, just at the very moment when she is on the point of getting the lovesick old fool under her thumb. For listen to what then happened. The way in which Marianna received the old fellow when we took him home has quite reformed him. He is fully convinced that she no longer loves you, but that she has given him at least one half of her heart, and that all he has to do is to win the other half. And Marianna, since she imbibed the poison of your kisses, has advanced three years in shrewdness, artfulness, and experience. She has convinced the old man, not only that she had no share in our trick, but that she hates our goings-on, and will meet with scorn every device on your part to approach her. In his excessive delight the old man was too hasty, and swore that if he could do anything to please his adored Marianna he would do it immediately, she had only to give utterance to her wish. Whereupon Marianna modestly asked for nothing except that her *zio carissimo* (dearest uncle) would take her to see Signor Formica in the theatre outside the Porta del Popolo. This rather posed Capuzzi; there were consultations with the Pyramid Doctor and with Pitichinaccio; at last Signor Pasquale and Signor Splendiano came to the resolution that they really would take Marianna to this theatre to-morrow. Pitichinaccio, it was resolved, should accompany them in the disguise of a handmaiden, to which he only gave his consent on condition that Signor Pasquale would make him a present, not only of the plush waistcoat, but also of a wig, and at night would, alternately with the Pyramid Doctor, carry him home. That bargain they finally made; and so the curious leash will certainly go along with pretty Marianna to see Signor Formica to-morrow, in the theatre outside the Porta del Popolo."

It is now necessary to say who Signor Formica was, and what he had to do with the theatre outside the Porta del Popolo.

At the time of the Carnival in Rome, nothing is more sad than when the theatre-managers have been unlucky in their choice of a musical composer, or when the first tenor at the Argentina theatre has lost his voice on the way, or when the male prima donna of the Valle theatre is laid up with a cold,—in brief, when the chief source of recreation which the Romans were hoping to find proves abortive, and then comes Holy Thursday and all at once cuts off all the hopes which might perhaps have been realized It was just after one of these unlucky Carnivals— almost before the strict fast-days were past, when a certain Nicolo Musso opened a theatre outside the Porta del Popolo, where he stated his intention of putting nothing but light impromptu comic sketches on the boards. The advertisement was drawn up in an ingenious and witty style, and consequently the Romans formed a favourable preconception of Musso's enterprise; but independently of this they would in their longing to still their dramatic hunger have greedily snatched at any the poorest pabulum of this description. The interior arrangements of the theatre, or rather of the small booth, did not say much for the pecuniary resources of the enterprising manager. There was no orchestra, nor were there boxes. Instead, a gallery was put up at the back, where the arms of the house of Colonna were conspicuous—a sign that Count Colonna had taken Musso and his theatre under his especial protection. A platform of slight elevation, covered with carpets and hung round with curtains, which, according to the requirements of the piece, had to represent a wood or a room or a street—this was the stage. Add to this that the spectators had to content themselves with hard uncomfortable wooden benches, and it was no wonder that Signor Musso's patrons on first entering were pretty loud in their grumblings at him for calling a paltry wooden booth a theatre. But no sooner had the first two actors who appeared exchanged a few words together than the attention of the audience was arrested; as the piece proceeded their interest took the form of applause, their applause grew to admiration, their admiration to the wildest pitch of enthusiastic excitement, which found vent in loud and continuous laughter, clapping of hands, and screams of "Bravo! Bravo!"

And indeed it would not have been very easy to find anything more perfect than these extemporised representations of Nicolo Musso; they overflowed with wit, humour, and genius, and lashed the follies of the day with an unsparing scourge. The audience were quite carried away by the incomparable characterisation which distinguished all the actors, but particularly by the inimitable mimicry of Pasquarello, by his marvellously natural imitations of the voice, gait, and postures of well-known personages. By his inexhaustible humour, and the point and appositeness of his impromptus, he quite carried his audience away. The man who played the *rôle* of Pasquarello, and who called himself Signor Formica, seemed to be animated by a spirit of singular originality; often there was something so strange in either tone or gesture, that the audience, even in the midst of the most unrestrained burst of laughter, felt a cold shiver run through them. He was excellently supported by Dr. Gratiano, who in pantomimic action, in voice, and in his talent for saying the most delightful things mixed up with apparently the most extravagant nonsense, had perhaps no equal in the world. This *rôle* was played by an old Bolognese named Maria Agli. Thus in a short time all educated Rome was seen hastening in a continuous stream to Nicolo Musso's little theatre outside the Porta del Popolo, whilst Formica's name was on everybody's lips, and people shouted with wild enthusiasm, "*Oh! Formica! Formica benedetto! Oh! Formicissimo!*"—not only in the theatre but also in the streets. They regarded him as a supernatural visitant, and many an old lady who had split her sides with laughing in the theatre, would suddenly look grave and say solemnly, "*Scherza coi fanti e lascia star santi*" (Jest with children but let the saints alone), if anybody ventured to say the least thing in disparagement of Formica's acting. This arose from the fact that outside the theatre Signor Formica was an inscrutable mystery. Never was he seen anywhere, and all efforts to discover traces of him were vain, whilst Nicolo Musso on his part maintained an inexorable silence respecting his retreat.

And this was the theatre that Marianna was anxious to go to.

"Let us make a decisive onslaught upon our foes," said Salvator; "we couldn't have a finer opportunity than when they're returning home from the theatre." Then he imparted to Antonio the details of a plan, which, though appearing adventurous and daring, Antonio nevertheless embraced with joy, since it held out to him a prospect that he should be able to carry off his Marianna from the hated old Capuzzi. He also heard with approbation that Salvator was especially concerned to chastise the Pyramid Doctor.

When night came, Salvator and Antonio each took a guitar and went to the Via Ripetta, where, with the express view of causing old Capuzzi annoyance, they complimented lovely Marianna with the finest serenade that ever was heard. For Salvator played and sang in masterly style, whilst Antonio, as far as the capabilities of his fine tenor would allow him, almost rivalled Odoardo Ceccarelli. Although Signor Pasquale appeared on the balcony and tried to silence the singers with abuse, his neighbours, attracted to their windows by the good singing, shouted to him that he and his companions howled and screamed like so many cats and dogs, and yet he wouldn't listen to good music when it did come into the street; he might just go inside and stop up his ears if he didn't want to listen to good singing. And so Signor Pasquale had to bear nearly all night long the torture of hearing Salvator and Antonio sing songs which at one time were the sweetest of love-songs and at another mocked at the folly of amorous old fools. They plainly saw Marianna standing at the window, notwithstanding that Signor Pasquale besought her in the sweetest phrases and protestations not to expose herself to the noxious night air.

Next evening the most remarkable company that ever was seen proceeded down the Via Ripetta towards the Porta del Popolo. All eyes were turned upon them, and people asked each other if these were maskers left from the Carnival. Signor Pasquale Capuzzi, spruce and smug, all elegance and politeness, wearing his gay Spanish suit well brushed, parading a new yellow feather in his conical hat, and stepping along in shoes too little for him, as if he were walking amongst eggs, was leading pretty Marianna on his arm; her slender figure could not be seen, still less her face, since she was smothered up to an unusual extent in her veil and wraps. On the other side marched Doctor Splendiano Accoramboni in his great wig, which covered the whole of his back, so that to look at him from behind there appeared to be a huge head walking along on two little legs. Close behind Marianna, and almost clinging to her, waddled the little monster Pitichinaccio, dressed in fiery red petticoats, and having his head covered all over in hideous fashion with bright-coloured flowers.

This evening Signor Formica outdid himself even, and, what he had never done before, introduced short songs into his performance, burlesquing the style of certain well-known singers. Old Capuzzi's passion for the stage, which in his youth had almost amounted to infatuation, was now stirred up in him anew. In a rapture of delight he kissed Marianna's hand time after time, and protested that he would not miss an evening visiting Nicolo Musso's theatre with her. Signor Formica he extolled to the very skies, and joined hand and foot in the boisterous applause of the rest of the spectators. Signor Splendiano was less satisfied, and kept continually admonishing Signor Capuzzi and lovely Marianna not to laugh so immoderately. In a single breath he ran over the names of twenty or more diseases which might arise from splitting the sides with laughing. But neither Marianna nor Capuzzi heeded him in the least. As for Pitichinaccio, he felt very uncomfortable. He had been obliged to sit behind the Pyramid Doctor, whose great wig completely overshadowed him. Not a single thing could he see on the stage, nor any of the actors, and was, moreover, repeatedly bothered and annoyed by two forward women who had placed themselves near him. They called him a dear, comely little lady, and asked him if he was married, though to be sure, he was very young, and whether he had any children, who they dare be bound were sweet little creatures, and so forth. The cold sweat stood in beads on poor Pitichinaccio's brow; he whined and whimpered, and cursed the day he was born.

After the conclusion of the performance, Signor Pasquale waited until the spectators had withdrawn from the theatre. The last light was extinguished just as Signor Splendiano had lit a small piece of a wax torch at it; and then Capuzzi, with his worthy friends and Marianna, slowly and circumspectly set out on their return journey.

Pitichinaccio wept and screamed; Capuzzi, greatly to his vexation, had to take him on his left arm, whilst with the right he led Marianna. Doctor Splendiano showed the way with his miserable little bit of torch, which only burned with difficulty, and even then in a feeble sort of a way, so that the wretched light it cast merely served to reveal to them the thick darkness of the night.

Whilst they were still a good distance from the Porta del Popolo they all at once saw themselves surrounded by several tall figures closely enveloped in mantles. At this moment the torch was knocked out of the Doctor's hand, and went out on the ground. Capuzzi, as well as the Doctor, stood still without uttering a sound. Then, without their knowing where it came from, a pale reddish light fell upon the muffled figures, and four grisly skulls riveted their hollow ghastly eyes upon the Pyramid Doctor. "Woe—woe—woe betide thee, Splendiano Accoramboni!" thus the terrible spectres shrieked in deep, sepulchral tones. Then one of them wailed, "Do you know me? do you know me, Splendiano? I am Cordier, the French painter, who was buried last week, and whom your medicaments brought to his grave." Then the second, "Do you know me, Splendiano? I am Küfner, the German painter, whom you poisoned with your infernal electuary." Then the third, "Do you know me, Splendiano? I am Liers, the Fleming, whom you killed with your pills, and whose brother you defrauded of a picture." Then the fourth, "Do you know me, Splendiano? I am Ghigi, the Neapolitan painter, whom you despatched with your powders." And lastly all four together, "Woe—woe—woe upon thee, Splendiano Accoramboni, cursed Pyramid Doctor! We bid you come—come down to us beneath the earth. Away—away—away with you! Hallo! hallo!" and so saying they threw themselves upon the unfortunate Doctor, and, raising him in their arms, whisked him away like a whirlwind.

Now, although Signor Pasquale was a good deal overcome by terror, yet it is surprising with what remarkable promptitude he recovered courage so soon as he saw that it was only his friend Accoramboni with whom the spectres were concerned. Pitichinaccio had stuck his head, with the flower-bed that was on it, under Capuzzi's mantle, and clung so fast round his neck that all efforts to shake him off proved futile.

"Pluck up your spirits," Capuzzi exhorted Marianna, when nothing more was to be seen of the spectres or of the Pyramid Doctor; "pluck up your spirits, and come to me, my sweet little ducky bird! As for my worthy friend Splendiano, it's all over with him. May St. Bernard, who also was an able physician and gave many a man a lift on the road to happiness, may he help him, if the revengeful painters whom he hastened to get to his Pyramid break his neck! But who'll sing the bass of my canzonas now? And this booby, Pitichinaccio, is squeezing my throat so, that, adding in the fright caused by Splendiano's abduction, I fear I shall not be able to produce a pure note for perhaps six weeks to come. Don't be alarmed, my Marianna, my darling! It's all over now."

She assured him that she had quite recovered from her alarm, and begged him to let her walk alone without support, so that he could free himself from his troublesome pet. But Signor Pasquale only took faster hold of her, saying that he wouldn't suffer her to leave his side a yard in that pitch darkness for anything in the world.

In the very same moment as Signor Pasquale, now at his ease again, was about to proceed on his road, four frightful fiend-like figures rose up just in front of him as if out of the earth; they wore short flaring red mantles and fixed their keen glittering eyes upon him, at the same time making horrible noises—yelling and whistling. "Ugh! ugh! Pasquale Capuzzi! You cursed fool! You amorous old devil! We belong to your fraternity; we are the evil spirits of love, and have come to carry you off to hell—to hell-fire—you and your crony Pitichinaccio." Thus screaming, the Satanic figures fell upon the old man. Capuzzi fell heavily to the ground and Pitichinaccio along with him, both raising a shrill piercing cry of distress and fear, like that of a whole troop of cudgelled asses.

Marianna had meanwhile torn herself away from the old man and leapt aside. Then one of the devils clasped her softly in his arms, whispering the sweet glad words, "O Marianna! my Marianna! At last we've managed it! My friends will carry the old man a long, long way from here, whilst we seek a better place of safety."

"O my Antonio!" whispered Marianna softly.

But suddenly the scene was illuminated by the light of several torches, and Antonio felt a stab in his shoulder. Quick as lightning he turned round, drew his sword, and attacked the fellow, who with his stiletto upraised was just preparing to aim a second blow. He perceived that his three companions were defending themselves against a superior number of gendarmes. He managed to beat off the fellow who had attacked him, and joined his friends. Although they were maintaining their ground bravely, the contest was yet too unequal; the gendarmes would infallibly have proved victorious had not two others suddenly ranged themselves with a shout on the side of the young men, one of them immediately cutting down the fellow who was pressing Antonio the hardest.

In a few minutes more the contest was decided against the police. Several lay stretched on the ground seriously wounded; the rest fled with loud shouts towards the Porta del Popolo.

Salvator Rosa (for he it was who had hastened to Antonio's assistance and cut down his opponent) wanted to take Antonio and the young painters who were disguised in the devils' masks and there and then pursue the gendarmes into the city.

Maria Agli, however, who had come along with him, and, notwithstanding his advanced age, had tackled the police as stoutly as any of the rest, urged that this would be imprudent, for the guard at the Porta del Popolo would be certain to have intelligence of the affair and would arrest them. So they all betook themselves to Nicolo Musso, who gladly received them into his narrow little house not far from the theatre. The artists took off their devils' masks and laid aside their mantles, which had been rubbed over with phosphorus, whilst Antonio, who, beyond the insignificant scratch on his shoulder, was not wounded at all, exercised his surgical skill in binding up the wounds of the rest—Salvator, Agli, and his young comrades—for they had none of them got off without being wounded, though none of them in the least degree dangerously.

The adventure, notwithstanding its wildness and audacity, would undoubtedly have been successful, had not Salvator and Antonio overlooked one person, who upset everything. The *ci-devant* bravo and gendarme Michele, who dwelt below in Capuzzi's house, and was in a certain sort his general servant, had, in accordance with Capuzzi's directions, followed them to the theatre, but at some distance off, for the old gentleman was ashamed of the tattered reprobate. In the same way Michele was following them homewards. And when the spectres appeared, Michele who, be it remarked, feared neither death nor devil, suspecting that something was wrong, hurried back as fast as he could run in the darkness to the Porta del Popolo, raised an alarm, and returned with all the gendarmes he could find, just at the moment when, as we know, the devils fell upon Signor Pasquale, and were about to carry him off as the dead men had the Pyramid Doctor.

In the very hottest moment of the fight, one of the young painters observed distinctly how one of the fellows, taking Marianna in his arms (for she had fainted), made off to the gate, whilst Signor Pasquale ran after him with incredible swiftness, as if he had got quicksilver in his legs. At the same time, by the light of the torches, he caught a glimpse of something gleaming, clinging to his mantle and whimpering; no doubt it was Pitichinaccio.

Next morning Doctor Splendiano was found near the Pyramid of Cestius, fast asleep, doubled up like a ball and squeezed into his wig, as if into a warm soft nest. When he was awakened, he rambled in his talk, and there was some difficulty in convincing him that he was still on the surface of the earth, and in Rome to boot. And when at length he reached his own house, he returned thanks to the Virgin and all the saints for his rescue, threw all his tinctures, essences, electuaries, and powders out of the window, burnt his prescriptions, and vowed to heal his patients in the future by no other means than by anointing and laying on of hands, as some celebrated physician of former ages, who was at the same time a saint (his name I cannot recall just at this moment), had with great success done before him. For his patients died as well as the patients of other people, and then they already saw the gates of heaven open before them ere they died, and in fact everything else that the saint wanted them to see.

"I can't tell you," said Antonio next day to Salvator, "how my heart boils with rage since my blood has been spilled. Death and destruction overtake that villain Capuzzi! I tell you, Salvator, that I am determined to *force* my way into his house. I will cut him down if he opposes me and carry off Marianna."

"An excellent plan!" replied Salvator, laughing. "An excellent plan! Splendidly contrived! Of course I presume you have also found some means for transporting Marianna through the air to the Spanish Square, so that they shall not seize you and hang you before you can reach that place of refuge. No, my dear Antonio, violence can do nothing for you this time. You may lay your life on it too that Signor Pasquale will now take steps to guard against any open attack. Moreover, our adventure has made a good deal of noise, and the irrepressible laughter of the people at the absurd way in which we have read a lesson to Splendiano and Capuzzi has roused the police out of their light slumber, and they, you may be sure, will now exert all their feeble efforts to entrap us. No, Antonio, let us have recourse to craft. *Con arte e con inganno si vive mezzo l'anno, con inganno e con arte si vive l'altra parte* (If cunning and scheming will help us six months through, scheming and cunning will help us the other six too), says Dame Caterina, nor is she far wrong. Besides, I can't help laughing to see how we've gone and acted for all the world like thoughtless boys, and I shall have to bear most of the blame, for I am a good bit older than you. Tell me now, Antonio, supposing our scheme had been successful, and you had actually carried off Marianna from the old man, where would you have fled to, where would you have hidden her, and how would you have managed to get united to her by the priest before the old man could interfere to prevent it? You shall, however, in a few days, really and truly run away with your Marianna. I have let Nicolo Musso as well as Signor Formica into all the secret, and in common with them devised a plan which can scarcely fail. So cheer up, Antonio; Signor Formica will help you."

"Signor Formica?" replied Antonio in a tone of indifference which almost amounted to contempt. "Signor Formica! In what way can that buffoon help me?"

"Ho! ho!" laughed Salvator. "Please to bear in mind, I beg you, that Signor Formica is worthy of your respect. Don't you know that he is a sort of magician who in secret is master of the most mysterious arts? I tell you, Signor Formica will help you. Old Maria Agli, the clever Bolognese Doctor Gratiano, is also a sharer in the plot, and will, moreover, have an important part to play in it. You shall abduct your Marianna, Antonio, from Musso's theatre."

"You are flattering me with false hopes, Salvator," said Antonio. "You have just now said yourself that Signor Pasquale will take care to avoid all open attacks. How can you suppose then, after his recent unpleasant experience, that he can possibly make up his mind to visit Musso's theatre again?"

"It will not be such a difficult thing as you imagine to entice the old man there," replied Salvator. "What will be more difficult to effect, will be, to get him in the theatre without his satellites. But, be that as it may, what you have now got to do, Antonio, is to have everything prepared and arranged with Marianna, so as to flee from Rome the moment the favourable opportunity comes. You must go to Florence; your skill as a painter will, after your arrival, in itself recommend you there; and you shall have no lack of acquaintances, nor of honourable patronage and assistance—that you may leave to me to provide for. After we have had a few days' rest, we will then see what is to be done further. Once more, Antonio—live in hope; Formica will help you."

V.

Of the new mishap which befalls Signor Pasquale Capussi. Antonio Scacciati successfully carries out his plan in Nicolo Musso's theatre, and flees to Florence.

Signor Pasquale was only too well aware who had been at the bottom of the mischief that had happened to him and the poor Pyramid Doctor near the Porta del Popolo, and so it may be imagined how enraged he was against Antonio, and against Salvator Rosa, whom he rightly judged to be the ringleader in it all. He was untiring in his efforts to comfort poor Marianna, who was quite ill from fear,—so she said; but in reality she was mortified that the scoundrel Michele with his gendarmes had come up, and torn her from her Antonio's arms. Meanwhile Margaret was very active in bringing her tidings of her lover; and she based all her hopes upon the enterprising mind of Salvator. With impatience she waited from day to day for something fresh to happen, and by a thousand petty tormenting ways let the old gentleman feel the effects of this impatience; but though she thus tamed his amorous folly and made him humble enough, she failed to reach the evil spirit of love that haunted his heart. After she had made him experience to the full all the tricksy humours of the most wayward girl, and then suffered him just once to press his withered lips upon her tiny hand, he would swear in his excessive delight that he would never cease fervently kissing the Pope's toe until he had obtained dispensation to wed his niece, the paragon of beauty and amiability. Marianna was particularly careful not to interrupt him in these outbreaks of passion, for by encouraging these gleams of hope in the old man's breast she fanned the flame of hope in her own, for the more he could be lulled into the belief that he held her fast in the indissoluble chains of love, the more easy it would be for her to escape him.

Some time passed, when one day at noon Michele came stamping upstairs, and, after he had had to knock a good many times to induce Signor Pasquale to open the door, announced with considerable prolixity that there was a gentleman below who urgently requested to see Signor Pasquale Capuzzi, who he knew lived there.

"By all the blessed saints of Heaven!" cried the old gentleman, exasperated; "doesn't the knave know that on no account do I receive strangers in my own house?"

But the gentleman was of very respectable appearance, reported Michele, rather oldish, talked well, and called himself Nicolo Musso.

"Nicolo Musso," murmured Capuzzi reflectively; "Nicolo Musso, who owns the theatre beyond the Porta del Popolo; what can he want with me?" Whereupon, carefully locking and bolting the door, he went downstairs with Michele, in order to converse with Nicolo in the street before the house.

"My dear Signor Pasquale," began Nicolo, approaching to meet him, and bowing with polished ease, "that you deign to honour me with your acquaintance affords me great pleasure. You lay me under a very great obligation. Since the Romans saw you in my theatre—you, a man of the most approved taste, of the soundest knowledge, and a master in art, not only has my fame increased, but my receipts have doubled. I am therefore all the more deeply pained to learn that certain wicked wanton boys made a murderous attack upon you and your friends as you were returning from my theatre at night. But I pray you, Signor Pasquale, by all the saints, don't cherish any grudge against me or my theatre on account of this outrage, which shall be severely punished. Don't deprive me of the honour of your company at my performances!"

"My dear Signor Nicolo," replied the old man, simpering, "be assured that I never enjoyed myself more than I did when I visited your theatre. Your Formica and your Agli—why, they are actors who cannot be matched anywhere. But the fright almost killed my friend Signor Splendiano Accoramboni, nay, it almost proved the death of me—no, it was too great; and though it has not made me averse from your theatre, it certainly has from the road there. If you will put up your theatre in the Piazza del Popolo, or in the Via Babuina, or in the Via Ripetta, I certainly will not fail to visit you a single evening; but there's no power on earth shall ever get me outside the Porta del Popolo at night-time again."

Nicolo sighed deeply, as if greatly troubled. "That is very hard upon me," said he then, "harder perhaps than you will believe, Signor Pasquale. For unfortunately—I had based all my hopes upon you. I came to solicit your assistance."

"My assistance?" asked the old gentleman in astonishment "My assistance, Signor Nicolo? In what way could it profit you?"

"My dear Signor Pasquale," replied Nicolo, drawing his handkerchief across his eyes, as if brushing away the trickling tears, "my most excellent Signor Pasquale, you will remember that my actors are in the habit of interspersing songs through their performances. This practice I was thinking of extending imperceptibly more and more, then to get together an orchestra, and, in a word, at last, eluding all prohibitions to the contrary, to establish an opera-house. You, Signor Capuzzi, are the first composer in all Italy; and we can attribute it to nothing but the inconceivable frivolity of the Romans and the malicious envy of your rivals that we hear anything else but your pieces exclusively at all the theatres. Signor Pasquale, I came to request you on my bended knees to allow me to put your immortal works, as far as circumstances will admit, on my humble stage."

"My dear Signor Nicolo," said the old gentleman, his face all sunshine, "what are we about to be talking here in the public street? Pray deign to have the goodness to climb up one or two rather steep flights of stairs. Come along with me up to my poor dwelling."

Almost before Nicolo got into the room, the old gentleman brought forward a great pile of dusty music manuscript, opened it, and, taking his guitar in his hands, began to deliver himself of a series of frightful high-pitched screams which he denominated singing.

Nicolo behaved like one in raptures. He sighed; he uttered extravagant expressions of approval; he exclaimed at intervals, "*Bravo! Bravissimo! Benedettissimo Capuzzi!*" until at last he threw himself at the old man's feet as if utterly beside himself with ecstatic delight, and grasped his knees. But he nipped them so hard that the old gentleman jumped off his seat, calling out with pain, and saying to Nicolo, "By the saints! Let me go, Signor Nicolo; you'll kill me."

"Nay," replied Nicolo, "nay, Signor Pasquale, I will not rise until you have promised that Formica may sing in my theatre the day after to-morrow the divine arias which you have just executed."

"You are a man of taste," groaned Pasquale,—"a man of deep insight. To whom could I better intrust my compositions than to you? You shall take all my arias with you. Only let me go. But, good God! I shall not hear them—my divine masterpieces! Oh! let me go, Signor Nicolo."

"No," cried Nicolo, still on his knees, and tightly pressing the old gentleman's thin spindle-shanks together, "no, Signor Pasquale, I will not let you go until you give me your word that you will be present in my theatre the night after to-morrow. You need not fear any new attack! Why, don't you think that the Romans, once they have heard your work, will bring you home in triumph by the light of hundreds of torches? But in case that does not happen, I myself and my faithful comrades will take our arms and accompany you home ourselves."

"You yourself will accompany me home, with your comrades?" asked Pasquale; "and how many may that be?"

"Eight or ten persons will be at your command, Signor Pasquale. Do yield to my intercession and resolve to come."

"Formica has a fine voice," lisped Pasquale. "How finely he will execute my arias."

"Do come, oh! do come!" exhorted Nicolo again, giving the old gentleman's knees an extra grip.

"You will pledge yourself that I shall reach my own house without being molested?" asked the old gentleman.

"I pledge my honour and my life," was Nicolo's reply, as he gave the knees a still sharper grip.

"Agreed!" cried the old gentleman; "I will be in your theatre the day after to-morrow."

Then Nicolo leapt to his feet and pressed Pasquale in so close an embrace that he gasped and panted quite out of breath.

At this moment Marianna entered the room. Signor Pasquale tried to frighten her away again by the look of resentment which he hurled at her; she, however, took not the slightest notice of it, but going straight up to Musso, addressed him as if in anger,—"It is in vain for you, Signor Nicolo, to attempt to entice my dear uncle to go to your theatre. You are forgetting that the infamous trick lately played by some reprobate seducers, who were lying in wait for me, almost cost the life of my dearly beloved uncle, and of his worthy friend Splendiano; nay, that it almost cost my life too. Never will I give my consent to my uncle's again exposing himself to such danger. Desist from your entreaties, Nicolo. And you, my dearest uncle, you will stay quietly at home, will you not, and not venture out beyond the Porta del Popolo again at night-time, which is a friend to nobody?"

Signor Pasquale was thunderstruck. He opened his eyes wide and stared at his niece. Then he rewarded her with the sweetest endearments, and set forth at considerable length how that Signor Nicolo had pledged himself so to arrange matters as to avoid every danger on the return home.

"None the less," said Marianna, "I stick to my word, and beg you most earnestly, my dearest uncle, not to go to the theatre outside the Porta del Popolo. I ask your pardon, Signor Nicolo, for speaking out frankly in your presence the dark suspicion that lurks in my mind. You are, I know, acquainted with Salvator Rosa and also with Antonio Scacciati. What if you are acting in concert with our enemies? What if you are only trying with evil intent to entice my dear uncle into your theatre in order that they may the more safely carry out some fresh villainous scheme, for I know that my uncle will not go without me?"

"What a suspicion!" cried Nicolo, quite alarmed. "What a terrible suspicion, Signora! Have you such a bad opinion of me? Have I such an ill reputation that you conceive I could be guilty of this the basest treachery? But if you think so unfavourably of me, if you mistrust the assistance I have promised you, why then let Michele, who I know rescued you out of the hands of the robbers—let Michele accompany you, and let him take a large body of gendarmes with him, who can wait for you outside the theatre, for you cannot of course expect me to fill my auditorium with police."

Marianna fixed her eyes steadily upon Nicolo's, and then said, earnestly and gravely, "What do you say? That Michele and gendarmes shall accompany us? Now I see plainly, Signor Nicolo, that you mean honestly by us, and that my nasty suspicion is unfounded. Pray forgive me my thoughtless words. And yet I cannot banish my nervousness and anxiety about my dear uncle; I must still beg him not to take this dangerous step."

Signor Pasquale had listened to all this conversation with such curious looks as plainly served to indicate the nature of the struggle that was going on within him. But now he could no longer contain himself; he threw himself on his knees before his beautiful niece, seized her hands, kissed them, bathed them with the tears which ran down his cheeks, exclaiming as if beside himself, "My adored, my angelic Marianna! Fierce and devouring are the flames of the passion which burns at my heart Oh! this nervousness, this anxiety—it is indeed the sweetest confession that you love me." And then he besought her not to give way to fear, but to go and listen in the theatre to the finest arias which the most divine of composers had ever written.

Nicolo too abated not in his entreaties, plainly showing his disappointment, until Marianna permitted her scruples to be overcome; and she promised to lay all fear aside and accompany the best and dearest of uncles to the theatre outside the Porta del Popolo. Signor Pasquale was in ectasies, was in the seventh heaven of delight. He was convinced that Marianna loved him; and he now might hope to hear his music on the stage, and win the laurel wreath which had so long been the vain object of his desires; he was on the point of seeing his dearest dreams fulfilled. Now he would let his light shine in perfect glory before his true and faithful friends, for he never thought for a moment but that Signor Splendiano and little Pitichinaccio would go with him as on the first occasion.

The night that Signor Splendiano had slept in his wig near the Pyramid of Cestius he had had, besides the spectres who ran away with him, all sorts of sinister apparitions to visit him. The whole cemetery was alive, and hundreds of corpses had stretched out their skeleton arms towards him, moaning and wailing that even in their graves they could not get over the torture caused by his essences and electuaries. Accordingly the Pyramid Doctor, although he could not contradict Signor Pasquale that it was only a wild freakish trick played upon him by a parcel of godless boys, grew melancholy; and, albeit not ordinarily superstitiously inclined, he yet now saw spectres everywhere, and was tormented by forebodings and bad dreams.

As for Pitichinaccio, he could not be convinced that they were not real devils come straight from the flames of hell who had fallen upon Signor Pasquale and upon himself, and the bare mention of that dreadful night was enough to make him scream. All the asseverations of Signor Pasquale that there had been nobody behind the masks but Antonio Scacciati and Salvator Rosa were of none effect, for Pitichinaccio wept and swore that in spite of his terror and apprehension he had clearly recognised both the voice and the behaviour of the devil Fanfarelli in the one who had pinched his belly black and blue.

It may therefore be imagined what an almost endless amount of trouble it cost Signor Pasquale to persuade the two to go with him once more to Nicolo Musso's theatre. Splendiano was the first to make the resolve to go,—after he had procured from a monk of St. Bernard's order a small consecrated bag of musk, the perfume of which neither dead man nor devil could endure; with this he intended to arm himself against all assaults. Pitichinaccio could not resist the temptation of a promised box of candied grapes, but Signor Pasquale had besides expressly to give his consent that he might wear his new abbot's coat, instead of his petticoats, which he affirmed had proved an immediate source of attraction to the devil.

What Salvator feared seemed therefore as if it would really take place; and yet his plan depended entirely, he continued to repeat, upon Signor Pasquale's being in Nicolo's theatre alone with Marianna, without his faithful satellites. Both Antonio and Salvator greatly racked their brains how they should prevent Splendiano and Pitichinaccio from going along with Signor Pasquale. Every scheme that occurred to them for the accomplishment of this desideratum had to be given up owing to want of time, for the principal plan in Nicolo's theatre had to be carried out on the evening of the following day.

But Providence, which often employs the most unlikely instruments for the chastisement of fools, interposed on behalf of the distressed lovers, and put it into Michele's head to practise some of his blundering, thus accomplishing what Salvator and Antonio's craft was unable to accomplish.

That same night there was heard in the Via Ripetta before Signor Pasquale's house such a chorus of fearful screams and of cursing and raving and abuse that all the neighbours were startled up out of their sleep, and a body of gendarmes, who had been pursuing a murderer as far as the Spanish Square, hastened up with torches, supposing that some fresh deed of violence was being committed. But when they, and a crowd of other people whom the noise had attracted, came upon the anticipated scene of murder, they found poor little Pitichinaccio lying as if dead on the ground, whilst Michele was thrashing the Pyramid Doctor with a formidable bludgeon. And they saw the Doctor reel to the floor just at the moment when Signor Pasquale painfully scrambled to his feet, drew his rapier, and furiously attacked Michele. Round about were lying pieces of broken guitars. Had not several people grasped the old man's arm he would assuredly have run Michele right through the heart. The ex-bravo, on now becoming aware by the light of the torches whom he had been molesting, stood as if petrified, his eyes almost starting out of his heady "a painted desperado, on the balance between will and power," as it is said somewhere. Then, uttering a fearful scream, he tore his hair and begged for pardon and mercy. Neither the Pyramid Doctor nor Pitichinaccio was seriously injured, but they had been so soundly cudgelled that they could neither move nor stir, and had to be carried home.

Signor Pasquale had himself brought this mishap upon his own shoulders.

We know that Salvator and Antonio complimented Marianna with the finest serenade that could be heard; but I have forgotten to say that to the old gentleman's very exceeding indignation they repeated it during several successive nights. At length Signor Pasquale whose rage was kept in check by his neighbours, was foolish enough to have recourse to the authorities of the city, urging them to forbid the two painters to sing in the Via Ripetta. The authorities, however, replied that it would be a thing unheard of in Rome to prevent anybody from singing and playing the guitar where he pleased, and it was irrational to ask such a thing. So Signor Pasquale determined to put an end to the nuisance himself, and promised Michele a large reward if he seized the first opportunity to fall upon the singers and give them a good sound drubbing. Michele at once procured a stout bludgeon, and lay in wait every night behind the door. But it happened that Salvator and Antonio judged it prudent to omit their serenading in the Via Ripetta for some nights preceding the carrying into execution of their plan, so as not to remind the old gentleman of his adversaries. Marianna remarked quite innocently that though she hated Antonio and Salvator, yet she liked their singing, for nothing was so nice as to hear music floating upwards in the night air.

This Signor Pasquale made a mental note of, and as the essence of gallantry purposed to surprise his love with a serenade on his part, which he had himself composed and carefully practised up with his faithful friends. On the very night preceding that in which he was hoping to celebrate his greatest triumph in Nicolo Musso's theatre, he stealthily slipped out of the house and went and fetched his associates, with whom he had previously arranged matters. But no sooner had they sounded the first few notes on their guitars than Michele, whom Signor Pasquale had thoughtlessly forgotten to apprise of his design, burst forth from behind the door, highly delighted at finding that the opportunity which was to bring him in the promised reward had at last come, and began to cudgel the musicians most unmercifully, with the results of which we are already acquainted. Of course there was no further mention made of either Splendiano or Pitichinaccio's accompanying Signor Pasquale to Nicolo's theatre, for they were both confined to their bed beplastered all over. Signor Pasquale, however, was unable to stay away, although his back and shoulders were smarting not a little from the drubbing he had himself received; every note in his arias was a cord which drew him thither with irresistible power.

"Well now," said Salvator to Antonio, "since the obstacle which we took to be insurmountable has been removed out of our way of itself, it all depends now entirely upon your address not to let the favourable moment slip for carrying off your Marianna from Nicolo's theatre. But I needn't talk, you'll not fail; I will greet you now as the betrothed of Capuzzi's lovely niece, who in a few days will be your wife. I wish you happiness, Antonio, and yet I feel a shiver run through me when I think upon your marriage."

"What do you mean, Salvator?" asked Antonio, utterly astounded.

"Call it a crotchet, call it a foolish fancy, or what you will, Antonio," rejoined Salvator,—"at any rate I love the fair sex; but there is not one, not even she on whom I foolishly dote, for whom I would gladly die, but what excites in my heart, so soon as I think of a union with her such as marriage is, a suspicion that makes me tremble with a most unpleasant feeling of awe. That which is inscrutable in the nature of woman mocks all the weapons of man. She whom we believe to have surrendered herself to us entirely, heart and soul, whom we believe to have unfolded all her character to us, is the first to deceive us, and along with the sweetest of her kisses we imbibe the most pernicious of poisons."

"And my Marianna?" asked Antonio, amazed.

"Pardon me, Antonio," continued Salvator, "even your Marianna, who is loveliness and grace personified, has given me a fresh proof of how dangerous the mysterious nature of woman is to us. Just call to mind what was the behavior of that innocent, inexperienced child when we carried her uncle home, how at a single glance from me she divined everything—everything, I tell you, and, as you yourself admitted, proceeded to play her part with the utmost sagacity. But that is not to be at all compared with what took place on the occasion of Musso's visit to the old gentleman. The most practised address, the most impenetrable cunning,—in short, all the inventive arts of the most experienced woman of the world could not have done more than little Marianna did, in order to deceive the old gentleman with perfect success. She could not have acted in any better way to prepare the road for us for any kind of enterprise. Our feud with the cranky old fool—any sort of cunning scheme seems justified, but—come, my dear Antonio, never mind my fanciful crotchets, but be happy with your Marianna; as happy as you can."

If a monk had taken his place beside Signor Pasquale when he set out along with his niece to go to Nicolo Musso's theatre, everybody would have thought that the strange pair were being led to execution. First went valiant Michele, repulsive in appearance, and armed to the teeth; then came Signor Pasquale and Marianna, followed by fully twenty gendarmes.

Nicolo received the old gentleman and his lady with every mark of respect at the entrance to the theatre, and conducted them to the seats which had been reserved for them, immediately in front of the stage. Signor Pasquale felt highly flattered by this mark of honour, and gazed about him with proud and sparkling eyes, whilst his pleasure, his joy, was greatly enhanced to find that all the seats near and behind Marianna were occupied by women alone. A couple of violins and a bass-fiddle were being tuned behind the curtains of the stage; the old gentleman's heart beat with expectation; and when all at once the orchestra struck up the *ritornello* of his work, he felt an electric thrill tingling in every nerve.

Formica came forward in the character of Pasquarello, and sang—sang in Capuzzi's own voice, and with all his characteristic gestures, the most hopeless aria that ever was heard. The theatre shook with the loud and boisterous laughter of the audience. They shouted; they screamed wildly, "O Pasquale Capuzzi! Our most illustrious composer and artist! Bravo! Bravissimo!" The old gentleman, not perceiving the ridicule and irony of the laughter, was in raptures of delight. The aria came to an end, and the people cried "Sh! sh!" for Doctor Gratiano, played on this occasion by Nicolo Musso himself, appeared on the stage, holding his hands over his ears and shouting to Pasquarello for goodness' sake to stop his ridiculous screeching.

Then the Doctor asked Pasquarello how long he had taken to the confounded habit of singing, and where he had got that execrable piece from.

Whereupon Pasquarello replied, that he didn't know what the Doctor would have; he was like the Romans, and had no taste for real music, since he failed to recognise the most talented of musicians. The aria had been written by the greatest of living composers, in whose service he had the good fortune to be, receiving instruction in both music and singing from the master himself.

Gratiano then began guessing, and mentioned the names of a great number of well-known composers and musicians, but at every distinguished name Pasquarello only shook his head contemptuously.

At length Pasquarello said that the Doctor was only exposing gross ignorance, since he did not know the name of the greatest composer of the time. It was no other than Signor Pasquale Capuzzi, who had done him the honour of taking him into his service. Could he not see that he was the friend and servant of Signor Pasquale?

Then the Doctor broke out into a loud long roar of laughter, and cried. What! Had he (Pasquarello) after running away from him (the Doctor), with whom, besides getting his wages and food, he had had his palm tickled with many a copper, had he gone and taken service with the biggest and most inveterate old coxcomb who ever stuffed himself with macaroni, to the patched Carnival fool who strutted about like a satisfied old hen after a shower of rain, to the snarling skinflint, the love-sick old poltroon, who infected the air of the Via Ripetta with the disgusting bleating which he called singing? &c., &c.

To which Pasquarello, quite incensed, made reply that it was nothing but envy which spoke in the Doctor's words; he (Pasquarello) was of course speaking with his heart in his mouth (*parla col cuore in mano*); the Doctor was not at all the man to pass an opinion upon Signor Pasquale Capuzzi di Senigaglia; he was speaking with his heart in his mouth. The Doctor himself had a strong tang of all that he blamed in the excellent Signor Pasquale; but he was speaking with his heart in his mouth; he (Pasquarello) had himself often heard fully six hundred people at once laugh most heartily at Doctor Gratiano, and so forth. Then Pasquarello spoke a long panegyric upon his new master, Signor Pasquale, attributing to him all the virtues under the sun; and he concluded with a description of his character, which he portrayed as being the very essence of amiability and grace.

"Heaven bless you, Formica!" lisped Signor Capuzzi to himself; "Heaven bless you, Formica! I perceive you have designed to make my triumph perfect, since you are upbraiding the Romans for all their envious and ungrateful persecution of me, and are letting them know *who* I really am."

"Ha! here comes my master himself," cried Pasquarello at this moment, and there entered on the stage—Signor Pasquale Capuzzi himself, just as he breathed and walked, his very clothes, face, gestures, gait, postures, in fact so perfectly like Signor Capuzzi in the auditorium, that the latter, quite aghast, let go Marianna's hand, which hitherto he had held fast in his own, and tapped himself, his nose, his wig, in order to discover whether he was not dreaming, or seeing double, whether he was really sitting in Nicolo Musso's theatre and dare credit the miracle.

Capuzzi on the stage embraced Doctor Gratiano with great kindness, and asked how he was. The Doctor replied that he had a good appetite, and slept soundly, at his service (*per servirlo*); and as for his purse—well, it was suffering from a galloping consumption. Only yesterday he had spent his last ducat for a pair of rosemary-coloured stockings for his sweetheart, and was just going to walk round to one or two bankers to see if he could borrow thirty ducats"——

"But how can you pass over your best friends?" said Capuzzi. "Here, my dear sir, here are fifty ducats, come take them."

"Pasquale, what are you about?" said the real Capuzzi in an undertone.

Dr. Gratiano began to talk about a bond and about interest; but Signor Capuzzi declared that he could not think of asking for either from such a friend as the Doctor was.

"Pasquale, have you gone out of your senses?" exclaimed the real Capuzzi a little louder.

After many grateful embraces Doctor Gratiano took his leave. Now Pasquarello drew near with a good many bows, and extolled Signor Capuzzi to the skies, adding, however, that his purse was suffering from the same complaint as Gratiano's, and he begged for some of the same excellent medicine that had cured his. Capuzzi on the stage laughed, and said he was pleased to find that Pasquarello knew how to turn his good humour to advantage, and threw him several glittering ducats.

"Pasquale, you must be mad, possessed of the devil," cried the real Capuzzi aloud. He was bidden be still.

Pasquarello went still further in his eulogy of Capuzzi, and came at last to speak, of the aria which he (Capuzzi) had composed, and with which he (Pasquarello) hoped to enchant everybody. The fictitious Capuzzi clapped Pasquarello heartily on the back, and went on to say that he might venture to tell him (Pasquarello), his faithful servant, in confidence, that in reality he knew nothing whatever of the science of music, and in respect to the aria of which he had just spoken, as well as all pieces that he had ever composed, why, he had stolen them out of Frescobaldi's canzonas and Carissimi's motets.

"I tell you you're lying in your throat, you knave," shouted the Capuzzi off the stage, rising from his seat. Again he was bidden keep still, and the woman who sat next him drew him down on the bench.

"It's now time to think about other and more important matters," continued Capuzzi on the stage. He was going to give a grand banquet the next day, and Pasquarello must look alive and have everything that was necessary prepared. Then he produced and read over a list of all the rarest and most expensive dishes, making Pasquarello tell him how much each would cost, and at the same time giving him the money for them.

"Pasquale! You're insane! You've gone mad! You good-for-nothing scamp! You spendthrift!" shouted the real Capuzzi at intervals, growing more and more enraged the higher the cost of this the most nonsensical of dinners rose.

At length, when the list was finished, Pasquarello asked what had induced him to give such a splendid banquet.

"To-morrow will be the happiest and most joyous day of my life," replied the fictitious Capuzzi. "For know, my good Pasquarello, that I am going to celebrate to-morrow the auspicious marriage of my dear niece Marianna. I am going to give her hand to that brave young fellow, the best of all artists, Scacciati."

Hardly had the words fallen from his lips when the real Capuzzi leapt to his feet, utterly beside himself, quite out of his mind, his face all aflame with the most fiendish rage, and doubling his fists and shaking them at his counterpart on the stage, he yelled at the top of his voice, "No, you won't, no, you won't, you rascal! you scoundrel, you,—Pasquale! Do you mean to cheat yourself out of your Marianna, you hound? Are you going to throw her in the arms of that scoundrel,—sweet Marianna, thy life, thy hope, thy all? Ah! look to it! Look to it! you infatuated fool. Just remember what sort of a reception you will meet with from yourself. You shall beat yourself black and blue with your own hands, so that you will have no relish to think about banquets and weddings!"

But the Capuzzi on the stage doubled his fists like the Capuzzi below, and shouted in exactly the same furious way, and in the same high-pitched voice, "May all the spirits of hell sit at your heart, you abominable nonsensical Pasquale, you atrocious skinflint—you love-sick old fool—you gaudy tricked-out ass with the cap and bells dangling about your ears. Take care lest I snuff out the candle of your life, and so at length put an end to the infamous tricks which you try to foist upon the good, honest, modest Pasquale Capuzzi."

Amidst the most fearful cursing and swearing of the real Capuzzi, the one on the stage dished up one fine anecdote after the other about him.

"You'd better attempt," shouted at last the fictitious Capuzzi, "you only dare, Pasquale, you amorous old ape, to interfere with the happiness of these two young people, whom Heaven has destined for each other."

At this moment there appeared at the back of the stage Antonio Scacciati and Marianna locked in each other's arms. Albeit the old gentleman was at other times somewhat feeble on his legs, yet now fury gave him strength and agility. With a single bound he was on the stage, had drawn his sword, and was charging upon the pretended Antonio. He found, however, that he was held fast behind. An officer of the Papal guard had stopped him, and said in a serious voice, "Recollect where you are, Signor Pasquale; you are in Nicolo Musso's theatre. Without intending it, you have today played a most ridiculous *rôle*. You will not find either Antonio or Marianna here."

The two persons whom Capuzzi had taken for his niece and her lover now drew near, along with the rest of the actors. The faces were all completely strange to him. His rapier escaped from his trembling hand; he took a deep breath as if awakening out of a bad dream; he grasped his brow with both hands; he opened his eyes wide. The presentiment of what had happened suddenly struck him, and he shouted, "Marianna!" in such a stentorian voice that the walls rang again.

But she was beyond reach of his shouts. Antonio had taken advantage of the opportunity whilst Pasquale, oblivious of all about him and even of himself, was quarrelling with his double, to make his way to Marianna, and back with her through the audience, and out at a side door, where a carriage stood ready waiting; and away they went as fast as their horses could gallop towards Florence.

"Marianna!" screamed the old man again, "Marianna! she is gone. She has fled. That knave Antonio has stolen her from me. Away! after them! Have pity on me, good people, and take torches and help me to look for my little darling. Oh! you serpent!"

And he tried to make for the door. But the officer held him fast, saying, "Do you mean that pretty young lady who sat beside you? I believe I saw her slip out with a young man—I think Antonio Scacciati—a long time ago, when you began your idle quarrel with one of the actors who wore a mask like your face. You needn't make a trouble of it; every inquiry shall at once be set on foot, and Marianna shall be brought back to you as soon as she is found. But as for yourself, Signor Pasquale, your behaviour here and your murderous attempt upon the life of that actor compel me to arrest you."

Signor Pasquale, his face as pale as death, incapable of uttering a single word or even a sound, was led away by the very same gendarmes who were to have protected him against masked devils and spectres. Thus it came to pass that on the selfsame night on which he had hoped to celebrate his triumph, he was plunged into the midst of trouble and of all the frantic despondency which amorous old fools feel when they are deceived.

VI.

Salvator Rosa leaves Rome and goes to Florence. Conclusion of the history.

Everything here below beneath the sun is subject to continual change; and perhaps there is nothing which can be called more inconstant than human opinion, which turns round in an everlasting circle like the wheel of fortune. He who reaps great praise to-day is overwhelmed with biting censure to-morrow; to-day we trample under foot the man who to-morrow will be raised far above us.

Of all those who in Rome had ridiculed and mocked at old Pasquale Capuzzi, with his sordid avarice, his foolish amorousness, his insane jealousy, who did not wish poor tormented Marianna her liberty? But now that Antonio had successfully carried off his mistress, all their ridicule and mockery was suddenly changed into pity for the old fool, whom they saw wandering about the streets of Rome with his head hanging on his breast, utterly disconsolate. Misfortunes seldom come singly; and so it happened that Signor Pasquale, soon after Marianna had been taken from him, lost his best bosom-friends also. Little Pitichinaccio choked himself in foolishly trying to swallow an almond-kernel in the middle of a cadenza; but a sudden stop was put to the life of the illustrious Pyramid Doctor Signor Splendiano Accoramboni by a slip of the pen, for which he had only himself to blame. Michele's drubbing made such work with him that he fell into a fever. He determined to make use of a remedy which he claimed to have discovered, so, calling for pen and ink, he wrote down a prescription in which, by employing a wrong sign, he increased the quantity of a powerful substance to a dangerous extent. But scarcely had he swallowed the medicine than he sank back on the pillows and died, establishing, however, by his own death in the most splendid and satisfactory manner the efficacy of the last tincture which he ever prescribed.

As already remarked, all those whose laughter had been the loudest, and who had repeatedly wished Antonio success in his schemes, had now nothing but pity for the old gentleman; and the bitterest blame was heaped, not so much upon Antonio, as upon Salvator Rosa, whom, to be sure, they regarded as the instigator of the whole plan.

Salvator's enemies, of whom he had a goodly number, exerted all their efforts to fan the flame. "See you," they said, "he was one of Masaniello's doughty partisans, and is ready to turn his hand to any deed of mischief, to any disreputable enterprise; we shall be the next to suffer from his presence in the city; he is a dangerous man."

And the jealous faction who had leagued together against Salvator did actually succeed in stemming the tide of his prosperous career. He sent forth from his studio one picture after the other, all bold in conception, and splendidly executed; but the so-called critics shrugged their shoulders, now pointing out that the hills were too blue, the trees too green, the figures now too long, now too broad, finding fault everywhere where there was no fault to be found, and seeking to detract from his hard-earned reputation in all the ways they could think of. Especially bitter in their persecution of him were the Academicians of St. Luke, who could not forget how he took them in about the surgeon; they even went beyond the limits of their own profession, and decried the clever stanzas which Salvator at that time wrote, hinting very plainly that he did not cultivate his fruit on his own garden soil, but plundered that of his neighbours. For these reasons, therefore, Salvator could not manage to surround himself with the splendour which he had lived amidst formerly in Rome. Instead of being visited by the most eminent of the Romans in a large studio, he had to remain with Dame Caterina and his green fig-tree; but amid these poor surroundings he frequently found both consolation and tranquillity of mind.

Salvator took the malicious machinations of his enemies to heart more than he ought to have done; he even began to feel that an insidious disease, resulting from chagrin and dejection, was gnawing at his vitals. In this unhappy frame of mind he designed and executed two large pictures which excited quite an uproar in Rome. Of these one represented the transitoriness of all earthly things, and in the principal figure, that of a wanton female bearing all the indications of her degrading calling about her, was recognised the mistress of one of the cardinals; the other portrayed the Goddess of Fortune dispensing her rich gifts. But cardinals' hats, bishops' mitres, gold medals, decorations of orders, were falling upon bleating sheep, braying asses, and other such like contemptible animals, whilst well-made men in ragged clothes were vainly straining their eyes upwards to get even the smallest gift. Salvator had given free rein to his embittered mood, and the animals' heads bore the closest resemblance to the features of various eminent persons. It is easy to imagine, therefore, how the tide of hatred against him rose, and that he was more bitterly persecuted than ever.

Dame Caterina warned him, with tears in her eyes, that as soon as it began to be dark she had observed suspicious characters lurking about the house and apparently dogging his every footstep. Salvator saw that it was time to leave Rome; and Dame Caterina and her beloved daughters were the only people whom it caused him pain to part from. In response to the repeated invitations of the Duke of Tuscany, he went to Florence; and here at length he was richly indemnified for all the mortification and worry which he had had to struggle against in Rome, and here all the honour and all the fame which he so truly deserved were freely conferred upon him. The Duke's presents and the high prices which he received for his pictures soon enabled him to remove into a large house and to furnish it in the most magnificent style. There he was wont to gather round him the most illustrious authors and scholars of the day, amongst whom it will be sufficient to mention Evangelista Toricelli, Valerio Chimentelli, Battista Ricciardi, Andrea Cavalcanti, Pietro Salvati, Filippo Apolloni, Volumnio Bandelli, Francesco Rovai. They formed an association for the prosecution of artistic and scientific pursuits, whilst Salvator was able to contribute an element of whimsicality to the meetings, which had a singular effect in animating and enlivening the mind. The banqueting-hall was like a beautiful grove with fragrant bushes and flowers and splashing fountains; and the dishes even, which were served up by pages in eccentric costumes, were very wonderful to look at, as if they came from some distant land of magic. These meetings of writers and savans in Salvator Rosa's house were called at that time the Accademia de' Percossi.

Though Salvator's mind was in this way devoted to science and art, yet his real true nature came to life again when he was with his friend Antonio Scacciati, who, along with his lovely Marianna, led the pleasant *sans souci* life of an artist. They often recalled poor old Signor Pasquale whom they had deceived, and all that had taken place in Nicolo Musso's theatre. Antonio asked Salvator how he had contrived to enlist in his cause the active interest not only of Musso but of the excellent Formica, and of Agli too. Salvator replied that it had been very easy, for Formica was his most intimate friend in Rome, so that it had been a work of both pleasure and love to him to arrange everything on the stage in accordance with the instructions Salvator gave him. Antonio protested that, though still he could not help laughing over the scene which had paved the way to his happiness, he yet wished with all his heart to be reconciled to the old gentleman, even if he should never touch a penny of Marianna's fortune, which the old gentleman had confiscated; the practice of his art brought him in a sufficient income. Marianna too was often unable to restrain her tears when she thought that her father's brother might go down to his grave without having forgiven her the trick which she had played upon him; and so Pasquale's hatred overshadowed like a dark cloud the brightness of their happiness. Salvator comforted them both—Antonio and Marianna—by saying that time had adjusted still worse difficulties, and that chance would perhaps bring the old gentleman near them in some less dangerous way than if they had remained in Rome, or were to return there now.

We shall see that a prophetic spirit spoke in Salvator.

A considerable time elapsed, when one day Antonio burst into Salvator's studio breathless and pale as death. "Salvator!" he cried, "Salvator, my friend, my protector! I am lost if you do not help me. Pasquale Capuzzi is here; he has procured a warrant for my arrest for the seduction of his niece."

"But what can Signor Pasquale do against you now?" asked Salvator. "Have you not been united to Marianna by the Church?"

"Oh!" replied Antonio, giving way completely to despair, "the blessing of the Church herself cannot save me from ruin. Heaven knows by what means the old man has been able to approach the Pope's nephew. At any rate the Pope's nephew has taken the old man under his protection, and has infused into him the hope that the Holy Father will declare my marriage with Marianna to be null and void; nay, yet further, that he will grant him (the old man) dispensation to marry his niece."

"Stop!" cried Salvator, "now I see it all; now I see it all. What threatens to be your ruin, Antonio, is this man's hatred against me. For I must tell you that this nephew of the Pope's, a proud, coarse, boorish clown, was amongst the animals in my picture to whom the Goddess of Fortune is dispensing her gifts. That it was I who helped you to win your Marianna, though indirectly, is well known, not only to this man, but to all Rome,—which is quite reason enough to persecute you since they cannot do anything to me. And so, Antonio, having brought this misfortune upon you, I must make every effort to assist you, and all the more that you are my dearest and most intimate friend. But, by the saints! I don't see in what way I can frustrate your enemies' little game"——

Therewith Salvator, who had continued to paint at a picture all the time, laid aside brush, palette, and maulstick, and, rising up from his easel, began to pace the room backwards and forwards, his arms crossed over his breast, Antonio meanwhile being quite wrapt up in his own thoughts, and with his eyes fixed unchangeably upon the floor.

At length Salvator paused before him and said with a smile, "See here, Antonio, I cannot do anything myself against your powerful enemies, but I know one who can help you, and who will help you, and that is—Signor Formica."

"Oh!" said Antonio, "don't jest with an unhappy man, whom nothing can save."

"What! you are despairing again?" exclaimed Salvator, who was now all at once in the merriest humour, and he laughed aloud. "I tell you, Antonio, my friend Formica shall help you in Florence as he helped you in Rome. Go away quietly home and comfort your Marianna, and calmly wait and see how things will turn out. I trust you will be ready at the shortest notice to do what Signor Formica, who is really here in Florence at the present time, shall require of you." This Antonio promised most faithfully, and hope revived in him again, and confidence.

Signor Pasquale Capuzzi was not a little astonished at receiving a formal invitation from the Accademia de' Percossi. "Ah!" he exclaimed, "Florence is the place then where a man's merits are recognised, where Pasquale Capuzzi di Senigaglia, a man gifted with the most excellent talents, is known and valued." Thus the thought of his knowledge and his art, and the honour that was shown him on their account, overcame the repugnance which he would otherwise have felt against a society at the head of which stood Salvator Rosa. His Spanish gala-dress was more carefully brushed than ever; his conical hat was equipped with a new feather; his shoes were provided with new ribbons; and so Signor Pasquale appeared at Salvator's as brilliant as a rose-chafer, and his face all sunshine. The magnificence which he saw on all sides of him, even Salvator himself, who had received him dressed in the richest apparel, inspired him with deep respect, and, after the manner of little souls, who, though at first proud and puffed up, at once grovel in the dust whenever they come into contact with what they feel to be superior to themselves, Pasquale's behaviour towards Salvator, whom he would gladly have done a mischief to in Rome, was nothing but humility and submissive deference.

So much attention was paid to Signor Pasquale from all sides, his judgment was appealed to so unconditionally, and so much was said about his services to art, that he felt new life infused into his veins; and an unusual spirit was awakened within him, so that his utterances on many points were more sensible than might have been expected. If it be added that never in his life before had he been so splendidly entertained, and never had he drunk such inspiring wine, it will readily be conceived that his pleasure was intensified from moment to moment, and that he forgot all the wrong which had been done him at Rome as well as the unpleasant business which had brought him to Florence. Often after their banquets the Academicians were wont to amuse themselves with short impromptu dramatic representations, and so this evening the distinguished playwright and poet Filippo Apolloni called upon those who generally took part in them to bring the festivities to a fitting conclusion with one of their usual performances. Salvator at once withdrew to make all the necessary preparations.

Not long afterwards the bushes at the farther end of the banqueting-hall began to move, the branches with their foliage were parted, and a little theatre provided with seats for the spectators became visible.

"By the saints!" exclaimed Pasquale Capuzzi, terrified, "where am I? Surely that's Nicolo Musso's theatre."

Without heeding his exclamation, Evangelista Toricelli and Andrea Cavalcanti—both of them grave, respectable, venerable men—took him by the arm and led him to a seat immediately in front of the stage, taking their places on each side of him.

This was no sooner done than there appeared on the boards—Formica in the character of Pasquarello.

"You reprobate, Formica!" shouted Pasquale, leaping to his feet and shaking his doubled fist at the stage. Toricelli and Cavalcanti's stern, reproving glances bade him sit still and keep quiet.

Pasquarello wept and sobbed, and cursed his destiny, which brought him nothing but grief and heart-breaking, declared he didn't know how he should ever set about it if he wanted to laugh again, and concluded by saying that if he could look upon blood without fainting, he should certainly cut his throat, or should throw himself in the Tiber if he could only let that cursed swimming alone when he got into the water.

Doctor Gratiano now joined him, and inquired what was the cause of his trouble.

Whereupon Pasquarello asked him whether he did not know anything about what had taken place in the house of his master, Signor Pasquale Capuzzi di Senigaglia, whether he did not know that an infamous scoundrel had carried off pretty Marianna, his master's niece?

"Ah!" murmured Capuzzi, "I see you want to make your excuses to me, Formica; you wish for my pardon—well, we shall see."

Doctor Gratiano expressed his sympathy, and observed that the scoundrel must have gone to work very cunningly to have eluded all the inquiries which had been instituted by Capuzzi.

"Ho! ho!" rejoined Pasquarello. "The Doctor need not imagine that the scoundrel, Antonio Scacciati, had succeeded in escaping the sharpness of Signor Pasquale Capuzzi, supported as he was, moreover, by powerful friends. Antonio had been arrested, his marriage with Marianna annulled, and Marianna herself had again come into Capuzzi's power.

"Has he got her again?" shouted Capuzzi, beside himself; "has he got her again, good Pasquale? Has he got his little darling, his Marianna? Is the knave Antonio arrested? Heaven bless you, Formica!"

"You take a too keen interest in the play, Signor Pasquale," said Cavalcanti, quite seriously. "Pray permit the actors to proceed with their parts without interrupting them in this disturbing fashion."

Ashamed of himself, Signor Pasquale resumed his seat, for he had again risen to his feet.

Doctor Gratiano asked what had taken place then.

A wedding, continued Pasquarello, a wedding had taken place. Marianna had repented of what she had done; Signor Pasquale had obtained the desired dispensation from the Holy Father, and had married his niece.

"Yes, yes," murmured Pasquale Capuzzi to himself, whilst his eyes sparkled with delight, "yes, yes, my dear, good Formica; he will marry his sweet Marianna, the happy Pasquale. He knew that the dear little darling had always loved him, and that it was only Satan who had led her astray."

"Why then, everything is all right," said Doctor Gratiano, "and there's no cause for lamentation."

Pasquarello began, however, to weep and sob more violently than before, till at length, as if overcome by the terrible nature of his pain, he fainted away. Doctor Gratiano ran backwards and forwards in great distress, was so sorry he had no smelling-bottle with him, felt in all his pockets, and at last produced a roasted chestnut, and put it under the insensible Pasquarello's nose. He at once recovered, sneezing violently, and begging him to attribute his faintness to his weak nerves, he related how that, immediately after the marriage, Marianna had been afflicted with the saddest melancholy, continually calling upon Antonio, and treating the old gentleman with contempt and aversion. But the old fellow, quite infatuated by his passion and jealousy, had not ceased to torment the poor girl with his folly in the most abominable way. And here Pasquarello mentioned a host of mad tricks which Pasquale had done, and which were really current in Rome about him. Signor Capuzzi sat on thorns; he murmured at intervals, "Curse you, Formica! You are lying! What evil spirit is in you?" He was only prevented from bursting out into a violent passion by Toricelli and Cavalcanti, who sat watching him with an earnest gaze.

Pasquarello concluded his narration by telling that Marianna had at length succumbed to her unsatisfied longing for her lover, her great distress of mind, and the innumerable tortures which were inflicted upon her by the execrable old fellow, and had died in the flower of her youth.

At this moment was heard a mournful *De profundis* sung by hollow, husky voices, and men clad in long black robes appeared on the stage, bearing an open coffin, within which was seen the corpse of lovely Marianna wrapped in white shrouds. Behind it came Signor Pasquale Capuzzi in the deepest mourning, feebly staggering along and wailing aloud, beating his breast, and crying in a voice of despair, "O Marianna! Marianna!"

So soon as the real Capuzzi caught sight of his niece's corpse he broke out into loud lamentations, and both Capuzzis, the one on the stage and the one off, gave vent to their grief in the most heartrending wails and groans, "O Marianna! O Marianna! O unhappy me! Alas! Alas for me!"

Let the reader picture to himself the open coffin with the corpse of the lovely child, surrounded by the hired mourners singing their dismal *De profundis* in hoarse voices, and then the comical masks of Pasquarello and Dr. Gratiano, who were expressing their grief in the most ridiculous gestures, and lastly the two Capuzzis, wailing and screeching in despair. Indeed, all who were witnesses of the extraordinary spectacle could not help feeling, even in the midst of the unrestrained laughter they had burst out into at sight of the wonderful old gentleman, that their hearts were chilled by a most uncomfortable feeling of awe.

Now the stage grew dark, and it thundered and lightened, and there rose up from below a pale ghostly figure, which bore most unmistakably the features of Capuzzi's dead brother, Pietro of Senigaglia, Marianna's father.

"O you infamous brother, Pasquale! what have you done with my daughter? what have you done with my daughter?" wailed the figure, in a dreadful and hollow voice. "Despair, you atrocious murderer of my child. You shall find your reward in hell."

Capuzzi on the stage dropped on the floor as if struck by lightning, and at the same moment the real Capuzzi reeled from his seat unconscious. The bushes rustled together again, and the stage was gone, and also Marianna and Capuzzi and the ghastly spectre Pietro. Signor Pasquale Capuzzi lay in such a dead faint that it cost a good deal of trouble to revive him.

At length he came to himself with a deep sigh, and, stretching out both hands before him as if to ward off the horror that had seized him, he cried in a husky voice, "Leave me alone, Pietro." Then a torrent of tears ran down his cheeks, and he sobbed and cried, "Oh! Marianna, my darling child—my—my Marianna." "But recollect yourself," said now Cavalcanti, "recollect yourself, Signor Pasquale, it was only on the stage that you saw your niece dead. She is alive; she is here to crave pardon for the thoughtless step which love and also your own inconsiderate conduct drove her to take."

And Marianna, and behind her Antonio Scacciati, now ran forward from the back part of the hall and threw themselves at the old gentleman's feet,—for he had meanwhile been placed in an easy chair. Marianna, looking most charming and beautiful, kissed his hands and bathed them with scalding tears, beseeching him to pardon both her and Antonio, to whom she had been united by the blessing of the Church.

Suddenly the hot blood surged into the old man's pallid face, fury flashed from his eyes, and he cried in a half-choked voice, "Oh! you abominable scoundrel! You poisonous serpent whom I nourished in my bosom!" Then old Toricelli, with grave and thoughtful dignity, put himself in front of Capuzzi, and told him that he (Capuzzi) had seen a representation of the fate that would inevitably and irremediably overtake him if he had the hardihood to carry out his wicked purpose against Antonio and Marianna's peace and happiness. He depicted in startling colours the folly and madness of amorous old men, who call down upon their own heads the most ruinous mischief which Heaven can inflict upon a man, since all the love which might have fallen to their share is lost, and instead hatred and contempt shoot their fatal darts at them from every side.

At intervals lovely Marianna cried in a tone that went to everybody's heart, "O my uncle, I will love and honour you as my own father; you will kill me by a cruel death if you rob me of my Antonio." And all the eminent men by whom the old gentleman was surrounded cried with one accord that it would not be possible for a man like Signor Pasquale Capuzzi di Senigaglia, a patron of art and himself an artist, not to forgive the young people, and assume the part of father to the most lovely of ladies, not possible that he could refuse to accept with joy as his son-in-law such an artist as Antonio Scacciati, who was highly esteemed throughout all Italy and richly crowned with fame and honour.

Then it was patent to see that a violent struggle went on within the old gentleman. He sighed, moaned, clasped his hands before his face, and, whilst Toricelli was continuing to speak in a most impressive manner, and Marianna was appealing to him in the most touching accents, and the rest were extolling Antonio all they knew how, he kept looking down—now upon his niece, now upon Antonio, whose splendid clothes and rich chains of honour bore testimony to the truth of what was said about the artistic fame he had earned.

Gone was all rage out of Capuzzi's countenance; he sprang up with radiant eyes, and pressed Marianna to his heart, saying, "Yes, I forgive you, my dear child; I forgive you, Antonio. Far be it from me to disturb your happiness. You are right, my worthy Signor Toricelli; Formica has shown me in the tableau on the stage all the mischief and ruin that would have befallen me had I carried out my insane design. I am cured, quite cured of my folly. But where is Signor Formica, where is my good physician? let me thank him a thousand times for my cure; it is he alone who has accomplished it. The terror that he has caused me to feel has brought about a complete revolution within me."

Pasquarello stepped forward. Antonio threw himself upon his neck, crying, "O Signor Formica, you to whom I owe my life, my all—oh! take off this disfiguring mask, that I may see your face, that Formica may not be any longer a mystery to me."

Pasquarello took off his cap and his artificial mask, which looked like a natural face, since it offered not the slightest hindrance to the play of countenance, and this Formica, this Pasquarello, was transformed into—Salvator Rosa.

"Salvator!" exclaimed Marianna, Antonio, and Capuzzi, utterly astounded.

"Yes," said that wonderful man, "it is Salvator Rosa, whom the Romans would not recognise as painter and poet, but who in the character of Formica drew from them, without their being aware of it, almost every evening for more than a year, in Nicolo Musso's wretched little theatre, the most noisy and most demonstrative storms of applause, from whose mouth they willingly took all the scorn, and all the satiric mockery of what is bad, which they would on no account listen to and see in Salvator's poems and pictures. It is Salvator Formica who has helped you, dear Antonio."

"Salvator," began old Capuzzi, "Salvator Rosa, albeit I have always regarded you as my worst enemy, yet I have always prized your artistic skill very highly, and now I love you as the worthiest friend I have, and beg you to accept my friendship in return."

"Tell me," replied Salvator, "tell me, my worthy Signor Pasquale, what service I can render you, and accept my assurances beforehand, that I will leave no stone unturned to accomplish whatever you may ask of me."

And now the genial smile which had not been seen upon Capuzzi's face since Marianna had been carried off, began to steal back again. Taking Salvator's hand he lisped in a low voice, "My dear Signor Salvator, you possess an unlimited influence over good Antonio; beseech him in my name to permit me to spend the short rest of my days with him, and my dear daughter Marianna, and to accept at my hands the inheritance left her by her mother, as well as the good dowry which I was thinking of adding to it. And he must not look jealous if I occasionally kiss the dear sweet child's little white hand; and ask him—every Sunday at least when I go to Mass, to trim up my rough moustache, for there's nobody in all the wide world understands it so well as he does."

It cost Salvator an effort to repress his laughter at the strange old man; but before he could make any reply, Antonio and Marianna, embracing the old gentleman, assured him that they should not believe he was fully reconciled to them, and should not be really happy, until he came to live with them as their dear father, never to leave them again. Antonio added that not only on Sunday, but every other day, he would trim Capuzzi's moustache as elegantly as he knew how, and accordingly the old gentleman was perfectly radiant with delight. Meanwhile a splendid supper had been prepared, to which the entire company now turned in the best of spirits.

In taking my leave of you, beloved reader, I wish with all my heart that, whilst you have been reading the story of the wonderful Signor Formica, you have derived as much pure pleasure from it as Salvator and all his friends felt on sitting down to their supper.

* * * * * * *

THE SAND-MAN.

NATHANAEL TO LOTHAIR.

I know you are all very uneasy because I have not written for such a long, long time. Mother, to be sure, is angry, and Clara, I dare say, believes I am living here in riot and revelry, and quite forgetting my sweet angel, whose image is so deeply engraved upon my heart and mind. But that is not so; daily and hourly do I think of you all, and my lovely Clara's form comes to gladden me in my dreams, and smiles upon me with her bright eyes, as graciously as she used to do in the days when I went in and out amongst you. Oh! how could I write to you in the distracted state of mind in which I have been, and which, until now, has quite bewildered me! A terrible thing has happened to me. Dark forebodings of some awful fate threatening me are spreading themselves out over my head like black clouds, impenetrable to every friendly ray of sunlight. I must now tell you what has taken place; I must, that I see well enough, but only to think upon it makes the wild laughter burst from my lips. Oh! my dear, dear Lothair, what shall I say to make you feel, if only in an inadequate way, that that which happened to me a few days ago could thus really exercise such a hostile and disturbing influence upon my life? Oh that you were here to see for yourself! but now you will, I suppose, take me for a superstitious ghost-seer. In a word, the terrible thing which I have experienced, the fatal effect of which I in vain exert every effort to shake off, is simply that some days ago, namely, on the 30th October, at twelve o'clock at noon, a dealer in weather-glasses came into my room and wanted to sell me one of his wares. I bought nothing, and threatened to kick him downstairs, whereupon he went away of his own accord.

You will conclude that it can only be very peculiar relations— relations intimately intertwined with my life— that can give significance to this event, and that it must be the person of this unfortunate hawker which has had such a very inimical effect upon me. And so it really is. I will summon up all my faculties in order to narrate to you calmly and patiently as much of the early days of my youth as will suffice to put matters before you in such a way that your keen sharp intellect may grasp everything clearly and distinctly, in bright and living pictures. Just as I am beginning, I hear you laugh and Clara say, "What's all this childish nonsense about!" Well, laugh at me, laugh heartily at me, pray do. But, good God! my hair is standing on end, and I seem to be entreating you to laugh at me in the same sort of frantic despair in which Franz Moor entreated Daniel to laugh him to scorn. But to my story.

Except at dinner we, *i.e.*, I and my brothers and sisters, saw but little of our father all day long. His business no doubt took up most of his time. After our evening meal, which, in accordance with an old custom, was served at seven o'clock, we all went, mother with us, into father's room, and took our places around a round table. My father smoked his pipe, drinking a large glass of beer to it. Often he told us many wonderful stories, and got so excited over them that his pipe always went out; I used then to light it for him with a spill, and this formed my chief amusement. Often, again, he would give us picture-books to look at, whilst he sat silent and motionless in his easy-chair, puffing out such dense clouds of smoke that we were all as it were enveloped in mist. On such evenings mother was very sad; and directly it struck nine she said, "Come, children! off to bed! Come! The 'Sand-man' is come I see." And I always did seem to hear something trampling upstairs with slow heavy steps; that must be the Sand-man. Once in particular I was very much frightened at this dull trampling and knocking; as mother was leading us out of the room I asked her, "O mamma! but who is this nasty Sand-man who always sends us away from papa? What does he look like?" "There is no Sand-man, my dear child," mother answered; "when I say the Sand-man is come, I only mean that you are sleepy and can't keep your eyes open, as if somebody had put sand in them." This answer of mother's did not satisfy me; nay, in my childish mind the thought clearly unfolded itself that mother denied there was a Sand-man only to prevent us being afraid,—why, I always heard him come upstairs. Full of curiosity to learn something more about this Sand-man and what he had to do with us children, I at length asked the old woman who acted as my youngest sister's attendant, what sort of a man he was—the Sand-man? "Why, 'thanael, darling, don't you know?" she replied. "Oh! he's a wicked man, who comes to little children when they won't go to bed and throws handfuls of sand in their eyes, so that they jump out of their heads all bloody; and he puts them into a bag and takes them to the half-moon as food for his little ones; and they sit there in the nest and have hooked beaks like owls, and they pick naughty little boys' and girls' eyes out with them." After this I formed in my own mind a horrible picture of the cruel Sand-man. When anything came blundering upstairs at night I trembled with fear and dismay; and all that my mother could get out of me were the stammered words "The Sandman! the Sand-man!" whilst the tears coursed down my cheeks. Then I ran into my bedroom, and the whole night through tormented myself with the terrible apparition of the Sand-man. I was quite old enough to perceive that the old woman's tale about the Sand-man and his little ones' nest in the half-moon couldn't be altogether true; nevertheless the Sand-man continued to be for me a fearful incubus, and I was always seized with terror—my blood always ran cold, not only when I heard anybody come up the stairs, but when I heard anybody noisily open my father's room door and go in. Often he stayed away for a long season altogether; then he would come several times in close succession.

 This went on for years, without my being able to accustom myself to this fearful apparition, without the image of the horrible Sand-man growing any fainter in my imagination. His intercourse with my father began to occupy my fancy ever more and more; I was restrained from asking my father about him by an unconquerable shyness; but as the years went on the desire waxed stronger and stronger within me to fathom the mystery myself and to see the fabulous Sand-man. He had been the means of disclosing to me the path of the wonderful and the adventurous, which so easily find lodgment in the mind of the child. I liked nothing better than to hear or read horrible stories of goblins, witches, Tom Thumbs, and so on; but always at the head of them all stood the Sand-man, whose picture I scribbled in the most extraordinary and repulsive forms with both chalk and coal everywhere, on the tables, and cupboard doors, and walls. When I was ten years old my mother removed me from the nursery into a little chamber off the corridor not far from my father's room. We still had to withdraw hastily whenever, on the stroke of nine, the mysterious unknown was heard in the house. As I lay in my little chamber I could hear him go into father's room, and soon afterwards I fancied there was a fine and peculiar smelling steam spreading itself through the house. As my curiosity waxed stronger, my resolve to make somehow or other the Sand-man's acquaintance took deeper root. Often when my mother had gone past, I slipped quickly out of my room into the corridor, but I could never see anything, for always before I could reach the place where I could get sight of him, the Sand-man was well inside the door. At last, unable to resist the impulse any longer, I determined to conceal myself in father's room and there wait for the Sand-man.

 One evening I perceived from my father's silence and mother's sadness that the Sand-man would come; accordingly, pleading that I was excessively tired, I left the room before nine o'clock and concealed myself in a hiding-place close beside the door. The street door creaked, and slow, heavy, echoing steps crossed the passage towards the stairs. Mother hurried past me with my brothers and sisters. Softly—softly—I opened father's room door. He sat as usual, silent and motionless, with his back towards it; he did not hear me; and in a moment I was in and behind a curtain drawn before my father's open wardrobe, which stood just inside the room. Nearer and nearer and nearer came the echoing footsteps. There was a strange coughing and shuffling and mumbling outside. My heart beat with expectation and fear. A quick step now close, close beside the door, a noisy rattle of the handle, and the door flies open with a bang. Recovering my courage with an effort, I take a cautious peep out. In the middle of the room in front of my father stands the Sand-man, the bright light of the lamp falling full upon his face. The Sand-man, the terrible Sand-man, is the old advocate *Coppelius* who often comes to dine with us.

But the most hideous figure could not have awakened greater trepidation in my heart than this Coppelius did. Picture to yourself a large broad-shouldered man, with an immensely big head, a face the colour of yellow-ochre, grey bushy eyebrows, from beneath which two piercing, greenish, cat-like eyes glittered, and a prominent Roman nose hanging over his upper lip. His distorted mouth was often screwed up into a malicious smile; then two dark-red spots appeared on his cheeks, and a strange hissing noise proceeded from between his tightly clenched teeth. He always wore an ash-grey coat of an old-fashioned cut, a waistcoat of the same, and nether extremities to match, but black stockings and buckles set with stones on his shoes. His little wig scarcely extended beyond the crown of his head, his hair was curled round high up above his big red ears, and plastered to his temples with cosmetic, and a broad closed hair-bag stood out prominently from his neck, so that you could see the silver buckle that fastened his folded neck-cloth. Altogether he was a most disagreeable and horribly ugly figure; but what we children detested most of all was his big coarse hairy hands; we could never fancy anything that he had once touched. This he had noticed; and so, whenever our good mother quietly placed a piece of cake or sweet fruit on our plates, he delighted to touch it under some pretext or other, until the bright tears stood in our eyes, and from disgust and loathing we lost the enjoyment of the tit-bit that was intended to please us. And he did just the same thing when father gave us a glass of sweet wine on holidays. Then he would quickly pass his hand over it, or even sometimes raise the glass to his blue lips, and he laughed quite sardonically when all we dared do was to express our vexation in stifled sobs. He habitually called us the "little brutes;" and when he was present we might not utter a sound; and we cursed the ugly spiteful man who deliberately and intentionally spoilt all our little pleasures. Mother seemed to dislike this hateful Coppelius as much as we did; for as soon as he appeared her cheerfulness and bright and natural manner were transformed into sad, gloomy seriousness. Father treated him as if he were a being of some higher race, whose ill-manners were to be tolerated, whilst no efforts ought to be spared to keep him in good-humour. He had only to give a slight hint, and his favourite dishes were cooked for him and rare wine uncorked.

As soon as I saw this Coppelius, therefore, the fearful and hideous thought arose in my mind that he, and he alone, must be the Sand-man; but I no longer conceived of the Sand-man as the bugbear in the old nurse's fable, who fetched children's eyes and took them to the half-moon as food for his little ones—no! but as an ugly spectre-like fiend bringing trouble and misery and ruin, both temporal and everlasting, everywhere wherever he appeared.

I was spell-bound on the spot. At the risk of being discovered, and, as I well enough knew, of being severely punished, I remained as I was, with my head thrust through the curtains listening. My father received Coppelius in a ceremonious manner. "Come, to work!" cried the latter, in a hoarse snarling voice, throwing off his coat. Gloomily and silently my father took off his dressing-gown, and both put on long black smock-frocks. Where they took them from I forgot to notice. Father opened the folding-doors of a cupboard in the wall; but I saw that what I had so long taken to be a cupboard was really a dark recess, in which was a little hearth. Coppelius approached it, and a blue flame crackled upwards from it. Round about were all kinds of strange utensils. Good God! as my old father bent down over the fire how different he looked! His gentle and venerable features seemed to be drawn up by some dreadful convulsive pain into an ugly, repulsive Satanic mask. He looked like Coppelius. Coppelius plied the red-hot tongs and drew bright glowing masses out of the thick smoke and began assiduously to hammer them. I fancied that there were men's faces visible round about, but without eyes, having ghastly deep black holes where the eyes should have been. "Eyes here! Eyes here!" cried Coppelius, in a hollow sepulchral voice. My blood ran cold with horror; I screamed and tumbled out of my hiding-place into the floor. Coppelius immediately seized upon me. "You little brute! You little brute!" he bleated, grinding his teeth. Then, snatching me up, he threw me on the hearth, so that the flames began to singe my hair. "Now we've got eyes—eyes—a beautiful pair of children's eyes," he whispered, and, thrusting his hands into the flames he took out some red-hot grains and was about to strew them into my eyes. Then my father clasped his hands and entreated him, saying, "Master, master, let my Nathanael keep his eyes—oh! do let him keep them." Coppelius laughed shrilly and replied, "Well then, the boy may keep his eyes and whine and pule his way through the world; but we will now at any rate observe the mechanism of the hand and the foot." And therewith he roughly laid hold upon me, so that my joints cracked, and twisted my hands and my feet, pulling them now this way, and now that, "That's not quite right altogether! It's better as it was!—the old fellow knew what he was about." Thus lisped and hissed Coppelius; but all around me grew black and dark; a sudden convulsive pain shot through all my nerves and bones; I knew nothing more.

I felt a soft warm breath fanning my cheek; I awakened as if out of the sleep of death; my mother was bending over me. "Is the Sand-man still there?" I stammered. "No, my dear child; he's been gone a long, long time; he'll not hurt you." Thus spoke my mother, as she kissed her recovered darling and pressed him to her heart. But why should I tire you, my dear Lothair? why do I dwell at such length on these details, when there's so much remains to be said? Enough—I was detected in my eavesdropping, and roughly handled by Coppelius. Fear and terror had brought on a violent fever, of which I lay ill several weeks. "Is the Sand-man still there?" these were the first words I uttered on coming to myself again, the first sign of my recovery, of my safety. Thus, you see, I have only to relate to you the most terrible moment of my youth for you to thoroughly understand that it must not be ascribed to the weakness of my eyesight if all that I see is colourless, but to the fact that a mysterious destiny has hung a dark veil of clouds about my life, which I shall perhaps only break through when I die.

Coppelius did not show himself again; it was reported he had left the town.

It was about a year later when, in pursuance of the old unchanged custom, we sat around the round table in the evening. Father was in very good spirits, and was telling us amusing tales about his youthful travels. As it was striking nine we all at once heard the street door creak on its hinges, and slow ponderous steps echoed across the passage and up the stairs. "That is Coppelius," said my mother, turning pale. "Yes, it is Coppelius," replied my father in a faint broken voice. The tears started from my mother's eyes. "But, father, father," she cried, "must it be so?" "This is the last time," he replied; "this is the last time he will come to me, I promise you. Go now, go and take the children. Go, go to bed—good-night."

As for me, I felt as if I were converted into cold, heavy stone; I could not get my breath. As I stood there immovable my mother seized me by the arm. "Come, Nathanael! do come along!" I suffered myself to be led away; I went into my room. "Be a good boy and keep quiet," mother called after me; "get into bed and go to sleep." But, tortured by indescribable fear and uneasiness, I could not close my eyes. That hateful, hideous Coppelius stood before me with his glittering eyes, smiling maliciously down upon me; in vain did I strive to banish the image. Somewhere about midnight there was a terrific crack, as if a cannon were being fired off. The whole house shook; something went rustling and clattering past my door; the house-door was pulled to with a bang. "That is Coppelius," I cried, terror-struck, and leapt out of bed. Then I heard a wild heartrending scream; I rushed into my father's room; the door stood open, and clouds of suffocating smoke came rolling towards me. The servant-maid shouted, "Oh! my master! my master!" On the floor in front of the smoking hearth lay my father, dead, his face burned black and fearfully distorted, my sisters weeping and moaning around him, and my mother lying near them in a swoon. "Coppelius, you atrocious fiend, you've killed my father," I shouted. My senses left me. Two days later, when my father was placed in his coffin, his features were mild and gentle again as they had been when he was alive. I found great consolation in the thought that his association with the diabolical Coppelius could not have ended in his everlasting ruin.

Our neighbours had been awakened by the explosion; the affair got talked about, and came before the magisterial authorities, who wished to cite Coppelius to clear himself. But he had disappeared from the place, leaving no traces behind him.

Now when I tell you, my dear friend, that the weather-glass hawker I spoke of was the villain Coppelius, you will not blame me for seeing impending mischief in his inauspicious reappearance. He was differently dressed; but Coppelius's figure and features are too deeply impressed upon my mind for me to be capable of making a mistake in the matter. Moreover, he has not even changed his name. He proclaims himself here, I learn, to be a Piedmontese mechanician, and styles himself Giuseppe Coppola.

I am resolved to enter the lists against him and revenge my father's death, let the consequences be what they may.

Don't say a word to mother about the reappearance of this odious monster. Give my love to my darling Clara; I will write to her when I am in a somewhat calmer frame of mind. Adieu, &c.

* * * * * *

CLARA TO NATHANAEL.

You are right, you have not written to me for a very long time, but nevertheless I believe that I still retain a place in your mind and thoughts. It is a proof that you were thinking a good deal about me when you were sending off your last letter to brother Lothair, for instead of directing it to him you directed it to me. With joy I tore open the envelope, and did not perceive the mistake until I read the words, "Oh! my dear, dear Lothair." Now I know I ought not to have read any more of the letter, but ought to have given it to my brother. But as you have so often in innocent raillery made it a sort of reproach against me that I possessed such a calm, and, for a woman, cool-headed temperament that I should be like the woman we read of—if the house was threatening to tumble down, I should, before hastily fleeing, stop to smooth down a crumple in the window-curtains—I need hardly tell you that the beginning of your letter quite upset me. I could scarcely breathe; there was a bright mist before my eyes. Oh! my darling Nathanael! what could this terrible thing be that had happened? Separation from you—never to see you again, the thought was like a sharp knife in my heart. I read on and on. Your description of that horrid Coppelius made my flesh creep. I now learnt for the first time what a terrible and violent death your good old father died. Brother Lothair, to whom I handed over his property, sought to comfort me, but with little success.

That horrid weather-glass hawker Giuseppe Coppola followed me everywhere; and I am almost ashamed to confess it, but he was able to disturb my sound and in general calm sleep with all sorts of wonderful dream-shapes. But soon—the next day—I saw everything in a different light. Oh! do not be angry with me, my best-beloved, if, despite your strange presentiment that Coppelius will do you some mischief, Lothair tells you I am in quite as good spirits, and just the same as ever.

I will frankly confess, it seems to me that all that was fearsome and terrible of which you speak, existed only in your own self, and that the real true outer world had but little to do with it. I can quite admit that old Coppelius may have been highly obnoxious to you children, but your real detestation of him arose from the fact that he hated children.

Naturally enough the gruesome Sand-man of the old nurse's story was associated in your childish mind with old Coppelius, who, even though you had not believed in the Sand-man, would have been to you a ghostly bugbear, especially dangerous to children. His mysterious labours along with your father at night-time were, I daresay, nothing more than secret experiments in alchemy, with which your mother could not be over well pleased, owing to the large sums of money that most likely were thrown away upon them; and besides, your father, his mind full of the deceptive striving after higher knowledge, may probably have become rather indifferent to his family, as so often happens in the case of such experimentalists. So also it is equally probable that your father brought about his death by his own imprudence, and that Coppelius is not to blame for it. I must tell you that yesterday I asked our experienced neighbour, the chemist, whether in experiments of this kind an explosion could take place which would have a momentarily fatal effect. He said, "Oh, certainly!" and described to me in his prolix and circumstantial way how it could be occasioned, mentioning at the same time so many strange and funny words that I could not remember them at all. Now I know you will be angry at your Clara, and will say, "Of the Mysterious which often clasps man in its invisible arms there's not a ray can find its way into this cold heart. She sees only the varied surface of the things of the world, and, like the little child, is pleased with the golden glittering fruit; at the kernel of which lies the fatal poison."

Oh! my beloved Nathanael, do you believe then that the intuitive prescience of a dark power working within us to our own ruin cannot exist also in minds which are cheerful, natural, free from care? But please forgive me that I, a simple girl, presume in any way to indicate to you what I really think of such an inward strife. After all, I should not find the proper words, and you would only laugh at me, not because my thoughts were stupid, but because I was so foolish as to attempt to tell them to you.

If there is a dark and hostile power which traitorously fixes a thread in our hearts in order that, laying hold of it and drawing us by means of it along a dangerous road to ruin, which otherwise we should not have trod—if, I say, there is such a power, it must assume within us a form like ourselves, nay, it must be ourselves; for only in that way can we believe in it, and only so understood do we yield to it so far that it is able to accomplish its secret purpose. So long as we have sufficient firmness, fortified by cheerfulness, to always acknowledge foreign hostile influences for what they really are, whilst we quietly pursue the path pointed out to us by both inclination and calling, then this mysterious power perishes in its futile struggles to attain the form which is to be the reflected image of ourselves. It is also certain, Lothair adds, that if we have once voluntarily given ourselves up to this dark physical power, it often reproduces within us the strange forms which the outer world throws in our way, so that thus it is we ourselves who engender within ourselves the spirit which by some remarkable delusion we imagine to speak in that outer form. It is the phantom of our own self whose intimate relationship with, and whose powerful influence upon our soul either plunges us into hell or elevates us to heaven. Thus you will see, my beloved Nathanael, that I and brother Lothair have well talked over the subject of dark powers and forces; and now, after I have with some difficulty written down the principal results of our discussion, they seem to me to contain many really profound thoughts. Lothair's last words, however, I don't quite understand altogether; I only dimly guess what he means; and yet I cannot help thinking it is all very true, I beg you, dear, strive to forget the ugly advocate Coppelius as well as the weather-glass hawker Giuseppe Coppola. Try and convince yourself that these foreign influences can have no power over you, that it is only the belief in their hostile power which can in reality make them dangerous to you. If every line of your letter did not betray the violent excitement of your mind, and if I did not sympathise with your condition from the bottom of my heart, I could in truth jest about the advocate Sand-man and weather-glass hawker Coppelius. Pluck up your spirits! Be cheerful! I have resolved to appear to you as your guardian-angel if that ugly man Coppola should dare take it into his head to bother you in your dreams, and drive him away with a good hearty laugh. I'm not afraid of him and his nasty hands, not the least little bit; I won't let him either as advocate spoil any dainty tit-bit I've taken, or as Sand-man rob me of my eyes.

My darling, darling Nathanael,
Eternally your, &c. &c.

* * * * * *

NATHANAEL TO LOTHAIR.

I am very sorry that Clara opened and read my last letter to you; of course the mistake is to be attributed to my own absence of mind. She has written me a very deep philosophical letter, proving conclusively that Coppelius and Coppola only exist in my own mind and are phantoms of my own self, which will at once be dissipated, as soon as I look upon them in that light. In very truth one can hardly believe that the mind which so often sparkles in those bright, beautifully smiling, childlike eyes of hers like a sweet lovely dream could draw such subtle and scholastic distinctions. She also mentions your name. You have been talking about me. I suppose you have been giving her lectures, since she sifts and refines everything so acutely. But enough of this! I must now tell you it is most certain that the weather-glass hawker Giuseppe Coppola is not the advocate Coppelius. I am attending the lectures of our recently appointed Professor of Physics, who, like the distinguished naturalist, is called Spalanzani, and is of Italian origin. He has known Coppola for many years; and it is also easy to tell from his accent that he really is a Piedmontese. Coppelius was a German, though no honest German, I fancy. Nevertheless I am not quite satisfied. You and Clara will perhaps take me for a gloomy dreamer, but nohow can I get rid of the impression which Coppelius's cursed face made upon me. I am glad to learn from Spalanzani that he has left the town. This Professor Spalanzani is a very queer fish. He is a little fat man, with prominent cheek-bones, thin nose, projecting lips, and small piercing eyes. You cannot get a better picture of him than by turning over one of the Berlin pocket-almanacs and looking at Cagliostro's portrait engraved by Chodowiecki; Spalanzani looks just like him.

Once lately, as I went up the steps to his house, I perceived that beside the curtain which generally covered a glass door there was a small chink. What it was that excited my curiosity I cannot explain; but I looked through. In the room I saw a female, tall, very slender, but of perfect proportions, and splendidly dressed, sitting at a little table, on which she had placed both her arms, her hands being folded together. She sat opposite the door, so that I could easily see her angelically beautiful face. She did not appear to notice me, and there was moreover a strangely fixed look about her eyes, I might almost say they appeared as if they had no power of vision; I thought she was sleeping with her eyes open. I felt quite uncomfortable, and so I slipped away quietly into the Professor's lecture-room, which was close at hand. Afterwards I learnt that the figure which I had seen was Spalanzani's daughter, Olimpia, whom he keeps locked in a most wicked and unaccountable way, and no man is ever allowed to come near her. Perhaps, however, there is after all, something peculiar about her; perhaps she's an idiot or something of that sort. But why am I telling you all this? I could have told you it all better and more in detail when I see you. For in a fortnight I shall be amongst you. I must see my dear sweet angel, my Clara, again. Then the little bit of ill-temper, which, I must confess, took possession of me after her fearfully sensible letter, will be blown away. And that is the reason why I am not writing to her as well to-day. With all best wishes, &c.

* * * * * *

Nothing more strange and extraordinary can be imagined, gracious reader, than what happened to my poor friend, the young student Nathanael, and which I have undertaken to relate to you. Have you ever lived to experience anything that completely took possession of your heart and mind and thoughts to the utter exclusion of everything else? All was seething and boiling within you; your blood, heated to fever pitch, leapt through your veins and inflamed your cheeks. Your gaze was so peculiar, as if seeking to grasp in empty space forms not seen of any other eye, and all your words ended in sighs betokening some mystery. Then your friends asked you, "What is the matter with you, my dear friend? What do you see?" And, wishing to describe the inner pictures in all their vivid colours, with their lights and their shades, you in vain struggled to find words with which to express yourself. But you felt as if you must gather up all the events that had happened, wonderful, splendid, terrible, jocose, and awful, in the very first word, so that the whole might be revealed by a single electric discharge, so to speak. Yet every word and all that partook of the nature of communication by intelligible sounds seemed to be colourless, cold, and dead. Then you try and try again, and stutter and stammer, whilst your friends' prosy questions strike like icy winds upon your heart's hot fire until they extinguish it. But if, like a bold painter, you had first sketched in a few audacious strokes the outline of the picture you had in your soul, you would then easily have been able to deepen and intensify the colours one after the other, until the varied throng of living figures carried your friends away, and they, like you, saw themselves in the midst of the scene that had proceeded out of your own soul.

Strictly speaking, indulgent reader, I must indeed confess to you, nobody has asked me for the history of young Nathanael; but you are very well aware that I belong to that remarkable class of authors who, when they are bearing anything about in their minds in the manner I have just described, feel as if everybody who comes near them, and also the whole world to boot, were asking, "Oh! what is it? Oh! do tell us, my good sir?" Hence I was most powerfully impelled to narrate to you Nathanael's ominous life. My soul was full of the elements of wonder and extraordinary peculiarity in it; but, for this very reason, and because it was necessary in the very beginning to dispose you, indulgent reader, to bear with what is fantastic—and that is not a little thing—I racked my brain to find a way of commencing the story in a significant and original manner, calculated to arrest your attention. To begin with "Once upon a time," the best beginning for a story, seemed to me too tame; with "In the small country town S—— lived," rather better, at any rate allowing plenty of room to work up to the climax; or to plunge at once *in medias res*, "'Go to the devil!' cried the student Nathanael, his eyes blazing wildly with rage and fear, when the weather-glass hawker Giuseppe Coppola"—well, that is what I really had written, when I thought I detected something of the ridiculous in Nathanael's wild glance; and the history is anything but laughable. I could not find any words which seemed fitted to reflect in even the feeblest degree the brightness of the colours of my mental vision. I determined not to begin at all. So I pray you, gracious reader, accept the three letters which my friend Lothair has been so kind as to communicate to me as the outline of the picture, into which I will endeavour to introduce more and more colour as I proceed with my narrative. Perhaps, like a good portrait-painter, I may succeed in depicting more than one figure in such wise that you will recognise it as a good likeness without being acquainted with the original, and feel as if you had very often seen the original with your own bodily eyes. Perhaps, too, you will then believe that nothing is more wonderful, nothing more fantastic than real life, and that all that a writer can do is to present it as a dark reflection from a dim cut mirror.

In order to make the very commencement more intelligible, it is necessary to add to the letters that, soon after the death of Nathanael's father, Clara and Lothair, the children of a distant relative, who had likewise died, leaving them orphans, were taken by Nathanael's mother into her own house. Clara and Nathanael conceived a warm affection for each other, against which not the slightest objection in the world could be urged. When therefore Nathanael left home to prosecute his studies in G——, they were betrothed. It is from G—— that his last letter is written, where he is attending the lectures of Spalanzani, the distinguished Professor of Physics.

I might now proceed comfortably with my narration, did not at this moment Clara's image rise up so vividly before my eyes that I cannot turn them away from it, just as I never could when she looked upon me and smiled so sweetly. Nowhere would she have passed for beautiful; that was the unanimous opinion of all who professed to have any technical knowledge of beauty. But whilst architects praised the pure proportions of her figure and form, painters averred that her neck, shoulders, and bosom were almost too chastely modelled, and yet, on the other hand, one and all were in love with her glorious Magdalene hair, and talked a good deal of nonsense about Battoni-like colouring. One of them, a veritable romanticist, strangely enough likened her eyes to a lake by Ruisdael, in which is reflected the pure azure of the cloudless sky, the beauty of woods and flowers, and all the bright and varied life of a living landscape. Poets and musicians went still further and said, "What's all this talk about seas and reflections? How can we look upon the girl without feeling that wonderful heavenly songs and melodies beam upon us from her eyes, penetrating deep down into our hearts, till all becomes awake and throbbing with emotion? And if we cannot sing anything at all passable then, why, we are not worth much; and this we can also plainly read in the rare smile which flits around her lips when we have the hardihood to squeak out something in her presence which we pretend to call singing, in spite of the fact that it is nothing more than a few single notes confusedly linked together." And it really was so. Clara had the powerful fancy of a bright, innocent, unaffected child, a woman's deep and sympathetic heart, and an understanding clear, sharp, and discriminating. Dreamers and visionaries had but a bad time of it with her; for without saying very much—she was not by nature of a talkative disposition—she plainly asked, by her calm steady look, and rare ironical smile, "How can you imagine, my dear friends, that I can take these fleeting shadowy images for true living and breathing forms?" For this reason many found fault with her as being cold, prosaic, and devoid of feeling; others, however, who had reached a clearer and deeper conception of life, were extremely fond of the intelligent, childlike, large-hearted girl But none had such an affection for her as Nathanael, who was a zealous and cheerful cultivator of the fields of science and art. Clara clung to her lover with all her heart; the first clouds she encountered in life were when he had to separate from her. With what delight did she fly into his arms when, as he had promised in his last letter to Lothair, he really came back to his native town and entered his mother's room! And as Nathanael had foreseen, the moment he saw Clara again he no longer thought about either the advocate Coppelius or her sensible letter; his ill-humour had quite disappeared.

Nevertheless Nathanael was right when he told his friend Lothair that the repulsive vendor of weather-glasses, Coppola, had exercised a fatal and disturbing influence upon his life. It was quite patent to all; for even during the first few days he showed that he was completely and entirely changed. He gave himself up to gloomy reveries, and moreover acted so strangely; they had never observed anything at all like it in him before. Everything, even his own life, was to him but dreams and presentiments. His constant theme was that every man who delusively imagined himself to be free was merely the plaything of the cruel sport of mysterious powers, and it was vain for man to resist them; he must humbly submit to whatever destiny had decreed for him. He went so far as to maintain that it was foolish to believe that a man could do anything in art or science of his own accord; for the inspiration in which alone any true artistic work could be done did not proceed from the spirit within outwards, but was the result of the operation directed inwards of some Higher Principle existing without and beyond ourselves.

This mystic extravagance was in the highest degree repugnant to Clara's clear intelligent mind, but it seemed vain to enter upon any attempt at refutation. Yet when Nathanael went on to prove that Coppelius was the Evil Principle which had entered into him and taken possession of him at the time he was listening behind the curtain, and that this hateful demon would in some terrible way ruin their happiness, then Clara grew grave and said, "Yes, Nathanael. You are right; Coppelius is an Evil Principle; he can do dreadful things, as bad as could a Satanic power which should assume a living physical form, but only—only if you do not banish him from your mind and thoughts. So long as you believe in him he exists and is at work; your belief in him is his only power." Whereupon Nathanael, quite angry because Clara would only grant the existence of the demon in his own mind, began to dilate at large upon the whole mystic doctrine of devils and awful powers, but Clara abruptly broke off the theme by making, to Nathanael's very great disgust, some quite commonplace remark. Such deep mysteries are sealed books to cold, unsusceptible characters, he thought, without being clearly conscious to himself that he counted Clara amongst these inferior natures, and accordingly he did not remit his efforts to initiate her into these mysteries. In the morning, when she was helping to prepare breakfast, he would take his stand beside her, and read all sorts of mystic books to her, until she begged him—"But, my dear Nathanael, I shall have to scold you as the Evil Principle which exercises a fatal influence upon my coffee. For if I do as you wish, and let things go their own way, and look into your eyes whilst you read, the coffee will all boil over into the fire, and you will none of you get any breakfast." Then Nathanael hastily banged the book to and ran away in great displeasure to his own room.

Formerly he had possessed a peculiar talent for writing pleasing, sparkling tales, which Clara took the greatest delight in listening to; but now his productions were gloomy, unintelligible, and wanting in form, so that, although Clara out of forbearance towards him did not say so, he nevertheless felt how very little interest she took in them. There was nothing that Clara disliked so much as what was tedious; at such times her intellectual sleepiness was not to be overcome; it was betrayed both in her glances and in her words. Nathanael's effusions were, in truth, exceedingly tedious. His ill-humour at Clara's cold prosaic temperament continued to increase; Clara could not conceal her distaste of his dark, gloomy, wearying mysticism; and thus both began to be more and more estranged from each other without exactly being aware of it themselves. The image of the ugly Coppelius had, as Nathanael was obliged to confess to himself, faded considerably in his fancy, and it often cost him great pains to present him in vivid colours in his literary efforts, in which he played the part of the ghoul of Destiny. At length it entered into his head to make his dismal presentiment that Coppelius would ruin his happiness the subject of a poem. He made himself and Clara, united by true love, the central figures, but represented a black hand as being from time to time thrust into their life and plucking out a joy that had blossomed for them. At length, as they were standing at the altar, the terrible Coppelius appeared and touched Clara's lovely eyes, which leapt into Nathanael's own bosom, burning and hissing like bloody sparks. Then Coppelius laid hold upon him, and hurled him into a blazing circle of fire, which spun round with the speed of a whirlwind, and, storming and blustering, dashed away with him. The fearful noise it made was like a furious hurricane lashing the foaming sea-waves until they rise up like black, white-headed giants in the midst of the raging struggle. But through the midst of the savage fury of the tempest he heard Clara's voice calling, "Can you not see me, dear? Coppelius has deceived you; they were not my eyes which burned so in your bosom; they were fiery drops of your own heart's blood. Look at me, I have got my own eyes still." Nathanael thought, "Yes, that is Clara, and I am hers for ever." Then this thought laid a powerful grasp upon the fiery circle so that it stood still, and the riotous turmoil died away rumbling down a dark abyss. Nathanael looked into Clara's eyes; but it was death whose gaze rested so kindly upon him.

Whilst Nathanael was writing this work he was very quiet and sober-minded; he filed and polished every line, and as he had chosen to submit himself to the limitations of metre, he did not rest until all was pure and musical. When, however, he had at length finished it and read it aloud to himself he was seized with horror and awful dread, and he screamed, "Whose hideous voice is this?" But he soon came to see in it again nothing beyond a very successful poem, and he confidently believed it would enkindle Clara's cold temperament, though to what end she should be thus aroused was not quite clear to his own mind, nor yet what would be the real purpose served by tormenting her with these dreadful pictures, which prophesied a terrible and ruinous end to her affection.

Nathanael and Clara sat in his mother's little garden. Clara was bright and cheerful, since for three entire days her lover, who had been busy writing his poem, had not teased her with his dreams or forebodings. Nathanael, too, spoke in a gay and vivacious way of things of merry import, as he formerly used to do, so that Clara said, "Ah! now I have you again. We have driven away that ugly Coppelius, you see." Then it suddenly occurred to him that he had got the poem in his pocket which he wished to read to her. He at once took out the manuscript and began to read. Clara, anticipating something tedious as usual, prepared to submit to the infliction, and calmly resumed her knitting. But as the sombre clouds rose up darker and darker she let her knitting fall on her lap and sat with her eyes fixed in a set stare upon Nathanael's face. He was quite carried away by his own work, the fire of enthusiasm coloured his cheeks a deep red, and tears started from his eyes. At length he concluded, groaning and showing great lassitude; grasping Clara's hand, he sighed as if he were being utterly melted in inconsolable grief, "Oh! Clara! Clara!" She drew him softly to her heart and said in a low but very grave and impressive tone, "Nathanael, my darling Nathanael, throw that foolish, senseless, stupid thing into the fire." Then Nathanael leapt indignantly to his feet, crying, as he pushed Clara from him, "You damned lifeless automaton!" and rushed away. Clara was cut to the heart, and wept bitterly. "Oh! he has never loved me, for he does not understand me," she sobbed.

Lothair entered the arbour. Clara was obliged to tell him all that had taken place. He was passionately fond of his sister; and every word of her complaint fell like a spark upon his heart, so that the displeasure which he had long entertained against his dreamy friend Nathanael was kindled into furious anger. He hastened to find Nathanael, and upbraided him in harsh words for his irrational behaviour towards his beloved sister. The fiery Nathanael answered him in the same style. "A fantastic, crack-brained fool," was retaliated with, "A miserable, common, everyday sort of fellow." A meeting was the inevitable consequence. They agreed to meet on the following morning behind the garden-wall, and fight, according to the custom of the students of the place, with sharp rapiers. They went about silent and gloomy; Clara had both heard and seen the violent quarrel, and also observed the fencing-master bring the rapiers in the dusk of the evening. She had a presentiment of what was to happen. They both appeared at the appointed place wrapped up in the same gloomy silence, and threw off their coats. Their eyes flaming with the bloodthirsty light of pugnacity, they were about to begin their contest when Clara burst through the garden door. Sobbing, she screamed, "You savage, terrible men! Cut me down before you attack each other; for how can I live when my lover has slain my brother, or my brother slain my lover?" Lothair let his weapon fall and gazed silently upon the ground, whilst Nathanael's heart was rent with sorrow, and all the affection which he had felt for his lovely Clara in the happiest days of her golden youth was awakened within him. His murderous weapon, too, fell from his hand; he threw himself at Clara's feet. "Oh! can you ever forgive me, my only, my dearly loved Clara? Can you, my dear brother Lothair, also forgive me?" Lothair was touched by his friend's great distress; the three young people embraced each other amidst endless tears, and swore never again to break their bond of love and fidelity.

Nathanael felt as if a heavy burden that had been weighing him down to the earth was now rolled from off him, nay, as if by offering resistance to the dark power which had possessed him, he had rescued his own self from the ruin which had threatened him. Three happy days he now spent amidst the loved ones, and then returned to G——, where he had still a year to stay before settling down in his native town for life.

Everything having reference to Coppelius had been concealed from the mother, for they knew she could not think of him without horror, since she as well as Nathanael believed him to be guilty of causing her husband's death.

* * * * * * *

When Nathanael came to the house where he lived he was greatly astonished to find it burnt down to the ground, so that nothing but the bare outer walls were left standing amidst a heap of ruins. Although the fire had broken out in the laboratory of the chemist who lived on the ground-floor, and had therefore spread upwards, some of Nathanael's bold, active friends had succeeded in time in forcing a way into his room in the upper storey and saving his books and manuscripts and instruments. They had carried them all uninjured into another house, where they engaged a room for him; this he now at once took possession of. That he lived opposite Professor Spalanzani did not strike him particularly, nor did it occur to him as anything more singular that he could, as he observed, by looking out of his window, see straight into the room where Olimpia often sat alone. Her figure he could plainly distinguish, although her features were uncertain and confused. It did at length occur to him, however, that she remained for hours together in the same position in which he had first discovered her through the glass door, sitting at a little table without any occupation whatever, and it was evident that she was constantly gazing across in his direction. He could not but confess to himself that he had never seen a finer figure. However, with Clara mistress of his heart, he remained perfectly unaffected by Olimpia's stiffness and apathy; and it was only occasionally that he sent a fugitive glance over his compendium across to her—that was all.

He was writing to Clara; a light tap came at the door. At his summons to "Come in," Coppola's repulsive face appeared peeping in. Nathanael felt his heart beat with trepidation; but, recollecting what Spalanzani had told him about his fellow-countryman Coppola, and what he had himself so faithfully promised his beloved in respect to the Sand-man Coppelius, he was ashamed at himself for this childish fear of spectres. Accordingly, he controlled himself with an effort, and said, as quietly and as calmly as he possibly could, "I don't want to buy any weather-glasses, my good friend; you had better go elsewhere." Then Coppola came right into the room, and said in a hoarse voice, screwing up his wide mouth into a hideous smile, whilst his little eyes flashed keenly from beneath his long grey eyelashes, "What! Nee weather-gless? Nee weather-gless? 've got foine oyes as well—foine oyes!" Affrighted, Nathanael cried, "You stupid man, how can you have eyes?—eyes—eyes?" But Coppola, laying aside his weather-glasses, thrust his hands into his big coat-pockets and brought out several spy-glasses and spectacles, and put them on the table. "Theer! Theer! Spect'cles! Spect'cles to put 'n nose! Them's my oyes—foine oyes." And he continued to produce more and more spectacles from his pockets until the table began to gleam and flash all over. Thousands of eyes were looking and blinking convulsively, and staring up at Nathanael; he could not avert his gaze from the table. Coppola went on heaping up his spectacles, whilst wilder and ever wilder burning flashes crossed through and through each other and darted their blood-red rays into Nathanael's breast. Quite overcome, and frantic with terror, he shouted, "Stop! stop! you terrible man!" and he seized Coppola by the arm, which he had again thrust into his pocket in order to bring out still more spectacles, although the whole table was covered all over with them. With a harsh disagreeable laugh Coppola gently freed himself; and with the words "So! went none! Well, here foine gless!" he swept all his spectacles together, and put them back into his coat-pockets, whilst from a breast-pocket he produced a great number of larger and smaller perspectives. As soon as the spectacles were gone Nathanael recovered his equanimity again; and, bending his thoughts upon Clara, he clearly discerned that the gruesome incubus had proceeded only from himself, as also that Coppola was a right honest mechanician and optician, and far from being Coppelius's dreaded double and ghost And then, besides, none of the glasses which Coppola now placed on the table had anything at all singular about them, at least nothing so weird as the spectacles; so, in order to square accounts with himself, Nathanael now really determined to buy something of the man. He took up a small, very beautifully cut pocket perspective, and by way of proving it looked through the window. Never before in his life had he had a glass in his hands that brought out things so clearly and sharply and distinctly. Involuntarily he directed the glass upon Spalanzani's room; Olimpia sat at the little table as usual, her arms laid upon it and her hands folded. Now he saw for the first time the regular and exquisite beauty of her features. The eyes, however, seemed to him to have a singular look of fixity and lifelesness. But as he continued to look closer and more carefully through the glass he fancied a light like humid moonbeams came into them. It seemed as if their power of vision was now being enkindled; their glances shone with ever-increasing vivacity. Nathanael remained standing at the window as if glued to the spot by a wizard's spell, his gaze rivetted unchangeably upon the divinely beautiful Olimpia. A coughing and shuffling of the feet awakened him out of his enchaining dream, as it were. Coppola stood behind him, "Tre zechini" (three ducats). Nathanael had completely forgotten the optician; he hastily paid the sum demanded. "Ain't 't? Foine gless? foine gless?" asked Coppola in his harsh unpleasant voice, smiling sardonically. "Yes, yes, yes," rejoined Nathanael impatiently; "adieu, my good friend." But Coppola did not leave the room without casting many peculiar side-glances upon Nathanael; and the young student heard him laughing loudly on the stairs. "Ah well!" thought he, "he's laughing at me because I've paid him too much for this little perspective—because I've given him too much money—that's it" As he softly murmured these words he fancied he detected a gasping sigh as of a dying man stealing awfully through the room; his heart stopped beating with fear. But to be sure he had heaved a deep sigh himself; it was quite plain. "Clara is quite right," said he to himself, "in holding me to be an incurable ghost-seer; and yet it's very ridiculous—ay, more than ridiculous, that the stupid thought of having paid Coppola too much for his glass should cause me this strange anxiety; I can't see any reason for it."

Now he sat down to finish his letter to Clara; but a glance through the window showed him Olimpia still in her former posture. Urged by an irresistible impulse he jumped up and seized Coppola's perspective; nor could he tear himself away from the fascinating Olimpia until his friend and brother Siegmund called for him to go to Professor Spalanzani's lecture. The curtains before the door of the all-important room were closely drawn, so that he could not see Olimpia. Nor could he even see her from his own room during the two following days, notwithstanding that he scarcely ever left his window, and maintained a scarce interrupted watch through Coppola's perspective upon her room. On the third day curtains even were drawn across the window. Plunged into the depths of despair,—goaded by longing and ardent desire, he hurried outside the walls of the town. Olimpia's image hovered about his path in the air and stepped forth out of the bushes, and peeped up at him with large and lustrous eyes from the bright surface of the brook. Clara's image was completely faded from his mind; he had no thoughts except for Olimpia. He uttered his love-plaints aloud and in a lachrymose tone, "Oh! my glorious, noble star of love, have you only risen to vanish again, and leave me in the darkness and hopelessness of night?"

Returning home, he became aware that there was a good deal of noisy bustle going on in Spalanzani's house. All the doors stood wide open; men were taking in all kinds of gear and furniture; the windows of the first floor were all lifted off their hinges; busy maid-servants with immense hair-brooms were driving backwards and forwards dusting and sweeping, whilst within could be heard the knocking and hammering of carpenters and upholsters.

Utterly astonished, Nathanael stood still in the street; then Siegmund joined him, laughing, and said, "Well, what do you say to our old Spalanzani?" Nathanael assured him that he could not say anything, since he knew not what it all meant; to his great astonishment, he could hear, however, that they were turning the quiet gloomy house almost inside out with their dusting and cleaning and making of alterations. Then he learned from Siegmund that Spalanzani intended giving a great concert and ball on the following day, and that half the university was invited. It was generally reported that Spalanzani was going to let his daughter Olimpia, whom he had so long so jealously guarded from every eye, make her first appearance.

Nathanael received an invitation. At the appointed hour, when the carriages were rolling up and the lights were gleaming brightly in the decorated halls, he went across to the Professor's, his heart beating high with expectation. The company was both numerous and brilliant. Olimpia was richly and tastefully dressed. One could not but admire her figure and the regular beauty of her features. The striking inward curve of her back, as well as the wasp-like smallness of her waist, appeared to be the result of too-tight lacing. There was something stiff and measured in her gait and bearing that made an unfavourable impression upon many; it was ascribed to the constraint imposed upon her by the company. The concert began. Olimpia played on the piano with great skill; and sang as skilfully an *aria di bravura*, in a voice which was, if anything, almost too sharp, but clear as glass bells. Nathanael was transported with delight; he stood in the background farthest from her, and owing to the blinding lights could not quite distinguish her features. So, without being observed, he took Coppola's glass out of his pocket, and directed it upon the beautiful Olimpia. Oh! then he perceived how her yearning eyes sought him, how every note only reached its full purity in the loving glance which penetrated to and inflamed his heart. Her artificial *roulades* seemed to him to be the exultant cry towards heaven of the soul refined by love; and when at last, after the *cadenza*, the long trill rang shrilly and loudly through the hall, he felt as if he were suddenly grasped by burning arms and could no longer control himself,—he could not help shouting aloud in his mingled pain and delight, "Olimpia!" All eyes were turned upon him; many people laughed. The face of the cathedral organist wore a still more gloomy look than it had done before, but all he said was, "Very well!"

The concert came to an end, and the ball began. Oh! to dance with her—with her—that was now the aim of all Nathanael's wishes, of all his desires. But how should he have courage to request her, the queen of the ball, to grant him the honour of a dance? And yet he couldn't tell how it came about, just as the dance began, he found himself standing close beside her, nobody having as yet asked her to be his partner; so, with some difficulty stammering out a few words, he grasped her hand. It was cold as ice; he shook with an awful, frosty shiver. But, fixing his eyes upon her face, he saw that her glance was beaming upon him with love and longing, and at the same moment he thought that the pulse began to beat in her cold hand, and the warm life-blood to course through her veins. And passion burned more intensely in his own heart also; he threw his arm round her beautiful waist and whirled her round the hall. He had always thought that he kept good and accurate time in dancing, but from the perfectly rhythmical evenness with which Olimpia danced, and which frequently put him quite out, he perceived how very faulty his own time really was. Notwithstanding, he would not dance with any other lady; and everybody else who approached Olimpia to call upon her for a dance, he would have liked to kill on the spot. This, however, only happened twice; to his astonishment Olimpia remained after this without a partner, and he failed not on each occasion to take her out again. If Nathanael had been able to see anything else except the beautiful Olimpia, there would inevitably have been a good deal of unpleasant quarrelling and strife; for it was evident that Olimpia was the object of the smothered laughter only with difficulty suppressed, which was heard in various corners amongst the young people; and they followed her with very curious looks, but nobody knew for what reason. Nathanael, excited by dancing and the plentiful supply of wine he had consumed, had laid aside the shyness which at other times characterised him. He sat beside Olimpia, her hand in his own, and declared his love enthusiastically and passionately in words which neither of them understood, neither he nor Olimpia. And yet she perhaps did, for she sat with her eyes fixed unchangeably upon his, sighing repeatedly, "Ach! Ach! Ach!" Upon this Nathanael would answer, "Oh, you glorious heavenly lady! You ray from the promised paradise of love! Oh! what a profound soul you have! my whole being is mirrored in it!" and a good deal more in the same strain. But Olimpia only continued to sigh "Ach! Ach!" again and again.

Professor Spalanzani passed by the two happy lovers once or twice, and smiled with a look of peculiar satisfaction. All at once it seemed to Nathanael, albeit he was far away in a different world, as if it were growing perceptibly darker down below at Professor Spalanzani's. He looked about him, and to his very great alarm became aware that there were only two lights left burning in the hall, and they were on the point of going out. The music and dancing had long ago ceased. "We must part—part!" he cried, wildly and despairingly; he kissed Olimpia's hand; he bent down to her mouth, but ice-cold lips met his burning ones. As he touched her cold hand, he felt his heart thrilled with awe; the legend of "The Dead Bride" shot suddenly through his mind. But Olimpia had drawn him closer to her, and the kiss appeared to warm her lips into vitality. Professor Spalanzani strode slowly through the empty apartment, his footsteps giving a hollow echo; and his figure had, as the flickering shadows played about him, a ghostly, awful appearance. "Do you love me? Do you love me, Olimpia? Only one little word—Do you love me?" whispered Nathanael, but she only sighed, "Ach! Ach!" as she rose to her feet. "Yes, you are my lovely, glorious star of love," said Nathanael, "and will shine for ever, purifying and ennobling my heart" "Ach! Ach!" replied Olimpia, as she moved along. Nathanael followed her; they stood before the Professor. "You have had an extraordinarily animated conversation with my daughter," said he, smiling; "well, well, my dear Mr. Nathanael, if you find pleasure in talking to the stupid girl, I am sure I shall be glad for you to come and do so." Nathanael took his leave, his heart singing and leaping in a perfect delirium of happiness.

During the next few days Spalanzani's ball was the general topic of conversation. Although the Professor had done everything to make the thing a splendid success, yet certain gay spirits related more than one thing that had occurred which was quite irregular and out of order. They were especially keen in pulling Olimpia to pieces for her taciturnity and rigid stiffness; in spite of her beautiful form they alleged that she was hopelessly stupid, and in this fact they discerned the reason why Spalanzani had so long kept her concealed from publicity. Nathanael heard all this with inward wrath, but nevertheless he held his tongue; for, thought he, would it indeed be worth while to prove to these fellows that it is their own stupidity which prevents them from appreciating Olimpia's profound and brilliant parts? One day Siegmund said to him, "Pray, brother, have the kindness to tell me how you, a sensible fellow, came to lose your head over that Miss Wax-face—that wooden doll across there?" Nathanael was about to fly into a rage, but he recollected himself and replied, "Tell me, Siegmund, how came it that Olimpia's divine charms could escape your eye, so keenly alive as it always is to beauty, and your acute perception as well? But Heaven be thanked for it, otherwise I should have had you for a rival, and then the blood of one of us would have had to be spilled." Siegmund, perceiving how matters stood with his friend, skilfully interposed and said, after remarking that all argument with one in love about the object of his affections was out of place, "Yet it's very strange that several of us have formed pretty much the same opinion about Olimpia. We think she is—you won't take it ill, brother?—that she is singularly statuesque and soulless. Her figure is regular, and so are her features, that can't be gainsaid; and if her eyes were not so utterly devoid of life, I may say, of the power of vision, she might pass for a beauty. She is strangely measured in her movements, they all seem as if they were dependent upon some wound-up clock-work. Her playing and singing has the disagreeably perfect, but insensitive time of a singing machine, and her dancing is the same. We felt quite afraid of this Olimpia, and did not like to have anything to do with her; she seemed to us to be only acting *like* a living creature, and as if there was some secret at the bottom of it all." Nathanael did not give way to the bitter feelings which threatened to master him at these words of Siegmund's; he fought down and got the better of his displeasure, and merely said, very earnestly, "You cold prosaic fellows may very well be afraid of her. It is only to its like that the poetically organised spirit unfolds itself. Upon me alone did her loving glances fall, and through my mind and thoughts alone did they radiate; and only in her love can I find my own self again. Perhaps, however, she doesn't do quite right not to jabber a lot of nonsense and stupid talk like other shallow people. It is true, she speaks but few words; but the few words she docs speak are genuine hieroglyphs of the inner world of Love and of the higher cognition of the intellectual life revealed in the intuition of the Eternal beyond the grave. But you have no understanding for all these things, and I am only wasting words." "God be with you, brother," said Siegmund very gently, almost sadly, "but it seems to me that you are in a very bad way. You may rely upon me, if all—No, I can't say any more." It all at once dawned upon Nathanael that his cold prosaic friend Siegmund really and sincerely wished him well, and so he warmly shook his proffered hand.

Nathanael had completely forgotten that there was a Clara in the world, whom he had once loved—and his mother and Lothair. They had all vanished from his mind; he lived for Olimpia alone. He sat beside her every day for hours together, rhapsodising about his love and sympathy enkindled into life, and about psychic elective affinity—all of which Olimpia listened to with great reverence. He fished up from the very bottom of his desk all the things that he had ever written—poems, fancy sketches, visions, romances, tales, and the heap was increased daily with all kinds of aimless sonnets, stanzas, canzonets. All these he read to Olimpia hour after hour without growing tired; but then he had never had such an exemplary listener. She neither embroidered, nor knitted; she did not look out of the window, or feed a bird, or play with a little pet dog or a favourite cat, neither did she twist a piece of paper or anything of that kind round her finger; she did not forcibly convert a yawn into a low affected cough—in short, she sat hour after hour with her eyes bent unchangeably upon her lover's face, without moving or altering her position, and her gaze grew more ardent and more ardent still. And it was only when at last Nathanael rose and kissed her lips or her hand that she said, "Ach! Ach!" and then "Good-night, dear." Arrived in his own room, Nathanael would break out with, "Oh! what a brilliant—what a profound mind! Only you—you alone understand me." And his heart trembled with rapture when he reflected upon the wondrous harmony which daily revealed itself between his own and his Olimpia's character; for he fancied that she had expressed in respect to his works and his poetic genius the identical sentiments which he himself cherished deep down in his own heart in respect to the same, and even as if it was his own heart's voice speaking to him. And it must indeed have been so;

for Olimpia never uttered any other words than those already mentioned. And when Nathanael himself in his clear and sober moments, as, for instance, directly after waking in a morning, thought about her utter passivity and taciturnity, he only said, "What are words—but words? The glance of her heavenly eyes says more than any tongue of earth. And how can, anyway, a child of heaven accustom herself to the narrow circle which the exigencies of a wretched mundane life demand?"

Professor Spalanzani appeared to be greatly pleased at the intimacy that had sprung up between his daughter Olimpia and Nathanael, and showed the young man many unmistakable proofs of his good feeling towards him; and when Nathanael ventured at length to hint very delicately at an alliance with Olimpia, the Professor smiled all over his face at once, and said he should allow his daughter to make a perfectly free choice. Encouraged by these words, and with the fire of desire burning in his heart, Nathanael resolved the very next day to implore Olimpia to tell him frankly, in plain words, what he had long read in her sweet loving glances,—that she would be his for ever. He looked for the ring which his mother had given him at parting; he would present it to Olimpia as a symbol of his devotion, and of the happy life he was to lead with her from that time onwards. Whilst looking for it he came across his letters from Clara and Lothair; he threw them carelessly aside, found the ring, put it in his pocket, and ran across to Olimpia. Whilst still on the stairs, in the entrance-passage, he heard an extraordinary hubbub; the noise seemed to proceed from Spalanzani's study. There was a stamping—a rattling—pushing—knocking against the door, with curses and oaths intermingled. "Leave hold—leave hold—you monster—you rascal—staked your life and honour upon it?—Ha! ha! ha! ha!—That was not our wager—I, I made the eyes—I the clock-work.—Go to the devil with your clock-work—you damned dog of a watch-maker—be off—Satan—stop—you paltry turner—you infernal beast!—stop—begone—let me go." The voices which were thus making all this racket and rumpus were those of Spalanzani and the fearsome Coppelius. Nathanael rushed in, impelled by some nameless dread. The Professor was grasping a female figure by the shoulders, the Italian Coppola held her by the feet; and they were pulling and dragging each other backwards and forwards, fighting furiously to get possession of her. Nathanael recoiled with horror on recognising that the figure was Olimpia. Boiling with rage, he was about to tear his beloved from the grasp of the madmen, when Coppola by an extraordinary exertion of strength twisted the figure out of the Professor's hands and gave him such a terrible blow with her, that he reeled backwards and fell over the table all amongst the phials and retorts, the bottles and glass cylinders, which covered it: all these things were smashed into a thousand pieces. But Coppola threw the figure across his shoulder, and, laughing shrilly and horribly, ran hastily down the stairs, the figure's ugly feet hanging down and banging and rattling like wood against the steps. Nathanael was stupefied;—he had seen only too distinctly that in Olimpia's pallid waxed face there were no eyes, merely black holes in their stead; she was an inanimate puppet. Spalanzani was rolling on the floor; the pieces of glass had cut his head and breast and arm; the blood was escaping from him in streams. But he gathered his strength together by an effort.

"After him—after him! What do you stand staring there for? Coppelius—Coppelius—he's stolen my best automaton—at which I've worked for twenty years—staked my life upon it—the clock-work— speech—movement—mine—your eyes—stolen your eyes—damn him—curse him—after him—fetch me back Olimpia—there are the eyes." And now Nathanael saw a pair of bloody eyes lying on the floor staring at him; Spalanzani seized them with his uninjured hand and threw them at him, so that they hit his breast Then madness dug her burning talons into him and swept down into his heart, rending his mind and thoughts to shreds. "Aha! aha! aha! Fire-wheel—fire-wheel! Spin round, fire-wheel! merrily, merrily! Aha! wooden doll! spin round, pretty wooden doll!" and he threw himself upon the Professor, clutching him fast by the throat. He would certainly have strangled him had not several people, attracted by the noise, rushed in and torn away the madman; and so they saved the Professor, whose wounds were immediately dressed. Siegmund, with all his strength, was not able to subdue the frantic lunatic, who continued to scream in a dreadful way, "Spin round, wooden doll!" and to strike out right and left with his doubled fists. At length the united strength of several succeeded in overpowering him by throwing him on the floor and binding him. His cries passed into a brutish bellow that was awful to hear; and thus raging with the harrowing violence of madness, he was taken away to the madhouse.

Before continuing my narration of what happened further to the unfortunate Nathanael, I will tell you, indulgent reader, in case you take any interest in that skilful mechanician and fabricator of automata, Spalanzani, that he recovered completely from his wounds. He had, however, to leave the university, for Nathanael's fate had created a great sensation; and the opinion was pretty generally expressed that it was an imposture altogether unpardonable to have smuggled a wooden puppet instead of a living person into intelligent tea-circles,—for Olimpia had been present at several with success. Lawyers called it a cunning piece of knavery, and all the harder to punish since it was directed against the public; and it had been so craftily contrived that it had escaped unobserved by all except a few preternaturally acute students, although everybody was very wise now and remembered to have thought of several facts which occurred to them as suspicious. But these latter could not succeed in making out any sort of a consistent tale. For was it, for instance, a thing likely to occur to any one as suspicious that, according to the declaration of an elegant beau of these tea-parties, Olimpia had, contrary to all good manners, sneezed oftener than she had yawned? The former must have been, in the opinion of this elegant gentleman, the winding up of the concealed clock-work; it had always been accompanied by an observable creaking, and so on. The Professor of Poetry and Eloquence took a pinch of snuff, and, slapping the lid to and clearing his throat, said solemnly, "My most honourable ladies and gentlemen, don't you see then where the rub is? The whole thing is an allegory, a continuous metaphor. You understand me? *Sapienti sat.*" But several most honourable gentlemen did not rest satisfied with this explanation; the history of this automaton had sunk deeply into their souls, and an absurd mistrust of human figures began to prevail. Several lovers, in order to be fully convinced that they were not paying court to a wooden puppet, required that their mistress should sing and dance a little out of time, should embroider or knit or play with her little pug, &c., when being read to, but above all things else that she should do something more than merely listen—that she should frequently speak in such a way as to really show that her words presupposed as a condition some thinking and feeling. The bonds of love were in many cases drawn closer in consequence, and so of course became more engaging; in other instances they gradually relaxed and fell away. "I cannot really be made responsible for it," was the remark of more than one young gallant. At the tea-gatherings everybody, in order to ward off suspicion, yawned to an incredible extent and never sneezed. Spalanzani was obliged, as has been said, to leave the place in order to escape a criminal charge of having fraudulently imposed an automaton upon human society. Coppola, too, had also disappeared.

When Nathanael awoke he felt as if he had been oppressed by a terrible nightmare; he opened his eyes and experienced an indescribable sensation of mental comfort, whilst a soft and most beautiful sensation of warmth pervaded his body. He lay on his own bed in his own room at home; Clara was bending over him, and at a little distance stood his mother and Lothair. "At last, at last, O my darling Nathanael; now we have you again; now you are cured of your grievous illness, now you are mine again." And Clara's words came from the depths of her heart; and she clasped him in her arms. The bright scalding tears streamed from his eyes, he was so overcome with mingled feelings of sorrow and delight; and he gasped forth, "My Clara, my Clara!" Siegmund, who had staunchly stood by his friend in his hour of need, now came into the room. Nathanael gave him his hand—"My faithful brother, you have not deserted me." Every trace of insanity had left him, and in the tender hands of his mother and his beloved, and his friends, he quickly recovered his strength again. Good fortune had in the meantime visited the house; a niggardly old uncle, from whom they had never expected to get anything, had died, and left Nathanael's mother not only a considerable fortune, but also a small estate, pleasantly situated not far from the town. There they resolved to go and live, Nathanael and his mother, and Clara, to whom he was now to be married, and Lothair. Nathanael was become gentler and more childlike than he had ever been before, and now began really to understand Clara's supremely pure and noble character. None of them ever reminded him, even in the remotest degree, of the past. But when Siegmund took leave of him, he said, "By heaven, brother! I was in a bad way, but an angel came just at the right moment and led me back upon the path of light. Yes, it was Clara." Siegmund would not let him speak further, fearing lest the painful recollections of the past might arise too vividly and too intensely in his mind.

The time came for the four happy people to move to their little property. At noon they were going through the streets. After making several purchases they found that the lofty tower of the town-house was throwing its giant shadows across the market-place. "Come," said Clara, "let us go up to the top once more and have a look at the distant hills." No sooner said than done. Both of them, Nathanael and Clara, went up the tower; their mother, however, went on with the servant-girl to her new home, and Lothair, not feeling inclined to climb up all the many steps, waited below. There the two lovers stood arm-in-arm on the topmost gallery of the tower, and gazed out into the sweet-scented wooded landscape, beyond which the blue hills rose up like a giant's city.

"Oh! do look at that strange little grey bush, it looks as if it were actually walking towards us," said Clara. Mechanically he put his hand into his sidepocket; he found Coppola's perspective and looked for the bush; Clara stood in front of the glass. Then a convulsive thrill shot through his pulse and veins; pale as a corpse, he fixed his staring eyes upon her; but soon they began to roll, and a fiery current flashed and sparkled in them, and he yelled fearfully, like a hunted animal. Leaping up high in the air and laughing horribly at the same time, he began to shout, in a piercing voice, "Spin round, wooden doll! Spin round, wooden doll!" With the strength of a giant he laid hold upon Clara and tried to hurl her over, but in an agony of despair she clutched fast hold of the railing that went round the gallery. Lothair heard the madman raging and Clara's scream of terror: a fearful presentiment flashed across his mind. He ran up the steps; the door of the second flight was locked. Clara's scream for help rang out more loudly. Mad with rage and fear, he threw himself against the door, which at length gave way. Clara's cries were growing fainter and fainter,—"Help! save me! save me!" and her voice died away in the air. "She is killed—murdered by that madman," shouted Lothair. The door to the gallery was also locked. Despair gave him the strength of a giant; he burst the door off its hinges. Good God! there was Clara in the grasp of the madman Nathanael, hanging over the gallery in the air; she only held to the iron bar with one hand. Quick as lightning,

64

Lothair seized his sister and pulled her back, at the same time dealing the madman a blow in the face with his doubled fist, which sent him reeling backwards, forcing him to let go his victim.

Lothair ran down with his insensible sister in his arms. She was saved. But Nathanael ran round and round the gallery, leaping up in the air and shouting, "Spin round, fire-wheel! Spin round, fire-wheel!" The people heard the wild shouting, and a crowd began to gather. In the midst of them towered the advocate Coppelius, like a giant; he had only just arrived in the town, and had gone straight to the market-place. Some were going up to overpower and take charge of the madman, but Coppelius laughed and said, "Ha! ha! wait a bit; he'll come down of his own accord;" and he stood gazing upwards along with the rest. All at once Nathanael stopped as if spell-bound; he bent down over the railing, and perceived Coppelius. With a piercing scream, "Ha! foine oyes! foine oyes!" he leapt over.

When Nathanael lay on the stone pavement with a broken head, Coppelius had disappeared in the crush and confusion.

Several years afterwards it was reported that, outside the door of a pretty country house in a remote district, Clara had been seen sitting hand in hand with a pleasant gentleman, whilst two bright boys were playing at her feet. From this it may be concluded that she eventually found that quiet domestic happiness which her cheerful, blithesome character required, and which Nathanael, with his tempest-tossed soul, could never have been able to give her.

* * * * * * *

THE ENTAIL.

Not far from the shore of the Baltic Sea is situated the ancestral castle of the noble family Von R——, called R—sitten. It is a wild and desolate neighbourhood, hardly anything more than a single blade of grass shooting up here and there from the bottomless drift-sand; and instead of the garden that generally ornaments a baronial residence, the bare walls are approached on the landward side by a thin forest of firs, that with their never-changing vesture of gloom despise the bright garniture of Spring, and where, instead of the joyous carolling of little birds awakened anew to gladness, nothing is heard but the ominous croak of the raven and the whirring scream of the storm-boding sea-gull. A quarter of a mile distant Nature suddenly changes. As if by the wave of a magician's wand you are transported into the midst of thriving fields, fertile arable land, and meadows. You see, too, the large and prosperous village, with the land-steward's spacious dwelling-house; and at the angle of a pleasant thicket of alders you may observe the foundations of a large castle, which one of the former proprietors had intended to erect. His successors, however, living on their property in Courland, left the building in its unfinished state; nor would Freiherr Roderick von R—— proceed with the structure when he again took up his residence on the ancestral estate, since the lonely old castle was more suitable to his temperament, which was morose and averse to human society. He had its ruinous walls repaired as well as circumstances would admit, and then shut himself up within them along with a cross-grained house-steward and a slender establishment of servants.

He was seldom seen in the village, but on the other hand he often walked and rode along the sea-beach; and people claimed to have heard him from a distance, talking to the waves and listening to the rolling and hissing of the surf, as though he could hear the answering voice of the spirit of the sea. Upon the topmost summit of the watch-tower he had a sort of study fitted up and supplied with telescopes—with a complete set of astronomical apparatus, in fact. Thence during the daytime he frequently watched the ships sailing past on the distant horizon like white-winged sea-gulls; and there he spent the starlight nights engaged in astronomical, or, as some professed to know, with astrological labours, in which the old house-steward assisted him. At any rate the rumour was current during his own lifetime that he was devoted to the occult sciences or the so-called Black Art, and that he had been driven out of Courland in consequence of the failure of an experiment by which an august princely house had been most seriously offended. The slightest allusion to his residence in Courland filled him with horror; but for all the troubles which had there unhinged the tenor of his life he held his predecessors entirely to blame, in that they had wickedly deserted the home of their ancestors. In order to fetter, for the future, at least the head of the family to the ancestral castle, he converted it into a property of entail. The sovereign was the more willing to ratify this arrangement since by its means he would secure for his country a family distinguished for all chivalrous virtues, and which had already begun to ramify into foreign countries.

Neither Roderick's son Hubert, nor the next Roderick, who was so called after his grandfather, would live in their ancestral castle; both preferred Courland. It is conceivable, too, that, being more cheerful and fond of life than the gloomy astrologer, they were repelled by the grim loneliness of the place. Freiherr Roderick had granted shelter and subsistence on the property to two old maids, sisters of his father, who were living in indigence, having been but niggardly provided for. They, together with an aged serving-woman, occupied the small warm rooms of one of the wings; besides them and the cook, who had a large apartment on the ground floor adjoining the kitchen, the only other person was a worn-out *chasseur*, who tottered about through the lofty rooms and halls of the main building, and discharged the duties of castellan. The rest of the servants lived in the village with the land-steward. The only time at which the desolated and deserted castle became the scene of life and activity was late in autumn, when the snow first began to fall and the season for wolf-hunting and boar-hunting arrived. Then came Freiherr Roderick with his wife, attended by relatives and friends and a numerous retinue, from Courland. The neighbouring nobility, and even amateur lovers of the chase who lived in the town hard by, came down in such numbers that the main building, together with the wings, barely sufficed to hold the crowd of guests. Well-served fires roared in all the stoves and fireplaces, while the spits were creaking from early dawn until late at night, and hundreds of light-hearted people, masters and servants, were running up and down stairs; here was heard the jingling and rattling of drinking glasses and jovial hunting choruses, there the footsteps of those dancing to the sound of the shrill music,—everywhere loud mirth and jollity; so that for four or five weeks together the castle was more like a first-rate hostelry situated on a main highroad than the abode of a country gentleman. This time Freiherr Roderick devoted, as well as he was able, to serious business, for, withdrawing from the revelry of his guests, he discharged the duties attached to his position as lord of the entail. He not only had a complete statement of the revenues laid before him, but he listened to every proposal for improvement and to every the least complaint of his tenants, endeavouring to establish order in everything, and check all wrongdoing and injustice as far as lay in his power.

In these matters of business he was honestly assisted by the old advocate V——, who had been law agent of the R—— family and Justitiarius of their estates in P—— from father to son for many years; accordingly, V—— was wont to set out for the estate at least a week before the day fixed for the arrival of the Freiherr. In the year 179- the time came round again when old V—— was to start on his journey for R—sitten. However strong and healthy the old man, now seventy years of age, might feel, he was yet quite assured that a helping hand would prove beneficial to him in his business. So he said to me one day as if in jest, "Cousin!" (I was his great-nephew, but he called me "cousin," owing to the fact that his own Christian name and mine were both the same)—"Cousin, I was thinking it would not be amiss if you went along with me to R—sitten and felt the sea-breezes blow about your ears a bit. Besides giving me good help in my often laborious work, you may for once in a while see how you like the rollicking life of a hunter, and how, after drawing up a neatly-written protocol one morning, you will frame the next when you come to look in the glaring eyes of such a sturdy brute as a grim shaggy wolf or a wild boar gnashing his teeth, and whether you know how to bring him down with a well-aimed shot." Of course I could not have heard such strange accounts of the merry hunting parties at R—sitten, or entertain such a true heartfelt affection for my excellent old great-uncle as I did, without being highly delighted that he wanted to take me with him this time. As I was already pretty well skilled in the sort of business he had to transact, I promised to work with unwearied industry, so as to relieve him of all care and trouble.

Next day we sat in the carriage on our way to R—sitten, well wrapped up in good fur coats, driving through a thick snowstorm, the first harbinger of the coming winter. On the journey the old gentleman told me many remarkable stories about the Freiherr Roderick, who had established the estate-tail and appointed him (V——), in spite of his youth, to be his Justitiarius and executor. He spoke of the harsh and violent character of the old nobleman, which seemed to be inherited by all the family, since even the present master of the estate, whom he had known as a mild-tempered and almost effeminate youth, acquired more and more as the years went by the same disposition. He therefore recommended me strongly to behave with as much resolute self-reliance and as little embarrassment as possible, if I desired to possess any consideration in the Freiherr's eyes; and at length he began to describe the apartments in the castle which he had selected to be his own once for all, since they were warm and comfortable, and so conveniently retired that we could withdraw from the noisy convivialities of the hilarious company whenever we pleased. The rooms, namely, which were on every visit reserved for him, were two small ones, hung with warm tapestry, close beside the large hall of justice, in the wing opposite that in which the two old maids resided.

At last, after a rapid but wearying journey, we arrived at R—sitten, late at night. We drove through the village; it was Sunday, and from the alehouse proceeded the sounds of music, and dancing, and merrymaking; the steward's house was lit up from basement to garret, and music and song were there too. All the more striking therefore was the inhospitable desolation into which we now drove. The sea-wind howled in sharp cutting dirges as it were about us, whilst the sombre firs, as if they had been roused by the wind from a deep magic trance, groaned hoarsely in a responsive chorus. The bare black walls of the castle towered above the snow-covered ground; we drew up at the gates, which were fast locked. But no shouting or cracking of whips, no knocking or hammering, was of any avail; the whole castle seemed to be dead; not a single light was visible at any of the windows. The old gentleman shouted in his strong stentorian voice, "Francis, Francis, where the deuce are you? In the devil's name rouse yourself; we are all freezing here outside the gates. The snow is cutting our faces till they bleed. Why the devil don't you stir yourself?" Then the watch-dog began to whine, and a wandering light was visible on the ground floor. There was a rattling of keys, and soon the ponderous wings of the gate creaked back on their hinges. "Ha! a hearty welcome, a hearty welcome, Herr Justitiarius. Ugh! it's rough weather!" cried old Francis, holding the lantern above his head, so that the light fell full upon his withered face, which was drawn up into a curious grimace, that was meant for a friendly smile. The carriage drove into the court, and we got out; then I obtained a full view of the old servant's extraordinary figure, almost hidden in his wide old-fashioned chasseur livery, with its many extraordinary lace decorations. Whilst there were only a few grey locks on his broad white forehead, the lower part of his face wore the ruddy hue of health; and, notwithstanding that the cramped muscles of his face gave it something of the appearance of a whimsical mask, yet the rather stupid good-nature which beamed from his eyes and played about his mouth compensated for all the rest.

"Now, old Francis," began my great-uncle, knocking the snow from his fur coat in the entrance hall, "now, old man, is everything prepared? Have you had the hangings in my room well dusted, and the beds carried in? and have you had a big roaring fire both yesterday and to-day?" "No," replied Francis, quite calmly, "no, my worshipful Herr Justitiarius, we've got none of that done." "Good Heavens!" burst out my great-uncle, "I wrote to you in proper time; you know that I always come at the time I fix. Here's a fine piece of stupid carelessness! I shall have to sleep in rooms as cold as ice." "But you see, worshipful Herr Justitiarius," continued Francis, most carefully clipping a burning thief from the wick of the candle with the snuffers and stamping it out with his foot, "but, you see, sir, all that would not have been of much good, especially the fires, for the wind and the snow have taken up their quarters too much in the rooms, driving in through the broken windows, and then"—— "What!" cried my uncle, interrupting him as he spread out his fur coat and placing his arms akimbo, "do you mean to tell me the windows are broken, and you, the castellan of the house, have done nothing to get them mended?" "But, worshipful Herr Justitiarius," resumed the old servant calmly and composedly, "but we can't very well get at them owing to the great masses of stones and rubbish lying all over the room." "Damn it all, how come there to be stones and rubbish in my room?" cried my uncle. "Your lasting health and good luck, young gentleman!" said the old man, bowing politely to me, as I happened to sneeze; but he immediately added, "They are the stones and plaster of the partition wall which fell in at the great shock." "Have you had an earthquake?" blazed up my uncle, now fairly in a rage. "No, not an earthquake, worshipful Herr Justitiarius," replied the old man, grinning all over his face, "but three days ago the heavy wainscot ceiling of the justice-hall fell in with a tremendous crash." "Then may the"—— My uncle was about to rip out a terrific oath in his violent passionate manner, but jerking up his right arm above his head and taking off his fox-skin cap with his left, he suddenly checked himself; and turning to me, he said with a hearty laugh, "By my troth, cousin, we must hold our tongues; we mustn't ask any more questions, or else we shall hear of some still worse misfortune, or have the whole castle tumbling to pieces about our ears." "But," he continued, wheeling round again to the old servant, "but, bless me, Francis, could you not have had the common sense to get me another room cleaned and warmed? Could you not have quickly fitted up a room in the main building for the court-day?" "All that has been already done," said the old man, pointing to the staircase with a gesture that invited us to follow him, and at once beginning to ascend them. "Now there's a most curious noodle for you!" exclaimed my uncle as we followed old Francis. The way led through long lofty vaulted corridors, in the dense darkness of which Francis's flickering light threw a strange reflection. The pillars, capitals, and vari-coloured arches seemed as if they were floating before us in the air; our own shadows stalked along beside us in gigantic shape, and the grotesque paintings on the walls over which they glided seemed all of a tremble and shake; whilst their voices, we could imagine, were whispering in the sound of our echoing footsteps, "Wake us not, oh! wake us not—us whimsical spirits who sleep here in these old stones." At last, after we had traversed a long suite of cold and gloomy apartments, Francis opened the door of a hall in which a fire blazing brightly in the grate offered us as it were a home-like welcome with its pleasant crackling. I felt quite comfortable the moment I entered, but my uncle, standing still in the middle of the hall, looked round him and said in a tone which was so very grave as to be almost solemn, "And so this is to be the justice-hall!" Francis held his candle above his head, so that my eye fell upon a light spot in the wide dark wall about the size of a door; then he said in a pained and muffled voice, "Justice has been already dealt out here." "What possesses you, old man?" asked my uncle, quickly throwing aside his fur coat and drawing near to the fire. "It slipped over my lips, I couldn't help it," said Francis; then he lit the great candles and opened the door of the adjoining room, which was very snugly fitted up for our reception. In a short time a table was spread for us before the fire, and the old man served us with several well-dressed dishes, which were followed by a brimming bowl of punch, prepared in true Northern style,—a very acceptable sight to two weary travellers like my uncle and myself. My uncle then, tired with his journey, went to bed as soon as he had finished supper; but my spirits were too much excited by the novelty and strangeness of the place, as well as by the punch, for me to think of sleep. Meanwhile, Francis cleared the table, stirred up the fire, and bowing and scraping politely, left me to myself.

Now I sat alone in the lofty spacious *Rittersaal* or Knight's Hall. The snow-flakes had ceased to beat against the lattice, and the storm had ceased to whistle; the sky was clear, and the bright full moon shone in through the wide oriel-windows, illuminating with magical effect all the dark corners of the curious room into which the dim light of my candles and the fire could not penetrate. As one often finds in old castles, the walls and ceiling of the hall were ornamented in a peculiar antique fashion, the former with fantastic paintings and carvings, gilded and coloured in gorgeous tints, the latter with heavy wainscoting. Standing out conspicuously from the great pictures, which represented for the most part wild bloody scenes in bear-hunts and wolf-hunts, were the heads of men and animals carved in wood and joined on to the painted bodies, so that the whole, especially in the flickering light of the fire and the soft beams of the moon, had an effect as if all were alive and instinct with terrible reality. Between these pictures reliefs of knights had been inserted, of life size, walking along in hunting costume; probably they were the ancestors of the family who had delighted in the chase. Everything, both in the paintings and in the carved work, bore the dingy hue of extreme old age; so much the more conspicuous therefore was the bright bare place on that one of the walls through which were two doors leading into adjoining apartments. I soon concluded that there too there must have been a door, that had been bricked up later; and hence it was that this new part of the wall, which had neither been painted like the rest, nor yet ornamented with carvings, formed such a striking contrast with the others. Who does not know with what mysterious power the mind is enthralled in the midst of unusual and singularly strange circumstances? Even the dullest imagination is aroused when it comes into a valley girt around by fantastic rocks, or within the gloomy walls of a church or an abbey, and it begins to have glimpses of things it has never yet experienced. When I add that I was twenty years of age, and had drunk several glasses of strong punch, it will easily be conceived that as I sat thus in the *Rittersaal* I was in a more exceptional frame of mind than I had ever been before. Let the reader picture to himself the stillness of the night within, and without the rumbling roar of the sea—the peculiar piping of the wind, which rang upon my ears like the tones of a mighty organ played upon by spectral hands—the passing scudding clouds which, shining bright and white, often seemed to peep in through the rattling oriel-windows like giants sailings past—in very truth, I felt, from the slight shudder which shook me, that possibly a new sphere of existences might now be revealed to me visibly and perceptibly. But this feeling was like the shivery sensations that one has on hearing a graphically narrated ghost story, such as we all like. At this moment it occurred to me that I should never be in a more seasonable mood for reading the book which, in common with every one who had the least leaning towards the romantic, I at that time carried about in my pocket,—I mean Schiller's "Ghost-seer." I read and read, and my imagination grew ever more and more excited. I came to the marvellously enthralling description of the wedding feast at Count Von V——'s.

Just as I was reading of the entrance of Jeronimo's bloody figure, the door leading from the gallery into the antechamber flew open with a tremendous bang. I started to my feet in terror; the book fell from my hands. In the very same moment, however, all was still again, and I began to be ashamed of my childish fears. The door must have been burst open by a strong gust of wind or in some other natural manner. It is nothing; my over-strained fancy converts every ordinary occurrence into the supernatural. Having thus calmed my fears, I picked up my book from the ground, and again threw myself in the arm-chair; but there came a sound of soft, slow, measured footsteps moving diagonally across the hall, whilst there was a sighing and moaning at intervals, and in this sighing and moaning there was expressed the deepest trouble, the most hopeless grief, that a human being can know. "Ha! it must be some sick animal locked up somewhere in the basement storey. Such acoustic deceptions at night time, making distant sounds appear close at hand, are well known to everybody. Who will suffer himself to be terrified at such a thing as that?" Thus I calmed my fears again. But now there was a scratching at the new portion of the wall, whilst louder and deeper sighs were audible, as if gasped out by some one in the last throes of mortal anguish. "Yes, yes; it is some poor animal locked up somewhere; I will shout as loudly as I can, I will stamp violently on the floor, then all will be still, or else the animal below will make itself heard more distinctly, and in its natural cries," I thought. But the blood ran cold in my veins; the cold sweat, too, stood upon my forehead, and I remained sitting in my chair as if transfixed, quite unable to rise, still less to cry out. At length the abominable scratching ceased, and I again heard the footsteps. Life and motion seemed to be awakened in me; I leapt to my feet, and went two or three steps forward. But then there came an ice-cold draught of wind through the hall, whilst at the same moment the moon cast her bright light upon the statue of a grave if not almost terrible-looking man; and then, as though his warning voice rang through the louder thunders of the waves and the shriller piping of the wind, I heard distinctly, "No further, no further! or you will sink beneath all the fearful horrors of the world of spectres." Then the door was slammed too with the same violent bang as before, and I plainly heard the footsteps in the anteroom, then going down the stairs. The main door of the castle was opened with a creaking noise, and afterwards closed again. Then it seemed as if a horse were brought out of the stable, and after a while taken back again, and finally all was still.

At that same moment my attention was attracted to my old uncle in the adjoining room; he was groaning and moaning painfully. This brought me fully to consciousness again; I seized the candles and hurried into the room to him. He appeared to be struggling with an ugly, unpleasant dream. "Wake up, wake up!" I cried loudly, taking him gently by the hand, and letting the full glare of the light fall upon his face. He started up with a stifled shout, and then, looking kindly at me, said, "Ay, you have done quite right—that you have, cousin, to wake me. I have had a very ugly dream, and it's all solely owing to this room and that hall, for they made me think of past times and many wonderful things that have happened here. But now let us turn to and have a good sound sleep." Therewith the old gentleman rolled himself in the bed-covering and appeared to fall asleep at once. But when I had extinguished the candles and likewise crept into bed, I heard him praying in a low tone to himself.

Next morning we began work in earnest; the land-steward brought his account-books, and various other people came, some to get a dispute settled, some to get arrangements made about other matters. At noon my uncle took me with him to the wing where the two old Baronesses lived, that we might pay our respects to them with all due form. Francis having announced us, we had to wait some time before a little old dame, bent with the weight of her sixty years, and attired in gay-coloured silks, who styled herself the noble ladies' lady-in-waiting, appeared and led us into the sanctuary. There we were received with comical ceremony by the old ladies, whose curious style of dress had gone out of fashion years and years before. I especially was an object of astonishment to them when my uncle, with considerable humour, introduced me as a young lawyer who had come to assist him in his business. Their countenances plainly indicated their belief that, owing to my youth, the welfare of the tenants of R—sitten was placed in jeopardy. Although there was a good deal that was truly ridiculous during the whole of this interview with the old ladies, I was nevertheless still shivering from the terror of the preceding night; I felt as if I had come in contact with an unknown power, or rather as if I had grazed against the outer edge of a circle, one step across which would be enough to plunge me irretrievably into destruction, as though it were only by the exertion of all the power of my will that I should be able to guard myself against *that* awful dread which never slackens its hold upon you until it ends in incurable insanity. Hence it was that the old Baronesses, with their remarkable towering head-dresses, and their peculiar stuff gowns, tricked off with gay flowers and ribbons, instead of striking me as merely ridiculous, had an appearance that was both ghostly and awe-inspiring. My fancy seemed to glean from their yellow withered faces and blinking eyes, ocular proof of the fact that they had succeeded in establishing themselves on at least a good footing with the ghosts who haunted the castle, as it derived auricular confirmation of the same fact from the wretched French which they croaked, partly between their tightly-closed blue lips and partly through their long thin noses, and also that they themselves possessed the power of setting trouble and dire mischief at work. My uncle, who always had a keen eye for a bit of fun, entangled the old dames in his ironical way in such a mish-mash of nonsensical rubbish that, had I been in any other mood, I should not have known how to swallow down my immoderate laughter; but, as I have just said, the Baronesses and their twaddle were, and continued to be, in my regard, ghostly, so that my old uncle, who was aiming at affording me an especial diversion, glanced across at me time after time utterly astonished. So after dinner, when we were alone together in our room, he burst out, "But in Heaven's name, cousin, tell me what is the matter with you? You don't laugh; you don't talk; you don't eat; and you don't drink. Are you ill, or is anything else the matter with you?" I now hesitated not a moment to tell him circumstantially all my terrible, awful experiences of the previous night I did not conceal anything, and above all I did not conceal that I had drunk a good deal of punch, and had been reading Schiller's "Ghostseer." "This I must confess to," I add, "for only so can I credibly explain how it was that my over-strained and active imagination could create all those ghostly spirits, which only exist within the sphere of my own brain." I fully expected that my uncle would now pepper me well with the stinging pellets of his wit for this my fanciful ghost-seeing; but, on the contrary, he grew very grave, and his eyes became riveted in a set stare upon the floor, until he jerked up his head and said, fixing me with his keen fiery eyes, "Your book I am not acquainted with, cousin; but your ghostly visitants were due neither to it nor to the fumes of the punch. I must tell you that I dreamt exactly the same things that you saw and heard. Like you, I sat in the easy-chair beside the fire (at least I dreamt so); but what was only revealed to you as slight noises I saw and distinctly comprehended with the eye of my mind. Yes, I beheld that foul fiend come in, stealthily and feebly step across to the bricked-up door, and scratch at the wall in hopeless despair until the blood gushed out from beneath his torn finger-nails; then he went downstairs, took a horse out of the stable, and finally put him back again. Did you also hear the cock crowing in a distant farmyard up at the village? You came and awoke me, and I soon resisted the baneful ghost of that terrible man, who is still able to disturb in this fearful way the quiet lives of the living." The old gentleman stopped; and I did not like to ask him further questions, being well aware that he would explain everything to me when he deemed that the proper time was come for doing so. After sitting for a while, deeply absorbed in his own thoughts, he went on, "Cousin, do you think you have courage enough to encounter the ghost again now that you know all that happens,—that is to say, along with me?" Of course I declared that I now felt quite strong enough, and ready for what he wished. "Then let us watch together during the coming night," the old gentleman went on to say. "There is a voice within me telling me that this evil spirit must fly, not so much before the power of my will as before my courage, which rests upon a basis of firm conviction. I feel that it is not at all presumption in me, but rather a good and pious deed, if I venture life and limb to exorcise this foul fiend that is banishing the sons from the old castle of their ancestors. But what am I thinking about? There can be no risk in the case at all, for with such a firm, honest mind and pious trust that I feel I possess, I and everybody cannot fail to be, now and always, victorious over such ghostly antagonists. And yet if, after all, it should be God's will that this evil power be enabled to work me mischief, then you must bear witness, cousin, that I fell in honest Christian fight against the spirit of hell which was here busy about its fiendish work. As for yourself, keep at a distance; no harm will happen to you then."

Our attention was busily engaged with divers kinds of business until evening came. As on the day before, Francis had cleared away the remains of the supper, and brought us our punch. The full moon shone brightly through the gleaming clouds, the sea-waves roared, and the night-wind howled and shook the oriel window till the panes rattled. Although inwardly excited, we forced ourselves to converse on indifferent topics. The old gentleman had placed his striking watch on the table; it struck twelve. Then the door flew open with a terrific bang, and, just as on the preceding night, soft slow footsteps moved stealthily across the hall in a diagonal direction, whilst there were the same sounds of sighing and moaning. My uncle turned pale, but his eyes shone with an unusual brilliance. He rose from his arm-chair, stretching his tall figure up to its full height, so that as he stood there with his left arm propped against his side and with his right stretched out towards the middle of the hall, he had the appearance of a hero issuing his commands. But the sighing and moaning were growing every moment louder and more perceptible, and then the scratching at the wall began more horribly even than on the previous night. My uncle strode forwards straight towards the walled-up door, and his steps were so firm that they echoed along the floor. He stopped immediately in front of the place, where the scratching noise continued to grow worse and worse, and said in a strong solemn voice, such as I had never before heard from his lips, "Daniel, Daniel! what are you doing here at this hour?" Then there was a horrible unearthly scream, followed by a dull thud as if a heavy weight had fallen to the ground. "Seek for pardon and mercy at the throne of the Almighty; that is your place. Away with you from the scenes of this life, in which you can nevermore have part." And as the old gentleman uttered these words in a tone still stronger than before, a feeble wail seemed to pass through the air and die away in the blustering of the storm, which was just beginning to rage. Crossing over to the door, the old gentleman slammed it to, so that the echo rang loudly through the empty anteroom. There was something so supernatural almost in both his language and his gestures that I was deeply struck with awe. On resuming his seat in his arm-chair his face was as if transfigured; he folded his hands and prayed inwardly. In this way several minutes passed, when he asked me in that gentle tone which always went right to my heart, and which he always had so completely at his command, "Well, cousin?" Agitated and shaken by awe, terror, fear, and pious respect and love, I threw myself upon my knees and rained down my warm tears upon the hand he offered me. He clasped me in his arms, and pressing me fervently to his heart said very tenderly, "Now we will go and have a good quiet sleep, good cousin;" and we did so. And as nothing of an unusual nature occurred on the following night, we soon recovered our former cheerfulness, to the prejudice of the old Baronesses; for though there did still continue to be something ghostly about them and their odd manners, yet it emanated from a diverting ghost which the old gentleman knew how to call up in a droll fashion.

At length, after the lapse of several days, the Baron put in his appearance, along with his wife and a numerous train of servants for the hunting; the guests who had been invited also arrived, and the castle, now suddenly awakened to animation, became the scene of the noisy life and revelry which have been before described. When the Baron came into our hall soon after his arrival, he seemed to be disagreeably surprised at the change in our quarters. Casting an ill-tempered glance towards the bricked-up door, he turned abruptly round and passed his hand across his forehead, as if desirous of banishing some disagreeable recollection. My great-uncle mentioned the damage done to the justice-hall and the adjoining apartments; but the Baron found fault with Francis for not accommodating us with better lodgings, and he good-naturedly requested the old gentleman to order anything he might want to make his new room comfortable; for it was much less satisfactory in this respect than that which he had usually occupied. On the whole, the Baron's bearing towards my old uncle was not merely cordial, but largely coloured by a certain deferential respect, as if the relation in which he stood towards him was that of a younger relative. But this was the sole trait that could in any way reconcile me to his harsh, imperious character, which was now developed more and more every day. As for me, he seemed to notice me but little; if he did notice me at all, he saw in me nothing more than the usual secretary or clerk. On the occasion of the very first important memorandum that I drew up, he began to point out mistakes, as he conceived, in the wording. My blood boiled, and I was about to make a caustic reply, when my uncle interposed, informing him briefly that I did my work exactly in the way he wished, and that in legal matters of this kind he alone was responsible. When we were left alone, I complained bitterly of the Baron, who would, I said, always inspire me with growing aversion. "I assure you, cousin," replied the old gentleman, "that the Baron, notwithstanding his unpleasant manner, is really one of the most excellent and kind-hearted men in the world. As I have already told you, he did not assume these manners until the time he became lord of the entail; previous to then he was a modest, gentle youth. Besides, he is not, after all, so bad as you make him out to be; and further, I should like to know why you are so averse to him." As my uncle said these words he smiled mockingly, and the blood rushed hotly and furiously into my face. I could not pretend to hide from myself—I saw it only too clearly, and felt it too unmistakably—that my peculiar antipathy to the Baron sprang out of the fact that I loved, even to madness, a being who appeared to me to be the loveliest and most fascinating of her sex who had ever trod the earth. This lady was none other than the Baroness herself. Her appearance exercised a powerful and irresistible charm upon me at the very moment of her arrival, when I saw her traversing the apartments in her Russian sable cloak, which fitted close to the exquisite symmetry of her shape, and with a rich veil wrapped about her head. Moreover, the circumstance that the two old aunts, with still more extraordinary gowns and be-ribboned head-dresses than I had yet seen them wear, were sweeping along one on each side of her and cackling their welcomes in French, whilst the Baroness was looking about her in a way so gentle as to baffle all description, nodding graciously first to one and then to another, and then adding in her flute-like voice a few German words in the pure sonorous dialect of Courland—all this formed a truly remarkable and unusual picture, and my imagination involuntarily connected it with the ghostly midnight visitant,—the Baroness being the angel of light who was to break the ban of the spectral powers of evil. This wondrously lovely lady stood forth in startling reality before my mind's eye. At that time she could hardly be nineteen years of age, and her face, as delicately beautiful as her form, bore the impression of the most angelic good-nature; but what I especially noticed was the indescribable fascination of her dark eyes, for a soft melancholy gleam of aspiration shone in them like dewy moonshine, whilst a perfect elysium of rapture and delight was revealed in her sweet and beautiful smile. She often seemed completely lost in her own thoughts, and at such moments her lovely face was swept by dark and fleeting shadows. Many observers would have concluded that she was affected by some distressing pain; but it rather seemed to me that she was struggling with gloomy apprehensions of a future pregnant with dark misfortunes; and with these, strangely enough, I connected the apparition of the castle, though I could not give the least explanation of why I did so.

On the morning following the Baron's arrival, when the company assembled to breakfast, my old uncle introduced me to the Baroness; and, as usually happens with people in the frame of mind in which I then was, I behaved with indescribable absurdity. In answer to the beautiful lady's simple inquiries how I liked the castle, &c., I entangled myself in the most extraordinary and nonsensical phrases, so that the old aunts ascribed my embarrassment simply and solely to my profound respect for the noble lady, and thought they were called upon condescendingly to take my part, which they did by praising me in French as a very nice and clever young man, as a *garçon très joli* (handsome lad). This vexed me; so suddenly recovering my self-possession, I threw out a *bonmot* in better French than the old dames were mistresses of; whereupon they opened their eyes wide in astonishment, and pampered their long thin noses with a liberal supply of snuff. From the Baroness's turning from me with a more serious air to talk to some other lady, I perceived that my *bonmot* bordered closely upon folly; this vexed me still more, and I wished the two old ladies to the devil. My old uncle's irony had long before brought me through the stage of the languishing love-sick swain, who in childish infatuation coddles his love-troubles; but I knew very well that the Baroness had made a deeper and more powerful impression upon my heart than any other woman had hitherto done. I saw and heard nothing but her; nevertheless I had a most explicit and unequivocal consciousness that it would be not only absurd, but even utter madness to dream of an amour, albeit I perceived no less clearly the impossibility of gazing and adoring at a distance like a love-lorn boy. Of such conduct I should have been perfectly ashamed. But what I could do, and what I resolved to do, was to become more intimate with this beautiful girl without allowing her to get any glimpse of my real feelings, to drink the sweet poison of her looks and words, and then, when far away from her, to bear her image in my heart for many, many days, perhaps for ever. I was excited by this romantic and chivalric attachment to such a degree, that, as I pondered over it during sleepless nights, I was childish enough to address myself in pathetic monologues, and even to sigh lugubriously, "Seraphina! O Seraphina!" till at last my old uncle woke up and cried, "Cousin, cousin! I believe you are dreaming aloud. Do it by daytime, if you can possibly contrive it, but at night have the goodness to let me sleep." I was very much afraid that the old gentleman, who had not failed to remark my excitement on the Baroness's arrival, had heard the name, and would overwhelm me with his sarcastic wit. But next morning all he said, as we went into the justice-hall, was, "God grant every man the proper amount of common sense, and sufficient watchfulness to keep it well under hand. It's a bad look-out when a man becomes converted into a fantastic coxcomb without so much as a word of warning." Then he took his seat at the great table and added, "Write neatly and distinctly, good cousin, that I may be able to read it without any trouble."

The respect, nay, the almost filial veneration which the Baron entertained towards my uncle, was manifested on all occasions. Thus, at the dinner-table he had to occupy the seat—which many envied him—beside the Baroness;

as for me, chance threw me first in one place and then in another; but for the most part, two or three officers from the neighbouring capital were wont to attach me to them, in order that they might empty to their own satisfaction their budget of news and amusing anecdotes, whilst diligently passing the wine about. Thus it happened that for several days in succession I sat at the bottom of the table at a great distance from the Baroness. At length, however, chance brought me nearer to her. Just as the doors of the dining-hall were thrown open for the assembled company, I happened to be in the midst of a conversation with the Baroness's companion and confidante,—a lady no longer in the bloom of youth, but by no means ill-looking, and not without intelligence,— and she seemed to take some interest in my remarks. According to etiquette, it was my duty to offer her my arm, and I was not a little pleased when she took her place quite close to the Baroness, who gave her a friendly nod. It may be readily imagined that all that I now said was intended not only for my fair neighbour, but also mainly for the Baroness. Whether it was that the inward tension of my feelings imparted an especial animation to all I said, at any rate my companion's attention became more riveted with every succeeding moment; in fact, she was at last entirely absorbed in the visions of the kaleidoscopic world which I unfolded to her gaze. As remarked, she was not without intelligence, and it soon came to pass that our conversation, completely independent of the multitude of words spoken by the other guests (which rambled about first to this subject and then to that), maintained its own free course, launching an effective word now and again whither I wanted it. For I did not fail to observe that my companion shot a significant glance or two across to the Baroness, and that the latter took pains to listen to us. And this was particularly the case when the conversation turned upon music and I began to speak with enthusiasm of this glorious and sacred art; nor did I conceal that, despite the fact of my having devoted myself to the dry tedious study of the law, I possessed tolerable skill on the harpsichord, could sing, and had even set several songs to music.

The majority of the company had gone into another room to take coffee and liqueurs; but, unawares, without knowing how it came about, I found myself near the Baroness, who was talking with her confidante. She at once addressed me, repeating in a still more cordial manner and in the tone in which one talks to an acquaintance, her inquiries as to how I liked living in the castle, &c. I assured her that for the first few days, not only the dreary desolation of the situation, but the ancient castle itself had affected me strangely, but even in this mood I had found much of deep interest, and that now my only wish was to be excused from the stirring scenes of the hunt, for I had not been accustomed to them. The Baroness smiled and said, "I can readily believe that this wild life in our fir forests cannot be very congenial to you. You are a musician, and, unless I am utterly mistaken, a poet as well. I am passionately fond of both arts. I can also play the harp a little, but I have to do without it here in R—— sitten, for my husband does not like me to bring it with me. Its soft strains would harmonize but ill with the wild shouts of the hunters and the ringing blare of their bugles, which are the only sounds that ought to be heard here. And O heaven! how I should like to hear a little music!" I protested that I would exert all the skill I had at my command to fulfil her wish, for there must surely without doubt be an instrument of some kind in the castle, even though it were only an old harpsichord. Then the Lady Adelheid (the Baroness's confidante) burst out into a silvery laugh and asked, did I not know that within the memory of man no other instrument had ever been heard in the castle except cracked trumpets, and hunting-horns which in the midst of joy would only sound lugubrious notes, and the twanging fiddles, untuned violoncellos, and braying oboes of itinerant musicians. The Baroness reiterated her wish that she should like to have some music, and especially should like to hear me; and both she and Adelheid racked their brains all to no purpose to devise some scheme by which they could get a decent pianoforte brought to the Castle. At this moment old Francis crossed the room. "Here's the man who always can give the best advice, and can procure everything, even things before unheard of and unseen." With these words the Lady Adelheid called him to her, and as she endeavoured to make him comprehend what it was that was wanted, the Baroness listened with her hands clasped and her head bent forward, looking upon the old man's face with a gentle smile. She made a most attractive picture, like some lovely, winsome child that is all eagerness to have a wished-for toy in its hands. Francis, after having adduced in his prolix manner several reasons why it would be downright impossible to procure such a wonderful instrument in such a big hurry, finally stroked his beard with an air of self-flattery and said, "But the land-steward's lady up at the village performs on the manichord, or whatever is the outlandish name they now call it, with uncommon skill, and sings to it so fine and mournful-like that it makes your eyes red, just like onions do, and makes you feel as if you would like to dance with both legs at once." "And you say she has a pianoforte?" interposed Lady Adelheid. "Aye, to be sure," continued the old man; "it comed straight from Dresden; a"—("Oh, that's fine!" interrupted the Baroness)—"a beautiful instrument," went on the old man, "but a little weakly; for not long ago, when the organist began to play on it the hymn 'In all Thy works,' he broke it all to pieces, so that"—("Good gracious!" exclaimed both the Baroness and Lady Adelheid)—"so that," went on the old man again, "it had to be taken to R—— to be mended, and cost a lot of money." "But has it come back again?" asked Lady Adelheid impatiently. "Aye, to be sure, my lady, and the steward's lady will reckon it a high honouR——" At this moment the Baron chanced to pass. He looked across at our group rather astonished, and whispered with a sarcastic smile to the Baroness, "So you have to take counsel of Francis again, I see?" The Baroness cast down her eyes blushing, whilst old Francis breaking off terrified, suddenly threw himself into military posture, his head erect, and his arms close and straight down his side. The old aunts came sailing down upon us in their stuff gowns and carried off the Baroness. Lady Adelheid followed her, and I was left alone as if spell-bound. A struggle began to rage within me between my rapturous anticipations of now being able to be near her whom I adored, who completely swayed all my thoughts and feelings, and my sulky ill-humour and annoyance at the Baron, whom I regarded as a barbarous tyrant. If he were not, would the grey-haired old servant have assumed such a slavish attitude?

"Do you hear? Can you see, I say?" cried my great-uncle, tapping me on the shoulder;—we were going upstairs to our own apartments. "Don't force yourself so on the Baroness's attention," he said when we reached the room. "What good can come of it? Leave that to the young fops who like to pay court to ladies; there are plenty of them to do it." I related how it had all come about, and challenged him to say if I had deserved his reproof. His only reply to this, however, was, "Humph! humph!" as he drew on his dressing-gown. Then, having lit his pipe, he took his seat in his easy-chair and began to talk about the adventures of the hunt on the preceding day, bantering me on my bad shots. All was quiet in the castle; all the visitors, both gentlemen and ladies, were busy in their own rooms dressing for the evening. For the musicians with the twanging fiddles, untuned violoncellos, and braying oboes, of whom Lady Adelheid had spoken, were come, and a merrymaking of no less importance than a ball, to be given in the best possible style, was in anticipation. My old uncle, preferring a quiet sleep to such foolish pastimes, stayed in his chamber. I, however, had just finished dressing when there came a light tap at our door, and Francis entered. Smiling in his self-satisfied way, he announced to me that the manichord had just arrived from the land-steward's lady in a sledge, and had been carried into the Baroness's apartments. Lady Adelheid sent her compliments and would I go over at once. It may be conceived how my pulse beat, and also with what a delicious tremor at heart I opened the door of the room in which I was to find *her*. Lady Adelheid came to meet me with a joyful smile. The Baroness, already in full dress for the ball, was sitting in a meditative attitude beside the mysterious case or box, in which slumbered the music that I was called upon to awaken. When she rose, her beauty shone upon me with such glorious splendour that I stood staring at her unable to utter a word. "Come, Theodore"—(for, according to the kindly custom of the North, which is found again farther south, she addressed everybody by his or her Christian name)—"Come, Theodore," she said pleasantly, "here's the instrument come. Heaven grant it be not altogether unworthy of your skill!" As I opened the lid I was greeted by the rattling of a score of broken strings, and when I attempted to strike a chord, the effect was hideous and abominable, for all the strings which were not broken were completely out of tune. "I doubt not our friend the organist has been putting his delicate little hands upon it again," said Lady Adelheid laughing; but the Baroness was very much annoyed and said, "Oh, it really is a slice of bad luck! I am doomed, I see, never to have any pleasure here." I searched in the case of the instrument, and fortunately found some coils of strings, but no tuning-key anywhere. Hence fresh laments. "Any key will do if the ward will fit on the pegs," I explained; then both Lady Adelheid and the Baroness ran backwards and forwards in gay spirits, and before long a whole magazine of bright keys lay before me on the sounding-board.

Then I set to work diligently, and both the ladies assisted me all they could, trying first one peg and then another. At length one of the tiresome keys fitted, and they exclaimed joyfully, "This will do! it will do!" But when I had drawn the first creaking string up to just proper pitch, it suddenly snapped, and the ladies recoiled in alarm. The Baroness, handling the brittle wires with her delicate little fingers, gave me the numbers as I wanted them, and carefully held the coil whilst I unrolled it. Suddenly one of them coiled itself up again with a whirr, making the Baroness utter an impatient "Oh!" Lady Adelheid enjoyed a hearty laugh, whilst I pursued the tangled coil to the corner of the room. After we had all united our efforts to extract a perfectly straight string from it, and had tried it again, to our mortification it again broke; but at last—at last we found some good coils; the strings began to hold, and gradually the discordant jangling gave place to pure melodious chords. "Ha! it will go! it will go! The instrument is getting in tune!" exclaimed the Baroness, looking at me with her lovely smile. How quickly did this common interest banish all the strangeness and shyness which the artificial manners of social intercourse impose. A kind of confidential familiarity arose between us, which, burning through me like an electric current, consumed the timorous nervousness and constraint which had lain like ice upon my heart. That peculiar mood of diffused melting sadness which is engendered of such love as mine was had quite left me; and accordingly, when the pianoforte was brought into something like tune, instead of interpreting my deeper feelings in dreamy improvisations, as I had intended, I began with those sweet and charming canzonets which have reached us from the South. During this or the other *Senza di te* (Without thee), or *Sentimi idol mio* (Hear me, my darling), or *Almen se nonpos'io* (At least if I cannot), with numberless *Morir mi sentos* (I feel I am dying), and *Addios* (Farewell), and *O dios!* (O Heaven!), a brighter and brighter brilliancy shone in Seraphina's eyes. She had seated herself close beside me at the instrument; I felt her breath fanning my cheek; and as she placed her arm behind me on the chair-back, a white ribbon, getting disengaged from her beautiful ball-dress, fell across my shoulder, where by my singing and Seraphina's soft sighs it was kept in a continual flutter backwards and forwards, like a true love-messenger. It is a wonder how I kept from losing my head.

As I was running my fingers aimlessly over the keys, thinking of a new song, Lady Adelheid, who had been sitting in one of the corners of the room, ran across to us, and, kneeling down before the Baroness, begged her, as she took both her hands and clasped them to her bosom, "Oh, dear Baroness! darling Seraphina! now you must sing too." To this she replied, "Whatever are you thinking about, Adelheid? How could I dream of letting our virtuoso friend hear such poor singing as mine?" And she looked so lovely, as, like a shy good child, she cast down her eyes and blushed, timidly contending with the desire to sing. That I too added my entreaties can easily be imagined; nor, upon her making mention of some little Courland *Volkslieder* or popular songs, did I desist from my entreaties until she stretched out her left hand towards the instrument and tried a few notes by way of introduction. I rose to make way for her at the piano, but she would not permit me to do so, asserting that she could not play a single chord, and for that reason, since she would have to sing without accompaniment, her performance would be poor and uncertain. She began in a sweet voice, pure as a bell, that came straight from her heart, and sang a song whose simple melody bore all the characteristics of those *Volkslieder* which proceed from the lips with such a lustrous brightness, so to speak, that we cannot help perceiving in the glad light which surrounds us our own higher poetic nature. There lies a mysterious charm in the insignificant words of the text which converts them into a hieroglyphic scroll representative of the unutterable emotions which throng our hearts. Who does not know that Spanish canzonet the substance of which is in words little more than, "With my maiden I embarked on the sea; a storm came on, and my timid maiden was tossed up and down: nay, I will never again embark on the sea with my maiden?" And the Baroness's little song contained nothing more than, "Lately I was dancing with my sweetheart at a wedding; a flower fell out of my hair; he picked it up and gave it me, and said, 'When, sweetheart mine, shall we go to a wedding again?'" When, on her beginning the second verse of the song, I played an *arpeggio* accompaniment, and further when, in the inspiration which now took possession of me, I at once stole from the Baroness's own lips the melodies of the other songs she sang, I doubtless appeared in her eyes, and in those of the Lady Adelheid, to be one of the greatest of masters in the art of music, for they overwhelmed me with enthusiastic praise. The lights and illuminations from the ball-room, situated in one of the wings of the castle, now shone across into the Baroness's chamber, whilst a discordant bleating of trumpets and French horns announced that it was time to gather for the ball. "Oh, now I must go," said the Baroness. I started up from the pianoforte. "You have afforded me a delightful hour; these have been the pleasantest moments I have ever spent in R—sitten," she added, offering me her hand; and as in the extreme intoxication of delight I pressed it to my lips, I felt her fingers close upon my hand with a sudden convulsive tremor. I do not know how I managed to reach my uncle's chamber, and still less how I got into the ball-room. There was a certain Gascon who was afraid to go into battle since he was all heart, and every wound would be fatal to him. I might be compared to him; and so might everybody else who is in the same mood that I was in; every touch was then fatal. The Baroness's hand—her tremulous fingers—had affected me like a poisoned arrow; my blood was burning in my veins.

On the following morning my old uncle, without asking any direct questions, had soon drawn from me a full account of the hour I had spent in the Baroness's society, and I was not a little abashed when the smile vanished from his lips and the jocular note from his words, and he grew serious all at once, saying, "Cousin, I beg you will resist this folly which is taking such a powerful hold upon you. Let me tell you that your present conduct, as harmless as it now appears, may lead to the most terrible consequences. In your thoughtless fatuity you are standing on a thin crust of ice, which may break under you ere you are aware of it, and let you in with a plunge. I shall take good care not to hold you fast by the coat-tails, for I know you will scramble out again pretty quick, and then, when you are lying sick unto death, you will say, 'I got this little bit of a cold in a dream.' But I warn you that a malignant fever will gnaw at your vitals, and years will pass before you recover yourself, and are a man again. The deuce take your music if you can put it to no better use than to cozen sentimental young women out of their quiet peace of mind." "But," I began, interrupting the old gentleman, "but have I ever thought of insinuating myself as the Baroness's lover?" "You puppy!" cried the old gentleman, "if I thought so I would pitch you out of this window." At this juncture the Baron entered, and put an end to the painful conversation; and the business to which I now had to turn my attention brought me back from my love-sick reveries, in which I saw and thought of nothing but Seraphina.

In general society the Baroness only occasionally interchanged a few friendly words with me; but hardly an evening passed in which a secret message was not brought to me from Lady Adelheid, summoning me to Seraphina. It soon came to pass that our music alternated with conversations on divers topics. Whenever I and Seraphina began to get too absorbed in sentimental dreams and vague aspirations, the Lady Adelheid, though now hardly young enough to be so naïve and droll as she once was, yet intervened with all sorts of merry and somewhat chaotic nonsense. From several hints she let fall, I soon discovered that the Baroness really had something preying upon her mind, even as I thought I had read in her eyes the very first moment I saw her; and I clearly discerned the hostile influence of the apparition of the castle. Something terrible had happened or was to happen. Although I was often strongly impelled to tell Seraphina in what way I had come in contact with the invisible enemy, and how my old uncle had banished him, undoubtedly for ever, I yet felt my tongue fettered by a hesitation which was inexplicable to myself even, whenever I opened my mouth to speak.

One day the Baroness failed to appear at the dinner table; it was said that she was a little unwell, and could not leave her room. Sympathetic inquiries were addressed to the Baron as to whether her illness was of a grave nature. He smiled in a very disagreeable way, in fact, it was almost like bitter irony, and said, "Nothing more than a slight catarrh, which she has got from our blustering sea-breezes. They can't tolerate any sweet voices; the only sounds they will endure are the hoarse 'Halloos' of the chase." At these words the Baron hurled a keen searching look at me across the table, for I sat obliquely opposite to him. He had not spoken to his neighbour, but to me. Lady Adelheid, who sat beside me, blushed a scarlet red. Fixing her eyes upon the plate in front of her, and scribbling about on it with her fork, she whispered, "And yet you must see Seraphina to-day; your sweet songs shall to-day also bring soothing and comfort to her poor heart." Adelheid addressed these words to me; but at this moment it struck me that I was almost apparently entangled in a base and forbidden intrigue with the Baroness, which could only end in some terrible crime. My old uncle's warning fell heavily upon my heart. What should I do? Not see her again? That was impossible so long as I remained in the castle; and even if I might leave the castle and return to K——, I had not the will to do it Oh! I felt only too deeply that I was not strong enough to shake myself out of this dream, which was mocking one with delusive hopes of happiness. Adelheid I almost regarded in the light of a common go-between; I would despise her, and yet, upon second thoughts, I could not help being ashamed of my folly. Had anything ever happened during those blissful evening hours which could in the least degree lead to any nearer relation with Seraphina than was permissible by propriety and morality? How dare I let the thought enter my mind that the Baroness would ever entertain any warm feeling for me? And yet I was convinced of the danger of my situation.

We broke up from dinner earlier than usual, in order to go again after some wolves which had been seen in the fir-wood close by the castle. A little hunting was just the thing I wanted in the excited frame of mind in which I then was. I expressed to my uncle my resolve to accompany the party; he gave me an approving smile and said, "That's right; I am glad you are going out with them for once. I shall stay at home, so you can take my firelock with you, and buckle my whinger round your waist; in case of need it is a good and trusty weapon, if you only keep your presence of mind." That part of the wood in which the wolves were supposed to lie was surrounded by the huntsmen. It was bitterly cold; the wind howled through the firs, and drove the light snow-flakes right in my face, so that when at length it came on to be dusk I could scarcely see six paces before me. Quite benumbed by the cold, I left the place that had been assigned to me and sought shelter deeper in the wood. There, leaning against a tree, with my firelock under my arm, I forgot the wolf-hunt entirely; my thoughts had travelled back to Seraphina's cosy room. After a time shots were heard in the far distance; but at the same moment there was a rustling in the reed-bank, and I saw not ten paces from me a huge wolf about to run past me. I took aim, and fired, but missed. The brute sprang towards me with glaring eyes; I should have been lost had I not had sufficient presence of mind to draw my hunting-knife, and, just as the brute was flying at me, to drive it deep into his throat, so that the blood spurted out over my hand and arm. One of the Baron's keepers, who had stood not far from me, came running up with a loud shout, and at his repeated "Halloo!" all the rest soon gathered round us. The Baron hastened up to me, saying, "For God's sake, you are bleeding—you are bleeding. Are you wounded?" I assured him that I was not Then he turned to the keeper who had stood nearest to me, and overwhelmed him with reproaches for not having shot after me when I missed. And notwithstanding that the man maintained this to have been perfectly impossible, since in the very same moment the wolf had rushed upon me, and any shot would have been at the risk of hitting me, the Baron persisted in saying that he ought to have taken especial care of me as a less experienced hunter. Meanwhile the keepers had lifted up the dead animal; it was one of the largest that had been seen for a long time; and everybody admired my courage and resolution, although to myself what I had done appeared quite natural I had not for a moment thought of the danger I had run. The Baron in particular seemed to take very great interest in the matter; I thought he would never be done asking me whether, though I was not wounded by the brute, I did not fear the ill effects that would follow from the fright As we went back to the castle, the Baron took me by the arm like a friend, and I had to give my firelock to a keeper to carry. He still continued to talk about my heroic deed, so that eventually I came to believe in my own heroism, and lost all my constraint and embarrassment, and felt that I had established myself in the Baron's eyes as a man of courage and uncommon resolution. The schoolboy had passed his examination successfully, was now no longer a schoolboy, and all the submissive nervousness of the schoolboy had left him. I now conceived I had earned a right to try and gain Seraphina's favour. Everybody knows of course what ridiculous combinations the fancy of a love-sick youth is capable of. In the castle, over the smoking punchbowl, by the fireside, I was the hero of the hour. Besides myself the Baron was the only one of the party who had killed a wolf—also a formidable one; the rest had to be content with ascribing their bad shots to the weather and the darkness, and with relating thrilling stories of their former exploits in hunting and the dangers they had escaped. I thought, too, that I might reap an especial share of praise and admiration from my old uncle as well; and so, with a view to this end, I related to him my adventure at pretty considerable length, nor did I forget to paint the savage brute's wild and bloodthirsty appearance in very startling colours. The old gentleman, however, only laughed in my face and said, "God is powerful even in the weak."

Tired of drinking and of the company, I was going quietly along the corridor towards the justice-hall when I saw a figure with a light slip in before me. On entering the hall I saw it was Lady Adelheid. "This is the way we have to wander about like ghosts or night-walkers in order to catch you, my brave slayer of wolves," she whispered, taking my arm. The words "ghosts" and "sleep-walkers," pronounced in the place where we were, fell like lead upon my heart; they immediately brought to my recollection the ghostly apparitions of those two awful nights. As then, so now, the wind came howling in from the sea in deep organ-like cadences, rattling the oriel windows again and again and whistling fearfully through them, whilst the moon cast her pale gleams exactly upon the mysterious part of the wall where the scratching had been heard. I fancied I discerned stains of blood upon it. Doubtless Lady Adelheid, who still had hold of my hand, must have felt the cold icy shiver which ran through me. "What's the matter with you?" she whispered softly; "what's the matter with you? You are as cold as marble. Come, I will call you back into life. Do you know how very impatient the Baroness is to see you? And until she does see you she will not believe that the ugly wolf has not really bitten you. She is in a terrible state of anxiety about you. Why, my friend,—oh! how have you awakened this interest in the little Seraphina? I have never seen her like this. Ah!—so now the pulse is beginning to prickle; see how quickly the dead man comes to life! Well, come along— but softly, still! Come, we must go to the little Baroness." I suffered myself to be led away in silence. The way in which Adelheid spoke of the Baroness seemed to me undignified, and the innuendo of an understanding between us positively shameful. When I entered the room along with Adelheid, Seraphina, with a low-breathed "Oh!" advanced three or four paces quickly to meet me; but then, as if recollecting herself, she stood still in the middle of the room. I ventured to take her hand and press it to my lips. Allowing it to rest in mine, she asked, "But, for Heaven's sake! is it your business to meddle with wolves? Don't you know that the fabulous days of Orpheus and Amphion are long past, and that wild beasts have quite lost all respect for even the most admirable of singers?" But this gleeful turn, by which the Baroness at once effectually guarded against all misinterpretation of her warm interest in me, I was put immediately into the proper key and the proper mood. Why I did not take my usual place at the pianoforte I cannot explain, even to myself, nor why I sat down beside the Baroness on the sofa. Her question, "And what were you doing then to get into danger?" was an indication of our tacit agreement that conversation, not music, was to engage our attention for that evening. After I had narrated my adventure in the wood, and mentioned the warm interest which the Baron had taken in it, delicately hinting that I had not thought him capable of so much feeling, the Baroness began in a tender and almost melancholy tone, "Oh! how violent and rude you must think the Baron; but I assure you it is only whilst we are living within these gloomy, ghostly walls, and during the time there is hunting going on in the dismal fir-forests, that his character completely changes, at least his outward behaviour does. What principally disquiets him in this unpleasant way is the thought, which constantly haunts him, that something terrible will happen here. And that undoubtedly accounts for the fact of his being so greatly agitated by your adventure, which fortunately has had no ill consequences. He won't have the meanest of his servants exposed to danger, if he knows it, still less a new-won friend whom he has come to like; and I am perfectly certain that Gottlieb, whom he blames for having left you in the lurch, will be punished; even if he escapes being locked up in a dungeon, he will yet have to suffer the punishment, so mortifying to a hunter, of going out the next time there is a hunt with only a club in his hand instead of a rifle. The circumstance that hunts like those which are held here are always attended with danger, and the fact that the Baron, though always fearing some sad accident, is yet so fond of hunting that he cannot desist from provoking the demon of mischief, make his existence here a kind of conflict, the ill effects of which I also have to feel. Many queer stories are current about his ancestor who established the entail; and I know myself that there is some dark family secret locked within these walls like a horrible ghost which drives away the owners, and makes it impossible for them to bear with it longer than a few weeks at a time—and that only amid a tumult of jovial guests. But I—Oh! how lonely I am in the midst of this noisy, merry company! And how the ghostly influences which breathe upon me from the walls stir and excite my very heart! You, my dear friend, have given me, through your musical skill, the first cheerful moments I have spent here. How can I thank you sufficiently for your kindness!" I kissed the hand she offered to me, saying, that even on the very first day, or rather during the very first night, I had experienced the ghostliness of the place in all its horrors. The Baroness fixed her staring eyes upon my face, as I went on to describe the ghostly character of the building, discernible everywhere throughout the castle, particularly in the decorations of the justice-hall, and to speak of the roaring of the wind from the sea, &c. Possibly my voice and my expressions indicated that I had something more in my mind than what I said; at any rate when I concluded, the

Baroness cried vehemently, "No, no; something dreadful has happened to you in that hall, which I never enter without shuddering. I beg you—pray, pray, tell me all."

Seraphina's face had grown deadly pale; and I saw plainly that it would be more advisable to give her a faithful account of all that I had experienced than to leave her excited imagination to conjure up some apparition that might perhaps, in a way I could not foresee, be far more horrible than what I had actually encountered. As she listened to me her fear and strained anxiety increased from moment to moment; and when I mentioned the scratching on the wall she screamed, "It's horrible! Yes, yes, it's in that wall that the awful secret is concealed!" But as I went on to describe with what spiritual power and superiority of will my old uncle had banished the ghost, she sighed deeply, as though she had shaken off a heavy burden that had weighed oppressively upon her. She leaned back in the sofa and held her hands before her face. Now I first noticed that Adelheid had left us. A considerable pause ensued, and as Seraphina still continued silent, I softly rose, and going to the pianoforte, endeavoured in swelling chords to invoke the bright spirits of consolation to come and deliver Seraphina from the dark influence to which my narration had subjected her. Then I soon began to sing as softly as I was able one of the Abbé Steffani's canzonas. The melancholy strains of the *Ochi, perchè piangete* (O eyes, why weep you?) roused Seraphina out of her reverie, and she listened to me with a gentle smile upon her face, and bright pearl-like tears in her eyes. How am I to account for it that I kneeled down before her, that she bent over towards me, that I threw my arms about her, that a long ardent kiss was imprinted on my lips? How am I to account for it that I did not lose my senses when she drew me softly towards her, how that I tore myself from her arms, and, quickly rising to my feet, hurried to the pianoforte? Turning from me, the Baroness took a few steps towards the window, then she turned round again and approached me with an air of almost proud dignity, which was not at all usual with her. Looking me straight in the face, she said, "Your uncle is the most worthy old man I know; he is the guardian-angel of our family. May he include me in his pious prayers!" I was unable to utter a word; the subtle poison that I had imbibed with her kiss burned and boiled in every pulse and nerve. Lady Adelheid came in. The violence of my inward conflict burst out at length in a passionate flood of tears, which I was unable to repress. Adelheid looked at me with wonder and smiled dubiously;—I could have murdered her. The Baroness gave me her hand, and said with inexpressible gentleness, "Farewell, my dear friend. Fare you right well; and remember that nobody perhaps has ever understood your music better than I have. Oh! these notes! they will echo long, long in my heart." I forced myself to utter a few stupid, disconnected words, and hurried up to my uncle's room. The old gentleman had already gone to bed. I stayed in the hall, and falling upon my knees, I wept aloud; I called upon my beloved by name, I gave myself up completely and regardlessly to all the absurd folly of a love-sick lunatic, until at last the extravagant noise I made awoke my uncle. But his loud call, "Cousin, I believe you have gone cranky, or else you're having another tussle with a wolf. Be off to bed with you if you will be so very kind"—these words compelled me to enter his room, where I got into bed with the fixed resolve to dream only of Seraphina.

It would be somewhere past midnight when I thought I heard distant voices, a running backwards and forwards, and an opening and banging of doors—for I had not yet fallen asleep. I listened attentively; I heard footsteps approaching the corridor; the hall door was opened, and soon there came a knock at our door. "Who is there?" I cried. A voice from without answered, "Herr Justitiarius, Herr Justitiarius, wake up, wake up!" I recognised Francis's voice, and as I asked, "Is the castle on fire?" the old gentleman woke up in his turn and asked, "Where—where is there a fire? Is it that cursed apparition again? where is it?" "Oh! please get up, Herr Justitiarius," said Francis, "Please get up; the Baron wants you." "What does the Baron want me for?" inquired my uncle further; "what does he want me for at this time of night? does he not know that all law business goes to bed along with the lawyer, and sleeps as soundly as he does?" "Oh!" cried Francis, now anxiously; "please, Herr Justitiarius, good sir, please get up. My lady the Baroness is dying." I started up with a cry of dismay. "Open the door for Francis," said the old gentleman to me. I stumbled about the room almost distracted, and could find neither door nor lock; my uncle had to come and help me. Francis came in, his face pale and troubled, and lit the candles. We had scarcely thrown on our clothes when we heard the Baron calling in the hall, "Can I speak to you, good V——?" "But what have you dressed for, cousin? the Baron only wanted me," asked the old gentleman, on the point of going out. "I must go down—I must see her and then die," I replied tragically, and as if my heart were rent by hopeless grief. "Ay, just so; you are right, cousin," he said, banging the door to in my face, so that the hinges creaked, and locking it on the outside. At the first moment, deeply incensed at this restraint, I thought of bursting the door open; but quickly reflecting that this would entail the disagreeable consequences of a piece of outrageous insanity, I resolved to await the old gentleman's return; then however, let the cost be what it might, I would escape his watchfulness. I heard him talking vehemently with the Baron, and several times distinguished my own name, but could not make out anything further. Every moment my position grew more intolerable. At length I heard that some one brought a message to the Baron, who immediately hurried off. My old uncle entered the room again. "She is dead!" I cried, running towards him, "And you are a stupid fool," he interrupted coolly; then he laid hold upon me and forced me into a chair. "I must go down," I cried, "I must go down and see her, even though it cost me my life." "Do so, good cousin," said he, locking the door, taking out the key, and putting it in his pocket. I now flew into a perfectly frantic rage; stretching out my hand towards the rifle, I screamed, "If you don't instantly open the door I will send this bullet through my brains." Then the old gentleman planted himself immediately in front of me, and fixing his keen piercing eyes upon me said, "Boy, do you think you can frighten me with your idle threats? Do you think I should set much value on your life if you can go and throw it away in childish folly like a broken plaything? What have you to do with the Baron's wife? who has given you the right to insinuate yourself, like a tiresome puppy, where you have no claim to be, and where you are not wanted? do you wish to go and act the love-sick swain at the solemn hour of death?" I sank back in my chair utterly confounded After a while the old gentleman went on more gently, "And now let me tell you that this pretended illness of the Baroness is in all probability nothing. Lady Adelheid always loses her head at the least little thing. If a rain-drop falls upon her nose, she screams, 'What fearful weather it is!' Unfortunately the noise penetrated to the old aunts, and they, in the midst of unseasonable floods of tears, put in an appearance armed with an entire arsenal of strengthening drops, elixirs of life, and the deuce knows what. A sharp fainting-fit"—— The old gentleman checked himself; doubtless he observed the struggle that was going on within me. He took a few turns through the room; then again planting himself in front of me, he had a good hearty laugh and said, "Cousin, cousin, what nonsensical folly have you now got in your head? Ah well! I suppose it can't be helped; the devil is to play his pretty games here in divers sorts of ways. You have tumbled very nicely into his clutches, and now he's making you dance to a sweet tune," He again took a few turns up and down, and again went on, "It's no use to think of sleep now; and it occurred to me that we might have a pipe, and so spend the few hours that are left of the darkness and the night." With these words he took a clay pipe from the cupboard, and proceeded to fill it slowly and carefully, humming a song to himself; then he rummaged about amongst a heap of papers, until he found a sheet, which he picked out and rolled into a spill and lighted. Blowing the tobacco-smoke from him in thick clouds, he said, speaking between his teeth, "Well, cousin, what was that story about the wolf?"

I know not how it was, but this calm, quiet behaviour of the old gentleman operated strangely upon me. I seemed to be no longer in R—sitten, and the Baroness was so far, far distant from me that I could only reach her on the wings of thought. The old gentleman's last question, however, annoyed me. "But do you find my hunting exploit so amusing?" I broke in,—"so well fitted for banter?" "By no means," he rejoined, "by no means, cousin mine; but you've no idea what a comical face such a whipper-snapper as you cuts, and how ludicrously he acts as well, when Providence for once in a while honours him by putting him in the way to meet with something out of the usual run of things. I once had a college friend who was a quiet, sober fellow, and always on good terms with himself. By accident he became entangled in an affair of honour,—I say by accident, because he himself was never in any way aggressive; and although most of the fellows looked upon him as a poor thing, as a poltroon, he yet showed so much firm and resolute courage in this affair as greatly to excite everybody's admiration. But from that time onwards he was also completely changed. The sober and industrious youth became a bragging, insufferable bully. He was always drinking and rioting, and fighting about all sorts of childish trifles, until he was run through in a duel by the Senior of an exclusive corps. I merely tell you the story, cousin; you are at liberty to think what you please about it But to return to the Baroness and her illness"—— At this moment light footsteps were heard in the hall; I fancied, too, there was an unearthly moaning in the air. "She is dead!" the thought shot through me like a fatal flash of lightning. The old gentleman quickly rose to his feet and called out, "Francis, Francis!" "Yes, my good Herr Justitiarius," he replied from without. "Francis," went on my uncle, "rake the fire together a bit in the grate, and if you can manage it, you had better make us a good cup or two of tea." "It is devilish cold," and he turned to me, "and I think we had better go and sit round the fire and talk a little." He opened the door, and I followed him mechanically. "How are things going on below?" he asked. "Oh!" replied Francis; "there was not much the matter. The Lady Baroness is all right again, and ascribes her bit of a fainting-fit to a bad dream." I was going to break out into an extravagant manifestation of joy and gladness, but a stern glance from my uncle kept me quiet "And yet, after all, I think it would be better if we lay down for an hour or two. You need not mind about the tea, Francis." "As you think well, Herr Justitiarius," replied Francis, and he left the room with the wish that we might have a good night's rest, albeit the cocks were already crowing. "See here, cousin," said the old gentleman, knocking the ashes out of his pipe on the grate, "I think, cousin, that it's a very good thing no harm has happened to you either from wolves or from loaded rifles." I now saw things in the right light, and was ashamed at myself to have thus given the old gentleman good grounds for treating me like a spoiled child.

Next morning he said to me, "Be so good as to step down, good cousin, and inquire how the Baroness is. You need only ask for Lady Adelheid; she will supply you with a full budget, I have no doubt" You may imagine how eagerly I hastened downstairs. But just as I was about to give a gentle knock at the door of the Baroness's anteroom, the Baron came hurriedly out of the same. He stood still in astonishment, and scrutinised me with a gloomy searching look. "What do you want here?" burst from his lips. Notwithstanding that my heart beat, I controlled myself and replied in a firm tone, "To inquire on my uncle's behalf how my lady, the Baroness, is?" "Oh! it was nothing—one of her usual nervous attacks. She is now having a quiet sleep, and will, I am sure, make her appearance at the dinner-table quite well and cheerful. Tell him that—tell him that." This the Baron said with a certain degree of passionate vehemence, which seemed to me to imply that he was more concerned about the Baroness than he was willing to show. I turned to go back to my uncle, when the Baron suddenly seized my arm and said, whilst his eyes flashed fire, "I have a word or two to say to you, young man." Here I saw the deeply injured husband before me, and feared there would be a scene which would perhaps end ignominiously for me. I was unarmed; but at that moment I remembered I had in my pocket the ingeniously-made hunting-knife which my uncle had presented to me after we got to R—sitten. I now followed the Baron, who led the way rapidly, with the determination not even to spare his life if I ran any risk of being treated dishonourably.

We entered the Baron's own room, the door of which he locked behind him. Now he began to pace restlessly backwards and forwards, with his arms folded one over the other; then he stopped in front of me and repeated, "I have a word or two to say to you, young man." I had wound myself up to a pitch of most daring courage, and I replied, raising my voice, "I hope they will be words which I may hear without resentment." He stared hard at me in astonishment, as though he had failed to understand me. Then, fixing his eyes gloomily upon the floor, he threw his arms behind his back, and again began to stride up and down the room. He took down a rifle and put the ramrod down the barrel to see whether it were loaded or not. My blood boiled in my veins; grasping my knife, I stepped close up to him, so as to make it impossible for him to take aim at me. "That's a handsome weapon," he said, replacing the rifle in the corner. I retired a few paces, the Baron following me. Slapping me on the shoulder, perhaps a little more violently than was necessary, he said, "I daresay I seem to you, Theodore, to be excited and irritable; and I really am so, owing to the anxieties of a sleepless night. My wife's nervous attack was not in the least dangerous; that I now see plainly. But here—here in this castle, which is haunted by an evil spirit, I always dread something terrible happening; and then it's the first time she has been ill here. And you—you alone were to blame for it." "How that can possibly be I have not the slightest conception," I replied calmly. "I wish," continued the Baron, "I wish that damned piece of mischief, my steward's wife's instrument, were chopped up into a thousand pieces, and that you—but no, no; it was to be so, it was inevitably to be so, and I alone am to blame for all. I ought to have told you, the moment you began to play music in my wife's room, of the whole state of the case, and to have informed you of my wife's temper of mind." I was about to speak; "Let me go on," said the Baron, "I must prevent your forming any rash judgment. You probably regard me as an uncultivated fellow, averse to the arts; but I am not so by any means. There is a particular consideration, however, based upon deep conviction, which constrains me to forbid the introduction here as far as possible of such music as can powerfully affect any person's mind, and to this I of course am no exception. Know that my wife suffers from a morbid excitability, which will finally destroy all the happiness of her life. Within these strange walls she is never quit of that strained over-excited condition, which at other times occurs but temporarily, and then generally as the forerunner of a serious illness. You will ask me, and quite reasonably too, why I do not spare my delicate wife the necessity of coming to live in this weird castle, and mix amongst the wild confusion of a hunting-party. Well, call it weakness—be it so; in a word, I cannot bring myself to leave her behind. I should be tortured by a thousand fears, and quite incapable of any serious business, for I am perfectly sure that I should be haunted everywhere, in the justice-hall as well as in the forest, by the most horrid ideas of all kinds of fatal mischief happening to her. And, on the other hand, I believe that the sort of life led here cannot fail to operate upon the weakly woman like strengthening chalybeate waters. By my soul, the sea-breezes, sweeping keenly after their peculiar fashion through the fir-trees, and the deep baying of the hounds, and the merry ringing notes of our hunting-horns *must* get the better of all your sickly languishing sentimentalisings at the piano, which no man ought play in *that way*. I tell you, you are deliberately torturing my wife to death." These words he uttered with great emphasis, whilst his eyes flashed with a restless fire. The blood mounted to my head; I made a violent gesture against the Baron with my hand; I was about to speak, but he cut me short "I know what you are going to say," he began, "I know what you are going to say, and I repeat that you are going the right road to kill my wife. But that you intended this I cannot of course for a moment maintain; and yet you will understand that I must put a stop to the thing. In short, by your playing and singing you work her up to a high pitch of excitement, and then, when she drifts without anchor and rudder on the boundless sea of dreams and visions and vague aspirations which your music, like some vile charm, has summoned into existence, you plunge her down into the depths of horror with a tale about a fearful apparition which you say came and played pranks with you up in the justice-hall. Your great-uncle has told me everything; but, pray, repeat to me all you saw, or did not see, heard, felt, divined by instinct."

I braced myself up and narrated calmly how everything had happened from beginning to end, the Baron merely interposing at intervals a few words expressive of his astonishment. When I came to the part where my old uncle had met the ghost with trustful courage and had exorcised him with a few powerful words, the Baron clasped his hands, raised them folded towards Heaven, and said with deep emotion, "Yes, he is the guardian-angel of the family. His mortal remains shall rest in the vault of my ancestors." When I finished my narration, the Baron murmured to himself, "Daniel, Daniel, what are you doing here at this hour?" as he folded his arms and strode up and down the room. "And was that all, Herr Baron?" I asked, making a movement as though I would retire. Starting up as if out of a dream, the Baron took me kindly by the hand and said, "Yes, my good friend, my wife, whom you have dealt so hardly by without intending it—you must cure her again; you alone can do so." I felt I was blushing, and had I stood opposite a mirror should undoubtedly have seen in it a very blank and absurd face. The Baron seemed to exult in my embarrassment; he kept his eyes fixed intently upon my face, smiling with perfectly galling irony. "How in the world can I cure her?" I managed to stammer out at length with an effort "Well," he said, interrupting me, "you have no dangerous patient to deal with at any rate. I now make an express claim upon your skill. Since the Baroness has been drawn into the enchanted circle of your music, it would be both foolish and cruel to drag her out of it all of a sudden. Go on with your music therefore. You will always be welcome during the evening hours in my wife's apartments. But gradually select a more energetic kind of music, and effect a clever alternation of the cheerful sort with the serious; and above all things, repeat your story of the fearful ghost very very often. The Baroness will grow familiar with it; she will forget that a ghost haunts this castle; and the story will have no stronger effect upon her than any other tale of enchantment which is put before her in a romance or a ghost-story book. Pray, do this, my good friend." With these words the Baron left me. I went away. I felt as if I were annihilated, to be thus humiliated to the level of a foolish and insignificant child. Fool that I was to suppose that jealousy was stirring his heart! He himself sends me to Seraphina; he sees in me only the blind instrument which, after he has made use of it, he can throw away if he thinks well. A few minutes previously I had really feared the Baron; deep down within my heart lurked the consciousness of guilt; but it was a consciousness which allowed me to feel distinctly the beauty of the higher life for which I was ripe. Now all had disappeared in the blackness of night; and I saw only the stupid boy who in childish obstinacy had persisted in taking the paper crown which he had put on his hot temples for a real golden one. I hurried away to my uncle, who was waiting for me. "Well, cousin, why have you been so long? Where have you been staying?" he cried as soon as he saw me. "I have been having some words with the Baron!" I quickly replied, carelessly and in a low voice, without being able to look at the old gentleman. "God damn it all," said he, feigning astonishment "Good gracious, boy! that's just what I thought. I suppose the Baron has challenged you, cousin?" The ringing peal of laughter which the old gentleman immediately afterwards broke out into taught me that this time too, as always, he had seen me through and through. I bit my lip, and durst not speak a word, for I knew very well that it would only be the signal for the old gentleman to overwhelm me beneath the torrent of teasing which was already hovering on the tip of his tongue.

 The Baroness appeared at the dinner-table in an elegant morning-robe, the dazzling whiteness of which exceeded that of fresh-fallen snow. She looked worn and low-spirited; but she began to speak in her soft and melodious accents, and on raising her dark eyes there shone a sweet and yearning look full of aspiration in their voluptuous glow, and a fugitive blush flitted across her lily-white cheeks. She was more beautiful than ever. But who can fathom the follies of a young man who has got too hot blood in his head and heart? The bitter pique which the Baron had stirred up within me I transferred to the Baroness. The entire business seemed to me like a foul mystification; and I would now show that I was possessed of alarmingly good common-sense and also of extraordinary sagacity. Like a petulant child, I shunned the Baroness and escaped Adelheid when she pursued me, and found a place where I wished, right at the bottom end of the table between the two officers, with whom I began to carouse right merrily. We kept our glasses going gaily during dessert, and I was, as so frequently is the case in moods like mine, extremely noisy and loud in my joviality. A servant brought me a plate with some bonbons on it, with the words, "From Lady Adelheid." I took them; and observed on one of them, scribbled in pencil, "and Seraphina." My blood coursed tumultuously in my veins. I sent a glance in Adelheid's direction, which she met with a most sly and archly cunning look; and taking her glass in her hand, she gave me a slight nod. Almost mechanically I murmured to myself, "Seraphina!" then taking up my glass in my turn, I drained it at a single draught. My glance fell across in *her* direction; I perceived that she also had drunk at the very same moment and was setting down her glass. Our eyes met, and a malignant demon whispered in my ear, "Unhappy wretch, she does love you!" One of the guests now rose, and, in conformity with the custom of the North, proposed the health of the lady of the house. Our glasses rang in the midst of a tumult of joy. My heart was torn with rapture and despair; the wine burned like fire within me; everything spun round in circles; I felt as if I must hasten and throw myself at her feet and there sigh out my life. "What's the matter with you, my friend?" asked my neighbour, thus recalling me to myself; but Seraphina had left the hall. We rose from the table. I was making for the door, but Adelheid held me fast, and began to talk about divers matters; I neither heard nor understood a single word. She grasped both my hands and, laughing, shouted something in my ear. I remained dumb and motionless, as though affected by catalepsy. All I remember is that I finally took a glass of liqueur out of Adelheid's hand in a mechanical way and drank it off, and then I recollect being alone in a window, and after that I rushed out of the hall, down the stairs, and ran out into the wood. The snow was falling in thick flakes; the fir-trees were moaning as they waved to and fro in the wind. Like a maniac I ran round and round in wide circles, laughing and screaming loudly, "Look, look and see. Aha! Aha! The devil is having a fine dance with the boy who thought he would taste of strictly forbidden fruit!" Who can tell what would have been the end of my mad prank if I had not heard my name called loudly from the outside of the wood? The storm had abated; the moon shone out brightly through the broken clouds; I heard dogs barking, and perceived a dark figure approaching me. It was the old man Francis. "Why, why, my good Herr Theodore," he began, "you have quite lost your way in the rough snow-storm. The Herr Justitiarius is awaiting you with much impatience." I followed the old man in silence. I found my great-uncle working in the justice-hall. "You have done well," he cried, on seeing me, "you have done a very wise thing to go out in the open air a little and get cool. But don't drink quite so much wine; you are far too young, and it's not good for you." I did not utter a word in reply, and also took my place at the table in silence. "But now tell me, good cousin, what it was the Baron really wanted you for?" I told him all, and concluded by stating that I would not lend myself for the doubtful cure which the Baron had proposed. "And it would not be practicable," the old gentleman interrupted, "for to-morrow morning early we set off home, cousin." And so it was that I never saw Seraphina again.

As soon as we arrived in K—— my old uncle complained that he felt the effects of the wearying journey this time more than ever. His moody silence, broken only by violent outbreaks of the worst possible ill-humour, announced the return of his attacks of gout. One day I was suddenly called in; I found the old gentleman confined to his bed and unable to speak, suffering from a paralytic stroke. He held a letter in his hand, which he had crumpled up tightly in a spasmodic fit. I recognised the hand-writing of the land-steward of R—sitten; but, quite upset by my trouble, I did not venture to take the letter out of the old gentleman's hand. I did not doubt that his end was near. But his pulse began to beat again, even before the physician arrived; the old gentleman's remarkably tough constitution resisted the mortal attack, although he was in his seventieth year. That selfsame day the doctor pronounced him out of danger.

We had a more severe winter than usual; this was followed by a rough and stormy spring; and hence it was more the gout—a consequence of the inclemency of the season—than his previous accident which kept him for a long time confined to his bed. During this period he made up his mind to retire altogether from all kinds of business. He transferred his office of Justitiarius to others; and so I was cut off from all hope of ever again going to R—sitten. The old gentleman would allow no one to attend him but me; and it was to me alone that he looked for all amusement and every cheerful diversion. And though, in the hours when he was free from pain, his good spirits returned, and he had no lack of broad jests, even making mention of hunting exploits, so that I fully expected every minute to hear him make a butt of my heroic deed, when I had killed the wolf with my whinger, yet never once did he allude to our visit to R—sitten, and as may well be imagined, I was very careful, from natural shyness, not to lead him directly up to the subject. My harassing anxiety and continual attendance upon the old gentleman had thrust Seraphina's image into the background. But as soon as his sickness abated somewhat, my thoughts returned with more liveliness to that moment in the Baroness's room, which I now looked upon as a star—a bright star—that had set, for me at least, for ever. An occurrence which now happened, by making me shudder with an ice-cold thrill as at sight of a visitant from the world of spirits, revived all the pain I had formerly felt. One evening, as I was opening the pocket-book which I had carried whilst at R—sitten, there fell out of the papers I was unfolding a dark curl, wrapped about with a white ribbon; I immediately recognised it as Seraphina's hair. But, on examining the ribbon more closely, I distinctly perceived the mark of a spot of blood on it! Perhaps Adelheid had skilfully contrived to secrete it about me during the moments of conscious insanity by which I had been affected during the last days of our visit; but why was the spot of blood there? It excited forebodings of something terrible in my mind, and almost converted this too pastoral love-token into an awful admonition, pointing to a passion which might entail the expenditure of precious blood. It was the same white ribbon that had fluttered about me in light wanton sportiveness as it were the first time I sat near Seraphina, and which Mysterious Night had stamped as an emblem of mortal injury. Boys ought not to play with weapons with the dangerous properties of which they are not familiar.

At last the storms of spring had ceased to bluster, and summer asserted her rights; and if the cold had formerly been unbearable, so now too was the heat when July came in. The old gentleman visibly gathered strength, and following his usual custom, went out to a garden in the suburbs. One still, warm evening, as we sat in the sweet-smelling jasmine arbour, he was in unusually good spirits, and not, as was generally the case, overflowing with sarcasm and irony, but in a gentle and almost soft and melting mood. "Cousin," he began, "I don't know how it is, but I feel so nice and warm and comfortable all over to-day; I have not felt like it for many years. I believe it is an augury that I shall die soon." I exerted myself to drive these gloomy thoughts from his mind. "Never mind, cousin," he said, "in any case I'm not long for this world; and so I will now discharge a debt I owe you. Do you still remember our autumn in R—sitten?" This question thrilled through me like a lightning-flash, so before I was able to make any reply he continued, "It was Heaven's will that your entrance into that castle should be signalised by memorable circumstances, and that you should become involved against your own will in the deepest secrets of the house. The time has now come when you must learn all. We have often enough talked about things which you, cousin, rather dimly guessed at than really understood. In the alternation of the seasons nature represents symbolically the cycle of human life. That is a trite remark; but I interpret it differently from everybody else. The dews of spring fall, summer's vapours fade away, and it is the pure atmosphere of autumn which clearly reveals the distant landscape, and then finally earthly existence is swallowed in the night of winter. I mean that the government of the Power Inscrutable is more plainly revealed in the clear-sightedness of old age. It is granted glimpses of the promised land, the pilgrimage to which begins with the death on earth. How clearly do I see at this moment the dark destiny of that house, to which I am knit by firmer ties than blood relationship can weave! Everything lies disclosed to the eyes of my spirit. And yet the things which I now see, in the form in which I see them—the essential substance of them, that is—this I cannot tell you in words; for no man's tongue is able to do so. But listen, my son, I will tell you as well as I am able, and do you think it is some remarkable story that might really happen; and lay up carefully in your soul the knowledge that the mysterious relations into which you ventured to enter, not perhaps without being summoned, might have ended in your destruction—but—that's all over now."

The history of the R—— entail, which my old uncle told me, I retain so faithfully in my memory even now that I can almost repeat it in his own words (he spoke of himself in the third person).

One stormy night in the autumn of 1760 the servants of R—sitten were startled out of the midst of their sleep by a terrific crash, as if the whole of the spacious castle had tumbled into a thousand pieces. In a moment everybody was on his legs; lights were lit; the house-steward, his face deadly pale with fright and terror, came up panting with his keys; but as they proceeded through the passages and halls and rooms, suite after suite, and found all safe, and heard in the appalling silence nothing except the creaking rattle of the locks, which occasioned some difficulty in opening, and the ghost-like echo of their own footsteps, they began one and all to be utterly astounded. Nowhere was there the least trace of damage. The old house-steward was impressed by an ominous feeling of apprehension. He went up into the great Knight's Hall, which had a small cabinet adjoining where Freiherr Roderick von R—— used to sleep when engaged in making his astronomical observations. Between the door of this cabinet and that of a second was a postern, leading through a narrow passage immediately into the astronomical tower. But directly Daniel (that was the house-steward's name) opened this postern, the storm, blustering and howling terrifically, drove a heap of rubbish and broken pieces of stones all over him, which made him recoil in terror; and, dropping the candles, which went out with a hiss on the floor, he screamed, "O God! O God! The Baron! he's miserably dashed to pieces!" At the same moment he heard sounds of lamentation proceeding from the Freiherr's sleeping-cabinet, and on entering it he saw the servants gathered around their master's corpse. They had found him fully dressed and more magnificently than on any previous occasion, and with a calm earnest look upon his unchanged countenance, sitting in his large and richly decorated arm-chair as though resting after severe study. But his rest was the rest of death. When day dawned it was seen that the crowning turret of the tower had fallen in. The huge square stones had broken through the ceiling and floor of the observatory-room, and then, carrying down in front of them a powerful beam that ran across the tower, they had dashed in with redoubled impetus the lower vaulted roof, and dragged down a portion of the castle walls and of the narrow connecting-passage. Not a single step could be taken beyond the postern threshold without risk of falling at least eighty feet into a deep chasm.

The old Freiherr had foreseen the very hour of his death, and had sent intelligence of it to his sons. Hence it happened that the very next day saw the arrival of Wolfgang, Freiherr von R——, eldest son of the deceased, and now lord of the entail. Relying confidently upon the probable truth of the old man's foreboding, he had left Vienna, which city he chanced to have reached in his travels, immediately he received the ominous letter, and hastened to R—sitten as fast as he could travel. The house-steward had draped the great hall in black, and had had the old Freiherr laid out in the clothes in which he had been found, on a magnificent state-bed, and this he had surrounded with tall silver candlesticks with burning wax-candles. Wolfgang ascended the stairs, entered the hall, and approached close to his father's corpse, without speaking a word. There he stood with his arms folded on his chest, gazing with a fixed and gloomy look and with knitted brows, into his father's pale countenance. He was like a statue; not a tear came from his eyes. At length, with an almost convulsive movement of the right arm towards the corpse, he murmured hoarsely, "Did the stars compel you to make the son whom you loved miserable?" Throwing his hands behind his back and stepping a short pace backwards, the Baron raised his eyes upwards and said in a low and well-nigh broken voice, "Poor, infatuated old man! Your carnival farce with its shallow delusions is now over. Now you no doubt see that the possessions which are so niggardly dealt out to us here on earth have nothing in common with Hereafter beyond the stars. What will—what power can reach over beyond the grave?" The Baron was silent again for some seconds, then he cried passionately, "No, your perversity shall not rob me of a grain of my earthly happiness, which you strove so hard to destroy," and therewith he took a folded paper out of his pocket and held it up between two fingers to one of the burning candles that stood close beside the corpse. The paper was caught by the flame and blazed up high; and as the reflection flickered and played upon the face of the corpse, it was as though its muscles moved and as though the old man uttered toneless words, so that the servants who stood some distance off were filled with great horror and awe. The Baron calmly finished what he was doing by carefully stamping out with his foot the last fragment of paper that fell on the floor blazing. Then, casting yet another moody glance upon his father, he hurriedly left the hall.

On the following day Daniel reported to the Freiherr the damage that had been done to the tower, and described at great length all that had taken place on the night when their dear dead master died; and he concluded by saying that it would be a very wise thing to have the tower repaired at once, for, if a further fall were to take place, there would be some danger of the whole castle—well, if not tumbling down, at any rate suffering serious damage.

"Repair the tower?" the Freiherr interrupted the old servant curtly, whilst his eyes flashed with anger, "Repair the tower? Never, never! Don't you see, old man," he went on more calmly, "don't you see that the tower could not fall in this way without some special cause? How if it was my father's own wish that the place where he carried on his unhallowed astrological labours should be destroyed—how if he had himself made certain preparations by which he was enabled to bring down the turret whenever he pleased and so occasion the ruin of the interior of the tower! But be that as it may. And if the whole castle tumbles down, I shan't care; I shall be glad. Do you imagine I am going to dwell in this weird owls' nest? No; my wise ancestor who had the foundations of a new castle laid in the beautiful valley yonder—he has begun a work which I intend to finish." Daniel said crestfallen, "Then will all your faithful old servants have to take up their bundles and go?" "That I am not going to be waited upon by helpless, weak-kneed old fellows like you is quite certain; but for all that I shall turn none away. You may all enjoy the bread of charity without working for it." "And am I," cried the old man, greatly hurt, "am I, the house-steward, to be forced to lead such a life of inactivity?" Then the Freiherr, who had turned his back upon the old man and was about to leave the room, wheeled suddenly round, his face perfectly ablaze with passion, strode up to the old man as he stretched out his doubled fist towards him, and shouted in a thundering voice, "You, you hypocritical old villain, it's you who helped my old father in his unearthly practices up yonder; you lay upon his heart like a vampire; and perhaps it was you who basely took advantage of the old man's mad folly to plant in his mind those diabolical ideas which brought me to the brink of ruin. I ought, I tell you, to kick you out like a mangy cur." The old man was so terrified at these harsh terrible words that he threw himself upon his knees beside the Freiherr; but the Baron, as he spoke these last words, threw forward his right foot, perhaps quite unintentionally (as is frequently the case in anger, when the body mechanically obeys the mind, and what is in the thought is imitatively realised in action) and hit the old man so hard on the chest that he rolled over with a stifled scream. Rising painfully to his feet and uttering a most singular sound, like the howling whimper of an animal wounded to death, he looked the Freiherr through and through with a look that glared with mingled rage and despair. The purse of money which the Freiherr threw down as he went out of the room, the old man left lying on the floor where it fell.

Meanwhile all the nearest relatives of the family who lived in the neighbourhood had arrived, and the old Freiherr was interred with much pomp in the family vault in the church at R—sitten; and now, after the invited guests had departed, the new lord of the entail appeared to shake off his gloomy mood, and to be prepared to duly enjoy the property that had fallen to him. Along with V——, the old Freiherr's Justitiarius, who won his full confidence in the very first interview they had, and who was at once confirmed in his office, the Baron made an exact calculation of his sources of income, and considered how large a part he could devote to making improvements and how large a part to building a new castle. V—— was of opinion that the old Freiherr could not possibly have spent all his income every year, and that there must certainly be money concealed somewhere, since he had found nothing amongst his papers except one or two bank-notes for insignificant sums, and the ready-money in the iron safe was but very little more than a thousand thalers, or about £150. Who would be so likely to know anything about it as Daniel, who in his obstinate self-willed way was perhaps only waiting to be asked about it? The Baron was now not a little concerned at the thought that Daniel, whom he had so grossly insulted, might let large sums moulder somewhere sooner than discover them to him, not so much, of course, from any motives of self-interest,—for of what use could even the largest sum of money be to him, a childless old man, whose only wish was to end his days in the castle of R—sitten?—as from a desire to take vengeance for the affront put upon him. He gave V—— a circumstantial account of the entire scene with Daniel, and concluded by saying that from several items of information communicated to him he had learned that it was Daniel alone who had contrived to nourish in the old Freiherr's mind such an inexplicable aversion to ever seeing his sons in R—sitten. The Justitiarius declared that this information was perfectly false, since there was not a human creature on the face of the earth who would have been able to guide the Freiherr's thoughts in any way, far less determine them for him; and he undertook finally to draw from Daniel the secret, if he had one, as to the place in which they would be likely to find money concealed. His task proved far easier than he had anticipated, for no sooner did he begin, "But how comes it, Daniel, that your old master has left so little ready-money?" than Daniel replied, with a repulsive smile, "Do you mean the few trifling thalers, Herr Justitiarius, which you found in the little strong box? Oh! the rest is lying in the vault beside our gracious master's sleeping-cabinet. But the best," he went on to say, whilst his smile passed over into an abominable grin, and his eyes flashed with malicious fire, "but the best of all—several thousand gold pieces—lies buried at the bottom of the chasm beneath the ruins." The Justitiarius at once summoned the Freiherr; they proceeded there, and then into the sleeping-cabinet, where Daniel pushed aside the wainscot in one of the corners, and a small lock became visible. Whilst the Freiherr was regarding the polished lock with covetous eyes, and making preparations to try and unlock it with the keys of the great bunch which he dragged with some difficulty out of his pocket, Daniel drew himself up to his full height, and looked down with almost malignant pride upon his master, who had now stooped down in order to see the lock better. Daniel's face was deadly pale, and he said, his voice trembling, "If I am a dog, my lord Freiherr, I have also at least a dog's fidelity." Therewith he held out a bright steel key to his master, who greedily snatched it out of his hand, and with it he easily succeeded in opening the door. They stepped into a small and low-vaulted apartment, in which stood a large iron coffer with the lid open, containing many money-bags, upon which lay a strip of parchment, written in the old Freiherr's familiar handwriting, large and old-fashioned.

One hundred and fifty thousand Imperial thalers in old *Fredericks d'or*, money saved from the revenues of the estate-tail of R—sitten; this sum has been set aside for the building of the castle. Further, the lord of the entail who succeeds me in the possession of this money shall, upon the highest hill situated eastward from the old tower of the castle (which he will find in ruins), erect a high beacon tower for the benefit of mariners, and cause a fire to be kindled on it every night. R—sitten, on Michaelmas Eve of the year 1760.

RODERICK, FREIHERR VON R.

The Freiherr lifted up the bags one after the other and let them fall again into the coffer, delighted at the ringing clink of so much gold coin; then he turned round abruptly to the old house-steward, thanked him for the fidelity he had shown, and assured him that they were only vile tattling calumnies which had induced him to treat him so harshly in the first instance. He should not only remain in the castle, but should also continue to discharge his duties, uncurtailed in any way, as house-steward, and at double the wages he was then having. "I owe you a large compensation; if you will take money, help yourself to one of these bags." As he concluded with these words, the Baron stood before the old man, with his eyes bent upon the ground, and pointed to the coffer; then, approaching it again, he once more ran his eyes over the bags. A burning flush suddenly mounted into the old house-steward's cheeks, and he uttered that awful howling whimper—a noise as of an animal wounded to death, according to the Freiherr's previous description of it to the Justitiarius. The latter shuddered, for the words which the old man murmured between his teeth sounded like, "Blood for gold." Of all this the Freiherr, absorbed in the contemplation of the treasure before him, had heard not the least. Daniel tottered in every limb, as if shaken by an ague fit; approaching the Freiherr with bowed head in a humble attitude, he kissed his hand, and drawing his handkerchief across his eyes under the pretence of wiping away his tears, said in a whining voice, "Alas! my good and gracious master, what am I, a poor childless old man, to do with money? But the doubled wages I accept with gladness, and will continue to do my duty faithfully and zealously."

The Freiherr, who had paid no particular heed to the old man's words, now let the heavy lid of the coffer fall to with a bang, so that the whole room shook and cracked, and then, locking the coffer and carefully withdrawing the key, he said carelessly, "Very well, very well, old man." But after they entered the hall he went on talking to Daniel, "But you said something about a quantity of gold pieces buried underneath the ruins of the tower?" Silently the old man stepped towards the postern, and after some difficulty unlocked it. But so soon as he threw it open the storm drove a thick mass of snow-flakes into the hall; a raven was disturbed and flew in croaking and screaming and dashed with its black wings against the window, but regaining the open postern it disappeared downwards into the chasm. The Freiherr stepped out into the corridor; but one single glance downwards, and he started back trembling. "A fearful sight!—I'm giddy!" he stammered as he sank almost fainting into the Justitiarius' arms. But quickly recovering himself by an effort, he fixed a sharp look upon the old man and asked, "Down there, you say?" Meanwhile the old man had been locking the postern, and was now leaning against it with all his bodily strength, and was gasping and grunting to get the great key out of the rusty lock. This at last accomplished, he turned round to the Baron, and, changing the huge key about backwards and forwards in his hands, replied with a peculiar smile, "Yes, there are thousands and thousands down there—all my dear dead master's beautiful instruments—telescopes, quadrants, globes, dark mirrors, they all lie smashed to atoms underneath the ruins between the stones and the big balk." "But money—coined money," interrupted the Baron, "you spoke of gold pieces, old man?" "I only meant things which had cost several thousand gold pieces," he replied; and not another word could be got out of him.

The Baron appeared highly delighted to have all at once come into possession of all the means requisite for carrying out his favourite plan, namely, that of building a new and magnificent castle. The Justitiarius indeed stated it as his opinion that, according to the will of the deceased, the money could only be applied to the repair and complete finishing of the interior of the old castle, and further, any new erection would hardly succeed in equalling the commanding size and the severe and simple character of the old ancestral castle. The Freiherr, however, persisted in his intention, and maintained that in the disposal of property respecting which nothing was stated in the deeds of the entail the irregular will of the deceased could have no validity. He at the same time led V—— to understand that he should conceive it to be his duty to embellish R—sitten as far as the climate, soil, and environs would permit, for it was his intention to bring home shortly as his dearly loved wife a lady who was in every respect worthy of the greatest sacrifices.

The air of mystery with which the Freiherr spoke of this alliance, which possibly had been already consummated in secret, cut short all further questions from the side of the Justitiarius. Nevertheless he found in it to some extent a redeeming feature, for the Freiherr's eager grasping after riches now appeared to be due not so much to avarice strictly speaking as to the desire to make one dear to him forget the more beautiful country she was relinquishing for his sake. Otherwise he could not acquit the Baron of being avaricious, or at any rate insufferably close-fisted, seeing that, even though rolling in money and even when gloating over the old *Fredericks d'or*, he could not help bursting out with the peevish grumble, "I know the old rascal has concealed from us the greatest part of his wealth, but next spring I will have the ruins of the tower turned over under my own eyes."

The Freiherr had architects come, and discussed with them at great length what would be the most convenient way to proceed with his castle-building. He rejected one drawing after another; in none of them was the style of architecture sufficiently rich and grandiose. He now began to draw plans himself, and, inspirited by this employment, which constantly placed before his eyes a sunny picture of the happiest future, brought himself into such a genial humour that it often bordered on wild exuberance of spirits, and even communicated itself to all about him. His generosity and profuse hospitality belied all imputations of avarice at any rate. Daniel also seemed to have now forgotten the insult that had been put upon him. Towards the Freiherr, although often followed by him with mistrustful eyes on account of the treasure buried in the chasm, his bearing was both quiet and humble. But what struck everybody as extraordinary was that the old man appeared to grow younger from day to day. Possibly this might be, because he had begun to forget his grief for his old master, which had stricken him sore, and possibly also because he had not now, as he once had, to spend the cold nights in the tower without sleep, and got better food and good wine such as he liked; but whatever the cause might be, the old greybeard seemed to be growing into a vigorous man with red cheeks and well-nourished body, who could walk firmly and laugh loudly whenever he heard a jest to laugh at.

The pleasant tenor of life at R—sitten was disturbed by the arrival of a man whom one would have judged to be quite in his element there. This was Wolfgang's younger brother Hubert, at the sight of whom Wolfgang had screamed out, with his face as pale as a corpse's, "Unhappy wretch, what do you want here?" Hubert threw himself into his brother's arms, but Wolfgang took him and led him away up to a retired room, where he locked himself in with him. They remained closeted several hours, at the end of which time Hubert came down, greatly agitated, and called for his horses. The Justitiarius intercepted him; Hubert tried to pass him; but V——, inspired by the hope that he might perhaps stifle in the bud what might else end in a bitter life-long quarrel between the brothers, besought him to stay, at least a few hours, and at the same moment the Freiherr came down calling, "Stay here, Hubert! you will think better of it." Hubert's countenance cleared up; he assumed an air of composure, and quickly pulling off his costly fur coat, and throwing it to a servant behind him, he grasped V——'s hand and went with him into the room, saying with a scornful smile, "So the lord of the entail will tolerate my presence here, it seems." V—— thought that the unfortunate misunderstanding would assuredly be smoothed away now, for it was only separation and existence apart from each other that would, he conceived, be able to foster it. Hubert took up the steel tongs which stood near the fire-grate, and as he proceeded to break up a knotty piece of wood that would only sweal, not burn, and to rake the fire together better, he said to V——, "You see what a good-natured fellow I am, Herr Justitiarius, and that I am skilful in all domestic matters. But Wolfgang is full of the most extraordinary prejudices, and—a bit of a miser." V—— did not deem it advisable to attempt to fathom further the relations between the brothers, especially as Wolfgang's face and conduct and voice plainly showed that he was shaken to the very depths of his nature by diverse violent passions.

Late in the evening V—— had occasion to go up to the Freiherr's room in order to learn his decision about some matter or other connected with the estate-tail. He found him pacing up and down the room with long strides, his arms crossed on his back, and much perturbation in his manner. On perceiving the Justitiarius he stood still, and then, taking him by both hands and looking him gloomily in the face, he said in a broken voice, "My brother is come. I know what you are going to say," he proceeded almost before V—— had opened his mouth to put a question. "Unfortunately you know nothing. You don't know that my unfortunate brother—yes, I will not call him anything worse than unfortunate—that, like a spirit of evil, he crosses my path everywhere, ruining my peace of mind. It is not his fault that I have not been made unspeakably miserable; he did his best to make me so, but Heaven willed it otherwise. Ever since he has known of the conversion of the property into an entail, he has persecuted me with deadly hatred. He envies me this property, which in his hands would only be scattered like chaff. He is the wildest spendthrift I ever heard of. His load of debt exceeds by a long way the half of the unentailed property in Courland that fell to him, and now, pursued by his creditors, who fail not to worry him for payment, he hurries here to me to beg for money." "And you, his brother, refuse to give him any?" V—— was about to interrupt him; but the Freiherr, letting V——'s hands fall, and taking a long step backwards, went on in a loud and vehement tone. "Stop! yes; I refuse. I neither can nor will give away a single thaler of the revenues of the entail. But listen, and I will tell you what was the proposal which I made the insane fellow a few hours ago, and made in vain, and then pass judgment upon the feelings of duty by which I am actuated. Our unentailed possessions in Courland are, as you are aware, considerable; the half that falls to me I am willing to renounce, but in favour of his family. For Hubert has married, in Courland, a beautiful lady, but poor. She and the children she has borne him are starving. The estates should be put under trust; sufficient should be set aside out of the revenues to support him, and his creditors be paid by arrangement. But what does he care for a quiet life—a life free of anxiety?—what does he care for wife and child? Money, ready-money, and large quantities, is what he will have, that he may squander it in infamous folly. Some demon has made him acquainted with the secret of the hundred and fifty thousand thalers, half of which he in his mad way demands, maintaining that this money is movable property and quite apart from the entailed portion. This, however, I must and will refuse him, but the feeling haunts me that he is plotting my destruction in his heart."

No matter how great the efforts which V—— made to persuade the Freiherr out of this suspicion against his brother, in which, of course, not being initiated into the more circumstantial details of the disagreement, he could only appeal to broad and somewhat superficial moral principles, he yet could not boast of the smallest success. The Freiherr commissioned him to treat with his hostile and avaricious brother Hubert. V—— proceeded to do so with all the circumspection he was master of, and was not a little gratified when Hubert at length declared, "Be it so then; I will accept my brother's proposals, but upon condition that he will now, since I am on the point of losing both my honour and my good name for ever through the severity of my creditors, make me an advance of a thousand *Fredericks d'or* in hard cash, and further grant that in time to come I may take up my residence, at least for a short time occasionally, in our beautiful R—sitten, along with my good brother." "Never, never!" exclaimed the Freiherr violently, when V—— laid his brother's amended counter-proposals before him. "I will never consent that Hubert stay in my house even a single minute after I have brought home my wife. Go, my good friend, tell this mar-peace that he shall have two thousand *Fredericks d'or*, not as an advance, but as a gift—only, bid him go, bid him go." V—— now learned at one and the same time that the ground of the quarrel between the two brothers must be sought for in this marriage. Hubert listened to the Justitiarius proudly and calmly, and when he finished speaking replied in a hoarse and hollow tone, "I will think it over; but for the present I shall stay a few days in the castle." V—— exerted himself to prove to the discontented Hubert that the Freiherr, by making over his share of their unentailed property, was really doing all he possibly could do to indemnify him, and that on the whole he had no cause for complaint against his brother, although at the same time he admitted that all institutions of the nature of primogeniture, which vested such preponderant advantages in the eldest-born to the prejudice of the remaining children, were in many respects hateful. Hubert tore his waistcoat open from top to bottom like a man whose breast was cramped and he wanted to relieve it by fresh air. Thrusting one hand into his open shirt-frill and planting the other in his side, he spun round on one foot in a quick pirouette and cried in a sharp voice, "Pshaw! What is hateful is born of hatred." Then bursting out into a shrill fit of laughter, he said, "What condescension my lord of the entail shows in being thus willing to throw his gold pieces to the poor beggar!" V—— saw plainly that all idea of a complete reconciliation between the brothers was quite out of the question.

To the Freiherr's annoyance, Hubert established himself in the rooms that had been appointed for him in one of the side wings of the castle as if with the view to a very long stay. He was observed to hold frequent and long conversations with the house-steward; nay, the latter was sometimes even seen to accompany him when he went out wolf-hunting. Otherwise he was very little seen, and studiously avoided meeting his brother alone, at which the latter was very glad. V—— felt how strained and unpleasant this state of things was, and was obliged to confess to himself that the peculiar uneasiness which marked all that Hubert both said and did was such as to destroy intentionally and effectually all the pleasure of the place. He now perfectly understood why the Freiherr had manifested so much alarm on seeing his brother.

One day as V—— was sitting by himself in the justice-room amongst his law-papers, Hubert came in with a grave and more composed manner than usual, and said in a voice that bordered upon melancholy, "I will accept my brother's last proposals. If you will contrive that I have the two thousand *Fredericks d'or* today, I will leave the castle this very night—on horseback—alone." "With the money?" asked V——. "You are right," replied Hubert; "I know what you would say—the weight! Give it me in bills on Isaac Lazarus of K——. For to K—— I am going this very night. Something is driving me away from this place. The old fellow has bewitched it with evil spirits." "Do you mean your father, Herr Baron?" asked V—— sternly. Hubert's lips trembled; he had to cling to the chair to keep from falling; but then suddenly recovering himself, he cried, "To-day then, please, Herr Justitiarius," and staggered to the door, not, however, without some exertion. "He now sees that no deceptions are any longer of avail, that he can do nothing against my firm will," said the Freiherr whilst drawing up the bills on Isaac Lazarus in K——. A burden was lifted off his heart by the departure of his inimical brother; and for a long time he had not been in such cheerful spirits as he was at supper. Hubert had sent his excuses; and there was not one who regretted his absence.

The room which V—— occupied was somewhat retired, and its windows looked upon the castle-yard. In the night he was suddenly startled up out of his sleep, and was under the impression that he had been awakened by a distant and pitiable moan. But listen as he would, all remained still as the grave, and so he was obliged to conclude that the sound which had fallen upon his ears was the delusion of a dream. But at the same time he was seized with such a peculiar feeling of breathless anxiety and terror that he could not stay in bed. He got up and approached the window. It was not long, however, before the castle door was opened, and a figure with a blazing torch came out of the castle and went across the court-yard. V—— recognised the figure as that of old Daniel, and saw him open the stable-door and go in, and soon afterwards bring out a saddle horse. Now a second figure came into view out of the darkness, well wrapped in furs, and with a fox-skin cap on his head. V—— perceived that it was Hubert; but after he had spoken excitedly with Daniel for some minutes, he returned into the castle. Daniel led back the horse into the stable and locked the door, and also that of the castle, after he had returned across the court-yard in the same way in which he crossed it before. It was evident Hubert had intended to go away on horseback, but had suddenly changed his mind; and no less evident was it that there was a dangerous understanding of some sort between Hubert and the old house-steward. V—— looked forward to the morning with burning impatience; he would acquaint the Freiherr with the occurrences of the night. Really it was now time to take precautionary measures against the attacks of Hubert's malice, which V—— was now convinced, had been betrayed in his agitated behaviour of the day before.

Next morning, at the hour when the Freiherr was in the habit of rising, V—— heard people running backwards and forwards, doors opened and slammed to, and a tumultuous confusion of voices talking and shouting. On going out of his room he met servants everywhere, who, without heeding him, ran past him with ghastly pale faces, upstairs, downstairs, in and out the rooms. At length he ascertained that the Freiherr was missing, and that they had been looking for him for hours in vain. As he had gone to bed in the presence of his personal attendant, he must have afterwards got up and gone away somewhere in his dressing-gown and slippers, taking the large candlestick with him, for these articles were also missed. V——, his mind agitated with dark forebodings, ran up to the ill-fated hall, the cabinet adjoining which Wolfgang had chosen, like his father, for his own bedroom. The postern leading to the tower stood wide open, with a cry of horror V—— shouted, "There—he lies dashed to pieces at the bottom of the ravine." And it was so. There had been a fall of snow, so that all they could distinctly make out from above was the rigid arm of the unfortunate man protruding from between the stones. Many hours passed before the workmen succeeded, at great risk of life, in descending by means of ladders bound together, and drawing up the corpse by the aid of ropes. In the last agonies of death the Baron had kept a tight hold upon the silver candlestick; the hand in which it was clenched was the only uninjured part of his whole body, which had been shattered in the most hideous way by rebounding on the sharp stones.

Just as the corpse was drawn up and carried into the hall, and laid upon the very same spot on the large table where a few weeks before old Roderick had lain dead, Hubert burst in, his face distorted by the frenzy of despair. Quite overpowered by the fearful sight he wailed, "Brother! O my poor brother! No; this I never prayed for from the demons who had entered into me." This suspicious self-exculpation made V—— tremble; he felt impelled to proceed against Hubert as the murderer of his brother. Hubert, however, had fallen on the floor senseless; they carried him to bed; but on taking strong restoratives he soon recovered. Then he appeared in V——'s room, pale and sorrow-stricken, and with his eyes half clouded with grief; and unable to stand owing to his weakness, he slowly sank down into an easy-chair, saying, "I have wished for my brother's death, because my father had made over to him the best part of the property through the foolish conversion of it into an entail. He has now found a fearful death. I am now lord of the estate-tail, but my heart is rent with pain—I can—I shall never be happy. I confirm you in your office; you shall be invested with the most extensive powers in respect to the management of the estate, upon which I cannot bear to live." Hubert left the room, and in two or three hours was on his way to K——.

It appeared that the unfortunate Wolfgang had got up in the night, probably with the intention of going into the other cabinet where there was a library. In the stupor of sleep he had mistaken the door, and had opened the postern, taken a step out, and plunged headlong down. But after all had been said, there was nevertheless a good deal that was strained and unlikely in this explanation. If the Baron was unable to sleep and wanted to get a book out of the library, this of itself excluded all idea of sleep-stupor; but this condition alone could account for any mistaking of the postern for the door of the cabinet. Then again, the former was fast locked, and required a good deal of exertion to unlock it. These improbabilities V—— accordingly put before the domestics, who had gathered round him, and at length the Freiherr's body-servant, Francis by name, said, "Nay, nay, my good Herr Justitiarius; it couldn't have happened in that way." "Well, how then?" asked V—— abruptly and sharply. But Francis, a faithful, honest fellow, who would have followed his master into his grave, was unwilling to speak out before the rest; he stipulated that what he had to say about the event should be confided to the Justitiarius alone in private. V—— now learned that the Freiherr used often to talk to Francis about the vast treasure which he believed lay buried beneath the ruins of the tower, and also that frequently at night, as if goaded by some malicious fiend, he would open the postern, the key of which Daniel had been obliged to give him, and would gaze with longing eyes down into the chasm where the supposed riches lay. There was now no doubt about it; on that ill-omened night the Freiherr, after his servant had left him, must have taken one of his usual walks to the postern, where he had been most likely suddenly seized with dizziness, and had fallen over. Daniel, who also seemed much upset by the Freiherr's terrible end, thought it would be a good thing to have the dangerous postern walled up; and this was at once done.

Freiherr Hubert von R——, who had then succeeded to the entail, went back to Courland without once showing himself at R—sitten again. V—— was invested with full powers for the absolute management of the property. The building of the new castle was not proceeded with; but on the other hand the old structure was put in as good a state of repair as possible. Several years passed before Hubert came again to R—sitten, late in the autumn, but after he had remained shut up in his room with V—— for several days, he went back to Courland. Passing on his way through K——, he deposited his will with the government authorities there.

The Freiherr, whose character appeared to have undergone a complete revolution, spoke more than once during his stay at R—sitten of presentiments of his approaching death. And these apprehensions were really not unfounded, for he died in the very next year. His son, named, like the deceased Baron, Hubert, soon came over from Courland to take possession of the rich inheritance; and was followed by his mother and his sister. The youth seemed to unite in his own person all the bad qualities of his ancestors: he proved himself to be proud, arrogant, impetuous, avaricious, in the very first moments after his arrival at R—sitten. He wanted to have several things which did not suit his notions of what was right and proper altered there and then: the cook he kicked out of doors; and he attempted to thrash the coachman, in which, however, he did not succeed, for the big brawny fellow had the impudence not to submit to it. In fact, he was on the high road to assuming the *rôle* of a harsh and severe lord of the entail, when V—— interposed in his firm earnest manner, declaring most explicitly that not a single chair should be moved, that not even a cat should leave the house if she liked to stay in it, until after the will had been opened. "You have the presumption to tell me, the lord of the entail," began the Baron. V——, however, cut short the young man, who was foaming with rage, and said, whilst he measured him with a keen searching glance, "Don't be in too great a hurry, Herr Baron. At all events, you have no right to exercise authority here until after the opening of your father's will. It is I—I alone—who am now master here; and I shall know how to meet violence with violent measures. Please to recollect that by virtue of my powers as executor of your father's will, as well as by virtue of the arrangements which have been made by the court, I am empowered to forbid your remaining in R—sitten if I think fit to do so; and so, if you wish to spare me this disagreeable step, I would advise you to go away quietly to K——." The lawyer's earnestness, and the resolute tone in which he spoke, lent the proper emphasis to his words. Hence the young Baron, who was charging with far two sharp-pointed horns, felt the weakness of his weapons against the firm bulwark, and found it convenient to cover the shame of his retreat with a burst of scornful laughter.

Three months passed and the day was come on which, in accordance with the expressed wish of the deceased, his will was to be opened at K——, where it had been deposited. In the chambers there was, besides the officers of the court, the Baron, and V——, a young man of noble appearance, whom V—— had brought with him, and who was taken to be V——'s clerk, since he had a parchment deed sticking out from the breast of his buttoned-up coat. Him the Baron treated as he did nearly all the rest, with scornful contempt; and he demanded with noisy impetuosity that they should make haste and get done with all their tiresome needless ceremonies as quickly as possible and without over many words and scribblings. He couldn't for the life of him make out why any will should be wanted at all with respect to the inheritance, and especially in the case of entailed property; and no matter what provisions were made in the will, it would depend entirely upon his decision as to whether they should be observed or not. After casting a hasty and surly glance at the handwriting and the seal, the Baron acknowledged them to be those of his dead father. Upon the clerk of the court preparing to read the will aloud, the young Baron, throwing his right arm carelessly over the back of his chair and leaning his left on the table, whilst he drummed with his fingers on its green cover, sat staring with an air of indifference out of the window. After a short preamble the deceased Freiherr Hubert von R—— declared that he had never possessed the estate-tail as its lawful owner, but that he had only managed it in the name of the deceased Freiherr Wolfgang von R——'s only son, called Roderick after his grandfather; and he it was to whom, according to the rights of family priority, the estate had fallen on his father's death. Amongst Hubert's papers would be found an exact account of all revenues and expenditure, as well as of existing movable property, &c. The will went on to relate that Wolfgang von R—— had, during his travels, made the acquaintance of Mdlle. Julia de St. Val in Geneva, and had fallen so deeply in love with her that he resolved never to leave her side again. She was very poor; and her family, although noble and of good repute, did not, however, rank amongst the most illustrious, for which reason Wolfgang dared not expect to receive the consent of old Roderick to a union with her, for the old Freiherr's aim and ambition was to promote by all possible means the establishment of a powerful family. Nevertheless he ventured to write from Paris to his father, acquainting him with the fact that his affections were engaged. But what he had foreseen was actually realised; the old Baron declared categorically that he had himself chosen the future mistress of the entail, and therefore there could never be any mention made of any other. Wolfgang, instead of crossing the Channel into England, as he was to have done, returned into Geneva under the assumed name of Born, and married Julia, who after the lapse of a year bore him a son, and this son became on Wolfgang's death the real lord of the entail. In explanation of the facts why Hubert, though acquainted with all this, had kept silent so long and had represented himself as lord of the entail, various reasons were assigned, based upon agreements formerly made with Wolfgang, but they seemed for the most part insufficient and devoid of real foundation.

The Baron sat staring at the clerk of the court as if thunderstruck, whilst the latter went on proclaiming all this bad news in a provokingly monotonous and jarring tone. When he finished, V—— rose, and taking the young man whom he had brought with him by the hand, said, as he bowed to the assembled company, "Here I have the honour to present to you, gentlemen, Freiherr Roderick von R——, lord of the entail of R—sitten." Baron Hubert looked at the youth, who had, as it were, fallen from the clouds to deprive him of the rich inheritance together with half the unentailed Courland estates, with suppressed fury in his gleaming eyes; then, threatening him with his doubled fist, he ran out of the court without uttering a word. Baron Roderick, on being challenged by the court-officers, produced the documents by which he was to establish his identity as the person whom he represented himself to be. He handed in an attested extract from the register of the church where his father was married, which certified that on such and such a day Wolfgang Born, merchant, born in K——, had been united in marriage with the blessing of the Church to Mdlle. Julia de St. Val, in the presence of certain witnesses, who were named. Further, he produced his own baptismal certificate (he had been baptized in Geneva as the son of the merchant Born and his wife Julia, *née* De St. Val, begotten in lawful wedlock), and various letters from his father to his mother, who was long since dead, but they none of them had any other signature than W.

V—— looked through all these papers with a cloud upon his face; and as he put them together again, he said, somewhat troubled, "Ah well! God will help us!"

The very next morning Freiherr Hubert von R—— presented, through an advocate whose services he had succeeded in enlisting in his cause, a statement of protest to the government authorities in K——, actually calling upon them to effectuate the immediate surrender to him of the entail of R—sitten. It was incontestable, maintained the advocate, that the deceased Freiherr Hubert Von R—— had not had the power to dispose of entailed property either by testament or in any other way. The testament in question, therefore, was nothing more than an evidential statement, written down and deposited with the court, to the effect that Freiherr Wolfgang von R—— had bequeathed the estate-tail to a son who was at that time still living; and accordingly it had as evidence no greater weight than that of any other witness, and so could not by any possibility legitimately establish the claims of the person who had announced himself to be Freiherr Roderick von R——. Hence it was rather the duty of this new claimant to prove by action at law his alleged rights of inheritance, which were hereby expressly disputed and denied, and so also to take proper steps to maintain his claim to the estate-tail, which now, according to the laws of succession, fell to Baron Hubert von R——. By the father's death the property came at once immediately into the hands of the son. There was no need for any formal declaration to be made of his entering into possession of the inheritance, since the succession could not be alienated; at any rate, the present owner of the estate was not going to be disturbed in his possession by claims which were perfectly groundless. Whatever reasons the deceased might have had for bringing forward another heir of entail were quite irrelevant. And it might be remarked that he had himself had an intrigue in Switzerland, as could be proved if necessary from the papers he had left behind him; and it was quite possible that the person whom he alleged to be his brother's son was his own son, the fruit of an unlawful love, for whom in a momentary fit of remorse he had wished to secure the entail.

However great was the balance of probability in favour of the truth of the circumstances as stated in the will, and however revolted the judges were, particularly by the last clauses of the protest, in which the son felt no compunction at accusing his dead father of a crime, yet the views of the case there stated were after all the right ones; and it was only due to V——'s restless exertions, and his explicit and solemn assurance that the proofs which were necessary to establish legitimately the identity of Freiherr Roderick von R—— should be produced in a very short time, that the surrender of the estate to the young Baron was deferred, and the contrivance of the administration of it in trust agreed to, until after the case should be settled.

V—— was only too well aware how difficult it would be for him to keep his promise. He had turned over all old Roderick's papers without finding the slightest trace of a letter or any kind of a statement bearing upon Wolfgang's relation to Mdlle. de St. Val. He was sitting wrapt in thought in old Roderick's sleeping-cabinet, every hole and corner of which he had searched, and was working at a long statement of the case that he intended despatching to a certain notary in Geneva, who had been recommended to him as a shrewd and energetic man, to request him to procure and forward certain documents which would establish the young Freiherr's cause on firm ground. It was midnight; the full moon shone in through the windows of the adjoining hall, the door of which stood open. Then V—— fancied he heard a noise as of some one coming slowly and heavily up the stairs, and also at the same time a jingling and rattling of keys. His attention was arrested; he rose to his feet and went into the hall, where he plainly made out that there was some one crossing the ante-room and approaching the door of the hall where he was. Soon afterwards the door was opened and a man came slowly in, dressed in night-clothes, his face ghastly pale and distorted; in the one hand he bore a candle-stick with the candles burning, and in the other a huge bunch of keys. V—— at once recognised the house-steward, and was on the point of addressing him and inquiring what he wanted so late at night, when he was arrested by an icy shiver; there was something so unearthly and ghost-like in the old man's manner and bearing as well as in his set, pallid face. He perceived that he was in presence of a somnambulist. Crossing the hall obliquely with measured strides, the old man went straight to the walled-up postern that had formerly led to the tower. He came to a halt immediately in front of it, and uttered a wailing sound that seemed to come from the bottom of his heart, and was so awful and so loud that the whole apartment rang again, making V—— tremble with dread. Then, setting the candlestick down on the floor and hanging the keys on his belt, Daniel began to scratch at the wall with both hands, so that the blood soon burst out from beneath his finger-nails, and all the while he was moaning and groaning as if tortured by nameless agony. After placing his ear against the wall in a listening attitude, he waved his hand as if hushing some one, stooped down and picked up the candlestick, and finally stole back to the door with soft measured footsteps. V—— took his own candle in his hand and cautiously followed him. They both went downstairs; the old man unlocked the great main door of the castle, V—— slipped cleverly through. Then they went to the stable, where old Daniel, to V——'s perfect astonishment, placed his candlestick so skilfully that the entire interior of the building was sufficiently lighted without the least danger. Having fetched a saddle and bridle, he put them on one of the horses which he had loosed from the manger, carefully tightening the girth and taking up the stirrup-straps. Pulling the tuft of hair on the horse's forehead outside the front strap, he took him by the bridle and led him out of the stable, clicking with his tongue and patting his neck with one hand. On getting outside in the courtyard he stood several seconds in the attitude of one receiving commands, which he promised by sundry nods to carry out. Then he led the horse back into the stable, unsaddled him, and tied him to the manger. This done, he took his candlestick, locked the stable, and returned to the castle, finally disappearing in his own room, the door of which he carefully bolted. V—— was deeply agitated by this scene; the presentiment of some fearful deed rose up before him like a black and fiendish spectre, and refused to leave him. Being so keenly alive as he was to the precarious position of his *protégé*, he felt that it would at least be his duty to turn what he had seen to his account.

Next day, just as it was beginning to be dusk, Daniel came into the Justitiarius's room to receive some instructions relating to his department of the household. V—— took him by the arms, and forcing him into a chair, in a confidential way began, "See you here, my old friend Daniel, I have long been wishing to ask you what you think of all this confused mess into which Hubert's peculiar will has tumbled us. Do you really think that the young man is Wolfgang's son, begotten in lawful marriage?" The old man, leaning over the arm of his chair, and avoiding V——'s eyes, for V—— was watching him most intently, replied doggedly, "Bah! Maybe he is; maybe he is not. What does it matter to me? It's all the same to me who's master here now." "But I believe," went on V——, moving nearer to the old man and placing his hand on his shoulder, "but I believed you possessed the old Freiherr's full confidence, and in that case he assuredly would not conceal from you the real state of affairs with regard to his sons. He told you, I dare say, about the marriage which Wolfgang had made against his will, did he not?" "I don't remember to have ever heard him say anything of that sort," replied the old man, yawning with the most ill-mannered loudness. "You are sleepy, old man," said V——; "perhaps you have had a restless night?"

"Not that I am aware," he rejoined coldly; "but I must go and order supper." Whereupon he rose heavily from his chair and rubbed his bent back, yawning again, and that still more loudly than before. "Stay a little while, old man," cried V——, taking hold of his hand and endeavouring to force him to resume his seat; but Daniel preferred to stand in front of the study-table; propping himself upon it with both hands, and leaning across towards V——, he asked sullenly, "Well, what do you want? What have I to do with the will? What do I care about the quarrel over the estate?" "Well, well," interposed V——, "we'll say no more about that now. Let us turn to some other topic, Daniel. You are out of humour and yawning, and all that is a sign of great weariness, and I am almost inclined to believe that it really was *you* last night, who"—— "Well, what did I do last night?" asked the old man without changing his position. V—— went on, "Last night, when I was sitting up above in your old master's sleeping-cabinet next the great hall, you came in at the door, your face pale and rigid; and you went across to the bricked-up postern and scratched at the wall with both your hands, groaning as if in very great pain. Do you walk in your sleep, Daniel?" The old man dropped back into the chair which V—— quickly managed to place for him; but not a sound escaped his lips. His face could not be seen, owing to the gathering dusk of the evening; V—— only noticed that he took his breath short and that his teeth were rattling together. "Yes," continued V—— after a short pause, "there is one thing that is very strange about sleep-walkers. On the day after they have been in this peculiar state in which they have acted as if they were perfectly wide awake, they don't remember the least thing, that they did." Daniel did not move. "I have come across something like what your condition was yesterday once before in the course of my experience," proceeded V——. "I had a friend who regularly began to wander about at night as you do whenever it was full moon,—nay, he often sat down and wrote letters. But what was most extraordinary was that if I began to whisper softly in his ear I could soon manage to make him speak; and he would answer correctly all the questions I put to him; and even things that he would most jealously have concealed when awake now fell from his lips unbidden, as though he were unable to offer any resistance to the power that was exerting its influence over him. Deuce take it! I really believe that, if a man who's given to walking in his sleep had ever committed any crime, and hoarded it up as a secret ever so long, it could be extracted from him by questioning when he was in this peculiar state. Happy are they who have a clean conscience like you and me, Daniel! We may walk as much as we like in our sleep; there's no fear of anybody extorting the confession of a crime from us. But come now, Daniel! when you scratch so hideously at the bricked-up postern, you want, I dare say, to go up the astronomical tower, don't you? I suppose you want to go and experiment like old Roderick—eh? Well, next time you come, I shall ask you what you want to do." Whilst V—— was speaking, the old man was shaken with continually increasing agitation; but now his whole frame seemed to heave and rock convulsively past all hope of cure, and in a shrill voice he began to utter a string of unmeaning gibberish. V—— rang for the servants. They brought lights; but as the old man's fit did not abate, they lifted him up as though he had been a mere automaton, not possessed of the power of voluntary movement, and carried him to bed. After continuing in this frightful state for about an hour, he fell into a profound sleep resembling a dead faint When he awoke he asked for wine; and, after he had got what he wanted, he sent away the man who was going to sit with him, and locked himself in his room as usual.

V—— had indeed really resolved to make the attempt he spoke of to Daniel, although at the same time he could not forget two facts. In the first place, Daniel, having now been made aware of his propensity to walk in his sleep, would probably adopt every measure of precaution to avoid him; and on the other hand, confessions made whilst in this condition would not be exactly fitted to serve as a basis for further proceedings. In spite of this, however, he repaired to the hall on the approach of midnight, hoping that Daniel, as frequently happens to those afflicted in this way, would be constrained to act involuntarily. About midnight there arose a great noise in the courtyard. V—— plainly heard a window broken in; then he went downstairs, and as he traversed the passages he was met by rolling clouds of suffocating smoke, which, he soon perceived were pouring out of the open door of the house-steward's room. The steward himself was just being carried out, to all appearance dead, in order to be taken and put to bed in another room. The servants related that about midnight one of the under-grooms had been awakened by a strange hollow knocking; he thought something had befallen the old man, and was preparing to get up and go and see if he could help him, when the night watchman in the court shouted, "Fire! Fire! The Herr House-Steward's room is all of a bright blaze!" At this outcry several servants at once appeared on the scene; but all their efforts to burst open the room door were unavailing. Whereupon they hurried out into the court, but the resolute watchman had already broken in the window, for the room was low and on the basement story, had torn down the burning curtains, and by pouring a few buckets of water on them had at once extinguished the fire. The house-steward they found lying on the floor in the middle of the room in a swoon. In his hand he still held the candlestick tightly clenched, the burning candles of which had caught the curtains, and so occasioned the fire. Some of the blazing rags had fallen upon the old man, burning his eyebrows and a large portion of the hair of his head. If the watchman had not seen the fire the old man must have been helplessly burned to death. The servants, moreover, to their no little astonishment found the room door secured on the inside by two quite new bolts, which had been fastened on since the previous evening, for they had not been there then. V—— perceived that the old man had wished to make it impossible for him to get out of his room; for the blind impulse which urged him to wander in his sleep he could not resist. The old man became seriously ill; he did not speak; he took but little nourishment; and lay staring before him with the reflection of death in his set eyes, just as if he were clasped in the vice-like grip of some hideous thought. V—— believed he would never rise from his bed again.

V—— had done all that could be done for his client; and he could now only await the result in patience; and so he resolved to return to K——. His departure was fixed for the following morning. As he was packing his papers together late at night, he happened to lay his hand upon a little sealed packet which Freiherr Hubert von R—— had given him, bearing the inscription, "To be read after my will has been opened," and which by some unaccountable means had hitherto escaped his notice. He was on the point of breaking the seal when the door opened and Daniel came in with still, ghostlike step. Placing upon the table a black portfolio which he carried under his arm, he sank upon his knees with a deep groan, and grasping V——'s hands with a convulsive clutch he said, in a voice so hollow and hoarse that it seemed to come from the bottom of a grave, "I should not like to die on the scaffold! There is One above who judges!" Then, rising with some trouble and with many painful gasps, he left the room as he had come.

V—— spent the whole of the night in reading what the black portfolio and Hubert's packet contained. Both agreed in all circumstantial particulars, and suggested naturally what further steps were to be taken. On arriving at K——, V—— immediately repaired to Freiherr Hubert von R——, who received him with ill-mannered pride. But the remarkable result of the interview, which began at noon and lasted on without interruption until late at night, was that the next day the Freiherr made a declaration before the court to the effect that he acknowledged the claimant to be, agreeably to his father's will, the son of Wolfgang von R——, eldest son of Freiherr Roderick von R——, and begotten in lawful wedlock with Mdlle. Julia de St. Val, and furthermore acknowledged him as rightful and legitimate heir to the entail. On leaving the court he found his carriage, with post-horses, standing before the door; he stepped in and was driven off at a rapid rate, leaving his mother and his sister behind him. They would perhaps never see him again, he wrote, along with other perplexing statements. Roderick's astonishment at this unexpected turn which the case had taken was very great; he pressed V—— to explain to him how this wonder had been brought about, what mysterious power was at work in the matter. V——, however, evaded his questions by giving him hopes of telling him all at some future time, and when he should have come into possession of the estate. For the surrender of the entail to him could not be effected immediately, since the court, not content with Hubert's declaration, required that Roderick should also first prove his own identity to their satisfaction. V—— proposed to the Baron that he should go and live at R—sitten, adding that Hubert's mother and sister, momentarily embarrassed by his sudden departure, would prefer to go and live quietly on the ancestral property rather than stay in the dear and noisy town. The glad delight with which Roderick welcomed the prospect of dwelling, at least for a time, under the same roof with the Baroness and her daughter, betrayed the deep impression which the lovely and graceful Seraphina had made upon him. In fact, the Freiherr made such good use of his time in R—sitten that, at the end of a few weeks, he had won Seraphina's love as well as her mother's cordial approval of her marriage with him. All this was for V—— rather too quick work, since Roderick's claims to be lord of the entail still continued to be rather doubtful. The life of idyllic happiness at the castle was interrupted by letters from Courland. Hubert had not shown himself at all at the estates, but had travelled direct to St Petersburg, where he had taken military service and was now in the field against the Persians, with whom Russia happened to be just then waging war. This obliged the Baroness and her daughter to set off immediately for their Courland estates, where everything was in confusion and disorder. Roderick, who regarded himself in the light of an accepted son-in-law, insisted upon accompanying his beloved; and hence, since V—— likewise returned to K——, the castle was left in its previous loneliness. The house-steward's malignant complaint grew worse and worse, so that he gave up all hopes of ever getting about again; and his office was conferred upon an old *chasseur*, Francis by name, Wolfgang's faithful servant.

At last, after long waiting, V—— received from Switzerland information of the most favourable character. The priest who had married Roderick was long since dead; but there was found in the church register a memorandum in his hand writing, to the effect that the man of the name of Born, whom he had joined in the bonds of wedlock with Mdlle. Julia de St. Val, had established completely to his satisfaction his identity as Freiherr Wolfgang von R——, eldest son of Freiherr Roderick von R—— of R—sitten. Besides this, two witnesses of the marriage had been discovered, a merchant of Geneva and an old French captain, who had moved to Lyons; to them also Wolfgang had in confidence stated his real name; and their affidavits confirmed the priest's notice in the church register. With these memoranda in his hands, drawn up with proper legal formalities, V—— now succeeded in securing his client in the complete possession of his rights; and as there was now no longer any hindrance to the surrender to him of the entail, it was to be put into his hands in the ensuing autumn. Hubert had fallen in his very first engagement, thus sharing the fate of his younger brother, who had likewise been slain in battle a year before his father's death. Thus the Courland estates fell to Baroness Seraphina von R——, and made a handsome dowry for her to take to the too happy Roderick.

November had already come in when the Baroness, along with Roderick and his betrothed, arrived at R—sitten. The formal surrender of the estate-tail to the young Baron took place, and then his marriage with Seraphina was solemnised. Many weeks passed amid a continual whirl of pleasure; but at length the wearied guests began gradually to depart from the castle, to V——'s great satisfaction, for he had made up his mind not to take his leave of R—sitten until he had initiated the young lord of the entail in all the relations and duties connected with his new position down to the minutest particulars. Roderick's uncle had kept an account of all revenues and disbursements with the most detailed accuracy; hence, since Hubert had only retained a small sum annually for his own support, the surplus revenues had all gone to swell the capital left by the old Freiherr, till the total now amounted to a considerable sum. Hubert had only employed the income of the entail for his own purposes during the first three years, but to cover this he had given a mortgage on the security of his share of the Courland property.

From the time when old Daniel had revealed himself to V—— as a somnambulist, V—— had chosen old Roderick's bed-room for his own sitting-room, in order that he might the more securely gather from the old man what he afterwards voluntarily disclosed. Hence it was in this room and in the adjoining great hall that the Freiherr transacted business with V——. Once they were both sitting at the great table by the bright blazing fire; V—— had his pen in his hand, and was noting down various totals and calculating the riches of the lord of the entail, whilst the latter, leaning his head on his hand, was blinking at the open account-books and formidable-looking documents. Neither of them heard the hollow roar of the sea, nor the anxious cries of the sea-gulls as they dashed against the windowpanes, flapping their wings and flying backwards and forwards, announcing the oncoming storm. Neither of them heeded the storm, which arose about midnight, and was now roaring and raging with wild fury round the castle walls, so that all the sounds of ill omen in the fire-grates and narrow passages awoke, and began to whistle and shriek in a weird, unearthly way. At length, after a terrific blast, which made the whole castle shake, the hall was completely lit up by the murky glare of the full moon, and V—— exclaimed, "Awful weather!" The Freiherr, quite absorbed in the consideration of the wealth which had fallen to him, replied indifferently, as he turned over a page of the receipt-book with a satisfied smile, "It is indeed; very stormy!" But, as if clutched by the icy hand of Dread, he started to his feet as the door of the hall flew open and a pale spectral figure became visible, striding in with the stamp of death upon its face. It was Daniel, who, lying helpless under the power of disease, was deemed in the opinion of V—— as of everybody else incapable of the ability to move a single limb; but, again coming under the influence of his propensity to wander in his sleep at full moon, he had, it appeared, been unable to resist it. The Freiherr stared at the old man without uttering a sound; and when Daniel began to scratch at the wall, and moan as though in the painful agonies of death, Roderick's heart was filled with horrible dread. With his face ashy pale and his hair standing straight on end, he leapt to his feet and strode towards the old man in a threatening attitude and cried in a loud firm voice, so that the hall rang again, "Daniel, Daniel, what are you doing here at this hour?" Then the old man uttered that same unearthly howling whimper, like the death-cry of a wounded animal, which he had uttered when Wolfgang had offered to reward his fidelity with gold; and he fell down on the floor. V—— summoned the servants; they raised the old man up; but all attempts to restore animation proved fruitless. Then the Freiherr cried, almost beside himself, "Good God! Good God! Now I remember to have heard that a sleepwalker may die on the spot if anybody calls him by his name. Oh! oh! unfortunate wretch that I am! I have killed the poor old man! I shall never more have a peaceful moment so long as I live." When the servants had carried the corpse away and the hall was again empty, V—— took the Freiherr, who was still continuing his self-reproaches, by the hand and led him in impressive silence to the walled-up postern, and said, "The man who fell down dead at your feet, Freiherr Roderick, was the atrocious murderer of your father." The Freiherr fixed his staring eyes upon V—— as though he saw the foul fiends of hell. But V—— went on, "The time has come now for me to reveal to you the hideous secret which, weighing upon the conscience of this monster and burthening him with curses, compelled him to roam abroad in his sleep. The Eternal Power has seen fit to make the son take vengeance upon the murderer of his father. The words which you thundered in the ears of that fearful night-walker were the last words which your unhappy father spoke." V—— sat down in front of the fire, and the Freiherr, trembling and unable to utter a word, took his seat beside him. V—— began to tell him the contents of the document which Hubert had left behind him, and the seal of which he (V——) was not to break until after the opening of the will Hubert lamented, in expressions testifying to the deepest remorse, the implacable hatred against his elder brother which took root in him from the moment that old Roderick established the entail. He was deprived of all weapons; for, even if he succeeded in maliciously setting the son at variance with the father, it would serve no purpose, since even Roderick himself had not the power to deprive his eldest son of his birth-right, nor would he on principle have ever done so, no matter how his affections had been alienated from him. It was only when Wolfgang formed his connection with Julia de St. Val in Geneva that

Hubert saw his way to effecting his brother's ruin. And that was the time when he came to an understanding with Daniel, to provoke the old man by villainous devices to take measures which should drive his son to despair.

He was well aware of old Roderick's opinion that the only way to ensure an illustrious future for the family to all subsequent time was by means of an alliance with one of the oldest families in the country. The old man had read this alliance in the stars, and any pernicious derangement of the constellation would only entail destruction upon the family he had founded. In this way it was that Wolfgang's union with Julia seemed to the old man like a sinful crime, committed against the ordinances of the Power which had stood by him in all his worldly undertakings; and any means that might be employed for Julia's ruin he would have regarded as justified for the same reason, for Julia had, he conceived, ranged herself against him like some demoniacal principle. Hubert knew that his brother loved Julia passionately, almost to madness in fact, and that the loss of her would infallibly make him miserable, perhaps kill him. And Hubert was all the more ready to assist the old man in his plans as he had himself conceived an unlawful affection for Julia, and hoped to win her for himself. It was, however, determined by a special dispensation of Providence that all attacks, even the most virulent, were to be thwarted by Wolfgang's resoluteness; nay, that he should contrive to deceive his brother: the fact that his marriage was actually solemnised and that of the birth of a son were kept secret from Hubert In Roderick's mind also there occurred, along with the presentiment of his approaching death, the idea that Wolfgang had really married the Julia who was so hostile to him. In the letter which commanded his son to appear at R——sitten on a given day to take possession of the entail, he cursed him if he did not sever his connection with her. This was the letter that Wolfgang burnt beside his father's corpse. To Hubert the old man wrote, saying that Wolfgang had married Julia, but that he would part from her. This Hubert took to be a fancy of his visionary father's; accordingly he was not a little dismayed when on reaching R——sitten Wolfgang with perfect frankness not only confirmed the old man's supposition, but also went on to add that Julia had borne him a son, and that he hoped in a short time to surprise her with the pleasant intelligence of his high rank and great wealth, for she had hitherto taken him for Born, a merchant from M——. He intended going to Geneva himself to fetch his beloved wife. But before he could carry out this plan he was overtaken by death. Hubert carefully concealed what he knew about the existence of a son born to Wolfgang in lawful wedlock with Julia, and so usurped the property that really belonged to his nephew. But only a few years passed before he became a prey to bitter remorse. He was reminded of his guilt in terrible wise by destiny, in the hatred which grew up and developed more and more between his two sons. "You are a poor starving beggar!" said the elder, a boy of twelve, to the younger, "but I shall be lord of R——sitten when father dies, and then you will have to be humble and kiss my hand when you want me to give you money to buy a new coat." The younger, goaded to ungovernable fury by his brother's proud and scornful words, threw the knife at him which he happened to have in his hand, and almost killed him. Hubert, for fear of some dire misfortune, sent the younger away to St. Petersburg; and he served afterwards as officer under Suwaroff, and fell fighting against the French. Hubert was prevented revealing to the world the dishonest and deceitful way in which he had acquired possession of the estate-tail by the shame and disgrace which would have come upon him; but he would not rob the rightful owner of a single penny more. He caused inquiries to be set on foot in Geneva, and learned that Madame Born had died of grief at the incomprehensible disappearance of her husband, but that young Roderick Born was being brought up by a worthy man who had adopted him. Hubert then caused himself to be introduced under an assumed name as a relative of Born the merchant, who had perished at sea, and he forwarded at given times sufficient sums of money to give the young heir of entail a good and respectable education. How he carefully treasured up the surplus revenues from the estate, and how he drew up the terms of his will, we already know. Respecting his brother's death, Hubert spoke in strangely obscure terms, but they allowed this much to be inferred, that there must be some mystery about it, and that he had taken part, indirectly, at least, in some heinous crime.

The contents of the black portfolio made everything clear. Along with Hubert's traitorous correspondence with Daniel was a sheet of paper written and signed by Daniel. V—— read a confession at which his very soul trembled, appalled. It was at Daniel's instigation that Hubert had come to R——sitten; and it was Daniel again who had written and told him about the one hundred and fifty thousand thalers that had been found. It has been already described how Hubert was received by his brother, and how, deceived in all his hopes and wishes, he was about to go off when he was prevented by V——, Daniel's heart was tortured by an insatiable thirst for vengeance, which he was determined to take on the young man who had proposed to kick him out like a mangy cur. He it was who relentlessly and incessantly fanned the flame of passion by which Hubert's desperate heart was consumed. Whilst in the fir forests hunting wolves, out in the midst of a blinding snowstorm, they agreed to effect his destruction. "Make away with him!" murmured Hubert, looking askance and taking aim with his rifle. "Yes, make away with him," snarled Daniel, "but not in *that way*, not in *that way!*" And he made the most solemn asseverations that he would murder the Freiherr and not a soul in the world should be the wiser. When, however, Hubert had got his money, he repented of the plot; he determined to go away in order to shun all further temptation. Daniel himself saddled his horse and brought it out of the stable; but as the Baron was about to mount, Daniel said to him in a sharp, strained voice, "I thought you would stay on the entail, Freiherr Hubert, now that it has just fallen to you, for the proud lord of the entail lies dashed to pieces at the bottom of the ravine, below the tower." The steward had observed that Wolfgang, tormented by his thirst for gold, often used to rise in the night, go to the postern which formerly led to the tower, and stand gazing with longing eyes down into the chasm, where, according to his (Daniel's) testimony, vast treasures lay buried. Relying upon this habit, Daniel waited near the hall-door on that ill-omened night; and as soon as he heard the Freiherr open the postern leading to the tower, he entered the hall and proceeded to where the Freiherr was standing, close by the brink of the chasm. On becoming aware of the presence of his villainous servant, in whose eyes the gleam of murder shone, the Freiherr turned round and said with a cry of terror, "Daniel, Daniel, what are you doing here at this hour?" But then Daniel shrieked wildly, "Down with you, you mangy cur!" and with a powerful push of his foot he hurled the unhappy man over into the deep chasm.

Terribly agitated by this awful deed, Freiherr Roderick found no peace in the castle where his father had been murdered. He went to his Courland estates, and only visited R—sitten once a year, in autumn. Francis—old Francis—who had strong suspicions as to Daniel's guilt, maintained that he often haunted the place at full moon, and described the nature of the apparition much as V—- afterwards experienced it for himself when he exorcised it. It was the disclosure of these circumstances, also, which stamped his father's memory with dishonour, that had driven young Freiherr Hubert out into the world.

This was my old great-uncle's story. Now he took my hand, and whilst his eyes filled with tears, he said, in a broken voice, "Cousin, cousin! And she too—the beautiful lady—has fallen a victim to the dark destiny, the grim, mysterious power which has established itself in that old ancestral castle. Two days after we left R—sitten the Freiherr arranged an excursion on sledges as the concluding event of the visit. He drove his wife himself; but as they were going down the valley the horses, for some unexplained reason, suddenly taking fright, began to snort and kick and plunge most savagely. 'The old man! The old man is after us!' screamed the Baroness in a shrill, terrified voice. At this same moment the sledge was overturned with a violent jerk, and the Baroness was hurled to a considerable distance. They picked her up lifeless—she was quite dead. The Freiherr is perfectly inconsolable, and has settled down into a state of passivity that will kill him. We shall never go to R—sitten again, cousin!"

Here my uncle paused. As I left him my heart was rent by emotion; and nothing but the all-soothing hand of Time could assuage the deep pain which I feared would cost me my life.

Years passed. V—— was resting in his grave, and I had left my native country. Then I was driven northwards, as far as St. Petersburg, by the devastating war which was sweeping over all Germany. On my return journey, not far from K——, I was driving one dark summer night along the shore of the Baltic, when I perceived in the sky before me a remarkably large bright star. On coming nearer I saw by the red flickering flame that what I had taken for a star must be a large fire, but could not understand how it could be so high up in the air. "Postilion, what fire is that before us yonder?" I asked the man who was driving me. "Oh! why, that's not a fire; it's the beacon tower of R—sitten." "R—sitten!" Directly the postilion mentioned the name all the experiences of the eventful autumn days which I had spent there recurred to my mind with lifelike reality. I saw the Baron—Seraphina—and also the remarkably eccentric old aunts—myself as well, with my bare milk-white face, my hair elegantly curled and powdered, and wearing a delicate sky-blue coat—nay, I saw myself in my love-sick folly, sighing like a furnace, and making lugubrious odes on my mistress's eyebrows. The sombre, melancholy mood into which these memories plunged me was relieved by the bright recollection of V——'s genial jokes, shooting up like flashes of coloured light, and I found them now still more entertaining than they had been so long ago. Thus agitated by pain mingled with much peculiar pleasure, I reached R—sitten early in the morning and got out of the coach in front of the post-house, where it had stopped I recognised the house as that of the land-steward; I inquired after him. "Begging your pardon," said the clerk of the post-house, taking his pipe from his mouth and giving his night-cap a tilt, "begging your pardon; there is no land-steward here; this is a Royal Government office, and the Herr Administrator is still asleep." On making further inquiries I learnt that Freiherr Roderick von R——, the last lord of the entail, had died sixteen years before without descendants, and that the entail in accordance with the terms of the original deeds had now escheated to the state. I went up to the castle; it was a mere heap of ruins. I was informed by an old peasant, who came out of the fir-forest, and with whom I entered into conversation, that a large portion of the stones had been employed in the construction of the beacon-tower. He also could tell the story of the ghost which was said to have haunted the castle, and he affirmed that people often heard unearthly cries and lamentations amongst the stones, especially at full moon.

Poor short-sighted old Roderick! What a malignant destiny did you conjure up to destroy with the breath of poison, in the first moments of its growth, that race which you intended to plant with firm roots to last on till eternity!

* * * * * * *

ARTHUR'S HALL.

You must of course, indulgent reader, have heard a good deal about the remarkable old commercial town of Dantzic. Perhaps you may be acquainted from abundant descriptions with all the sights to be seen there; but I should like it best of all if you have ever been there yourself in former times, and seen with your own eyes the wonderful hall into which I will now take you—I mean Arthur's Hall.

At the hour of noon the hall was crammed full of men of the most diverse nations, all pushing about and immersed to the eyes in business, so that the ears were deafened by the confused din. But when the exchange hours were over, and the merchants had gone to dinner, and only a few odd individuals hurried through the hall on business (for it served as a means of communication between two streets), that I dare say was the time when you, gracious reader, liked to visit Arthur's Hall best, whenever you were in Dantzic. For then a kind of magical twilight fell through the dim windows, and all the strange reliefs and carvings, with which the wall was too profusely decorated, became instinct with life and motion. Stags with immense antlers, together with other wonderful animals, gazed down upon you with their fiery eyes till you could hardly look at them; and the marble statue of the king, also in the midst of the hall, caused you to shiver more in proportion as the dusk of evening deepened. The great picture representing an assemblage of all the Virtues and Vices, with their respective names attached, lost perceptibly in moral effect; for the Virtues, being high up, were blended unrecognisably in a grey mist, whilst the Vices—wondrously beautiful ladies in gay and brilliant costumes—stood out prominently and very seductively, threatening to enchant you with their sweet soft words. You preferred to turn your eyes upon the narrow border which went almost all round the hall, and on which were represented in pleasing style long processions of gay-uniformed militia of the olden time, when Dantzic was an Imperial town. Honest burgomasters, their features stamped with shrewdness and importance, ride at the head on spirited horses with handsome trappings, whilst the drummers, pipers, and halberdiers march along so jauntily and life-like, that you soon begin to hear the merry music they play, and look to see them all defile out of that great window up there into the Langemarkt.

While, then, they are marching off, you, indulgent reader,—if you were, that is, a tolerable sketcher,—would not be able to do otherwise than copy with pen and ink yon magnificent burgomaster with his remarkably handsome page. Pen and ink and paper, provided at public cost, were always to be found lying about on the tables; accordingly the material would be all ready at hand, and you would have felt the temptation irresistible. This you would have been permitted to do, but not so the young merchant Traugott, who, on beginning to do anything of this kind, encountered a thousand difficulties and vexations. "Advise our friend in Hamburg at once that that business has been settled, my good Herr Traugott," said the wholesale and retail merchant, Elias Roos, with whom Traugott was about to enter upon an immediate partnership, besides marrying his only daughter, Christina. After a little trouble, Traugott found a place at one of the crowded tables; he took a sheet of paper, dipped his pen in the ink, and was about to begin with a free caligraphic flourish, when, running over once more in his mind what he wished to say, he cast his eyes upwards. Now it happened that he sat directly opposite a procession of figures, at the sight of which he was always, strangely enough, affected with an inexplicable sadness. A grave man, with something of dark melancholy in his face, and with a black curly beard and dressed in sumptuous clothing, was riding a black horse, which was led by the bridle by a marvellous youth: his rich abundance of hair and his gay and graceful costume gave him almost a feminine appearance. The face and form of the man made Traugott shudder inwardly, but a whole world of sweet vague aspirations beamed upon him from the youth's countenance. He could never tear himself away from looking at these two; and hence, on the present occasion, instead of writing Herr Elias Roos's letter of advice to Hamburg, he sat gazing at the wonderful picture, absently scribbling all over his paper. After this had lasted some time, a hand clapped him on the shoulder from behind, and a gruff voice said, "Nice—very nice; that's what I like; something maybe made of that." Traugott, awakening out of his dreamy reverie, whisked himself round; but, as if struck by a lightning flash, he remained speechless with amazement and fright, for he was staring up into the face of the dark melancholy man who was depicted on the wall before him. He it was who uttered the words stated above; at his side stood the delicate and wonderfully beautiful youth, smiling upon him with indescribable affection. "Yes, it is they—the very same!" was the thought that flashed across Traugott's mind. "I expect they will at once throw off their unsightly mantles and stand forth in all the splendours of their antique costume." The members of the crowd pushed backwards and forwards amongst each other, and the strangers had soon disappeared in the crush; but even after the hours of 'Change were long over, and only a few odd individuals crossed the hall, Traugott still remained in the self-same place with the letter of advice in his hand, as though he were converted into a solid stone statue.

At length he perceived Herr Elias Roos coming towards him with two strangers. "What are you about, cogitating here so long after noon, my respected Herr Traugott?" asked Elias Roos; "have you sent off the letter all right?" Mechanically Traugott handed him the paper; but Herr Elias Roos struck his hands together above his head, stamping at first gently, but then violently, with his right foot, as he cried, making the hall ring again, "Good God! Good God! what childish tricks are these? Nothing but sheer childishness, my respected Traugott,—my good-for-nothing son-in-law—my imprudent partner. Why, the devil must be in your honour! The letter—the letter! O God! the post!" Herr Elias Roos was almost choking with vexation, whilst the two strangers were laughing at the singular letter of advice, which could hardly be said to be of much use. For, immediately after the words, "In reply to yours of the 20th inst. respecting——" Traugott had sketched the two extraordinary figures of the old man and the youth in neat bold outlines. The two strangers sought to pacify Herr Elias Roos by addressing him in the most affectionate manner; but Herr Elias Roos tugged his round wig now on this side and now on that, struck his cane against the floor, and cried, "The young devil!—was to write letter of advice—makes drawings—ten thousand marks gone—dam!" He blew through his fingers and then went on lamenting, "Ten thousand marks!" "Don't make a trouble of it, my dear Herr Roos," said at length the elder of the two strangers. "The post is of course gone; but I am sending off a courier to Hamburg in an hour. Let me give him your letter, and it will then reach its destination earlier than it would have done by the post" "You incomparable man!" exclaimed Herr Elias, his face a perfect blaze of sunshine. Traugott had recovered from his awkward embarrassment; he was hastening to the table to write the letter, but Herr Elias pushed him away, casting a right malicious look upon him, and murmuring between his teeth, "No need for you, my good son!"

Whilst Herr Elias was studiously busy writing, the elder gentleman approached young Traugott, who was standing silent with shame, and said to him, "You don't seem to be exactly in your place, my good sir. It would never have come into a true merchant's head to make drawings instead of writing a business letter as he ought" Traugott could not help feeling that this reproach was only too well founded. Much embarrassed, he replied, "By my soul, this hand has already written many admirable letters of advice; it is only, occasionally that such confoundedly odd ideas come into my mind." "But, my good sir," continued the stranger smiling, "these are not confoundedly odd ideas at all. I can really hardly believe that all your business letters taken together have been so admirable as these sketches, outlined so neatly and boldly and firmly. There is, I am sure, true genius in them." With these words the stranger took out of Traugott's hand the letter—or rather what was begun as a letter but had ended in sketches—carefully folded it together, and put it in his pocket. This awakened in Traugott's mind the firm conviction that he had done something far more excellent than write a business letter. A strange spirit took possession of him; so that, when Herr Elias Roos, who had now finished writing, addressed him in an angry tone, "Your childish folly might have cost me ten thousand marks," he replied louder and with more decision than was his habit, "Will your worship please not to behave in such an extraordinary way, else I will never write you another letter of advice so long as I live, and we will separate." Herr Elias pushed his wig right with both hands and stammered, as he stared hard at Traugott, "My estimable colleague, my dear, dear son, what proud words you are using!" The old gentleman again interposed, and a few words sufficed to restore perfect peace; and so they all went to Herr Elias's house to dinner, for he had invited the strangers home with him. Fair Christina received them in holiday attire, all clean and prim and proper; and soon she was wielding the excessively heavy silver soup-ladle with a practised hand.

Whilst these five persons are sitting at table, I could, gracious reader, bring them pictorially before your eyes; but I shall only manage to give a few general outlines, and those certainly worse than the sketches which Traugott had the audacity to scribble in the inauspicious letter; for the meal will soon be over; and besides, I am urged by an impulse I cannot resist to go on with the remarkable history of the excellent Traugott, which I have undertaken to relate to you.

That Herr Elias Roos wears a round wig you already know from what has been stated above; and I have no need to add anything more; for after what he has said, you can now see the round little man with his liver-coloured coat, waistcoat, and trousers, with gilt buttons, quite plainly before your eyes. Of Traugott I have a very great deal to say, because this is his history which I am telling, and so of course he occurs in it. If now it be true that a man's thoughts and feelings and actions, making their influence felt from within him outwards, so model and shape his bodily form as to give rise to that wonderful harmony of the whole man, that is not to be explained but only felt, which we call character, then my words will of themselves have already shown you Traugott himself in the flesh. If this is not the case, then all my gossip is wasted, and you may forthwith regard my story as unread. The two strangers are uncle and nephew, formerly retail dealers, but now merchants trading on their gains, and friends of Herr Elias Roos, that is to say, they had a good many business transactions together. They live at Königsberg, dress entirely in the English fashion, carry about with them a mahogany boot-jack which has come from London, possess considerable taste for art, and are, in a word, experienced, well-educated people. The uncle has a gallery of art objects and collects hand-sketches (witness the pilfered letter of advice).

But properly my chief business was to give you, kindly reader, a true and life-like description of Christina; for her nimble person will, I observe, soon disappear; and it will be as well for me to get a few traits jotted down at once. Then she may willingly go! Picture to yourself a medium-sized stoutish female of from two to three and twenty years of age, with a round face, a short and rather turned-up nose, and friendly light-blue eyes, which smile most prettily upon everybody, saying, "I shall soon be married now." Her skin is dazzling white, her hair is not altogether of a too reddish tinge; she has lips which were certainly made to be kissed, and a mouth which, though indeed rather wide, she yet screws up small in some extraordinary way, but so as to display then two rows of pearly teeth. If we were to suppose that the flames from the next-door neighbour's burning house were to dart in at her chamber-window, she would make haste to feed the canary and lock up the clean linen from the wash, and then assuredly hasten down into the office and inform Herr Elias Roos that by that time his house also was on fire. She has never had an almond-cake spoilt, and her melted-butter always thickens properly, owing to the fact that she never stirs the spoon round towards the left, but always towards the right. But since Herr Elias Roos has poured out the last bumper of old French wine, I will only hasten to add that pretty Christina is uncommonly fond of Traugott because he is going to marry her; for what in the name of wonder should she do if she did not get married?

After dinner Herr Elias Roos proposed to his friends to take a walk on the ramparts. Although Traugott, whose mind had never been stirred by so many wonderful and extraordinary things as to-day, would very much have liked to escape the company, he could not contrive it; for, just as he was going out of the door, without having even kissed his betrothed's hand, Herr Elias caught him by the coat-tails, crying, "My honoured son-in-law, my good colleague, but you're not going to leave us?" And so he had to stay.

A certain professor of physics once stated the theory that the *Anima Mundi*, or Spirit of the World, had, as a skilful experimentalist, constructed somewhere an excellent electric machine, and from it proceed certain very mysterious wires, which pass through the lives of us all; these we do our best to creep round and avoid, but at some moment or other we must tread upon them, and then there passes a flash and a shock through our souls, suddenly altering the forms of everything within them. Upon this thread Traugott must surely have trod in the moment that he was unconsciously sketching the two persons who stood in living shape behind him, for the singular appearance of the strangers had struck him with all the violence of a lightning-flash; and he now felt as if he had very clear conceptions of all those things which he had hitherto only dimly guessed at and dreamt about. The shyness which at other times had always fettered his tongue so soon as the conversation turned upon things which lay concealed like holy secrets at the bottom of his heart had now left him; and hence it was that, when the uncle attacked the curious half-painted, half-carved pictures in Arthur's Hall as wanting in taste, and then proceeded more particularly to condemn the little pictures representing the soldiers as being whimsical, Traugott boldly maintained that, although it was very likely true that all these things did not harmonize with the rules of good taste, nevertheless he had experienced, what indeed several others had also experienced, viz., a wonderful and fantastic world had been unfolded to him in Arthur's Hall, and some few of the figures had reminded him in even lifelike looks, nay, even in plain distinct words, that he also was a great master, and could paint and wield the chisel as well as the man out of whose unknown studio they themselves had proceeded Herr Elias certainly looked more stupid than usual whilst the young fellow was saying such grand things, but the uncle made answer in a very malicious manner, "I repeat once more, I do not comprehend why you want to be a merchant, why you haven't rather devoted yourself altogether to art."

Traugott conceived an extreme repugnance to the man, and accordingly he joined the nephew for the walk, and found his manner very friendly and confidential. "O Heaven!" said the latter, "how I envy you your beautiful and glorious talent! I wish I could only sketch like you! I am not at all wanting in genius; I have already sketched some deucedly pretty eyes and noses and ears, ay, and even three or four entire heads;—but, dash it all! the business, you know! the business!" "I always thought," said Traugott, "that as soon as a man detected the spark of true genius—of a genuine love for art—within him, he ought not to know anything about any other business." "You mean he ought to be an artist!" rejoined the nephew. "Ah! how can you say so? See you here, my estimable friend! I have, I believe, reflected more upon these things than many others; in fact, I am such a decided admirer of art, and have gone into the real essential nature of the thing far deeper than I am even able to express, and so I can only make use of hints and suggestions." The nephew, as he expressed these opinions, looked so learned and so profound that Traugott really began to feel in awe of him. "You will agree with me," continued the nephew, after he had taken a pinch of snuff and had sneezed twice, "you will agree with me that art embroiders our life with flowers; amusement, recreation after serious business—that is the praiseworthy end of all effort in art; and the attainment of this end is the more perfect in proportion as the art products assume a nearer approach to excellence. This end is very clearly seen in life; for it is only the man who pursues art in the spirit I have just mentioned who enjoys comfort and ease; whilst these for ever and eternally flee away from the man who, directly contrary to the nature of the case, regards art as a true end in itself—as the highest aim in life. And so, my good friend, don't take to heart what my uncle said to try and persuade you to turn aside from the serious business of life, and rely upon a way of employing your energies which, if without support, will only make you stagger about like a helpless child." Here the nephew paused as if expecting Traugott's reply; but Traugott did not know for the life of him what he ought to say. All that the nephew had said struck him as indescribably stupid talk. He contented himself with asking, "But what do you really mean by the serious business of life?" The nephew looked at him somewhat taken aback. "Well, by my soul, you can't help conceding to me that a man who is alive must live, and that's what your artist by profession hardly ever succeeds in doing, for he's always hard up." And he went on with a long rigmarole of bosh, which he clothed in fine words and stereotyped phrases. The end of it all appeared to be pretty much this—that by living he meant little else than having no debts but plenty of money, plenty to eat and drink, a beautiful wife, and also well-behaved children, who never got any grease-stains on their nice Sunday-clothes, and so on. This made Traugott feel a tightness in his throat, and he was glad when the clever nephew left him, and he found himself alone in his own room.

"What a wretched miserable life I lead, to be sure!" he soliloquised. "On beautiful mornings in the glorious golden spring-time, when into even the obscure streets of the town the warm west wind finds its way, and its faint murmurings and rustlings seem to be telling of all the wonders which are to be seen blooming in the woods and fields, then I have to crawl down sluggishly and in an ill-temper into Herr Elias Roos's smoke-begrimed office. And there sit pale faces before huge ugly-shaped desks; all are working on amidst gloomy silence, which is only broken by the rustle of leaves turned over in the big books, by the chink of money that is being counted, and by unintelligible sounds at odd intervals. And then again what work it is! What is the good of all this thinking and all this writing? Merely that the pile of gold pieces may increase in the coffers, and that the Fafnir's treasure, which always brings mischief, may glitter and sparkle more and more! Oh, how gladly a painter or a sculptor must go out into the air, and with head erect imbibe all the refreshing influences of spring, until they people the inner world of his mind with beautiful images pulsing with glad and energetic life! Then from the dark bushes step forth wonderful figures, which his own mind has created, and which continue to be his own, for within him dwells the mysterious wizard power of light, of colour, of form; hence he is able to give abiding shape to what he has seen with the eye of his mind, in that he represents it in a material substitute. What is there to prevent me tearing myself loose from this hated mode of life? That remarkable old man assured me that I am called to be an artist, and still more so did the nice handsome youth. For although he did not speak a word, it yet somehow struck me that his glance said plainly what I had for such a long time felt like a vague emotional pulsation within me, and what, oppressed by a multitude of doubts, has hitherto been unable to rise to the level of consciousness. Instead of going on in this miserable way, could I not make myself a good painter?"

Traugott took out all the things that he had ever drawn and examined them with critical eyes. Several things looked quite different to-day from what they had ever done before, and that not worse, but better. His attention was especially attracted by one of his childish attempts, of the time when he was quite a boy; it was a sketch of the old burgomaster and the handsome page, the outlines very much wanting in firmness, of course, but nevertheless recognisable. And he remembered quite well that these figures had made a strange impression upon him even at that time, and how one evening at dusk they enticed him with such an irresistible power of attraction, that he had to leave his playmates and go into Arthur's Hall, where he took almost endless pains to copy the picture. The contemplation of this drawing filled him with a feeling of very deep yearning sadness. According to his usual habit, he ought to go and work a few hours in the office; but he could not do it; he went out to the Carlsberg instead. There he stood and gazed out over the heaving sea, striving to decipher in the waves and in the grey misty clouds which had gathered in wonderful shapes over Hela, as in a magic mirror, his own destiny in days to come.

Don't you too believe, kindly reader, that the sparks which fall into our hearts from the higher regions of Love are first made visible to us in the hours of hopeless pain? And so it is with the doubts that storm the artist's mind. He sees the Ideal and feels how impotent are his efforts to reach it; it will flee before him, he thinks, always unattainable. But then again he is once more animated by a divine courage; he strives and struggles, and his despair is dissolved into a sweet yearning, which both strengthens him and spurs him on to strain after his beloved idol, so that he begins to see it continually nearer and nearer, but never reaches it.

Traugott was now tortured to excess by this state of hopeless pain. Early next morning, on again looking over his drawings, which he had left lying on the table he thought them all paltry and foolish, and he now called to mind the oft-repeated words of one of his artistic friends, "A great deal of the mischief done by dabblers in art of moderate abilities arises from the fact that so many people take a somewhat keen superficial excitement for a real essential vocation to pursue art." Traugott felt strongly urged to look upon Arthur's Hall and his adventure with the two mysterious personages, the old man and the young one, for one of these states of superficial excitement;

so he condemned himself to go back to the office again; and he worked so assiduously at Herr Elias Roos's, without heeding the disgust which frequently so far overcame him that he had to break off suddenly and rush off out into the open air. With sympathetic concern, Herr Elias Roos set this down to the indisposition which, according to his opinion, the fearfully pale young man must be suffering from.

Some time passed; Dominic's Fair came, after which Traugott was to marry Christina and be introduced to the mercantile world as Herr Elias Roos's partner. This period he regarded as that of a sad leave-taking from all his high hopes and aspirations; and his heart grew heavy whenever he saw dear Christina as busy as a bee superintending the scrubbing and polishing that was going on everywhere in the middle story, folding curtains with her own hands, and giving the final polish to the brass pots and pans, &c.

One day, in the thick of the surging crowd of strangers in Arthur's Hall, Traugott heard close behind him a voice whose well-known tones made his heart jump. "And do you really mean to say that this stock stands at such a low figure?" Traugott whisked himself quickly round, and saw, as he had expected, the remarkable old man, who had appealed to a broker to get him to buy some stock, the price of which had at that moment fallen to an extremely low figure. Behind the old man stood the youth, who greeted Traugott with a friendly but melancholy smile. Then Traugott hastened to address the old man. "Excuse me, sir; the price of the stock which you are desirous of selling is really no higher than what you have been told; nevertheless, it may with confidence be anticipated that in a few days the price will rise considerably. If, therefore, you take my advice, you will postpone the conversion of your stock for a little time longer." "Eh! sir?" replied the old man rather coldly and roughly, "what have you to do with my business? How do you know that just now a silly bit of paper like this is of no use at all to me, whilst ready money is what I have great need of?" Traugott, not a little abashed because the old man had taken his well-meant intention in such ill part, was on the point of retiring, when the youth looked at him with tears in his eyes, as if in entreaty. "My advice was well meant, sir," he replied quickly; "I cannot suffer you to inflict upon yourself an important loss. Let me have your stock, but on the condition that I afterwards pay for it the higher price which it will be worth in a few day's time." "Well, you are an extraordinary man," said the old man. "Be it so then; although I can't understand what induces you to want to enrich me." So saying, he shot a keen flashing glance at the youth, who cast down his beautiful blue eyes in shy confusion. They both followed Traugott to the office, where the money was paid over to the old man, whose face was dark and sullen as he put it in his purse. Whilst he was doing so, the youth whispered softly to Traugott, "Are you not the gentleman who was sketching such pretty figures several weeks ago in Arthur's Hall?" "Certainly I am," replied Traugott, and he felt how the remembrance of the ridiculous episode of the letter of advice drove the hot blood into his face. "Oh then, I don't at all wonder," the youth was continuing, when the old man gave him an angry look, which at once made him silent. In the presence of these strangers Traugott could not get rid of a certain feeling of awkward constraint; and so they went away before he could muster courage enough to inquire further into their circumstances and mode of life.

In fact there was something so quite out of the ordinary in the appearance of these two persons that even the clerks and others in the office were struck by it. The surly book-keeper had stuck his pen behind his ear, and leaning on his arms, which he clasped behind his head, he sat watching the old man with keen glittering eyes. "God forgive me," he said when the strangers had left the office, "if he didn't look like an old picture of the year 1400 in St. John's parish church, with his curly beard and black mantle." Herr Elias set him down without more ado as a Polish Jew, notwithstanding his noble bearing and his extremely grave old-German face, and cried with a simper, "Silly fellow! sells his stock now; might make at least ten per cent, more in a week." Of course he knew nothing about the additional price which had been agreed upon, and which Traugott intended to pay out of his own pocket. And this he really did do when some days later he again met the old man and the youth in Arthur's Hall.

The old man said, "My son has reminded me that you are an artist also, and so I will accept what I should have otherwise refused." They were standing close beside one of the four granite pillars which support the vaulted roof of the hall, and immediately in front of the two painted figures which Traugott had formerly sketched in the letter of advice. Without reserve he spoke of the great resemblance between these figures and the old man himself and the youth. The old man smiled a peculiar smile, and laying his hand on Traugott's shoulder, said in a low and deliberate tone, "Then you didn't know that I am the German painter Godofredus Berklinger, and that it was I who painted the pictures which seem to give you so much pleasure, a long time ago, whilst still a learner in art. That burgomaster I copied in commemoration of myself, and that the page who is leading the horse is my son you can of course very easily see by comparing the faces and figures of the two." Traugott was struck dumb with astonishment. But he very soon came to the conclusion that the old man, who took himself to be the artist of a picture more than two hundred years old must be labouring under some peculiar delusion. The old man went on, lifting up his head and looking proudly about him, "Ay, that was an artistic age if you like—glorious, vigorous, flourishing, when I decorated this hall with all these gay pictures in honour of the wise King Arthur and his Round Table. I verily believe that the tall stately figure who once came to me as I was working here, and exhorted me to go on and gain my mastership—for at that time I had not reached that dignity,—was King Arthur himself." Here the young man interposed, "My father is an artist, sir, who has few equals; and you would have no cause to be sorry if he would allow you to inspect his works." Meanwhile the old man was taking a turn through the hall, which had now become empty; he now called to the youth to go, and then Traugott begged him to show him his pictures. The old man fixed his eyes upon him and regarded him for some time with a keen and searching glance, and at length said with much gravity, "You are, I must say, rather audacious to be wanting to enter the inner shrine before you have begun your probationary years. But—be it so! If your eyes are still too dull to see, you may at least dimly feel. Come and see me early to-morrow morning," and he indicated where he lived. Next morning Traugott did not fail to get away from business early and hasten to the retired street where the remarkable old man lived. The youth, dressed in old-German style, opened the door to receive him and led him into a spacious room, in the centre of which he found the old man sitting on a little stool in front of a large piece of outstretched grey primed canvas. "You have come exactly at the right time, sir," the old man cried by way of greeting, "for I have just put the finishing-touch to yon large picture, which has occupied me more than a year and cost me no small amount of trouble. It is the fellow of a picture of the same size, representing 'Paradise Lost,' which I completed last year and which I can also show you here. This, as you will observe, is 'Paradise Regained,' and I should be very sorry for you if you begin to put on critical airs and try to get some allegory out of it Allegorical pictures are only painted by duffers and bunglers; my picture is not to *signify* but to *be*. You perceive how all these varied groups of men and animals and fruits and flowers and stones unite to form one harmonic whole, whose loud and excellent music is the divinely pure chord of glorification." And the old man began to dwell more especially upon the individual groups; he called Traugott's attention to the secrets of the division of light and shade, to the glitter of the flowers and the metals, to the singular shapes which, rising up out of the calyx of the lilies, entwined themselves about the forms of the divinely beautiful youths and maidens who were dancing to the strains of music, and he called his attention to the bearded men who, with all the strong pride of youth in their eyes and movements, were apparently talking to various kinds of curious animals. The old man's words, whilst they grew continually more emphatic, grew also continually more incomprehensible and confused. "That's right, old greybeard, let thy diamond crown flash and sparkle," he cried at last, riveting a fixed but fiery glance upon the canvas. "Throw off the Isis veil which thou didst put over thy head when the profane approached thee. What art thou folding thy dark robe so carefully over thy breast for? I want to see thy heart; that is the philosopher's stone through which the mystery is revealed. Art thou not I? Why dost thou put on such a bold and mighty air before me? Wilt thou contend with thy master? Thinkest thou that the ruby, thy heart, which sparkles so, can crush my breast? Up then—step forward—come here! I have created thee, for I am"—— Here the old man suddenly fell on the floor like one struck by lightning. Whilst Traugott lifted him up, the youth quickly wheeled up a small arm-chair, into which they placed the old man, who soon appeared to have fallen into a gentle sleep.

"Now you know, my kind sir, what is the matter with my good old father," said the youth softly and gently. "A cruel destiny has stripped off all the blossoms of his life; and for several years past he has been insensible to the art for which he once lived. He spends days and days sitting in front of a piece of outstretched primed canvas, with his eyes fixed upon it in a stare; that he calls painting. Into what an overwrought condition the description of such a picture brings him, you have just seen for yourself. Besides this he is haunted by another unhappy thought, which makes my life to be a sad and agitated one; but I regard it as a fatality by which I am swept along in the same stream that has caught him. You would like something to help you to recover from this extraordinary scene; please follow me then into the adjoining room, where you will find several pictures of my father's early days, when he was still a productive artist."

And great was Traugott's astonishment to find a row of pictures apparently painted by the most illustrious masters of the Netherlands School. For the most part they represented scenes taken from real life; for example, a company returning from hunting, another amusing themselves with singing and playing, and such like subjects. They bore evidences of great thought, and particularly the expression of the heads, which were realised with especially vigorous life-like power. Just as Traugott was about to return into the former room, he noticed another picture close beside the door, which held him fascinated to the spot. It was a remarkably pretty maiden dressed in old-German style, but her face was exactly like the youth's, only fuller and with a little more colour in it, and she seemed to be somewhat taller too. A tremor of nameless delight ran through Traugott at the sight of this beautiful girl. In strength and vitality the picture was quite equal to anything by Van Dyk. The dark eyes were looking down upon Traugott with a soft yearning look, whilst her sweet lips appeared to be half opened ready to whisper loving words. "O heaven! Good heaven!" sighed Traugott with a sigh that came from the very bottom of his heart; "where—oh! where can I find her?" "Let us go," said the youth. Then Traugott cried in a sort of rapturous frenzy, "Oh! it is indeed she!—the beloved of my soul, whom I have so long carried about in my heart, but whom I only knew in vague stirrings of emotion. Where—oh! where is she?" The tears started from young Berklinger's eyes; he appeared to be shaken by a convulsive and sudden attack of pain, and to control himself with difficulty. "Come along," he at length said, in a firm voice, "that is a portrait of my unhappy sister Felicia. She has gone for ever. You will never see her."

Like one in a dream, Traugott suffered himself to be led into the other room. The old man was still sleeping; but all at once he started up, and staring at Traugott with eyes flashing with anger, he cried, "What do you want? What do you want, sir?" Then the youth stepped forward and reminded him that he had just been showing his new picture to Traugott, had he forgotten? At this Berklinger appeared to recollect all that had passed; it was evident that he was much affected; and he replied in an undertone, "Pardon an old man's forgetfulness, my good sir." "Your new piece is an admirable—an excellent work. Master Berklinger," Traugott proceeded; "I have never seen anything equal to it. I am sure it must cost a great deal of study and an immense amount of labour before a man can advance so far as to turn out a work like that. I discern that I have an inextinguishable propensity for art, and I earnestly entreat you, my good old master, to accept me as your pupil; you will find me industrious." The old man grew quite cheerful and amiable; and embracing Traugott, he promised that he would be a faithful master to him.

Thus it came to pass that Traugott visited the old painter every day that came, and made very rapid progress in his studies. He now conceived an unconquerable disgust of business, and was so careless that Herr Elias Roos had to speak out and openly find fault with him; and finally he was very glad when Traugott kept away from the office altogether, on the pretext that he was suffering from a lingering illness. For this same reason the wedding, to Christina's no little annoyance, was indefinitely postponed. "Your Herr Traugott seems to be suffering from some secret trouble," said one of Herr Elias Roos's merchant-friends to him one day; "perhaps it's the balance of some old love-affair that he's anxious to settle before the wedding-day. He looks very pale and distracted." "And why shouldn't he then?" rejoined Herr Elias. "I wonder now," he continued after a pause,—"I wonder now if that little rogue Christina has been having words with him? My book-keeper—the love-smitten old ass—he is always kissing and squeezing her hand. Traugott's devilishly in love with my little girl, I know. Can there be any jealousy? Well, I'll sound my young gentleman."

But however carefully he sounded he could find no satisfactory bottom, and he said to his merchant-friend, "That Traugott is a most peculiar fellow; well, I must just let him go his own way; though if he had not fifty thousand thalers in my business I know what I should do, since now he never does a stroke of anything."

Traugott, absorbed in art, would now have led a real bright sunshiny life, had his heart not been torn with passionate love for the beautiful Felicia, whom he often saw in wonderful dreams. The picture had disappeared; the old man had taken it away; and Traugott durst not ask him about it without risk of seriously offending him. On the whole, old Berklinger continued to grow more confidential; and instead of taking any honorarium for his instruction, he permitted Traugott to help out his narrow house-keeping in many ways. From young Berklinger Traugott learned that the old man had been obviously taken in in the sale of a little cabinet, and that the stock which Traugott had realised for them was all that they had left of the price received for it, as well as all the money they possessed. But it was only seldom that Traugott was allowed to have any confidential conversation with the youth; the old man watched over him with the most singular jealousy, and at once scolded him sharply if he began to converse freely and cheerfully with their friend. This Traugott felt all the more painfully since he had conceived a deep and heart-felt affection for the youth, owing to his striking likeness to Felicia. Indeed he often fancied, when he stood near the young man, that he was standing beside the picture he loved so much, now alive and breathing, and that he could feel her soft breath on his cheek; and then he would like to have drawn the youth, as if he really were his darling Felicia herself, to his swelling heart.

Winter was past; beautiful spring was filling the woods and fields with brightness and blossoms. Herr Elias Roos advised Traugott either to drink whey for his health's sake or to go somewhere to take the baths. Fair Christina was again looking forward with joy to the wedding, although Traugott seldom showed himself—and thought still less of his relations with her.

Once Traugott was confined to the office the whole day long, making a requisite squaring up of his accounts, &c.; he had been obliged to neglect his meals, and it was beginning to get very dark when he reached Berklinger's remote dwelling. He found nobody in the first room, but from the one adjoining he heard the music of a lute. He had never heard the instrument there before. He listened; a song, from time to time interrupted, accompanied the music like a low soft sigh. He opened the door. O Heaven! with her back towards him sat a female figure, dressed in old-German style with a high lace ruff, exactly like the picture. At the noise which Traugott unavoidably made on entering, the figure rose, laid the lute on the table, and turned round. It was she, Felicia herself! "Felicia!" cried Traugott enraptured; and he was about to throw himself at the feet of his beloved divinity when he felt a powerful hand laid upon his collar behind, and himself dragged out of the room by some one with the strength of a giant. "You abandoned wretch! you incomparable villain!" screamed old Berklinger, pushing him on before him, "so that was your love for art? Do you mean to murder me?" And therewith he hurled him out at the door, whilst a knife glittered in his hand. Traugott flew downstairs and hurried back home stupefied; nay, half crazy with mingled delight and terror.

He tossed restlessly on his couch, unable to sleep. "Felicia! Felicia!" he exclaimed time after time, distracted with pain and the pangs of love. "You are there, you are there, and I may not see you, may not clasp you in my arms! You love me, oh yes! that I know. From the pain which pierces my breast so savagely I feel that you love me."

The morning sun shone brightly into Traugott's chamber; then he got up, and determined, let the cost be what it might, that he would solve the mystery of Berklinger's house. He hurried off to the old man's, but his feelings may not be described when he saw all the windows wide open and the maid-servants busy sweeping out the rooms. He was struck with a presentiment of what had happened. Berklinger had left the house late on the night before along with his son, and was gone nobody knew where. A carriage drawn by two horses had fetched away the box of paintings and the two little trunks which contained all Berklinger's scanty property. He and his son had followed half an hour later. All inquiries as to where they had gone remained fruitless: no livery-stable keeper had let out horses and carriage to persons such as Traugott described, and even at the town gates he could learn nothing for certain;—in short, Berklinger had disappeared as if he had flown away on the mantle of Mephistopheles.

Traugott went back home prostrated by despair. "She is gone! She is gone! The beloved of my soul! All—all is lost!" Thus he cried as he rushed past Herr Elias Roos (for he happened to be just at that moment in the entrance hall) towards his own room. "God bless my soul!" cried Herr Elias, pulling and tugging at his wig. "Christina! Christina!" he shouted, till the whole house echoed. "Christina! You disgraceful girl! My good-for-nothing daughter!" The clerks and others in the office rushed out with terrified faces; the book-keeper asked amazed, "But Herr Roos?" Herr Roos, however, continued to scream without stopping, "Christina! Christina!" At this point Miss Christina stepped in through the house-door, and raising her broad-brimmed straw-hat just a little and smiling, asked what her good father was bawling in this outrageous way for. "I strictly beg you will let such unnecessary running away alone," Herr Elias began to storm at her. "My son-in-law is a melancholy fellow and as jealous as a Turk. You'd better stay quietly at home, or else there'll be some mischief done. My partner is in there screaming and crying about his betrothed, because she will gad about so." Christina looked at the book-keeper astounded; but he gave a significant glance in the direction of the cupboard in the office where Herr Roos was in the habit of keeping his cinnamon water. "You'd better go in and console your betrothed," he said as he strode away. Christina went up to her own room, only to make a slight change in her dress, and give out the clean linen, and discuss with the cook what would have to be done about the Sunday roast-joint, and at the same time pick up a few items of town-gossip, then she would go at once and see what really was the matter with her betrothed.

You know, kindly, reader, that we all of us, when in Traugott's case, have to go through our appointed stages; we can't help ourselves. Despair is succeeded by a dull dazed sort of moody reverie, in which the crisis is wont to occur; and this then passes over into a milder pain, in which Nature is able to apply her remedies with effect.

It was in this stage of sad but beneficial pain that, some days later, Traugott again sat on the Carlsberg, gazing out as before upon the sea-waves and the grey misty clouds which had gathered over Hela; but he was not seeking as before to discover the destiny reserved for him in days to come; no, for all that he had hoped for, all that he had dimly dreamt of, had vanished. "Oh!" said he, "my call to art was a bitter, bitter deception. Felicia was the phantom who deluded me into the belief in that which never had any other existence but in the insane fancy of a fever-stricken mind. It's all over. I will give it all up, and go back—into my dungeon. I have made up my mind; I will go back." Traugott again went back to his work in the office, whilst the wedding-day with Christina was once more fixed. On the day before the wedding was to come off, Traugott was standing in Arthur's Hall, looking, not without a good deal of heart-rending sadness, at the fateful figures of the old burgomaster and his page, when his eye fell upon the broker to whom Berklinger was trying to sell his stock. Without pausing to think, almost mechanically in fact, he walked up to him and asked, "Did you happen to know the strikingly curious old man with the black curly beard who some time ago frequently used to be seen here along with a handsome youth?" "Why, to be sure I did," answered the broker; "that was the crack-brained old painter Gottfried Berklinger." "Then don't you know where he has gone to and where he is now living?" asked Traugott again. "Ay, that I do," replied the broker; "he has now for a long time been living quietly at Sorrento along with his daughter." "With his daughter Felicia?" asked Traugott so vehemently and so loudly that everybody turned round to look at him. "Why, yes," went on the broker calmly, "that was, you know, the pretty youth who always followed the old man about everywhere. Half Dantzic knew that he was a girl, notwithstanding that the crazy old fellow thought there was not a single soul could guess it. It had been prophesied to him that if his daughter were ever to get married he would die a shameful death; and accordingly he determined never to let anybody know anything about her, and so he passed her off everywhere as his son." Traugott stood like a statue; then he ran off through the streets—away out of the town-gates—into the open country, into the woods, loudly lamenting, "Oh! miserable wretch that I am! It was she—she, herself; I have sat beside her scores and hundreds of times—have breathed her breath—pressed her delicate hands—looked into her beautiful eyes—heard her sweet words—and now I have lost her! No; not lost I will follow her into the land of art. I acknowledge the finger of destiny. Away—away to Sorrento."

He hurried back home. Herr Elias Roos got in his way; Traugott laid hold of him and carried him along with him into the room. "I shall never marry Christina, never!" he screamed. "She looks like *Voluptas* (Pleasure) and *Luxuries* (Wantonness), and her hair is like that of *Ira* (Wrath), in the picture in Arthur's Hall. O Felicia! Felicia! My beautiful darling! Why do you stretch out your arms so longingly towards me? I am coming, I am coming. And now let me tell you, Herr Elias," he continued, again laying hold of the pale merchant, "you will never see me in your damned office again. What do I care for your cursed ledgers and day-books? I am a painter, ay, and a good painter too. Berklinger is my master, my father, my all, and you are nothing—nothing at all." And therewith he gave Herr Elias a good shaking. Herr Elias, however, began to shout at the top of his voice, "Help! help! Come here, folks! Help! My son-in-law's gone mad. My partner's in a raging fit Help! help!" Everybody came running out of the office. Traugott had released his hold upon Elias and now sank down exhausted in a chair. They all gathered round him; but when he suddenly leapt to his feet and cried with a wild look, "What do you all want?" they all hurried off out of the room in a string, Herr Elias in the middle.

Soon afterwards there was a rustling of a silk dress, and a voice asked, "Have you really gone crazed, my dear Herr Traugott, or are you only jesting?" It was Christina. "I am not the least bit crazed, my angel," replied Traugott, "nor is it one whit truer that I am jesting. Pray compose yourself, my dear, but our wedding won't come off to-morrow; I shall never marry you, neither to-morrow, nor at any other time." "There is not the least need of it," said Christina very calmly. "I have not been particularly pleased with you for some time, and some one I know will value it far differently if he may only lead home as his bride the rich and pretty Miss Christina Roos. Adieu!" Therewith she rustled off. "She means the book-keeper," thought Traugott. As soon as he had calmed down somewhat he went to Herr Elias and explained to him in convincing terms that he need not expect to have him either as his son-in-law or as his partner in the business. Herr Elias reconciled himself to the inevitable; and repeated with downright honest joy in the office again and again that he thanked God to have got rid of that crazy-headed Traugott—even after the latter was a long, long way distant from Dantzic.

On at length arriving at the longed-for country, Traugott found a new life awaiting him, bright and brilliant. At Rome he was introduced to the circle of the German colony of painters and shared in their studies. Thus it came to pass that he stayed there longer than would seem to have been permissible in the face of his longing to find Felicia again, by which he had hitherto been so restlessly urged onwards. But his longing was now grown weaker; it shaped itself in his heart like a fascinating dream, whose misty shimmer enveloped his life on all sides, so that he believed that all he did and thought, and all his artistic practice, were turned towards the higher supernatural regions of blissful intuitions. All the female figures which his now experienced artistic skill enabled him to create bore lovely Felicia's features. The young painters were greatly struck by the exquisitely beautiful face, the original of which they in vain sought to find in Rome; they overwhelmed Traugott with multitudes of questions as to where he had seen the beauty. Traugott however was very shy of telling of his singular adventure in Dantzic, until at last, after the lapse of several months, an old Königsberg friend, Matuszewski by name, who had come to Rome to devote himself entirely to art, declared joyfully that he had seen there—in Rome, the girl whom Traugott copied in all his pictures. Traugott's wild delight may be imagined. He no longer concealed what it was that had attracted him so strongly to art, and urged him on with such irresistible power into Italy; and his Dantzic adventure proved so singular and so attractive that they all promised to search eagerly for the lost loved one.

Matuszewski's efforts were the most successful. He had soon found out where the girl lived, and discovered moreover that she really was the daughter of a poor old painter, who just at that period was busy putting a new coat on the walls of the church Trinita del Monte. All these things agreed nicely. Traugott at once hastened to the church in question along with Matuszewski; and in the painter, whom he saw working up on a very high scaffolding, he really thought he recognised old Berklinger. Thence the two friends hurried off to the old man's dwelling, without having been noticed by him. "It is she," cried Traugott, when he saw the painter's daughter standing on the balcony, occupied with some sort of feminine work. "Felicia, my Felicia!" he exclaimed aloud in his joy, as he burst into the room. The girl looked up very much alarmed. She had Felicia's features; but it was not Felicia. In his bitter disappointment poor Traugott's wounded heart was rent as if from innumerable dagger-thrusts. In a few words Matuszewski explained all to the girl. In her pretty shy confusion, with her cheeks deep crimson, and her eyes cast down upon the ground, she made a marvellously attractive picture to look at; and Traugott, whose first impulse had been quickly to retire, nevertheless, after casting but a single pained glance at her, remained standing where he was, as though held fast by silken bonds. His friend was not backward in saying all sorts of complimentary things to pretty Dorina, and so helped her to recover from the constraint and embarrassment into which she had been thrown by the extraordinary manner of their entrance. Dorina raised the "dark fringed curtains of her eyes" and regarded the stranger with a sweet smile, and said that her father would soon come home from his work, and would be very pleased to see some German painters, for he esteemed them very highly. Traugott was obliged to confess that, exclusive of Felicia, no girl had ever excited such a warm interest in him as Dorina did. She was in fact almost a second Felicia; the only differences were that Dorina's features seemed to him less delicate and more sharply cut, and her hair was darker. It was the same picture, only painted by Raphael instead of by Rubens.

It was not long before the old gentleman came in; and Traugott now plainly saw that he had been greatly misled by the height of the scaffolding in the church, on which the old man had stood. Instead of his being the strong Berklinger, he was a thin, mean-looking little old man, timid and crushed by poverty. A deceptive accidental light in the church had given his clean-shaved chin an appearance similar to Berklinger's black curly beard. In conversing about art matters the old man unfolded considerable ripe practical knowledge; and Traugott made up his mind to cultivate his acquaintance; for though his introduction to the family had been so painful, their society now began to exercise a more and more agreeable influence upon him.

Dorina, the incarnation of grace and child-like ingenuousness, plainly allowed her preference for the young German painter to be seen. And Traugott warmly returned her affection. He grew so accustomed to the society of the pretty child (she was but fifteen), that he often spent the whole day with the little family; his studio he transferred to the spacious apartment which stood empty next their rooms; and finally he established himself in the family itself. Hence he was able of his prosperity to do much in a delicate way to relieve their straitened circumstances; and the old man could not very well think otherwise than that Traugott would marry Dorina; and he even said so to him without reservation. This put Traugott in no little consternation: for he now distinctly recollected the object of his journey, and perceived where it seemed likely to end. Felicia again stood before his eyes instinct with life; but, on the other hand, he felt that he could not leave Dorina. His vanished darling he could not, for some extraordinary reason, conceive of as being his wife. She was pictured in his imagination as an intellectual vision, that he could neither lose nor win. Oh! to be immanent in his beloved intellectually for ever! never to have her and own her physically! But Dorina was often in his thoughts as his dearly loved wife; and as often as he contemplated the idea of again binding himself in the indissoluble bonds of betrothal, he felt a delicious tremor run through him and a gentle warmth pervade his veins; and yet he regarded it as unfaithfulness to his first love. Thus Traugott's heart was the scene of contest between the most contradictory feelings; he could not make up his mind what to do. He avoided the old painter; and *he* accordingly feared Traugott intended to receive his dear child. He had moreover already spoken of Traugott's wedding as a settled thing; and it was only under this impression that he had tolerated Dorina's familiar intimacy with Traugott, which otherwise would have given the girl an ill name. The blood of the Italian boiled within him, and one day he roundly declared to Traugott that he must either marry Dorina or leave him, for he would not tolerate this familiar intercourse an hour longer. Traugott was tormented by the keenest annoyance as well as by the bitterest vexation. The old man he viewed in the light of a vile match-maker; his own actions and behaviour were contemptible; and that he had ever deserted Felicia he now judged to be sinful and abominable. His heart was sore wounded at parting from Dorina; but with a violent effort he tore himself free from the sweet bonds. He hastened away to Naples, to Sorrento.

He spent a whole year in making the strictest inquiries after Berklinger and Felicia; but all was in vain; nobody knew anything about them. The sole gleam of intelligence that he could find was a vague sort of presumption, which was founded merely upon the tradition that an old German painter had been seen in Sorrento several years before—and that was all. After being driven backwards and forwards like a boat on the restless sea, Traugott at length came to a stand in Naples; and in proportion as his industry in art pursuits again awakened, the longing for Felicia which he cherished in his bosom grew softer and milder. But he never saw any pretty girl, if she was the least like Dorina in figure, movement, or bearing, without feeling most bitterly the loss of the dear sweet child. Yet when he was painting he never thought of Dorina, but always of Felicia; she continued to be his constant ideal.

At length he received letters from his native town. Herr Elias Roos had departed this life, his business agent wrote, and Traugott's presence was required in order to settle matters with the book-keeper, who had married Miss Christina and undertaken the business. Traugott hurried back to Dantzic by the shortest route.

Again he was standing in Arthur's Hall, leaning against the granite pillar, opposite the burgomaster and the page; he dwelt upon the wonderful adventure which had had such a painful influence upon his life; and, a prey to deep and hopeless sadness, he stood and looked with a set fixed gaze upon the youth, who greeted him with living eyes, as it were, and whispered in a sweet and charming voice, "And so you could not desert me then after all?"

"Can I believe my eyes? Is it really your own respected self come back again safe and sound, and quite cured of your unpleasant melancholy?" croaked a voice near Traugott. It was the well-known broker. "I have not found her," escaped Traugott involuntarily. "Whom do you mean? Whom has your honour not found?" asked the broker. "The painter Godofredus Berklinger and his daughter Felicia," rejoined Traugott. "I have searched all Italy for them; not a soul knew anything about them in Sorrento." This made the broker open his eyes and stare at him, and he stammered, "Where do you say you have searched for Berklinger and Felicia? In Italy? in Naples? in Sorrento?" "Why, yes; to be sure," replied Traugott, very testily. Whereupon the broker struck his hands together several times in succession, crying as he did so, "Did you ever now? Did you ever hear tell of such a thing? But

Herr Traugott! Herr Traugott!" "Well, what is there to be so much astonished at?" rejoined Traugott, "don't behave in such a foolish fashion, pray. Of course a man will travel as far as Sorrento for his sweetheart's sake. Yes, yes; I loved Felicia and followed her." But the broker skipped about on one foot, and continued to say, "Well, now, did you ever? did you ever?" until Traugott placed his hand earnestly upon his arm and asked, "Come, tell me then, in heaven's name! what is it that you find so extraordinary?" The broker began, "But, my good Herr Traugott, do you mean to say you don't know that Herr Aloysius Brandstetter, our respected town-councillor and the senior of our guild, calls his little villa, in that small fir-wood at the foot of Carlsberg, in the direction of Conrad's Hammer, by the name of Sorrento? He bought Berklinger's pictures of him and took the old man and his daughter into his house, that is, out to Sorrento. And there they lived for several years; and if you, my respected Herr Traugott, had only gone and planted your own two feet on the middle of the Carlsberg, you could have had a view right into the garden, and could have seen Miss Felicia walking about there dressed in curious old-German style, like the women in those pictures—there was no need for you to go to Italy. Afterwards the old man—but that is a sad story" "Never mind; go on," said Traugott, hoarsely. "Yes," continued the broker. "Young Brandstetter came back from England, saw Miss Felicia, and fell in love with her. Coming unexpectedly upon the young lady in the garden, he fell upon his knees before her in romantic fashion, and swore that he would wed her and deliver her from the tyrannical slavery in which her father kept her. Close behind the young people, without their having observed it, stood the old man; and the very self-same moment in which Felicia said, 'I will be yours,' he fell down with a stifled scream, and was dead as a door nail. It's said he looked very very hideous—all blue and bloody, because he had by some inexplicable means burst an artery. After that Miss Felicia could not bear young Brandstetter at all, and at last she married Mathesius, criminal and aulic counsellor, of Marienwerder. Your honour, as an old flame, should go and see the *Frau Kriminalräthin*. Marienwerder is not so far, you know, as your real Italian Sorrento. The good lady is said to be very comfortable and to have enriched the world with divers children."

Silent and crushed, Traugott hastened from the Hall. This issue of his adventure filled him with awe and dread. "No, it is not she—it is not she!" he cried. "It is not Felicia, that divine image which enkindled an infinite longing in my bosom, whom I followed into yon distant land, seeing her before me everywhere where I went like my star of fortune, twinkling and glittering with sweet hopes. Felicia—*Kriminalräthin* Mathesius! Ha! Ha! Ha!—*Kriminalräthin* Mathesius!" Traugott, shaken by extreme sensations of misery, laughed aloud and hastened in his usual way through the Oliva Gate along the Langfuhr to the Carlsberg. He looked down into Sorrento, and the tears gushed from his eyes. "Oh!" he cried, "Oh! how deep, how incurably deep an injury, O thou eternal ruling Power, does thy bitter irony inflict upon poor man's soft heart! But no, no! But why should the child cry over the incurable pain when instead of enjoying the light and warmth he thrusts his hand into the flames? Destiny visibly laid its hand upon me, but my dimmed vision did not recognise the higher nature at work; and I had the presumption to delude myself with the idea that the forms, created by the old master and mysteriously awakened to life, which stepped down to meet me, were my own equals, and that I could draw them down into the miserable transitoriness of earthly existence. No, no, Felicia, I have never lost you; you are and will be mine for ever, for you yourself are the creative artistic power dwelling within me. Now,—and only now have I first come to know you. What have you—what have I to do with the *Kriminalräthin* Mathesius? I fancy, nothing at all."

"Neither did I know what you should have to do with her, my respected Herr Traugott," a voice broke in. Traugott awakened out of his dream. Strange to say, he found himself, without knowing how he got there, again leaning against the granite pillar in Arthur's Hall. The person who had spoken the abovementioned words was Christina's husband. He handed to Traugott a letter that had just arrived from Rome. Matuszewski wrote:—

"Dorina is prettier and more charming than ever, only pale with longing for you, my dear friend. She is expecting you every hour, for she is most firmly convinced that you could never be untrue to her. She loves you with all her heart. When shall we see you again?"

"I am very pleased that we settled all our business this morning," said Traugott to Christina's husband after he had read this, "for to-morrow I set out for Rome, where my bride is most anxiously longing for me."

Weird Tales, Vol. II.
THE DOGE AND DOGESS

This was the title that distinguished in the art-catalogue of the works exhibited by the Berlin Academy of Arts in September, 1816, a picture which came from the brush of the skilful clever Associate of the Academy, C. Kolbe. There was such a peculiar charm in the piece that it attracted all observers. A Doge, richly and magnificently dressed, and a Dogess at his side, as richly adorned with jewellery, are stepping out on to a balustered balcony; *he* is an old man, with a grey beard and rusty red face, his features indicating a peculiar blending of expressions, now revealing strength, now weakness, again pride and arrogance, and again pure good-nature; *she* is a young woman, with a far-away look of yearning sadness and dreamy aspiration not only in her eyes but also in her general bearing. Behind them is an elderly lady and a man holding an open sun-shade. At one end of the balcony is a young man blowing a conch-shaped horn, whilst in front of it a richly decorated gondola, bearing the Venetian flag and having two gondoliers, is rocking on the sea. In the background stretches the sea itself studded with hundreds and hundreds of sails, whilst the towers and palaces of magnificent Venice are seen rising out of its waves. To the left is Saint Mark's, to the right, more in the front, San Giorgio Maggiore. The following words were cut in the golden frame of the picture.

Ah! senza amare,
Andare sul mare
Col sposo del mare,
Non puo consolare.
To go on the sea
With the spouse of the sea,
When loveless I be,
Is no comfort to me.

One day there arose before this picture a fruitless altercation as to whether the artist really intended it for anything more than a mere picture, that is, the temporary situation, sufficiently indicated by the verse, of a decrepit old man who with all his splendour and magnificence is unable to satisfy the desires of a heart filled with yearning aspirations, or whether he intended to represent an actual historical event. One after the other the visitors left the place, tired of the discussion, so that at length there were only two men left, both very good friends to the noble art of painting. "I can't understand," said one of them, "how people can spoil all their enjoyment by eternally hunting after some jejune interpretation or explanation. Independently of the fact that I have a pretty accurate notion of what the relations in life between this Doge and Dogess were, I am more particularly struck by the subdued richness and power that characterises the picture as a whole. Look at this flag with the winged lions, how they flutter in the breeze as if they swayed the world. O beautiful Venice!" He began to recite Turandot's riddle of Lion of the Adriatic, "*Dimmi, qual sia quella terribil fera*," &c. He had hardly come to the end when a sonorous masculine voice broke in with Calaf's solution, "*Tu quadrupede fera*," &c. Unobserved by the friends, a man of tall and noble appearance, his grey mantle thrown picturesquely across his shoulder, had taken up a position behind them, and was examining the picture with sparkling eyes. They got into conversation, and the stranger said almost in atone of solemnity, "It is indeed a singular mystery, how a picture often arises in the mind of an artist, the figures of which, previously indistinguishable, incorporate mist driving about in empty space, first seem to shape themselves into vitality in his mind, and there seem to find their home. Suddenly the picture connects itself with the past, or even with the future, representing something that has really happened or that will happen. Perhaps it was not known to Kolbe himself that the persons he was representing in this picture are none other than the Doge Marino Falieriand his lady Annunciata."

The stranger paused, but the two friends urgently entreated him to solve for them this riddle as he had solved that of the Lion of the Adriatic. Whereupon he replied, "If you have patience, my inquisitive sirs, I will at once explain the picture to you by telling you Falieri's history. But have you patience? I shall be very circumstantial, for I cannot speak otherwise of things which stand so life-like before my eyes that I seem to have seen them myself. And that may very well be the case, for all historians--amongst whom I happen to be one--are properly a kind of talking ghost of past ages."

The friends accompanied the stranger into a retired room, when, without further preamble, he began as follows:--

It is now a long time ago, and if I mistake not, it was in the month of August, 1354, that the valiant Genoese captain, Paganino Doria by name, utterly routed the Venetians and took their town of Parenzo. And his well-manned galleys were now cruising backwards and forwards in the Lagune, close in front of Venice, like ravenous beasts of prey which, goaded by hunger, roam restlessly up and down spying out where they may most safely pounce upon their victims; and both people and seignory were panic-stricken with fear. All the male population, liable to military service, and everybody who could lift an arm, flew to their weapons or seized an oar. The harbour of Saint Nicholas was the gathering-place for the bands. Ships and trees were sunk, and chains riveted to chains, to lock the harbour-mouth against the enemy. Whilst there was heard the rattle of arms and the wild tumult of preparation, and whilst the ponderous masses thundered down into the foaming sea, on the Rialto the agents of the seignory were wiping the cold sweat from their pale brows, and with troubled countenances and hoarse voices offering almost fabulous percentage for ready money, for the straitened republic was in want of this necessary also. Moreover, it was determined by the inscrutable decree of Providence that just at this period of extreme distress and anxiety, the faithful shepherd should be taken away from his troubled flock. Completely borne down by the burden of the public calamity, the Doge Andrea Dandolo died; the people called him the "dear good count" (*il caro contino*), because he was always cordial and kind, and never crossed Saint Mark's Square without speaking a word of comfort to those in need of good advice, or giving a few sequins to those who were in want of money. And as every blow is wont to fall with double sharpness upon those who are discouraged by misfortune, when at other times they would hardly have felt it at all, so now, when the people heard the bells of Saint Mark's proclaim in solemn muffled tones the death of their Duke, they were utterly undone with sorrow and grief. Their support, their hope, was now gone, and they would have to bend their necks to the Genoese yoke, they cried, in despite of the fact that Dandolo's loss did not seem to have any very counteractive effect upon the progress that was being made with all necessary warlike preparations. The "dear good count" had loved to live in peace and quietness, preferring to follow the wondrous courses of the stars rather than the problematical complications of state policy; he understood how to arrange a procession on Easter Day better than how to lead an army.

The object now was to elect a Doge who, endowed at one and the same time with the valour and genius of a war captain, and with skill in statecraft, should save Venice, now tottering on her foundations, from the threatening power of her bold and ever-bolder enemy. But when the senators assembled there was none but what had a gloomy face, hopeless looks, and head bent earthwards and resting on his supporting hand. Where were they to find a man who could seize the unguided helm and direct the bark of the state aright? At last the oldest of the councillors, called Marino Bodoeri, lifted up his voice and said, "You will not find him here around us, or amongst us; direct your eyes to Avignon, upon Marino Falieri, whom we sent to congratulate Pope Innocent on his elevation to the Papal dignity; he can find better work to do now; he's the man for us; let us choose him Doge to stem this current of adversity. You will urge by way of objection that he is now almost eighty years old, that his hair and beard are white as silver, that his blithe appearance, fiery eye, and the deep red of his nose and cheeks are to be ascribed, as his traducers maintain, to good Cyprus wine rather than to energy of character; but heed not that. Remember what conspicuous bravery this Marino Falieri showed as admiral of the fleet in the Black Sea, and bear in mind the great services which prevailed with the Procurators of Saint Mark to invest this Falieri with the rich countship of Valdemarino." Thus highly did Bodoeri extol Falieri's virtues; and he had a ready answer for all objections, so that at length all voices were unanimous in electing Falieri. Several, however, still continued to allude to his hot, passionate temper, his ambition, and his self-will; but they were met with the reply: "And it is exactly because all these have gone from the old man, that we choose the *grey-beard* Falieri and not the *youth* Falieri." And these censuring voices were completely silenced when the people, learning upon whom the choice had fallen, greeted it with the loudest and most extravagant demonstrations of delight. Do we not know that in such dangerous times, in times of such tension and unrest, any resolution that really is a resolution is accepted as an inspiration from Heaven? Thus it came to pass that the "dear good count" and all his gentleness and piety were forgotten, and every one cried, "By Saint Mark, this Marino ought long ago to have been our Doge, and then we should not have yon arrogant Doria before our very doors." And crippled soldiers painfully lifted up their wounded arms and cried, "That is Falieri who beat the Morbassan--the valiant captain whose victorious banners waved in the Black Sea." Wherever a knot of people gathered, there was one amongst them telling of Falieri's heroic deeds; and, as though Doria were already defeated, the air rang with wild shouts of triumph. An additional reason for this was that Nicolo Pisani who, Heaven knows why! instead of going to meet Doria with his fleet, had coolly sailed away to Sardinia, was now returned. Doria withdrew from the Lagune; and what was really due to the approach of Pisani's fleet was ascribed to the formidable name of Marino Falieri. Then the people and the seignory were seized by a kind of frantic ecstasy that such an auspicious choice had been made; and as an uncommon way of testifying the same, it was determined to welcome the newly elected Doge as if he were a messenger from heaven bringing honour, victory, and abundance of riches. Twelve nobles, each accompanied by a numerous retinue in rich dresses, had been sent by the Seignory to Verona, where the ambassadors of the Republic were again to announce to Falieri, on his arrival, with all due ceremony, his elevation to the supreme office in the state. Then fifteen richly decorated vessels of state, equipped by the Podesta of Chioggia, and under the command of his own son Taddeo Giustiniani, took the Doge and his attendant company on board at Chiozza; and now they moved on like the triumphal procession of a most mighty and victorious monarch to St. Clement's, where the Bucentaur was awaiting the Doge.

At this very moment, namely, when Marino Falieri was about to set foot on board the Bucentaur,--and that was on the evening of the 3d of October about sunset--a poor unfortunate man lay stretched at full length on the hard marble pavement in front of the Customhouse. A few rags of striped linen, of a colour now no longer recognisable, the remains of what apparently had once been a sailor's dress, such as was worn by the very poorest of the people--porters and assistant oarsmen, hung about his lean starved body. There was not a trace of a shirt to be seen, except the poor fellow's own skin, which peeped through his rags almost everywhere, and was so white and delicate that the very noblest need not have been shy or ashamed of it Accordingly, his leanness only served to display more fully the perfect proportions of his well-knit frame. A careful scrutiny of the unfortunate's light-chestnut hair, now hanging all tangled and dishevelled about his exquisitely beautiful forehead, his blue eyes dimmed with extreme misery, his Roman nose, his fine formed lips--he seemed to be not more than twenty years old at the most--inevitably suggested that he was of good birth, and had by some adverse turn of fortune been thrown amongst the meanest classes of the people.

As remarked, the youth lay in front of the pillars of the Custom-house, his head resting on his right arm, and his eyes riveted in a vacant stare upon the sea, without movement or change of posture. An observer might well have fancied that he was devoid of life, or that death had fixed him there whilst turning him into an image of stone, had not a deep sigh escaped him from time to time, as if wrung from him by unutterable pain. And they were in fact occasioned by the pain of his left arm, which had apparently been seriously wounded, and was lying stretched out on the pavement, wrapped up in bloody rags.

All labour had ceased; the hum of trade was no longer heard; all Venice, in thousands of boats and gondolas, was gone out to meet the much-lauded Falieri. Hence it was that the unhappy youth was sighing away his pain in utter helplessness. But just as his weary head fell back upon the pavement, and he seemed on the point of fainting, a hoarse and very querulous voice cried several times in succession, "Antonio, my dear Antonio." At length Antonio painfully raised himself partly up; and, turning his head towards the pillars of the Custom- house, whence the voice seemed to proceed, he replied very faintly, and in a scarce intelligible voice, "Who is calling me? Who has come to cast my dead body into the sea, for it will soon be all over with me." Then a little shrivelled wrinkled crone came up panting and coughing, hobbling along by the aid of her staff; she approached the wounded youth, and squatting down beside him, she burst out into a most repulsive chuckling and laughing. "You foolish child, you foolish child," whispered the old woman, "are you going to perish here--will you stay here to die, while a golden fortune is waiting for you? Look yonder, look yonder at yon blazing fire in the west; there are sequins for you! But you must eat, dear Antonio, eat and drink; for it's only hunger which has made you fall down here on this cold pavement. Your arm is now quite well again, yes, that it is." Antonio recognised in the old crone the singular beggar-woman who was generally to be seen on the steps of the Franciscan Church, chuckling to herself and laughing, and soliciting alms from the worshippers; he himself, urged by some inward inexplicable propensity, had often thrown her a hard-earned penny, which he had not had to spare. "Leave me, leave me in peace, you insane old woman," he said; "but you are right, it is hunger more than my wound which has made me weak and miserable; for three days I have not earned a farthing. I wanted to go over to the monastery and see if I could get a spoonful or two of the soup that is made for invalids; but all my companions have gone; there is not one to have compassion upon me and take me in his *barca*; and now I have fallen down here, and shall, I expect, never get up again." "Hi! hi! hi! hi!" chuckled the old woman; "why do you begin to despair so soon? Why lose heart so quickly? You are thirsty and hungry, but I can help you. Here are a few fine dried fish which I bought only to-day in the Mint; here is lemon-juice and a piece of nice white bread; eat, my son; and then we will look at the wounded arm." And the old woman proceeded to bring forth fish, bread, and lemon juice from the bag which hung like a hood down her back, and also projected right above her bent head. As soon as Antonio had moistened his parched and burning lips with the cool drink, he felt the pangs of hunger return with double fury, and he greedily devoured the bread and the fish.

Meanwhile the old woman was busy unwrapping the rags from his wounded arm, and it was found that, though it was badly crushed, the wound was progressing favourably towards healing. The old woman took a salve out of a little box and warmed it with the breath of her mouth, and as she rubbed it on the wound she asked, "But who then has given you such a nasty blow, my poor boy?" Antonio was so refreshed and charged anew with vital energy that he had raised himself completely up; his eyes flashed, and he shook his doubled fist above his head, crying, "Oh! that rascal Nicolo; he tried to maim me, because he envies me every wretched penny that any generous hand bestows upon me. You know, old dame, that I barely managed to hold body and soul together by helping to carry bales of goods from ships and freight-boats to the *dépôt* of the Germans, the so-called Fontego-- of course you know the building"--Directly Antonio uttered the word Fontego, the old woman began to chuckle and laugh most abominably, and to mumble, "Fontego-- Fontego--Fontego." "Have done with your insane laughing if I am to go on with my story," added Antonio angrily. At once the old woman grew quiet, and Antonio continued, "after a time I saved a little bit of money, and bought a new jerkin, so that I looked quite fine; and then I got enrolled amongst the gondoliers. As I was always in a blithe humour, worked hard, and knew a great many good songs, I soon earned a good deal more than the rest. This, however, awakened my comrades' envy. They blackened my character to my master, so that he turned me adrift; and everywhere where I went or where I stood they cried after me, 'German cur! Cursed heretic!' Three days ago, as I was helping to unload a boat near St. Sebastian, they fell upon me with sticks and stones. I defended myself stoutly, but that malicious Nicolo dealt me a blow with his oar, which grazed my head and severely injured my arm, and knocked me on the ground. Ay, you've given me a good meal, old woman, and I am sure I feel that your salve has done my arm a world of good. See, I can already move it easily--now I shall be able to row bravely again." Antonio had risen up from the ground, and was swinging his arm violently backwards and forwards, but the old woman again fell to chuckling and laughing loudly, whilst she hobbled round about him in the most extraordinary fashion--dancing with short tripping steps as it were--and she cried, "My son, my good boy, my good lad--row on bravely--he is coming--he is coming. The gold is shining red in the bright flames. Row on stoutly, row on; but only once more, only once more; and then never again."

But Antonio was not paying the slightest heed to the old woman's words, for the most splendid of spectacles was unfolding itself before his eyes. The Bucentaur, with the Lion of the Adriatic on her fluttering standard, was coming along from St. Clement's to the measured stroke of the oars like a mighty winged golden swan. Surrounded by innumerable *barcas* and gondolas, and with her head proudly and boldly raised, she appeared like a princess commanding a triumphing army, that had emerged from the depths of the sea, wearing bright and gaily decked helmets. The evening sun was sending down his fiery rays upon the sea and upon Venice, so that everything appeared to have been plunged into a bath of blazing fire; but whilst Antonio, completely forgetful of all his unhappiness, was standing gazing with wonder and delight, the gleams of the sun grew more bloody and more bloody. The wind whistled shrilly and harshly, and a hollow threatening echo came rolling in from the open sea outside. Down burst the storm in the midst of black clouds, and enshrouded all in thick darkness, whilst the waves rose higher and higher, pouring in from the thundering sea like foaming hissing monsters, threatening to engulf everything. The gondolas and *barcas* were driven in all directions like scattered feathers. The Bucentaur, unable to resist the storm owing to its flat bottom, was yawing from side to side. Instead of the jubilant notes of trumpets and cornets, there was heard through the storm the anxious cries of those in distress.

Antonio gazed upon the scene like one stupefied, without sense and motion. But then there came a rattling of chains immediately in front of him; he looked down, and saw a little canoe, which was chained to the wall, and was being tossed up and down by the waves; and a thought entered his mind like a flash of lightning. He leaped into the canoe, unfastened it, seized the oar which he found in it, and pushed out boldly and confidently into the sea, directly towards the Bucentaur. The nearer he came to it the more distinctly could he hear shouts for help. "Here, here, come here--save the Doge, save the Doge." It is well known that little fisher-canoes are safer and better to manage in the Lagune when it is stormy than are larger boats; and accordingly these little craft were hastening from all sides to the rescue of Marino Falieri's invaluable person. But it is an invariable principle in life that the Eternal Power reserves every bold deed as a brilliant success to the one specially chosen for it, and hence all others have all their pains for nothing. And as on this occasion it was poor Antonio who was destined to achieve the rescue of the newly elected Doge, he alone succeeded in working his way on to the Bucentaur in his little insignificant fisher-canoe. Old Marino Falieri, familiar with such dangers, stepped firmly, without a moment's hesitation, from the sumptuous but treacherous Bucentaur into poor Antonio's little craft, which, gliding smoothly over the raging waves like a dolphin, brought him in a few minutes to St. Mark's Square. The old man, his clothing saturated with wet, and with large drops of sea-spray in his grey beard, was conducted into the church, where the nobles with blanched faces concluded the ceremonies connected with the Doge's public entry. But the people, as well as the seignory, confounded by this unfortunate *contretemps*, to which was also added the fact that the Doge, in the hurry and confusion, had been led between the two columns where common malefactors were generally executed, grew silent in the midst of their triumph, and thus the day that had begun in festive fashion ended in gloom and sadness.

Nobody seemed to think about the Doge's rescuer; nor did Antonio himself think about it, for he was lying in the peristyle of the Ducal Palace, half dead with fatigue, and fainting with the pain caused by his wound, which had again burst open. He was therefore all the more surprised when just before midnight a Ducal halberdier took him by the shoulders, saying, "Come along, friend," and led him into the palace, where he pushed him into the Duke's chamber. The old man came to meet him with a kindly smile, and said, pointing to a couple of purses lying on the table, "You have borne yourself bravely, my son. Here; take these three thousand sequins, and if you want more ask for them; but have the goodness never to come into my presence again." As he said these last words the old man's eyes flashed with fire, and the tip of his nose grew a darker red Antonio could not fathom the old man's mind; he did not, however, trouble himself overmuch about it, but with some little difficulty took up the purses, which he believed he had honestly and rightly earned.

Next morning old Falieri, conspicuous in the splendours of his newly acquired dignity, stood in one of the lofty bay windows of the palace, watching the bustling scene below, where the people were busy engaged in practising all kinds of weapons, when Bodoeri, who from the days when he was a youth had enjoyed the intimate and unchangeable friendship of the Doge, entered the apartment. As, however, the Doge was quite wrapped up in himself and his dignity, and did not appear to notice his entrance, Bodoeri clapped his hands together and cried with a loud laugh, "Come, Falieri, what are all these sublime thoughts that are being hatched and nourished in your mind since you first put the Doge's bent bonnet on?" Falieri, coming to himself like one awakening from a dream, stepped forward to meet his old friend with an air of forced amiability. He felt that he really owed his bonnet to Bodoeri, and the words of the latter seemed to be a reminder of the fact. But since every obligation weighed like a burden upon Falieri's proud ambitious spirit, and he could not dismiss the oldest member of the Council, and his tried friend to boot, as he had dismissed poor Antonio, he constrained himself to utter a few words of thanks, and immediately began to speak of the measures to be adopted to meet their enemy, who was now developing so great an activity in every direction. Bodoeri interrupted him and said, cunningly smiling, "That, and all else that the state demands of you, we will maturely weigh and consider an hour or two hence in a full meeting of the Great Council. I have not come to you thus early in order to invent a plan for defeating yon presumptuous Doria or bringing to reason Louis the Hungarian, who is again setting his longing eyes upon our Dalmatian seaports. No, Marino, I was thinking solely about you, and about what you perhaps would not guess-- your marriage." "How came you to think of such a thing as *that*?" replied the Doge, greatly annoyed; and rising to his feet, he turned his back upon Bodoeri and looked out of the window. "It's a long time to Ascension Day. By that time I hope the enemy will be routed, and that victory, honour, additional riches, and a wider extension of power will have been won for the sea-born lion of the Adriatic. The chaste bride shall find her bridegroom worthy of her." "Pshaw! pshaw!" interrupted Bodoeri, impatiently; "you are talking about that memorable ceremony on Ascension Day, when you will throw the gold ring from the Bucentaur into the waves under the impression that you are wedding the Adriatic Sea. But do you not know,--you, Marino, you, kinsman to the sea,--of any other bride than the cold, damp, treacherous element which you delude yourself into the belief that you rule, and which only yesterday revolted against you in such dangerous fashion? Marry, how can you fancy lying in the arms of such a bride of such a wild, wayward thing? Why when you only just skimmed her lips as you rode along in the Bucentaur she at once began to rage and storm. Would an entire Vesuvius of fiery passion suffice to warm the icy bosom of such a false bride as that? Continually faithless, she is wedded time after time, nor does she receive the ring as a treasured symbol of love, but she extorts it as a tribute from a slave? No, Marino, I was thinking of your marriage to the most beautiful child of the earth than can be found." "You are prating utter nonsense, utter nonsense, I tell you, old man," murmured Falieri without turning away from the window. "I, a grey-haired old man, eighty years of age, burdened with toil and trouble, who have never been married, and now hardly capable of loving"---- "Stop," cried Bodoeri, "don't slander yourself. Does not the Winter, however rough and cold he may be, at last stretch out his longing arms towards the beautiful goddess who comes to meet him borne by balmy western winds? And when he presses her to his benumbed bosom, when a gentle glow pervades his veins, where then is his ice and his snow? You say you are eighty years old; that is true; but do you measure old age then by years merely? Don't you carry your head as erect and walk with as firm a step as you did forty summers ago? Or do you perhaps feel that your strength is failing you, that you must carry a lighter sword, that you grow faint when you walk fast, or get short of breath when you ascend the steps of the Ducal Palace?" "No, by Heaven, no," broke in Falieri upon his friend, as he turned away from the window with an abrupt passionate movement and approached him, "no, I feel no traces of age upon me." "Well then," continued Bodoeri, "take deep draughts in your old age of all the delights of earth which are now destined for you. Elevate the woman whom I have chosen for you to be your Dogess; and then all the ladies of Venice will be constrained to admit that she stands first of all in beauty and in virtue, even as the Venetians recognise in you their captain in valour, intellect, and power."

Bodoeri now began to sketch the picture of a beautiful woman, and in doing so he knew how to mix his colours so cleverly, and lay them on with so much vigour and effect, that old Falieri's eyes began to sparkle, and his face grew redder and redder, whilst he puckered up his mouth and smacked his lips as if he were draining sundry glasses of fiery Syracuse. "But who is this paragon of loveliness of whom you are speaking?" said he at last with a smirk. "I mean nobody else but my dear niece--it's she I mean," replied Bodoeri. "What! your niece?" interrupted

Falieri. "Why, she was married to Bertuccio Nenolo when I was Podesta of Treviso." "Oh! you are thinking about my niece Francesca," continued Bodoeri, "but it is her sweet daughter whom I intend for you. You know how rude, rough Nenolo was enticed to the wars and drowned at sea. Francesca buried her pain and grief in a Roman nunnery, and so I had little Annunciata brought up in strict seclusion at my villa in Treviso"---- "What!" cried Falieri, again impatiently interrupting the old man, "you mean me to raise your niece's daughter to the dignity of Dogess? How long is it since Nenolo was married? Annunciata must be a child--at the most only ten years old. When I was Podesta in Treviso, Nenolo had not even thought of marrying, and that's"---- "Twenty-five years ago," interposed Bodoeri, laughing; "come, you are getting all at sea with your memory of the flight of time, it goes so rapidly with you. Annunciata is a maiden of nineteen, beautiful as the sun, modest, submissive, inexperienced in love, for she has hardly ever seen a man. She will cling to you with childlike affection and unassuming devotion." "I will see her, I will see her," exclaimed the Doge, whose eyes again beheld the picture of the beautiful Annunciata which Bodoeri had sketched.

His desire was gratified the self-same day; for immediately he got back to his own apartments from the meeting of the Great Council, the crafty Bodoeri, who no doubt had many reasons for wishing to see his niece Dogess at Falieri's side, brought the lovely Annunciata to him secretly. Now, when old Falieri saw the angelic maiden, he was quite taken aback by her wonderful beauty, and was scarcely able to stammer out a few unintelligible words as he sued for her hand. Annunciata, no doubt well instructed by Bodoeri beforehand, fell upon her knees before the princely old man, her cheeks flushing crimson. She grasped his hand and pressed it to her lips, softly whispering, "O sir, will you indeed honour me by raising me to a place at your side on your princely throne? Oh! then I will reverence you from the depths of my soul, and will continue your faithful handmaiden as long as I have breath." Old Falieri was beside himself with happiness and delight. As Annunciata took his hand he felt a convulsive throb in every limb; and then his head and all his body began to tremble and totter to such a degree that he had to sink hurriedly into his great arm-chair. It seemed as if he were about to refute Bodoeri's good opinion as to the strength and toughness of his eighty summers. Bodoeri, in fact, could not keep back the peculiar smile that darted across his lips; innocent, un* sophisticated Annunciata observed nothing; and happily no one else was present Finally it was resolved for some reason--either because old Falieri felt in what an uncomfortable position he would appear in the eyes of the people as the betrothed of a maiden of nineteen, or because it occurred to him as a sort of presentiment that the Venetians, who were so prone to mockery, ought not to be so directly challenged to indulge in it, or because he deemed it better to say nothing at all about the critical period of betrothal--at any rate, it was resolved, with Bodoeri's consent, that the marriage should be celebrated with the greatest secrecy, and that then some days later the Dogess should be introduced to the seignory and the people as if she had been some time married to Falieri, and had just arrived from Treviso, where she had been staying during Falieri's mission to Avignon.

Let us now turn our eyes upon yon neatly dressed handsome youth who is going up and down the Rialto with his purse of sequins in his hand, conversing with Jews, Turks, Armenians, Greeks. He turns away his face with a frown, walks on further, stands still, turns round, and ultimately has himself rowed by a gondolier to St. Mark's Square. There he walks up and down with uncertain hesitating steps, his arms folded and his eyes bent upon the ground; nor does he observe, or even have any idea, that all the whispering and low coughing from various windows and various richly draped balconies are love-signals which are meant for him. Who would have easily recognised in this youth the same Antonio who a few days before had lain on the marble pavement in front of the Custom-house, poor, ragged, and miserable? "My dear boy! My dear golden boy, Antonio, good day, good day!" Thus he was greeted by the old beggar-woman, who sat on the steps leading to St. Mark's Church, and whom he was going past without observing. Turning abruptly round, he recognised the old woman, and, dipping his hand into his purse, took out a handful of sequins with the intention of throwing them to her. "Oh! keep your gold in your purse," chuckled and laughed the old woman; "what should I do with your money? am I not rich enough? But if you want to do me a kindness, get me a new hood made, for this which I am now wearing is no longer any protection against wind and weather. Yes, please get me one, my dear boy, my dear golden boy,--but keep away from the Fontego,--keep away from the Fontego." Antonio stared into the old woman's pale yellow face, the deep wrinkles in which twitched convulsively in a strange awe-inspiring way. And when she clapped her lean bony hands together so that the joints cracked, and continued her disagreeable laugh, and went on repeating in a hoarse voice, "Keep away from the Fontego," Antonio cried, "Can you not have done with that mad insane nonsense, you old witch?"

As Antonio uttered this word, the old woman, as if struck by a lightning-flash, came rolling down the high marble steps like a ball. Antonio leapt forward and grasped her by both hands, and so prevented her from falling heavily. "O my good lad, my good lad," said the old crone in a low, querulous voice, "what a hideous word that was which you uttered. Kill me rather than repeat that word to me again. Oh! you don't know how deeply you have cut me to the heart, me--who have such a true affection for you--no, you don't know"---- Abruptly breaking off, she wrapped up her head in the dark brown cloth flaps which covered her shoulders like a short mantle, and sighed and moaned as if suffering unspeakable pain. Antonio felt his heart strangely moved; lifting up the old woman, he carried her up into the vestibule of the church, and set her down upon one of the marble benches which were there. "You have been kind to me, old woman," he began, after he had liberated her head from the ugly cloth flaps, "you have been kind to me, since it is to you that I really owe all my prosperity; for if you had not stood by me in the hour of need, I should long ere this have been at the bottom of the sea, nor should I have rescued the old Doge, and received these good sequins. But even if you had not shown that kindness to me, I yet feel that I should have a special liking for you as long as I live, in spite of the fact that your insane behaviour-- chuckling and laughing so horribly--strikes my heart with awe. To tell you the truth, old dame, even when I had hard work to get a living by carrying merchandise and rowing, I always felt as if I must work still harder that I might have a few pence to give you." "O son of my heart, my golden Tonino," cried the old woman, raising her shrivelled arms above her head, whilst her staff fell rattling on the marble floor and rolled away from her, "O Tonino mine, I know it; yes, I know it; you must cling to me with all your soul, you may do as you will, for--but hush! hush! hush!" The old woman stooped painfully down in order to reach her staff, but Antonio picked it up and handed it to her.

Leaning her sharp chin on her staff, and riveting her eyes in a set stare upon the ground, she began to speak in a reserved but hollow voice, "Tell me, my child, have you no recollection at all of any former time, of what you did or where you were before you found yourself here, a poor wretch hardly able to keep body and soul together?" With a deep sigh, Antonio took his seat beside the old crone and then began, "Alas! mother, only too well do I know that I was born of parents living in the most prosperous circumstances; but who they were and how I came to leave them, of this I have not the slightest notion, nor could I have. I remember very well a tall handsome man, who often took me in his arms and smothered me with kisses and put sweets in my mouth. And I can also in the same way call to mind a pleasant and pretty lady, who used to dress and undress me and place me in a soft little bed every night, and who in fact was very kind to me in every way. They used to talk to me in a foreign, sonorous language, and I also stammered several words of the same tongue after them. Whilst I was an oarsman my jealous rivals used to say I must be of German origin, from the colour of my hair and eyes, and from my general build. And this I believe myself, for the language which that man spoke (he must have been my father) was German. But the most vivid recollection which I have of that time is that of one terrible night, when I was awakened out of deep sleep by a fearful scream of distress. People were running about the house; doors were being opened and banged to; I grew terribly frightened, and began to cry loudly. Then the lady who used to dress me and take care of me burst into the room, snatched me out of bed, stopped my mouth, enveloped me in shawls, and ran off with me. From that moment I can remember nothing more, until I found myself again in a splendid house, situated in a most charming district. Then there rises up the image of a man whom I called 'father,' a majestic man of noble but benevolent appearance. Like all the rest in the house, he spoke Italian.

"For several weeks I had not seen my father, when one day several ugly- looking strangers came and kicked up a great deal of noise in the house, rummaging about and turning out everything. When they saw me they asked who I was, and what I was doing there? 'Don't you know I'm Antonio, and belong to the house?' I replied; but they laughed in my face and tore off all my fine clothes and turned me out of doors, threatening to have me whipped if I dared to show myself again. I ran away screaming and crying. I had not gone a hundred yards from the house when I met an old man, whom I recognised as being one of my foster-father's servants. 'Come along, Antonio,' he said, taking hold of my hand, 'come along, my poor boy, that house is now closed to us both for ever. We must both look out and see how we can earn a crust of bread.'

"The old man brought me along with him here. He was not so poor as he seemed to be from his mean clothing. Directly we arrived I saw him rip up his jerkin and produce a bag of sequins; and he spent the whole day running about on the Rialto, now acting as broker, now dealing on his own account. I had always to be close at his heels; and whenever he had made a bargain he had a habit of begging a trifle for the *figliuolo* (little boy). Every one whom I looked boldly in the face was glad to pull out a few pence, which the old man pocketed with infinite satisfaction, affirming, as he stroked my cheeks, that he was saving it up to buy me a new jerkin. I was very comfortable with the old man, whom the people called Old Father Bluenose, though for what reason I don't know. But this life did not last long. You will remember that terrible time, old woman, when one day the earth began to tremble, and towers and palaces were shaken to their very foundations and began to reel and totter, and the bells to ring as if tolled by the arms of invisible giants. Hardly seven years have passed since that day. Fortunately I escaped along with my old man out of the house before it fell in with a crash behind us. There was no business doing; everybody on the Rialto seemed stunned, and everything lifeless. But this dreadful event was only the precursor of another approaching monster, which soon breathed out its poisonous breath over the town and the surrounding country. It was known that the pestilence, which had first made its way from the Levant into Sicily, was committing havoc in Tuscany. As yet Venice had been spared. One day Old Father Bluenose was dealing with an Armenian on the Rialto; they were agreed over their bargain, and warmly shook hands. Father Bluenose had sold the Armenian certain good wares at a very low price, and now asked for the usual trifle for the *figliuolo*. The stranger, a big stalwart man with a thick curly beard (I can see him now), bent a kind look upon me, and then kissed me, pressing a few sequins into my hand, which I hastily pocketed. We took a gondola to St. Mark's. On the way the old man asked me for the sequins, but for some reason or other, I don't know what induced me to do it, I maintained that I must keep them myself, since the Armenian had wished me to do so. The old man got angry; but whilst he was quarrelling with me I noticed a disagreeable dirty yellow colour spreading over his face, and that he was mixing up all sorts of incoherent nonsense in his talk. When we reached the Square he reeled about like a drunken man, until he fell to the ground in front of the Ducal Palace--dead. With a loud wail I threw myself upon the corpse. The people came running round us, but as soon as the dreaded cry 'The pestilence! the pestilence!' was heard, they scattered and flew apart in terror. At the same moment I was seized by a dull numbing pain, and my senses left me.

"When I awoke I found I was in a spacious room, lying on a plain mattress, and covered with a blanket. Round about me there were fully twenty or thirty other pale ghastly forms lying on similar mattresses. As I learned later, certain compassionate monks, who happened to be just coming out of St. Mark's, had, on finding signs of life in me, put me in a gondola and got me taken over to Giudecca into the monastery of San Giorgio Maggiore, where the Benedictines had established a hospital. How can I describe to you, old woman, this moment of re-awakening? The violence of the plague had completely robbed me of all recollections of the past. Just as if the spark of life had been suddenly dropped into a lifeless statue, I had but a momentary kind of existence, so to speak, linked on to nothing. You may imagine what trouble, what distress this life occasioned me in which my consciousness seemed to swim in empty space without an anchorage. All that the monks could tell me was that I had been found beside Father Bluenose, whose son I was generally accounted to be. Gradually and slowly I gathered my thoughts together, and tried to reflect upon my previous life, but what I have told you, old dame, is all that I can remember of it, and that consists only of certain individual disconnected pictures. Oh! this miserable being-alone-in-the-world! I can't be gay and happy, no matter what may happen!" "Tonino, my dear Tonino," said the old woman, "be contented with what the present moment gives you."

"Say no more, old woman, say no more," interrupted Antonio; "there is still something else which embitters my life, following me about incessantly everywhere; I know it will be the utter ruin of me in the end. An unspeakable longing,--a consuming aspiration for something,--I can neither say nor even conceive what it is--has taken complete possession of my heart and mind since I awoke to renewed life in the hospital. Whilst I was still poor and wretched, and threw myself down at night on my hard couch, weary and worn out by the hard heavy labour of the day, a dream used to come to me, and, fanning my hot brow with balmy rustling breezes, shed about my heart all the inexpressible bliss of some single happy moment, in which the Eternal Power had been pleased to grant me in thought a glimpse of the delights of heaven, and the memory of which was treasured up in the recesses of my soul I now rest on soft cushions, and no labour consumes my strength: but if I awaken out of a dream, or if in my waking hours the recollection of that great moment returns to my mind, I feel that the lonely wretched existence I lead is just as much an oppressive burden now as it was then, and that it is vain for me to try and shake it off. All my thinking and all my inquiries are fruitless; I cannot fathom what this glorious thing is which formerly happened in my life. Its mysterious and alas! to me, unintelligible echo, as it were, fills me with such great happiness; but will not this happiness pass over into the most agonising pain, and torture me to death, when I am obliged to acknowledge that all my hope of ever finding that unknown Eden again, nay, that even the courage to search for it, is lost? Can there indeed remain traces of that which has vanished without leaving any sign behind it?" Antonio ceased speaking, and a deep and painful sigh escaped his breast.

During his narrative the old crone had behaved like one who sympathised fully with his trouble, and felt all that he felt, and like a mirror reflected every movement and gesture which the pain wrung from him. "Tonino," she now began in a tearful voice, "my dear Tonino, do you mean to tell me that you let your courage sink because the remembrance of some glorious moment in your life has perished out of your mind? You foolish child! You foolish child! Listen to--hi! hi! hi!" The old woman began to chuckle and laugh in her usual disagreeable way, and to hop about on the marble floor. Some people came; she cowered down in her accustomed posture; they threw her alms. "Antonio--lead me away, Antonio--away to the sea," she croaked Almost involuntarily--he could not explain how it came about--he took her by the arm and led her slowly across St. Mark's Square. On the way the old woman muttered softly and solemnly, "Antonio, do you see these dark stains of blood here on the ground? Yes, blood--much blood--much blood everywhere! But, hi! hi! hi! Roses will spring up out of the blood--beautiful red roses for a wreath for you--for your sweetheart. O good Lord of all, what lovely angel of light is this, who is coming to meet you with such grace and such a bright starry smile? Her lily-white arms are stretched out to embrace you. O Antonio, you lucky, lucky lad! bear yourself bravely! bear yourself bravely! And at the sweet hour of sunset you may pluck myrtle-leaves--myrtle-leaves for the bride--for the maiden-widow--hi! hi! hi!

Myrtle-leaves plucked at the hour of sunset, but these will not be blossoms until midnight! Do you hear the whisperings of the night-winds? the longing moaning swell of the sea? Row away bravely, my bold oarsman, row away bravely!" Antonio's heart was deeply thrilled with awe as he listened to the old crone's wonderful words, which she mumbled to herself in a very peculiar and extraordinary way, mingled with an incessant chuckling.

They came to the pillar which bears the Lion of the Adriatic. The old woman was going on right past it, still muttering to herself; but Antonio, feeling very uncomfortable at the old crone's behaviour, and being, moreover, stared at in astonishment by the passers-by, stopped and said roughly, "Here--sit you down on these steps, old woman, and have done with your talk; it will drive me mad. It is a fact that you saw my sequins in the fiery images in the clouds; but, for that very reason, what do you mean by prating about angels of light--bride-- maiden-widow--roses and myrtle-leaves? Do you want to make a fool of me, you fearful woman, till some insane attempt hurries me to destruction? You shall have a new hood--bread--sequins--all that you want, but leave me alone." And he was about to make off hastily; but the old woman caught him by the mantle, and cried in a shrill piercing voice, "Tonino, my Tonino, do take a good look at me for once, or else I must go to the very edge of the Square yonder and in despair throw myself over into the sea." In order to avoid attracting more eyes upon him than he was already doing, Antonio actually stood still. "Tonino," went on the old woman, "sit down here beside me; my heart is bursting, I must tell you--Oh! do sit down here beside me." Antonio sat down on the steps, but so as to turn his back upon her; and he took out his account-book, whose white pages bore witness to the zeal with which he did business on the Rialto.

The old woman now whispered very low, "Tonino, when you look upon my shrivelled features, does there not dawn upon your mind the slightest, faintest recollection of having known me formerly a long, long time ago?" "I have already told you, old woman," replied Antonio in the same low tones, and without turning round, "I have already told you, that I feel drawn towards you in a way that I can't explain to myself, but I don't attribute it to your ugly shrivelled face. Nay, when I look at your strange black glittering eyes and sharp nose, at your blue lips and long chin, and bristly grey hair, and when I hear your abominable chuckling and laughing, and your confused talk, I rather turn away from you with disgust, and am even inclined to believe that you possess some execrable power for attracting me to you." "O God! God! God!" whined the old dame, a prey to unspeakable pain, "what fiendish spirit of darkness has put such fearful thoughts into your head? O Tonino, my darling Tonino, the woman who took such tender loving care of you when a child, and who saved your life from the most threatening danger on that awful night--it was I."

In the first moments of startled surprise Antonio turned round as if shot; but then he fixed his eyes upon the old woman's hideous face and cried angrily, "So that is the way you think you are going to befool me, you abominable insane old crone! The few recollections which I have retained of my childhood are fresh and lively. That kind and pretty lady who tended me--Oh! I can see her plainly now! She had a full bright face with some colour in it--eyes gently smiling-beautiful dark- brown hair--dainty hands; she could hardly be thirty years old, and you--you, an old woman of ninety!" "O all ye saints of Heaven!" interrupted the old dame, sobbing, "all ye blessed ones, what shall I do to make my Tonino believe in me, his faithful Margaret?" "Margaret!" murmured Antonio, "Margaret! That name falls upon my ears like music heard a long long time ago, and for a long long time forgotten. But-- no, it is impossible--impossible." Then the old dame went on more calmly, dropping her eyes, and scribbling as it were with her staff on the ground, "You are right; the tall handsome man who used to take you in his arms and kiss you and give you sweets was your father, Tonino; and the language in which we spoke to each other was the beautiful sonorous German. Your father was a rich and influential merchant in Augsburg. His young and lovely wife died in giving birth to you. Then, since he could not settle down in the place where his dearest lay buried, he came hither to Venice, and brought me, your nurse, with him to take care of you. That terrible night an awful fate overtook your father, and also threatened you. I succeeded in saving you. A noble Venetian adopted you; I, deprived of all means of support, had to remain in Venice.

"My father, a barber-surgeon, of whom it was said that he practised forbidden science as well, had made me familiar from my earliest childhood with the mysterious virtues of Nature's remedies. By him I was taught to wander through the fields and woods, learning the properties of many healing herbs, of many insignificant mosses, the hours when they should be plucked and gathered, and how to mix the juices of the various simples. But to this knowledge there was added a very special gift, which Heaven has endowed me with for some inscrutable purpose. I often see future events as if in a dim and distant mirror; and almost without any conscious effort of will, I declare in expressions which are unintelligible to myself what I have seen; for some unknown Power compels me, and I cannot resist it. Now when I had to stay behind in Venice, deserted of all the world, I resolved to earn a livelihood by means of my tried skill. In a brief time I cured the most dangerous diseases. And furthermore, as my presence alone had a beneficial effect upon my patients, and the soft stroking of my hand often brought them past the crisis in a few minutes, my fame necessarily soon spread through the town, and money came pouring in in streams. This awakened the jealousy of the physicians, quacks who sold their pills and essences in St. Mark's Square, on the Rialto, and in the Mint, poisoning their patients instead of curing them. They spread abroad that I was in league with the devil himself; and they were believed by the superstitious folk. I was soon arrested and brought before the ecclesiastical tribunal. O my Tonino, what horrid tortures did they inflict upon me in order to force from me a confession of the most damnable of all alliances! I remained firm. My hair turned white; my body withered up to a mummy; my feet and hands were paralysed. But there was still the terrible rack left--the cunningest invention of the foul fiend,--and it extorted from me a confession at which I shudder even now. I was to be burnt alive; but when the earthquake shook the foundations of the palaces and of the great prison, the door of the underground dungeon in which I lay confined sprang open of itself, and I staggered up out of my grave as it were through rubbish and ruins. O Tonino, you called me an old woman of ninety; I am hardly more than fifty. This lean, emaciated body, this hideously distorted face, this icicle-like hair, these lame feet--no, it was not the lapse of years, it was only unspeakable tortures which could in a few months change me thus from a strong woman into the monstrous creature I now am. And my hideous chuckling and laughing--this was forced from me by the last strain on the rack, at the memory of which my hair even now stands on an end, and I feel altogether as if I were locked in a red-hot coat of mail; and since that time I have been constantly subject to it; it attacks me without my being able to check it. So don't stand any longer in awe of me, Tonino, Oh! it was indeed your heart which told you that as a little boy you lay on my bosom." "Woman," said Antonio hoarsely, wrapped up in his own thoughts, "woman, I feel as if I must believe you. But who was my father? What was he called? What was the awful fate which overtook him on that terrible night? Who was it who adopted me? And--what was that occurrence in my life which now, like some potent magical spell from a strange and unknown world, exercises an irresistible sway over my soul, so that all my thoughts are dissipated into a dark night-like sea, so to speak? When you tell me all this, you mysterious woman, then I will believe you." "Tonino," replied the old crone, sighing, "for your own sake I must keep silent; but the time when I may speak will soon come. The Fontego--the Fontego--keep away from the Fontego."

"Oh!" cried Antonio angrily, "you need not begin to speak your dark sentences again to enchant me by some devilish wile or other. My heart is rent, you must speak, or"---- "Stop," interrupted she, "no threats--am I not your faithful nurse, who tended you?"---- Without waiting to hear what the old woman had got further to say, he picked himself up and ran away swiftly. From a distance he shouted to her, "You shall nevertheless have a new hood, and as many sequins besides as you like."

It was in truth a remarkable spectacle, to see the old Doge Marino Falieri and his youthful wife: he, strong enough and robust enough in very truth, but with a grey beard, and innumerable wrinkles in his rusty brown face, with some difficulty bearing his head erect, forming a pathetic figure as he strode along; she, a perfect picture of grace, with the pure gentleness of an angel in her divinely beautiful face, an irresistible charm in her longing glances, a queenly dignity enthroned upon her open lily-white brow, shadowed by her dark locks, a sweet smile upon her cheeks and lips, her pretty head bent with winsome submissiveness, her slender form moving with ease, scarce seeming to touch the earth--a beautiful lady in fact, a native of another and a higher world. Of course you have seen angelic forms like this, conceived and painted by the old masters. Such was Annunciata. How then could it be otherwise but that every one who saw her was astonished and enraptured with her beauty, and all the fiery youths of the Seignory were consumed with passion, measuring the old Doge with mocking looks, and swearing in their hearts that they would be the Mars to this Vulcan, let the consequences be what they might? Annunciata soon found herself surrounded with admirers, to whose flattering and seductive words she listened quietly and graciously, without thinking anything in particular about them. The conception which her pure angelic spirit had formed of her relation to her aged and princely husband was that she ought to honour him as her supreme lord, and cling to him with all the unquestioning fidelity of a submissive handmaiden. He treated her kindly, nay tenderly; he pressed her to his ice-cold heart and called her his darling; he heaped up all the jewels he could find upon her; what else could she wish for from him, what other rights could she have upon him? In this way, therefore, it was impossible for the thought of unfaithfulness to the old man ever in any way to find lodgment in her mind; all that lay beyond the narrow circle of these limited relations was to this good child an unknown region, whose forbidden borders were wrapped in dark mists, unseen and unsuspected by her. Hence all efforts to win her love were fruitless.

But the flames of passion--of love for the beautiful Dogess--burned in none so violently and so uncontrolled as in Michele Steno. Notwithstanding his youth, he was invested with the important and influential post of Member of the Council of Forty. Relying upon this fact, as well as upon his personal beauty, he felt confident of success. Old Marino Falieri he did not fear in the least; and, indeed, the old man seemed to indulge less frequently in his violent outbreaks of furious passion, and to have laid aside his rugged untamable fierceness, since his marriage. There he sat beside his beautiful Annunciata, spruce and prim, in the richest, gayest apparel, smirking and smiling, challenging in the sweet glances of his grey eyes,--from which a treacherous tear stole from time to time,--those who were present to say if any one of them could boast of such a wife as his. Instead of speaking in the rough arrogant tone of voice in which he had formerly been in the habit of expressing himself, he whispered, scarce moving his lips, addressed every one in the most amiable manner, and granted the most absurd petitions. Who would have recognised in this weak amorous old man the same Falieri who had in a fit of passion buffeted the bishop on Corpus Christi Day at Treviso, and who had defeated the valiant Morbassan. This growing weakness spurred on Michele Steno to attempt the most extravagant schemes. Annunciata did not understand why he was constantly pursuing her with his looks and words; she had no conception of his real purpose, but always preserved the same gentle, calm, and friendly bearing towards him. It was just this quiet unconscious behaviour, however, which drove him wild, which drove him to despair almost. He determined to effect his end by sinister means. He managed to involve Annunciata's most confidential maid in a love intrigue, and she at last permitted him to visit her at night. Thus he believed he had paved a way to Annunciata's unpolluted chamber; but the Eternal Power willed that this treacherous iniquity should recoil upon the head of its wicked author.

One night it chanced that the Doge, who had just received the ill tidings of the battle which Nicolo Pisani had lost against Doria off Porto Longo, was unable to sleep owing to care and anxiety, and was rambling through the passages of the Ducal Palace. Then he became aware of a shadow stealing apparently out of Annunciata's apartments and creeping towards the stairs. He at once rushed towards it; it was Michele Steno leaving his mistress. A terrible thought flashed across Falieri's mind; with the cry "Annunciata!" he threw himself upon Steno with his drawn dagger in his hand. But Steno, who was stronger and more agile than the old man, averted the thrust, and knocked him down with a violent blow of his fist; then, laughing loudly and shouting, "Annunciata! Annunciata!" he rushed downstairs. The old man picked himself up and stole towards Annunciata's apartments, his heart on fire with the torments of hell. All was quiet, as still as the grave. He knocked; a strange maid opened the door--not the one who was in the habit of sleeping near Annunciata's chamber. "What does my princely husband command at this late and unusual hour?" asked Annunciata in a calm and sweetly gentle tone, for she had meanwhile thrown on a light night-robe and was now come forward. Old Falieri stared at her speechless; then, raising both hands above his head, he cried, "No, it is not possible, it is not possible." "What is not possible, my princely sir?" asked Annunciata, startled at the deep solemn tones of the old man's voice. But Falieri, without answering her question, turned to the maid, "Why are *you* sleeping here? why does not Luigia sleep here as usual?" "Oh!" replied the little one, "Luigia would make me exchange places with her to-night; she is sleeping in the ante-room close by the stairs." "Close by the stairs!" echoed Falieri, delighted; and he hurried away to the ante-room. At his loud knocking Luigia opened the door; and when she saw the Doge, her master's face inflamed with rage, and his flashing eyes, she threw herself upon her bare knees and confessed her shame, which was set beyond all doubt by a pair of elegant gentleman's gloves lying on the easy-chair, whilst the sweet scent about them betrayed their dandified owner. Hotly incensed at Steno's unheard-of impudence, the Doge wrote to him next morning, forbidding him, on pain of banishment from the town, to approach the Ducal Palace, or the presence of the Doge and Dogess.

Michele Steno was wild with fury at the failure of his well-planned scheme, and at the disgrace of being thus banished from the presence of his idol. Now when he had to see from a distance how gently and kindly the Dogess spoke to other young men of the Seignory--that was indeed her natural manner--his envy and the violence of his passion filled his mind with evil thoughts. The Dogess had without doubt only scorned him because he had been anticipated by others with better luck; and he had the hardihood to utter his thoughts openly and publicly. Now whether it was that old Falieri had tidings of this shameless talk, or whether he came to look upon the occurrence of that memorable night as the warning finger of destiny, or whether now, in spite of all his calmness and equanimity, and his perfect confidence in the fidelity of his wife, he saw clearly the danger of the unnatural position in which he stood in respect to her--at any rate he became ill-tempered and morose. He was plagued and tortured by all the fiends of jealousy, and confined Annunciata to the inner apartments of the Ducal Palace, so that no man ever set eyes upon her. Bodoeri took his niece's part, and soundly rated old Falieri; but he would not hear of any change in his conduct.

All this took place shortly before Holy Thursday. On the occasion of the popular sports which take place on this day in St. Mark's Square, it was customary for the Dogess to take her seat beside the Doge, under a canopy erected on the balcony which lies opposite to the Piazetti. Bodoeri reminded the Doge of this custom, and told him that it would be very absurd, and sure to draw down upon him the mocking laughter of both populace and Seignory, if, in the teeth of custom and usage, he let his perverse jealousy exclude Annunciata from this honour. "Do you think," replied old Falieri, whose pride was immediately aroused, "do you think I am such an idiotic old fool that I am afraid to show my most precious jewel for fear of thievish hands, and that I could not prevent her being stolen from me with my good sword? No, old man, you are mistaken; to-morrow Annunciata shall go with me in solemn procession across St. Mark's Square, that the people may see their Dogess, and on Holy Thursday she shall receive the nosegay from the bold sailor who comes sailing down out of the air to her." The Doge was thinking of a very ancient custom as he said these words. On Holy Thursday a bold fellow from amongst the people is drawn up from the sea to the summit of the tower of St. Mark's, in a machine that resembles a little ship and is suspended on ropes, then he shoots from the top of the tower with the speed of an arrow down to the Square where the Doge and Dogess are sitting, and presents a nosegay of flowers to the Dogess, or to the Doge if he is alone.

The next day the Doge carried out his intention. Annunciata had to don her most magnificent robes; and surrounded by the Seignory and attended by pages and guards, she and Falieri crossed the Square when it was swarming with people. They pushed and squeezed themselves to death almost to see the beautiful Dogess; and he who succeeded in setting eyes upon her thought he had taken a peep into Paradise and had beheld the loveliest of the bright and beautiful angels. But according to Venetian habits, in the midst of the wildest outbreaks of their frantic admiration, here and there were heard all sorts of satiric phrases and rhymes--and coarse enough too-- aimed at old Falieri and his young wife. Falieri, however, appeared not to notice them, but strode along as pathetically as possible at Annunciata's side, smirking and smiling all over his face, and free on this occasion from all jealousy, although he must have seen the glances full of burning passion which were directed upon his beautiful lady from all sides. Arrived before the principal entrance to the Palace, the guards had some difficulty in driving back the crowd, so that the Doge and Dogess might go in; but here and there were still standing isolated knots of better-dressed citizens, who could not very well be refused entrance into even the inner quadrangle of the Palace. Now it happened just at the moment that the Dogess entered the quadrangle, that a young man, who with a few others stood under the portico, fell down suddenly upon the hard marble floor, as if dead, with the loud scream, "O good God! good God!" The people ran together from every side and surrounded the dead man, so that the Dogess could not see him; yet, as the young man fell, she felt as if a red-hot knife were suddenly thrust into her heart; she grew pale; she reeled, and was only prevented from fainting by the smelling-bottles of the ladies who hastened to her assistance. Old Falieri, greatly alarmed and put out by the accident, wished the young man and his fit anywhere; and he carried his Annunciata, who hung her pretty head on her bosom and closed her eyes like a sick dove, himself up the steps into her own apartments in the interior of the Palace, although it was very hard work for him to do so.

Meanwhile the people, who had increased to crowds in the inner quadrangle, had been spectators of a remarkable scene. They were about to lift up the young man, whom they took to be quite dead, and carry him away, when an ugly old beggar-woman, all in rags, came limping up with a loud wail of grief; and punching their sides and ribs with her sharp elbows she made a way for herself through the thick of the crowd. When she at length saw the senseless youth, she cried, "Let him be, fools; you stupid people, let him be; he is not dead." Then she squatted down beside him; and taking his head in her lap she gently rubbed and stroked his forehead, calling him by the sweetest of names. As the people noted the old woman's ugly apish face, and the repulsive play of its muscles, bending over the young fellow's fine handsome face, his soft features now stiff and pale as in death, when they saw her filthy rags fluttering about over the rich clothing the young man wore, and her lean brownish-yellow arms and long hands trembling upon his forehead and exposed breast--they could not in truth resist shuddering with awe. It looked as if it were the grinning form of death himself in whose arms the young man lay. Hence the crowd standing round slipped away quietly one after the other, till there were only a few left They, when the young man opened his eyes with a deep sigh, took him up and carried him, at the old woman's request, to the Grand Canal, where a gondola took them both on board, the old woman and the youth, and brought them to the house which she had indicated as his dwelling. Need it be said that the young man was Antonio, and that the old woman was the beggar of the steps of the Franciscan Church, who wanted to make herself out to be his nurse?

When Antonio was quite recovered from his stupefaction and perceived the old woman at his bed-side, and knew that she had just been giving him some strengthening drops, he said brokenly in a hoarse voice, bending a long gloomy melancholy gaze upon her, "*You* with me, Margaret--that is good; what more faithful nurse could I have found than you? Oh! forgive me, mother, that I, a doltish, senseless boy, doubted for an instant what you discovered to me. Yes, you are *the* Margaret who reared me, who cared for me and tended me; I knew it all the time, but some evil spirit bewildered my thoughts. I have seen her; it is she--it is she. Did I not tell you there was some mysterious magical power dwelling in me, which exercised an uncontrollable supremacy over me? It has emerged from its obscurity dazzling with light, to effect my destruction through nameless joy. I now know all-- everything. Was not my foster-father Bertuccio Nenolo, and did he not bring me up at his country-seat near Treviso?" "Yes, yes," replied the old woman, "it was indeed Bertuccio Nenolo, the great sea-captain, whom the sea devoured as he was about to adorn his temples with the victor's wreath." "Don't interrupt me," continued Antonio; "listen patiently to what I have to say.

"With Bertuccio Nenolo I lived in clover. I wore fine clothes; the table was always covered when I was hungry; and after I had said my three prayers properly I was allowed to run about the woods and fields just as I pleased. Close beside the villa there was a little wood of sweet pines, cool and dark, and filled with sweet scents and songs. There one evening, when the sun began to sink, I threw me down beneath a big tree, tired with running and jumping about, and stared up at the blue sky. Perhaps I was stupefied by the fragrant smell of the flowering herbs in the midst of which I lay; at any rate, my eyes closed involuntarily, and I sank into a state of dreamy reverie, from which I was awakened by a rustling, as if some one had struck a blow in the grass beside me. I started up into a sitting posture; an angelic child with heavenly eyes stood near me and looked down upon me, smiling most sweetly and bewitchingly. 'O good boy,' she said, in a low soft voice, 'how beautiful and calmly you sleep, and yet death, nasty death, was so near to you.' Close beside my breast I saw a small black snake with its head crushed; the little girl had killed the poisonous reptile with a switch from a nut-tree, and just as it was wriggling on to my destruction. Then a trembling of sweet awe fell upon me; I knew that angels often came down from heaven above to rescue men in person from the threatening attack of some evil enemy. I fell upon my knees and raised my folded hands. 'Oh! you are surely an angel of light, sent by God to save my life,' I cried. The pretty creature stretched out both arms towards me and said softly, whilst a deeper flush mantled upon her cheeks, 'No, good boy; I am not an angel, but a girl--a child like you.' Then my feeling of awe gave place to a nameless delight, which spread like a gentle warmth through all my limbs. I rose to my feet; we clasped each other in our arms, our lips met, and we were speechless, weeping, sobbing with sweet unutterable sadness.

"Then a clear silvery voice cried through the wood, 'Annunciata! Annunciata!' 'I must go now, darling boy, mother is calling me,' whispered the little girl. My heart was rent with unspeakable pain. 'Oh! I love you so much,' I sobbed, and the scalding tears fell from the little girl's eyes upon my cheeks. 'I am so--so fond of you, good boy,' she cried, pressing a last kiss upon my lips. 'Annunciata,' the voice cried again; and the little girl disappeared behind the bushes. Now that, Margaret, was the moment when the mighty spark of love fell upon my soul, and it will gather strength, and, enkindling flame after flame, will continue to burn there for ever. A few days afterwards I was turned out of the house.

"Father Bluenose told me, since I did not cease talking about the lovely child who had appeared to me, and whose sweet voice I thought I heard in the rustling of the trees, in the gushing murmurs of the springs, and in the mysterious soughing of the sea--yes, then Father Bluenose told me that the girl could be none other than Nenolo's daughter Annunciata, who had come to the villa with her mother Francesca, but had left it again on the following day. O mother-- Margaret--help me. Heaven! This Annunciata--is the Dogess." And Antonio buried his face in the pillows, weeping and sobbing with unspeakable emotion.

"My dear Tonino," said the old woman, "rouse yourself and be a man; come, do resist bravely this foolish emotion. Come, come, how can you think of despairing when you are in love? For whom does the golden flower of hope blossom if not for the lover? You do not know in the evening what the morning may bring; what you have beheld in your dreams comes to meet you in living form. The castle that hovered in the air stands all at once on the earth, a substantial and splendid building. See here, Tonino, you are not paying the least heed to my words; but my little finger tells me, and so does somebody else as well, that the bright standard of love is gaily waving for you out at sea. Patience, Tonino--patience, my boy!" Thus the old woman sought to comfort poor Antonio; and her words did really sound like sweet music. He would not let her leave him again. The beggar-woman had disappeared from the steps of the Franciscan Church, and in her stead people saw Signor Antonio's housekeeper, dressed in becoming matronly style, limping about St. Mark's Square and buying the requisite provisions for his table.

Holy Thursday was come. It was to be celebrated on this occasion in more magnificent fashion than it had ever been before. In the middle of the Piazzetta of St. Mark's a high staging was erected for a special kind of artistic fire--something perfectly new, which was to be exhibited by a Greek--a man experienced in such matters. In the evening old Falieri came out on the balcony along with his beautiful lady, reflecting his pride and happiness in the magnificence of his surroundings, and with radiant eyes challenging all who stood near to admire and wonder. As he was about to take his seat on the chair of state he perceived Michele Steno actually on the same balcony with him, and saw that he had chosen a position whence he could keep his eyes constantly fixed upon the Dogess, and must of necessity be observed by her. Completely overmastered by furious rage, and wild with jealousy, Falieri shouted in a loud and commanding tone that Steno was to be at once removed from the balcony. Michele Steno raised his hand against Falieri, but that same moment the guards appeared, and compelled him to quit his place, which he did, foaming with rage and grinding his teeth, and threatening revenge in the most horrible imprecations.

Meanwhile Antonio, utterly beside himself at sight of his beloved Annunciata, had made his way out through the crowd, and was striding backwards and forwards in the darkness of the night alone along the edge of the sea, his heart rent by unutterable anguish. He debated within himself whether it would not be better to extinguish the consuming fire within him in the ice-cold waves than to be slowly tortured to death by hopeless pain. But little was wanting, and he had leapt into the sea; he was already standing on the last step that goes down to the water, when a voice called to him from a little boat, "Ay, a very good evening to you, Signor Antonio." By the reflection cast by the illuminations of the Square, he recognised that it was merry Pietro, one of his former comrades. He was standing in the boat, his new cap adorned with feathers and tinsel, and his new striped jacket gaily decorated with ribbons, whilst he held in his hand a large and beautiful nosegay of sweet-scented flowers. "Good evening, Pietro," shouted Antonio back, "what grand folks are you going to row to-night that you are decked off so fine?" "Oh!" replied Pietro, dancing till his boat rocked; "see you, Signor Antonio, I am going to earn my three sequins to-day; for I'm going to make the journey up to St. Mark's Tower and then down again, to take this nosegay to the beautiful Dogess." "But isn't that a risky and break-neck adventure, Pietro, my friend?" asked Antonio. "Well," he replied, "there is some little chance of breaking one's neck, especially as we go to-day right through the middle of the artificial fire. The Greek says, to be sure, that he has arranged everything so that the fire will not hurt a hair of anybody's head, but"---- Pietro shrugged his shoulders.

Antonio stepped down to Pietro in the boat, and now perceived that he stood close in front of the machine, which was fastened to a rope coming out of the sea. Other ropes, by means of which the machine was to be drawn up, were lost in the night. "Now listen, Pietro," began Antonio, after a silent pause, "see here, comrade, if you could earn ten sequins to-day without exposing your life to danger, would it not be more agreeable to you?" "Why, of course," and Pietro burst into a good hearty laugh. "Well then," continued Antonio, "take these ten sequins and change clothes with me, and let me take your place, I will go up instead of you. Do, my good friend and comrade, Pietro, let me go up." Pietro shook his head dubiously, and weighing the money in his hand, said, "You are very kind, Signor Antonio, to still call a poor devil like me your comrade, and you are generous as well. The money I should certainly like very much; but, on the other hand, to place this nosegay in our beautiful Dogess's hand myself, to hear her sweet voice--and after all that's really why I am ready to risk my life. Well, since it is you, Signor Antonio, I close with your offer." They both hastily changed their clothes; and hardly was Antonio dressed when Pietro cried, "Quick, into the machine; the signal is given." At the same moment the sea was lit up with the reflection of thousands of bright flashes, and all the air along the margin of the sea rang with loud reverberating thunders. Right through the midst of the hissing crackling flames of the artificial fire, Antonio rose up into the air with the speed of a hurricane, and shot down uninjured upon the balcony, hovering in front of the Dogess. She had risen to her feet and stepped forward; he felt her breath on his cheeks; he gave her the nosegay. But in the unspeakable delirious delight of the moment he was clasped as if in red-hot arms by the fiery pain of hopeless love. Senseless, insane with longing, rapture, anguish, he grasped her hand, and covered it with burning kisses, crying in the sharp tone of despairing misery, "O Annunciata!" Then the machine, like a blind instrument of fate, whisked him away from his beloved back to the sea, where he sank down stunned, quite exhausted, into Pietro's arms, who was waiting for him in the boat.

Meanwhile the Doge's balcony was the scene of tumult and confusion. A small strip of paper had been found fastened to the Doge's seat, containing in the common Venetian dialect the words:

Il Dose Falier della bella muier,
I altri la gode é lui la mantien.

(The Doge Falieri, the husband of the beautiful lady; others kiss her, and he--he keeps her.)

Old Falieri burst into a violent fit of passion, and swore that the severest punishment should overtake the man who had been guilty of this audacious offence. As he cast his eyes about they fell upon Michele Steno standing beneath the balcony in the Square, in the full light of the torches; he at once commanded his guards to arrest him as the instigator of the outrage. This command of the Doge's provoked a universal cry of dissent; in giving way to his overmastering rage he was offering insult to both Seignory and populace, violating the rights of the former, and spoiling the latter's enjoyment of their holiday. The members of the Seignory left their places; but old Marino Bodoeri mixed among the people, actively representing the grave nature of the outrage that had been done to the head of the state, and seeking to direct the popular hatred upon Michele Steno. Nor had Falieri judged wrongly; for Michele Steno, on being expelled from the Duke's balcony, had really hurried off home, and there written the above-mentioned slanderous words; then when all eyes were fixed upon the artificial fire, he had fastened the strip of paper to the Doge's seat, and withdrawn from the gallery again unobserved. He maliciously hoped it would be a galling blow for them, for both the Doge and the Dogess, and that the wound would rankle deeply--so deeply as to touch a vital part. Willingly and openly he admitted the deed, and transferred all blame to the Doge, since he had been the first to give umbrage to *him*.

The Seignory had been for some time dissatisfied with their chief, for instead of meeting the just expectations of the state, he gave proofs daily that the fiery warlike courage in his frozen and worn-out heart was merely like the artificial fire which bursts with a furious rush out of the rocket-apparatus, but immediately disappears in black lifeless flakes, and has accomplished nothing. Moreover, since his union with his young and beautiful wife (it had long before leaked out that he was married to her directly after attaining to the Dogate) old Falieri's jealousy no longer let him appear in the character of heroic captain, but rather of *vechio Pantalone* (old fool); hence it was that the Seignory, nursing their swelling resentment, were more inclined to condone Michele Steno's fault, than to see justice done to their deeply-wounded chief. The matter was referred by the Council of Ten to the Forty, one of the leaders of which Michele had formerly been. The verdict was that Michele Steno had already suffered sufficiently, and a month's banishment was quite punishment enough for the offence. This sentence only served to feed anew and more fully old Falieri's bitterness against a Seignory which, instead of protecting their own head, had the impudence to punish insults that were offered to him as they would offences of merely the most insignificant description.

As generally happens in the case of lovers, once a single ray of the happiness of love has fallen upon them, they are surrounded for days and weeks and months by a sort of golden veil, and dream dreams of Paradise; and so Antonio could not recover himself from the stupefying rapture of that happy moment; he could hardly breathe for delirious sadness. He had been well scolded by the old woman for running such a great risk; and she never ceased mumbling and grumbling about exposure to unnecessary danger.

But one day she came hopping and dancing with her staff in the strange way she had when apparently affected by some foreign magical influence. Without heeding Antonio's words and questions, she began to chuckle and laugh, and kindling a small fire in the stove, she put a little pan on it, into which she poured several ingredients from many various-coloured phials, and made a salve, which she put into a little box; then she limped out of the house again, chuckling and laughing. She did not return until late at night, when she sat down in the easy-chair, panting and coughing for breath; and after she had in a measure recovered from her great exhaustion, she at length began, "Tonino, my boy Tonino, whom do you think I have come from? See--try if you can guess. Whom do I come from? where have I been?" Antonio looked at her, and a singular instinctive feeling took possession of him. "Well now," chuckled the old woman, "I have come from her--her herself, from the pretty dove, lovely Annunciata." "Don't drive me mad, old woman!" shouted Antonio. "What do you say?" continued she, "I am always thinking about you, my Tonino.

"This morning, whilst I was haggling for some fine fruit under the peristyle of the Palace, I heard the people talking with bated breath of the accident that had befallen the beautiful Dogess. I inquired again and again of several people, and at last a big, uncultivated, red haired fellow, who stood leaning against a column, yawning and chawing lemons, said to me, 'Oh well, a young scorpion has been trying its little teeth on the little finger of her left hand, and there's been a drop or two of blood shed--that's all. My master, Signor Doctor Giovanni Basseggio, is now in the palace, and he has, no doubt, before this cut off her pretty hand, and the finger with it.' Just as the fellow was telling me this there arose a great noise on the broad steps, and a little man--such a tiny little man-- came rolling down at our feet, screaming and lamenting, for the guards had kicked him down as if he had been a nine pin. The people gathered round him, laughing heartily; the little man struggled and fought with his legs in the air without being able to get up; but the red-haired fellow rushed forward, snatched up the little doctor, tucked him under his arm, and ran off with him as fast as his legs could carry him to the Canal, where he got into a gondola with him and rowed away--the little doctor screaming and yelling with all his might the whole time. I knew how it was; just as Signor Basseggio was getting his knife ready to cut off the pretty hand, the Doge had had him kicked down the steps. I also thought of something else--quick--quick as you can--go home make a salve--and then come back here to the Ducal Palace.

"And I stood on the great stairs with my bright little phial in my hand. Old Falieri was just coming down; he darted a glance at me, and, his choler rising, said, 'What does this old woman want here?' Then I curtsied low-- quite down to the ground--as well as I could, and told him that I had a nice remedy which would very soon cure the beautiful Dogess. When the old man heard that, he fixed a terrible keen look upon me, and stroked his grey beard into order; then he seized me by both shoulders and pushed me upstairs and on into the chamber, where I nearly fell all my length. O Tonino, there was the pretty child reclining on a couch, as pale as death, sighing and moaning with pain and softly lamenting, 'Oh! I am poisoned in every vein.' But I at once set to work and took off the simple doctor's silly plaster. O just Heaven! her dear little hand--all red as red--and swollen. Well, well, my salve cooled it--soothed it. 'That does it good; yes, that does it good,' softly whispered the sick darling. Then Marino cried quite delighted, 'You shall have a thousand sequins, old woman, if you save me the Dogess;' and therewith he left the room.

"For three hours I sat there, holding her little hand in mine, stroking and attending to it. Then the darling woman woke up out of the gentle slumber into which she had fallen, and no longer felt any pain. After I had made a fresh poultice, she looked at me with eyes brimming with gladness. Then I said, 'O most noble lady, you once saved a boy's life when you killed the little snake that was about to attack him as he slept.' O Tonino, you should have seen the hot blood rush into her pale face, as if a ray of the setting sun had fallen upon it--and how her eyes flashed with the fire of joy. 'Oh! yes, old woman,' she said, 'oh! I was quite a child then--it was at my father's country villa. Oh! he was a dear pretty boy--I often think of him now. I don't think I have ever had a single happy experience since that time.' Then I began to talk about you, that you were in Venice, that your heart still beat with the love and rapture of that moment, that, in order to gaze *once* more in the heavenly eyes of the angel who saved you, you had faced the risk of the dangerous aerial voyage, that you it was who had given her the nosegay on Holy Thursday. 'O Tonino, Tonino,' she cried in an ecstasy of delight, 'I felt it, I felt it; when he pressed my hand

121

to his lips, when he named my name, I could not conceive why it went so strangely to my heart; it was indeed pleasure, but pain as well. Bring him here, bring him to me--the pretty boy.'" As the old woman said this Antonio threw himself upon his knees and cried like one insane, "O good God! pray let no dire fate overtake me now--now at least until I have seen her, have pressed her to my heart." He wanted the old woman to take him to the Palace the very next day; but she flatly refused, since old Falieri was in the habit of paying visits to his sick wife nearly every hour that came.

Several days went by; the old woman had completely cured the Dogess; but as yet it had been quite impossible to take Antonio to see her. The old woman soothed his impatience as well as she could, always repeating that she was constantly talking to beautiful Annunciata about the Antonio whose life she had saved, and who loved her so passionately. Tormented by all the pangs of desire and yearning love, Antonio spent his time in going about in his gondola and restlessly traversing the squares. But his footsteps involuntarily turned time after time in the direction of the Ducal Palace. One day he saw Pietro standing on the bridge close to the back part of the Palace, opposite the prisons, leaning on a gay-coloured oar, whilst a gondola, fastened to one of the pillars, was rocking on the Canal. Although small, it had a comfortable little deck, was adorned with tasteful carvings, and even decorated with the Venetian flag, so that it bore some resemblance to the Bucentaur. As soon as Pietro saw his former comrade he shouted out to him, "Hi! Signor Antonio, the best of good greetings to you; your sequins have brought me good luck." Antonio asked somewhat absently what sort of good luck he meant, and learned the important intelligence that nearly every evening Pietro had to take the Doge and Dogess in his gondola across to Giudecca, where the Doge had a nice house not far from San Giorgio Maggiore. Antonio stared at Pietro, and then burst out spasmodically, "Comrade, you may earn another ten sequins and more if you like. Let me take your place; I will row the Doge over." But Pietro informed him that he could not think of doing so, for the Doge knew him and would not trust himself with anybody else. At length when Antonio, his mind excited by all the tortures of love, began to give way to unbridled anger, and violently importune him, and to swear in an insane and ridiculous fashion that he would leap after the gondola and drag it down under the sea, Pietro replied laughing, "Why, Signor Antonio, Signor Antonio, why, I declare you have quite lost yourself in the Dogess's beautiful eyes." But he consented to allow Antonio to go with him as his assistant in rowing; he would excuse it to old Falieri on the ground of the weight of the boat, as well, as being himself a little weak and unwell, and old Falieri did always think the gondola went too slowly on this trip. Off Antonio ran, and he only just returned to the bridge in time, dressed in coarse oarsman's clothing, his face stained, and with a long moustache stuck above his lips, for the Doge came down from the Palace with the Dogess, both attired most splendidly and magnificently. "Who's that stranger fellow there?" began the Doge angrily to Pietro; and it required all Pietro's most solemn asseverations that he really required an assistant, before the old man could be induced to allow Antonio to help row the gondola.

It often happens that in the midst of the wildest delirium of delight and rapture the soul, strengthened as it were by the power of the moment, is able to impose fetters upon itself, and to control the flames of passion which threaten to blaze out from the heart. In a similar way Antonio, albeit he was close beside the lovely Annunciata and the seam of her dress touched him, was able to hide his consuming passion by maintaining a firm and powerful hold upon his oar, and, whilst avoiding any greater risk, by only glancing at her momentarily now and then. Old Falieri was all smirks and smiles; he kissed and fondled beautiful Annunciata's little white hands, and threw his arm around her slender waist. In the middle of the channel, when St. Mark's Square and magnificent Venice with all her proud towers and palaces lay extended before them, old Falieri raised his head and said, gazing proudly about him, "Now, my darling, is it not a grand thing to ride on the sea with the lord--the husband of the sea? Yes, my darling, don't be jealous of my bride, who is submissively bearing us on her broad bosom. Listen to the gentle splashing of the wavelets; are they not words of love which she is whispering to the husband who rules her? Yes, yes, my darling, you indeed wear my ring on your finger, but she below guards in the depths of her bosom the ring of betrothal which I threw to her." "Oh! my princely Sir," began Annunciata, "oh! how can this cold treacherous water be your bride? it quite makes me shiver to think that you are married to this proud imperious element." Old Falieri laughed till his chin and beard tottered and shook. "Don't distress yourself, my pet," he said, "it's far better, of course, to rest in your soft warm arms than in the ice-cold lap of my bride below there; but it's a grand thing to ride on the sea with the lord of the sea!" Just as the Doge was saying these words, the faint strains of music at a distance came floating towards them. The notes of a soft male voice, gliding along the waves of the sea, came nearer and nearer; the words that were sung were--

Ah! senza amare,
Andare sul mare,
Col sposo del' mare
Non puo consolare.

Other voices took up the strain, and the same words were repeated again and again in every-varying alternation, until the song died away like the soft breath of the wind as it were. Old Falieri appeared not to pay the slightest heed to the song; on the contrary, he was relating to the Dogess with much prolixity the meaning and history of the solemnity which takes place on Ascension Day when the Doge throws his ring from the Bucentaur and is married to the sea.

He spoke of the victories of the republic, and how she had formerly conquered Istria and Dalmatia under the rule of Peter Urseolus the Second, and how this ceremony had its origin in that conquest But if old Falieri heeded not the song, so now his tales were lost upon the Dogess. She sat with her mind completely wrapped up in the sweet sounds which came floating along the sea. When the song came to an end her eyes wore a strange far-off look, as if she were awakening from a profound dream and striving to see and interpret the images which sportively mocked her efforts to hold them fast. "*Senza amare, senza amare, non puo consolare,*" she whispered softly, whilst the tears glistened like bright pearls in her heavenly eyes, and sighs escaped her breast as it heaved and sank with the violence of her emotions. Still smirking and smiling and talking away, the old man, with the Dogess at his side, stepped out upon the balcony of his house near San Giorgio Maggiore, without noticing that Annunciata stood at his side like one in a dream, speechless, her tearful eyes fixed upon some far-off land, whilst her heart was agitated by feelings of a singular and mysterious character. A young man in gondolier's costume blew a blast on a conch-shaped horn, till the sounds echoed far away over the sea. At this signal another gondola drew near. Meanwhile an attendant bearing a sunshade and a maid had approached the Doge and Dogess; and thus attended they went towards the palace. The second gondola came to shore, and from it stepped forth Marino Bodoeri and several other persons, amongst whom were merchants, artists, nay people out of the lowest classes of the populace even; and they followed the Doge.

Antonio could hardly wait until the following evening, since he hoped then to have the desired message from his beloved Annunciata. At last-- at last the old woman came limping in, dropped panting into the arm-chair, and clapped her thin bony hands together again and again, crying. "Tonino, O Tonino! what in the world has happened to our dear darling? When I went into her room, there she lay on the couch with her eyes half closed, her pretty head resting on her arm, neither slumbering nor awake, neither sick nor well. I approached her: 'Oh! noble lady,' said I, 'what misfortune has happened to you? Does your scarce-healed wound hurt you still?' But she looked at me, oh! with such eyes, Antonio--I have never seen anything like them. And directly I looked down into the humid moonlight that was in them, they withdrew behind the dark clouds of their silken lashes. Then sighing a sigh that came from the depths of her heart, she turned her lovely pale face to the wall and whispered softly--so softly, but oh! so sadly! that I was cut right to the heart, '*Amare--amare--ah! senza amare!*' I fetched a little chair and sat down beside her, and began to talk about you. She buried herself in the cushions; and her breathing, coming quicker and quicker and quicker, turned to sighing. I told her candidly that you had been in the gondola disguised, and that I would now at once without delay take you, who were dying of love and longing, to see her. Then she suddenly started up from the cushions, and whilst the scalding tears streamed down her cheeks, she exclaimed vehemently, 'For God's sake! By all the Holy Saints! no--no--I cannot see him, old woman. I conjure you, tell him he is never--never again to come near me--never. Tell him he is to leave Venice, to go away at once!' 'So then you will let my poor Antonio die?' I interposed. Then she sank back upon the cushions, apparently smarting from the most unutterable anguish, and her voice was almost choked with tears as she sobbed out, 'Shall not I also die the bitterest of deaths?' At this point old Falieri entered the room, and at a sign from him I had to withdraw." "She has rejected me--away--away into the sea!" cried Antonio, giving way to utter despair. The old woman chuckled and laughed in her usual way, and went on, "You simple child! you simple child! don't you see that lovely Annunciata loves you with all the intensity, with all the agonised love of which a woman's heart is capable? You simple boy! Late to-morrow evening slip into the Ducal Palace; you will find me in the second gallery on the right from the great staircase, and then we will see what's to be done."

The following evening as Antonio, trembling with expectant happiness, stole up the great staircase, his conscience suddenly smote him, as though he were about to commit some great crime. He was so dazed, and he trembled and shook so, that he was scarcely able to climb the stairs. He had to stop and rest by leaning himself against a column immediately in front of the gallery that had been indicated to him. All at once he was plunged in the midst of a bright glare of torches, and before he could move from the place old Bodoeri stood in front of him, accompanied by some servants, who bore the torches. Bodoeri fixed his eyes upon the young man, and then said, "Ha! you are Antonio; you have been assigned this post, I know; come, follow me." Antonio, convinced that his proposed interview with the Dogess was betrayed, followed, not without trembling. But imagine his astonishment when, on entering a remote room, Bodoeri embraced him and spoke of the importance of the post that had been assigned to him, and which he would have to maintain with courage and firm resolution that very night. But his amazement increased to anxious fear and dismay when he learned that a conspiracy had been long ripening against the Seignory, and that at the head of it was the Doge himself. And this was the night in which, agreeably to the resolutions come to in Falieri's house on Giudecca, the Seignory was to fall and old Marino Falieri was to be proclaimed sovereign Duke of Venice.

Antonio stared at Bodoeri without uttering a word; Bodoeri interpreted the young man's silence as a refusal to take part in the execution of the formidable conspiracy, and he cried incensed, "You cowardly fool! You shall not leave this palace again; you shall either take up arms on our side or die--but talk to this man first" A tall and noble figure stepped forward from the dark background of the apartment. As soon as Antonio saw the man's face, which he could not do until he came into the light of the torches, and recognised it, he threw himself upon his knees and cried, completely losing his presence of mind at seeing him whom he never dreamt of seeing again, "O good God! my father, Bertuccio Nenolo! my dear foster-parent." Nenolo raised the young man up, clasped him in his arms, and said in a gentle voice, "Aye, of a verity I am Bertuccio Nenolo, whom you perhaps thought lay buried at the bottom of the sea, but I have only quite recently escaped from my shameful captivity at the hands of the savage Morbassan. Yes, I am the Bertuccio Nanolo who adopted you. And I never for a moment dreamt that the stupid servants whom Bodoeri sent to take possession of the villa, which he had bought of me, would turn you out of the house. You infatuated youth! Do you hesitate to take up arms against a despotic caste whose cruelty robbed you of a father? Ay! go down to the quadrangle of the Fontego, and the stains which you will there see on the stone pavements are the stains of your father's blood. The Seignory when making over to the German merchants the *dépôt* and exchange which you know under the name of the Fontego, forbade all those who had offices assigned to them to take the keys with them when they went away; they were to leave them with the official in charge of the Fontego. Your father acted contrary to this law, and had therefore incurred a heavy penalty. But now when the offices were opened on your father's return, there was found amongst his wares a chest of false Venetian coins. He vainly protested his innocence; it was only too evident that some malicious fiend, perhaps the official in charge himself, had smuggled in the chest in order to ruin your father. The inexorable judges, satisfied that the chest had been found in your father's offices, condemned him to death. He was executed in the quadrangle of the Fontego; nor would you now be living if faithful Margaret had not saved you. I, your father's truest friend, adopted you; and in order that you might not betray yourself to the Seignory, you were not told what was your father's name. But now-- now, Anthony Dalbirger,--now is the time--now, to seize your arms and revenge upon the heads of the Seignory your father's shameful death."

Antonio, fired by the spirit of vengeance, swore to be true to the conspirators and to act with invincible courage. It is well known that it was the affront put upon Bertuccio Nenolo by Dandulo when he was appointed to superintend the naval preparations, and on the occasion of a quarrel struck Nenolo in the face, that induced him to join with his ambitious son-in-law in his conspiracy against the Seignory. Both Nenolo and Bodoeri were desirous for old Falieri to assume the princely mantle in order that they might themselves rise along with him. The conspirators' plan was to spread abroad the news that the Genoese fleet lay before the Lagune. Then when night came the great bell in St. Mark's Tower was to be rung, and the town summoned to arms, under the false pretext of defence. This was to be the signal for the conspirators, whose numbers were considerable, and who were scattered throughout all Venice, to occupy St. Mark's Square, make themselves masters of the remaining principal squares of the town, murder the leading men of the Seignory, and proclaim the Doge sovereign Duke of Venice.

But it was not the will of Heaven that this murderous scheme should succeed, nor that the fundamental constitution of the harassed state should be trampled in the dust by old Falieri--a man inflamed with pride and haughtiness. The meetings in Falieri's house on Giudecca had not escaped the watchfulness of the Ten; but they failed altogether to learn any reliable intelligence. But the conscience of one of the conspirators, a fur-merchant of Pisa, Bentian by name, pricked him; he resolved to save from destruction his friend and gossip, Nicolas Leoni, a member of the Council of Ten. When twilight came on, he went to him and besought him not to leave his house during the night, no matter what occurred. Leoni's suspicion was aroused; he detained the fur-merchant, and on pressing him closely learned the whole scheme. In conjunction with Giovanni Gradenigo and Marco Cornaro he called the Council of Ten together in St. Salvador's (church); and there, in less than three hours, measures were taken calculated to stifle all the efforts of the conspirators on the first sign of movement.

Antonio's commission was to take a body of men and go to St. Mark's Tower, and see that the bell was tolled. Arrived there, he found the tower occupied by a large force of Arsenal troops, who, on his attempting to approach, charged upon him with their halberds. His own band, seized with a sudden panic, scattered like chaff; and he himself slipped away in the darkness of the night. But he heard the footsteps of a man following close at his heels; he felt him lay hands upon him, and he was just on the point of cutting his pursuer down when by means of a sudden flash of light he recognised Pietro. "Save yourself," cried he, "save yourself, Antonio,--here in my gondola. All is betrayed. Bodoeri--Nenolo--are in the power of the Seignory; the doors of the Ducal Palace are closed; the Doge is confined a prisoner in his own apartment--watched like a criminal by his own faithless guards. Come along--make haste--get away." Almost stupefied, Antonio suffered himself to be dragged into the gondola. Muffled voices--the clash of weapons--single cries for help--then with the deepest blackness of the night there followed a breathless awful silence. Next morning the populace, stricken with terror, beheld a fearful sight; it made every man's blood run cold in his veins. The Council of the Ten had that very same night passed sentence of death upon the leaders of the conspiracy who had been seized. They were strangled, and suspended from the balcony at the side of the Palace overlooking the Piazzetta, the one whence the Doge was in the habit of witnessing all ceremonies,--and where, alas! Antonio had hovered in the air before the lovely Annunciata, and where she had received from him the nosegay of flowers. Amongst the corpses were those of Marino Bodoeri and Bertuccio Nenolo. Two days later old Marino Falieri was sentenced to death by the Council of Ten, and executed on the so-called Giant Stairs of the Palace.

Antonio wandered about unconsciously, like a man in a dream; no one laid hands upon him, for no one recognised him as having been of the number of the conspirators. On seeing old Falieri's grey head fall, he started up, as it were, out of his death-like trance. With a most unearthly scream--with the shout, "Annunciata!" he rushed storming in the Palace, and along the passages. Nobody stopped him; the guards, as if stupefied by the terrible thing that had just taken place, only stared after him. The old crone came to meet him, loudly lamenting and complaining; she seized his hand and--a few steps more, and along with her he entered Annunciata's room. There she lay, poor thing, on the couch, as if already dead. Antonio rushed towards her and covered her hands with burning kisses, calling her by the sweetest and tenderest names.

Then she slowly opened her lovely heavenly eyes and saw Antonio; at first, however, it appeared as if it cost her an effort to call him to mind; but speedily she raised herself up, threw both her arms around his neck, and drew him to her bosom, showering down her hot tears upon him and kissing his cheeks--his lips. "Antonio--my Antonio--I love you, oh! more than I can tell you--yes, yes, there *is* a heaven on earth. What are my father's and my uncle's and my husband's death in comparison with the blissful joy of your love? Oh! let us flee--flee from this scene of blood and murder." Thus spake Annunciata, her heart rent by the bitterest anguish, as well as by the most passionate love. Amid thousands of kisses and never-ending tears, the two lovers mutually swore eternal fidelity; and, forgetting the fearful events of the terrible day that was past, they turned their eyes from the earth and looked up into the heaven which the spirit of love had unfolded to their view. The old woman advised them to flee to Chiozza; thence Antonio intended to travel in an opposite direction by land towards his own native country.

His friend, Pietro, procured him a small boat and had it brought to the bridge behind the Palace. When night came, Annunciata, enveloped in a thick shawl, crept stealthily down the steps with her lover, attended by old Margaret, who bore some valuable jewel caskets in her hood. They reached the bridge unobserved, and unobserved they embarked in their small craft. Antonio seized the oar, and away they went at a quick and vigorous rate. The bright moonlight danced along the waves in front of them like a gladsome messenger of love. They reached the open sea. Then began a peculiar whistling and howling of the wind far above their heads; black shadows came trooping up and hung themselves like a dark veil over the bright face of the moon. The dancing moonshine, the gladsome messenger of love, sank in the black depths of the sea amongst its muttering thunders. The storm came on and drove the black piled-up masses of clouds in front of it with wrathful violence. Up and down tossed the boat. "O help us! God, help us!" screamed the old woman. Antonio, no longer master of the oar, clasped his darling Annunciata in his arms, whilst she, aroused by his fiery kisses, strained him to her bosom in the intensity of her rapturous affection. "O my Antonio!"--"O my Annunciata!" they whispered, heedless of the storm which raged and blustered ever more furiously. Then the sea, the jealous widow of the beheaded Doge Falieri, stretched up her foaming waves as if they were giant arms, and seized upon the lovers, and dragged them, along with the old woman, down, down into her fathomless depths.

As soon as the man in the mantle had thus concluded his narrative, he jumped up quickly and left the room with strong rapid strides. The friends followed him with their eyes, silently and very much astonished; then they went to take another look at the picture. The old Doge again looked down upon them with a smirk, in his ridiculous finery and foppish vanity; but when they carefully looked into the Dogess's face they perceived quite plainly that the shadow of some unknown pain--a pain of which she only had a foreboding--was throned upon her lily brow, and that dreamy aspirations of love gleamed from behind her dark lashes, and hovered around her sweet lips. The Hostile Power seemed to be threatening death and destruction from out the distant sea and the vaporous clouds which enshrouded St. Mark's. They now had a clear conception of the deeper significance of the charming picture; but so often as they looked upon it again, all the sympathetic sorrow which they had felt at the history of Antonio and Annunciata's love returned upon them and filled the deepest recesses of their souls with its pleasurable awe.

MASTER MARTIN, THE COOPER, AND HIS JOURNEYMAN.

Well may your heart swell in presentient sadness, indulgent reader, when your footsteps wander through places where the splendid monuments of Old German Art speak, like eloquent tongues, of the magnificence, good steady industry, and sterling honesty of an illustrious age now long since passed away. Do you not feel as if you were entering a deserted house? The Holy Book in which the head of the household read is still lying open on the table, and the gay rich tapestry that the mistress of the house spun with her own hands is still hanging on the walls; whilst round about in the bright clean cupboards are ranged all kinds of valuable works of art, gifts received on festive occasions. You could almost believe a member of the household will soon enter and receive you with genuine hearty hospitality. But you will wait in vain for those whom the eternally revolving wheel of Time has whirled away; you may therefore surrender yourself to the sweet dream in which the old Masters rise up before you and speak honest and weighty words that sink deeply into your heart Then for the first time will you be able to grasp the profound significance of their works, for you will then not only live in, but you will also understand the age which could produce such masters and such works. But, alas! does it not happen that, as you stretch out your loving arms to clasp the beautiful image of your dream, it shyly flees away on the light morning clouds before the noisy bustle of the day, whilst you, your eyes filling with scalding tears, gaze after the bright vision as it gradually disappears? And so, rudely disturbed by the life that is pulsing about you, you are suddenly wakened out of your pleasant dream, retaining only the passionate longing that thrills your breast with its delicious awe.

Such sentiments as these, indulgent reader, have always animated the breast of him who is about to pen these pages for you, whenever his path has led him through the world-renowned city of Nuremberg. Now lingering before that wonderful structure, the fountain in the market-place, now contemplating St. Sebald's shrine, and the ciborium in St. Lawrence's Church, and Albert Dürer's grand pictures in the castle and in the town-house, he used to give himself up entirely to the delicious reveries which transported him into the midst of all the glorious splendours of the old Imperial Town. He thought of the true-hearted words of Father Rosenblüth--

O Nuremberg, thou glorious spot,
Thy honour's bolt was aimed aright,
Sticks in the mark whereat wisdom shot;
And truth in thee hath come to light.

Many a picture of the life of the worthy citizens of that period, when art and manual industry went loyally and industriously hand in hand, rose up brightly before his mind's eye, impressing itself upon his soul in especially cheerful and pleasing colours. Graciously be pleased, therefore, that he put one of these pictures before you. Perhaps, as you gaze upon it, it may afford you gratification, perhaps it may draw from you a good-natured smile, perhaps you may even come to feel yourself at home in Master Martin's house, and may linger willingly amongst his casks and tubs. Well!--Then the writer of these pages will have effected what is the sincere and honest wish of his heart.

How Master Martin was elected "Candle-master" and how he returned thanks therefor.

On the 1st of May, 1580, in accordance with traditionary custom and usage, the honourable guild of coopers, or wine-cask makers, of the free Imperial Town of Nuremberg, held with all due ceremony a meeting of their craft. A short time previously one of the presidents, or "Candle-masters," as they were called, had been carried to his grave; it was therefore necessary to elect a successor. Choice fell upon Master Martin. And in truth there was scarcely another who could be measured against him in the building of strong and well-made casks; none understood so well as he the management of wine in the cellar; hence he counted amongst his customers very many men of distinction, and lived in the most prosperous circumstances--nay, almost rolled in riches. Accordingly, after Martin had been elected, the worthy Councillor Jacobus Paumgartner, who, in his official character of syndic, presided over the meeting, said, "You have done bravely well, friends, to choose Master Martin as your president, for the office could not be in better hands. He is held in high esteem by all who know him, not only on account of his great skill, but on account of his ripe experience in the art of keeping and managing the rich juice of the grape. His steady industry and upright life, in spite of all the wealth he has amassed, may serve as an example to you all. Welcome then a thousand times, goodman Master Martin, as our honoured president."

With these words Paumgartner rose to his feet and took a few steps forward, with open arms, expecting that Martin would come to meet him. The latter immediately placed both his hands upon the arms of his chair and raised himself as expeditiously as his portly person would permit him to rise,--which was only slowly and heavily. Then just as slowly he strode into Paumgartner's hearty embrace, which, however, he scarcely returned. "Well," said Paumgartner, somewhat nettled at this, "well, Master Martin, are you not altogether well pleased that we have elected you to be our 'Candle-master'?" Master Martin, as was his wont, threw his head back into his neck, played with his fingers upon his capacious belly, and, opening his eyes wide and thrusting forward his under-lip with an air of superior astuteness, let his eyes sweep round the assembly. Then, turning to Paumgartner, he began, "Marry, my good and worthy sir, why should I not be altogether well pleased, seeing that I receive what is my due? Who refuses to take the reward of his honest labour? Who turns away from his threshold the defaulting debtor when at length he comes to pay his long standing debt? What! my good sirs," and Martin turned to the masters who sat around, "what! my good sirs, has it then occurred to you at last that I--I *must* be president of our honourable guild? What do you look for in your president? That he be the most skilful in workmanship? Go look at my two-tun cask made without fire, my brave masterpiece, and then come and tell me if there's one amongst you dare boast that, so far as concerns thoroughness and finish, he has ever turned out anything like it. Do you desire that your president possess money and goods? Come to my house and I will throw open chests and drawers, and you shall feast your eyes on the glitter of the sparkling gold and silver. Will you have a president who is respected by noble and base-born alike? Only ask our honoured gentlemen of the Council, ask the princes and noblemen around our good town of Nuremberg, ask his Lordship, the Bishop of Bamberg, ask what they all think of Master Martin? Oh! I--I don't think you'll hear much said against him." At the same time Master Martin struck his big fat belly with the greatest self-satisfaction, smiling with his eyes half-closed. Then, as all remained silent, nothing being heard except a dubious clearing of the throat here and there, he continued, "Ay! ay! I see. I ought, I know very well, to thank you all handsomely that in this election the good Lord above has at last seen fit to enlighten your minds. Well, when I receive the price of my labour, when my debtor repays me the borrowed money, I write at the bottom of the bill or of the receipt my 'Paid with thanks, Thomas Martin, Master-cooper here.' Let me then thank you all from my heart, since in electing me to be your president and 'Candle-master' you have wiped out an old debt. As for the rest, I pledge you that I will discharge the duties of my office with all fidelity and uprightness. In the hour of need I will stand by the guild and by each of you to the very best of my abilities with word and deed. I will exert the utmost diligence to uphold the honour and fame of our celebrated handicraft, without bating one jot of its present credit. My honoured syndic, and all you, my good friends and masters, I invite to come and partake of good cheer with me on the coming Sunday. Then, with blithesome hearts and minds, let us deliberate over a glass of good Hochheimer] or Johannisberger, or any other choice wine in my cellar that your palates may crave, what can be done for the furtherance of our common weal. Once again, I say you shall be all heartily welcome."

The honest masters' countenances, which had perceptibly clouded on hearing Master Martin's proud words, now recovered their serenity, whilst the previous dead silence was followed by the cheerful buzz of conversation, in which a good deal was said about Master Martin's great deserts, and also about his choice cellar. All promised to be present on the Sunday, and offered their hands to the newly-elected "Candle- master," who took them and shook them warmly, also drawing a few of the masters a little towards him, as if desirous of embracing them. The company separated in blithe good-humour.

What afterwards took place in Master Martin's house.

Now it happened that Councillor Jacobus Paumgartner had to pass by Master Martin's in order to reach his own home; and as they both stood outside Master Martin's door, and Paumgartner was about to proceed on his way, his friend, doffing his low bonnet, and bowing respectfully and as low as he was able, said to him, "I should be very glad, my good and worthy sir, if you would not disdain to step in and spend an hour or so in my humble house. Be pleased to suffer me to derive both profit and entertainment from your wise conversation." "Ay, ay! Master Martin, my friend," replied Paumgartner smiling, "gladly enough will I stay a while with you; but why do you call your house a humble house? I know very well that there's none of the richest of our citizens who can excel you in jewels and valuable furniture. Did you not a short time ago complete a handsome building which makes your house one of the ornaments of our renowned Imperial Town? In respect of its interior fittings I say nothing, for no patrician even need be ashamed of it."

Old Paumgartner was right; for on opening the door, which was brightly polished and richly ornamented with brass-work, they stepped into a spacious entrance hall almost resembling a state-room; the floor was tastefully inlaid, fine pictures hung on the walls, and the cupboards and chairs were all artistically carved. And all who came in willingly obeyed the direction inscribed in verses, according to olden custom, on a tablet which hung near the door:--

Let him who will the stairs ascend
See that his shoes be rubbed well clean.

Or taken off were better, I ween;
He thus avoids what might offend.
A thoughtful man is well aware
How he indoors himself should bear.

It had been a hot day, and now as the hour of twilight was approached it began to be close and stuffy in the rooms, so Master Martin led his eminent guest into the cool and spacious parlour-kitchen. For this was the name applied at that time to a place in the houses of the rich citizens which, although furnished as a kitchen, was never used as such--all kinds of valuable utensils and other necessaries of housekeeping being there set out on show. Hardly had they got inside the door when Master Martin shouted in a loud voice, "Rose, Rose!" Then the door was immediately opened, and Rose, Master Martin's only daughter, came in.

I should like you, dear reader, to awaken at this moment a vivid recollection of our great Albrecht Dürer's masterpieces; I would wish that the glorious maidens whom we find in them, with all their noble grace, their sweet gentleness and piety, should recur to your mind, endowed with living form. Recall the noble and delicate figure, the beautifully arched, lily-white forehead, the carnation flitting like a breath of roses across the cheek, the full sweet cherry-red lips,-- recall the eyes full of pious aspirations, half-veiled by their dark lashes, like moonlight seen through dusky foliage,--recall the silky hair, artfully gathered into graceful plaits,--recall the divine beauty of these maidens, and you will see lovely Rose. How else than in this way could the narrator sketch the dear, darling child? And yet permit me to remind you here of an admirable young artist into whose heart a quickening ray has fallen from these beautiful old times. I mean the German painter Cornelius, in Rome. Just as Margaret looks in Cornelius's drawings to Goethe's mighty *Faust* when she utters the words, "Bin weder Fräulein noch schön" (I am neither a lady of rank, nor yet beautiful), so also may Rose have looked when in the shyness of her pure chaste heart she felt compelled to shun addresses that smacked somewhat too much of freedom.

Rose bowed low with child-like respect before Paumgartner, and taking his hand, pressed it to her lips. The crimson colour rushed into the old gentleman's pale cheeks, as the sun when setting shoots up a dying flash, suddenly converting the dark foliage into gold, so the fire of a youth now left far behind gleamed once more in his eyes. "Ay! ay!" he cried in a blithesome voice, "marry, my good friend Master Martin, you are a rich and a prosperous man, but the best of all the blessings which the good Lord has given you is your lovely daughter Rose. If the hearts of old gentlemen like us who sit in the Town Council are so stirred that we cannot turn away our purblind eyes from the dear child, who can find fault with the young folks if they stop and stand like blocks of wood, or as if spell-bound, when they meet your daughter in the street, or see her at church, though we have a word of blame for our clerical gentry, because on the Allerwiese, or wherever else a festival is held, they all crowd round your daughter, with their sighs, and loving glances, and honied words, to the vexation of all other girls? Well, well, Master Martin, you can choose you your son-in-law amongst any of our young patricians, or wherever else you may list."

A dark frown settled on Master Martin's face; he bade his daughter fetch some good old wine; and after she had left the room, the hot blushes mantling thick and fast upon her cheeks, and her eyes bent upon the floor, he turned to old Paumgartner, "Of a verity, my good sir, Heaven has dowered my daughter with exceptional beauty, and herein too I have been made rich; but how can you speak of it in the girl's presence? And as for a patrician son-in-law, there'll never be anything of that sort." "Enough, Master Martin, say no more," replied Paumgartner, laughing. "Out of the fulness of the heart the mouth must speak. Don't you believe, then, that when I set eyes on Rose the sluggish blood begins to leap in my old heart also? And if I do honestly speak out what she herself must very well know, surely there's no very great mischief done."

Rose brought the wine and two beautiful drinking-glasses. Then Martin pushed the heavy table, which was ornamented with some remarkable carving, into the middle of the kitchen. Scarcely, however, had the old gentlemen taken their places and Master Martin had filled the glasses when a trampling of horses was heard in front of the house. It seemed as if a horseman had pulled up, and as if his voice was heard in the entrance-passage below. Rose hastened down and soon came back with the intelligence that old Junker Heinrich von Spangenberg was there and wished to speak to Master Martin. "Marry!" cried Martin, "now this is what I call a fine lucky evening, which brings me my best and oldest customer. New orders of course, I see I shall have to 'cask' out again"--Therewith he hastened down as fast as he was able to meet his welcome guest.

How Master Martin extols his trade above all others.

The Hochheimer sparkled in the beautiful cut drinking-glasses, and loosened the tongues and opened the hearts of the three old gentlemen. Old Spangenberg especially, who, though advanced in years, was yet brimming with freshness and vivacity, had many a jolly prank out of his merry youth to relate, so that Master Martin's belly wabbled famously, and again and again he had to brush the tears out of his eyes, caused by his loud and hearty laughing. Herr Paumgartner, too, forgot more than was customary with him the dignity of the Councillor, and enjoyed right well the noble liquor and the merry conversation. But when Rose again made her appearance with the neat housekeeper's basket under her arm, out of which she took a tablecloth as dazzling white as fresh- fallen snow,--when she tripped backwards and forwards busy with household matters, laying the cloth, and placing a plentiful supply of appetising dishes on the table,--when, with a winning smile she invited the gentlemen not to despise what had been hurriedly prepared, but to turn to and eat--during all this time their conversation and laughter ceased. Neither Paumgartner nor Spangenberg averted their sparkling eyes from the fascinating maiden, whilst Master Martin too, leaning back in his chair, and folding his hands, watched her busy movements with a gratified smile. Rose was withdrawing, but old Spangenberg was on his feet in a moment, quick as a youth; he took the girl by both shoulders and cried, again and again, as the bright tears trickled from his eyes, "Oh you good, you sweet little angel! What a dear darling girl you are!" then he kissed her twice--three times on the forehead, and returned to his seat, apparently in deep thought.

Paumgartner proposed the toast of Rose's health. "Yes," began Spangenberg, after she had gone out of the room, "yes, Master Martin, Providence has given you a precious jewel in your daughter, whom you cannot well over-estimate. She will yet bring you to great honour. Who is there, let him be of what rank in life he may, who would not willingly be your son-in-law?" "There you are," interposed Paumgartner; "there you see, Master Martin, the noble Herr von Spangenberg is exactly of my opinion. I already see our dear Rose a patrician's bride with the rich jewellery of pearls in her beautiful flaxen hair." "My dear sirs," began Martin, quite testily, "why do you, my dear sirs, keep harping upon this matter--a matter to which I have not as yet directed my thoughts? My Rose has only just reached her eighteenth year; it's not time for such a young thing to be looking out for a lover. How things may turn out afterwards--well, that I leave entirely to the will of the Lord; but this I do at any rate know, that none shall touch my daughter's hand, be he patrician or who he may, except the cooper who approves himself the cleverest and skilfullest master in his trade--presuming, of course, that my daughter will have him, for never will I constrain my dear child to do anything in the world, least of all to make a marriage that she does not like." Spangenberg and Paumgartner looked at each other, perfectly astonished at this extraordinary decision of the Master's. At length, after some clearing of his throat, Spangenberg began, "So, then, your daughter is not to wed out of her own station?" "God forbid she should," rejoined Martin. "But," continued Spangenberg, "if now a skilled master of a higher trade, say a goldsmith, or even a brave young artist, were to sue for your Rose and succeeded in winning her favour more than all other young journeymen, what then?" "I should say," replied Master Martin, throwing his head back into his neck, "show me, my excellent young friend, the fine two-tun cask which you have made as your masterpiece; and if he could not do so, I should kindly open the door for him and very politely request him to try his luck elsewhere." "Ah! but," went on Spangenberg again, "if the young journeyman should reply, 'A little structure of that kind I cannot show you, but come with me to the market-place and look at yon beautiful house which is sending up its slender gable into the free open air--that's my masterpiece.'" "Ah! my good sir, my good sir," broke in Master Martin impatiently, "why do you give yourself all this trouble to try and make me alter my conviction? Once and for all, my son-in-law must be of *my* trade; for my trade I hold to be the finest trade there is in the world. Do you think we've nothing to do but to fix the staves into the trestles (hoops), so that the cask may hold together? Marry, it's a fine thing and an admirable thing that our handiwork requires a previous knowledge of the way in which that noble blessing of Heaven, good wine, must be kept and managed, that it may acquire strength and flavour so as to go through all our veins and warm our blood like the true spirit of life! And then as for the construction of the casks--if we are to turn out a successful piece of work, must we not first draw out our plans with compass and rule? We must be arithmeticians and geometricians of no mean attainments, how else can we adapt the proportion and size of the cask to the measure of its contents? Ay, sir, my heart laughs in my body when we've bravely laboured at the staves with jointer and adze and have gotten a brave cask in the vice; and then when my journeymen swing their mallets and down it comes on the drivers clipp! clapp! clipp! clapp!--that's merry music for you; and there stands your well- made cask. And of a verity I may look a little proudly about me when I take my marking-tool in my hand and mark the sign of my handiwork, that is known and honoured of all respectable wine-masters, on the bottom of the cask. You spoke of house-building, my good sir. Well, a beautiful house is in truth a glorious piece of work, but if I were a house- builder and went past a house I had built, and saw a dirty fellow or good-for-nothing rascal who had got possession of it looking down upon me from the bay-window, I should feel thoroughly ashamed,--I should feel, purely out of vexation and annoyance, as if I should like to pull down and destroy my own work. But nothing like that can happen with the structures I build. Within them there comes and lives once for all nothing but the purest spirit on earth--good wine. God prosper my handiwork!"

"That's a fine eulogy," said Spangenberg, "and honestly and well meant. It does you honour to think so highly of your craft; but--do not get impatient if I keep harping upon the same string--now if a patrician really came and sued for your daughter? When a thing is brought right home to a man it often looks very different from what he thought it would." "Why, i' faith," cried Master Martin somewhat vehemently, "why, what else could I do but make a polite bow and say, 'My dear sir, if you were a brave cooper, but as it is'"---- "Stop a bit," broke in Spangenberg again; "but if now some fine day a handsome Junker on a gallant horse, with a brilliant retinue dressed in magnificent silks and satins, were to pull up before your door and ask you for Rose to wife?" "Marry, by my faith," cried Master Martin still more vehemently than before, "why, marry, I should run down as fast as I could and lock and bolt the door, and I should shout 'Ride on farther! Ride on farther! my worshipful Herr Junker; roses like mine don't blossom for you. My wine-cellar and my money-bags would, I dare say, suit you passing well--and you would take the girl in with the bargain; but ride on! ride on farther.'" Old Spangenberg rose to his feet, his face hot and red all over; then, leaning both hands on the table, he stood looking on the floor before him. "Well," he began after a pause, "and now the last question, Master Martin. If the Junker before your door were my own son, if I myself stopped at your door, would you shut it then, should you believe then that we were only come for your wine- cellar and your money-bags?" "Not at all, not at all, my good and honoured sir," replied Master Martin. "I would gladly throw open my door, and everything in my house should be at your and your son's service; but as for my Rose, I should say to you, 'If it had only pleased Providence to make your gallant son a brave cooper, there would be no more welcome son-in-law on earth than he; but now'---- But, my dear good sir, why do you tease and worry me with such curious questions? See you, our merry talk has come abruptly to an end, and look! our glasses are all standing full. Let's put all sons-in-law and Rose's marriage aside; here, I pledge you to the health of your son, who is, I hear, a handsome young knight." Master Martin seized his glass; Paumgartner followed his example, saying, "A truce to all captious conversation, and here's a health to your gallant son." Spangenberg touched glasses with them, and said with a forced smile, "Of course you know I was only speaking in jest; for nothing but wild head-strong passion could ever lead my son, who may choose him a wife from amongst the noblest families in the land, so far to disregard his rank and birth as to sue for your daughter. But methinks you might have answered me in a somewhat more friendly way." "Well, but, my good sir," replied Master Martin, "even in jest I could only speak as I should act if the wonderful things you are pleased to imagine were really to happen. But you *must* let me have my pride; for you cannot but allow that I am the skilfullest cooper far and near, that I understand the management of wine, that I observe strictly and truly the admirable wine-regulations of our departed Emperor Maximilian (may he rest in peace!), that as beseems a pious man I abhor all godlessness, that I never burn more than one small half-ounce of pure sulphur in one of my two-tun casks, which is necessary to preserve it--the which, my good and honoured sirs, you will have abundantly remarked from the flavour of my wine." Spangenberg resumed his seat, and tried to put on a cheerful countenance, whilst Paumgartner introduced other topics of conversation. But, as it so often happens, when once the strings of an instrument have got out of tune, they are always getting more or less warped, so that the player in vain tries to entice from them again the full-toned chords which they gave at first, thus it was with the three old gentlemen; no remark, no word, found a sympathetic response. Spangenberg called for his grooms, and left Master Martin's house quite in an ill-humour after he had entered it in gay good spirits.

The old Grandmother's Prophecy.

Master Martin was rather ill at ease because his brave old customer had gone away out of humour in this way, and he said to Paumgartner, who had just emptied his last glass and rose to go too, "For the life of me, I can't understand what the old gentleman meant by his talk, and why he should have got testy about it at last." "My good friend Master Martin," began Paumgartner, "you are a good and honest man; and a man has verily a right to set store by the handiwork he loves and which brings him wealth and honour; but he ought not to show it in boastful pride, that's against all right Christian feeling. And in our guild- meeting to-day you did not act altogether right in putting yourself before all the other masters. It may true that you understand more about your craft than all the rest; but that you go and cast it in their teeth can only provoke ill-humour and black looks. And then you must go and do it again this evening! You could not surely be so infatuated as to look for anything else in Spangenberg's talk beyond a jesting attempt to see to what lengths you would go in your obstinate pride. No wonder the worthy gentleman felt greatly annoyed when you told him you should only see common covetousness in any Junker's wooing of your daughter. But all would have been well if, when Spangenberg began to speak of his son, you had interposed--if you had said, 'Marry, my good and honoured sir, if you yourself came along with your son to sue for my daughter--why, i' faith, that would be far too high an honour for me, and I should then have wavered in my firmest principles.' Now, if you had spoken to him like that, what else could old Spangenberg have done but forget his former resentment, and smile cheerfully and in good humour as he had done before?" "Ay, scold me," said Master Martin, "scold me right well, I have well deserved it; but when the old gentleman would keep talking such stupid nonsense I felt as if I were choking, I could not make any other answer." "And then," went on Paumgartner, "what a ridiculous resolve to give your daughter to nobody but a cooper! You will commit, you say, your daughter's destiny to Providence, and yet with human shortsightedness you anticipate the decree of the Almighty in that you obstinately determine beforehand that your son-in-law is to come from within a certain narrow circle. That will prove the ruin of you and your Rose, if you are not careful Have done, Master Martin, have done with such unchristian childish folly; leave the Almighty, who will put a right choice in your daughter's honest heart when the right time comes--leave Him to manage it all in his own way." "O my worthy friend," said Master Martin, quite crest-fallen, "I now see how wrong I was not to tell you everything at first. You think it is nothing but overrating my handiwork that has brought me to take this unchangeable resolve of wedding Rose to none but a master-cooper; but that is not so; there is another reason, a more wonderful and mysterious reason. I can't let you go until you have learned all; you shall not bear ill-will against me over-night. Sit down, I earnestly beg you, stay a few minutes longer. See here; there's still a bottle of that old wine left which the ill-tempered Junker has despised; come, let's enjoy it together." Paumgartner was astonished at Master Martin's earnest, confidential tone, which was in general perfectly foreign to his nature; it seemed as if there was something weighing heavy upon the man's heart that he wanted to get rid of.

And when Paumgartner had taken his seat and drunk a glass of wine, Master Martin began as follows. "You know, my good and honoured friend, that soon after Rose was born I lost my beloved wife; Rose's birth was her death. At that time my old grandmother was still living, if you can call it living when one is blind, deaf as a post, scarce able to speak, lame in every limb, and lying in bed day after day and night after night Rose had been christened; and the nurse sat with the child in the room where my old grandmother lay. I was so cut up with grief, and when I looked upon my child, so sad and yet so glad--in fact I was so greatly shaken that I felt utterly unfitted for any kind of work, and stood quite still and wrapped up in my own thoughts beside my old grandmother's bed; and I counted her happy, since now all her earthly pain was over. And as I gazed upon her face a strange smile began to steal across it, her withered features seemed to be smoothed out, her pale cheeks became flushed with colour. She raised herself up in bed; she stretched out her paralysed arms, as if suddenly animated by some supernatural power,--for she had never been able to do so at other times. She called distinctly in a low pleasant voice, 'Rose, my darling Rose!' The nurse got up and brought her the child, which she rocked up and down in her arms. But then, my good sir, picture my utter astonishment, nay, my alarm, when the old lady struck up in a clear strong voice a song in the *Hohe fröhliche Lobweis* of Herr Hans Berchler, mine host of the Holy Ghost in Strasburg, which ran like this--

Maiden tender, with cheeks so red,
Rose, listen to the words I say;
Wouldst guard thyself from fear and ill?
Then put thy trust in God alway;
Let not thy tongue at aught make mock,
Nor foolish longings feed at heart.
A vessel fair to see he'll bring,
In which the spicy liquid foams,
And bright, bright angels gaily sing.
And then in reverent mood
Hearken to the truest love,
Oh! hearken to the sweet love-words.
The vessel fair with golden grace--
Lo! him who brings it in the house
Thou wilt reward with sweet embrace;
And an thy lover be but true,
Thou need'st nor wait thy father's kiss.
The vessel fair will always bring
All wealth and joy and peace and bliss;
So, virgin fair, with the bright, bright eyes,
Let aye thy little ear be ope
To all true words. And henceforth live,
And with God's richest blessing thrive.

"And after she had sung this song through, she laid the child gently and carefully down upon the coverlet; and, placing her trembling withered hand upon her forehead, she muttered something to herself, to us, however, unintelligible; but the rapt countenance of the old lady showed in every feature that she was praying. Then her head sank back upon the pillows, and just as the nurse took up the child my old grandmother took a deep breath; she was dead." "That is a wonderful story," said Paumgartner when Master Martin ceased speaking; "but I don't exactly see what is the connection between your old grandmother's prophetic song and your obstinate resolve to give Rose to none but a master-cooper." "What!" replied Master Martin, "why, what can be plainer than that the old lady, especially inspired by the Lord at the last moments of her life, announced in a prophetic voice what must happen if Rose is to be happy? The lover who is to bring wealth and joy and peace and bliss into the house with his vessel fair, who is that but a lusty cooper who has made his vessel fair, his masterpiece with me? In what other vessel does the spicy liquid foam, if not in the wine-cask? And when the wine works, it bubbles and even murmurs and splashes; that's the lovely angels chasing each other backwards and forwards in the wine and singing their gay songs. Ay, ay, I tell you, my old grandmother meant none other lover than a master-cooper; and it shall be so, it shall be so." "But, my good Master Martin," said Paumgartner, "you are interpreting the words of your old grandmother just in your own way. Your interpretation is far from satisfactory to my mind; and I repeat that you ought to leave all simply to the ordering of Providence and your daughter's heart, in which I dare be bound the right choice lies hidden away somewhere." "And I repeat," interrupted Martin impatiently, "that my son-in-law *shall* be,--I am resolved,--*shall* be none other than a skilful cooper." Paumgartner almost got angry at Master Martin's stubbornness; he controlled himself, however, and, rising from his seat, said, "It's getting late, Master Martin, let us now have done with our drinking and talking, for neither methinks will do us any more good."

When they came out into the entrance-hall, there stood a young woman with five little boys, the eldest scarce eight years old apparently, and the youngest scarce six months. She was weeping and sobbing bitterly. Rose hastened to meet the two old gentlemen and said, "Oh father, father! Valentine is dead; there is his wife and the children." "What! Valentine dead?" cried Master Martin, greatly startled. "Oh! that accident! that accident! Just fancy," he continued, turning to Paumgartner, "just fancy, my good sir, Valentine was the cleverest journeyman I had on the premises; and he was industrious, and a good honest man as well. Some time ago he wounded himself dangerously with the adze in building a large cask; the wound got worse and worse; he was seized with a violent fever, and now he has had to die of it in the prime of life." Thereupon Master Martin approached the poor disconsolate woman, who, bathed in tears, was lamenting that she had nothing but misery and starvation staring her in the face. "What!" said Master Martin, "what do you think of me then? Your husband got his dangerous wound whilst working for me, and do you think I am going to let you perish of want? No, you all belong to my house from now onwards. To-morrow, or whenever you like, we'll bury your poor husband, and then do you and your boys go to my farm outside the Ladies Gate, where my fine open workshop is, and where I work every day with my journeymen. You can install yourself as housekeeper there to look after things for me, and your fine boys I will educate as if they were my own sons. And, I tell you what, I'll take your old father as well into my house. He was a sturdy journeyman cooper once upon a time whilst he still had muscle in his arms. And now--if he can no longer wield the mallet, or the beetle or the beak iron, or work at the bench, he yet can do something with croze-adze, or can hollow out staves for me with the draw-knife. At any rate he shall come along with you and be taken into my house." If Master Martin had not caught hold of the woman, she would have fallen on the floor at his feet in a dead swoon, she was so affected by grief and emotion. The eldest of the boys clung to his doublet, whilst the two youngest, whom Rose had taken in her arms, stretched out their tiny hands towards him, as if they had understood it all. Old Paumgartner said, smiling and with bright tears standing in his eyes, "Master Martin, one can't bear you any ill-will;" and he betook himself to his own home.

How the two young journeymen Frederick and Reinhold became acquainted with each other.

Upon a beautiful, grassy, gently-sloping hill, shaded by lofty trees, lay a fine well-made young journeyman, whose name was Frederick. The sun had already set, and rosy tongues of light were stretching upwards from the furthest verge of the horizon. In the distance the famed imperial town of Nuremberg could be plainly seen, spreading across the valley and boldly lifting up her proud towers against the red glow of the evening, its golden rays gilding their pinnacles. The young journeyman was leaning his arm on his bundle, which lay beside him, and contained his necessaries whilst on the travel, and was gazing with looks full of longing down into the valley. Then he plucked some of the flowers which grew among the grass within reach of him and tossed them into the air towards the glorious sunset; afterwards he sat gazing sadly before him, and the burning tears gathered in his eyes. At length he raised his head, and spreading out his arms as if about to embrace some one dear to him, he sang in a clear and very pleasant voice the following song:--

My eyes now rest once more
On thee, O home, sweet home!
My true and honest heart
Has ne'er forgotten thee.
O rosy glow of evening come,
I fain would naught but roses see.
Ye sweetest buds and flowers of love,

Bend down and touch my heart
With winsome sweet caresses.
O swelling bosom, wilt thou burst?
Yet hold in pain and sweet joy fast.
O golden evening red!
O beauteous ray, be my sweet messenger,
And bear to her my sighs and tears--
My tears and sighs on faithfully to her.
And were I now to die,
And roses then did ask thee--say,
"His heart with love--it pined away."

Having sung this song, Frederick took a little piece of wax out of his bundle, warmed it in his bosom, and began in a neat and artistic manner to model a beautiful rose with scores of delicate petals. Whilst busy with this work he hummed to himself some of the lines of the song he had just sung, and so deeply absorbed was he in his occupation that he did not observe the handsome youth who had been standing behind him for some time and attentively watching his work.

"Marry, my friend," began now the youth, "by my troth, that is a dainty piece of work you are making there." Frederick looked round in alarm; but when he looked into the dark friendly eyes of the young stranger, he felt as if he had known him for a long time. Smiling, he replied, "Oh! my dear sir, how can you notice such trifling? it only serves me for pastime on my journey." "Well then," went on the stranger youth, "if you call that delicately formed flower, which is so faithful a reproduction of Nature, trifling, you must be a skilful practised modeller. You have afforded me a pleasant surprise in two ways. First, I was quite touched to the heart by the song you sang so admirably to Martin Häscher's *Zarte Buchstabenweis*; and now I cannot but admire your artistic skill in modelling. How much farther do you intend to travel to-day?" Frederick replied, "Yonder lies the goal of my journey before our eyes. I am going home, to the famed imperial town of Nuremberg. But as the sun has now been set some time, I shall pass the night in the village below there, and then by being up and away in the early morning I can be in Nuremberg at noon." "Marry," cried the youth, delighted, "how finely things will fit; we are both going the same way, for I want to go to Nuremberg. I will spend the night with you here in the village, and then we'll proceed on our way again to-morrow. And now let us talk a little." The youth, Reinhold by name, threw himself down beside Frederick on the grass, and continued, "If I mistake not, you are a skilful artist-caster, are you not? I infer it from your style of modelling; or perhaps you are a worker in gold and silver?" Frederick cast down his eyes sadly, and said dejectedly, "Marry, my dear sir, you are taking me for something far better and higher than I really am. Well, I will speak candidly; I have learned the trade of a cooper, and am now going to work for a well-known master in Nuremberg. You will no doubt look down upon me with contempt since, instead of being able to mould and cast splendid statues, and such like, all I can do is to hoop casks and tubs." Reinhold burst out laughing, and cried, "Now that I call droll. I shall look down upon you--eh? because you are a cooper; why man, that's what I am; I'm nothing but a cooper." Frederick opened his eyes wide in astonishment; he did not know what to make of it, for Reinhold's dress was in keeping with anything sooner than a journeyman cooper's on travel. His doublet of fine black cloth, trimmed with slashed velvet, his dainty ruff, his short broadsword, and baretta with a long drooping feather, seemed rather to point to a prosperous merchant; and yet again there was a strange something about the face and form of the youth which completely negatived the idea of a merchant. Reinhold, noticing Frederick's doubting glances, undid his travelling-bundle and produced his cooper's apron and knife-belt, saying, "Look here, my friend, look here. Have you any doubts now as to my being a comrade? I perceive you are astonished at my clothing, but I have just come from Strasburg, where the coopers go about the streets as fine as noblemen. Certainly I did once set my heart upon something else like you, but now to be a cooper is the topmost height of my ambition, and I have staked many a grand hope upon it. Is it not the same with you, comrade? But I could almost believe that a dark cloud-shadow had been hung unawares about the brightness of your youth, so that you are no longer able to look freely and gladly about you. The song which you were just singing was full of pain and of the yearning of love; but there were strains in it that seemed as if they proceeded from my own heart, and I somehow fancy I know all that is locked up within your breast. You may therefore all the more put confidence in me, for shall we not then be good comrades in Nuremberg?" Reinhold threw his arm around Frederick and looked kindly into his eyes. Whereupon Frederick said, "The more I look at you, honest friend, the stronger I feel drawn towards you; I clearly discern within my breast the wonderful voice which faithfully echoes the cry that you are a sympathetic spirit I must tell you all--not that a poor fellow like me has any important secrets to confide to you, but simply because there is room in the heart of the true friend for *his* friend's pain, and during the first moments of our new acquaintance even I acknowledge you to be my truest friend.

"I am now a cooper, and may boast that I understand my work; but all my thoughts have been directed to another and a nobler art since my very childhood. I wished to become a great master in casting statues and in silver-work, like Peter Fischer or the Italian Benvenuto Cellini; and so I worked with intense ardour along with Herr Johannes Holzschuer, the well-known worker in silver in my native town yonder. For although he did not exactly cast statues himself, he was yet able to give me a good introduction to the art. And Herr Tobias Martin, the master-cooper, often came to Herr Holzschuer's with his daughter, pretty Rose. Without being consciously aware of it, I fell in love with her. I then left home and went to Augsburg in order to learn properly the art of casting, but this first caused my smouldering passion to burst out into flames. I saw and heard nothing but Rose; every exertion and all labour that did not tend to the winning of her grew hateful to me. And so I adopted the only course that would bring me to this goal. For Master Martin will only give his daughter to the cooper who shall make the very best masterpiece in his house, and who of course finds favour in his daughter's eyes as well. I deserted my own art to learn cooperage. I am now going to Nuremberg to work for Master Martin. But now that my home lies before me and Rose's image rises up before my eyes, I feel overcome with anxiety and nervousness, and my heart sinks within me. Now I see clearly how foolishly I have acted; for I don't even know whether Rose loves me or whether she ever will love me." Reinhold had listened to Frederick's story with increasing attention. He now rested his head on his arm, and, shading his eyes with his hand, asked in a hollow moody voice, "And has Rose never given you any signs of her love?" "Nay," replied Frederick, "nay, for when I left Nuremberg she was more a child than a maiden. No doubt she liked me; she smiled upon me most sweetly when I never wearied plucking flowers for her in Herr Holzschuer's garden and weaving them into wreaths, but----" "Oh! then all hope is not yet lost," cried Reinhold suddenly, and so vehemently and in such a disagreeably shrill voice that Frederick was almost terrified. At the same time he leapt to his feet, his sword rattling against his side, and as he stood upright at his full stature the deep shadows of the night fell upon his pale face and distorted his gentle features in a most unpleasant way, so that Frederick cried, perfectly alarmed, "What's happened to you all at once?" and stepping back, his foot knocked against Reinhold's bundle. There proceeded from it the jarring of some stringed instrument, and Reinhold cried angrily, "You ill-mannered fellow, don't break my lute all to pieces." The instrument was fastened to the bundle; Reinhold unbuckled it and ran his fingers wildly over the strings as if he would break them all. But his playing soon grew soft and melodious. "Come, brother," said he in the same gentle tone as before, "let us now go down into the village. I've got a good means here in my hands to banish the evil spirits who may cross our path, and who might in particular have any dealings with me." "Why, brother," replied Frederick, "what evil spirits will be likely to have anything to do with us on the way? But your playing is very, very nice; please go on with it."

The golden stars were beginning to dot the dark azure sky. The night breezes in low murmurous whispers swept lightly over the fragrant meadows. The brooks babbled louder, and the trees rustled in the distant woods round about Then Frederick and Reinhold went down the slope playing and singing, and the sweet notes of their songs, so full of noble aspirations, swelled up clear and sharp in the air, as if they had been plumed arrows of light. Arrived at their quarters for the night, Reinhold quickly threw aside lute and bundle and strained Frederick to his heart; and Frederick felt on his cheeks the scalding tears which Reinhold shed.

How the two young journeymen, Reinhold and Frederick, were taken into Master Martin's house.

Next morning when Frederick awoke he missed his new-won friend, who had the night before thrown himself down upon the straw pallet at his side; and as his lute and his bundle were likewise missing, Frederick quite concluded that Reinhold, from reasons which were unknown to him, had left him and gone another road. But directly he stepped out of the house Reinhold came to meet him, his bundle on his back and his lute under his arm, and dressed altogether differently from what he had been the day before. He had taken the feather out of his baretta, and laid aside his sword, and had put on a plain burgher's doublet of an unpretentious colour, instead of the fine one with the velvet trimmings. "Now, brother," he cried, laughing merrily to his astonished friend, "you will acknowledge me for your true comrade and faithful work-mate now, eh? But let me tell you that for a youth in love you have slept most soundly. Look how high the sun is. Come, let us be going on our way." Frederick was silent and busied with his own thoughts; he scarcely answered Reinhold's questions and scarcely heeded his jests. Reinhold, however, was full of exuberant spirits; he ran from side to side, shouted, and waved his baretta in the air. But he too became more and more silent the nearer they approached the town. "I can't go any farther, I am so full of nervousness and anxiety and sweet sadness; let us rest a little while beneath these trees." Thus spake Frederick just before they reached the gate; and he threw himself down quite exhausted in the grass. Reinhold sat down beside him, and after a while began, "I daresay you thought me extremely strange yesterday evening, good brother mine. But as you told me about your love, and were so very dejected, then all kinds of foolish nonsense flooded my mind and made me quite confused, and would have made me mad in the end if your good singing and my lute had not driven away the evil spirits. But this morning when the first ray of sunlight awoke me, all my gaiety of heart returned, for all nasty feelings had already left me last evening. I ran out, and whilst wandering among the undergrowth a crowd of fine things came into my mind: how I had found you, and how all my heart felt drawn towards you. There also occurred to me a pretty little story which happened some time ago when I was in Italy; I will tell it to you, since it is a remarkable illustration of what true friendship can do.

"It chanced that a noble prince, a warm patron and friend of the Fine Arts, offered a very large prize for a painting, the subject of which was definitely fixed, and which, though a splendid subject, was one difficult to treat. Two young painters, united by the closest bond of friendship and wont to work together, resolved to compete for the prize. They communicated their designs to each other and had long talks as to how they should overcome the difficulties connected with the subject. The elder, more experienced in drawing and in arrangement and grouping, had soon formed a conception of the picture and sketched it; then he went to the younger, whom he found so discouraged in the very designing that he would have given the scheme up, had not the elder constantly encouraged him, and imparted to him good advice. But when they began to paint, the younger, a master in colour, was able to give his friend many a hint, which he turned to the best account; and eventually it was found that the younger had never designed a better picture, nor the elder coloured one better. The pieces being finished, the two artists fell upon each other's neck; each was delighted, enraptured, with the other's work, and each adjudged the prize, which they both deserved, to his friend. But when, eventually, the prize was declared to have fallen to the younger, he cried, ashamed, 'Oh! how can I have gained the prize? What is my merit in comparison with that of my friend? I should never have produced anything at all good without his advice and valuable assistance.' Then said the elder, 'And did not you too stand by me with invaluable counsel? My picture is certainly not bad; but yours has carried off the prize as it deserved. To strive honestly and openly towards the same goal, that is the way of true friends; the wreath which the victor wins confers honour also upon the vanquished. I love you now all the more that you have so bravely striven, and in your victory I also reap fame and honour.' And the painter was right, was he not, Frederick? Honest contention for the same prize, without any malicious reserve, ought to unite true friends still more and knit their hearts still closer, instead of setting them at variance. Ought there to be any room in noble minds for petty envy or malicious hate?" "Never, certainly not," replied Frederick. "We are now faithful loving brothers, and shall both in a short time construct our masterpiece in Nuremburg, a good two-tun cask, made without fire; but Heaven forbid that I should feel the least spark of envy if yours, dear brother Reinhold, turned out to be better than mine." "Ha! ha! ha!" laughed Reinhold heartily, "go on with you and your masterpiece; you'll soon manage that to the joy of all good coopers. And let me tell you that in all that concerns calculation of size and proportion, and drawing plans of sections of circles, you'll find I'm your man. And then in choosing your wood you may rely fully upon me. Staves of the holm oak felled in winter, without worm-holes, without either red or white streaks, and without blemish, that's what we must look for; you may trust my eyes. I will stand by you with all the help I can, in both deed and counsel; and my own masterpiece will be none the worse for it." "But in the name of all that's holy," broke in Frederick here, "why are we chattering about who is to make the best masterpiece? Are we to have any contest about the matter?--the best masterpiece--to gain Rose! What are we thinking about? The very thought makes me giddy." "Marry, brother," cried Reinhold, still laughing, "there was no thought at all of Rose. You are a dreamer. Come along, let us go on if we are to get into the town." Frederick leapt to his feet, and went on his way, his mind in a whirl of confusion.

As they were washing and brushing off the dust of travel in the hostelry, Reinhold said to Frederick, "To tell you the truth, I for my part don't know for what master I shall work; I have no acquaintances here at all; and I thought you would perhaps take me along with you to Master Martin's, brother? Perhaps I may get taken on by him." "You remove a heavy load from my heart," replied Frederick, "for if you will only stay with me, it will be easier for me to conquer my anxiety and nervousness." And so the two young apprentices trudged sturdily on to the house of the famed cooper, Master Martin.

It happened to be the very Sunday on which Master Martin gave his feast in honour of his election as "Candle-master;" and the two arrived just as they were partaking of the good cheer. So it was that as Reinhold and Frederick entered into Master Martin's house they heard the ringing of glasses and the confused buzz and rattle of a merry company at a feast. "Oh!" said Frederick quite cast down, "we have, it seems, come at an unseasonable time." "Nay, I think we have come exactly at the right time," replied Reinhold, "for Master Martin is sure to be in good humour after a good feast, and well disposed to grant our wishes." They caused their arrival to be announced to Master Martin, and soon he appeared in the entrance-passage, dressed in holiday garb and with no small amount of colour in his nose and on his cheeks. On catching sight of Frederick he cried, "Holla! Frederick, my good lad, have you come home again? That's fine! And so you have taken up the best of all trades--cooperage. Herr Holzschuer cuts confounded wry faces when your name is mentioned, and says a great artist is ruined in you, and that you could have cast little images and espaliers as fine as those in St. Sebald's or on Fugger's house at

Augsburg. But that's all nonsense; you have done quite right to step across the way here. Welcome, lad, welcome with all my heart." And therewith Herr Martin took him by the shoulders and drew him to his bosom, as was his wont, thoroughly well pleased. This kind reception by Master Martin infused new spirits into Frederick; all his nervousness left him, so that unhesitatingly and without constraint he was able not only to prefer his own request but also warmly to recommend Reinhold. "Well, to tell you the truth," said Master Martin, "you could not have come at a more fortunate time than just now, for work keeps increasing and I am bankrupt of workmen. You are both heartily welcome. Put your bundles down and come in; our meal is indeed almost finished, but you can come and take your seats at the table, and Rose shall look after you and get you something." And Master Martin and the two journeymen went into the room. There sat the honest masters, the worthy syndic Jacobus Paumgartner at their head, all with hot red faces. Dessert was being served, and a better brand of wine was sparkling in the glasses. Every master was talking about something different from all his neighbours and in a loud voice, and yet they all thought they understood each other; and now and again some of them burst out in a hearty laugh without exactly knowing why. When, however. Master Martin came back, leading the two young men by the hand, and announced aloud that he brought two journeymen who had come to him well provided with testimonials just at the time he wanted them, then all grew silent, each master scrutinising the smart young fellows with a smile of comfortable satisfaction, whilst Frederick cast his eyes down and twisted his baretta about in his hands. Master Martin directed the youths to places at the very bottom of the table; but these were soon the very best of all, for Rose came and took her seat between the two, and served them attentively both with dainty dishes and with good rich wine. There was Rose, a most winsome picture of grace and loveliness, seated between the two handsome youths, all in midst of the bearded old men--it was a right pleasant sight to see; the mind instantly recalled a bright morning cloud rising solitary above the dim dark horizon, or beautiful spring flowers lifting up their bright heads from amidst the uniform colourless grass. Frederick was so very happy and so very delighted that his breath almost failed him for joy; and only now and again did he venture to steal a glance at her who filled his heart so fully. His eyes were fixedly bent upon his plate; how could he possibly dream of eating the least morsel? Reinhold, on the other hand, could not turn his sparkling, radiant eyes away from the lovely maiden. He began to talk about his long journeys in such a wonderful way that Rose had never heard anything like it. She seemed to see everything of which he spoke rise up vividly before her in manifold ever-changing forms. She was all eyes and ears; and when Reinhold, carried away by the fire of his own words, grasped her hand and pressed it to his heart, she didn't know where she was. "But bless me," broke off Reinhold all at once, "why, Frederick, you are quite silent and still. Have you lost your tongue? Come, let us drink to the weal of the lovely maiden who has so hospitably entertained us." With a trembling hand Frederick seized the huge drinking-glass that Reinhold had filled to the brim and now insisted on his draining to the last drop. "Now here's long life to our excellent master," cried Reinhold, again filling the glasses and again compelling Frederick to empty his. Then the fiery juices of the wine permeated his veins and stirred up his stagnant blood until it coursed as it were triumphantly through his every limb. "Oh! I feel so indescribably happy," he whispered, the burning blushes mounting into his cheeks. "Oh! I have never felt so happy in all my life before." Rose, who undoubtedly gave another interpretation to his words, smiled upon him with incomparable gentleness. Then, quit of all his embarrassing shyness, Frederick said, "Dear Rose, I suppose you no longer remember me, do you?" "But, dear Frederick," replied Rose, casting down her eyes, "how could I possibly forget you in so short a time? When you were at Herr Holzschuer's--true, I was only a mere child then, yet you did not disdain to play with me, and always had something nice and pretty to talk about. And that dear little basket made of fine silver wire that you gave me at Christmas-time, I've got it still, and I take care of it and keep it as a precious memento." Frederick was intoxicated with delight and tears glittered in his eyes. He tried to speak, but there only burst from his breast, like a deep sigh, the words, "O Rose--dear, dear Rose." "I have always really from my heart longed to see you again," went on Rose; "but that you would become a cooper, that I never for a moment dreamed. Oh! when I call to mind the beautiful things that you made whilst you were with Master Holzschuer--oh! it really is a pity that you have not stuck to your art." "O Rose," said Frederick, "it is only for your sake that I have become unfaithful to it." No sooner had he uttered these words than he could have sunk into the earth for shame and confusion. He had most thoughtlessly let the confession slip over his lips. Rose, as if divining all, turned her face away from him; whilst he in vain struggled for words.

Then Herr Paumgartner struck the table a bang with his knife, and announced to the company that Herr Vollrad, a worthy *Meistersinger*, would favour them with a song. Herr Vollrad at once rose to his feet, cleared his throat, and sang such an excellent song in the *Güldne Tonweis* of Herr Vogelgesang that everybody's heart leapt with joy, and even Frederick recovered himself from his awkward embarrassment again. After Herr Vollrad had sung several other excellent songs to several other excellent tunes, such as the *Süsser Ton*, the *Krummzinkenweis*, the *Geblümte Paradiesweis*, the *Frisch Pomeranzenweis*, &c., he called upon any one else at the table who understood anything of the sweet and delectable art of the *Meistersinger* also to honour them with a song. Then Reinhold rose to his feet and said that if he might be allowed to accompany himself on his lute in the Italian fashion he would give them a song, keeping, however, strictly to the German tune. As nobody had any objection he fetched his instrument, and, after a little tuneful prelude, began the following song:--

Where is the little fount
Where sparkles the spicy wine?
From forth its golden depths
Its golden sparkles mount
And dance 'fore the gladdened eye.
This beautiful little fount
Wherein the golden wine
Sparkles--who made it,
With thoughtful skill and fine,
With such high art and industry,
That praise deserve so well?
This little fount so gay,
Wrought with high art and fine,
Was fashioned by one
Who ne'er an artist was--
But a brave young cooper he,
His veins with rich wine glowing,
His heart with true love singing,
And ever lovingly--
For that's young cooper's way
In all the things he does.

This song pleased them all down to the ground, but none more so than Master Martin, whose eyes sparkled with pleasure and delight. Without heeding Vollrad, who had almost too much to say about Hans Müller's *Stumpfe Schossweis*, which the youth had caught excellently well,-- Master Martin, without heeding him, rose from his seat, and, lifting his *passglas* above his head, called aloud, "Come here, honest cooper and *Meistersinger*, come here and drain this glass with me, your Master Martin." Reinhold had to do as he was bidden. Returning to his place, he whispered into Frederick's ear, who was looking very pensive, "Now, you must sing--sing the song you sang last night." "Are you mad?" asked Frederick, quite angry. But Reinhold turned to the company and said in a loud voice, "My honoured gentlemen and masters, my dear brother Frederick here can sing far finer songs, and has a much pleasanter voice than I have, but his throat has got full of dust from his travels, and he will treat you to some of his songs another time, and then to the most admirable tunes." And they all began to shower down their praises upon Frederick, as if he had already sung. Indeed, in the end, more than one of the masters was of opinion that his voice was really more agreeable than journeyman Reinhold's, and Herr Vollrad also, after he had drunk another glass, was convinced that Frederick could use the beautiful German tunes far better than Reinhold, for the latter had too much of the Italian style about him. And Master Martin, throwing his head back into his neck, and giving his round belly a hearty slap, cried, "Those are *my* journeymen, *my* journeymen, I tell you--mine, master-cooper Tobias Martin's of Nuremberg." And all the other masters nodded their heads in assent, and, sipping the last drops out of the bottom of their tall glasses, said, "Yes, yes. Your brave, honest journeymen, Master Martin--that they are." At length it was time to retire to rest Master Martin led Reinhold and Frederick each into a bright cheerful room in his own house.

*How the third journeyman came into Master Martin's house,
and what followed in consequence.*

After the two journeymen had worked for some weeks in Master Martin's workshop, he perceived that in all that concerned measurement with rule and compass, and calculation, and estimation of measure and size by eyesight, Reinhold could hardly find his match, but it was a different thing when it came to hard work at the bench or with the adze or the mallet. Then Reinhold soon grew tired, and the work did not progress, no matter how great efforts he might make. On the other hand, Frederick planed and hammered away without growing particularly tired. But one thing they had in common with each other, and that was their well-mannered behaviour, marked, principally at Reinhold's instance, by much natural cheerfulness and good-natured enjoyment. Besides, even when hard at work, they did not spare their throats, especially when pretty Rose was present, but sang many an excellent song, their pleasant voices harmonising well together. And whenever Frederick, glancing shyly across at Rose, seemed to be falling into his melancholy mood, Reinhold at once struck up a satirical song that he composed, beginning, "The cask is not the cither, nor is the cither the cask," so that old Herr Martin often had to let the croze-adze which he had raised, sink again without striking and hold his big belly as it wabbled from his internal laughter. Above all, the two journeymen, and mainly Reinhold, had completely won their way into Martin's favour; and it was not difficult to observe that Rose found a good many pretexts for lingering oftener and longer in the workshop than she certainly otherwise would have done.

One day Master Martin entered his open workshop outside the town-gate, where work was carried on all the summer through, with his brow weighted with thought Reinhold and Frederick were in the act of setting up a small cask. Then Master Martin planted himself before them with his arms crossed over his chest and said, "I can't tell you how pleased I am with you, my good journeymen, but I am just now in a great difficulty. They write me from the Rhine that this will be a more prosperous wine-year than there ever has been before. A learned man says that the comet which has been seen in the heavens will fructify the earth with its wonderful tail, so that the glowing heat which fabricates the precious metals down in the deepest mines will all stream upwards and evaporate into the thirsty vines, till they prosper and thrive and put forth multitudes of grapes, and the liquid fire with which they are filled will be poured out into the grapes. It will be almost three hundred years before such a favourable constellation occurs again. So now we shall all have our hands full of work. And then there's his Lordship the Bishop of Bamberg has written to me and ordered a large cask. That we can't get done; and I shall have to look about for another useful journeyman. Now I should not like to take the first fellow I meet off the street amongst us, and yet the matter is very urgent. If you know of a good journeyman anywhere whom you would be willing to work with, you have only to tell me, and I will get him here, even though it should cost me a good sum of money."

Hardly had Master Martin finished speaking when a young man, tall and stalwart, shouted to him in a loud voice, "Hi! you there! is this Master Martin's workshop?" "Certainly," replied Master Martin, going towards the young man, "certainly it is; but you needn't shout so deuced loud and lumber in like that; that's not the way to find people." "Ha! ha! ha!" laughed the young fellow, "marry, you are Master Martin himself, for--fat belly--stately double-chin--sparkling eyes, and red nose--yes, that's just how he was described to me. I bid you good hail, Master Martin." "Well, and what do you want from Master Martin?" he asked, indignantly. The young fellow replied, "I am a journeyman cooper, and merely wanted to ask if I could find work with you." Marvelling that just as he was thinking about looking out for a journeyman one should come to him like this, Master Martin drew back a few paces and eyed the young man from head to foot. He, however, met the scrutiny unabashed and with sparkling eyes. Noting his broad chest, stalwart build, and powerful arms, Master Martin thought within himself, it's just such a lusty fellow as this that I want, and he at once asked him for his trade testimonials. "I haven't them with me just at this present moment," replied the young man, "but I will get them in a short time; and I give you now my word of honour that I will work well and honestly, and that must suffice you." Thereupon, without waiting for Master Martin's reply, the young journeyman stepped into the workshop. He threw down his baretta and bundle, took off his doublet, put on his apron, and said, "Come, Master Martin, tell me at once what I am to begin with." Master Martin, completely taken aback by the young stranger's resolute vigour and promptitude, had to think a little; then he said, "Come then, my fine fellow, and show me at once that you are a good cooper; take this croze-adze and finish the groove of that cask lying in the vice yonder." The stranger performed what he had been bidden with remarkable strength, quickness, and skill; and then he cried, laughing loudly, "Now, Master Martin, have you any doubts now as to my being a good cooper? But," he continued, going backwards and forwards through the shop, and examining the instruments and tools, and supply of wood, "but though you are well supplied with useful stores and--but what do you call this little thing of a mallet? I suppose it's for your children to play with; and this little adze here--why it must be for your apprentices when they first begin," and he swung round his head the huge heavy mallet which Reinhold could not lift and which Frederick had great difficulty in wielding; and then he did the same with the ponderous adze with which Master Martin himself worked. Then he rolled a couple of huge casks on one side as if they had been light balls, and seized one of the large thick beams which had not yet been worked at "Marry, master," he cried, "marry, this is good sound oak; I wager it will snap like glass." And thereupon he struck the stave against the grindstone so that it broke clean in half with a loud crack. "Pray be so kind," said Master Martin, "pray have the kindness, my good fellow, to kick that two-tun cask about or to pull down the whole shop. There, you can take that balk for a mallet, and that you may have an adze to your mind I will have Roland's sword, which is three yards long, fetched for you from the town-house." "Ay, do, that's just the thing," said the young man, his eyes flashing; but the next minute he cast them down upon the ground and said, lowering his voice, "I only thought, good master, that you wanted right strong journeymen for your heavy work, and now I have, I see, been too forward, too swaggering, in displaying my bodily strength. But do take me on to work, I will faithfully do whatever you shall require of me." Master Martin scanned the youth's features, and could not but admit that he had never seen more nobility and at the same time more downright honesty in any man's face. And yet, as he looked upon the young fellow, there stole into his mind a dim recollection of some man whom he had long esteemed and honoured, but he could not clearly call to mind who it was. For this reason he granted the young man's request on the spot, only enjoining upon him to produce at the earliest opportunity the needful credible trade attestations.

Meanwhile Reinhold and Frederick had finished setting up their cask and were now busy driving on the first hoops. Whilst doing this they were always in the habit of striking up a song; and on this occasion they began a good song in Adam Puschmann's *Stieglitzweis*. Then Conrad (that was the name of the new journeyman) shouted across from the bench where Master Martin had placed him, "By my troth, what squalling do you call that? I could fancy I hear mice squeaking somewhere about the shop. An you mean to sing at all, sing so that it will cheer the heart and make the work go down well. That's how I sing a bit now and again." And he began to bellow out a noisy hunting ditty with its hollas! and hoy, boys! and he imitated the yelping of the hounds and the shrill shouts of the hunters in such a clear, keen, stentorian voice that the huge casks rang again and all the workshop echoed. Master Martin held his hands over his ears, and Dame Martha's (Valentine's widow) little boys, who were playing in the shop, crept timorously behind the piled-up staves. Just at this moment Rose came in, amazed, nay, frightened at the terrible noise; it could not be called singing anyhow. As soon as Conrad observed her, he at once stopped, and leaving his bench he approached her and greeted her with the most polished grace. Then he said in a gentle voice, whilst an ardent fire gleamed in his bright brown eyes, "Lovely lady, what a sweet rosy light shone into this humble workman's hut when you came in! Oh! had I but perceived you sooner, I had not outraged your tender ears with my wild hunting ditty." Then, turning to Master Martin and the other journeymen, he cried, "Oh! do stop your abominable knocking and rattling. As long as this gracious lady honours us with her presence, let mallets and drivers rest. Let us only listen to her sweet voice, and with bowed head hearken to what she may command us, her humble servants." Reinhold and Frederick looked at each other utterly amazed; but Master Martin burst out laughing and said, "Well, Conrad, it is now plain that you are the most ridiculous donkey who ever put on apron. First you come here and want to break everything to pieces like an uncultivated giant; then you bellow in such a way as to make our ears tingle; and, as a fitting climax to all your foolishness, you take my little daughter Rose for a lady of rank and act like a love-smitten Junker." Conrad replied, coolly, "Your lovely daughter I know very well, my worthy Master Martin; but I tell you that she is the most peerless lady who treads the earth, and if Heaven grant it she would honour the very noblest of Junkers by permitting him to be her Paladin in faithful knightly love." Master Martin held his sides, and it was only by giving vent to his laughter in hums and haws that he prevented himself from choking. As soon as he could at all speak, he stammered, "Good, very good, my most excellent youth; you may continue to regard my daughter as a lady of high rank, I shall not hinder you; but, irrespective of that, will you have the goodness to go back to your bench?" Conrad stood as if spell-bound, his eyes cast down upon the ground; and rubbing his forehead, he said in a low voice, "Ay, it is so," and did as he was bidden. Rose, as she always did in the shop, sat down upon a small cask, which Frederick placed for her, and which Reinhold carefully dusted. At Master Martin's express desire they again struck up the admirable song in which they had been so rudely interrupted by Conrad's bluster; but he went on with his work at the bench, quite still, and entirely wrapped up in his own thoughts.

When the song came to an end Master Martin said, "Heaven has endowed you with a noble gift, my brave lads; you would not believe how highly I value the delectable art of song. Why, once I wanted to be a *Meistersinger* myself, but I could not manage it, even though I tried all I knew how. All that I gained by my efforts was ridicule and mockery. In 'Voluntary Singing' I either got into false 'appendages,' or 'double notes,' or a wrong 'measure,' or an unsuitable 'embellishment,' or started the wrong melody altogether. But you will succeed better, and it shall be said, what the master can't do, his journeymen can. Next Sunday after the sermon there will be a singing contest by the *Meistersinger* at the usual time in St. Catherine's Church. But before the 'Principal Singing' there will be a 'Voluntary,' in which you may both of you win praise and honour in your beautiful art, for any stranger who can sing at all, may freely take part in this. And, he! Conrad, my journeyman Conrad," cried Master Martin across to the bench, "would not you also like to get into the singing-desk and treat our good folk to your fine hunting-chorus?" Without looking up, Conrad replied, "Mock not, good master, mock not; everything in its place. Whilst you are being edified by the *Meistersinger*, I shall enjoy myself in my own way on the Allerwiese."

And what Master Martin anticipated came to pass. Reinhold got into the singing-desk and sang divers songs to divers tunes, with which all the *Meistersingers* were well pleased; and although they were of opinion that the singer had not made any mistake, yet they had a slight objection to urge against him--a sort of something foreign about his style, but yet they could not say exactly in what it consisted. Soon afterwards Frederick took his seat in the singing-desk; and doffing his baretta, he stood some seconds looking silently before him; then after sending a glance at the audience which entered lovely Rose's bosom like a burning arrow, and caused her to fetch a deep sigh, he began such a splendid song in Heinrich Frauenlob's *Zarter Ton*, that all the masters agreed with one accord there was none amongst them who could surpass the young journeyman.

The singing-school came to an end towards evening, and Master Martin, in order to finish off the day's enjoyment in proper style, betook himself in high good-humour to the Allerwiese along with Rose. The two journeymen, Reinhold and Frederick, were permitted to accompany them; Rose was walking between them. Frederick, radiant with delight at the masters' praise, and intoxicated with happiness, ventured to breathe many a daring word in Rose's ear which she, however, casting down her eyes in maidenly coyness, pretended not to hear. Rather she turned to Reinhold, who, according to his wont, was running on with all sorts of merry nonsense; nor did he hesitate to place his arm in Rose's. Whilst even at a considerable distance from the Allerwiese they could hear noisy shouts and cries. Arrived at the place where the young men were amusing themselves in all kinds of games, partly chivalric, they heard the crowd shout time after time, "Won again! won again! He's the strongest again! Nobody can compete with him." Master Martin, on working his way through the crowd, perceived that it was nobody else but his journeyman Conrad who was reaping all this praise and exciting the people to all this applause. He had beaten everybody in racing and boxing and throwing the spear. As Martin came up, Conrad was shouting out and inquiring if there was anybody who would have a merry bout with him with blunt swords. This challenge several stout young patricians, well accustomed to this species of pastime, stepped forward and accepted. But it was not long before Conrad had again, without much trouble or exertion, overcome all his opponents; and the applause at his skill and strength seemed as if it would never end.

The sun had set; the last glow of evening died away, and twilight began to creep on apace. Master Martin, with Rose and the two journeymen, had thrown themselves down beside a babbling spring of water. Reinhold was telling of the wonders of distant Italy, but Frederick, quiet and happy, had his eyes fixed on pretty Rose's face. Then Conrad drew near with slow hesitating steps, as if rather undecided in his own mind whether he should join them or not Master Martin called to him, "Come along, Conrad, come along, come along; you have borne yourself bravely on the meadow; that's what I like in my journeymen, and it's what becomes them. Don't be shy, lad; come and join us, you have my permission." Conrad cast a withering glance at his master, who however met it with a condescending nod; then the young journeyman said moodily, "I am not the least bit shy of you, and I have not asked your permission whether I may lie down here or not,--in fact, I have not come to *you* at all. All my opponents I have stretched in the sand in the merry knightly sports, and all I now wanted was to ask this lovely lady whether she would not honour me with the beautiful flowers she wears in her bosom, as the prize of the chivalric contest." Therewith he dropped upon one knee in front of Rose, and looked her straight and honestly in the face with his clear brown eyes, and he begged, "O give me those beautiful flowers, sweet Rose, as the prize of victory; you cannot refuse me that." Rose at once took the flowers from her bosom and gave them to him, laughing and saying, "Ay, I know well that a brave knight like you deserves a token of honour from a lady; and so here, you may have my withered flowers." Conrad kissed the flowers that were given him, and then fastened them in his baretta; but Master Martin, rising to his feet, cried, "There's another of your silly tricks--come, let us be going home; it is getting dark." Herr Martin strode on first; Conrad with modest courtly grace took Rose's arm; whilst Reinhold and Frederick followed them considerably out of humour. People who met them, stopped and turned round to look after them, saying, "Marry, look now, look; that's the rich cooper Thomas Martin, with his pretty little daughter and his stout journeymen. A fine set of people I call them."

Of Dame Martha's conversation with Rose about the three journeymen, Conrad's quarrel with Master Martin.

Generally it is the morning following a holiday when young girls are wont to enjoy all the pleasure of it, and taste it, and thoroughly digest it; and this after celebration they seem to like far better than the actual holiday itself. And so next morning pretty Rose sat alone in her room with her hands folded on her lap, and her head bent slightly forward in meditation--her spindle and embroidery meanwhile resting. Probably she was now listening to Reinhold's and Frederick's songs, and now watching Conrad cleverly gaining the victory over his competitors, and now she saw him coming to her for the prize of victory; and then she hummed a few lines of a pretty song, and then she whispered, "Do you want my flowers?" whereat a deeper crimson suffused her cheeks, and brighter glances made their way through her downcast eyelashes, and soft sighs stole forth from her inmost heart. Then Dame Martha came in, and Rose was delighted to be able to tell at full length all that had taken place in St. Catherine's Church and on the Allerwiese. When Rose had done speaking, Dame Martha said, smiling, "Oh! so now, dear Rose, you will soon have to make your choice between your three handsome lovers." "For God's sake," burst out Rose, quite frightened, and flushing hotly all over her face, "for mercy's sake, Dame Martha, what do you mean by that? I--three lovers!" "Don't take on so," went on Dame Martha, "don't take on in that way, dear Rose, as if you knew nothing, as if you could guess nothing. Why, where do you put your eyes, girl? you must be quite blind not to see that our journeymen. Reinhold, Frederick, and Conrad--yes, all three of them--are madly in love with you." "What a fancy, to be sure, Dame Martha," whispered Rose, holding her hands before her face.

Then Dame Martha knelt down before her, and threw her arm about her, saying, "Come, my pretty, bashful child, take your hands away, and look me straight in the eyes, and then tell me you have not long ago perceived that you fill both the heart and the mind of each of our journeymen, deny that if you can. Nay, I tell you, you can't do it; and it would, i' faith, be a truly wonderful thing if a maiden's eyes did not see a thing of that sort. Why, when you go into the shop, their eyes are off their work and flying across to you in a minute, and they bustle and stir about with new life. And Reinhold and Frederick begin their best songs, and even wild Conrad grows quiet and gentle; each tries to invent some excuse to approach nearer to you, and when you honour one of them with a sweet look or a kindly word, how his eyes sparkle, and his face flushes! Come now, my pet, is it not nice to have such handsome fellows all making love to you? But whether you will choose one of the three or which it will be, that I cannot indeed say, for you are good and kind to them all alike, and yet--and yet--but I must not say more. Now an you come to me and said, 'O Dame Martha, give me your advice, to which of these young men, who are all wanting me, shall I give my hand and heart?' then I should of course answer, 'If your heart does not speak out loudly and distinctly. It's this or it's that, why, let them all three go.' I must say Reinhold pleases me right well, and so does Frederick, and so does Conrad; and then again on the other hand I have something to say against each of them. In fact, dear Rose, when I see them working away so bravely, I always think of my poor Valentine; and I must say that, if he could not perhaps produce any better work, there was yet quite a different kind of swing and style in all that he did do. You could see all his heart was in his work; but with these young fellows it always seems to me as if they only worked so, so--as if they had in their heads different things altogether from their work; nay, it almost strikes me as if it were a burden which they have voluntarily taken up, and were now bearing with sturdy courage. Of them all I can get on best with Frederick; he's such a faithful, affectionate fellow. He is the one who seems to belong to us most; I understand all that he says. And then his love for you is so still, and as shy as a good child's; he hardly dares to look at you, and blushes if you only say a single word to him; and that's what I like so much in the dear lad." A tear seemed to glisten in Rose's eye as Dame Martha said this. She stood up, and turning to the window, said, "I like Frederick very much, but you must not pass over Reinhold contemptuously." "I never dreamt of doing so," replied Dame Martha, "for Reinhold is by a long way the handsomest of all. And what eyes he has! And when he looks you through and through with his bright glances--no, it's more than you can endure. And yet there's something so strange and peculiar in his character, it quite makes me shiver at times, and makes me quite afraid of him. When Reinhold is working in the shop, I should think Herr Martin, when he tells him to do this or do that, must always feel as I should if anybody were to put a bright pan in my kitchen all glittering with gold and precious stones, and should bid me use it like any ordinary common pan--why, I should hardly dare to touch it at all. He tells his stories and talks and talks, and it all sounds like sweet music, and you are quite carried away by it, but when I sit down to think seriously about what he has been saying, I find I haven't understood a single word. And then when he now and again jests in the way we do, and I think now he's just like us, then all at once he looks so distinguished that I get really afraid of him. And yet I can't say that he puffs himself up in the way that many of our Junkers or patricians do; no, it's something else altogether different. In a word, it strikes me, by my troth, as if he held intercourse with higher spirits, as if he belonged, in fact, to another world. Conrad is a wild overbearing fellow, and yet there is something confoundedly distinguished about him as well; it doesn't agree with the cooper's apron somehow. And he always acts as if nobody but he had to give orders, and as if the others must obey him. In the short time that he has been here he has got so far that when he bellows at Master Martin in his loud ringing voice, his master generally does what he wishes. But at the same time he is so good-natured and so thoroughly honest that you can't bear ill-will against him; rather, I must say, that in spite of his wildness, I almost like him better than I do Reinhold, for even if he does speak fearfully grand, you can yet understand him very well. I wager he has once been a campaigner, he may say what he likes. That's why he knows so much about arms, and has even got something of knights' ways about him, which doesn't suit him at all badly. Now do tell me, Rose dear, without any ifs and ands, which of the three journeymen you like best?" "Don't ask me such searching questions, dear Dame Martha," answered Rose. "But of this I am quite sure, that Reinhold does not stir up in me the same feelings that he does in you. It's perfectly true, too, that he is altogether different from his equals; and when he talks I could fancy I enter into a beautiful garden full of bright and magnificent flowers and blossoms and fruits, such as are not to be found on earth, and I like to be amongst them. Since Reinhold has been here I see many things in a different light, and lots of things that were once dim and formless in my mind are now so bright and clear that I can easily distinguish them." Dame Martha rose to her feet, and shaking her finger at Rose as she went out of the room, said, "Ah! ah! Rose, so Reinhold is the favourite then? I didn't think it, I didn't even dream it." Rose made answer as she accompanied her as far as the door, "Pray, dear Dame Martha, think nothing, dream nothing, but leave all to the future. What *it* brings is the will of God, and to that everybody must bow humbly and gratefully."

Meanwhile it was becoming extremely lively in Master Martin's workshop. In order to execute all his orders he had engaged with ordinary labourers and taken in some apprentices, and they all hammered and knocked till the din could be heard far and wide. Reinhold had finished his calculations and measurements for the great cask that was to be built for the Bishop of Bamberg, whilst Frederick and Conrad had set it up so cleverly that Master Martin's heart laughed in his body, and he cried again and again, "Now that I call a grand piece of work; that'll be the best little cask I've ever made--except my masterpiece." Now the three apprentices stood driving the hoops on to the fitted staves, and the whole place rang again with the din of their mallets. Old Valentine was busy plying his draw-knife, and Dame Martha, her two youngest on her knee, sat just behind Conrad, whilst the other wideawake little rascals were shouting and making a noise, tumbling the hoops about, and chasing each other. In fact, there was so much hubbub and so much vigorous hard work going on that hardly anybody noticed old Herr Johannes Holzschuer as he stepped into the shop. Master Martin went to meet him, and politely inquired what he desired. "Why, in the first place," said Holzschuer, "I want to have a look at my dear Frederick again, who is working away so lustily yonder. And then, goodman Master Martin, I want a stout cask for my wine-cellar, which I will ask you to make for me. Why look you, that cask they are now setting up there is exactly the sort of thing I want; you can let me have that, you've only got to name the price." Reinhold, who had grown tired and had been resting a few minutes down in the shop, and was now preparing to ascend the scaffolding again, heard Holzschuer's words and said, turning his head towards the old gentleman, "Marry, my friend Herr Holzschuer, you need not set your heart upon this cask; we are making it for his Lordship the Bishop of Bamberg." Master Martin, his arms folded on his back, his left foot planted forward, his head thrown back in his neck, blinked at the cask and said proudly, "My dear master, you might have seen from the carefully selected wood and the great pains taken in the work that a masterpiece like that was meant for a prince's cellar. My journeyman Reinhold has said the truth; don't set your heart on a piece of work like that. But when the vintage is over I will get you a plain strong little cask made, such as will be suitable for your cellar." Old Holzschuer, incensed at Master Martin's pride, replied that his gold pieces weighed just as much as the Bishop of Bamberg's, and that he hoped he could get good work elsewhere for ready money. Master Martin, although fuming with rage, controlled himself with difficulty; he would not by any means like to offend old Herr Holzschuer, who stood so high in the esteem both of the Council and of all the burghers. At this moment Conrad struck mightier blows than ever with his mallet, so that the whole shop rang and cracked; then Master Martin's internal rage boiled over, and he shouted vehemently, "Conrad, you blockhead, what do you mean by striking so blindly and heedlessly? do you mean to break my cask in pieces?" "Ho! ho!" replied Conrad, looking round defiantly at his master, "Ho! ho! my comical little master, and why should I not?" And therewith he dealt such a terrible blow at the cask that the strongest hoop sprang, rattling, and knocked Reinhold down from the narrow plank on the scaffolding; and it was further evident from the hollow echo that a stave had been broken as well. Completely mastered by his furious anger, Master Martin snatched out of Valentine's hand the bar he was shaving, and striding towards the cask, dealt Conrad a good sound stroke with it on the back, shouting, "You cursed dog!" As soon as Conrad felt the blow he wheeled sharply round, and after standing for a moment as if bereft of his senses, his eyes blazed up with fury, he ground his teeth, and screamed, "Struck! struck!" Then at one bound he was down from the scaffolding, had snatched up an adze that lay on the floor, and aimed a powerful stroke at his master; had not Frederick pulled Martin on one side the blow would have split his head; as it was, the adze only grazed his arm, from which, however, the blood at once began to spurt out. Martin, fat and helpless as he was, lost his equilibrium and fell over the bench, at which one of the apprentices was working, into the floor. They all threw themselves upon Conrad, who was frantic, flourishing his bloody adze in the air, and shouting and screaming in a terrible voice, "Let him go to hell! To hell with him!" Hurling them all off with the strength of a giant, he was preparing to deal a second blow at his poor master, who was gasping for breath and groaning on the floor,--a blow that would have completely done for him--when Rose, pale as a corpse with fright, appeared in the shop-door. As soon as Conrad observed her he stood as if turned to a pillar of stone, the adze suspended in the air. Then he threw the tool away from him, struck his hands together upon his chest, and cried in a voice that went to everybody's heart, "Oh, good God! good God! what have I done?" and away he rushed out of the shop. No one thought of following him.

Now poor Master Martin was after some difficulty lifted up; it was found, however, that the adze had only penetrated into the thick fleshy part of the arm, and the wound could not therefore be called serious. Old Herr Holzschuer, whom Martin had involved with him in his fall, was pulled out from beneath the shavings, and Dame Martha's children, who ceased not to scream and cry over good Father Martin, were appeased as far as that could be done. As for Martin himself, he was quite dazed, and said if only that devil of a bad journeyman had not spoilt his fine cask he should not make much account of the wound.

Sedan chairs were brought for the old gentlemen, for Holzschuer also had bruised himself rather in his fall. He hurled reproaches at a trade in which they employed such murderous tools, and conjured Frederick to come back to his beautiful art of casting and working in the precious metals, and the sooner the better.

As soon as the dusk of evening began to creep up over the sky, Frederick, and along with him Reinhold, whom the hoop had struck rather sharply, and who felt as if every limb was benumbed, strode back into the town in very low spirits. Then they heard a soft sighing and groaning behind a hedge. They stood still, and a tall figure at once rose up; they immediately recognised Conrad, and began to withdraw timidly. But he addressed them in a tearful voice, saying, "You need not be so frightened at me, my good comrades; of course you take me for a devilish murderous brute, but I am not--indeed I am not so. I could not do otherwise; I *ought* to have struck down the fat old master, and by rights I ought to go along with you and do it *now*, if I only could. But no, no; it's all over. Remember me to pretty Rose, whom I love so above all reason. Tell her I will bear her flowers on my heart all my life long, I will adorn myself with them when I--but she will perhaps hear of me again some day. Farewell! farewell! my good, brave comrades." And Conrad ran away across the field without once stopping.

Reinhold said, "There is something peculiar about this young fellow; we can't weigh or measure this deed by any ordinary standard. Perhaps the future will unfold to us the secret that has lain heavy upon his breast."

Reinhold leaves Master Martin's house.

If formerly there had been merry days in Master Martin's workshop, so now they were proportionately dull. Reinhold, incapable of work, remained confined to his room; Martin, his wounded arm in a sling, was incessantly abusing the good-for-nothing stranger-apprentice, and railing at him for the mischief he had wrought Rose, and even Dame Martha and her children, avoided the scene of the rash savage deed, and so Frederick's blows fell dull and melancholy enough, like a woodcutter's in a lonely wood in winter time, for to Frederick it was now left to finish the big cask alone, and a hard task it was.

And soon his mind and heart were possessed by a profound sadness, for he believed he had now clear proofs of what he had for a long time feared. He no longer had any doubt that Rose loved Reinhold. Not only had she formerly shown many a kindness to Reinhold alone, and to him alone given many a sweet word, but now--it was as plain as noonday-- since Reinhold could no longer come to work. Rose too no longer thought of going out, but preferred to stay indoors, no doubt to wait upon and take good care of her lover. On Sundays, when all the rest set out gaily, and Master Martin, who had recovered to some extent of his wound, invited him to walk with him and Rose to the Allerwiese, he refused the invitation; but, burdened with trouble and the bitter pain of disappointed love, he hastened off alone to the village and the hill where he had first met with Reinhold. He threw himself down in the tall grass where the flowers grew, and as he thought how that the beautiful star of hope which had shone before him all along his homeward path had now suddenly set in the blackness of night after he had reached his goal, and as he thought how that this step which he had taken was like the vain efforts of a dreamer stretching out his yearning arms after an empty vision of air,--the tears fell from his eyes and dropped upon the flowers, which bent their little heads as if sorrowing for the young journeyman's great unhappiness. Without his being exactly conscious of it, the painful sighs which escaped his labouring breast assumed the form of words, of musical notes, and he sang this song:--

My star of hope,
Where hast thou gone?
Alas! thy glory rises up--
Thy glory sweet, far from me now--
And pours its light on others down.
Ye rustling evening breezes, rouse you,
Blow on my breast,
Awake all joy that kills,
Awake all pain that brings to death,
So that my sore and bleeding heart,
Steeped to the core in bitter tears,
May break in yearning comfortless.
Why whisper ye, ye darksome trees?
So softly and like friends together?
And why, O golden skirts of sky,
Look ye so kindly down on me?
Show me my grave;
For that is now my haven of hope,
Where I shall calmly, softly sleep.

And as it often happens that the very greatest trouble, if only it can find vent in tears and words, softens down into a gentle melancholy, mild and painless, and that often a faint glimmer of hope appears then in the soul, so it was with Frederick; when he had sung this song he felt wonderfully strengthened and comforted The evening breezes and the darksome trees that he had called upon in his song rustled and whispered words of consolation;

and like the sweet dreams of distant glory or of distant happiness, golden streaks of light worked their way up across the dusky sky. Frederick rose to his feet, and went down the hill into the village. He almost fancied that Reinhold was walking beside him as he did on the day they first found each other; and all the words which Reinhold had spoken again recurred to his mind. And as his thoughts dwelt upon Reinhold's story about the contest between the two painters who were friends, then the scales fell from his eyes. There was no doubt about it; Reinhold must have seen Rose before and loved her. It was only his love for her which had brought him to Nuremberg to Master Martin's, and by the contest between the two painters he meant simply and solely their own--Reinhold's and Frederick's--rival wooing of beautiful Rose. The words that Reinhold had then spoken rang again in his ears,--"Honest contention for the same prize, without any malicious reserve, ought to unite true friends and knit their hearts still closer together, instead of setting them at variance. There should never be any place in noble minds for petty envy or malicious hatred." "Yes," exclaimed Frederick aloud, "yes, friend of my heart, I will appeal to you without any reserve, you yourself shall tell me if all hope for me is lost."

It was approaching noon when Frederick tapped at Reinhold's door. As all remained still within, he pushed open the door, which was not locked as usual, and went in. But the moment he did so he stood rooted to the spot. Upon an easel, the glorious rays of the morning sun falling upon it, was a splendid picture, Rose in all the pride of her beauty and charms, and life size. The maul-stick lying on the table, and the wet colours of the palette, showed that some one had been at work on the picture quite recently. "O Rose, Rose!--By Heaven!" sighed Frederick. Reinhold, who had entered behind him unperceived, clapped him on the shoulder and asked, smiling, "Well, now, Frederick, what do you say to my picture!" Then Frederick pressed him to his heart and cried, "Oh you splendid fellow--you are indeed a noble artist. Yes, it's all clear to me now. You have won the prize--for which I--poor me!--had the hardihood to struggle. Oh! what am I in comparison with you? And what is my art against yours? And yet I too had some fine ideas in my head. Don't laugh at me, dear Reinhold; but, look you, I thought what a grand thing it would be to model Rose's lovely figure and cast it in the finest silver. But that's all childishness, whilst you--you--Oh! how sweetly she smiles upon you, and how delightfully you have brought out all her beauty. O Reinhold! Reinhold! you happy, happy fellow! Ay, and it has all come about as you said long ago. We have both striven for the prize and you have won it: you could not help but win it, and I shall still continue to be your friend with all my heart But I must leave this house--my home: I cannot bear it, I should die if I were to see Rose again. Please forgive me, my dear, dear, noble friend. To-day, this very moment, I will go--go away into the wide world, where my trouble, my unbearable misery, is sending me." And thus speaking, Frederick was hastening out of the apartment, but Reinhold held him fast, saying gently, "You shall not go; for things may turn out quite different from what you think. It is now time for me to tell you all that I have hitherto kept silence about. That I am not a cooper but a painter you are now well aware, and I hope a glance at this picture will convince you that I am not to be ranked amongst the inferior artists. Whilst still young I went to Italy, the land of art; there I had the good fortune to be accepted as a pupil by renowned masters, who fostered into living fire the spark which glowed within me. Thus it came to pass that I rapidly rose into fame, that my pictures became celebrated throughout all Italy, and the powerful Duke of Florence summoned me to his court. At that time I would not hear a word about German art, and without having seen any of your pictures, I talked a good deal of nonsense about the coldness, the bad drawing, and the hardness of your Dürer and your Cranach. But one day a picture-dealer brought a small picture of the Madonna by old Albrecht to the Duke's gallery, and it made a powerful and wonderful impression upon me, so that I turned away completely from the voluptuousness of Italian art, and from that very hour determined to go back to my native Germany and study there the masterpieces upon which my heart was now set I came to Nuremberg here, and when I beheld Rose I seemed to see the Madonna who had so wonderfully stirred my heart, walking in bodily form on earth. I had the same experiences as you, dear Frederick; the bright flames of love flashed up and consumed me, mind and heart and soul. I saw nothing, I thought of nothing, but Rose; all else had vanished from my mind; and even art itself only retained its hold upon me in so far as it enabled me to draw and paint Rose again and again-- hundreds of times. I would have approached the maiden in the free Italian way; but all my attempts proved fruitless. There was no means of securing a footing of intimacy in Master Martin's house in any insidious way. At last I made up my mind to sue for Rose directly, when I learned that Master Martin had determined to give his daughter only to a good master-cooper. Straightway I formed the adventurous resolve to go and learn the trade of cooperage in Strasburg, and then to come and work in Master Martin's work-shop. I left all the rest to the ordering of Providence. You know in what way I carried out my resolve; but I must now also tell you what Master Martin said to me some days ago. He said I should make a skilful cooper and should be a right dear and worthy son-in-law, for he saw plainly that I was seeking to gain Rose's favour, and that she liked me right well." "Can it then indeed well be otherwise?" cried Frederick, painfully agitated "Yes, yes, Rose will be *yours*; how came I, unhappy wretch that I am, ever to hope for such happiness?" "You are forgetting, my brother," Reinhold went on to say; "you are forgetting that Rose herself has not confirmed this, which our cunning Master Martin no doubt is well aware of. True it is that Rose has always shown herself kind and charming towards me, but a loving heart betrays itself in other ways. Promise me, brother, to remain quiet for three days longer, and to go to your work in the shop as usual. I also could now go to work again, but since I have been busy with, and wrapt up in this picture, I feel an indescribable disgust at that coarse rough work out yonder. And, what is more, I can never lay hand upon mallet again, let come what will. On the third day I will frankly tell you how matters stand between me and Rose. If I should really be the lucky one to whom she has given her love, then you may go your way and make trial of the experience that time can cure the deepest wounds." Frederick promised to await his fate.

On the third day Frederick's heart beat with fear and anxious expectation; he had in the meantime carefully avoided meeting Rose. Like one in a dream he crept about the workshop, and his awkwardness gave Master Martin, no doubt, just cause for his grumbling and scolding, which was not by any means customary with him. Moreover, the master seemed to have encountered something that completely spoilt all his good spirits. He talked a great deal about base tricks and ingratitude, without clearly expressing what he meant by it. When at length evening came, and Frederick was returning towards the town, he saw not far from the gate a horseman coming to meet him, whom he recognised to be Reinhold. As soon as the latter caught sight of Frederick he cried, "Ha! ha! I meet you just as I wanted." And leaping from his horse, he slung the rein over his arm, and grasped his friend's hand. "Let us walk along a space beside each other," he said. "Now I can tell you what luck I have had with my suit." Frederick observed that Reinhold wore the same clothes which he had worn when they first met each other, and that the horse bore a portmanteau. Reinhold looked pale and troubled. "Good luck to you, brother," he began somewhat wildly; "good luck to you. You can now go and hammer away lustily at your casks; I will yield the field to you. I have just said adieu to pretty Rose and worthy Master Martin." "What!" exclaimed Frederick, whilst an electric thrill, as it were, shot through all his limbs--"what! you are going away now that Master Martin is willing to take you for his son-in-law, and Rose loves you?" Reinhold replied, "That was only a delusion, brother, which your jealousy has led you into. It has now come out that Rose would have had me simply to show her dutifulness and obedience, but there's not a spark of love glowing in her ice-cold heart. Ha! ha! I should have made a fine cooper--that I should. Week-days scraping hoops and planing staves, Sundays walking beside my honest wife to St. Catherine's or St. Sebald's, and in the evening to the Allerwiese, year after year"---- "Nay, mock not," said Frederick, interrupting Reinhold's loud laughter, "mock not at the excellent burgher's simple, harmless life. If Rose does not really love you, it is not her fault; you are so passionate, so wild." "You are right," said Reinhold; "It is only the silly way I have of making as much noise as a spoilt child when I conceive I have been hurt. You can easily imagine that I spoke to Rose of my love and of her father's good-will. Then the tears started from her eyes, and her hand trembled in mine. Turning her face away, she whispered, 'I must submit to my father's will'--that was enough for me. My peculiar resentment, dear Frederick, will now let you see into the depths of my heart; I must tell you that my striving to win Rose was a deception, imposed upon me by my wandering mind. After I had finished Rose's picture my heart grew calm; and often, strange enough, I fancied that Rose was now the picture, and that the picture was become the real Rose. I detested my former coarse, rude handiwork; and when I came so intimately into contact with the incidents of common life, getting one's 'mastership' and getting married, I felt as if I were going to be confined in a dungeon and chained to the stocks. How indeed can the divine being whom I carry in my heart ever be my wife? No, she shall for ever stand forth glorious in youth, grace, and beauty, in the pictures--the masterpieces--which my restless spirit shall create. Oh! how I long for such things! How came I ever to turn away from my divine art? O thou glorious land, thou home of Art, soon again will I revel amidst thy cool and balmy airs." The friends had reached the place where the road which Reinhold intended to take turned to the left. "Here we will part," cried Reinhold, pressing Frederick to his heart in a long warm embrace; then he threw himself upon horseback and galloped away. Frederick stood watching him without uttering a word, and then, agitated by the most unaccountable feelings, he slowly wended his way homewards.

How Frederick was driven out of the workshop by Master Martin.

The next day Master Martin was working away at the great cask for the Bishop of Bamberg in moody silence, nor could Frederick, who now felt the full bitterness of parting from Reinhold, utter a word either, still less break out into song. At last Master Martin threw aside his mallet, and crossing his arms, said in a muffled voice, "Well, Reinhold's gone. He was a distinguished painter, and has only been making a fool of me with his pretence of being a cooper. Oh! that I had only had an inkling of it when he came into my house along with you and bore himself so smart and clever, wouldn't I just have shown him the door! Such an open honest face, and so much deceit and treachery in his mind! Well, he's gone, and now you will faithfully and honestly stick to me and my handiwork. Who knows whether you may not become something more to me still--when you have become a skilful master and Rose will have you--well, you understand me, and may try to win Rose's favour." Forthwith he took up his mallet and worked away lustily again. Frederick did not know how to account for it, but Master Martin's words rent his breast, and a strange feeling of anxiety arose in his mind, obscuring every glimmer of hope. After a long interval Rose made a first appearance again in the workshop, but was very reserved, and, as Frederick to his mortification could see, her eyes were red with weeping. She has been weeping for him, she does love him, thus he said within himself, and he was quite unable to raise his eyes to her whom he loved with such an unutterable love.

The mighty cask was finished, and now Master Martin began to be blithe and in good humour again as he regarded this very successful piece of work. "Yes, my son," said he, clapping Frederick on the shoulder, "yes, my son, I will keep my word: if you succeed in winning Rose's favour and build a good sound masterpiece, you shall be my son-in-law. And then you can also join the noble guild of the *Meistersinger*, and so win you great honour."

Master Martin's business now increased so very greatly that he had to engage two other journeymen, clever workmen, but rude fellows, quite demoralised by their long wanderings. Coarse jests now echoed in the workshop instead of the many pleasant talks of former days, and in place of Frederick and Reinhold's agreeable singing were now heard low and obscene ditties. Rose shunned the workshop, so that Frederick saw her but seldom, and only for a few moments at a time. And then when he looked at her with melancholy longing and sighed, "Oh! if I might talk to you again, dear Rose, if you were only as friendly again as at the time when Reinhold was still with us!" she cast down her eyes in shy confusion and whispered "Have you something to tell me, dear Frederick?" And Frederick stood like a statue, unable to speak a word, and the golden opportunity was quickly past, like a flash of lightning that darts across the dark red glow of the evening, and is gone almost before it is observed.

Master Martin now insisted that Frederick should begin his masterpiece. He had himself sought out the finest, purest oak wood, without the least vein or flaw, which had been over five years in his wood-store, and nobody was to help Frederick except old Valentine. Not only was Frederick put more and more out of taste with his work by the rough journeymen, but he felt a tightness in his throat as he thought that this masterpiece was to decide over his whole life long. The same peculiar feeling of anxiety which he had experienced when Master Martin was praising his faithful devotion to his handiwork now grew into a more and more distinct shape in a quite dreadful way. He now knew that he should fail miserably and disgracefully in his work; his mind, now once more completely taken up with his own art, was fundamentally averse to it. He could not forget Reinhold and Rose's picture. His own art now put on again her full glory in his eyes. Often as he was working, the crushing sense of the unmanliness of his conduct quite overpowered him, and, alleging that he was unwell, he ran off to St. Sebald's Church. There he spent hours in studying Peter Fischer's marvellous monument, and he would exclaim, as if ravished with delight, "Oh, good God! Is there anything on earth more glorious than to conceive and execute such a work?" And when he had to go back again to his staves and hoops, and remembered that in this way only was Rose to be won, he felt as if burning talons were rending his bleeding heart, and as if he must perish in the midst of his unspeakable agony. Reinhold often came to him in his dreams and brought him striking designs for artistic castings, into which Rose's form was worked in most ingenious ways, now as a flower, now as an angel, with little wings. But there was always something wanting; he discovered that it was Rose's heart which Reinhold had forgotten, and that he added to the design himself. Then he thought he saw all the flowers and leaves of the work move, singing and diffusing their sweet fragrances, and the precious metals showed him Rose's likeness in their glittering surface. Then he stretched out his arms longingly after his beloved, but the likeness vanished as if in dim mist, and Rose herself, pretty Rose, pressed him to her loving heart in an ecstasy of passionate love.

His condition with respect to the unfortunate cooperage grew worse and worse, and more and more unbearable, and he went to his old master Johannes Holzschuer to seek comfort and assistance. He allowed Frederick to begin in his shop a piece of work which he, Frederick, had thought out and for which he had for some time been saving up his earnings, so that he could procure the necessary gold and silver. Thus it happened that Frederick was scarcely ever at work in Martin's shop, and his deathly pale face gave credence to his pretext that he was suffering from a consuming illness. Months went past, and his masterpiece, his great two-tun cask, was not advanced any further. Master Martin was urgent upon him that he should at least do as much as his strength would allow, and Frederick really saw himself compelled to go to the hated cutting block again and take the adze in hand. Whilst he was working, Master Martin drew near and examined the staves at which he was working; and he got quite red in the face and cried, "What do you call this? What work is this, Frederick? Has a journeyman been preparing these staves for his 'mastership,' or a stupid apprentice who only put his nose into the workshop three days ago? Pull yourself together, lad: what devil has entered into you that you are making a bungle of things like this? My good oak wood,--and this your masterpiece! Oh! you awkward, imprudent boy!" Overmastered by the torture and agony which raged within him, Frederick was unable to contain himself any longer; so, throwing the adze from him he said, "Master, it's all over; no, even though it cost me my life, though I perish in unutterable misery, I cannot work any longer--no, I cannot work any longer at this coarse trade. An irresistible power is drawing me back to my own glorious art. Your daughter Rose I love unspeakably, more than anybody else on earth can ever love her. It is only for her sake that I ever entered upon this hateful work. I have now lost her, I know, and shall soon die of grief for love of her; but I can't help it, I must go back to my own glorious art, to my excellent old master, Johannes Holzschuer, whom I so shamefully deserted." Master Martin's eyes blazed like flashing candles. Scarce able to speak for rage, he stammered, "What! you too! Deceit and treachery! Dupe *me* like this! coarse trade--cooperage! Out of my eyes, you disgraceful fellow; begone with you!" And therewith he laid hold of poor Frederick by the shoulders and threw him out of the shop, which the rude journeymen and apprentices greeted with mocking laughter. But old Valentine folded his hands, and gazing thoughtfully before him, said, "I've noticed, that I have, the good fellow had something higher in his mind than our casks." Dame Martha shed many tears, and her boys cried and screamed for Frederick, who had often played kindly with them and brought them several lots of sweets.

Conclusion.

However angry Master Martin might feel towards Reinhold and Frederick, he could not but admit to himself that along with them all joy and all pleasure had disappeared from the workshop. Every day he was annoyed and provoked by the new journeymen. He had to look after every little trifle, and it cost him no end of trouble and exertion to get even the smallest amount of work done to his mind. Quite tired out with the cares of the day, he often sighed, "O Reinhold! O Frederick! I wish you had not so shamefully deceived me, I wish you had been good coopers." Things at last got so bad that he often contemplated the idea of giving up business altogether.

As he was sitting at home one evening in one of these gloomy moods, Herr Jacobus Paumgartner and along with him Master Johannes Holzschuer came in quite unexpectedly. He saw at once that they were going to talk about Frederick; and in fact Herr Paumgartner very soon turned the conversation upon him, and Master Holzschuer at once began to say all he could in praise of the young fellow. It was his opinion that Frederick with his industry and his gifts would certainly not only make an excellent goldsmith, but also a most admirable art-caster, and would tread in Peter Fischer's footsteps. And now Herr Paumgartner began to reproach Master Martin in no gentle terms for his unkind treatment of his poor journeyman Frederick, and they both urged him to give Rose to the young fellow to wife when he was become a skilful goldsmith and caster,--that is, of course, in case she looked with favour upon him,--for his affection for her tingled in every vein he had. Master Martin let them have their say out, then he doffed his cap and said, smiling, "That's right, my good sirs, I'm glad you stand up so bravely for the journeyman who so shamefully deceived me. That, however, I will forgive him; but don't ask that I should alter my fixed resolve for his sake; Rose can never be anything to him." At this moment Rose entered the room, pale and with eyes red with weeping, and she silently placed wine and glasses on the table. "Well then," began Herr Holzschuer, "I must let poor Frederick have his own way; he wants to leave home for ever. He has done a beautiful piece of work at my shop, which, if you, my good master, will allow, he will present to Rose as a keepsake; look at it." Whereupon Master Holzschuer produced a small artistically-chased silver cup, and handed it to Master Martin, who, a great lover of costly vessels and such like, took it and examined it on all sides with much satisfaction. And indeed a more splendid piece of silver work than this little cup could hardly be seen. Delicate chains of vine-leaves and roses were intertwined round about it, and pretty angels peeped up out of the roses and the bursting buds, whilst within, on the gilded bottom of the cup, were engraved angels lovingly caressing each other. And when the clear bright wine was poured into the cup, the little angels seemed to dance up and down as if playing prettily together. "It is indeed an elegant piece of work," said Master Martin, "and I will keep it if Frederick will take the double of what it is worth in good gold pieces." Thus speaking, he filled the cup and raised it to his lips. At this moment the door was softly opened, and Frederick stepped in, his countenance pale and stamped with the bitter, bitter pain of separating for ever from her he held dearest on earth. As soon as Rose saw him she uttered a loud piercing cry, "O my dearest Frederick!" and fell almost fainting on his breast. Master Martin set down the cup, and on seeing Rose in Frederick's arms opened his eyes wide as if he saw a ghost. Then he again took up the cup without speaking a word, and looked into it; but all at once he leapt from his seat and cried in a loud voice, "Rose, Rose, do you love Frederick?" "Oh!" whispered Rose, "I cannot any longer conceal it, I love him as I love my own life; my heart nearly broke when you sent him away." "Then embrace your betrothed, Frederick; yes, yes, your betrothed, Frederick," cried Master Martin. Paumgartner and Holzschuer looked at each other utterly bewildered with astonishment, but Master Martin, holding the cup in his hand, went on, "By the good God, has it not all come to pass as the old lady prophesied?--

'A vessel fair to see he'll bring,
In which the spicy liquid foams,
And bright, bright angels gaily sing.
... The vessel fair with golden grace,
Lo! him who brings it in the house,

Thou wilt reward with sweet embrace,
And, an thy lover be but true,
Thou need'st not wait thy father's kiss.'

O Stupid fool I have been! Here is the vessel fair to see, the angels-- the lover--Ay! ay! gentlemen; it's all right now, all right now; my son-in-law is found."

Whoever has had his mind ever confused by a bad dream, so that he thought he was lying in the deep cold blackness of the grave, and suddenly he awakens in the midst of the bright spring-tide full of fragrance and sunshine and song, and she whom he holds dearest on earth has come to him and has cast her arms about him, and he can look up into the heaven of her lovely face,--whoever has at any time experienced this will understand Frederick's feelings, will comprehend his exceeding great happiness. Unable to speak a word, he held Rose tightly clasped in his arms as though he would never let her leave him, until she at length gently disengaged herself and led him to her father. Then he found his voice, "O my dear master, is it all really true? You will give me Rose to wife, and I may go back to my art?" "Yes, yes," said Master Martin, "you may in truth believe it; can I do any other since you have fulfilled my old grandmother's prophecy? You need not now of course go on with your masterpiece." Then Frederick, perfectly radiant with delight, smiled and said, "No, my dear master, if it be pleasing to you I will now gladly and in good spirits finish my big cask--my last piece of work in cooperage--and then I will go back to the melting-furnace." "Yes, my good brave son," replied Master Martin, his eyes sparkling with joy, "yes, finish your masterpiece, and then we'll have the wedding."

Frederick kept his word faithfully, and finished the two-tun cask; and all the masters declared that it would be no easy task to do a finer piece of work, whereat Master Martin was delighted down to the ground, and was moreover of opinion that Providence could not have found for him a more excellent son-in-law.

At length the wedding day was come, Frederick's masterpiece stood in the entrance hall filled with rich wine, and crowned with garlands. The masters of the trade, with the syndic Jacobus Paumgartner at their head, put in an appearance along with their housewives, followed by the master goldsmiths. All was ready for the procession to begin its march to St. Sebald's Church, where the pair were to be married, when a sound of trumpets was heard in the street, and a neighing and stamping of horses before Martin's house. Master Martin hastened to the bay-window. It was Herr Heinrich von Spangenberg, in gay holiday attire, who had pulled up in front of the house; a few paces behind him, on a high- spirited horse, sat a young and splendid knight, his glittering sword at his side, and high-coloured feathers in his baretta, which was also adorned with flashing jewels. Beside the knight, Herr Martin perceived a wondrously beautiful lady, likewise splendidly dressed, seated on a jennet the colour of fresh-fallen snow. Pages and attendants in brilliant coats formed a circle round about them. The trumpet ceased, and old Herr von Spangenberg shouted up to him, "Aha! aha! Master Martin, I have not come either for your wine cellar or for your gold pieces, but only because it is Rose's wedding day. Will you let me in, good master?" Master Martin remembered his own words very well, and was a little ashamed of himself; but he hurried down to receive the Junker. The old gentleman dismounted, and after greeting him, entered the house. Some of the pages sprang forward, and upon their arms the lady slipped down from her palfrey; the knight gave her his hand and followed the old gentleman. But when Master Martin looked at the young knight he recoiled three paces, struck his hands together, and cried, "Good God! Conrad!" "Yes, Master Martin," said the knight, smiling, "I am indeed your journeyman Conrad. Forgive me for the wound I inflicted on you. But you see, my good master, that I ought properly to have killed you; but things have now all turned out different." Greatly confused, Master Martin replied, that it was after all better that he had not been killed; of the little bit of a cut with the adze he had made no account. Now when Master Martin with his new guests entered the room where the bridal pair and the rest were assembled, they were all agreeably surprised at the beautiful lady, who was so exactly like the bride, even down to the minutest feature, that they might have been taken for twin-sisters. The knight approached the bride with courtly grace and said, "Grant, lovely Rose, that Conrad be present here on this auspicious day. You are not now angry with the wild thoughtless journeyman who was nigh bringing a great trouble upon you, are you?" But as the bridegroom and the bride and Master Martin were looking at each other in great wonder and embarrassment, old Herr von Spangenberg said, "Well, well, I see I must help you out of your dream. This is my son Conrad, and here is his good, true wife, named Rose, like the lovely bride. Call our conversation to mind, Master Martin. I had a very special reason for asking you whether you would refuse your Rose to my son. The young puppy was madly in love with her, and he induced me to lay aside all other considerations and make up my mind to come and woo her on his behalf. But when I told him in what an uncourteous way I had been dismissed, he in the most nonsensical way stole into your house in the guise of a cooper, intending to win her favour and then actually to run away with her. But--you cured him with that good sound blow across his back; my best thanks for it. And now he has found a lady of rank who most likely is, after all, *the* Rose who was properly in his heart from the beginning."

Meanwhile the lady had with graceful kindness greeted the bride, and hung a valuable pearl necklace round her neck as a wedding present. "See here, dear Rose," she then said, taking a very withered bunch of flowers out from amongst the fresh blooming ones which she wore at her bosom--"see here, dear Rose, these are the flowers that you once gave my Conrad as the prize of victory; he kept them faithfully until he saw me, then he was unfaithful to you and gave them to me; don't be angry with me for it." Rose, her cheeks crimson, cast down her eyes in shy confusion, saying, "Oh! noble lady, how can you say so? Could the Junker then ever really love a poor maiden like me? You alone were his love, and it was only because I am called Rose, and, as they say here, something like you, that he wooed me, all the while thinking it was you."

A second time the procession was about to set out, when a young man entered the room, dressed in the Italian style, all in black slashed velvet, with an elegant lace collar and rich golden chains of honour hanging from his neck. "O Reinhold, my Reinhold!" cried Frederick, throwing himself upon the young man's breast. The bride and Master Martin also cried out excitedly, "Reinhold, our brave Reinhold is come!" "Did I not tell you," said Reinhold, returning Frederick's embrace with warmth,--"did I not tell you, my dear, dear friend, that things might turn out gloriously for you? Let me celebrate your wedding day with you; I have come a long way on purpose to do so; and as a lasting memento hang up in your house the picture which I have painted for you and brought with me." And then he called down to his two servants, who brought in a large picture in a magnificent gold frame. It represented Master Martin in his workshop along with his journeymen Reinhold, Frederick, and Conrad working at the great cask, and lovely Rose was just entering the shop. Everybody was astonished at the truth and magnificent colouring of the piece as a work of art. "Ay," said Frederick, smiling, "that is, I suppose, your masterpiece as cooper; mine is below yonder in the entrance-hall; but I shall soon make another." "I know all," replied Reinhold, "and rate you lucky. Only stick fast to your art; it can put up with more domesticity and such-like than mine."

At the marriage feast Frederick sat between the two Roses, and opposite him Master Martin between Conrad and Reinhold. Then Herr Paumgartner filled Frederick's cup up to the brim with rich wine, and drank to the weal of Master Martin and his brave journeymen. The cup went round; and first it was drained by the noble Junker Heinrich von Spangenberg, and after him by all the worthy masters who sat at the table--to the weal of Master Martin and his brave journeymen.

MADEMOISELLE DE SCUDÉRI.
A TALE OF THE TIMES OF LOUIS XIV.

The little house in which lived Madeleine de Scudéri, well known for her pleasing verses, and the favour of Louis XIV. and the Marchioness de Maintenon, was situated in the Rue St. Honorée.

One night almost at midnight--it would be about the autumn, of the year 1680--there came such a loud and violent knocking at the door of her house that it made the whole entrance-passage ring again. Baptiste, who in the lady's small household discharged at one and the same time the offices of cook, footman, and porter, had with his mistress's permission gone into the country to attend his sister's wedding; and thus it happened that La Martinière, Mademoiselle's lady-maid was alone, and the only person awake in the house. The knockings were repeated. She suddenly remembered that Baptiste had gone for his holiday, and that she and her mistress were left in the house without any further protection. All the outrages burglaries, thefts, and murders--which were then so common in Paris, crowded upon her mind; she was sure it was a band of cut-throats who were making all this disturbance outside; they must be well aware how lonely the house stood, and if let in would perpetrate some wicked deed against her mistress; and so she remained in her room, trembling and quaking with fear, and cursing Baptiste and his sister's wedding as well.

Meanwhile the hammering at the door was being continued; and she fancied she heard a voice shouting at intervals, "Oh! do open the door! For God's sake, do open the door!" At last La Martinière's anxiety rose to such a pitch that, taking up the lighted candle, she ran out into the passage. There she heard quite plainly the voice of the person knocking, "For God's sake! do open the door, please!" "Certainly," thought she, "that surely is not the way a robber would knock. Who knows whether it is not some poor man being pursued and wants protection from Mademoiselle, who is always ready to do an act of kindness? But let us be cautious." Opening a window, she called out, asking who was down making such a loud noise at the house-door so late at night, awakening everybody up out of their sleep; and she endeavoured to give her naturally deep voice as manly a tone as she possibly could.

By the glimmer of the moon, which now broke through the dark clouds, she could make out a tall figure, enveloped in a light-grey mantle, having his broad-brimmed hat pulled down right over his eyes. Then she shouted in a loud voice, so as to be heard by the man below, "Baptiste, Claude, Pierre, get up and go and see who this good-for-nothing vagabond is, who is trying to break into the house." But the voice from below made answer gently, and in a tone that had a plaintive ring in it, "Oh! La Martinière, I know quite well that it is you, my good woman, however much you try to disguise your voice; I also know that Baptiste has gone into the country, and that you are alone in the house with your mistress. You may confidently undo the door for me; you need have no fear. For I must positively speak with your mistress, and this very minute." "Whatever are you thinking about?" replied La Martinière. "You want to speak to Mademoiselle in the middle of the night? Don't you know that she has been gone to bed a long time, and that for no price would I wake her up out of her first sound sleep, which at her time of life she has so much need of?" The person standing below said, "But I know that your mistress has only just laid aside her new romance *Clélie*, at which she labours so unremittingly; and she is now writing certain verses which she intends to read to the Marchioness de Maintenon to-morrow. I implore you, Madame Martinière, have pity and open me the door. I tell you the matter involves the saving of an unfortunate man from ruin,--that the honour, freedom, nay, that the life of a man is dependent upon this moment, and I *must* speak to Mademoiselle. Recollect how your mistress's anger would rest upon you for ever, if she learned that you had had the hard-heartedness to turn an unfortunate man away from her door when he came to supplicate her assistance." "But why do you come to appeal to my mistress's compassion at this unusual hour? Come again early in the morning," said La Martinière. The person below replied, "Does Destiny, then, heed times and hours when it strikes, like the fatal flash, fraught with destruction? When there is but a single moment longer in which rescue is still possible, ought assistance to be delayed? Open me the door; you need have nothing to fear from a poor defenceless wretch, who is deserted of all the world, pursued and distressed by an awful fate, when he comes to beseech Mademoiselle to save him from threatening danger?" La Martinière heard the man below moaning and sobbing with anguish as he said these words, and at the same time the voice was the voice of a young man, gentle, and gifted with the power of appealing straight to the heart She was greatly touched; without much further deliberation she fetched the keys.

But hardly had she got the door opened when the figure enveloped in the mantle burst tumultuously in, and striding past Martinière into the passage, cried wildly, "Lead me to your mistress!" In terror Martinière lifted up the candle, and its light fell upon a young man's face, deathly pale and fearfully agitated. Martinière almost dropped on the floor with fright, for the man now threw open his mantle and showed the bright hilt of a stiletto sticking out of the bosom of his doublet. His eyes flashed fire as he fixed them upon her, crying still more wildly than before, "Lead me to your mistress, I tell you." Martinière now believed Mademoiselle was in the most imminent danger; and her affection for her beloved mistress, whom she honoured, moreover, as her good and faithful mother, burnt up stronger in her heart, enkindling a courage which she had not conceived herself capable of showing. Hastily pulling to the door of her chamber, which she had left standing open, she planted herself before it, and said in a strong firm voice, "I tell you what, your mad behaviour in the house here, corresponds but ill with your plaintive words outside; I see clearly that I let my pity be excited on a wrong occasion. You neither ought to, nor shall you, speak to my mistress now. If your intentions are not evil, you need not fear daylight; so come again to-morrow and state your business then. Now, begone with you out of the house." The man heaved a deep and painful sigh, and fixing Martinière with a formidable look, grasped his stiletto. She silently commended her soul to Heaven, but manfully stood her ground, and boldly met the man's gaze, at the same time drawing herself closer to the door, for through it the man would have to go to get to her mistress's chamber. "Let me go to your mistress, I tell you!" cried the man again. "Do what you will," replied Martinière, "I shall not stir from this place. Go on and finish your wicked deed; but remember that you also will die a shameful death at the Place Grève, like your atrocious partners in crime." "Ah! yes, you are right, La Martinière," replied the man, "I do look like a villainous robber and cut-throat, and am armed like one, but my partners have not been executed,--no, not yet." Therewith, hurling looks of furious wrath at the poor woman, who was almost dead with terror, he drew his stiletto. "O God! O God!" she exclaimed, expecting her death-blow; but at this moment there was heard a rattle of arms in the street, and the hoof-strokes of horses. "The *Maréchaussée*! the *Maréchaussée*! Help! Help!" screamed Martinière. "You abominable woman, you are determined to ruin me. All is lost now--it's all over. But here, here-- take this. Give that to your mistress this very night--to-morrow if you like." Whispering these words, he snatched the light from La Martinière, extinguished it, and then forced a casket into her hands. "By your hopes of salvation, I conjure you, give this casket to Mademoiselle," cried the man; and he rushed out of the house.

Martinière fell to the floor; at length she rose up with difficulty, and groped her way back in the darkness to her own room, where she sank down in an arm-chair completely exhausted, unable to utter a sound. Then she heard the keys rattle, which she had left in the lock of the street-door. The door was closed and locked, and she heard cautious, uncertain footsteps approaching her room. She sat riveted to the chair without power to move, expecting something terrible to happen. But her sensations may be imagined when the door opened, and by the light of the night-taper she recognised at the first glance that it was honest Baptiste, looking very pale and greatly troubled. "In the name of all the saints!" he began, "tell me, Dame Martinière, what has happened? Oh! the anxiety and fear I have had! I don't know what it was, but something drove me away from the wedding last evening. I couldn't help myself; I had to come. On getting into our street, I thought. Dame Martinière sleeps lightly, she'll be sure to hear me, thinks I, if I tap softly and gently at the door, and will come out and let me in. Then there comes a strong patrol on horseback as well as on foot, all armed to the teeth, and they stop me and won't let me go on. But luckily Desgrais the lieutenant of the *Maréchaussée*, is amongst them, who knows me quite well; and when they put their lanterns under my nose, he says, 'Why, Baptiste, where are you coming from at this time o' night? You'd better stay quietly in the house and take care of it There's some deviltry at work, and we are hoping to make a good capture to-night.' You wouldn't believe how heavy these words fell on my heart. Dame Martinière. And then when I put my foot on the threshold, there comes a man, all muffled up, rushing out of the house with a drawn dagger in his hand, and he runs over me--head over heels. The door was open, and the keys sticking in the lock. Oh! tell me what it all means." Martinière, relieved of her terrible fear and anxiety, related all that had taken place.

Then she and Baptiste went out into the passage, and there they found the candlestick lying on the floor where the stranger had thrown it as he ran away. "It is only too certain," said Baptiste, "that our Mademoiselle would have been robbed, ay, and even murdered, I make no doubt. The fellow knew, as you say, that you were alone with Mademoiselle,--why, he also knew that she was awake with her writings. I would bet anything it was one of those cursed rogues and thieves who force their way right into the houses, cunningly spying out everything that may be of use to them in carrying out their infernal plans. And as for that little casket, Dame Martinière--I think we'd better throw it into the Seine where it's deepest. Who can answer for it that there's not some wicked monster got designs on our good lady's life, and that if she opens the box she won't fall down dead like old Marquis de Tournay did, when he opened a letter that came from somebody he didn't know?"

After a long consultation the two faithful souls made up their minds to tell their mistress everything next morning, and also to place the mysterious casket in her hands, for of course it could be opened with proper precautions. After minutely weighing every circumstance connected with the suspicious stranger's appearance, they were both of the same opinion, namely, that there was some special mystery connected with the matter, which they durst not attempt to control single-handed; they must leave it to their good lady to unriddle.

Baptiste's apprehensions were well founded. Just at that time Paris was the scene of the most abominable atrocities, and exactly at the same period the most diabolical invention of Satan was made, to offer the readiest means for committing these deeds.

Glaser, a German apothecary, the best chemist of his age, had busied himself, as people of his profession were in the habit of doing, with alchemistical experiments. He had made it the object of his endeavour to discover the Philosopher's Stone. His coadjutor was an Italian of the name of Exili. But this man only practised alchemy as a blind. His real object was to learn all about the mixing and decoction and sublimating of poisonous compounds, by which Glaser on his part hoped to make his fortune; and at last he succeeded in fabricating that subtle poison that is without smell and without taste, that kills either on the spot or gradually and slowly, without ever leaving the slightest trace in the human body, and that deceives all the skill and art of the physicians, since, not suspecting the presence of poison, they fail not to ascribe the death to natural causes. Circumspectly as Exili went to work, he nevertheless fell under the suspicion of being a seller of poison, and was thrown into the Bastille. Soon afterwards Captain Godin de Sainte Croix was confined in the same dungeon. This man had for a long time been living in relations with the Marchioness de Brinvillier, which brought disgrace on all the family; so at last, as the Marquis continued indifferent to his wife's shameful conduct, her father, Dreux d'Aubray, *Civil Lieutenant* of Paris, compelled the guilty pair to part by means of a warrant which was executed upon the Captain. Passionate, unprincipled, hypocritically feigning to be pious, and yet inclined from his youth up to all kinds of vice, jealous, revengeful even to madness, the Captain could not have met with any more welcome information than that contained in Exili's diabolical secret, since it would give him the power to annihilate all his enemies. He became an eager scholar of Exili, and soon came to be as clever as his master, so that, on being liberated from the Bastille, he was in a position to work on unaided.

Before an abandoned woman, De Brinvillier became through Sainte Croix's instrumentality a monster. He contrived to induce her to poison successively her own father, with whom she was living, tending with heartless hypocrisy his declining days, and then her two brothers, and finally her sister,--her father out of revenge, and the others on account of the rich family inheritance. From the histories of several poisoners we have terrible examples how the commission of crimes of this class becomes at last an all-absorbing passion. Often, without any further purpose than the mere vile pleasure of the thing, just as chemists make experiments for their own enjoyment, have poisoners destroyed persons whose life or death must have been to them a matter of perfect indifference.

The sudden decease of several poor people in the Hotel Dieu some time afterwards excited the suspicion that the bread had been poisoned which Brinvillier, in order to acquire a reputation for piety and benevolence, used to distribute there every week. At any rate, it is undoubtedly true that she was in the habit of serving the guests whom she invited to her house with poisoned pigeon pie. The Chevalier de Guet and several other persons fell victims to these hellish banquets. Sainte Croix, his confederate La Chaussée, and Brinvillier were able for a long time to enshroud their horrid deeds behind an impenetrable veil. But of what avail is the infamous cunning of reprobate men when the Divine Power has decreed that punishment shall overtake the guilty here on earth?

The poisons which Sainte Croix prepared were of so subtle a nature that if the powder (called by the Parisians *Pondre de Succession*, or Succession Powder) were prepared with the face exposed, a single inhalation of it might cause instantaneous death. Sainte Croix therefore, when engaged in its manufacture, always wore a mask made of fine glass. One day, just as he was pouring a prepared powder into a phial, his mask fell off, and, inhaling the fine particles of the poison, he fell down dead on the spot. As he had died without heirs, the officers of the law hastened to place his effects under seal. Amongst them they found a locked box, which contained the whole of the infernal arsenal of poisons that the abandoned wretch Sainte Croix had had at command; they also found Brinvillier's letters, which left no doubt as to her atrocious crimes. She fled to Liége, into a convent there. Desgrais, an officer of the *Maréchaussée*, was sent after her. In the disguise of a monk he arrived at the convent where she had concealed herself, and contrived to engage the terrible woman in a love intrigue, and finally, under the pretext of a secret meeting, to entice her out to a lonely garden beyond the precincts of the town. Directly she arrived at the appointed place she was surrounded by Desgrais' satellites, whilst her monkish lover was suddenly converted into an officer of the *Maréchaussée*, who compelled her to get into the carriage which stood ready near the garden; and, surrounded by the police troop, she was driven straight off to Paris. La Chaussée had been already beheaded somewhat earlier; Brinvillier suffered the same death, after which her body was burned and the ashes scattered to the winds.

Now that the monster who had been able to direct his secret murderous weapons against both friend and foe alike unpunished was out of the world, the Parisians breathed freely once more. But it soon became known abroad that the villain Sainte Croix's abominable art had been handed down to certain successors. Like a malignant invisible spirit, murder insinuated itself into the most intimate circles, even the closest of those formed by relationship and love and friendship, and laid a quick sure grasp upon its unfortunate victims. He who was seen one day in the full vigour of health, tottered about the next a weak wasting invalid, and no skill of the physician could save him from death. Wealth, a lucrative office, a beautiful and perhaps too young a wife—any of these was sufficient to draw down upon the possessor this persecution unto death. The most sacred ties were severed by the cruellest mistrust. The husband trembled at his wife, the father at his son, the sister at the brother. The dishes remained untouched, and the wine at the dinner, which a friend put before his friends; and there where formerly jest and mirth had reigned supreme, savage glances were now spying about for the masked murderer. Fathers of families were observed buying provisions in remote districts with uneasy looks and movements, and preparing them themselves in the first dirty cook-shop they came to, since they feared diabolical treachery in their own homes. And yet even the greatest and most well-considered precautions were in many cases of no avail.

In order to put a stop to this iniquitous state of things, which continued to gain ground and grow greater day by day, the king appointed a special court of justice for the exclusive purpose of inquiring into and punishing these secret crimes. This was the so-called *Chambre Ardente*, which held its sittings not far from the Bastille, its acting president being La Regnie. For a considerable period all his efforts, however zealously they were prosecuted, remained fruitless; it was reserved for the crafty Desgrais to discover the most secret haunts of the criminals. In the Faubourg St. Germain there lived an old woman called Voisin, who made a regular business of fortune-telling and raising departed spirits; and with the help of her confederates Le Sage and Le Vigoureux, she managed to excite fear and astonishment in the minds of persons who could not be called exactly either weak or credulous. But she did more than this. A pupil of Exili, like La Croix, she, like him, concocted the same subtle poison that killed and left no trace behind it; and so she helped in this way profligate sons to get early possession of their inheritance, and depraved wives to another and younger husband. Desgrais wormed his way into her secret; she confessed all; the *Chambre Ardente* condemned her to be burned alive, and the sentence was executed in the Place Grève.

Amongst her effects was found a list of all the persons who had availed themselves of her assistance; and hence it was that not only did execution follow upon execution, but grave suspicion fell even upon persons of high position. Thus it was believed that Cardinal Bonzy had obtained from La Voisin the means of bringing to an untimely end all those persons to whom, as Archbishop of Narbonne, he was obliged to pay annuities. So also the Duchess de Bouillon, and the Countess de Soissons, whose names were found on the list, were accused of having had dealings with the diabolical woman; and even Francois Henri de Montmorenci, Boudebelle, Duke of Luxemburg, peer and marshal of the kingdom, was not spared. He too was prosecuted by the terrible *Chambre Ardente*. He voluntarily gave himself up to be imprisoned in the Bastille, where through Louvois' and La Regnie's hatred he was confined in a cell only six feet long. Months passed before it was made out satisfactorily that the Duke's transgression did not deserve any blame: he had once had his horoscope cast by Le Sage.

It is certain that the President La Regnie was betrayed by his blind zeal into acts of cruelty and arbitrary violence. The tribunal acquired the character of an Inquisition; the most trifling suspicion was sufficient to entail strict incarceration; and it was left to chance to establish the innocence of a person accused of a capital crime. Moreover, La Regnie was hideous in appearance, and of a malicious temperament, so that he soon drew down upon himself the hatred of those whose avenger or protector he was appointed to be. The Duchess de Bouillon, being asked by him during her trial if she had seen the devil, replied, "I fancy I can see him at this moment."

But whilst the blood of the guilty and the suspected alike was flowing in streams in the Place Grève, and after a time the secret poisonings became less and less frequent, a new kind of outrage came to light, and again filled the city with dismay. It seemed as if a band of miscreant robbers were in league together for the purpose of getting into their possession all the jewellery they could. No sooner was any valuable ornament purchased than, no matter how or where kept, it vanished in an inconceivable way. But what was still worse, any one who ventured to wear jewellery on his person at night was robbed, and often murdered even, either in the public street or in the dark passage of a house. Those who escaped with their lives declared that they had been knocked down by a blow on the head, which felled them like a lightning flash, and that on awaking from their stupor they had found that they had been robbed and were lying in quite a different place from that where they had received the blow. All who were murdered, some of whom were found nearly every morning lying either in the streets or in the houses, had all one and the same fatal wound,--a dagger-thrust in the heart, killing, according to the judgment of the surgeons, so instantaneously and so surely that the victim would drop down like a stone, unable to utter a sound. Who was there at the voluptuous court of Louis XIV. who was not entangled in some clandestine intrigue, and stole to his mistress at a late hour, often carrying a valuable present about him? The robbers, as if they were in league with spirits, knew almost exactly when anything of this sort was on foot. Often the unfortunate did not reach the house where he expected to meet with the reward of his passion; often he fell on the threshold, nay, at the very chamber door of his mistress, who was horrified at finding the bloody corpse.

In vain did Argenson, the Minister of Police, order the arrest of every person from amongst the populace against whom there was the least suspicion; in vain did La Regnie rage and try to extort confessions; in vain did they strengthen their watch and their patrols;--they could not find a trace of the evil-doers. The only thing that did to a certain extent avail was to take the precaution of going armed to the teeth and have a torch carried before one; and yet instances were not wanting in which the servant was annoyed by stones thrown at him, whilst at the same moment his master was murdered and robbed. It was especially remarkable that, in spite of all inquiries in every place where traffic in jewellery was in any way possible, not the smallest specimen of the stolen ornaments ever came to light, and so in this way also no clue was found which might have been followed.

Desgrais was furious that the miscreants should thus baffle all his cunning. The quarter of the town in which he happened to be stationed was spared; whilst in the others, where nobody apprehended any evil, these robberies and murders claimed their richest victims.

Desgrais hit upon the ruse of making several Desgrais one after the other, so exactly alike in gait, posture, speech, figure, and face, that the myrmidons of the police themselves did not know which was the real Desgrais. Meanwhile, at the risk of his own life, he used to watch alone in the most secret haunts and lairs of crime, and follow at a distance first this man and then that, who at his own instance carried some valuable jewellery about his person. These men, however, were not attacked; and hence the robbers must be acquainted with this contrivance also. Desgrais absolutely despaired.

One morning Desgrais came to President La Regnie pale and perturbed, quite distracted in fact. "What's the matter? What news? Have you got a clue?" cried the President "Oh! your excellency," began Desgrais, stammering with rage, "oh! your excellency--last night--not far from the Louvre--the Marquis de la Fare was attacked in my presence." "By Heaven then!" shouted La Regnie, exultant with joy, "we have them." "But first listen to me," interrupted Desgrais with a bitter smile, "and hear how it all came about. Well then, I was standing near the Louvre on the watch for these devils who mock me, and my heart was on fire with fury. Then there came a figure close past me without noticing me, walking with unsteady steps and looking behind him. By the faint moonlight I saw that it was Marquis de la Fare. I was not surprised to see him; I knew where he was stealing to. But he had not gone more than ten or twelve paces past me when a man started up right out of the earth as it seemed and knocked him down, and stooped over him. In the sudden surprise and on the impulse of the moment, which would else have delivered the murderer into my hands, I was thoughtless enough to cry out; and I was just bursting out of my hiding-place with a rush, intending to throw myself upon him, when I got entangled in my mantle and fell down. I saw the man hurrying away on the wings of the wind; I made haste and picked myself up and ran after him; and as I ran I blew my horn; from the distance came the answering whistles of the man; the streets were all alive; there was a rattle of arms and a trampling of horses in all directions. 'Here! here! Desgrais! Desgrais!' I shouted till the streets echoed. By the bright moonlight I could always see the man in front of me, doubling here and there to deceive me. We came to the Rue Nicaise, and there his strength appeared to fail him: I redoubled my efforts; and he only led me by fifteen paces at the most"---- "You caught him up; you seized him; the patrol came up?" cried La Regnie, his eyes flashing, whilst he seized Desgrais by the arm as though he were the flying murderer. "Fifteen paces," continued Desgrais in a hollow voice and with difficulty drawing his breath-- "fifteen paces from me the man sprang aside into the shade and disappeared through the wall." "Disappeared?-- through the wall? Are you mad?" cried La Regnie, taking a couple of steps backwards and striking his hands together.

"From this moment onwards," continued Desgrais, rubbing his brow like a man tormented by hateful thoughts, "your excellency may call me a madman or an insane ghost-seer, but it was just as I have told you. I was standing staring at the wall like one petrified when several men of the patrol hurried up breathless, and along with them Marquis de la Fare, who had picked himself up, with his drawn sword in his hand. We lighted the torches, and sounded the wall backwards and forwards,--not an indication of a door or a window or an opening. It was a strong stone wall bounding a yard, and was joined on to a house in which live people against whom there has never risen the slightest suspicion. To-day I have again taken a careful survey of the whole place. It must be the Devil himself who is mystifying us."

Desgrais' story became known in Paris. People's heads were full of the sorceries and incantations and compacts with Satan of Voisin, Vigoureuse, and the reprobate priest Le Sage; and as in the eternal nature of us men, the leaning to the marvellous and the wonderful so often outweighs all the authority of reason, so the public soon began to believe simply and solely that as Desgrais in his mortification had said, Satan himself really did protect the abominable wretches, who must have sold their souls to him. It will readily be believed that Desgrais' story received all sorts of ornamental additions. An account of the adventure, with a woodcut on the title-page representing a grim Satanic form before which the terrified Desgrais was sinking in the earth, was printed and largely sold at the street corners. This alone was enough to overawe the people, and even to rob the myrmidons of the police of their courage, who now wandered about the streets at night trembling and quaking, hung about with amulets and soaked in holy water.

Argenson perceived that the exertions of the *Chambre Ardente* were of no avail, and he appealed to the king to appoint a tribunal with still more extensive powers to deal with this new epidemic of crime, to hunt up the evil-doers, and to punish them. The king, convinced that he had already vested too much power in the *Chambre Ardente* and shaken with horror at the numberless executions which the bloodthirsty La Regnie had decreed, flatly refused to entertain the proposed plan.

Another means was chosen to stimulate the king's interest in the matter.

Louis was in the habit of spending the afternoon in Madame de Maintenon's salons, and also despatching state business therewith his ministers until a late hour at night. Here a poem was presented to him in the name of the jeopardised lovers, complaining that, whenever gallantry bid them honour their mistress with a present, they had always to risk their lives on the fulfilment of the injunction. There was always both honour and pleasure to be won in shedding their blood for their lady in a knightly encounter; but it was quite another thing when they had to deal with a stealthy malignant assassin, against whom they could not arm themselves. Would Louis, the bright polar star of all love and gallantry, cause the resplendent beams of his glory to shine and dissipate this dark night, and so unveil the black mystery that was concealed within it? The god-like hero, who had broken his enemies to pieces, would now (they hoped) draw his sword glittering with victory, and, as Hercules did against the Lernean serpent, or Theseus the Minotaur, would fight against the threatening monster which was gnawing away all the raptures of love, and darkening all their joy and converting it into deep pain and grief inconsolable.

Serious as the matter was, yet the poem did not lack clever and witty turns, especially in the description of the anxieties which the lovers had to endure as they stole by secret ways to their mistresses, and of how their apprehensions proved fatal to all the rapturous delights of love and to every dainty gallant adventure before it could even develop into blossom. If it be added that the poem was made to conclude with a magniloquent panegyric upon Louis XIV., the king could not fail to read it with visible signs of satisfaction. Having reached the end of it, he turned round abruptly to Madame de Maintenon, without lifting his eyes from the paper, and read the poem through again aloud; after which he asked her with a gracious smile what was her opinion with respect to the wishes of the jeopardised lovers.

De Maintenon, faithful to the serious bent of her mind, and always preserving a certain colour of piety, replied that those who walked along secret and forbidden paths were not worthy of any special protection, but that the abominable criminals did call for special measures to be taken for their destruction. The king, dissatisfied with this wavering answer, folded up the paper, and was going back to the Secretary of State, who was working in the next room, when on casting a glance sideways his eye fell upon Mademoiselle de Scudéri, who was present in the salon and had taken her seat in a small easy-chair not far from De Maintenon. Her he now approached, whilst the pleasant smile which at first had played about his mouth and on his cheeks, but had then disappeared, now won the upper hand again. Standing immediately in front of Mademoiselle, and unfolding the poem once more, he said softly, "Our Marchioness will not countenance in any way the gallantries of our amorous gentlemen, and give us evasive answers of a kind that are almost quite forbidden. But you, Mademoiselle, what is your opinion of this poetic petition?" De Scudéri rose respectfully from her chair, whilst a passing blush flitted like the purple sunset rays in evening across the venerable lady's pale cheeks, and she said, bowing gently and casting down her eyes,

"Un amant qui craint les voleurs
N'est point digne d'amour."
(A lover who is afraid of robbers is not worthy of love.)

The king, greatly struck by the chivalric spirit breathed in these few words, which upset the whole of the poem with its yards and yards of tirades, cried with sparkling eyes, "By St. Denis, you are right. Mademoiselle! Cowardice shall not be protected by any blind measures which would affect the innocent along with the guilty; Argenson and La Regnie must do their best as they are."

All these horrors of the day La Martinière depicted next morning in startling colours when she related to her mistress the occurrence of the previous night; and she handed over to her the mysterious casket in fear and trembling. Both she and Baptiste, who stood in the corner as pale as death, twisting and doubling up his night-cap, and hardly able to speak in his fear and anxiety,--both begged Mademoiselle in the most piteous terms and in the names of all the saints, to use the utmost possible caution in opening the box. De Scudéri, weighing the locked mystery in her hand, and subjecting it to a careful scrutiny, said smiling, "You are both of you ghost-seers! That I am not rich, that there are not sufficient treasures here to be worth a murder, is known to all these abandoned assassins, who, you yourself tell me, spy out all that there is in a house, as well as it is to me and you. You think they have designs upon my life? Who could make capital out of the death of an old lady of seventy-three, who never did harm to anybody in the world except the miscreants and peace-breakers in the romances which she writes herself, who makes middling verses which can excite nobody's envy, who will have nothing to leave except the state dresses of an old maid who sometimes went to court, and a dozen or two well-bound books with gilt edges? And then you, Martinière,--you may describe the stranger's appearance as frightful as you like, yet I cannot believe that his intentions were evil. So then----"

La Martinière recoiled some paces, and Baptiste, uttering a stifled "Oh!" almost sank upon his knees as Mademoiselle proceeded to press upon a projecting steel knob; then the lid flew back with a noisy jerk.

But how astonished was she to see a pair of gold bracelets, richly set with jewels, and a necklace to match. She took them out of the case; and whilst she was praising the exquisite workmanship of the necklace, Martinière was eyeing the valuable bracelets, and crying time after time, that the vain Lady Montespan herself had no such ornaments as these. "But what is it for? what does it all mean?" said De Scudéri. But at this same moment she observed a small slip of paper folded together, lying at the bottom of the casket. She hoped, and rightly, to find in it an explanation of the mystery. She had hardly finished reading the contents of the scrip when it fell from her trembling hands. She sent an appealing glance towards Heaven, and then fell back almost fainting into her chair. Terrified, Martinière sprang to her assistance, and so also did Baptiste. "Oh! what an insult!" she exclaimed, her voice half-choked with tears, "Oh! what a burning shame! Must I then endure this in my old age? Have I then gone and acted with wrong and foolish levity like some young giddy thing? O God, are words let fall half in jest capable of being stamped with such an atrocious interpretation? And am I, who have been faithful to virtue, and of blameless piety from my earliest childhood until now,--am I to be accused of the crime of making such a diabolical compact?"

Mademoiselle held her handkerchief to her eyes and wept and sobbed bitterly, so that Martinière and Baptiste were both of them confused and rendered helpless by embarrassed constraint, not knowing what to do to help their mistress in her great trouble.

Martinière picked up the ominous strip of paper from the floor. Upon it was written--

"Un amant qui craint les voleurs
N'est point digne d'amour.

"Your sagacious mind, honoured lady, has saved us from great persecution. We only exercise the right of the stronger over the weak and the cowardly in order to appropriate to ourselves treasures that would else be disgracefully squandered. Kindly accept these jewels as a token of our gratitude. They are the most brilliant that we have been enabled to meet with for a long time; and yet you, honoured lady, ought to be adorned with jewellery even still finer than this is. We trust you will not withdraw from us your friendship and kind remembrance.

"Is it possible?" exclaimed De Scudéri after she had to some extent recovered herself, "is it possible for men to carry their shameless insolence, their godless scorn, to such lengths?" The sun shone brightly through the dark-red silk window curtains and made the brilliants which lay on the table beside the open casket to sparkle in the reddish gleam. Chancing to cast her eyes upon them, De Scudéri hid her face with abhorrence, and bade Martinière take the fearful jewellery away at once, that very moment, for the blood of the murdered victims was still adhering to it. Martinière at once carefully locked the necklace and bracelets in the casket again, and thought that the wisest plan would be to hand it over to the Minister of Police, and to confide to him every thing connected with the appearance of the young man who had caused them so much uneasiness, and the way in which he had placed the casket in her hands.

De Scudéri rose to her feet and slowly paced up and down the room in silence, as if she were only now reflecting what was to be done. She then bade Baptiste fetch a sedan chair, while Martinière was to dress her, for she meant to go straight to the Marchioness de Maintenon.

She had herself carried to the Marchioness's just at the hour when she knew she should find that lady alone in her salons. The casket with the jewellery De Scudéri also took with her.

Of course the Marchioness was greatly astonished to see Mademoiselle, who was generally a pattern of dignity, amiability (notwithstanding her advanced age), and gracefulness, come in with tottering steps, pale, and excessively agitated. "By all the saints, what's happened to you?" she cried when she saw the poor troubled lady, who, almost distracted and hardly able to walk erect, hurried to reach the easy-chair which De Maintenon pushed towards her. At length, having recovered her power of speech somewhat, Mademoiselle related what a deep insult--she should never get over it--her thoughtless jest in answer to the petition of the jeopardised lovers had brought upon her. The Marchioness, after learning the whole of the story by fragments, arrived at the conclusion that De Scudéri took the strange occurrence far too much to heart, that the mockery of depraved wretches like these could never come home to a pious, noble mind like hers, and finally she requested to see the ornaments.

De Scudéri gave her the open casket; and the Marchioness, on seeing the costly jewellery, could not help uttering a loud cry of admiration. She took out the necklace and the bracelets, and approached the window with them, where first she let the sun play upon the stones, and then she held them up close to her eyes in order to see better the exquisite workmanship of the gold, and to admire the marvellous skill with which every little link in the elaborate chain was finished. All at once the Marchioness turned round abruptly towards Mademoiselle and cried, "I tell you what, Mademoiselle, these bracelets and necklace must have been made by no less a person than René Cardillac."

René Cardillac was at that time the most skilful goldsmith in Paris, and also one of the most ingenious as well as one of the most eccentric men of the age. Rather small than great, but broad-shouldered and with a strong and muscular frame, Cardillac, although considerably more than fifty, still possessed the strength and activity of youth. And his strength, which might be said to be something above the common, was further evidenced by his abundant curly reddish hair, and his thick-set features and the sultry gleam upon them. Had not Cardillac been known throughout all Paris, as one of the most honest and honourable of men, disinterested, frank, without any reserve, always ready to help, the very peculiar appearance of his eyes, which were small, deep-set, green, and glittering, might have drawn upon him the suspicion of lurking malice and viciousness.

As already said, Cardillac was the greatest master in his trade, not only in Paris, but also perhaps of his age. Intimately acquainted with the properties of precious stones, he knew how to treat them and set them in such a manner that an ornament which had at first been looked upon as wanting in lustre, proceeded out of Cardillac's shop possessing a dazzling magnificence. Every commission he accepted with burning avidity, and fixed a price that seemed to bear no proportion whatever to the work to be done--so small was it. Then the work gave him no rest; both night and day he was heard hammering in his work-shop, and often when the thing was nearly finished he would suddenly conceive a dislike to the form; he had doubts as to the elegance of the setting of some or other of the jewels, of a little link--quite a sufficient reason for throwing all into the crucible, and beginning the entire work over again. Thus every individual piece of jewellery that he turned out was a perfect and matchless masterpiece, utterly astounding to the person who had given the commission.

But it was now hardly possible to get any work that was once finished out of his hands. Under a thousand pretexts he put off the owner from week to week, and from month to month. It was all in vain to offer him double for the work; he would not take a single *Louis d'or* more than the price bargained for. When at last he was obliged to yield to the insistence of his customer, he could not help betraying all the signs of the greatest annoyance, nay, of even fury seething in his heart. If the piece of work which he had to deliver up was something of more than ordinary importance, especially anything of great value, worth many thousands owing to the costliness of the jewels or the extreme delicacy of the gold-work, he was capable of running about like a madman, cursing himself, his labour, and all about him. But then if any person came up behind him and shouted, "René Cardillac, would you not like to make a beautiful necklace for my betrothed?--bracelets for my sweet-heart," or so forth, he would suddenly stop still, and looking at him with his little eyes, would ask, as he rubbed his hands, "Well, what have you got?" Thereupon the other would produce a small jewel-case, and say, "Oh! some jewels--see; they are nothing particular, only common things, but in your hands"---- Cardillac does not let him finish what he has to say, but snatching the case out of his hand takes out the stones (which are in reality of but little value) and holds them up to the light, crying enraptured, "Ho! ho! common things, are they? Not at all! Pretty stones--magnificent stones; only let me make them up for you. And if you're not squeamish to a handful or two of *Louis d'or*, I can add a few more little gems, which shall sparkle in your eyes like the great sun himself." The other says, "I will leave it all to you, Master René, and pay you what you like."

Then, without making any difference whether his customer is a rich citizen only or an eminent nobleman of the court, Cardillac throws his arms impetuously round his neck and embraces him and kisses him, saying that now he is quite happy again, and the work will be finished in a week's time. Running off home with breathless speed and up into his workshop, he begins to hammer away, and at the week's end has produced a masterpiece of art But when the customer comes prepared to pay with joy the insignificant sum demanded, and expecting to take the finished ornament away with him, Cardillac gets testy, rude, obstinate, and hard to deal with. "But, Master Cardillac, recollect that my wedding is to-morrow."--"But what have I to do with your wedding? come again in a fortnight's time." "The ornament is finished; here is your money; and I must have it." "And I tell you that I've lots of things to alter in it, and I shan't let you have it to-day." "And I tell you that if you won't deliver up the ornament by fair means--of course I am willing to pay you double for it--you shall soon see me march up with Argenson's serviceable underlings."--"Well, then, may Satan torture you with scores of red-hot pincers, and hang three hundredweight on the necklace till it strangle your bride." And therewith, thrusting the jewellery into the bridegroom's breast pocket, Cardillac seizes him by the arm and turns him roughly out of the door, so that he goes stumbling all down the stairs. Then Cardillac puts his head out of the window and laughs like a demon on seeing the poor young man limp out of the house, holding his handkerchief to his bloody nose.

But one thing there was about him that was quite inexplicable. Often, after he had enthusiastically taken a piece of work in hand, he would implore his customer by the Virgin and all the saints, with every sign of deep and violent agitation, and with moving protestations, nay, amidst tears and sobs, that he might be released from his engagement. Several persons who were most highly esteemed of the king and the people had vainly offered large sums of money to get the smallest piece of work from him. He threw himself at the king's feet and besought as a favour at his hands that he might not be asked to do any work for him. In the same way he refused every commission from De Maintenon; he even rejected with aversion and horror the proposal she made him to fabricate for her a little ring with emblematic ornaments, which was to be presented to Racine.

Accordingly De Maintenon now said, "I would wager that if I sent for Cardillac to come here to tell me at least for whom he made these ornaments, he would refuse to come, since he would probably fear it was some commission; and he never will make anything for me on any account. And yet he has, it seems, dropped something of his inflexible obstinacy some time ago, for I hear that he now labours more industriously than ever, and delivers up his work at once, though still not without much inward vexation and turning away of his face." De Scudéri, who was greatly concerned that the ornaments should, if it could possibly be managed, come soon into the hands of the proper owner, thought they might send express word to Master Whimsicality that they did not want him to do any work, but only to pass his opinion upon some jewels. This commended itself to the Marchioness. Cardillac was sent for; and, as though he had been already on the way, after a brief interval he stepped into the room.

On observing De Scudéri he appeared to be embarrassed; and, like one confounded by something so utterly unexpected that he forgets the claims of propriety such as the moment demands, he first made a low and reverential obeisance to this venerable lady, and then only did he turn to the Marchioness. She, pointing to the jewellery, which now lay glittering on the dark-green table-cloth, asked him hastily if it was of his workmanship. Hardly glancing at it, and keeping his eyes steadily fixed upon De Maintenon, Cardillac hurriedly packed the necklace and bracelets into the casket, which stood beside them, and pushed it violently away from him. Then he said, whilst a forbidding smile gleamed in his red face, "By my honour, noble lady, he would have but a poor acquaintance with René Cardillac's workmanship who should believe for a single moment that any other goldsmith in the world could set a piece of jewellery like that is done. Of course it's my handiwork." "Then tell me," continued the Marchioness, "for whom you made these ornaments." "For myself alone," replied Cardillac. "Ah! I dare say your ladyship finds that strange," he continued, since both she and De Scudéri had fixed their eyes upon him astounded, the former full of mistrust, the latter of anxious suspense as to what turn the matter would take next; "but it is so. Merely out of love for my beautiful handicraft I picked out all my best stones and gladly set to work upon them, exercising more industry and care over them than I had ever done over any stones before. A short time ago the ornaments disappeared in some inconceivable way out of my workshop." "Thank Heaven!"

cried De Scudéri, whilst her eyes sparkled with joy, and she jumped up from her chair as quick and nimble as a young girl; then going up to Cardillac, she placed both her hands upon his shoulders, and said, "Here, Master René, take your property back again, which these rascally miscreants stole from you." And she related every detail of how she had acquired possession of the ornaments, to all of which Cardillac listened silently, with his eyes cast down upon the floor. Only now and again he uttered an indistinct "Hm!--So!--Ho! ho!" now throwing his hands behind his back, and now softly stroking his chin and cheeks.

When De Scudéri came to the end of her story, Cardillac appeared to be struggling with some new and striking thought which had occurred to him during the course of it, and as though he were labouring with some rebellious resolve that refused to conform to his wishes. He rubbed his forehead, sighed, drew his hand across his eyes, as if to check tears which were gushing from them. At length he seized the casket which De Scudéri was holding out towards him, and slowly sinking upon one knee, said, "These jewels have been decreed to you, my noble and respected lady, by Destiny. Yes, now I know that it was you I thought about when I was labouring at them, and that it was for you I worked. Do not disdain to accept these ornaments, nor refuse to wear them; they are indeed the best things I have made for a very long time." "Why, why, Master René," replied De Scudéri, in a charming, jesting manner; "what are you thinking about? Would it become me at my years to trick myself out with such bright gems? And what makes you think of giving me such an over-rich present? Nay, nay, Master René. Now if I were beautiful like the Marchioness de Fontange, and rich too, I assure you I should not let these ornaments pass out of my hands; but what do these withered arms want with vain show, and this covered neck with glittering ornaments?" Meanwhile Cardillac had risen to his feet again; and whilst persistently holding out the casket towards De Scudéri he said, like one distracted--and his looks were wild and uneasy,--"Have pity upon me, Mademoiselle, and take the ornaments. You don't know what great respect I cherish in my heart for your virtue and your high good qualities. Accept this little present as an effort on my behalf to show my deep respect and devotion." But as De Scudéri still continued to hesitate, De Maintenon took the casket out of Cardillac's hands, saying, "Upon my word, Mademoiselle, you are always talking about your great age. What have we, you and I, to do with years and their burdens? And aren't you acting just like a shy young thing, who would only too well like to take the sweet fruit that is offered to her if she could only do so without stirring either hand or finger? Don't refuse to accept from our good Master René as a free gift what scores of others could never get, in spite of all their gold and all their prayers and entreaties."

Whilst speaking De Maintenon had forced the casket into Mademoiselle's hand; and now Cardillac again fell upon his knees and kissed De Scudéri's gown and hands, sighing and gasping, weeping and sobbing; then he jumped up and ran off like a madman, as fast as he could run, upsetting chairs and tables in his senseless haste, and making the glasses and porcelain tumble together with a ring and jingle and clash.

De Scudéri cried out quite terrified, "Good Heavens! what's happened to the man?" But the Marchioness, who was now in an especially lively mood and in such a pert humour as was in general quite foreign to her, burst out into a silvery laugh, and said, "Now, I've got it, Mademoiselle. Master René has fallen desperately in love with you, and according to the established form and settled usage of all true gallantry, he is beginning to storm your heart with rich presents." She even pushed her raillery further, admonishing De Scudéri not to be too cruel towards her despairing lover, until Mademoiselle, letting her natural-born humour have play, was carried away by the bubbling stream of merry conceits and fancies. She thought that if that was really the state of the case, she should be at last conquered and would not be able to help affording to the world the unprecedented example of a goldsmith's bride, of untarnished nobility, of the age of three and seventy. De Maintenon offered her services to weave the wedding-wreath, and to instruct her in the duties of a good house-wife, since such a snippety bit of a girl could not of course know much about such things.

But when at length De Scudéri rose to say adieu to the Marchioness, she again, notwithstanding all their laughing jests, grew very grave as she took the jewel-case in her hand, and said, "And yet, Marchioness, do you know, I can never wear these ornaments. Whatever be their history, they have at some time or other been in the hands of those diabolical wretches who commit robbery and murder with all the effrontery of Satan himself; nay, I believe they must be in an unholy league with him. I shudder with awe at the sight of the blood which appears to adhere to the glittering stones. And then, I must confess, I cannot help feeling that there is something strangely uneasy and awe-inspiring about Cardillac's behaviour. I cannot get rid of the dark presentiment that behind all this there is lurking some fearful and terrible secret; but when, on the other hand, I pass the whole matter with all its circumstantial adjuncts in clear review before my mind, I cannot even guess what the mystery consists in, nor yet how our brave honest Master René, the pattern of a good industrious citizen, can have anything to do with what is bad or deserving of condemnation; but of this I am quite sure, that I shall never dare to put the ornaments on."

The Marchioness thought that this was carrying scruples too far. But when De Scudéri asked her on her conscience what she should really do in her (Scudéri's) place, De Maintenon replied earnestly and decisively, "Far sooner throw the ornaments into the Seine than ever wear them."

The scene with Master René was described by De Scudéri in charming verses, which she read to the king on the following evening in De Maintenon's salon. And of course it may readily be conceived that, conquering her uncomfortable feelings and forebodings of evil, she drew at Master René's expense a diverting picture, in bright vivacious colours, of the goldsmith's bride of three and seventy who was of such ancient nobility. At any rate the king laughed heartily, and swore that Boileau Despreux had found his master; hence De Scudéri's poem was popularly adjudged to be the wittiest that ever was written.

Several months had passed, when, as chance would have it, De Scudéri was driving over the Pont Neuf in the Duchess de Montansier's glass coach. The invention of this elegant class of vehicles was still so recent that a throng of the curious always gathered round it when one appeared in the streets. And so there was on the present occasion a gaping crowd round De Montansier's coach on the Pont Neuf, so great as almost to hinder the horses from getting on. All at once De Scudéri heard a continuous fire of abuse and cursing, and perceived a man making his way through the thick of the crowd by the help of his fists and by punching people in the ribs. And when he came nearer she saw that his piercing eyes were riveted upon her. His face was pale as death and distorted by pain; and he kept his eyes riveted upon her all the time he was energetically working his way onwards with his fists and elbows, until he reached the door. Pulling it open with impetuous violence, he threw a strip of paper into De Scudéri's lap, and again dealing out and receiving blows and punches, disappeared as he had come. Martinière, who was accompanying her mistress, uttered a scream of terror when she saw the man appear at the coach door, and fell back upon the cushions in a swoon. De Scudéri vainly pulled the cord and called out to the driver; he, as if impelled by the foul Fiend, whipped up his horses, so that they foamed at the mouth and tossed their heads, and kicked and plunged, and finally thundered over the bridge at a sharp trot. De Scudéri emptied her smelling-bottle over the insensible woman, who at length opened her eyes. Trembling and shaking, she clung convulsively to her mistress, her face pale with anxiety and terror as she gasped out, "For the love of the Virgin, what did that terrible man want? Oh! yes, it was he! it was he!--the very same who brought you the casket that awful night." Mademoiselle pacified the poor woman, assuring her that not the least mischief had been done, and that the main thing to do just then was to see what the strip of paper contained. She unfolded it and found these words--

"I am being plunged into the pit of destruction by an evil destiny which you may avert. I implore you, as the son does the mother whom he cannot leave, and with the warmest affection of a loving child, send the necklace and bracelets which you received from me to Master René Cardillac; any pretext will do, to get some improvement made--or to get something altered. Your welfare, your life, depend upon it. If you have not done so by the day after to-morrow I will force my way into your dwelling and kill myself before your eyes."

"Well now, it is at any rate certain," said De Scudéri when she had read it, "that this mysterious man, even if he does really belong to the notorious band of thieves and robbers, yet has no evil designs against me. If he had succeeded in speaking to me that night, who knows whether I should not have learnt of some singular event or some mysterious complication of things, respecting which I now try in vain to form even the remotest guess. But let the matter now take what shape it may, I shall certainly do what this note urgently requests me to do, if for no other reason than to get rid of those ill-starred jewels, which I always fancy are a talisman of the foul Fiend himself. And I warrant Cardillac, true to his rooted habit, won't let it pass out of his hands again so easily."

The very next day De Scudéri intended to go and take the jewellery to the goldsmith's. But somehow it seemed as if all the wits and intellects of entire Paris had conspired together to overwhelm Mademoiselle just on this particular morning with their verses and plays and anecdotes. No sooner had La Chapelle finished reading a tragedy, and had slyly remarked with some degree of confident assurance that he should now certainly beat Racine, than the latter poet himself came in, and routed him with a pathetic speech of a certain king, until Boileau appeared to let off the rockets of his wit into this black sky of Tragedy--in order that he might not be talked to death on the subject of the colonnade of the Louvre, for he had been penned up in it by Dr. Perrault, the architect.

It was high noon; De Scudéri had to go to the Duchess de Montansier's; and so the visit to Master René Cardillac's was put off until the next day. Mademoiselle, however, was tormented by a most extraordinary feeling of uneasiness. The young man's figure was constantly before her eyes; and deep down in her memory there was stirring a dim recollection that she had seen his face and features somewhere before. Her sleep, which was of the lightest, was disturbed by troublesome dreams. She fancied she had acted frivolously and even criminally in having delayed to grasp the hand which the unhappy wretch, who was sinking into the abyss of ruin, was stretching up towards her; nay, she was even haunted by the thought that she had had it in her power to prevent a fatal event from taking place or an enormous crime from being committed. So, as soon as the morning was fully come, she had Martinière finish her toilet, and drove to the goldsmith, taking the jewel-casket with her.

The people were pouring into the Rue Nicaise, to the house where Cardillac lived, and were gathering about his door, shouting, screaming, and creating a wild tumult of noise; and they were with difficulty prevented by the *Maréchaussée*, who had drawn a cordon round the house, from forcing their way in. Angry voices were crying in a wild confused hubbub, "Tear him to pieces! pound him to dust! the accursed murderer!" At length Desgrais appeared on the scene with a strong body of police, who formed a passage through the heart of the crowd. The house door flew open and a man stepped out loaded with chains; and he was dragged away amidst the most horrible imprecations of the furious mob.

At the moment that De Scudéri, who was half swooning from fright and her apprehensions that something terrible had happened, was witness of this scene, a shrill piercing scream of distress rang upon her ears. "Go on, go on, right forward," she cried to her coachman, almost distracted. Scattering the dense mass of people by a quick clever turn of his horses, he pulled up immediately in front of Cardillac's door. There De Scudéri observed Desgrais, and at his feet a young girl, as beautiful as the day, with dishevelled hair, only half dressed, and her countenance stamped with desperate anxiety and wild with despair. She was clasping his knees and crying in a tone of the most terrible, the most heart-rending anguish, "Oh! he is innocent! he is innocent." In vain were Desgrais' efforts, as well as those of his men, to make her leave hold and to raise her up from the floor. At last a strong brutal fellow laid his coarse rough hands upon the poor girl and dragged her away from Desgrais by main force, but awkwardly stumbling let her drop, so that she rolled down the stone steps and lay in the street, without uttering a single sound more; she appeared to be dead.

Mademoiselle could no longer contain herself. "For God's sake, what has happened? What's all this about?" she cried as she quickly opened the door of her coach and stepped out. The crowd respectfully made way for the estimable lady. She, on perceiving that two or three compassionate women had raised up the girl and set her on the steps, where they were rubbing her forehead with aromatic waters, approached Desgrais and repeated her question with vehemence. "A horrible thing has happened," said Desgrais. "René Cardillac was found this morning murdered, stabbed to the heart with a dagger. His journeyman Olivier Brusson is the murderer. That was he who was just led away to prison." "And the girl?" exclaimed Mademoiselle---- "Is Madelon, Cardillac's daughter," broke in Desgrais. "Yon abandoned wretch is her lover. And she's screaming and crying, and protesting that Olivier is innocent, quite innocent. But the real truth is she is cognisant of the deed, and I must have her also taken to the *conciergerie* (prison)."

Saying which, Desgrais cast a glance of such spiteful malicious triumph upon the girl that De Scudéri trembled. Madelon was just beginning to breathe again, but she still lay with her eyes closed incapable of either sound or motion; and they did not know what to do, whether to take her into the house or to stay with her longer until she came round again. Mademoiselle's eyes filled with tears, and she was greatly agitated, as she looked upon the innocent angel; Desgrais and his myrmidons made her shudder. Downstairs came a heavy rumbling noise; they were bringing down Cardillac's corpse. Quickly making up her mind. De Scudéri said loudly, "I will take the girl with me; you may attend to everything else, Desgrais." A muttered wave of applause swept through the crowd. They lifted up the girl, whilst everybody crowded round and hundreds of arms were proffered to assist them; like one floating in the air the young girl was carried to the coach and placed within it,--blessings being showered from the lips of all upon the noble lady who had come to snatch innocence from the scaffold.

The efforts of Seron, the most celebrated physician in Paris, to bring Madelon back to herself were at length crowned with success, for she had lain for hours in a dead swoon, utterly unconscious. What the physician began was completed by De Scudéri, who strove to excite the mild rays of hope in the girl's soul, till at length relief came to her in the form of a violent fit of tears and sobbing. She managed to relate all that had happened, although from time to time her heart- rending grief got the upper hand, and her voice was choked with convulsive sobs.

About midnight she had been awakened by a light tap at her chamber door, and heard Olivier's voice imploring her to get up at once, as her father was dying. Though almost stunned with dismay, she started up and opened the door, and saw Olivier with a light in his hand, pale and dreadfully agitated, and dripping with perspiration. He led the way into her father's workshop, with an unsteady gait, and she followed him. There lay her father with fixed staring eyes, his throat rattling in the agonies of death. With a loud wail she threw herself upon him, and then first noticed his bloody shirt. Olivier softly drew her away and set to work to wash a wound in her father's left breast with a traumatic balsam, and to bind it up. During this operation her father's senses came back to him; his throat ceased to rattle; and he bent, first upon her and then upon Olivier, a glance full of feeling, took her hand, and placed it in Olivier's, fervently pressing them together. She and Olivier both fell upon their knees beside her father's bed; he raised himself up with a cry of agony, but at once sank back again, and in a deep sigh breathed his last. Then they both gave way to their grief and sorrow, and wept aloud.

Olivier related how during a walk, on which he had been commanded by his master to attend him, the latter had been murdered in his presence, and how through the greatest exertions he had carried the heavy man home, whom he did not believe to have been fatally wounded.

When morning dawned the people of the house, who had heard the lumbering noises, and the loud weeping and lamenting during the night, came up and found them still kneeling in helpless trouble by her father's corpse. An alarm was raised; the *Maréchaussée* made their way into the house, and dragged off Olivier to prison as the murderer of his master. Madelon added the most touching description of her beloved Olivier's goodness, and steady industry, and faithfulness. He had honoured his master highly, as though he had been his own father; and the latter had fully reciprocated this affection, and had chosen Brusson, in spite of his poverty, to be his son-in-law, since his skill was equal to his faithfulness and the nobleness of his character. All this the girl related with deep, true, heart-felt emotion; and she concluded by saying that if Olivier had thrust his dagger into her father's breast in her own presence she should take it for some illusion caused by Satan, rather than believe that Olivier could be capable of such a horrible wicked crime.

De Scudéri, most deeply moved by Madelon's unutterable sufferings, and quite ready to regard poor Olivier as innocent, instituted inquiries, and she found that all Madelon had said about the intimate terms on which master and journeyman had lived was fully confirmed. The people in the same house, as well as the neighbours, unanimously agreed in commending Olivier as a pattern of goodness, morality, faithfulness, and industry; nobody knew anything evil about him, and yet when mention was made of his heinous deed, they all shrugged their shoulders and thought there was something passing comprehension in it.

Olivier, on being arraigned before the *Chambre Ardente* denied the deed imputed to him, as Mademoiselle learned, with the most steadfast firmness and with honest sincerity, maintaining that his master had been attacked in the street in his presence and stabbed, that then, as there were still signs of life in him, he had himself carried him home, where Cardillac had soon afterwards expired. And all this too harmonised with Madelon's account.

Again and again and again De Scudéri had the minutest details of the terrible event repeated to her. She inquired minutely whether there had ever been a quarrel between master and journeyman, whether Olivier was perhaps not subject occasionally to those hasty fits of passion which often attack even the most good-natured of men like a blind madness, impelling the commission of deeds which appear to be done quite independent of voluntary action. But in proportion as Madelon spoke with increasing heartfelt warmth of the quiet domestic happiness in which the three had lived, united by the closest ties of affection, every shadow of suspicion against poor Olivier, now being tried for his life, vanished away. Scrupulously weighing every point and starting with the assumption that Olivier, in spite of all the things which spoke so loudly for his innocence, was nevertheless Cardillac's murderer, De Scudéri did not find any motive within the bounds of possibility for the hideous deed; for from every point of view it would necessarily destroy his happiness. He is poor but clever. He has succeeded in gaining the good-will of the most renowned master of his trade; he loves his master's daughter; his master looks upon his love with a favourable eye; happiness and prosperity seem likely to be his lot through life. But now suppose that, provoked in some way that God alone may know, Olivier had been so overmastered by anger as to make a murderous attempt upon his benefactor, his father, what diabolical hypocrisy he must have practised to have behaved after the deed in the way in which he really did behave. Firmly convinced of Olivier's innocence, Mademoiselle made up her mind to save the unhappy young man at no matter what cost.

Before appealing, however, to the king's mercy, it seemed to her that the most advisable step to take would be to call upon La Regnie, and direct his attention to all the circumstances that could not fail to speak for Olivier's innocence, and so perhaps awaken in the President's mind a feeling of interest favourable to the accused, which might then communicate itself to the judges with beneficial results.

La Regnie received De Scudéri with all the great respect to which the venerable lady, highly honoured as she was by the king himself, might justly lay claim. He listened quietly to all that she had to adduce with respect to the terrible crime, and Olivier's relations to the victim and his daughter, and his character. Nevertheless the only proof he gave that her words were not falling upon totally deaf ears was a slight and well-nigh mocking smile; and in the same way he heard her protestations and admonitions, which were frequently interrupted by tears, that the judge was not the enemy of the accused, but must also duly give heed to anything that spoke in his favour. When at length Mademoiselle paused, quite exhausted, and dried the tears from her eyes. La Regnie began, "It does honour to the excellence of your heart. Mademoiselle, that, being moved by the tears of a young lovesick girl, you believe everything she tells you, and none the less so that you are incapable of conceiving the thought of such an atrocious deed; but not so is it with the judge, who is wont to rend asunder the mask of brazen hypocrisy. Of course I need not tell you that it is not part of my office to unfold to every one who asks me the various stages of a criminal trial. Mademoiselle, I do my duty and trouble myself little about the judgment of the world. All miscreants shall tremble before the *Chambre Ardente*, which knows no other punishment except the scaffold and the stake. But since I do not wish you, respected lady, to conceive of me as a monster of hard-heartedness and cruelty, suffer me in a few words to put clearly before you the guilt of this young reprobate, who, thank Heaven, has been overtaken by the avenging arm of justice. Your sagacious mind will then bid you look with scorn upon your own good kindness, which does you so much honour, but which would never under any circumstances be fitting in me.

"Well then! René Cardillac is found in the morning stabbed to the heart with a dagger. The only persons with him are his journeyman Olivier Brusson and his own daughter. In Olivier's room, amongst other things, is found a dagger covered with blood, still fresh, which dagger fits exactly into the wound. Olivier says, 'Cardillac was cut down at night before my eyes.' 'Somebody attempted to rob him?' 'I don't know.' 'You say you went with him, how then were you not able to keep off the murderer, or hold him fast, or cry out for help?' 'My master walked fifteen, nay, fully twenty paces in front of me, and I followed him.' 'But why, in the name of wonder, at such a distance?' 'My master would have it so.' 'But tell us then what Master Cardillac was doing out in the streets at so late an hour?' 'That I cannot say.' 'But you have never before known him to leave the house after nine o'clock in the evening, have you?' Here Olivier falters; he is confused; he sighs; he bursts into tears; he protests by all that is holy that Cardillac really went out on the night in question, and then met with his death. But now your particular attention, please, Mademoiselle. It has been proved to absolute certainty that Cardillac never left the house that night, and so, of course, Olivier's assertion that he went out with him is an impudent lie. The house door is provided with a ponderous lock, which on locking and unlocking makes a loud grating echoing noise; moreover, the wings of the door squeak and creak horribly on their hinges, so that, as we have proved by repeated experiments, the noise is heard all the way up to the garrets. Now in the bottom story, and so of course close to the street door, lives old Master Claude Patru and his housekeeper, a person of nearly eighty years of age, but still lively and nimble. Now these two people heard Cardillac come downstairs punctually at nine o'clock that evening, according to his usual practice, and lock and bolt the door with considerable noise, and then go up again, where they further heard him read the evening prayers aloud, and then, to judge by the banging of doors, go to his own sleeping-chamber. Master Claude, like many old people, suffers from sleeplessness; and that night too he could not close an eye. And so, somewhere about half-past nine it seems, his old housekeeper went into the kitchen (to get into which she had to cross the passage) for a light, and then came and sat down at the table beside Master Claude with an old Chronicle, out of which she read; whilst the old man, following the train of his thoughts, first sat down in his easy-chair, and then stood up again, and paced softly and slowly up and down the room in order to bring on weariness and sleepiness. All remained quiet and still until after midnight. Then they heard quick steps above them and a heavy fall like some big weight being thrown on the floor, and then soon after a muffled groaning. A peculiar feeling of uneasiness and dreadful suspense took possession of them both. It was horror at the bloody deed which had just been committed, which passed out beside them. The bright morning came and revealed to the light what had been begun in the hours of darkness."

"But," interrupted De Scudéri, "but by all the saints, tell me what motive for this diabolical deed you can find in any of the circumstances which I just now repeated to you at such length?" "Hm!" rejoined La Regnie, "Cardillac was not poor--he had some valuable stones in his possession." "But would not his daughter inherit everything?" continued De Scudéri. "You are forgetting that Olivier was to be Cardillac's son-in-law." "But perhaps he had to share or only do the murderous deed for others," said La Regnie. "Share? do a murderous deed for others?" asked De Scudéri, utterly astounded. "I must tell you, Mademoiselle," continued the President, "that Olivier's blood would long ago have been shed in the Place Grève, had not his crime been bound up with that deeply enshrouded mystery which has hitherto exercised such a threatening sway over all Paris. It is evident that Olivier belongs to that accursed band of miscreants who, laughing to scorn all the watchfulness, and efforts, and strict investigations of the courts, have been able to carry out their plans so safely and unpunished. Through him all shall--all must be cleared up. Cardillac's wound is precisely similar to those borne by all the persons who have been found murdered and robbed in the streets and houses. But the most decisive fact is that since the time Olivier Brusson has been under arrest all these murders and robberies have ceased The streets are now as safe by night as they are by day. These things are proof enough that Olivier probably was at the head of this band of assassins. As yet he will not confess it; but there are means of making him speak against his will." "And Madelon," exclaimed De Scudéri, "and Madelon, the faithful, innocent dove!" "Oh!" said La Regnie, with a venomous smile, "Oh! but who will answer to me for it that she also is not an accomplice in the plot? What does she care about her father's death? Her tears are only shed for this murderous rascal." "What do you say?" screamed De Scudéri; "it cannot possibly be. Her father--this girl!" "Oh!" went on La Regnie, "Oh, but pray recollect De Brinvillier. You will be so good as to pardon me if I perhaps soon find myself compelled to take your favourite from your protection, and have her cast into the Conciergerie."

This terrible suspicion made Mademoiselle shudder. It seemed to her as if no faithfulness, no virtue, could stand fast before this fearful man; he seemed to espy murder and blood-guiltiness in the deepest and most secret thoughts. She rose to go. "Be human!" was all that she could stammer out in her distress, and she had difficulty in breathing. Just on the point of going down the stairs, to the top of which the President had accompanied her with ceremonious courtesy, she was suddenly struck by a strange thought, at which she herself was surprised. "And could I be allowed to see this unhappy Olivier Brusson?" she asked, turning round quickly to the President. He, however, looked at her somewhat suspiciously, but his face was soon contracted into the forbidding smile so characteristic of him. "Of course, honoured lady," said he, "relying upon your feelings and the little voice within you more than upon what has taken place before our very eyes, you will yourself prove Olivier's guilt or innocence, I perceive. If you are not afraid to see the dark abodes of crime, and if you think there will be nothing too revolting in looking upon pictures of depravity in all its stages, then the doors of the Conciergerie shall be opened to you in two hours from now. You shall have this Olivier, whose fate excites your interest so much, presented to you."

To tell the truth, De Scudéri could by no means convince herself of the young man's guilt. Although everything spoke against him, and no judge in the world could have acted differently from what La Regnie did in face of such conclusive circumstantial evidence, yet all these base suspicions were completely outweighed by the picture of domestic happiness which Madelon had painted for her in such warm lifelike colours; and hence she would rather adopt the idea of some unaccountable mystery than believe in the truth of that at which her inmost heart revolted.

She was thinking that she would get Olivier to repeat once more all the events of that ill-omened night and worm her way as much as possible into any secret there might be which remained sealed to the judges, since for their purposes it did not seem worth while to give themselves any further trouble about the matter.

On arriving at the Conciergerie, De Scudéri was led into a large light apartment. She had not long to wait before she heard the rattle of chains. Olivier Brusson was brought in. But the moment he appeared in the doorway De Scudéri sank on the floor fainting. When she recovered, Olivier had disappeared. She demanded impetuously that she should be taken to her carriage; she would go--go at once, that very moment, from the apartments of wickedness and infamy. For oh! at the very first glance she had recognised in Olivier Brusson the young man who had thrown the note into the carriage on the Pont Neuf, and who had brought her the casket and the jewels. Now all doubts were at an end; La Regnie's horrible suspicion was fully confirmed. Olivier Brusson belonged to the atrocious band of assassins; undoubtedly he murdered his master. And Madelon? Never before had Mademoiselle been so bitterly deceived by the deepest promptings of her heart; and now, shaken to the very depths of her soul by the discovery of a power of evil on earth in the existence of which she had not hitherto believed, she began to despair of all truth. She allowed the hideous suspicion to enter her mind that Madelon was involved in the complot, and might have had a hand in the infamous deed of blood. As is frequently the case with the human mind, that, once it has laid hold upon an idea, it diligently seeks for colours, until it finds them, with which to deck out the picture in tints ever more vivid and ever more glaring; so also De Scudéri, on reflecting again upon all the circumstances of the deed, as well as upon the minutest features in Madelon's behaviour, found many things to strengthen her suspicion. And many points which hitherto she had regarded as a proof of innocence and purity now presented themselves as undeniable tokens of abominable wickedness and studied hypocrisy. Madelon's heartrending expressions of trouble, and her floods of piteous tears, might very well have been forced from her, not so much from fear of seeing her lover perish on the scaffold, as of falling herself by the hand of the executioner. To get rid at once of the serpent she was nourishing in her bosom, this was the determination with which Mademoiselle got out of her carriage.

When she entered her room, Madelon threw herself at her feet. With her lovely eyes--none of God's angels had truer--directed heavenwards, and with her hands folded upon her heaving bosom, she wept and wailed, craving help and consolation. Controlling herself by a painful effort, De Scudéri, whilst endeavouring to impart as much earnestness and calmness as she possibly could to the tone in which she spoke, said, "Go--go--comfort yourself with the thought that righteous punishment will overtake yon murderer for his villainous deeds. May the Holy Virgin forbid that you yourself come to labour under the heavy burden of blood-guiltiness." "Oh! all hope is now lost!" cried Madelon, with a piercing shriek, as she reeled to the floor senseless. Leaving La Martinière to attend to the girl, Mademoiselle withdrew into another room.

De Scudéri's heart was torn and bleeding; she felt herself at variance with all mankind, and no longer wished to live in a world so full of diabolical deceit! She reproached Destiny which in bitter mockery had so many years suffered her to go on strengthening her belief in virtue, and truth, only to destroy now in her old age the beautiful images which had been her guiding-stars through life.

She heard Martinière lead away Madelon, who was sighing softly and lamenting. "Alas! and she--she too--these cruel men have infatuated her. Poor, miserable me! Poor, unhappy Olivier!" The tones of her voice cut De Scudéri to the heart; again there stirred in the depths of her soul a dim presentiment that there was some mystery connected with the case, and also the belief in Olivier's innocence returned. Her mind distracted by the most contradictory feelings, she cried, "What spirit of darkness is it which has entangled me in this terrible affair? I am certain it will be the death of me." At this juncture Baptiste came in, pale and terrified, with the announcement that Desgrais was at the door. Ever since the trial of the infamous La Voisin the appearance of Desgrais in any house was the sure precursor of some criminal charge; hence came Baptiste's terror, and therefore it was that Mademoiselle asked him with a gracious smile, "What's the matter with you, Baptiste? The name Scudéri has been found on La Voisin's list, has it not, eh?" "For God's sake," replied Baptiste, trembling in every limb, "how can you speak of such a thing? But Desgrais, that terrible man Desgrais, behaves so mysteriously, and is so urgent; he seems as if he couldn't wait a moment before seeing you." "Well, then, Baptiste," said De Scudéri, "then bring him up at once--the man who is so terrible to you; in me, at least, he will excite no anxiety."

"The President La Regnie has sent me to you, Mademoiselle," said Desgrais on stepping into the room, "with a request which he would hardly dare hope you could grant, did he not know your virtue and your courage. But the last means of bringing to light a vile deed of blood lie in your hands; and you have already of your own accord taken an active part in the notorious trial which the *Chambre Ardente*, and in fact all of us, are watching with breathless interest. Olivier Brusson has been half a madman since he saw you. He was beginning to show signs of compliance and a readiness to make a confession, but he now swears again, by all the powers of Heaven, that he is perfectly innocent of the murder of Cardillac; and yet he says he is ready to die the death which he has deserved. You will please observe, Mademoiselle, that the last clause evidently has reference to other crimes which weigh upon his conscience. But vain are all our efforts to get him to utter a single word more; even the threat of torture has been of no avail. He begs and prays, and beseeches us to procure him an interview with you; for to *you*, to *you* only, will he confess all. Pray deign, Mademoiselle, to hear Brusson's confession." "What!" exclaimed De Scudéri indignantly, "am I to be made an instrument of by a criminal court, am I to abuse this unhappy man's confidence to bring him to the scaffold? No, Desgrais. However vile a murderer Brusson may be, I would never, never deceive him in that villainous way. I don't want to know anything about his secrets; in any case they would be locked up within my own bosom as if they were a holy confession made to a priest" "Perhaps," rejoined Desgrais with a subtle smile, "perhaps, Mademoiselle, you would alter your mind after you had heard Brusson. Did you not yourself exhort the President to be human? And he is being so, in that he gives way to Brusson's foolish request, and thus resorts to the last means before putting him to the rack, for which he was well ripe some time ago." De Scudéri shuddered involuntarily. "And then, honoured lady," continued Desgrais, "it will not be demanded of you that you again enter those dark gloomy rooms which filled you with such horror and aversion. Olivier shall be brought to you here in your own house as a free man, but at night, when all excitement can be avoided. Then, without being even listened to, though of course he would be watched, he may without constraint make a clean confession to you. That you personally will have nothing to fear from the wretch--for that I will answer to you with my life. He mentions your name with the intensest veneration. He reiterates again and again that it is nothing but his dark destiny, which prevented him seeing you before, that has brought his life into jeopardy in this way. Moreover, you will be at liberty to divulge what you think well of the things which Brusson confesses to you. And what more could we indeed compel you to do?"

De Scudéri bent her eyes upon the floor in reflection. She felt she must obey the Higher Power which was thus demanding of her that she should effect the disclosure of some terrible secret, and she felt, too, as though she could not draw back out of the tangled skein into which she had run without any conscious effort of will. Suddenly making up her mind, she replied with dignity, "God will give me firmness and self-command, Bring Brusson here; I will speak with him."

Just as on the previous occasion when Brusson brought the casket, there came a knock at De Scudéri's house door at midnight. Baptiste, forewarned of this nocturnal visit, at once opened the door. De Scudéri felt an icy shiver run through her as she gathered from the light footsteps and hollow murmuring voices that the guards who had brought Brusson were taking up their stations about the passages of the house.

At length the room door was softly opened. Desgrais came in, followed by Olivier Brusson, freed from his fetters, and dressed in his own neat clothing. The officer bowed respectfully and said, "Here is Brusson, honoured lady," and then left the room. Brusson fell upon his knees before Mademoiselle, and raised his folded hands in entreaty, whilst copious tears ran down his cheeks.

De Scudéri turned pale and looked down upon him without being able to utter a word. Though his features were now gaunt and hollow from trouble and anguish and pain, yet an expression of the truest staunchest honesty shone upon his countenance. The longer Mademoiselle allowed her eyes to rest upon his face, the more forcibly was she reminded of some loved person, whom she could not in any way clearly call to mind. All her feelings of shivery uncomfortableness left her; she forgot that it was Cardillac's murderer who was kneeling before her; she spoke in the calm pleasing tone of goodwill that was characteristic of her, "Well, Brusson, what have you to tell me?" He, still kneeling, heaved a sigh of unspeakable sadness, that came from the bottom of his heart, "Oh! honoured, highly esteemed lady, can you have lost all traces of recollection of me?" Mademoiselle scanned his features more narrowly, and replied that she had certainly discovered in his face a resemblance to some one she had once loved, and that it was entirely owing to this resemblance that she had overcome her detestation of the murderer, and was listening to him calmly.

Brusson was deeply hurt at these words; he rose hastily to his feet and took a step, backwards, fixing his eyes gloomily on the floor. "Then you have completely forgotten Anne Guiot?" he said moodily; "it is her son Olivier,--the boy whom you often tossed on your lap--who now stands before you." "Oh help me, good Heaven!" exclaimed Mademoiselle, covering her face with both hands and sinking back upon the cushions. And reason enough she had to be thus terribly affected. Anne Guiot, the daughter of an impoverished burgher, had lived in De Scudéri's house from a little girl, and had been brought up by Mademoiselle with all the care and faithfulness which a mother expends upon her own child. Now when she was grown up there came a modest good-looking young man, Claude Brusson by name, and he wooed the girl. And since he was a thoroughly clever watchmaker, who would be sure to find a very good living in Paris, and since Anne had also grown to be truly fond of him, De Scudéri had no scruples about giving her consent to her adopted daughter's marriage. The young people, having set up housekeeping, led a quiet life of domestic happiness; and the ties of affection were knit still closer by the birth of a marvellously pretty boy, the perfect image of his lovely mother.

De Scudéri made a complete idol of little Olivier, carrying him off from his mother for hours and days together to caress him and to fondle him. Hence the boy grew quite accustomed to her, and would just as willingly be with her as with his mother. Three years passed away, when the trade-envy of Brusson's fellow-artificers made them concert together against him, so that his business decreased day by day, until at last he could hardly earn enough for a bare subsistence. Along with this he felt an ardent longing to see once more his beautiful native city of Geneva; accordingly the small family moved thither, in spite of De Scudéri's opposition and her promises of every possible means of support Anne wrote two or three times to her foster-mother, and then nothing more was heard from her; so that Mademoiselle had to take refuge in the conclusion that the happy life they were leading in Brusson's native town prevented their memories dwelling upon the days that were past and gone. It was now just twenty-three years since Brusson had left Paris along with his wife and child and had gone to Geneva.

"Oh! horrible!" exclaimed De Scudéri when she had again recovered herself to some extent. "Oh! horrible! are you Olivier? my Anne's son? And now----" "Indeed, honoured lady," replied Olivier calmly and composedly, "indeed you never could, I suppose, have any the least idea that the boy whom you fondled with all a mother's tenderness, into whose mouth you never tired of putting sweets and candies as you tossed him on your lap, whom you called by the most caressing names, would, when grown up to be a young man, one day stand before you accused of an atrocious crime. I am not free from reproach; the *Chambre Ardente* may justly bring a charge against me; but by my hopes of happiness after death, even though it be by the executioner's hand, I am innocent of this bloody deed; the unhappy Cardillac did not perish through me, nor through any guilty connivance on my part." So saying, Olivier began to shake and tremble. Mademoiselle silently pointed to a low chair which stood beside him, and he slowly sank down upon it.

"I have had plenty of time to prepare myself for my interview with you," he began, "which I regard as the last favour to be granted me by Heaven in token of my reconciliation with it, and I have also had time enough to gain what calmness and composure are needful in order to relate to you the history of my fearful and unparalleled misfortunes. I entreat your pity, that you will listen calmly to me, however much you may be surprised--nay, even struck with horror, by the disclosure of a secret which I am sure you have never for a moment suspected. Oh! that my poor father had never left Paris! As far back as my recollections of Geneva go I remember how I felt the tears of my unhappy parents falling upon my cheeks; and how their complaints of misery, which I did not understand, provoked me also to tears. Later I experienced to the full and with keen consciousness in what a state of crushing want and of deep distress my parents lived. My father found all his hopes deceived. He died bowed to the earth with pain, and broken with trouble, immediately after he had succeeded in placing me as apprentice to a goldsmith. My mother talked much about you; she said she would pour out all her troubles to you; but then she fell a victim to that despondency which is born of misery. That, and also a feeling of false shame, which often preys upon a deeply wounded spirit, prevented her from taking any decisive step. Within a few months after my father's death my mother followed him to the grave." "Poor Anne! poor Anne!" exclaimed Mademoiselle, quite overcome by sorrow. "All praise and thanks to the Eternal Power of Heaven that she is gone to the better land; she will not see her darling son, branded with shame, fall by the hand of the executioner," cried Olivier aloud, casting his eyes upwards with a wild unnatural look of anguish.

The police grew uneasy outside; footsteps passed to an fro. "Ho! ho!" said Olivier, smiling bitterly, "Desgrais is waking up his myrmidons, as though I could make my escape *here*. But to continue--I led a hard life with my master, albeit I soon got to be the best workman, and at last even surpassed my master himself. One day a stranger happened to come into our shop to buy some jewellery. And when he saw a beautiful necklace which I had made he clapped me on the shoulder in a friendly way and said, eyeing the ornament, 'Ha! i' faith, my young friend, that's an excellent piece of work. To tell you the truth, I don't know who there is who could beat you, unless it were René Cardillac, who, you know, is the first goldsmith in the world. You ought to go to him; he would gladly take you into his workshop; for nobody but you could help him in his artistic labours; and on the other hand he is the only man from whom you could learn anything.' The stranger's words sank into my heart and took deep root there. I hadn't another moment's ease in Geneva; I felt a violent impulse to be gone. At last I contrived to get free from my master. I came to Paris. René Cardillac received me coldly and churlishly. I persevered in my purpose; he must give me some work, however insignificant it might be. I got a small ring to finish. On my taking the work to him, he fixed his keen glittering eyes upon me as if he would read the very depths of my soul. Then he said, 'You are a good clever journeyman; you may come to me and help me in my shop. I will pay you well; you shall be satisfied with me.' Cardillac kept his word. I had been several weeks with him before I saw Madelon; she was at that time, if I mistake not, in the country, staying, with a female relative of Cardillac's; but at length she came. O Heaven! O God! what did I feel when I saw the sweet angel? Has any man ever loved as I do? And now--O Madelon!"

Olivier was so distressed he could not go on. Holding both hands before his face, he sobbed violently, But at length, fighting down with an effort the sharp pain that shook him, he went on with his story.

"Madelon looked upon me with friendly eyes. Her visits into the workshop grew more and more frequent. I was enraptured to perceive that she loved me. Notwithstanding the strict watch her father kept upon us many a stolen pressure of the hand served as a token of the mutual understanding arrived at between us; Cardillac did not appear to notice anything. I intended first to win his favour, and, if I could gain my mastership, then to woo for Madelon. One day, as I was about to begin work, Cardillac came to me, his face louring darkly with anger and scornful contempt 'I don't want your services any longer,' he began, 'so out you go from my house this very hour; and never show yourself in my sight again. Why I can't do with you here any longer, I have no need to tell you. For you, you poor devil, the sweet fruit at which you are stretching out your hand hangs too high.' I attempted to speak, but he laid hold upon me with a powerful grasp and threw me out of doors, so that I fell to the floor and severely wounded my head and arm. I left the house hotly indignant and furious with the stinging pain; at last I found a good-natured acquaintance in the remotest corner of the Faubourg St. Martin, who received me into his garret. But I had neither ease nor rest. Every night I used to lurk about Cardillac's house deluding myself with the fancy that Madelon would hear my sighing and lamenting, and that she would perhaps find a way to speak to me out of the window unheard. All sorts of confused plans were revolving in my brain, which I hoped to persuade her to carry out.

"Now joining Cardillac's house in the Rue Nicaise there is a high wall, with niches and old stone figures in them, now half crumbled away. One night I was standing close beside one of these stone images and looking up at those windows of the house which looked out upon the court enclosed by the wall. All at once I observed a light in Cardillac's workshop. It was midnight; Cardillac never used to be awake at that hour; he was always in the habit of going to rest on the stroke of nine. My heart beat in uncertain trepidation; I began to think something might have happened which would perhaps pave the way for me to go back into the house once more. But soon the light vanished again. I squeezed myself into the niche close to the stone figure; but I started back in dismay on feeling a pressure against me, as if the image had become instinct with life. By the dusky glimmer of the night I perceived that the stone was slowly revolving, and a dark form slipped out from behind it and went away down the street with light, soft footsteps. I rushed towards the stone figure; it stood as before, close to the wall. Almost without thinking, rather as if impelled by some inward prompter, I stealthily followed the figure. Just beside an image of the Virgin he turned round; the light of the street lamp standing exactly in front of the image fell full upon his face. It was Cardillac.

"An unaccountable feeling of apprehension--an unearthly dread fell upon me. Like one subject to the power of magic, I had to go on--on--in the track of the spectre-like somnambulist. For that was what I took my master to be, notwithstanding that it was not the time of full moon, when this visitation is wont to attack the sleeper. Finally Cardillac disappeared into the deep shade on the side of the street. By a sort of low involuntary cough, which, however, I knew well, I gathered that he was standing in the entry to a house. 'What is the meaning of that? What is he going to do?' I asked myself, utterly astounded, pressing close against a house-wall. It was not long before a man came along with fluttering plumes and jingling spur, singing and gaily humming an air. Like a tiger leaping upon his prey, Cardillac burst out of his lurking-place and threw himself upon the man, who that very same instant fell to the ground, gasping in the agonies of death. I rushed up with a cry of horror; Cardillac was stooping over the man, who lay on the floor. 'Master Cardillac, what are you doing?' I shouted. 'Cursed fool!' growled Cardillac, running past me with lightning-like speed and disappearing from sight.

"Quite upset and hardly able to take a step, I approached the man who had been stabbed. I knelt down beside him. 'Perhaps,' thought I, 'he still may be saved;' but there was not the least sign of life. In my fearful agitation I had hardly noticed that the *Maréchausée* had surrounded me. 'What? already another assassinated by these demons! Hi! hi! Young man, what are you about here?--Are you one of the band?--Away with him!' Thus they cried one after another, and they laid hold of me. I was scarcely able to stammer out that I should never be capable of such an abominable deed, and that they might therefore let me go my way in peace. Then one of them turned his lamp upon my face and said laughing, 'Why, it's Olivier Brusson, the journeyman goldsmith, who works for our worthy honest Master René Cardillac. Ay, I should think so!--*he* murder people in the street--he looks like it indeed! It's just like murderous assassins to stoop lamenting over their victim's corpse till somebody comes and takes them into custody. Well, how was it, youngster? Speak out boldly?' 'A man sprang out immediately in front of me,' I said, 'and threw himself upon this man and stabbed him, and then ran away as quick as lightning when I shouted out. I only wanted to see if the stabbed man might still be saved.' 'No, my son,' cried one of those who had taken up the corpse; 'he's dead enough; the dagger has gone right through the heart as usual.' 'The Devil!' said another; 'we have come too late again, as we did yesterday.' Thereupon they went their way, taking the corpse with them.

"What my feelings were I cannot attempt to describe. I felt myself to make sure whether I were not being mocked by some hideous dream; I fancied I must soon wake up and wonder at the preposterous delusion. Cardillac, the father of my Madelon, an atrocious murderer! My strength failed me; I sank down upon the stone steps leading up to a house. The morning light began to glimmer and was stronger and stronger; an officer's hat decorated with feathers lay before me on the pavement. I saw again vividly Cardillac's bloody deed, which had been perpetrated on the spot where I sat. I ran off horrified.

"I was sitting in my garret, my thoughts in a perfect whirl, nay, I was almost bereft of my senses, when the door opened, and René Cardillac came in. 'For God's sake, what do you want?' I exclaimed on seeing him. Without heeding my words, he approached close to me, smiling with calmness and an air of affability which only increased my inward abhorrence. Pulling up a rickety old stool and taking his seat upon it close beside me, for I was unable to rise from the heap of straw upon which I had thrown myself, he began, 'Well, Olivier, how are you getting on, my poor fellow? I did indeed do an abominably rash thing when I turned you out of the house; I miss you at every step and turn. I have got a piece of work on hand just now which I cannot finish without your help. How would it be if you came back to work in my shop? Have you nothing to say? Yes, I know I have insulted you. I will not attempt to conceal it from you that I was angry on account of your love making to my Madelon. But since then I have ripely reflected upon the matter, and decided that, considering your skill and industry and faithful honesty, I could not wish for any better son-in-law than you. So come along with me, and see if you can win Madelon to be your bride.'

"Cardillac's words cut me to the very heart; I trembled with dread at his wickedness; I could not utter a word. 'Do you hesitate?' he continued in a sharp tone, piercing me through and through with his glittering eyes; 'do you hesitate? Perhaps you can't come along with me just to-day--perhaps you have some other business on hand! Perhaps you mean forsooth to pay a visit to Desgrais or get yourself admitted to an interview with D'Argenson or La Regnie. But you'd better take care, boy, that the claws which you entice out of their sheaths to other people's destruction don't seize upon you yourself and tear you to pieces!' Then my swelling indignation suddenly found vent 'Let those who are conscious of having committed atrocious crimes,' I cried,--'let them start at the names you just named. As for me, I have no reason to do so--I have nothing to do with them.' 'Properly speaking,' went on Cardillac, 'properly speaking, Olivier, it is an honour to you to work with me--with me, the most renowned master of the age, and highly esteemed everywhere for his faithfulness and honesty, so that all wicked calumnies would recoil upon the head of the backbiter. And as far as concerns Madelon, I must now confess that it is she alone to whom you owe this compliance on my part. She loves you with an intensity which I should not have credited the delicate child with. Directly you had gone she threw herself at my feet, clasped my knees, and confessed amid endless tears that she could not live without you. I thought she only fancied so, as so often happens with young and love-sick girls; they think they shall die at once the first time a milky-faced boy looks kindly upon them. But my Madelon did really become ill and begin to pine away; and when I tried to talk her out of her foolish silly notions, she only uttered your name scores of times. What on earth could I do if I didn't want her to die away in despair? Last evening I told her I would give my consent to her dearest wishes, and would come and fetch you to-day. And during the night she has blossomed up like a rose, and is now waiting for you with all the longing impatience of love.'

"May God in heaven forgive me! I don't know myself how it came about, but I suddenly found myself in Cardillac's house; and Madelon cried aloud with joy, 'Olivier! my Olivier! my darling! my husband!' as she rushed towards me and threw both her arms round my neck, pressing me close to her bosom, till in a perfect delirium of passionate delight I swore by the Virgin and all the saints that I would never, never leave her."

Olivier was so deeply agitated by the recollection of this fateful moment, that he was obliged to pause. De Scudéri, struck with horror at this foul iniquity in a man whom she had always looked upon as a model of virtue and honest integrity, cried, "Oh! it is horrible! So René Cardillac belongs to the murderous band which has so long made our good city a mere bandits' haunt?" "What do you say, Mademoiselle, to the *band*?" said Olivier. "There has never been such a band. It was Cardillac *alone* who, active in wickedness, sought for his victims and found them throughout the entire city. And it was because he acted alone that he was enabled to carry on his operations with so much security, and from the same cause arose the insuperable difficulty of getting a clue to the murderer. But let me go on with my story; the sequel will explain to you the secrets of the most atrocious but at the same time of the most unfortunate of men.

"The situation in which I now found myself fixed at my master's may be easily imagined. The step was taken; I could not go back. At times I felt as though I were Cardillac's accomplice in crime; the only thing that made me forget the inner anguish that tortured me was Madelon's love, and it was only in her presence that I succeeded in totally suppressing all external signs of the nameless trouble and anxiety I had in my heart. When I was working with the old man in the shop, I could never look him in the face; and I was hardly able to speak a word, owing to the awful dread with which I trembled whenever near the villain, who fulfilled all the duties of a faithful and tender father, and of a good citizen, whilst the night veiled his monstrous iniquity. Madelon, dutiful, pure, confiding as an angel, clung to him with idolatrous affection. The thought often struck like a dagger to my heart that, if justice should one day overtake the reprobate and unmask him, she, deceived by the diabolical arts of the foul Fiend, would assuredly die in the wildest agonies of despair. This alone would keep my lips locked, even though it brought upon me a criminal's death. Notwithstanding that I picked up a good deal of information from the talk of the *Maréchaussée* yet the motive for Cardillac's atrocities, as well as his manner of accomplishing them, still remained riddles to me; but I had not long to wait for the solution.

"One day Cardillac was very grave and preoccupied over his work, instead of being in the merriest of humours, jesting and laughing as he usually did, and so provoking my abhorrence of him. All of a sudden he threw aside the ornament he was working at, so that the pearls and other stones rolled across the floor, and starting to his feet he exclaimed, 'Olivier, things can't go on in this way between us; the footing we are now on is getting unbearable. Chance has played into your hands the knowledge of a secret which has baffled the most inventive cunning of Desgrais and all his myrmidons. You have seen me at my midnight work, to which I am goaded by my evil destiny; no resistance is ever of any avail. And your evil destiny it was which led you to follow me, which wrapped you in an impenetrable veil and gave you the lightness of foot which, enabled you to walk as noiselessly as the smallest insect, so that I, who in the blackest night see as plainly as a tiger and hear the slightest noise, the humming of midges, far away along the streets, did not perceive you near me. Your evil star has brought you to me, my associate. As you are now circumstanced there can be no thought of treachery on your part, and so you may now know all.' 'Never, never will I be your associate, you hypocritical reprobate,' I endeavoured to cry out, but I felt a choking sensation in my throat, caused by the dread which came upon me as Cardillac spoke. Instead of speaking words, I only gasped out certain unintelligible sounds. Cardillac again sat down on his bench, drying the perspiration from his brow. He appeared to be fearfully agitated by his recollections of the past and to have difficulty in preserving his composure. But at length he began.

"'Learned men say a good deal about the extraordinary impressions of which women are capable when *enceinte*, and of the singular influence which such a vivid involuntary external impression has upon the unborn child. I was told a surprising story about my mother. About eight months before I was born, my mother accompanied certain other women to see a splendid court spectacle in the Trianon. There her eyes fell upon a cavalier wearing a Spanish costume, who wore a flashing jewelled chain round his neck, and she could not keep her eyes off it. Her whole being was concentrated into desire to possess the glittering stones, which she regarded as something of supernatural origin. Several years previously, before my mother was married, the same cavalier had paid his insidious addresses to her, but had been repulsed with indignant scorn. My mother knew him again; but now by the gleam of the brilliant diamonds he appeared to her to be a being of a higher race--the paragon of beauty. He noticed my mother's looks of ardent desire. He believed he should now be more successful than formerly. He found means to approach her, and, yet more, to draw her away from her acquaintances to a retired place. Then he clasped her passionately in his arms, whilst she laid hold of the handsome chain; but in that moment the cavalier reeled backwards, dragging my mother to the ground along with him. Whatever was the cause--whether he had a sudden stroke, or whether it was due to something else--enough, the man was dead. All my mother's efforts to release herself from the stiffened arms of the corpse proved futile. His glazed eyes, their faculty of vision now extinguished, were fixed upon her; and she lay on the ground with the dead man. At length her piercing screams for help reached the ears of some people passing at a distance; they hurried up and freed her from the arms of her ghastly lover. The horror prostrated her in a serious illness. Her life, and mine too, was despaired of; but she recovered, and her accouchement was more favourable than could have been expected. But the terror of that fearful moment had left its stamp upon *me*. The evil star of my destiny had got in the ascendant and shot down its sparks upon me, enkindling in me a most singular but at the same time a most pernicious passion. Even in the earliest days of my childhood there was nothing I thought so much of as I did of flashing diamonds and ornaments of gold. It was regarded as an ordinary childish inclination. But the contrary was soon made manifest, for when a boy I stole all the gold and jewellery I could anywhere lay my hands on. Like the most experienced goldsmith I could distinguish by instinct false jewellery from real. The latter alone proved an attraction to me; objects made of imitated gold as well as gold coins I heeded not in the least. My inborn propensity had, however, to give way to the excessively cruel thrashings which I received at my father's hand.

"'I adopted the trade of a goldsmith, merely that I might be able to handle gold and precious stones. I worked with passionate enthusiasm and soon became the first master in the craft. But now began a period in which my innate propensity, so long repressed, burst forth with vehemence and grew most rapidly, imbibing nourishment from everything about it. So soon as I had completed a piece of jewellery, and had delivered it up to the customer,

I fell into a state of unrest, of desperate disquiet, which robbed me of sleep and health and courage for my daily life. Day and night the person for whom I had done the work stood before my eyes like a spectre, adorned with my jewellery, whilst a voice whispered in my ears, "Yes, it's yours; yes it's yours. Go and take it. What does a dead man want diamonds for?" Then I began to practise thievish arts. As I had access to the houses of the great, I speedily turned every opportunity to good account: no lock could baffle my skill; and I soon had the object which I had made in my hands again. But after a time even that did not banish my unrest. That unearthly voice still continued to make itself heard in my ears, mocking me to scorn, and crying, "Ho! ho! a dead man is wearing your jewellery." By some inexplicable means, which I do not understand, I began to conceive an unspeakable hatred of those for whom I made my ornaments. Ay, deep down in my heart there began to stir a murderous feeling against them, at which I myself trembled with apprehension.

"'About this time I bought this house. I had just struck a bargain with the owner; we were sitting in this room drinking a glass of wine together and enjoying ourselves over the settlement of our business. Night had come; I rose to go; then the vendor of the house said, "See here, Master René; before you go, I must make you acquainted with the secret of the place." Therewith he unlocked that press let into the wall there, pushed away the panels at the back, and stepped into a little room, where, stooping down, he lifted up a trap-door. We descended a flight of steep, narrow stairs, and came to a narrow postern, which he unlocked, and let us out into the court-yard. Then the old gentleman, the previous owner of the house, stepped up to the wall and pressed an iron knob, which projected only very triflingly from it; immediately a portion of the wall swung round, so that a man could easily slip through the opening, and in that way gain the street. I will show you the neat contrivance some day, Olivier; very likely it was constructed by the cunning monks of the monastery which formerly stood on this site, in order that they might steal in and out secretly. It is a piece of wood, plastered with mortar and white-washed on the outside only, and within it, on the side next the street, is fixed a statue, also of wood, but coloured to look exactly like stone, and the whole piece, together with the statue, moves upon concealed hinges. Dark thoughts swept into my mind when I saw this contrivance; it appeared to have been built with a predestined view to such deeds as yet remained unknown to myself.

"'I had just completed a valuable ornament for a courtier, and knew that he intended it for an opera-dancer. The ominous torture assailed me again; the spectre dogged my footsteps; the whispering fiend was at my ear. I took possession of my new house. I tossed sleeplessly on my couch, bathed in perspiration, caused by the hideous torments I was enduring. In imagination I saw the man gliding along to the dancer's abode with my ornament. I leapt up full of fury; threw on my mantle, went down by the secret stairs, through the wall, and into the Rue Nicaise. He is coming along; I throw myself upon him; he screams out; but I have seized him fast from behind, and driven my dagger right into his heart; the ornament is mine. This done I experienced a calmness, a satisfaction in my soul, which I had never yet experienced. The spectre had vanished; the voice of the fiend was still. Now I knew what my evil Destiny wanted; I had either to yield to it or to perish. And now too you understand the secret of all my conduct, Olivier. But do not believe, because I must do that for which there is no help, that therefore I have entirely lost all sense of pity, of compassion, which is said to be one of the essential properties of human nature. You know how hard it is for me to part with a finished piece of work, and that there are many for whom I refuse to work at all, because I do not wish their death; and it has also happened that when I felt my spectre would have to be exorcised on the following day by blood, I have satisfied it with a stout blow of the fist the same day, which stretched on the ground the owner of my jewel, and delivered the jewel itself into my hand.'

"Having told me all this Cardillac took me into his secret vault and granted me a sight of his jewel-cabinet; and the king himself has not one finer. A short label was attached to each article, stating accurately for whom it was made, when it was recovered, and whether by theft, or by robbery from the person accompanied with violence, or by murder. Then Cardillac said in a hollow and solemn voice, 'On your wedding-day, Olivier, you will have to lay your hand on the image of the crucified Christ and swear a solemn oath that after I am dead you will reduce all these riches to dust, through means which I shall then, before I die, disclose to you. I will not have any human creature, and certainly neither Madelon nor you, come into possession of this blood-bought treasure-store.' Entangled in this labyrinth of crime, and with my heart lacerated by love and abhorrence, by rapture and horror, I might be compared to the condemned mortal whom a lovely angel is beckoning upwards with a gentle smile, whilst on the other hand Satan is holding him fast in his burning talons, till the good angel's smiles of love, in which are reflected all the bliss of the highest heaven, become converted into the most poignant of his miseries. I thought of flight--ay, even of suicide--but Madelon! Blame me, reproach me, honoured lady, for my too great weakness in not fighting down by an effort of will a passion that was fettering me to crime; but am I not about to atone for my fault by a death of shame?

"One day Cardillac came home in uncommonly good spirits. He caressed Madelon, greeted me with the most friendly good-will, and at dinner drank a bottle of better wine, of a brand that he only produced on high holidays and festivals, and he also sang and gave vent to his feelings in exuberant manifestations of joy. When Madelon had left us I rose to return to the workshop. 'Sit still, lad,' said Cardillac; 'we'll not work any more to-day. Let us drink another glass together to the health of the most estimable and most excellent lady in Paris.' After I had joined glasses with him and had drained mine to the bottom, he went on, 'Tell me, Olivier, how do you like these verses,'

'Un amant qui craint les voleuis
N'est point digne d'amour.'

"Then he went on to relate the episode between you and the king in De Maintenon's salons, adding that he had always honoured you as he never had any other human creature, and that you were gifted with such lofty virtue as to make his ill-omened star of Destiny grow pale, and that if you were to wear the handsomest ornament he ever made it would never provoke in him either an evil spectre or murderous thoughts. 'Listen now, Olivier,' he said, 'what I have made up my mind to do. A long time ago I received an order for a necklace and a pair of bracelets for Henrietta of England, and the stones were given me for the purpose. The work turned out better than the best I had ever previously done; but my heart was torn at the thought of parting from the ornaments, for they had become my pet jewels. You are aware of the Princess's unhappy death by sinister means. The ornaments I retained, and will now send them to Mademoiselle de Scudéri in the name of the persecuted band of robbers as a token of my respect and gratitude. Not only will Mademoiselle receive an eloquent token of her triumph, but I shall also laugh Desgrais and his associates to scorn, as they deserve to be laughed at. You shall take her the ornaments.' As Cardillac mentioned your name, Mademoiselle, I seemed to see a dark veil thrown aside, revealing the fair, bright picture of my early happy childhood days in gay and cheerful colours. A wondrous source of comfort entered my soul, a ray of hope, before which all my dark spirits faded away. Possibly Cardillac noted the effect which his words had upon me and interpreted it in his own way, 'You appear to find pleasure in my plan,' he said. 'And I may as well state to you that I have been commanded to do this by an inward monitor deep down in my heart, very different from that which demands its holocaust of blood like some ravenous beast of prey. I often experience very remarkable feelings; I am powerfully affected by an inward apprehension, by fear of something terrible, the horrors of which breathe upon me in the air from a far-distant world of the Supernatural. I then feel even as if the crimes I commit as the blind instrument of my ill-starred Destiny may be charged upon my immortal soul, which has no share in them. During one such mood I vowed to make a diamond crown for the Holy Virgin in St. Eustace's Church. But so often as I thought seriously about setting to work upon it, I was overwhelmed by this unaccountable apprehension, so that I gave up the project altogether. Now I feel as if I must humbly offer an acknowledgment at the altar of virtue and piety by sending to De Scudéri the handsomest ornaments I have ever worked.'

"Cardillac, who was intimately acquainted with your habits and ways of life. Mademoiselle, gave me instructions respecting the manner and the hour--the how and the when--in which I was to deliver the ornaments, which he locked in an elegant case, into your hands. I was completely thrilled with delight, for Heaven itself now pointed out to me through the miscreant Cardillac, a way by which I might rescue myself from the hellish thraldom in which I, a sinner and outcast, was slowly perishing; these at least were my thoughts. In express opposition to Cardillac's will I resolved to force myself in to an interview with you. I intended to reveal myself as Anne Brusson's son, as your own adoptive child, and to throw myself at your feet and confess all--all. I knew that you would have been so touched by the overwhelming misery which would have threatened poor innocent Madelon by any disclosure that you would have respected the secret; whilst your keen, sagacious mind would, I felt assured, have devised some means by which Cardillac's infamous wickedness might have been prevented without any exposure. Pray do not ask me what shape these means would have taken; I do not know. But that you would save Madelon and me, of that I was most firmly convinced, as firmly as I believe in the comfort and help of the Holy Virgin. You know how my intention was frustrated that night, Mademoiselle. I still cherished the hope of being more successful another time. Soon after this Cardillac seemed suddenly to lose all his good-humour. He went about with a cloudy brow, fixed his eyes on vacancy in front of him, murmured unintelligible words, and gesticulated with his hands, as if warding off something hostile from him; his mind appeared to be tormented by evil thoughts. Thus he behaved during the course of one whole morning. Finally he sat down to his work-table; but he soon leapt up again peevishly and looked out of the window, saying moodily and earnestly, 'I wish after all that Henrietta of England had worn my ornaments.' These words struck terror to my heart. Now I knew that his warped mind was again enslaved by the abominable spectre of murder, and that the voice of the fiend was again ringing audibly in his ears. I saw your life was threatened by the villainous demon of murder. If Cardillac only had his ornaments in his hands again, you were saved.

"Every moment the danger increased. Then I met you on the Pont Neuf, and forced my way to your carriage, and threw you that note, beseeching you to restore the ornaments which you had received to Cardillac's hands at once. You did not come. My distress deepened to despair when on the following day Cardillac talked about nothing else but the magnificent ornaments which he had seen before his eyes during the night. I could only interpret that as having reference to your jewellery, and I was certain that he was brooding over some fresh murderous onslaught which he had assuredly determined to put into execution during the coming night. I must save you, even if it cost Cardillac's own life. So soon as he had locked himself in his own room after evening prayers, according to his wont, I climbed out of a window into the court-yard, slipped through the opening in the wall, and took up my station at no great distance, hidden in the deep shade. I had not long to wait before Cardillac appeared and stole softly up the street, me following him. He bent his steps towards the Rue St. Honoré; my heart trembled with apprehension. All of a sudden I lost sight of him. I made up my mind to take post at your house-door. Then there came an officer past me, without perceiving me, singing and gaily humming a tune to himself, as on the occasion when chance first made me a witness of Cardillac's bloody deeds. But that selfsame moment a dark figure leapt forward and fell upon the officer. It was Cardillac. This murder I would at any rate prevent. With a loud shout I reached the spot in two or three bounds, when, not the officer, but Cardillac, fell on the floor groaning. The officer let his dagger fall, and drawing his sword put himself in a posture for fighting, imagining that I was the murderer's accomplice; but when he saw that I was only concerned about the slain man, and did not trouble myself about him, he hurried away. Cardillac was still alive. After picking up and taking charge of the dagger which the officer had let fall, I loaded my master upon my shoulders and painfully hugged him home, carrying him up to the workshop by way of the concealed stairs. The rest you know.

"You see, honoured lady, that my only crime consists in the fact that I did not betray Madelon's father to the officers of the law, and so put an end to his enormities. My hands are clean of any deed of blood. No torture shall extort from me a confession of Cardillac's crimes. I will not, in defiance of the Eternal Power, which veiled the father's hideous bloodguiltiness from the eyes of the virtuous daughter, be instrumental in unfolding all the misery of the past, which would now have a far more disastrous effect upon her, nor do I wish to aid worldly vengeance in rooting up the dead man from the earth which covers him, nor that the executioner should now brand the mouldering bones with dishonour. No; the beloved of my soul will weep for me as one who has fallen innocent, and time will soften her sorrow; but how irretrievable a shock would it be if she learnt of the fearful and diabolical deeds of her dearly-loved father."

Olivier paused; but now a torrent of tears suddenly burst from his eyes, and he threw himself at De Scudéri's feet imploringly. "Oh! now you are convinced of my innocence--oh! surely you must be! have pity upon me; tell me how my Madelon bears it." Mademoiselle summoned La Martinière, and in a few moments more Madelon's arms were round Olivier's neck. "Now all is well again since you are here. I knew it, I knew this most noble-minded lady would save you," cried Madelon again and again; and Olivier forgot his situation and all that was impending over him, he was free and happy. It was most touching to hear the two mutually pour out all their troubles, and relate all that they had suffered for one another's sake; then they embraced one another anew, and wept with joy to see each other again.

If De Scudéri had not been already convinced of Olivier's innocence she would assuredly have been satisfied of it now as she sat watching the two, who forgot the world and their misery and their excessive sufferings in the happiness of their deep and genuine mutual affection. "No," she said to herself, "it is only a pure heart which is capable of such happy oblivion."

The bright beams of morning broke in through the window. Desgrais knocked softly at the room door, and reminded those within that it was time to take Olivier Brusson away, since this could not be done later without exciting a commotion. The lovers were obliged to separate.

The dim shapeless feelings which had taken possession of De Scudéri's mind on Olivier's first entry into the room, had now acquired form and content--and in a fearful way. She saw the son of her dear Anne innocently entangled in such a way that there hardly seemed any conceivable means of saving him from a shameful death. She honoured the young man's heroic purpose in choosing to die under an unjust burden of guilt rather than divulge a secret that would certainly kill his Madelon. In the whole region of possibility she could not find any means whatever to snatch the poor fellow out of the hands of the cruel tribunal. And yet she had a most clear conception that she ought not to hesitate at any sacrifice to avert this monstrous perversion of justice which was on the point of being committed. She racked her brain with a hundred different schemes and plans, some of which bordered upon the extravagant, but all these she rejected almost as soon as they suggested themselves. Meanwhile the rays of hope grew fainter and fainter, till at last she was on the verge of despair. But Madelon's unquestioning child-like confidence, the rapturous enthusiasm with which she spoke of her lover, who now, absolved of all guilt, would soon clasp her in his arms as his bride, infused De Scudéri with new hope and courage, exactly in proportion as she was the more touched by the girl's words.

At length, for the sake of doing something, De Scudéri wrote a long letter to La Regnie, in which she informed him that Olivier Brusson had proved to her in the most convincing manner his perfect innocence of Cardillac's death, and that it was only his heroic resolve to carry with him into the grave a secret, the revelation of which would entail disaster upon virtue and innocence, that prevented him making a revelation to the court which would undoubtedly free him, not only from the fearful suspicion of having murdered Cardillac, but also of having belonged to a band of vile assassins. De Scudéri did all that burning zeal, that ripe and spirited eloquence could effect, to soften La Regnie's hard heart. In the course of a few hours La Regnie replied that he was heartily glad to learn that Olivier Brusson had justified himself so completely in the eyes of his noble and honoured protectress. As for Olivier's heroic resolve to carry with him into the grave a secret that had an important bearing upon the crime under investigation, he was sorry to say that the *Chambre Ardente* could not respect such heroic courage, but would rather be compelled to adopt the strongest means to break it. At the end of three days he hoped to be in possession of this extraordinary secret, which it might be presumed would bring wonders to light.

De Scudéri knew only too well what those means were by which the savage La Regnie intended to break Brusson's heroic constancy. She was now sure that the unfortunate was threatened with the rack. In her desperate anxiety it at length occurred to her that the advice of a doctor of the law would be useful, if only to effectuate a postponement of the torture. The most renowned advocate in Paris at that time was Pierre Amaud d'Andilly; and his sound knowledge and liberal mind were only to be compared to his virtue and his sterling honesty. To him, therefore, De Scudéri had recourse, and she told him all, so far as she could, without violating Brusson's secret She expected that D'Andilly would take up the cause of the innocent man with zeal, but she found her hopes most bitterly deceived. The lawyer listened calmly to all she had to say, and then replied in Boileau's words, smiling as he did so, "*Le vrai peut quelque fois n'être pas vraisemblable*"(Sometimes truth wears an improbable garb). He showed De Scudéri that there were most noteworthy grounds for suspicion against Brusson, that La Regnie's proceedings could neither be called cruel nor yet hurried, rather they were perfectly within the law--nay, that he could not act otherwise without detriment to his duties as judge. He himself did not see his way to saving Brusson from torture, even by the cleverest defence. Nobody but Brusson himself could avert it, either by a candid confession or at least by a most detailed account of all the circumstances attending Cardillac's murder, and this might then perhaps furnish grounds for instituting fresh inquiries. "Then I will throw myself at the king's feet and pray for mercy," said De Scudéri, distracted, her voice half choked by tears. "For Heaven's sake, don't do it, Mademoiselle, don't do it. I would advise you to reserve this last resource, for if it once fail it is lost to you for ever. The king will never pardon a criminal of this class: he would draw down upon himself the bitterest reproaches of the people, who would believe their lives were always in danger. Possibly Brusson, either by disclosing his secret or by some other means, may find a way to allay the suspicions which are working against him. Then will be the time to appeal to the king for mercy, for he will not inquire what has been proved before the court, but be guided by his own inner conviction." De Scudéri had no help for it but to admit that D'Andilly with his great experience was in the right.

Late one evening she was sitting in her own room in very great trouble, appealing to the Virgin and the Holy Saints, and thinking whatever should she do to save the unhappy Brusson, when La Martinière came in to announce that Count de Miossens, colonel of the King's Guards, was urgently desiring to speak to Mademoiselle.

"Pardon me, Mademoiselle," said Miossens, bowing with military grace, "pardon me for intruding upon you so late, at such an inconvenient hour. We soldiers cannot do as we like, and then a couple of words will suffice to excuse me. It is on Olivier Brusson's account that I have come." De Scudéri's attention was at once on the stretch as to what was to follow, and she said, "Olivier Brusson?--that most unhappy of mortals? What have you to do with him?" "Yes, I did indeed think," continued Miossens smiling, "that your *protégé's* name would be sufficient to procure me a favourable hearing. All the public are convinced of Brusson's guilt. But you, I know, cling to another opinion, which is based, to be sure, upon the protestations of the accused, as it is said; with me, however, it is otherwise. Nobody can be more firmly convinced that Brusson is innocent of Cardillac's death than I am." "Oh! go on and tell me; go on, pray!" exclaimed De Scudéri, whilst her eyes sparkled with delight. Miossens continued, speaking with emphasis, "It was I--I who stabbed the old goldsmith not far from your house here in the Rue St. Honors." "By the Saints!--you--you?" exclaimed Mademoiselle. "And I swear to you, Mademoiselle," went on Miossens, "that I am proud of the deed. For let me tell you that Cardillac was the most abandoned and hypocritical of villains, that it was he who committed those dreadful murders and robberies by night, and so long escaped all traps laid for him. Somehow, I can't say how, a strong feeling of suspicion was aroused in my mind against the old reprobate when he brought me an ornament I had ordered and was so visibly disturbed on giving it to me; and then he inquired particularly for whom I wanted the ornament, and also questioned my valet in the most artful way as to when I was in the habit of visiting a certain lady. I had long before noticed that all the unfortunates who fell victims to this abominable epidemic of murder and robbery bore one and the same wound. I felt sure that the assassin had by practice grown perfect in inflicting it, and that it must prove instantaneously fatal, and upon this he relied implicitly. If it failed, then it would come to a fight on equal terms. This led me to adopt a measure of precaution which is so simple that I cannot comprehend why it did not occur to others, who might then have safeguarded themselves against any murderous assault that threatened them. I wore a light shirt of mail under my tunic. Cardillac attacked me from behind. He laid hold upon me with the strength of a giant, but the surely-aimed blow glanced aside from the iron. That same moment I wrested myself free from his grasp, and drove my dagger, which I held in readiness, into his heart." "And you maintained silence?" asked De Scudéri; "you did not notify to the tribunals what you had done?" "Permit me to remark," went on Miossens, "permit me to remark, Mademoiselle, that such an announcement, if it had not at once entailed disastrous results upon me, would at any rate have involved me in a most detestable trial. Would La Regnie, who ferrets out crime everywhere--would he have believed my unsupported word if I had accused honest Cardillac, the pattern of piety and virtue, of an attempted murder? What if the sword of justice had turned its point against me?" "That would not have been possible," said De Scudéri, "your birth--your rank"---- "Oh! remember Marshal de Luxembourg, whose whim for having his horoscope cast by Le Sage brought him under the suspicion of being a poisoner, and eventually into the Bastille. No! by St. Denis! I would not risk my freedom for an hour-- not even the lappet of my ear--in the power of that madman La Regnie, who only too well would like to have his knife at the throats of all of us." "But do you know you are bringing innocent Brusson to the scaffold?" "Innocent?" rejoined Miossens, "innocent? Are you speaking of the villain Cardillac's accomplice, Mademoiselle? he who helped him in his evil deeds? who deserves to die a hundred deaths? No, indeed! He would meet a just end on the scaffold. I have only disclosed to you, honoured lady, the details of the occurrence on the presupposition that, without delivering me into the hands of the *Chambre Ardent*, you will yet find a way to turn my secret to account on behalf of your *protégé*."

De Scudéri was so enraptured at finding her conviction of Brusson's innocence confirmed in such a decisive manner that she did not scruple to tell the Count all, since he already knew of Cardillac's iniquity, and to exhort him to accompany her to see D'Andilly. To *him* all should be revealed under the seal of secrecy, and he should advise them what was to be done.

After De Scudéri had related all to D'Andilly down to the minutest particulars, he inquired once more about several of the most insignificant features. In particular he asked Count Miossens whether he was perfectly satisfied that it was Cardillac who had attacked him, and whether he would be able to identify Olivier Brusson as the man who had carried away the corpse. De Miossens made answer, "Not only did I very well recognise Cardillac by the bright light of the moon, but I have also seen in La Regnie's hands the dagger with which Cardillac was stabbed; it is mine, distinguished by the elegant workmanship of the hilt. As I only stood one yard from the young man, and his hat had fallen off, I distinctly saw his features, and should certainly recognise him again."

After gazing thoughtfully before him for some minutes in silence, D'Andilly said, "Brusson cannot possibly be saved from the hands of justice in any ordinary and regular way. Out of consideration for Madelon he refuses to accuse Cardillac of being the thievish assassin. And he must continue to do so, for even if he succeeded in proving his statements by pointing out the secret exit and the accumulated store of stolen jewellery, he would still be liable to death as a partner in Cardillac's guilt. And the bearings of things would not be altered if Count Miossens were to state to the judges the real details of the meeting with Cardillac. The only thing we can aim at securing is a postponement of the torture. Let Count Miossens go to the *Conciergerie*, have Olivier Brusson brought forward, and recognise in him the man who carried away Cardillac's dead body. Then let him hurry off to La Regnie and say, 'I saw a man stabbed in the Rue St. Honoré, and as I stood close beside the corpse another man sprang forward and stooped down over the dead body; but on finding signs of life in him he lifted him on his shoulders and carried him away. This man I recognise in Olivier Brusson.' This evidence would lead to another hearing of Brusson and to his confrontation with Miossens. At all events the torture would be delayed and further inquiries would be instituted. Then will come the proper time to appeal to the king. It may be left to your sagacity, Mademoiselle, to do this in the adroitest manner. As far as my opinion goes, I think it would be best to disclose to him the whole mystery. Brusson's confessions are borne out by this statement of Count Miossens; and they may, perhaps, be still further substantiated by secret investigations at Cardillac's own house. All this could not afford grounds for a verdict of acquittal by the court, but it might appeal to the king's feelings, that it is his prerogative to speak mercy where the judge can only condemn, and so elicit a favourable decision from His Majesty." Count Miossens followed implicitly D'Andilly's advice; and the result was what the latter had foreseen.

But now the thing was to get at the king; and this was the most difficult part of all to accomplish, since he believed that Brusson alone was the formidable assassin who for so long a time had held all Paris enthralled by fear and anxiety, and accordingly he had conceived such an abhorrence of him that he burst into a violent fit of passion at the slightest allusion to the notorious trial. De Maintenon, faithful to her principle of never speaking to the king on any subject that was disagreeable, refused to take any steps in the affair; and so Brusson's fate rested entirely in De Scudéri's hands. After long deliberation she formed a resolution which she carried into execution as promptly as she had conceived it. Putting on a robe of heavy black, silk, and hanging Cardillac's valuable necklace round her neck, and clasping the bracelets on her arms, and throwing a black veil over her head, she presented herself in De Maintenon's salons at a time when she knew the king would be present there. This stately robe invested the venerable lady's noble figure with such majesty as could not fail to inspire respect, even in the mob of idle loungers who were wont to collect in anterooms, laughing and jesting in frivolous and irreverent fashion. They all shyly made way for her; and when she entered the salon the king himself in his astonishment rose and came to meet her. As his eyes fell upon the glitter of the costly diamonds in the necklace and bracelets, he cried, "'Pon my soul, that's Cardillac's jewellery!" Then, turning to De Maintenon, he added with an arch smile, "See, Marchioness, how our fair bride mourns for her bridegroom." "Oh! your Majesty," broke in De Scudéri, taking up the jest and carrying it on, "would it indeed beseem a deeply sorrowful bride to adorn herself in this splendid fashion? No, I have quite broken off with that goldsmith, and should never think about him more, were it not that the horrid recollection of him being carried past me after he had been murdered so often recurs to my mind." "What do you say?" asked the king. "What! you saw the poor devil?" De Scudéri now related in a few words how she chanced to be near Cardillac's house just as the murder was discovered--as yet she did not allude to Brusson's being mixed up in the matter. She sketched Madelon's excessive grief, told what a deep impression the angelic child made upon her, and described in what way she had rescued the poor girl out of Desgrais' hands, amid the approving shouts of the people. Then came the scenes with La Regnie, with Desgrais, with Brusson--the interest deepening and intensifying from moment to moment. The king was so carried away by the extraordinary graphic power and burning eloquence of Mademoiselle's narration that he did not perceive she was talking about the hateful trial of the abominable wretch Brusson; he was quite unable to utter a word; all he could do was to let off the excess of his emotion by an exclamation from time to time. Ere he knew where he was--he was so utterly confused by this unprecedented tale which he had heard that he was unable to order his thoughts--De Scudéri was prostrate at his feet, imploring pardon for Olivier Brusson. "What are you doing?" burst out the king, taking her by both hands and forcing her into a chair. "What do you mean, Mademoiselle? This is a strange way to surprise me. Oh! it's a terrible story. Who will guarantee me that Brusson's marvellous tale is true?" Whereupon De Scudéri replied, "Miossens' evidence--an examination of Cardillac's house--my heart-felt conviction--and oh! Madelon's virtuous heart, which recognised the like virtue in unhappy Brusson's." Just as the king was on the point of making some reply he was interrupted by a noise at the door, and turned round. Louvois, who during this time was working in the adjoining apartment, looked in with an expression of anxiety stamped upon his features. The king rose and left the room, following Louvois.

The two ladies, both De Scudéri and De Maintenon, regarded this interruption as dangerous, for having been once surprised the king would be on his guard against falling a second time into the trap set for him. Nevertheless after a lapse of some minutes the king came back again; after traversing the room once or twice at a quick pace, he planted himself immediately in front of De Scudéri and, throwing his arms behind his back, said in almost an undertone, yet without looking at her, "I should very much like to see your Madelon." Mademoiselle replied, "Oh! my precious liege! what a great--great happiness your condescension will confer upon the poor unhappy child. Oh! the little girl only waits a sign from you to approach, to throw herself at your feet." Then she tripped towards the door as quickly as she was able in her heavy clothing, and called out on the outside of it that the king would admit Madelon Cardillac; and she came back into the room weeping and sobbing with overpowering delight and gladness.

De Scudéri had foreseen that some such favour as this might be granted and so had brought Madelon along with her, and she was waiting with the Marchioness' lady-in-waiting with a short petition in her hands that had been drawn up by D'Andilly. After a few minutes she lay prostrate at the king's feet, unable to speak a word. The throbbing blood was driven quicker and faster through the poor girl's veins owing to anxiety, nervous confusion, shy reverence, love, and anguish. Her cheeks were died with a deep purple blush; her eyes shone with bright pearly tears, which from time to time fell through her silken eyelashes upon her beautiful lily-white bosom. The king appeared to be struck with the surprising beauty of the angelic creature. He softly raised her up, making a motion as if about to kiss the hand which he had grasped. But he let it go again and regarded the lovely girl with tears in his eyes, thus betraying how great was the emotion stirring within him. De Maintenon softly whispered to Mademoiselle, "Isn't she exactly like La Vallière, the little thing? There's hardly a pin's difference between them. The king luxuriates in the most pleasing memories. Your cause is won."

Notwithstanding the low tone in which De Maintenon spoke, the king appeared to have heard what she said. A fleeting blush passed across his face; his eye wandered past De Maintenon; he read the petition which Madelon had presented to him, and then said mildly and kindly, "I am quite ready to believe, my dear child, that you are convinced of your lover's innocence; but let us hear what the *Chambre Ardente* has got to say to it." With a gentle wave of the hand he dismissed the young girl, who was weeping as if her heart would break.

To her dismay De Scudéri observed that the recollection of La Vallière, however beneficial it had appeared to be at first, had occasioned the king to alter his mind as soon as De Maintenon mentioned her name. Perhaps the king felt he was being reminded in a too indelicate way of how he was about to sacrifice strict justice to beauty, or perhaps he was like the dreamer, when, on somebody's shouting to him, the lovely dream-images which he was about to clasp, quickly vanish away. Perhaps he no longer saw *his* La Vallière before his eyes, but only thought of

Sœur Louise de la Misèricorde (Louise the Sister of Mercy),--the name La Vallière had assumed on joining the Carmelite nuns--who worried him with her pious airs and repentance. What else could they now do but calmly wait for the king's decision?

Meanwhile Count Miossens' deposition before the *Chambre Ardente* had become publicly known; and as it frequently happens that the people rush so readily from one extreme to another, so on this occasion he whom they had at first cursed as a most abominable murderer and had threatened to tear to pieces, they now pitied, even before he ascended the scaffold, as the innocent victim of barbarous justice. Now his neighbours first began to call to mind his exemplary walk of life, his great love for Madelon, and the faithfulness and touching submissive affection which he had cherished for the old goldsmith. Considerable bodies of the populace began to appear in a threatening manner before La Regnie's palace and to cry out, "Give us Olivier Brusson; he is innocent;" and they even stoned the windows, so that La Regnie was obliged to seek shelter from the enraged mob with the *Maréchaussée*.

Several days passed, and Mademoiselle heard not the least intelligence about Olivier Brusson's trial. She was quite inconsolable and went off to Madame de Maintenon; but she assured her that the king maintained a strict silence about the matter, and it would not be advisable to remind him of it. Then when she went on to ask with a smile of singular import how little La Vallière was doing, De Scudéri was convinced that deep down in the heart of the proud lady there lurked some feeling of vexation at this business, which might entice the susceptible king into a region whose charm she could not understand. Mademoiselle need therefore hope for nothing from De Maintenon.

At last, however, with D'Andilly's help, De Scudéri succeeded in finding out that the king had had a long and private interview with Count Miossens. Further, she learned that Bontems, the king's most confidential valet and general agent, had been to the Conciergerie and had an interview with Brusson, also that the same Bontems had one night gone with several men to Cardillac's house, and there spent a considerable time. Claude Patru, the man who inhabited the lower storey, maintained that they were knocking about overhead all night long, and he was sure that Olivier had been with them, for he distinctly heard his voice. This much was, therefore, at any rate certain, that the king himself was having the true history of the circumstances inquired into; but the long delay before he gave his decision was inexplicable. La Regnie would no doubt do all he possibly could to keep his grip upon the victim who was to be taken out of his clutches. And this annihilated every hope as soon as it began to bud.

A month had nearly passed when De Maintenon sent word to Mademoiselle that the king wished to see her that evening in her salons.

De Scudéri's heart beat high; she knew that Brusson's case would now be decided. She told poor Madelon so, who prayed fervently to the Virgin and the saints that they would awaken in the king's mind a conviction of Brusson's innocence.

Yet it appeared as though the king had completely forgotten the matter, for in his usual way he dallied in graceful conversation with the two ladies, and never once made any allusion to poor Brusson. At last Bontems appeared, and approaching the king whispered certain words in his ear, but in so low a tone that neither De Maintenon nor De Scudéri could make anything out of them. Mademoiselle's heart quaked. Then the king rose to his feet and approached her, saying with brimming eyes, "I congratulate you, Mademoiselle. Your *protégé* Olivier Brusson, is free." The tears gushed from the old lady's eyes; unable to speak a word, she was about to throw herself at the king's feet. But he prevented her, saying, "Go, go, Mademoiselle. You ought to be my advocate in Parliament and plead my causes, for, by St. Denis, there's nobody on earth could withstand your eloquence; and yet," he continued, "and yet when Virtue herself has taken a man under her own protection, is he not safe from all base accusations, from the *Chambre Ardente* and all other tribunals in the world?" De Scudéri now found words and poured them out in a stream of glowing thanks. The king interrupted her, by informing her that she herself would find awaiting her in her own house still warmer thanks than he had a right to claim from her, for probably at that moment the happy Olivier was clasping his Madelon in his arms. "Bontems shall pay you a thousand *Louis d'or*," concluded the king. "Give them in my name to the little girl as a dowry. Let her marry her Brusson, who doesn't deserve such good fortune, and then let them both be gone out of Paris, for such is my will."

La Martinière came running forward to meet her mistress, and Baptiste behind her; the faces of both were radiant with joy; both cried delighted, "He is here! he is free! O the dear young people!" The happy couple threw themselves at Mademoiselle's feet. "Oh! I knew it! I knew it!" cried Madelon. "I knew that you, that nobody but you, would save my darling Olivier." "And O my mother," cried Olivier, "my belief in you never wavered." They both kissed the honoured lady's hands, and shed innumerable tears. Then they embraced each other again and again, affirming that the exquisite happiness of that moment outweighed all the unutterable sufferings of the days that were past; and they vowed never to part from each other till Death himself came to part them.

A few days later they were united by the blessing of the priest. Even though it had not been the King's wish, Brusson would not have stayed in Paris, where everything would have reminded him of the fearful time of Cardillac's crimes, and where, moreover, some accident might reveal in pernicious wise his dark secret, now become known to several persons, and so his peace of mind might be ruined for ever. Almost immediately after the wedding he set out with his young wife for Geneva, Mademoiselle's blessings accompanying them on the way. Richly provided with means through Madelon's dowry, and endowed with uncommon skill at his trade, as well as with every virtue of a good citizen, he led there a happy life, free from care. He realised the hopes which had deceived his father and had brought him at last to his grave.

A year after Brusson's departure there appeared a public proclamation, signed by Harloy de Chauvalon, Archbishop of Paris, and by the parliamentary advocate, Pierre Arnaud d'Andilly, which ran to the effect that a penitent sinner had, under the seal of confession, handed over to the Church a large and valuable store of jewels and gold ornaments which he had stolen. Everybody who up to the end of the year 1680 had lost ornaments by theft, particularly by a murderous attack in the public street, was to apply to D'Andilly, and then, if his description of the ornament which had been stolen from him tallied exactly with any of the pieces awaiting identification, and if further there existed no doubt as to the legitimacy of his claim, he should receive his property again. Many of those whose names stood on Cardillac's list as having been, not murdered, but merely stunned by a blow, gradually came one after the other to the parliamentary advocate, and received, to their no little amazement, their stolen property back again. The rest fell to the coffers of the Church of St. Eustace.

GAMBLER'S LUCK.

Pyrmont had a larger concourse of visitors than ever in the summer of 18--. The number of rich and illustrious strangers increased from day to day, greatly exciting the zeal of speculators of all kinds. Hence it was also that the owners of the faro-bank took care to pile up their glittering gold in bigger heaps, in order that this, the bait of the noblest game, which they, like good skilled hunters, knew how to decoy, might preserve its efficacy.

Who does not know how fascinating an excitement gambling is, particularly at watering-places, during the season, where every visitor, having laid aside his ordinary habits and course of life, deliberately gives himself up to leisure and ease and exhilarating enjoyment? then gambling becomes an irresistible attraction. People who at other times never touch a card are to be seen amongst the most eager players; and besides, it is the fashion, especially in higher circles, for every one to visit the bank in the evening and lose a little money at play.

The only person who appeared not to heed this irresistible attraction, and this injunction of fashion, was a young German Baron, whom we will call Siegfried. When everybody else hurried off to the play-house, and he was deprived of all means and all prospect of the intellectual conversation he loved, he preferred either to give reins to the flights of his fancy in solitary walks or to stay in his own room and take up a book, or even indulge in poetic attempts, in writing, himself.

As Siegfried was young, independent, rich, of noble appearance and pleasing disposition, it could not fail but that he was highly esteemed and loved, and that he had the most decisive good-fortune with the fair sex. And in everything that he took up or turned his attention to, there seemed to be a singularly lucky star presiding over his actions. Rumour spoke of many extraordinary love-intrigues which had been forced upon him, and out of which, however ruinous they would in all likelihood have been for many other young men, he escaped with incredible ease and success. But whenever the conversation turned upon him and his good fortune, the old gentlemen of his acquaintance were especially fond of relating a story about a watch, which had happened in the days of his early youth. For it chanced once that Siegfried, while still under his guardian's care, had quite unexpectedly found himself so straitened for money on a journey that he was absolutely obliged to sell his gold watch, which was set with brilliants, merely in order to get on his way. He had made up his mind that he would have to throw away his valuable watch for an old song; but as there happened to be in the hotel where he had put up at a young prince who was just in want of such an ornament, the Baron actually received for it more than it was really worth. More than a year passed and Siegfried had become his own master, when he read in the newspapers in another place that a watch was to be made the subject of a lottery. He took a ticket, which cost a mere trifle, and won--the same gold watch set with brilliants which he had sold. Not long afterwards he exchanged this watch for a valuable ring. He held office for a short time under the Prince of G----, and when he retired from his post the Prince presented to him as a mark of his good-will the very identical gold watch set with brilliants as before, together with a costly chain.

From this story they passed to Siegfried's obstinacy in never on any account touching a card; why, with his strongly pronounced good-luck he had all the more inducement to play; and they were unanimous in coming to the conclusion that the Baron, notwithstanding all his other conspicuous good qualities, was a miserly fellow, far too careful and far too stingy to expose himself to the smallest possible loss. That the Baron's conduct was in every particular the direct contrary of that of an avaricious man had no weight with them; and as is so often the case, when the majority have set their hearts upon tagging a questioning 'but' on to the good name of a talented man, and are determined to find this 'but' at any cost, even though it should be in their own imagination, so in the present case the sneering allusion to Siegfried's aversion to play afforded them infinite satisfaction.

Siegfried was not long in learning what was being said about him; and since, generous and liberal as he was, there was nothing he hated and detested more than miserliness, he made up his mind to put his traducers to shame by ransoming himself from this foul aspersion at the cost of a couple of hundred *Louis d'or*, or even more if need be, however much disgusted he might feel at gambling. He presented himself at the faro-bank with the deliberate intention of losing the large sum which he had put in his pocket; but in play also the good luck which stood by him in everything he undertook did not prove unfaithful. Every card he chose won. The cabalistic calculations of seasoned old players were shivered to atoms against the Baron's play. No matter whether he changed his cards or continued to stake on the same one, it was all the same: he was always a winner. In the Baron they had the singular spectacle of a punter at variance with himself because the cards fell favourable for him; and notwithstanding that the explanation of his behaviour was pretty patent, yet people looked at each other significantly and gave utterance in no ambiguous terms to the opinion that the Baron, carried along by his penchant for the marvellous, might eventually become insane, for any player who could be dismayed at his run of luck must surely be insane.

The very fact of having won a considerable sum of money made it obligatory upon the Baron to go on playing until he should have carried out his original purpose; for in all probability his large win would be followed by a still larger loss. But people's expectations were not in the remotest degree realised, for the Baron's striking good-luck continued to attend him.

Without his being conscious of it, there began to be awakened in his mind a strong liking for faro, which with all its simplicity is the most ominous of games; and this liking continued to increase more and more. He was no longer dissatisfied with his good-luck; gambling fettered his attention and held him fast to the table for nights and nights, so that he was perforce compelled to give credence to the peculiar attraction of the game, of which his friends had formerly spoken and which he would by no means allow to be correct, for he was attracted to faro not by the thirst for gain, but simply and solely by the game itself.

One night, just as the banker had finished a *taille*, the Baron happened to raise his eyes and observed that an elderly man had taken post directly opposite to him and had got his eyes fixed upon him in a set, sad, earnest gaze. And as long as play lasted, every time the Baron looked up, his eyes met the stranger's dark sad stare, until at last he could not help being struck with a very uncomfortable and oppressive feeling. And the stranger only left the apartment when play came to an end for the night. The following night he again stood opposite the Baron, staring at him with unaverted gaze, whilst his eyes had a dark mysterious spectral look. The Baron still kept his temper. But when on the third night the stranger appeared again and fixed his eyes, burning with a consuming fire, upon the Baron, the latter burst out, "Sir, I must beg you to choose some other place. You exercise a constraining influence upon my play."

With a painful smile the stranger bowed and left the table, and the hall too, without uttering a word.

But on the next night the stranger again stood opposite the Baron, piercing him through and through with his dark fiery glance. Then the Baron burst out still more angrily than on the preceding night, "If you think it a joke, sir, to stare at me, pray choose some other time and some other place to do so; and now have the"---- A wave of the hand towards the door took the place of the harsh words the Baron was about to utter. And as on the previous night, the stranger, after bowing slightly, left the hall with the same painful smile upon his lips.

Siegfried was so excited and heated by play, by the wine which he had taken, and also by the scene with the stranger, that he could not sleep. Morning was already breaking, when the stranger's figure appeared before his eyes. He observed his striking, sharp-cut features, worn with suffering, and his sad deep-set eyes just as he had stared at him; and he noticed his distinguished bearing, which, in spite of his mean clothing, betrayed a man of high culture. And then the air of painful resignation with which the stranger submitted to the harsh words flung at him, and fought down his bitter feelings with an effort, and left the hall! "No," cried Siegfried, "I did him wrong-- great wrong. Is it indeed at all like me to blaze up in this rude, ill- mannered way, like an uncultivated clown, and to offer insults to people without the least provocation?" The Baron at last arrived at the conviction that it must have been a most oppressive feeling of the sharp contrast between them which had made the man stare at him so; in the moment that he was perhaps contending with the bitterest poverty, he (the Baron) was piling up heaps and heaps of gold with all the superciliousness of the gambler. He resolved to find out the stranger that very morning and atone to him for his rudeness.

And as chance would have it, the very first person whom the Baron saw strolling down the avenue was the stranger himself.

The Baron addressed him, offered the most profuse apologies for his behaviour of the night before, and in conclusion begged the stranger's pardon in all due form. The stranger replied that he had nothing to pardon, since large allowances must be made for a player deeply intent over his game, and besides, he had only himself to blame for the harsh words he had provoked, since he had obstinately persisted in remaining in the place where he disturbed the Baron's play.

The Baron went further; he said there were often seasons of momentary embarrassment in life which weighed with a most galling effect upon a man of refinement, and he plainly hinted to the stranger that he was willing to give the money he had won, or even more still, if by that means he could perhaps be of any assistance to him.

"Sir," replied the stranger, "you think I am in want, but that is not indeed the case; for though poor rather than rich, I yet have enough to satisfy my simple wants. Moreover, you will yourself perceive that as a man of honour I could not possibly accept a large sum of money from you as indemnification for the insult you conceive you have offered me, even though I were not a gentleman of birth."

"I think I understand you," replied the Baron starting; "I am ready to grant you the satisfaction you demand."

"Good God!" continued the stranger--"Good God, how unequal a contest it would be between us two! I am certain that you think as I do about a duel, that it is not to be treated as a piece of childish folly; nor do you believe that a few drops of blood, which have perhaps fallen from a scratched finger, can ever wash tarnished honour bright again. There are many cases in which it is impossible for two particular individuals to continue to exist together on this earth, even though the one live in the Caucasus and the other on the Tiber; no separation is possible so long as the hated foe can be thought of as still alive. In this case a duel to decide which of the two is to give way to the other on this earth is a necessity. Between us now, as I have just said, a duel would be fought upon unequal terms, since nohow can my life be valued so highly as yours. If I run you through, I destroy a whole world of the finest hopes; and if I fall, then you have put an end to a miserable existence, that is harrowed by the bitterest and most agonising memories. But after all--and this is of course the main thing--I don't conceive myself to have been in the remotest degree insulted. You bade me go, and I went."

These last words the stranger spoke in a tone which nevertheless betrayed the sting in his heart. This was enough for the Baron to again apologise, which he did by especially dwelling upon the fact that the stranger's glance had, he did not know why, gone straight to his heart, till at last he could endure it no longer.

"I hope then," said the stranger, "that if my glance did really penetrate to your heart, it aroused you to a sense of the threatening danger on the brink of which you are hovering. With a light glad heart and youthful ingenuousness you are standing on the edge of the abyss of ruin; one single push and you will plunge headlong down without a hope of rescue. In a single word, you are on the point of becoming a confirmed and passionate gambler and ruining yourself."

The Baron assured him that he was completely mistaken. He related the circumstances under which he had first gone to the faro-table, and assured him that he entirely lacked the gambler's characteristic disposition; all he wished was to lose two hundred *Louis d'or* or so, and when he had succeeded in this he intended to cease punting. Up to that time, however, he had had the most conspicuous run of good-luck.

"Oh! but," cried the stranger, "oh! but it is exactly this run of good- luck wherein lies the subtlest and most formidable temptation of the malignant enemy. It is this run of good-luck which attends your play, Baron,--the circumstances under which you have begun to play,--nay, your entire behaviour whilst actually engaged in play, which only too plainly betray how your interest in it deepens and increases on each occasion; all--all this reminds me only too forcibly of the awful fate of a certain unhappy man, who, in many respects like you, began to play under circumstances similar to those which you have described in your own case. And therefore it was that I could not keep my eyes off you, and that I was hardly able to restrain myself from saying in words what my glances were meant to tell you. 'Oh! see--see--see the demons stretching out their talons to drag you down into the pit of ruin.' Thus I should like to have called to you. I was desirous of making your acquaintance; and I have succeeded. Let me tell you the history of the unfortunate man whom I mentioned; you will then perhaps be convinced that it is no idle phantom of the brain when I see you in the most imminent danger, and warn you."

The stranger and the Baron both sat down upon a seat which stood quite isolated, and then the stranger began as follows:--

"The same brilliant qualities which distinguish you, Herr Baron, gained Chevalier Menars the esteem and admiration of men and made him a favourite amongst women. In riches alone Fortune had not been so gracious to him as she has been to you; he was almost in want; and it was only through exercising the strictest economy that he was enabled to appear in a state becoming his position as the scion of a distinguished family. Since even the smallest loss would be serious for him and upset the entire tenor of his course of life, he dare not indulge in play; besides, he had no inclination to do so, and it was therefore no act of self-sacrifice on his part to avoid the tables. It is to be added that he had the most remarkable success in everything which he took in hand, so that Chevalier Menars' good-luck became a by-word.

"One night he suffered himself to be persuaded, contrary to his practice, to visit a play-house. The friends whom he had accompanied were soon deeply engaged in play.

"Without taking any interest in what was going forward, the Chevalier, busied with thoughts of quite a different character, first strode up and down the apartment and then stood with his eyes fixed upon the gaming-table, where the gold continued to pour in upon the banker from all sides. All at once an old colonel observed the Chevalier, and cried out, 'The devil! Here we've got Chevalier Menars and his good-luck amongst us, and yet we can win nothing, since he has declared neither for the banker nor for the punters. But we can't have it so any longer; he shall at once punt for me.'

"All the Baron's attempts to excuse himself on the ground of his lack of skill and total want of experience were of no avail; the Colonel was not to be denied; the Chevalier must take his place at the table.

"The Chevalier had exactly the same run of fortune that you have, Herr Baron. The cards fell favourable for him, and he had soon won a considerable sum for the Colonel, whose joy at his grand thought of claiming the loan of Chevalier Menars' steadfast good-luck knew no bounds.

"This good-luck, which quite astonished all the rest of those present, made not the slightest impression upon the Chevalier; nay, somehow, in a way inexplicable to himself, his aversion to play took deeper root, so that on the following morning when he awoke and felt the consequences of his exertion during the night, through which he had been awake, in a general relaxation both mental and physical, he took a most earnest resolve never again under any circumstances to visit a play-house.

"And in this resolution he was still further strengthened by the old Colonel's conduct; he had the most decided ill-luck with every card he took up; and the blame for this run of bad-luck he, with the most extraordinary infatuation, put upon the Chevalier's shoulders. In an importunate manner he demanded that the Chevalier should either punt for him or at any rate stand at his side, so as by his presence to banish the perverse demon who always put into his hands cards which never turned up right. Of course it is well known that there is more absurd superstition to be found amongst gamblers than almost anywhere else. The only way in which the Chevalier could get rid of the Colonel was by declaring in a tone of great seriousness that he would rather fight him than play for him, for the Colonel was no great friend of duels. The Chevalier cursed his good-nature in having complied with the old fool's request at first.

"Now nothing less was to be expected than that the story of the Baron's marvellously lucky play should pass from mouth to mouth, and also that all sorts of enigmatical mysterious circumstances should be invented and added on to it, representing the Chevalier as a man in league with supernatural powers. But the fact that the Chevalier in spite of his good-luck did not touch another card, could not fail to inspire the highest respect for his firmness of character, and so very much increase the esteem which he already enjoyed.

"Somewhere about a year later the Chevalier was suddenly placed in a most painful and embarrassing position owing to the non-arrival of the small sum of money upon which he relied to defray his current expenses. He was obliged to disclose his circumstances to his most intimate friend, who without hesitation supplied him with what he needed, at the same time twitting him with being the most hopelessly eccentric fellow that ever was. 'Destiny,' said he 'gives us hints in what way and where we ought to seek our own benefit; and we have only our own indolence to blame if we do not heed, do not understand these hints. The Higher Power that rules over us has whispered quite plainly in your ears, If you want money and property go and play, else you will be poor and needy, and never independent, as long as you live.'

"And now for the first time the thought of how wonderfully fortune had favoured him at the faro-bank took clear and distinct shape in his mind; and both in his dreams and when awake he heard the banker's monotonous *gagne*, *perd*, and the rattle of the gold pieces. 'Yes, it is undoubtedly so,' he said to himself, 'a single night like that one before would free me from my difficulties, and help me over the painful embarrassment of being a burden to my friends; it is my duty to follow the beckoning finger of fate.' The friends who had advised him to try play, accompanied him to the play-house, and gave him twenty *Louis d'or* more that he might begin unconcerned.

"If the Chevalier's play had been splendid when he punted for the old Colonel, it was indeed doubly so now. Blindly and without choice he drew the cards he staked upon, but the invisible hand of that Higher Power which is intimately related to Chance, or rather actually is what we call Chance, seemed to be regulating his play. At the end of the evening he had won a thousand *Louis d'or*.

"Next morning he awoke with a kind of dazed feeling. The gold pieces he had won lay scattered about beside him on the table. At the first moment he fancied he was dreaming; he rubbed his eyes; he grasped the table and pulled it nearer towards him. But when he began to reflect upon what had happened, when he buried his fingers amongst the gold pieces, when he counted them with gratified satisfaction, and even counted them through again, then delight in the base mammon shot for the first time like a pernicious poisonous breath through his every nerve and fibre, then it was all over with the purity of sentiment which he had so long preserved intact. He could hardly wait for night to come that he might go to the faro-table again. His good-luck continued constant, so that after a few weeks, during which he played nearly every night, he had won a considerable sum.

"Now there are two sorts of players. Play simply as such affords to many an indescribable and mysterious pleasure, totally irrespective of gain. The strange complications of chance occur with the most surprising waywardness; the government of the Higher Power becomes conspicuously evident; and this it is which stirs up our spirit to move its wings and see if it cannot soar upwards into the mysterious kingdom, the fateful workshop of this Power, in order to surprise it at its labours.

"I once knew a man who spent many days and nights alone in his room, keeping a bank and punting against himself; this man was, according to my way of thinking, a genuine player. Others have nothing but gain before their eyes, and look upon play as a means to getting rich speedily. This class the Chevalier joined, thus once more establishing the truth of the saying that the real deeper inclination for play must lie in the individual nature--must be born in it. And for this reason he soon found the sphere of activity to which the punter is confined too narrow. With the very large sum of money that he had won by gambling he established a bank of his own; and in this enterprise fortune favoured him to such an extent that within a short time his bank was the richest in all Paris. And agreeably to the nature of the case, the largest proportion of players flocked to him, the richest and luckiest banker.

"The heartless, demoralising life of a gambler soon blotted out all those advantages, as well mental as physical, which had formerly secured to the Chevalier people's affection and esteem. He ceased to be a faithful friend, a cheerful, easy guest in society, a chivalrous and gallant admirer of the fair sex. Extinguished was all his taste for science and art, and gone all striving to advance along the road to sound knowledge. Upon his deathly pale countenance, and in his gloomy eyes, where a dim, restless fire gleamed, was to be read the full expression of the extremely baneful passion in whose toils he was entangled. It was not fondness for play, no, it was the most abominable avarice which had been enkindled in his soul by Satan himself. In a single word, he was the most finished specimen of a faro-banker that may be seen anywhere.

"One night Fortune was less favourable to the Chevalier than usual, although he suffered no loss of any consequence. Then a little thin old man, meanly clad, and almost repulsive to look at, approached the table, drew a card with a trembling hand, and placed a gold piece upon it. Several of the players looked up at the old man at first greatly astonished, but after that they treated him with provoking contempt. Nevertheless his face never moved a muscle, far less did he utter a single word of complaint.

"The old man lost; he lost one stake after another; but the higher his losses rose the more pleased the other players got. And at last, when the new-comer, who continued to double his stake every time, placed five hundred *Louis d'or* at once upon a card and this the very next moment turned up on the losing side, one of the other players cried with a laugh, 'Good-luck, Signor Vertua, good-luck! Don't lose heart. Go on staking; you look to me as if you would finish with breaking the bank through your immense winnings.' The old man shot a basilisk-like look upon the mocker and hurried away, but only to return at the end of half an hour with his pockets full of gold. In the last *taille* he was, however, obliged to cease playing, since he had again lost all the money he had brought back with him.

"This scornful and contemptuous treatment of the old man had excessively annoyed the Chevalier, for in spite of all his abominable practices, he yet insisted on certain rules of good behaviour being observed at his table. And so on the conclusion of the game, when Signor Vertua had taken his departure, the Chevalier felt he had sufficient grounds to speak a serious word or two to the mocker, as well as to one or two other players whose contemptuous treatment of the old man had been most conspicuous, and whom the Chevalier had bidden stay behind for this purpose.

"'Ah! but, Chevalier,' cried one of them, 'you don't know old Francesco Vertua, or else you would have no fault to find with us and our behaviour towards him; you would rather approve of it. For let me tell you that this Vertua, a Neapolitan by birth, who has been fifteen years in Paris, is the meanest, dirtiest, most pestilent miser and usurer who can be found anywhere. He is a stranger to every human feeling; if he saw his own brother writhing at his feet in the agonies of death, it would be an utter waste of pains to try to entice a single *Louis d'or* from him, even if it were to save his brother's life. He has a heavy burden of curses and imprecations to bear, which have been showered down upon him by a multitude of men, nay, by entire families, who have been plunged into the deepest distress through his diabolical speculations. He is hated like poison by all who know him; everybody wishes that vengeance may overtake him for all the evil that he has done, and that it may put an end to his career of iniquity. He has never played before, at least since he has been in Paris; and so from all this you need not wonder at our being so greatly astounded when the old skin-flint appeared at your table. And for the same reasons we were, of course, pleased at the old fellow's serious losses, for it would have been hard, very hard, if the old rascal had been favoured by Fortune. It is only too certain. Chevalier, that the old fool has been deluded by the riches of your bank. He came intending to pluck you and has lost his own feathers. But yet it completely puzzles me how Vertua could act thus in a way so opposite to the true character of a miser, and could bring himself to play so high. Ah! well--you'll see he will not come again; we are now quit of him.'

"But this opinion proved to be far from correct, for on the very next night Vertua presented himself at the Chevalier's bank again, and staked and lost much more heavily than on the night preceding. But he preserved a calm demeanour through it all; he even smiled at times with a sort of bitter irony, as though foreseeing how soon things would be totally changed. But during each of the succeeding nights the old man's losses increased like a glacier at a greater and greater rate, till at last it was calculated that he had paid over thirty thousand *Louis d'or* to the bank. Finally he entered the hall one evening, long after play had begun, with a deathly pale face and troubled looks, and took up his post at some distance from the table, his eyes riveted in a set stare upon the cards which the Chevalier successively drew. At last, just as the Chevalier had shuffled the cards, had had them cut and was about to begin the *taille*, the old man cried in such a harsh grating voice, 'Stop!' that everybody looked round well-nigh dismayed. Then, forcing his way to the table close up to the Chevalier, he said in his ear, speaking in a hoarse voice, 'Chevalier, my house in the Rue St. Honoré, together with all the furniture and all the gold and silver and all the jewels I possess, are valued at eighty thousand francs, will you accept the stake?' 'Very good,' replied the Chevalier coldly, without looking round at the old man; and he began the *taille*.

"'The queen,' said Vertua; and at the next draw the queen had lost. The old man reeled back from the table and leaned against the wall motionless and paralysed, like a rigid stone statue. Nobody troubled himself any further about him.

"Play was over for the night; the players were dispersing; the Chevalier and his croupiers were packing away in the strong box the gold he had won. Then old Vertua staggered like a ghost out of the corner towards the Chevalier and addressed him in a hoarse, hollow voice, 'Yet a word with you, Chevalier,--only a single word.'

"'Well, what is it?' replied the Chevalier, withdrawing the key from the lock of the strong box and measuring the old man from head to foot with a look of contempt.

"'I have lost all my property at your bank, Chevalier,' went on the old man; 'I have nothing, nothing left I don't know where I shall lay my head tomorrow, nor how I shall appease my hunger. You are my last resource, Chevalier; lend me the tenth part of the sum I have lost to you that I may begin my business over again, and so work my way up out of the distressed state I now am in.'

"'Whatever are you thinking about,' rejoined the Chevalier, 'whatever are you thinking about, Signor Vertua? Don't you know that a faro- banker never dare lend of his winnings? That's against the old rule, and I am not going to violate it.'

"'You are right,' went on Vertua again. 'You are right, Chevalier. My request was senseless--extravagant--the tenth part! No, lend me the twentieth part.' 'I tell you,' replied the Chevalier impatiently, 'that I won't lend a farthing of my winnings.'

"'True, true,' said Vertua, his face growing paler and paler and his gaze becoming more and more set and staring, 'true, you ought not to lend anything--I never used to do. But give some alms to a beggar--give him a hundred *Louis d'or* of the riches which blind Fortune has thrown in your hands to-day.'

"'Of a verity you know how to torment people, Signor Vertua,' burst out the Chevalier angrily. 'I tell you you won't get so much as a hundred, nor fifty, nor twenty, no, not so much as a single *Louis d'or* from me. I should be mad to make you even the smallest advance, so as to help you begin your shameful trade over again. Fate has stamped you in the dust like a poisonous reptile, and it would simply be villainy for me to aid you in recovering yourself. Go and perish as you deserve.'

"Pressing both hands over his face, Vertua sank on the floor with a muffled groan. The Chevalier ordered his servant to take the strong-box down to his carriage, and then cried in a loud voice, 'When will you hand over to me your house and effects, Signor Vertua?'

"Vertua hastily picked himself up from the ground and said in a firm voice, 'Now, at once--this moment, Chevalier; come with me.'

"'Good,' replied the Chevalier, 'you may ride with me as far as your house, which you shall leave tomorrow for good.'

"All the way neither of them spoke a single word, neither Vertua nor the Chevalier. Arrived in front of the house in the Rue St. Honoré, Vertua pulled the bell; an old woman opened the door, and on perceiving it was Vertua cried, 'Oh! good heavens, Signor Vertua, is that you at last? Angela is half dead with anxiety on your account.'

"'Silence,' replied Vertua. 'God grant she has not heard this unlucky bell! She is not to know that I have come.' And therewith he took the lighted candle out of the old woman's hand, for she appeared to be quite stunned, and lighted the Chevalier up to his own room.

"'I am prepared for the worst,' said Vertua. 'You hate, you despise me, Chevalier. You have ruined me, to your own and other people's joy; but you do not know me. Let me tell you then that I was once a gambler like you, that capricious Fortune was as favourable to me as she is to you, that I travelled through half Europe, stopping everywhere where high play and the hope of large gains enticed me, that the piles of gold continually increased in my bank as they do in yours. I had a true and beautiful wife, whom I neglected, and she was miserable in the midst of all her magnificence and wealth. It happened once, when I had set up my bank in Genoa, that a young Roman lost all his rich patrimony at my bank. He besought me to lend him money, as I did you to-day, sufficient at least to enable him to travel back to Rome. I refused with a laugh of mocking scorn, and in the insane fury of despair he thrust the stiletto which he wore right into my breast. At great pains the surgeons succeeded in saving me; but it was a wearying painful time whilst I lay on the bed of sickness. Then my wife tended me, comforted me, and kept up my courage when I was ready to sink under my sufferings; and as I grew towards recovery a feeling began to glimmer within me which I had never experienced before, and it waxed ever stronger and stronger. A gambler becomes an alien to all human emotion, and hence I had not known what was the meaning of a wife's love and faithful attachment. The debt of what I owed my wife burned itself into my ungrateful heart, and also the sense of the villainous conduct to which I had sacrificed her. All those whose life's happiness, whose entire existence, I had ruined with heartless indifference were like tormenting spirits of vengeance, and I heard their hoarse hollow voices echoing from the grave, upbraiding me with all the guilt and criminality, the seed of which I had planted in their bosoms. It was only my wife who was able to drive away the unutterable distress and horror that then came upon me. I made a vow never to touch a card more. I lived in retirement; I rent asunder all the ties which held me fast to my former mode of life; I withstood the enticements of my croupiers, when they came and said they could not do without me and my good-luck. I bought a small country villa not far from Rome, and thither, as soon as I was recovered of my illness, I fled for refuge along with my wife. Oh! only one single year did I enjoy a calmness, a happiness, a peaceful content, such as I had never dreamt of! My wife bore me a daughter, and died a few weeks later. I was in despair; I railed at Heaven and again cursed myself and my reprobate life, for which Heaven was now exacting vengeance upon me by depriving me of my wife--she who had saved me from ruin, who was the only creature who afforded me hope and consolation. I was driven away from my country villa hither to Paris, like the criminal who fears the horrors of solitude. Angela grew up the lovely image of her mother; my heart was wholly wrapt up in her; for her sake I felt called upon not so much to obtain a large fortune for her as to increase what I had already got. It is the truth that I lent money at a high rate of interest; but it is a foul calumny to accuse me of deceitful usury. And who are these my accusers? Thoughtless, frivolous people who worry me to death until I lend them money, which they immediately go and squander like a thing of no worth, and then get in a rage if I demand inexorable punctuality in repayment of the money which does not indeed belong to me,--no, but to my daughter, for I merely look upon myself as her steward. It's not long since I saved a young man from disgrace and ruin by advancing him a considerable sum. As I knew he was terribly poor, I never mentioned a syllable about repayment until I knew he had got together a rich property. Then I applied to him for settlement of his debt Would you believe it, Chevalier? the dishonourable knave, who owed all he had to me, tried to deny the debt, and on being compelled by the court to pay me, reproached me with being a villainous miser? I could tell you more such like cases; and these things have made me hard and insensible to emotion when I have to deal with folly and baseness. Nay, more--I could tell you of the many bitter tears I have wiped away, and of the many prayers which have gone up to Heaven for me and my Angela, but you would only regard it as empty boasting, and pay not the slightest heed to it, for you are a gambler. I thought I had satisfied the resentment of Heaven; it was but a delusion, for Satan has been permitted to lead me astray in a more disastrous way than before. I heard of your good- luck. Chevalier. Every day I heard that this man and that had staked and staked at your bank until he became a beggar. Then the thought came into my mind that I was destined to try my gambler's luck, which had never hitherto deserted me, against yours, that the power was given me to put a stop to your practices; and this thought, which could only have been engendered by some extraordinary madness, left me no rest, no peace. Hence I came to your bank; and my terrible infatuation did not leave me until all my property--all my Angela's property--was yours. And now the end has come. I presume you will allow my daughter to take her clothing with her?'

"'Your daughter's wardrobe does not concern me,' replied the Chevalier. 'You may also take your beds and other necessary household utensils, and such like; for what could I do with all the old lumber? But see to it that nothing of value of the things which now belong to me get mixed up with it.'

"Old Vertua stared at the Chevalier a second or two utterly speechless; then a flood of tears burst from his eyes, and he sank upon his knees in front of the Chevalier, perfectly upset with trouble and despair, and raised his hands crying, 'Chevalier, have you still a spark of human feeling left in your breast? Be merciful, merciful. It is not I, but my daughter, my Angela, my innocent angelic child, whom you are plunging into ruin. Oh! be merciful to *her*; lend *her*, *her*, my Angela, the twentieth part of the property you have deprived her of. Oh! I know you will listen to my entreaty! O Angela! my daughter!' And therewith the old man sobbed and lamented and moaned, calling upon his child by name in the most heart-rending tones.

"'I am getting tired of this absurd theatrical scene,' said the Chevalier indifferently but impatiently; but at this moment the door flew open and in burst a girl in a white night-dress, her hair dishevelled, her face pale as death,-- burst in and ran to old Vertua, raised him up, took him in her arms, and cried, 'O father! O father! I have heard all, I know all! Have you really lost everything-- everything, really? Have you not your Angela? What need have we of money and property? Will not Angela sustain you and tend you? O father, don't humiliate yourself a moment longer before this despicable monster. It is not *we*, but *he*, who is poor and miserable in the midst of his contemptible riches; for see, he stands there deserted in his awful hopeless loneliness; there is not a heart in all the wide world to cling lovingly to his breast, to open out to him when he despairs of his own life, of himself. Come, father. Leave this house with me. Come, let us make haste and be gone, that this fearful man may not exult over your trouble.'

"Vertua sank half fainting into an easy-chair. Angela knelt down before him, took his hands, kissed them, fondled them, enumerated with childish loquacity all the talents, all the accomplishments, which she was mistress of, and by the aid of which she would earn a comfortable living for her father; she besought him from the midst of burning tears to put aside all his trouble and distress, since her life would now first acquire true significance, when she had to sew, embroider, sing, and play her guitar, not for mere pleasure, but for her father's sake.

"Who, however hardened a sinner, could have remained insensible at the sight of Angela, thus radiant in her divine beauty, comforting her old father with sweet soft words, whilst the purest affection, the most childlike goodness, beamed from her eyes, evidently coming from the very depths of her heart?

"Quite otherwise was it with the Chevalier. A perfect Gehenna of torment and of the stinging of conscience was awakened within him. Angela appeared to him to be the avenging angel of God, before whose splendour the misty veil of his wicked infatuation melted away, so that he saw with horror the repulsive nakedness of his own miserable soul. Yet right through the midst of the flames of this infernal pit that was blazing in the Chevalier's heart passed a divine and pure ray, whose emanations of light were the sweetest rapture, the very bliss of heaven; but the shining of this ray only made his unutterable torments the more terrible to bear.

"The Chevalier had never been in love. The moment in which he saw Angela was the moment in which he was to experience the most ardent passion, and also at the same time the crushing pain of utter hopelessness. For no man who had appeared before the pure angel-child, lovely Angela, in the way the Chevalier had done, could dream of hope. He attempted to speak, but his tongue seemed to be numbed by cramp. At last, controlling himself with an effort, he stammered with trembling voice, 'Signor Vertua, listen to me. I have not won anything from you-- nothing at all. There is my strong box; it is yours,--nay, I must pay you yet more than there is there. I am your debtor. There, take it, take it!'

"'O my daughter!' cried Vertua. But Angela rose to her feet, approached the Chevalier, and flashed a proud look upon him, saying earnestly and composedly, *'Chevalier, allow me to tell you that there is something higher than money and goods; there are sentiments to which you are a stranger, which, whilst sustaining our souls with the comfort of Heaven, bid us reject your gift, your favour, with contempt. Keep your mammon, which is burdened with the curse that pursues you, you heartless, depraved gambler.'

"'Yes,' cried the Chevalier in a fearful voice, his eyes flashing wildly, for he was perfectly beside himself, 'yes, accursed,--accursed will I be--down into the depths of damnation may I be hurled if ever again this hand touches a card. And if you then send me from you, Angela, then it will be you who will bring irreparable ruin upon me. Oh! you don't know--you don't understand me. You can't help but call me insane; but you will feel it--you will know all, when you see me stretched at your feet with my brains scattered. Angela! It's now a question of life or death! Farewell!'

"Therewith the Chevalier rushed off in a state of perfect despair. Vertua saw through him completely; he knew what change had come over him; he endeavoured to make his lovely Angela understand that certain circumstances might arise which would make it necessary to accept the Chevalier's present Angela trembled with dread lest she should understand her father. She did not conceive how it would ever be possible to meet the Chevalier on any other terms save those of contempt. Destiny, which often ripens into shape deep down in the human heart, without the mind being aware of it, permitted that to take place which had never been thought of, never been dreamed of.

"The Chevalier was like a man suddenly wakened up out of a fearful dream; he saw himself standing on the brink of the abyss of ruin, and stretched out his arms in vain towards the bright shining figure which had appeared to him, not, however, to save him--no--but to remind him of his damnation.

"To the astonishment of all Paris, Chevalier Menars' bank disappeared from the gambling-house; nobody ever saw him again; and hence the most diverse and extraordinary rumours were current, each of them more false than the rest. The Chevalier shunned all society; his love found expression in the deepest and most unconquerable despondency. It happened, however, that old Vertua and his daughter one day suddenly crossed his path in one of the dark and lonely alleys of the garden of Malmaison.

"Angela, who thought she could never look upon the Chevalier without contempt and abhorrence, felt strangely moved on seeing him so deathly pale, terribly shaken with trouble, hardly daring in his shy respect to raise his eyes. She knew quite well that ever since that ill-omened night he had altogether relinquished gambling and effected a complete revolution in his habits of life. She, she alone had brought all this about, she had saved the Chevalier from ruin--could anything be more flattering to her woman's vanity? Hence it was that, after Vertua had exchanged the usual complimentary remarks with the Chevalier, Angela asked in a tone of gentle and sympathetic pity, 'What is the matter with you, Chevalier Menars? You are looking very ill and full of trouble. I am sure you ought to consult a physician.'

"It is easy to imagine how Angela's words fell like a comforting ray of hope upon the Chevalier's heart. From that moment he was not like the same man. He lifted up his head; he was able to speak in those tones, full of the real inward nature of the man, with which he had formerly won all hearts. Vertua exhorted him to come and take possession of the house he had won.

"'Yes, Signor Vertua,' cried the Chevalier with animation, 'yes, that I will do. I will call upon you tomorrow; but let us carefully weigh and discuss all the conditions of the transfer, even though it should last some months.'

"'Be it so then, Chevalier,' replied Vertua, smiling. 'I fancy that there will arise a good many things to be discussed, of which we at the present moment have no idea.' The Chevalier, being thus comforted at heart, could not fail to develop again all the charms of manner which had once been so peculiarly his own before he was led astray by his insane, pernicious passion for gambling. His visits at old Vertua's grew more and more frequent; Angela conceived a warmer and warmer liking for the man whose safeguarding angel she had been, until finally she thought she loved him with all her heart; and she promised him her hand, to the great joy of old Vertua, who at last felt that the settlement respecting the property he had lost to the Chevalier could now be concluded.

"One day Angela, Chevalier Menars' happy betrothed, sat at her window wrapped up in varied thoughts of the delights and happiness of love, such as young girls when betrothed are wont to dwell upon. A regiment of *chasseurs* passed by to the merry sound of the trumpet, bound for a campaign in Spain. As Angela was regarding with sympathetic interest the poor men who were doomed to death in the wicked war, a young man wheeled his horse quickly to one side and looked up at her, and she sank back in her chair fainting.

"Oh! the *chasseur* who was riding to meet a bloody death was none other than young Duvernet, their neighbour's son, with whom she had grown up, who had run in and out of the house nearly every day, and had only kept away since the Chevalier had begun to visit them.

"In the young man's glance, which was charged with reproaches having all the bitterness of death in them, Angela became conscious for the first time, not only that he loved her unspeakably, but also how boundless was the love which she herself felt for him. Hitherto she had not been conscious of it; she had been infatuated, fascinated by the glitter which gathered ever more thickly about the Chevalier. She now understood, and for the first time, the youth's labouring sighs and quiet unpretending homage; and now too she also understood her own embarrassed heart for the first time, knew what had caused the fluttering sensation in her breast when Duvernet had come, and when she had heard his voice.

"'It is too late! I have lost him!' was the voice that spoke in Angela's soul. She had courage enough to beat down the feelings of wretchedness which threatened to distract her heart; and for that reason--namely, that she possessed the courage--she succeeded.

"Nevertheless it did not escape the Chevalier's acute perception that something had happened to powerfully affect Angela; but he possessed sufficient delicacy of feeling not to seek for a solution of the mystery, which it was evident she desired to conceal from him. He contented himself with depriving any dangerous rival of his power by expediting the marriage; and he made all arrangements for its celebration with such fine tact, and such a sympathetic appreciation of his fair bride's situation and sentiments, that she saw in them a new proof of the good and amiable qualities of her husband.

"The Chevalier's behaviour towards Angela showed him attentive to her slightest wish, and exhibited that sincere esteem which springs from the purest affection; hence her memory of Duvernet soon vanished entirely from her mind. The first cloud that dimmed the bright heaven of her happiness was the illness and death of old Vertua.

"Since the night when he had lost all his fortune at the Chevalier's bank he had never touched a card, but during the last moments of his life play seemed to have taken complete possession of his soul. Whilst the priest who had come to administer to him the consolation of the Church ere he died, was speaking to him of heavenly things, he lay with his eyes closed, murmuring between his teeth, '*perd, gagne,*' whilst his trembling half-dead hands went through the motions of dealing through a *taille*, of drawing the cards. Both Angela and the Chevalier bent over him and spoke to him in the tenderest manner, but it was of no use; he no longer seemed to know them, nor even to be aware of their presence. With a deep-drawn sigh '*gagne*,' he breathed his last.

"In the midst of her distressing grief Angela could not get rid of an uncomfortable feeling of awe at the way in which the old man had died. She again saw in vivid shape the picture of that terrible night when she had first seen the Chevalier as a most hardened and reprobate gambler; and the fearful thought entered her mind that he might again, in scornful mockery of her, cast aside his mask of goodness and appear in his original fiendish character, and begin to pursue his old course of life once more.

"And only too soon was Angela's dreaded foreboding to become reality. However great the awe which fell upon the Chevalier at old Francesco Vertua's death-scene, when the old man, despising the consolation of the Church, though in the last agonies of death, had not been able to turn his thoughts from his former sinful life--however great was the awe that then fell upon the Chevalier, yet his mind was thereby led, though how he could not explain, to dwell more keenly upon play than ever before, so that every night in his dreams he sat at the faro-bank and heaped up riches anew.

"In proportion as Angela's behaviour became more constrained, in consequence of her recollection of the character in which she had first seen the Chevalier, and as it became more and more impossible for her to continue to meet him upon the old affectionate, confidential footing upon which they had hitherto lived, so exactly in the same degree distrust of Angela crept into the Chevalier's mind, since he ascribed her constraint to the secret which had once disturbed her peace of mind and which had not been revealed to him. From this distrust were born displeasure and unpleasantness, and these he expressed in various ways which hurt Angela's feelings. By a singular cross-action of spiritual influence Angela's recollections of the unhappy Duvemet began to recur to her mind with fresher force, and along with these the intolerable consciousness of her ruined love,--the loveliest blossom that had budded in her youthful heart. The strained relations between the pair continued to increase until things got to such a pitch that the Chevalier grew disgusted with his simple mode of life, thought it dull, and was smitten with a powerful longing to enjoy the life of the world again. His star of ill omen began to acquire the ascendancy. The change which had been inaugurated by displeasure and great unpleasantness was completed by an abandoned wretch who had formerly been croupier in the Chevalier's faro-bank. He succeeded by means of the most artful insinuations and conversations in making the Chevalier look upon his present walk of life as childish and ridiculous. The Chevalier could not understand at last how, for a woman's sake, he ever came to leave a world which appeared to him to contain all that made life of any worth.

"It was not long ere Chevalier Menars' rich bank was flourishing more magnificently than ever. His good-luck had not left him; victim after victim came and fell; he amassed heaps of riches. But Angela's happiness--it was ruined--ruined in fearful fashion; it was to be compared to a short fair dream. The Chevalier treated her with indifference, nay even with contempt. Often, for weeks and months together, she never saw him once; the household arrangements were placed in the hands of a steward; the servants were being constantly changed to suit the Chevalier's whims; so that Angela, a stranger in her own house, knew not where to turn for comfort. Often during her sleepless nights the Chevalier's carriage stopped before the door, the heavy strong-box was carried upstairs, the Chevalier flung out a few harsh monosyllabic words of command, and then the doors of his distant room were sent to with a bang--all this she heard, and a flood of bitter tears started from her eyes. In a state of the most heart-rending anguish she called upon Duvernet time after time, and implored Providence to put an end to her miserable life of trouble and suffering.

"One day a young man of good family, after losing all his fortune at the Chevalier s bank, sent a bullet through his brain in the gambling-house, and in the very same room even in which the bank was established, so that the players were sprinkled by the blood and scattered brains, and started up aghast. The Chevalier alone preserved his indifference; and, as all were preparing to leave the apartment, he asked whether it was in accordance with their rules and custom to leave the bank before the appointed hour on account of a fool who had had no conduct in his play.

"The occurrence created a great sensation. The most experienced and hardened gamblers were indignant at the Chevalier's unexampled behaviour. The voice of the public was raised against him. The bank was closed by the police. He was, moreover, accused of false play; and his unprecedented good-luck tended to establish the truth of the charge. He was unable to clear himself. The fine he was compelled to pay deprived him of a considerable part of his riches. He found himself disgraced and looked upon with contempt; then he went back to the arms of the wife he had ill-used, and she willingly received him, the penitent, since the remembrance of how her own father had turned aside from the demoralising life of a gambler allowed a glimmer of hope to rise, that the Chevalier's conversion might this time, now that he was older, really have some stamina in it.

"The Chevalier left Paris along with his wife, and went to Genoa, Angela's birthplace. Here he led a very retired life at first. But all endeavours to restore the footing of quiet domesticity with Angela, which his evil genius had destroyed, were in vain. It was not long before his deep-rooted discontent awoke anew and drove him out of the house in a state of uneasy, unsettled restlessness. His evil reputation had followed him from Paris to Genoa; he dare not venture to establish a bank, although he was being goaded to do so by a power he could hardly resist.

"At that time the richest bank in Genoa was kept by a French colonel, who had been invalided owing to serious wounds. His heart burning with envy and fierce hatred, the Chevalier appeared at the Colonel's table, expecting that his usual good fortune would stand by him, and that he should soon ruin his rival. The Colonel greeted him in a merry humour, such as was in general not customary with him, and said that now the play would really be worth indulging in since they had got Chevalier Menars and his good-luck to join them, for now would come the struggle which alone made the game interesting.

"And in fact during the first *taille* the cards fell favourable to the Chevalier as they always had done. But when, relying upon his invincible luck, he at last cried '*Va banquet*,' he lost a very considerable sum at one stroke.

"The Colonel, at other times preserving the same even temperament whether winning or losing, now swept the money towards him with the most demonstrative signs of extreme delight. From this moment fortune turned away from the Chevalier utterly and completely. He played every night, and every night he lost, until his property had melted away to a few thousand ducats, which he still had in securities.

"The Chevalier had spent the whole day in running about to get his securities converted into ready money, and did not reach home until late in the evening. So soon as it was fully night, he was about to leave the house with his last gold pieces in his pocket, when Angela, who suspected pretty much how matters stood, stepped in his path and threw herself at his feet, whilst a flood of tears gushed from her eyes, beseeching him by the Virgin and all the saints to abandon his wicked purpose, and not to plunge her in want and misery.

"He raised her up and strained her to his heart with painful passionate intensity, saying in a hoarse voice, 'Angela, my dear sweet Angela! It can't be helped now, indeed it must be so; I must go on with it, for I can't let it alone. But to-morrow--to-morrow all your troubles shall be over, for by the Eternal Destiny that rules over us I swear that to-day shall be the last time I will play. Quiet yourself, my dear good child--go and sleep--dream of happy days to come, of a better life that is in store for you; that will bring good-luck. Herewith he kissed his wife and hurried off before she could stop him.

"Two *tailles*, and the Chevalier had lost all--all. He stood beside the Colonel, staring upon the faro-table in moody senselessness.

"'Are you not punting any more, Chevalier?' said the Colonel, shuffling the cards for a new *taille*, 'I have lost all,' replied the Chevalier, forcing himself with an effort to be calm.

"'Have you really nothing left?' asked the Colonel at the next *taille*.

"'I am a beggar,' cried the Chevalier, his voice trembling with rage and mortification; and he continued to stare fiercely upon the table without observing that the players were gaining more and more advantages over the banker.

"The Colonel went on playing quietly. But whilst shuffling the cards for the following *taille*, he said in a low voice, without looking at the Chevalier, 'But you have a beautiful wife.'

"'What do you mean by that?' burst out the Chevalier angrily. The Colonel drew his cards without making any answer.

"'Ten thousand ducats or--Angela!' said the Colonel, half turning round whilst the cards were being cut.

"'You are mad!' exclaimed the Chevalier, who now began to observe on coming more to himself that the Colonel continually lost and lost again.

"'Twenty thousand ducats against Angela!' said the Colonel in a low voice, pausing for a moment in his shuffling of the cards.

"The Chevalier did not reply. The Colonel went on playing, and almost all the cards fell to the players' side.

"'Taken!' whispered the Chevalier in the Colonel's ear, as the new *taille* began, and he pushed the queen on the table.

"In the next draw the queen had lost. The Chevalier drew back from the table, grinding his teeth, and in despair stood leaning in a window, his face deathly pale.

"Play was over. 'Well, and what's to be done now?' were the Colonel's mocking words as he stepped up to the Chevalier.

"'Ah!' cried the Chevalier, quite beside himself, 'you have made me a beggar, but you must be insane to imagine that you could win my wife. Are we on the islands? is my wife a slave, exposed as a mere *thing* to the brutal arbitrariness of a reprobate man, that he may trade with her, gamble with her? But it is true! You would have had to pay twenty thousand ducats if the queen had won, and so I have lost all right to raise a protest if my wife is willing to leave me to follow you. Come along with me, and despair when you see how my wife will repel you with detestation when you propose to her that she shall follow you as your shameless mistress.'

"'You will be the one to despair,' replied the Colonel, with a mocking, scornful laugh; 'you will be the one to despair, Chevalier, when Angela turns with abhorrence from you--you, the abandoned sinner, who have made her life miserable--and flies into my arms in rapture and delight; you will be the one to despair when you learn that we have been united by the blessing of the Church, and that our dearest wishes are crowned with happiness. You call me insane. Ho! ho! All I wanted to win was the right to claim her, for of Angela herself I am sure. Ho! ho! Chevalier, let me inform you that your wife loves *me--me*, with unspeakable love: let me inform you that I am that Duvernet, the neighbour's son, who was brought up along with Angela, bound to her by ties of the most ardent affection--he whom you drove away by means of your diabolical devices. Ah! it was not until I had to go away to the wars that Angela became conscious to herself of what I was to her; I know all. It was too late. The Spirit of Evil suggested to me the idea that I might ruin you in play, and so I took to gambling--followed you to Genoa,--and now I have succeeded. Away now to your wife.'

"The Chevalier was almost annihilated, like one upon whose head had fallen the most disastrous blows of fortune. Now he saw to the bottom of that mysterious secret, now he saw for the first time the full extent of the misfortune which he had brought upon poor Angela. 'Angela, my wife, shall decide,' he said hoarsely, and followed the Colonel, who was hurrying off at full speed.

"On reaching the house the Colonel laid his hand upon the latch of Angela's chamber; but the Chevalier pushed him back, saying, 'My wife is asleep. Do you want to rouse her up out of her sweet sleep?'

"'Hm!' replied the Colonel. 'Has Angela ever enjoyed sweet sleep since you brought all this nameless misery upon her?' Again the Colonel attempted to enter the chamber; but the Chevalier threw himself at his feet and screamed, frantic with despair, 'Be merciful. Let me keep my wife; you have made me a beggar, but let me keep my wife.'

"'That's how old Vertua lay at your feet, you miscreant dead to all feeling, and could not move your stony heart; may Heaven's vengeance overtake you for it.' Thus spoke the Colonel; and he again strode towards Angela's chamber.

"The Chevalier sprang towards the door, tore it open, rushed to the bed in which his wife lay, and drew back the curtains, crying, 'Angela! Angela!' Bending over her, he grasped her hand; but all at once he shook and trembled in mortal anguish and cried in a thundering voice, 'Look! look! you have won my wife's corpse.'

"Perfectly horrified, the Colonel approached the bed; no sign of life!--Angela was dead--dead.

"Then the Colonel doubled his fist and shook it heavenwards, and rushed out of the room uttering a fearful cry. Nothing more was ever heard of him."

This was the end of the stranger's tale; and the Baron was so shaken that before he could say anything the stranger had hastily risen from the seat and gone away.

A few days later the stranger was found in his room suffering from apoplexy of the nerves. He never opened his mouth up to the moment of his death, which ensued after the lapse of a few hours. His papers proved that, though he called himself Baudasson simply, he was no less a person than the unhappy Chevalier Menars himself.

The Baron recognised it as a warning from Heaven, that Chevalier Menars had been led across his path to save him just as he was approaching the brink of the precipice; he vowed that he would withstand all the seductions of the gambler's deceptive luck.

Up till now he has faithfully kept his word.

MASTER JOHANNES WACHT.

At the time when people in the beautiful and pleasant town of Bamberg lived, according to the well-known saying, well,*i.e.*, under the crook, namely in the end of the previous century, there was also one inhabitant, a man belonging to the burgher class, who might be called in every respect both singular and eminent His name was Johannes Wacht, and his trade was that of a carpenter.

Nature, in weighing and definitely determining her children's destinies, pursues her own dark inscrutable path; and all that is claimed by convenience, and by the opinions and considerations which prevail in man's narrow existence, as determining factors in settling the true tendency of every man's self. Nature regards as nothing more than the pert play of deluded children imagining themselves to be wise. But short-sighted man often finds an insuperable irony in the contradiction between the conviction of his own mind and the mysterious ordering of this inscrutable Power, who first nourished and fed him at her maternal bosom and then deserted him; and this irony fills him with terror and awe, since it threatens to annihilate his own self.

The mother of Life does not choose for her favourites either the palaces of the great or the state-apartments of princes. And so she made our Johannes, who, as the kindly reader will soon learn, might be called one of her most richly endowed favourites, first see the light of the world on a wretched heap of straw, in the workshop of an impoverished master turner in Augsburg. His mother died of want and from suffering soon after the child's birth, and his father followed her after the lapse of a few months.

The town government had to take charge of the helpless boy; and when the Council's master carpenter, a well-to-do, respectable man, who found in the child's face, notwithstanding that it was pinched with hunger, certain traits which pleased him,--when he would not suffer the boy to be lodged in a public institution, but took him into his own house, in order to bring him up along with his own children, then there dawned upon Johannes his first genial ray of sunshine, heralding a happier lot in the future.

In an incredibly short space of time the boy's frame developed, so that it was difficult to believe that the little insignificant creature in the cradle had really been the shapeless colourless chrysalis out of which this pretty, living, golden-locked boy had proceeded, like a beautiful butterfly. But--what seemed of more importance--along with this pleasing grace of physical form the boy soon displayed such eminent intellectual faculties as astonished both his foster-father and his teachers. Johannes grew up in a workshop which sent forth some of the best and highest work that mechanical skill was able to produce, since the master carpenter to the Council was constantly engaged upon the most important buildings. No wonder, therefore, that the child's mind, which caught up everything with such keen clear perception, should be excited thereby, and should feel all his heart drawn towards a trade the deeper significance of which, in so far as it was concerned with the material creation of great and bold ideas, he dimly felt deep down in his soul. The joy that this bent of the orphan's mind occasioned his foster-father may well be conceived; and hence he felt persuaded to teach the boy all practical matters himself with great care and attention, and furthermore, when he had grown into a youth, to have him instructed by the cleverest masters in all the higher branches of knowledge connected with the trade, both theoretical and practical, such as, for instance, drawing, architecture, mechanics, &c.

Our Johannes was four and twenty years of age when the old master carpenter died; and even at that time his foster-son was a thoroughly experienced and skilful journeyman in all branches of his craft, whose equal could not be found far and near. At this period Johannes set out, along with his true and faithful comrade Engelbrecht, on the usual journeyman's travels.

Herewith you know, indulgent reader, all that it is needful to know about the youth of our worthy Wacht; and it only remains to tell you in a few words how it was that he came to settle in Bamberg and how he became master there.

After being on the travel for a pretty long time he happened to arrive at Bamberg on his way home along with his comrade Engelbrecht; and there they found the Bishop's palace undergoing thorough repair, and particularly on that side of it where the walls rose up to a great height out of a very narrow alley or court. Here an entirely new roof was to be put up, of very great and very heavy beams; and they wanted a machine, which, whilst taking up the least possible room, would possess sufficient concentration of power to raise the heavy weights up to the required height. The Prince-bishop's builder, who knew how to calculate to a nicety how Trajan's Column in Rome had been made to stand, and also knew the hundred or more mistakes that had been made which he should never have laid himself open to the reproach of committing, had indeed constructed a machine--a sort of crane--which was very nice to look at, and was praised by everybody as a masterpiece of mechanical skill; but when the men tried to set the thing agoing, it turned out that the Herr builder had calculated upon downright Samsons and Herculeses. The wheels creaked and squeaked horribly; the huge beams which were hooked on to the crane did not budge an inch; the men declared, whilst shaking the sweat from their brows, that they would much sooner carry ships' mainmasts up steep stairs than strain themselves in this way, and waste all their best strength in vain over such a machine; and there matters remained.

Standing at some distance, Wacht and Engelbrecht looked on at what they were doing, or rather, not doing; and it is possible that Wacht may have smiled just a little at the builder's want of knowledge.

A grey-headed old foreman, recognising the strangers' handicraft from their clothing, stepped up to them without more ado, and asked Wacht if he understood how to manage the machine any better since he looked so cunning about it. "Ah, well!" replied Wacht, without being in the least disconcerted, "ah well; it's a doubtful point whether I know better, for every fool thinks he understands everything better than anybody else; but I can't help wondering that in this part of the country you don't seem to be acquainted with a certain simple contrivance, which would easily perform all that the Herr Builder yonder is vainly tormenting his men to accomplish."

The young man's bold answer nettled the grey-haired old foreman not a little; he turned away muttering to himself; and very soon it was known to them all that a young stranger, a carpenter's journeyman, had laughed the builder together with his machine to scorn, and boasted that he was acquainted with a more serviceable contrivance. As is usually the case, nobody paid any heed to it; but the worthy builder as well as the honourable guild of carpenters in Bamberg were of opinion that the stranger had not, it was to be presumed, devoured up all the wisdom of the world, nor would he presume to dictate to and teach old and experienced masters. "Now do you see, Johannes," said Engelbrecht to his comrade, "now do you see how your rash boldness has again provoked against you the people whom we must meet as comrades of the craft?"

"Who can, who may look on quietly," replied Johannes, whilst his eyes flashed, "when the poor labourers--I'm sure they're to be pitied--are tormented so and made to work beyond all reason, and that all to no purpose. And who knows whether my rash boldness may not, after all, have beneficial consequences?" And it really turned out to be so.

One single individual, of such pre-eminent intellectual capacity that no gleam of knowledge, however fugitive it might be, ever escaped his keen penetration, attached a quite different importance to the youth's words from what the rest did, for the builder had reported them to him as the presumptuous saying of a young fledgling carpenter. This man was the Prince-bishop himself. He had the young man summoned to his presence, that he might inquire further into the import of his words, and was not a little astonished both at his appearance and at his general bearing and character. My kindly reader ought to know what this astonishment was due to, and now is the time to tell him something more about Johannes Wacht's exterior and Johannes Wacht's mind and thoughts.

As far as his face and figure were concerned, he might justly be called a remarkably handsome young fellow, and yet his noble features and majestic stature did not attain to full perfection until after he had reached a riper manhood. Æsthetic canons of the cathedral credited Johannes with having the head of an old Roman; a younger member of the same fraternity, who even in the severest winter was in the habit of going about dressed in black silk, and who had read Schiller's *Fiesko*, maintained, on the contrary, that Johannes Wacht was Verrina in the flesh.

But the mysterious charm by means of which many highly-gifted men are enabled to win at once the confidence of those whom they approach does not consist in beauty and grace of external form alone. We in a certain sense feel their superiority; yet this feeling is by no means an oppressive feeling as might be imagined; but, whilst elevating the spirit, it also excites a certain kind of mental comfort that does us an incalculable amount of good. All the factors of the physical and intellectual organism are united into a whole by the most perfect harmony, so that the contact with the superior soul is like a pure strain of music; it suffers no discord. This harmony creates that inimitable deportment, that--one might almost say--comfort in the slightest movements, through which the consciousness of true human dignity is proclaimed. This deportment can be taught by no dancing-master, by no Prince's tutor; and well and rightly does it deserve its proper name of the distinguished deportment, since it is stamped as such by Nature herself. Here need only be added that Master Wacht, unflinchingly constant in generosity, truth, and faithfulness to his burgher standing, became as the years went on ever more a man of the people. He developed all the virtues, but at the same time all the unconquerable prejudices, which are generally wont to form the unfavourable sides of such men's characters. My kindly reader will soon learn of what these prejudices consisted.

I have now perhaps sufficiently explained why it was that the young man's appearance made such an uncommon impression upon the respected Prince-bishop. For a long time he observed the stalwart young workman in silence, but with visible satisfaction; then he questioned him about his previous life. Johannes answered all his questions candidly and modestly, and finally explained to the Prince with convincing clearness, that the master-builder's machine, though perhaps fitted for other purposes, would in the present case never effect what it was intended to do.

In reply to the Prince's inquiry whether he could indeed trust himself to specify a machine that would be more suitable for the purpose, namely, to raise the heavy weights, the young man replied that all he required to construct such a machine was a single day, and the help of his comrade Engelbrecht and a few skilful and willing labourers.

It may be conceived with what malicious and mischievous inward joy, and with what impatience the master-builder, and all who were connected with him, looked forward to the morrow, when the forward stranger would be sent off home covered with shame and ridicule. But things turned out different from what these good-hearted people had expected, or indeed had wished.

Three capsterns suitably situated and so arranged as to exert an effect one upon another, and each only manned by eight labourers, elevated the heavy beams up to the giddy level of the roof with so much ease that they appeared to dance in the air. From this moment the brave clever craftsman could date the foundation of his reputation in Bamberg. The Prince urged him seriously to stay in that town and secure his mastership; towards the attainment of this end he would lend him all the assistance he possibly could. Wacht, however, hesitated, notwithstanding that he was very well pleased with the pleasant and cheap town of Bamberg. The fact that several important buildings were just then in course of erection put a heavy weight into the scale for staying; but the final turn to the balance was given by a circumstance which is very often wont to decide matters in life; namely, Johannes Wacht found again quite unexpectedly in Bamberg the beautiful virtuous maiden whom he had seen several years previously in Erlangen, and into whose friendly blue eyes he had then peeped a little too much. In a few words, Johannes Wacht became master, married the virtuous maiden of Erlangen, and soon contrived through industry and skill to purchase a pretty house on the Kaulberg, which had a large tract of garden ground stretching away back up the hill, and there he settled down for life.

But upon whom does the friendly star of good fortune shine unchangeably with the same degree of splendour at all times? Providence had decreed that our honest Johannes should be submitted to a trial under which perhaps any other man, with less firmness of spirit, would have sunk. The first fruit of this very happy marriage was a son, an excellent youth, who appeared to be walking steadfastly in his father's footsteps. He was eighteen years of age when one night a large fire broke out not far from Wacht's house. Father and son hurried to the spot, agreeably to their calling, to help in extinguishing the flames. Along with other carpenters the son boldly clambered up to the roof in order to cut away its burning framework, as far as could be done. His father, who had remained below, as he always did, to direct the demolition of walls, &c., and to superintend the work of extinction, looked up and seeing the imminent danger shouted, "Johannes! men! come down! come down!" Too late—with a fearful crash the wall fell in; the son lay struck to death in the flames, which leapt up crackling louder as if in horrid triumph.

But this terrible blow was not the only one which was to fall upon poor Johannes. An inconsiderate maid-servant burst with a frantic cry of distress into her mistress' room, who was only partly convalescent from a distracting nervous disorder, and was in great uneasiness and anxiety about the fire, the dark-red reflection of which was flickering on the walls of her chamber. "Your son, your Johannes, is killed; the wall has buried him and his comrades in the middle of the flames," screamed the girl. As though stung with sharp, sudden pain, her mistress raised herself up in the bed; but breathing out a deep sigh, she sank back upon the cushions again. She was struck with paralysis of the nerves; she was dead.

"Now let us see," said the citizens, "how Master Wacht will bear his great trouble. He has often enough preached to us that a man ought not to succumb to the greatest misfortune, but ought to bear his head erect and strive with the strength which the Creator has planted in every man's breast to withstand the misery that threatens him, so long as the contrary is not evidently decreed in the Eternal counsels. Let us see now what sort of an example he will give us."

They were not a little astonished when, although the master himself was not seen in the workshop, yet his journeymen's activity continued without interruption, so that work never stood still for a single moment, but went on just as if the master had not experienced any trouble.

With steadfast courage and firm step, and with his face shining with all the consolation and all the hope that sprang from his belief—the true religion rooted deep down in his breast—he had followed the corpses of his wife and son; and on the noon of the same day after the funeral, which had taken place in the morning, he said to Engelbrecht, "Engelbrecht, it is now necessary for me to be alone with my grief, which is almost breaking my heart, in order that I may become acquainted with it and strengthen myself against it. You, brother, my honest, industrious foreman, will know what to do for a week; for that space I am going to shut myself up in my own chamber."

And indeed for a whole week Master Wacht never left his room. The maid frequently brought down his food again untouched; and they often heard in the passage his low, sad cry, cutting them to the quick, "O my wife! O my Johannes!"

Many of Wacht's acquaintances were of opinion that he ought not by any means to be left in this solitary state; by brooding constantly over his grief his mind might become unsettled Engelbrecht, however, met them with the reply, "Let him alone; you don't know my Johannes. Since Providence, in its inscrutable purposes, has sent him this hard trial, it has also given him strength to overcome it, and all earthly consolation would only outrage his feelings. I know in what manner he is working his way out of his deep grief." These last words Engelbrecht uttered with a well-nigh cunning look upon his face; but he would not give any further information as to what he meant. Wacht's acquaintances had to content themselves, and leave the unfortunate man in peace.

A week was passed, and early the next morning, which was a bright summer morning, at five o'clock Master Wacht came out unexpectedly into the workyard amongst his journeymen, who were all hard at work. Their axes and saws stopped, whilst they greeted him with a half-sorrowful cry, "Master Wacht! Our good Master Wacht!"

With a cheerful face, upon which the traces of the struggle against grief which he had gone through had deepened the expression of sterling good-nature and given it a most touching character, he stepped amongst his faithful workpeople and told them how the goodness of Heaven had sent down the spirit of mercy and consolation upon him, and that he was now filled with strength and courage to go on and discharge the duties of his calling. He betook himself to the building in the middle of the yard, which served for the storage of the tools at night, and for keeping the plans and memoranda of work, &c. Englebrecht, the journeymen, the apprentices, followed him in a string. On entering, Johannes stood rooted to the spot.

His poor boy's axe, which was identified by certain distinctive marks, had been found with half-charred handle under the ruins of the house that had been burnt down. His companions had fastened it high up on the wall directly opposite the door, and, in a rather rude attempt at art, had painted round it a wreath of roses and cypress-branches; and underneath the wreath they had placed their beloved comrade's name, together with the year of his birth and the date of the ill-omened night when he had met such a violent death.

"Poor Hans!" exclaimed Master Wacht on perceiving this touching monument of the true faithful spirits, whilst a flood of tears gushed from his eyes. "Poor Hans! the last time you wielded that tool was for the welfare of your brothers; but now you are resting in your grave, and will never more stand by my side and use your earnest industry in helping to forward a good piece of work."

Then Master Wacht went round the circle and gave each journeyman and each apprentice a good honest shake of the hand, saying, "Think of him." Then they all went back to their work, except Engelbrecht, whom Wacht bid stay with him.

"See here, my old comrade," cried Wacht, "what extraordinary means the Eternal Power has chosen to help me to overcome my great trouble. During the days when I was almost heart-broken with grief for my wife and child, whom I have lost in such a terrible way, there came into my mind the idea of a highly artistic and complicated trussed girder, which I had been thinking about for a long time without ever being able to see my way to the thing clearly. Look here."

Therewith Master Wacht unrolled the drawing at which he had worked during the past week, and Engelbrecht was greatly astonished at the boldness and originality of the invention no less than at its exceptional neatness in the finished state. The mechanical part of the contrivance was so skilfully and cleverly arranged that even Engelbrecht, with all his great experience, could not comprehend it at once; but the greater therefore was his glad admiration when Master Wacht explained to him the whole construction down to the minutest details, and he had convinced himself that the putting of the plan into execution could not fail to be successful.

At this time Wacht's household consisted of only two daughters besides himself; but it was very soon to be increased.

Albeit a clever and industrious workman, Master Engelbrecht had never been able to advance so far as that lowest grade of affluence which had been the reward of Wacht's very earliest undertakings. He had to contend with the worst enemy of life, against which no human power is of any avail; it not only threatened to destroy him, but really did destroy him--namely, consumption. He died, leaving a wife and two boys almost in want. His wife went back to her own home; and Master Wacht would willingly have taken both boys into his own house, but this could only be arranged in the case of the elder, who was called Sebastian. He was a strong intelligent lad, and having an inclination to follow his father's trade, promised to make a good clever carpenter. He had, however, a certain refractoriness of disposition, which at times seemed to border closely upon badness, as well as being somewhat rude in his manners, and even often wild and untamable; but these ill qualities Wacht hoped to conquer by wise training. The younger boy, Jonathan by name, was exactly the opposite of his elder brother; he was a very pretty little boy, but rather fragile, his blue eyes laughing with gentleness and kind-heartedness. This boy had been adopted during his father's lifetime by Herr Theophilus Eichheimer, a worthy doctor of law, as well as the first and oldest advocate in the place. Noticing the boy's remarkably good parts, as well as his most decided bent for knowledge, he had taken him to train him for a lawyer.

And here one of those unconquerable prejudices of our Wacht came to light which have been already spoken of above, namely, he was perfectly convinced in his own mind that everything understood under the name of law was nothing else but so many phrases artificially hammered out and put together by lawyers, with the sole purpose of perplexing the true feeling of right which had been planted in every virtuous man's breast. Since he could not exactly shut his eyes to the necessity for law-courts, he discharged all his hatred upon the advocates, whom as a class he conceived to be, if not altogether miserable deceivers, yet at any rate such contemptible men that they practised usury in shameful fashion with all that was most holy and venerable in the world. It will be seen presently how Wacht, who in all other relations of life was an intelligent and clear-sighted man, resembled in this particular the coarsest-minded amongst the lowest of the people. The further prejudice that he would not admit there was any piety or virtue amongst the adherents of the Roman Catholic Church, and that he trusted no Catholic, might perhaps be pardoned him, since he had imbibed the principles of a well-nigh fanatical Protestantism in Augsburg. It may be conceived, therefore, how it cut Master Wacht to the heart to see the son of his most faithful friend entering upon a career that he so bitterly detested.

The will of the deceased, however, was in his eyes sacred; and it was, moreover, at any rate certain that Jonathan with his weakly body could not be trained up to any handicraft that made any very large demand upon physical strength. Besides, when old Herr Theophilus Eichheimer talked to the master about the divine gift of knowledge, at the same time praising little Jonathan as a good intelligent boy, Wacht for the moment forgot the advocate, and law, and his own prejudice as well. He fastened all his hopes upon the belief that Jonathan, who bore his father's virtues in his heart, would give up his profession when he arrived at riper years, and was able to perceive all the disgrace that attached to it.

Though Jonathan was a good, quiet boy, fond of studying in-doors, Sebastian was all the oftener and all the deeper engaged in all kinds of wild foolish pranks. But since in respect to his handiwork he followed in his father's footsteps, and no fault could ever be found with his industry or with the neatness of his work, Master Wacht ascribed his at times too outrageous tricks to the unrefined untamed fire of youth, and he forgave the young fellow, observing that he would be sure to sow his wild oats when on his travels.

These travels Sebastian soon set out upon; and Master Wacht heard nothing more from him until Sebastian, on attaining his majority, wrote from Vienna, begging for his little patrimonial inheritance, which Master Wacht sent to him correct to the last farthing, receiving in return a receipt for it drawn up by one of the Vienna courts.

Just the same sort of difference in character as distinguished the Engelbrechts was noticeable also between Wacht's two daughters, of whom the elder was called Rettel and the younger Nanni.

It may here be hastily remarked in passing, that, according to the taste generally prevalent in Bamberg, the Christian name Nanni is the prettiest and finest a girl can well have. And so, kindly reader, if you ever ask a pretty child in Bamberg, "What is your name, my little angel?" the little thing will be sure to cast down her eyes in shy confusion and tug at her black silk apron, and whisper in friendly fashion with a slight blush upon her cheeks, "'N! 'N! Nanni, y'r honour."

Rettel, Wacht's elder daughter, was a fat little thing, with red rosy cheeks and right friendly black eyes, with which she looked boldly into the face of the sunshine of life, as it had dawned upon her, without blinking. In respect of her education and her character she had not risen a hair's breadth above the sphere of the handicraftsman. She gossiped with her female relatives and friends, and liked dressing herself, though in gay colours and without taste; but her own peculiar element, wherein she "lived and moved, and had her being," was the kitchen. Nobody's hare-ragout and geese giblets, not even those of the most experienced cook far and near, ever turned out so tasty as hers; in the preparation of sauces she was a perfect adept; vegetables, such as savoy and cauliflower, were dressed by Rettel's cunning hand in a way that could not be beaten, since she knew in a moment through a subtle unfailing instinct when there was too much or too little dripping; and her short cakes put in the shade the most successful productions of a similar kind at the most sumptuous of church feasts.

Father Wacht was very well satisfied with his daughter's cooking; and he once hazarded the opinion that the Prince-bishop could not have more delicious vermicelli noodles on his table than those which Rettel made. This remark sank so deeply into the good girl's pleased heart, that she was preparing to send a huge dish of the said vermicelli noodles up to the Prince-bishop, and that too on a fast day. Fortunately Master Wacht got scent of the plan in time, and amidst hearty laughter prevented the bold idea from being put into execution.

Not only was stout little Rettel a clever housekeeper, a perfect cook, and at the same time a pattern of good nature and childish affection and fidelity, but like a well-trained child she also loved her father very tenderly.

Now characters of Wacht's class, in spite of their earnestness, often display a certain ironical waggishness which comes into play on easy provocation, and lends an agreeable charm to life, just as the deep brook greets with its silver curling waves the light breeze that skims its surface.

It could not fail but that good Rettel's ways and doings frequently provoked this sly humour; and so the relations between Wacht and his daughter were invested with a curiously modified charm of colour. The indulgent reader will come across instances later on; for the present it may suffice to mention one such here, which certainly deserves to be called entertaining. In Master Wacht's house there was a quiet, good-looking young man, who held a post in the Prince's exchequer office and drew a very good income. In straightforward German fashion he sued the father for the hand of his elder daughter, and Master Wacht, if he would not do an injustice to the young man as well as to his Rettel, could not help but grant him permission to visit the house, that he might have opportunities to try and win the girl's affections. Rettel, informed of the man's purpose, received him with very friendly looks, in which might be read at times, "At our wedding, dear, I shall bake the cake myself."

Master Wacht, however, was not altogether well pleased with his daughter's growing liking for the Herr Administrator of the Prince's revenues, since the Herr Administrator himself didn't seem to him to be all that he should be. In the first place, the man was as a matter of course a Roman Catholic, and in the second place Wacht thought he perceived in him on nearer acquaintance a certain sneaking dissimulation of manner, which pointed to a mind ill at ease. He would willingly have got the undesirable suitor out of the house again if he could have done so without hurting Rettel's feelings. Master Wacht observed him closely, and knew how to make shrewd and cunning use of his observations. He perceived that the Herr Administrator did not set much store by well-cooked dishes, but swallowed down everything in the same indiscriminate fashion, and that, moreover, in a disagreeably repulsive way. One Sunday, when the Herr Administrator was dining at Master Wacht's, as he usually did on that day, the latter began to heap up praises and commendations upon every dish which busy Rettel caused to be served up; and not only did he call upon the Herr Administrator to join him in his encomiums, but he also asked him pointedly what he thought of various ways of dressing dishes. The Herr Administrator replied somewhat dryly that he was a temperate and abstemious man, accustomed from his youth up to the greatest frugality. At noon, for dinner, he was satisfied with a spoonful or two of soup and a little piece of beef, but the latter must be cooked hard, since so cooked a smaller quantity sufficed to satisfy the hunger, and there was no need to overload the stomach with large pieces. For his evening meal he generally managed upon a saucer of good egg and butter beaten up together and a very small glass of liquor; moreover, the only other refreshment he allowed himself was a glass of extra beer at six o'clock in the evening, taken if possible in the good fresh air. It may be imagined what looks Rettelchen fixed upon the unfortunate administrator. And yet the worst was still to come. Bavarian puffy noodles were next served, and they were swollen up to such a big, big size that they seemed to be the masterpiece of the table. The frugal Herr Administrator took his knife and with the most cool-blooded indifference cut the noodle which was passed to him into many pieces. Rettel rushed out of the room with a loud cry of despair.

I must inform the reader who does not know the secret of eating Bavarian puffy noodles that when eaten they must be cleverly pulled to pieces, since when cut they lose all taste and bring disgrace upon the professional pride of the cook who made them.

From that moment Rettel looked upon the frugal Herr Administrator as the most abominable man under the face of the sun. Master Wacht did not contradict her in any way; and so the reckless iconoclast in the province of cookery lost his bride for ever.

Though the chequered figure of little Rettel has cost almost too many words, yet a very few strokes will suffice to put clearly before my reader's eyes the face, figure, and character of pretty, graceful Nanni.

It is only in South Germany, particularly in Franconia, and almost exclusively in the burgher classes, that you can meet with such elegant and delicate figures, such good and pleasing angelic little faces, where there is a sweet heavenly yearning in the blue eyes and a divine smile upon the rosy lips, as Nanni's; from them we at once see that the old painters had not far to seek the originals of their Madonnas. Of exactly the same type in figure, face, and character was the Erlangen maiden whom Master Wacht had married; and Nanni was a most faithful copy of her mother. With respect to her genuine tender womanliness and with respect to that beneficial culture which is nothing but true tact under all conditions of life, her mother was the exact counterpart of what Master Wacht was with respect to his distinguishing qualities as man. Perhaps the daughter was less serious and firm than her mother, but on the other hand she was the perfection of maidenly sweetness; and the only fault that could be found with her was that her womanly tenderness of feeling and a sensitiveness which, as a consequence of her weakened organisation, was easily provoked to a tearful and unhealthy degree, made her too delicate and fragile for the realities of life.

Master Wacht could not look at the dear child without emotion, and he loved her in a way that is seldom found in the case of strong characters like his. It is possible that he may have always spoiled her a little; and it will soon be shown in what way her tenderness so often received that special material and encouragement which made it often degenerate into sickly sentimentality.

Nanni loved to dress with extreme simplicity, but in the finest stuffs and according to cuts which rose above the limits of her station in life. Wacht, however, let her do as she liked, since when dressed according to her own taste the dear child looked so very pretty and engaging.

I must now hasten to destroy an idea which perhaps might arise in the mind of any reader who should happen to have been in Bamberg several years ago, and so would call to mind the hideous and tasteless head-dress with which at that time even the prettiest maidens were wont to disfigure their faces--the flat hood fitting close to the head and not allowing the smallest little lock of hair to be seen, a black and not over-broad ribbon crossing close over the forehead, and meeting behind low down on the neck in an outrageously ugly bow. This ribbon afterwards continued to increase in width until it reached the preposterous breadth of nearly half an ell; hence it had to be specially ordered in the manufactory and strengthened inside with stiff card-board, so that it projected above the head like a steeple-hat; just above the hollow of the neck they wore a bow, which owing to its breadth stuck out far beyond the shoulders, and resembled the outspread wings of an eagle; and along the temples and about the ears tiny curls crept out from beneath the hood. And strange to say, many a fine Bamberg beauty looked quite charming in this head-covering.

It formed a very picturesque sight to stand behind a funeral procession and watch it set itself in motion. It is the custom in Bamberg for the burghers to be invited to attend the funeral procession of a deceased person by the so-called "death-woman," who in a croaking voice and in the name of the deceased screams out her invitation in the street, in front of the house of the persons she is inviting; as, for instance, "Herr so-and-so, or Frau so-and-so, beg you to pay them the last honours." The good gossips and the young maidens, who in general seldom get out into the open air, fail not to put in an appearance in great numbers; and when the troop of women sets itself in motion and the wind catches the immense ends of the bows, it can be likened to nothing else but a huge flock of black ravens or eagles suddenly startled and just beginning their rustling flight.

The indulgent reader is therefore requested not to picture pretty Nanni in any other head-dress except a neat little Erlangen hood.

However objectionable it was to Master Wacht that Jonathan was to belong to a class which he hated, he did not by any means make the boy, or later the youth, feel the consequences of his displeasure. Rather he was always very pleased to see the good quiet Jonathan look in after his day's work was done, to spend the evening with his daughters and old Barbara. But then Jonathan also wrote the finest hand that could be seen anywhere; and it afforded Master Wacht no little joy, for he was uncommonly fond of good handwriting, when his Nanni, whose writing-master Jonathan had installed himself to be, began gradually after a time to write the same elegant hand as her master.

In the evening Master Wacht himself was either busy in his own work-room, or, as was often the case, he visited a beer-house, where he met with his fellow-craftsmen and the gentlemen of the council, and in his way enlivened the company with his own rare wit. Meanwhile in the house at home Barbara busily kept her distaff on the whirl and whizz, whilst Rettel balanced the house-keeping accounts, or thought out the preparation of new and hitherto unheard-of dishes, or related again to the old woman, mingled with a good deal of loud laughter, what she had learned in confidence from her various gossips in the town.

And the youth Jonathan? He sat at the table with Nanni; and she also wrote and drew, of course under his guidance. And yet to sit writing and drawing the whole evening through is a downright tiring piece of business; hence it was no unfrequent occurrence for Jonathan to draw some neatly-bound book out of his pocket and read it to pretty, sensitive Nanni in a low softly-whispering tone.

Through old Eichheimer's influence Jonathan had won the patronage of the minor canon, who designated Master Wacht a real Verrina. The canon, Count von Kösel, a man of genius, lived and revelled in Goethe's and Schiller's works, which were just at that time beginning to rise like bright streaming meteors, overtopping all others, above the horizon of the literary sky. He thought, and rightly, that he discerned a similar tendency in his attorney's young clerk, and took a special delight not only in lending him the works in question, but in reading them in common with him, and so helping him to thoroughly digest them.

But Jonathan won his way to the Count's heart in an especial way, because he expressed a very favourable opinion of the verses which the Count patched together out of high-sounding phrases in the sweat of his own brow, and because he was, to the Count's unspeakable satisfaction, edified and touched by them to the proper pitch. Nevertheless it is a fact that Jonathan's taste in æsthetic matters was really greatly improved by his intercourse with the intellectual, though somewhat euphuistic, Count.

My kind reader now knows what class of books Jonathan used to take out of his pocket and read to pretty Nanni, and can form a just conception of the way in which this kind of writings would inevitably excite a girl mentally organised as Nanni was. "O star of the gloaming eve!" Would not Nanni's tears flow when her attractive writing-master began in this low and solemn fashion?

It is a fact of common experience that young people who are in the habit of singing tender love-duets together very easily put themselves in the places of the fictitious characters of the song, and come to look upon the duets in question as giving both the melody and the text for the whole of life; so also the youth who reads a love romance to a maiden very readily becomes the hero of the story, whilst the girl dreams herself into the role of the heroine. In the case of such fitly adapted spirits as Jonathan and Nanni such incitement as this even was not required to provoke them to love each other. They were one heart and one soul; the maiden and the youth were, so to speak, but one brightly burning flame of love, pure and inextinguishable. Of his daughter's tender passion Father Wacht had not the slightest inkling; but he was soon to learn all.

Through unwearied industry and genuine talent Jonathan succeeded in a brief space of time in completing his legal studies and qualifying for admission to the grade of advocate; and, as a matter of fact, his admission soon followed. He intended one Sunday to surprise Master Wacht with this glad news, which established him upon a secure footing for life. But imagine how he trembled with dismay when Wacht bent his eyes upon him, blazing with anger; he had never seen him look so passionately wrathful. "What!" cried Wacht, in a tone that made the walls ring again, "what! you miserable good-for-nothing fellow! Nature has neglected your body, but richly endowed you with splendid intellectual gifts, and these you are intending to abuse in a shameless way, like a bad crafty knave, and so putting your knife at your own mother's throat? You mean to say you are going to traffic in justice as in some cheap paltry ware in the public market, and weigh it out with false scales to the poor peasants and the oppressed burgher, who in vain utter their plaintive cries before the soft-cushioned seat of the inexorable judge, and going to get yourself paid with blood-stained pence which the poor man hands to you whilst bathed in tears? Will you fill your brains with lying laws of man's contriving, and practise knavish tricks and schemes, and make a lucrative business of it to fatten yourself upon? Is all your father's virtue, tell me, vanished from your heart? Your father--your name is Engelbrecht--no! when I hear you called so I will not believe that it is the name of my comrade, who was a pattern of virtue and honesty, but I must believe that it is Satan, who in the apish mockery of Hell is shouting the name across his grave, and so beguiling men to take the young lying lawyer's cub for the real son of that excellent carpenter Gottfried Engelbrecht. Begone! you are no longer my foster-son! You are a serpent whom I will pluck from my bosom, whom I will disown"----

At this point Nanni rushed in and threw herself at Master Wacht's feet with a piercing heart-rending cry of distress. "Father!" she cried, completely overcome by her incontrollable anguish and unbridled despair, "father, if you disown him, you will disown me also--me, your own favourite daughter; he is mine, my Jonathan; I can never, never part with him in this world."

The poor child fell down in a swoon and struck her head against the closet-door, so that the drops of blood trickled down her delicate white forehead. Barbara and Rettel ran in and carried the insensible girl to the sofa. Jonathan stood like a statue, as if thunderstruck, incapable of the slightest movement. It would be difficult to describe the inner emotions which revealed themselves on Wacht's countenance. His face, instead of being flushed with the redness of anger, was now pale as a corpse's; there only remained a dark fire gleaming in his fixed set eyes; the cold perspiration of death appeared to be standing on his forehead. After gazing unchangeably before him for some minutes without speaking, he relieved his labouring breast by saying in a significant tone, "So that was it!" then he strode slowly towards the door, where he again stood still, and turning half round towards the women, cried, "Dont' spare *eau de Cologne*, and this foolery will soon be over."

Shortly afterwards the Master was seen to leave the house at a quick pace and bend his steps towards the hills. It may be conceived in what great trouble and distress the family was plunged. Rettel and Barbara could not for the life of them imagine what terrible thing had happened; but when the Master did not return to dinner, but stayed out till late at night--a thing he had never done before--they were greatly agitated with anxiety and fear. At length they heard him coming, heard him open the street-door, bang it violently to, ascend the stairs with strong firm footsteps, and lock himself in his own chamber.

Poor Nanni soon recovered herself again and wept quietly to herself. But Jonathan did not stop short of wild outbreaks of inconsolable despair, and several times spoke of shooting himself. It is a fortunate thing that pistols are articles which do not necessarily belong to the furniture of sentimental young lawyers; or at least, if they are to be found amongst their effects, they generally have no lock or else won't go off.

After he had run through certain streets like a madman, Jonathan's course led him instinctively to his noble patron, to whom he lamented all his unheard-of misery in outbreaks of the most violent passion. It need hardly be added, it is so self-evident a thing, that the young love-smitten advocate was, according to his own desperate assertions, the first and only individual in all the wide world whom such a terrible fate had befallen, wherefore he reproached destiny and all the powers of enmity as having conspired together against him.

The canon listened to him calmly and with a certain share of interest; but nevertheless he did not appear to appreciate the full extent of the trouble which the young lawyer imagined he felt "My dear young friend," said the canon, taking the advocate by the hand in a friendly way, and leading him to a seat, "my dear young friend, hitherto I have looked upon our carpenter Herr Johannes Wacht as a great man in his way, but I now perceive that he is also a very great fool. Great fools are like jibbing horses; it's hard to make them move; but once they have been got to move, they trot merrily along the way they are wanted to go. In spite of the old man's senseless anger you ought not by any means to give up your beautiful Nanni in consequence of the unpleasant scene of today. But before proceeding to talk further about your love-affair, which is indeed very charming and romantic, let us turn to and discuss a little breakfast. It was noon when you went to old Wacht, and I don't dine until four o'clock in Seehof."

A very appetising breakfast indeed was served up on the little table at which they both sat--the canon and the advocate--Bayonne hams, garnished round about with slices of Portuguese onions, a cold larded partridge of the red kind and a foreigner to boot, truffles cooked in red wine, a dish of Strasburg *pâtés de foie gras*, finally a plate of genuine Strachinoand another with butter, as yellow and shining as lilies of the valley.

The indulgent reader who loves such dainty butter, and ever goes to Bamberg, will be pleased at getting there the finest and best, but will also at the same time be annoyed when he learns that the inhabitants, from mistaken notions of housekeeping, melt it down to a grease, which generally tastes rancid and spoils all the food.

Besides, good dry champagne was sending up its pearly sparkles in a beautifully-cut crystal decanter. The canon had not unloosed the napkin from his neck, but had let it stay where it was when he had received the young lawyer; and, after the footman had quickly supplied a second cover, he proceeded to place the choicest morsels before the despairing lover and to pour out wine for him; and then he set to work heartily himself. Some one once had the hardihood to maintain that the stomach is equivalent to all the other physical and intellectual parts of man put together. That is a profane and abominable doctrine; but this much is certain, that the stomach is like a despotic tyrant or ironical mystifier, and often carries through its own will. And this was the case in the present instance. For instinctively, without being clearly conscious of what he was about, the young lawyer had in a few minutes devoured a huge piece of Bayonne ham, created terrible devastation amongst the Portuguese garniture, put out of sight half a partridge, no inconsiderable quantity of trufles, and also more Strasburg *pâtés* than was exactly becoming in a young advocate full of trouble. Moreover, they both relished the champagne so much that the footman soon had to fill up the crystal decanter a second time.

The advocate felt a pleasant and beneficial degree of warmth penetrate his vitals, and all he experienced of his trouble was a singular sort of shiver, which exactly resembled electric shocks, causing pain but doing good. He proved himself susceptible to the consolations of his patron, who, after comfortably sipping up his last glass of wine and elegantly wiping his mouth, settled himself into position and began as follows:--

"In the first place, my dear good friend, you must not be so foolish as to imagine that you are the only man on earth to whom a father has refused the hand of his daughter. But that's nothing to do with the present case. As I have already told you, the old fool's reason for hating you is so preposterously absurd that it cannot last long; and whether it appear to you at this moment nonsensical or not, I can hardly bear the thought of all ending in a tame commonplace wedding, so that the whole thing may be summed up in the few words,--Peter has wooed Grete, and Peter and Grete are man and wife.

"The situation is, however, so far new and grand in that it is merely hatred against a class to which the beloved foster-son belongs that can furnish the sole lever for setting a new and special tragic development in motion; but to the real matter at issue! You are a poet, my friend, and that alters everything. Your love, your trouble, ought to appear in your eyes as something magnificent, in the full splendours of the sacred art of poesy. You will hear the strains of the lyre struck by the muse who is nearest akin to you, and in the divine gush of inspiration you will receive the winged words in which to express your love and your unhappiness. As a poet you might be called at this moment the happiest man on the earth, since, your heart having been really wounded as deep as it can be wounded, your heart's blood is now gushing out. You require, therefore, no artificial incitement to allure you to a poetic mood; and mark my words, this period of trouble will enable you to produce something great and admirable.

"I must draw your attention to the fact that in these first moments of your unhappiness there will be mingled with it a peculiar and very unpleasant feeling which cannot be woven into any poetry; but it is a feeling which soon vanishes away. Let me make you understand. For example, after the unfortunate lover has had a good sound drubbing from the enraged father, and has been kicked out of the house, and the outraged mamma has locked the young lady in her chamber, and repelled the attempted storming on the part of the desperate lover by the armed domestics of the house, and when plebeian fists have even entertained no shyness of the very finest cloth" (here the canon sighed somewhat), "then this fermented prose of miserable vulgarity must evaporate in order that the pure poetic unhappiness of love may settle as sediment You have been fearfully scolded, my dear young friend, this was the bitter prose that had to be surmounted; you have surmounted it, and so now give yourself up entirely to poetry. Here--here are Petrarch's *Sonnets* and Ovid's *Elegies*; take them, read them, write yourself, and come and read to me what you have written. Perhaps in the meantime I also may experience a disappointment in love, of which I am not altogether deprived of hopes, since I shall in all likelihood fall in love with a stranger lady who has stopped at the 'White Lamb' in the Steinweg, and whom Count Nesselstädt maintains to be a paragon of beauty and grace, albeit he has only caught a fugitive glimpse of her at the window. Then, my friend, like the Dioscuri, we will travel the same bright path of poetry and disappointed love. Note, my good fellow, what a great advantage my station in life gives me, for every affection which I conceive, being a longing and hoping which can never be gratified, rises to tragic intensity. But now, my friend, out, out, away into the woods as you ought to."

It would doubtless be very wearisome to my kind reader, if not unbearable, were I to describe here at length, in detail and with all sorts of over-choice and exquisite words and phrases, all that Jonathan and Nanni did in their trouble. Such things may be found in any indifferent romance; and it is often amusing enough to see into what postures the struggling author throws himself, merely in order to appear original. On the other hand, it seems to be of great importance to follow Master Wacht on his walks, or rather in his mental journeyings.

It must appear very remarkable that a man of such strong self-reliant spirit as Master Wacht, who had borne with unshaken courage and unbending steadfastness the most terrible misfortunes that had befallen him, and that would have crushed many less stouthearted spirits, could be thus put beside himself with passion at an occurrence which any other father of a family would have regarded as an ordinary event and one easy to remedy, and would in fact have set about remedying it in some way or other, good or bad. Of course the indulgent reader is well aware that this behaviour of Wacht's must be traced to some good psychological reason. The thought that poor Nanni's love for innocent Jonathan was a misfortune which would exercise a pernicious influence upon the whole course of his subsequent life was only due to the perverse discord in Wacht's soul. But the very fact that this discord was able to go on making itself heard in the otherwise harmonical character of this thoroughly noble man, embraced the impossibility of smothering it or reducing it completely to silence.

Wacht had made his acquaintance with the feminine character in one who possessed it in a simple but also at the same time grand and noble form. His own wife had enabled him to see into the depths of the real woman's nature, as in a bright mirror-like lake. He saw in her the true heroine who fought with weapons that were constantly unconquerable. His orphan wife had forfeited the inheritance of an immensely rich aunt, she had forfeited the love of all her relatives, and she had opposed with unshaken courage the persistent efforts of the Church, which embittered her life with many a hard trial, when, though herself trained up in the Catholic religion, she had married the Protestant Wacht, and shortly before had gone over to this faith in Augsburg, impelled thereto by the pure enthusiasm of conviction. All this now passed through Master Wacht's mind; and as he thought upon the sentiments he had felt when he led the maiden to the altar, the warm tears ran down his cheeks. Nanni was her mother over again; Wacht loved the child with an intensity of affection that was quite unparalleled, and this fact was of itself more than enough to make him reject as abominable, nay, as fiendishly cruel, any attempt to separate the lovers that appeared in the remotest degree to savour of violence. When, on the other hand, he reflected upon the whole course of Jonathan's previous life, he was obliged to admit that all the virtues of a good, industrious, and modest youth could not easily be so happily united in another as they were in Jonathan, albeit his handsome expressive face bore the impress of traits which were perhaps a little too soft, and almost effeminate, and his diminutive and weak but elegant bodily frame bespoke a tender intellectual spirit. When he reflected further that the two children had always been together, and how evident had been their mutual liking for each other, he was really puzzled to understand how it was that he had not expected beforehand what had now really happened, and so could have taken precautions in time. Now it was too late.

He was urged on through the hills by a mood of mind which set his whole being in a turmoil of distraction; such a state as this he had hitherto never experienced, and he was inclined to take it for a seduction of Satan, since several thoughts arose in his mind which in the very next minute he could not help regarding as diabolical. He could not recover his self-composure, still less form any decisive plan of action. The sun was beginning to set when he reached the village of Buch; turning into the hotel, he ordered something good to eat and a bottle of excellent beer from the rock.

"Ah! a very fine evening! Ah! what a remarkable occurrence to see our good Master Wacht here in beautiful Buch, on this glorious Sunday evening. To tell you the truth, I can hardly believe my eyes. Your respected family is, I presume, somewhere else in the country." Thus was Master Wacht addressed by some one with a shrill, squeaking voice. The man who thus interrupted his meditations was no less a personage than Herr Pickard Leberfink, a decorator and gilder by trade, and one of the drollest men in the world.

Leberfink's exterior struck everybody's eye as something eccentric and extraordinary. He was of small size, thick and stumpy, with a body too long, and with short bowed legs; his face was not at all ugly, but good-natured, with round red little cheeks and small grey eyes that were by no means wanting in vivacity. Pursuant to an old obsolete French fashion, he was elaborately curled and powdered every day; but it was on Sundays that his costume was especially striking. For then he wore, to take one example, a striped silk coat of a lilac and canary-yellow colour with immense silver-plated buttons, a waistcoat embroidered in gay tints, satin hose of a brilliant green, white and light-blue silk stockings, delicately striped, and shining black polished shoes, upon which glittered large buckles set with precious stones. If to this we add that his gait was the elegant gait of a dancing master, that he had a certain cat-like suppleness of body, and that his little legs had a strange knack of knocking the heels together on fitting occasions,--for instance, when leaping across a gutter,--it could not fail but that the little decorator got himself singled out everywhere as an extraordinary creature. With other aspects of his character my kindly reader will make an acquaintance presently.

Master Wacht was not altogether displeased at having his painful meditations interrupted in this way. Herr, or better Monsieur Pickard Leberfink, decorator and gilder, was a great fop, but at the same time the most honest and faithful soul in the world; he was a very liberal-minded man, was generous to the poor, and always ready to serve his friends. He only practised his calling now and again, merely out of love for it, since he had no need of business. He was rich; his father had left him some landed property, having a magnificent rock-cellar, which was only separated from Master Wacht's premises by a large garden. Master Wacht was fond of the droll little Leberfink on account of his downright genuineness, and also because he was a member of the small Protestant community which was permitted to exercise the rites of its faith in Bamberg. With conspicuous alacrity and willingness Leberfink accepted Wacht's invitation to join him at his table, and drink another bottle of beer from the rock along with him. He began the conversation by saying that for a long time he had been wanting to call upon Master Wacht at his own house, since he had two things he wished to talk to him about, one of which was almost making his heart burst. Wacht made answer, he thought Leberfink knew him, and must be aware that anybody who had anything to say to him, no matter what it was, might speak out his thoughts frankly. Leberfink now imparted to the Master in confidence that the wine-dealer who owned the beautiful garden, with the massive pavilion, which lay between their two properties, had privately offered to sell it to him. He thought he recollected having heard Wacht once express a wish how very much he should like to own this garden; if now the opportunity was come to satisfy this wish, he (Leberfink) offered his services as negotiator, and expressed his willingness to settle everything for him.

It was a fact that Master Wacht had for some time entertained a desire to enlarge his property by the addition of a good garden, and especially so since Nanni was always longing for the beautiful shrubs and trees which gave out such a luxurious abundance of sweet scents in this very garden. Moreover, it seemed to him now as if Fortune were graciously smiling upon him, and just at the time when poor Nanni had experienced such bitter trouble, an opportunity for affording her pleasure should present itself so unexpectedly. The Master at once settled all the needful particulars with the obliging decorator, who promised that on the following Sunday Wacht should be able to stroll through the garden as its owner. "Come now," cried Master Wacht, "come now, friend Leberfink, out with it--what is it that is making your heart burst?"

Then Herr Pickard Leberfink fell to sighing in the most pitiable manner; and he pulled the most extraordinary faces, and ran on with such a string of gibberish that nobody could make either head or tail of it. Master Wacht, however, knew what to make of it, for he shook his head, saying, "Ah! that may be contrived;" and he smiled to himself at the wonderful sympathy of their related spirits.

This meeting with Leberfink had certainly done Master Wacht good; he believed he had conceived a plan by virtue of which he should manage not only to stand against, but even to overcome, the severest and most terrible misfortune which, according to his infatuated way of thinking, had come upon him. The only thing that can declare the verdict of the tribunal within him is the course of action he adopted; and perhaps, kindly reader, this tribunal faltered for the first time. Here is the place to offer a brief remark, which, perhaps, would not very well lend itself for insertion later. As so frequently happens in such cases, old Barbara had interfered in the matter, and been very urgent in her accusations of the loving pair to Master Wacht, making it a special charge against them that they had always read worldly books together. The Master caused her to bring two or three of the books which Nanni had. One was a work of Goethe's; unfortunately it is not known which work it was. After turning over the leaves, he gave it back to Barbara, that she might restore it to the place whence she had secretly taken it. Not a single word about Nanni's reading ever escaped him; once only, when some seasonable occasion presented at dinner, did he say, "There is a remarkable mind rising up amongst us Germans; God grant him success! My days are over; such things are not for my age, nor yet for my calling; but you--Jonathan? I envy you many things that will come to light in the days to come." Jonathan understood Wacht's oracular words the more easily, since some days previously he had discovered by chance *Götz von Berlichingen* lying on the Master's work-table, half covered by other papers. Wacht's great mind, whilst acknowledging the uncommon genius of the new writer, had also perceived the impossibility of beginning a new flight himself.

Next day poor Nanni hung her head like a sick dove. "What's the matter with my dear child?" asked Master Wacht in the tender sympathetic tone that was so peculiarly his own, and with which he knew how to stir everybody's heart, "what's the matter with my dear child? are you ill? I can't believe it. You don't get out into the fresh air sufficiently. See here now; I have a long time been wishing you would for once in a way bring me my tea out to the workshop. Do so to-day; we may expect a most beautiful evening. You will come, won't you, Nanni, my darling? You will butter me some rolls yourself--that will make them ever so good." Therewith Master Wacht took the dear girl in his arms and stroked her brown curls back from her forehead, and he kissed her and pressed her to his heart, and tenderly caressed her,--treating her, in fact, in the most affectionate way that he knew how; and he was well aware of the irresistible charm of his manner at such times. A flood of tears gushed from Nanni's eyes, and with some difficulty all she could get out was, "Father! father!" "Well, well!" said Wacht, and a strain of embarrassment might have been detected in his voice, "all may yet turn out well."

A week passed; naturally enough Jonathan had not shown himself, and the Master had not mentioned him with a single syllable. On Sunday, when the soup was standing smoking on the table, and the family were about to take their seats for dinner. Master Wacht asked gaily, "And where is our Jonathan?" Rettel, with a view to sparing poor Nanni, replied in an undertone, "Father, don't you know then what's taken place? Wouldn't Jonathan of course be shy of showing himself here in your presence?" "Oh the monkey!" said Wacht, laughing; "let Christian run over at once and fetch him."

It need hardly be said that the young advocate failed not to put in an appearance immediately, nor that during the first moments after his arrival a dark oppressive thunder-cloud, as it were, hovered over them all. At length, however, Master Wacht's unconstrained good spirits, seconded by Leberfink's droll sallies, succeeded in calling forth a tone of conversation which, if it could not be called exactly merry, yet managed to maintain the balance of concord pretty evenly. After dinner Master Wacht said, "Let us get a little fresh air and stroll out to my workyard." And they did so.

Monsieur Pickard Leberfink deliberately kept close to Rettelchen's side, who was a pattern of friendliness towards him, since the polite decorator had exhausted himself in praising her dishes, and had confessed that never so long as he had lived, not even when dining with the ecclesiastics in Banz, had he enjoyed a more delicious meal. As Master Wacht now hurried on at a quick pace right across the middle of the workyard, with a large bundle of keys in his hand, the young lawyer was unintentionally brought close to Nanni. But all that the lovers ventured upon were stolen sighs and low soft-breathed love-plaints.

Master Wacht came to a halt in front of a fine newly-made door, which had been constructed in the wall parting his workyard from the merchant's garden. He unlocked the door and stepped in, inviting his family to follow him. They, none of them, knew exactly what to make of the old gentleman, except Herr Pickard Leberfink, who never laid aside his sly smile, or ceased his soft giggle. In the midst of the beautiful garden there was a very spacious pavilion; this too Master Wacht opened, and stepping in remained standing in its centre; from every one of its windows one obtained a different romantic view. "Yes," said Master Wacht in a voice that bore witness to a heart well pleased with itself, "here I am in my own property; this beautiful garden is mine. I was obliged to buy it, not so much to augment my own place or increase the value of my property, no! but because I knew that a certain darling little thing longed so for these shrubs and trees, and for these beautiful sweet-smelling flower-beds."

Then Nanni threw herself upon the old gentleman's breast and cried, "O father! father! You will break my heart with your kindness, with your goodness; do have pity"---- "There, there, say no more," Master Wacht interrupted his suffering child, "be a good girl, and all may be brought right in some marvellous way. You can find a great deal of comfort in this little paradise"---- "Oh! yes, yes, yes," exclaimed Nanni in a burst of enthusiasm, "O ye trees, ye shrubs, ye flowers, ye distant hills, you beautiful fleeting evening clouds--my spirit lives wholly in you all; I shall come to myself again when your sweet voices comfort me." Therewith Nanni ran out of the open door of the pavilion into the garden like a startled young roe; and Jonathan, the lawyer, delayed not to follow her at his fastest speed, for no power would then have been able to keep him back. Monsieur Pickard Leberfink requested permission to show Rettelchen round the new property.

Meanwhile old Wacht had beer and tobacco brought to a spot under the trees, close at the brow of the hill, whence he could look down into the valley; and there he sat in a right glad and comfortable humour, puffing the blue clouds of genuine Holland into the air. No doubt my kindly reader is wondering greatly at this frame of mind in Master Wacht, and is at a loss to explain to himself how a mood like this was at all possible to a temperament like Wacht's. He had arrived, not so much at any determined plan as at the conviction that the Eternal Power could not possibly let him live to experience such a very terrible misfortune as that of seeing his favourite child united to a lawyer; that is, to Satan himself. "Something will happen," he said to himself; "something must happen, by which either this unhappy affair will be broken off or Jonathan snatched from the pit of destruction. It would be rash temerity, nay, perhaps a ruinous piece of mischief, producing the exact contrary of what was wished, if with my feeble hand I were to attempt to control the fly-wheel of Destiny."

It is hard to credit what miserable, nay, often what absurd reasons a man will hunt up in order to represent the approaching misfortune as avertable. So there were moments in which Wacht built his hopes upon the arrival of wild Sebastian, whom he pictured to himself as a stalwart young fellow in the full flush and pride of youth, just on the point of attaining to manhood, and that he would bring about a change of direction in the drifting of circumstances, and make things different from what they then were. The very common, and alas! often too true idea came into his head, that woman is too greatly impressed by strong and striking manliness not to be conquered by it at last.

When the sun began to go down, Monsieur Pickard Leberfink invited the family to go into his garden, which adjoined their own, and take a little refreshment. Beside Wacht's new possession the noble decorator and gilder's garden formed a most ridiculous and extraordinary contrast. Whilst almost too small in size, so that the only thing it could perhaps boast in its favour was the good height at which it was situated, it was laid out in Dutch style, the trees and hedges clipped with the shears in the most scrupulous and pedantic fashion. The slender stems of the fruit-trees standing in the flower-beds looked very pretty in their coats of light blue and rose tints, and pale yellow, and other colours. Leberfink had varnished them, and so beautified Nature. Moreover they saw in the trees the apples of the Hesperides.

But yet several further surprises were in store. Leberfink bade the girls pluck themselves a nosegay each; but on gathering the flowers they perceived to their amazement that both stalks and leaves were gilded. It was also very remarkable that all the leaves which Rettel took into her hands were shaped like hearts.

The refreshment upon which Leberfink regaled his guests consisted of the choicest confectionery, the finest sweetmeats, and old Rhine wine and Muscatel. Rettel was quite beside herself over the confectionery, observing with special emphasis that such sweetmeats, which were for the most part splendidly silvered and gilded, were not, she knew made in Bamberg. Then Monsieur Pickard Leberfink assured her privately, with a most amorous smirk, that he himself knew a little about baking cakes and sweets, and that he was the happy maker of all these delicious dainties. Rettel almost fell upon her knees before him in reverence and astonishment; and yet the greatest surprise, was still in store for her.

In the deepening dusk Monsieur Pickard Leberfink very cleverly contrived to entice little Rettel into a small arbour. No sooner was he alone with her than he recklessly plumped himself down upon both knees in the wet grass, notwithstanding that he was wearing his brilliant green satin hose; and, amidst many strange and unintelligible sounds of distress--not very dissimilar to the midnight elegies of the tom-cat Hinz--he presented her with an immense nosegay of flowers, in the middle of which was the finest full-blown rose that could be found anywhere. Rettel did what everybody does who has a nosegay given to him; she raised it to her nose; but in the selfsame moment she felt a sharp prick. In her alarm she was about to throw the nosegay away. But see what charming wonder had revealed itself in the meantime! A beautifully varnished little cupid had leapt up out of the heart of the rose and was holding out a burning heart with both hands towards Rettel. From his mouth depended a small strip of paper on which were written the words, "Voilà le cœur de Monsieur Pickard Leberfink, que je vous offre" (Here I offer you the heart of Monsieur Pickard Leberfink).

"Good gracious!" exclaimed Rettel, very much alarmed. "Good gracious! what are you doing, my good Herr Leberfink? Don't kneel down in front of me as if I were a princess. You will make marks on your beautiful satin-- in the wet grass, and you will catch cold yourself; but elder tea and white sugar candy are good remedies."

"No!" exclaimed the desperate lover--"No, O Margaret, Pickard Leberfink, who loves you with all his heart, will not rise from the wet grass until you promise to be his"---- "You want to marry me?" asked Rettel. "Well then, up you get at once. Speak to my father, darling Leberfink, and drink one or two cups of elder tea this evening."

Why should the reader be longer wearied with Leberfink's and Rettel's folly? They were made for each other, and were betrothed, at which Father Wacht was right glad in his own teasing, humorous way.

A certain degree of life was introduced into Wacht's house by Rettel's betrothal; and even the disconsolate lovers had more freedom, since they were less observed. But something of a quite special character was to happen to put an abrupt end to this quiet and comfortable condition in which they were all living. The young lawyer seemed particularly preoccupied, and his thoughts busy with some affair or another that absorbed all his energies; his visits at Wacht's house even began to be less frequent, and he often stayed away in the evening--a thing he had never been wont to do previously. "What can be the matter with our Jonathan? He is completely preoccupied; he's quite another fellow from what he used to be," said Master Wacht, although he knew very well what was the cause, or rather the event, which was exercising such a visible influence upon the young lawyer, at least to all outward appearance. To tell the truth, he looked upon this event as the dispensation of Providence through which he should perhaps escape the great misfortune by which he believed himself threatened, and which he felt would completely upset all the happiness of his life.

Some few months previously a young and unknown lady had arrived in Bamberg, and under circumstances which could only be called singular and mysterious. She was staying at the "White Lamb." All the servants she had with her were an old grey-haired manservant and an old lady's- maid. Very various were the opinions current about her. Many maintained she was a distinguished and immensely rich Hungarian countess, who, owing to matrimonial dissensions, was compelled to take up her residence in solitary retirement in Bamberg for a time. Others, on the contrary, set her down as an ordinary forsaken Dido, and yet others as an itinerant singer, who would soon throw off her veil of nobility and announce herself as about to give a concert,--possibly she had no recommendations to the Prince-bishop. At any rate the majority were unanimous in making up their minds to regard the stranger, who, according to the statements of the few persons who had seen her, was of exceptional beauty, as an extremely ambiguous person.

It had been noticed that the stranger lady's old man-servant had followed the young lawyer about a long time, until one day he caught him at the spring in the market-place, which is ornamented with an image of Neptune (whom the honest folk of Bamberg are generally in the habit of calling the Fork-man); and there the old man stood talking to Jonathan a long, long time. Spirits alive to all that goes forward, who can never meet anybody without asking eagerly, "Wherever has he been? Wherever is he going? Whatever is he doing?" and so on, had made out that the young advocate very often visited the beautiful unknown, in fact almost every day and at night-time, when he spent several hours with her. It was soon the talk of the town that the lawyer Jonathan Engelbrecht had got entangled in the dangerous toils of the young unknown adventuress.

It would have been, both then and always, entirely contrary to Master Wacht's character to make use of this apparent erring conduct of the young advocate as a weapon against poor Nanni. He left it to Dame Barbara and her whole following of gossips to keep Nanni informed of all particulars; from them she would learn every item of intelligence, and that, he made no doubt, with a due amplification of all the details. The crisis of the whole affair was reached when one day the young lawyer suddenly set off on a journey along with the lady, nobody knew whither. "That's the way frivolity goes on; the forward young gentleman will lose his business," said the knowing ones. But this was not the case; for not a little to the astonishment of the public, old Eichheimer himself attended to his foster-son's business with the most painstaking care; he seemed to be initiated into the secret about the lady and to approve of all the steps taken by his foster-son.

Master Wacht never spoke a word about the matter, and once when poor Nanni could no longer hide her trouble, but moaned in a low tone, her voice half-choked with tears, "Why has Jonathan left us?" Master Wacht replied in an off-handed way, "Ay, that's just what lawyers do. Who knows what sort of an intrigue Jonathan has got entangled in with the stranger, thinking it will bring him money, and be to his advantage?" Then, however, Herr Pickard Leberfink was wont to take Jonathan's side, and to assert that he for his part was convinced the stranger could be nothing less than a princess, who had had recourse to the already world-renowned young advocate in an extremely delicate law-suit And therewith he also unearthed so many stories about lawyers who, through especial sagacity and especial penetration and skill, had unravelled the most complicated difficulties, and brought to light the most closely hidden things, till Master Wacht begged him for goodness' sake to hold his tongue, since he was feeling quite ill and sick; Nanni, on the contrary, derived inward comfort from all Leberfink's remarkable stories, and she plucked up her hopes again. With her trouble, however, there was united a perceptible mixture of annoyance and anger, and particularly at the moments when it seemed to her utterly impossible that Jonathan could have been untrue to her. From this it might be inferred that Jonathan had not sought to exculpate himself, but had obstinately maintained silence about his adventure.

After some months had elapsed the young lawyer came back to Bamberg in the highest good spirits; and Master Wacht, on seeing the bright glad light in Nanni's eyes when she looked at him, could not well do otherwise than conclude that Jonathan had fully justified his conduct to her. Doubtless it would not be disagreeable to the indulgent reader to have the history of what had taken place between the stranger lady and the young lawyer inserted here as an episodical *novella*.

Count Z----, a Hungarian, owner of more than a million, married from pure affection a miserably poor girl, who drew down upon her head the hatred of his family, not only because her own family was enshrouded in complete obscurity, but also because the only valuable treasures she possessed were her divine virtue, beauty, and grace. The Count promised his wife that at his death he would settle all his property upon her by will.

Once when he returned to Vienna into the arms of his wife, after having been summoned from Paris to St. Petersburg on diplomatic business, he related to her that he had been attacked by a severe illness in a little town, the name of which he had quite forgotten; there he had seized the opportunity whilst recovering from his illness to draw up a will in her favour and deposit it with the court. Some miles farther on the road he must have been seized with a new and doubly virulent attack of his grave nervous complaint, so that the name of the place where he had made his will and that of the court where he had deposited it had completely slipped his memory; moreover, he had lost the document of receipt from the court acknowledging the deposition of the testament. As so often happens in similar cases the Count postponed the making of a new will from day to day, until he was overtaken by death. Then his relatives did not neglect to lay claim to all the property he left behind him, so that the poor Countess saw her too rich inheritance melted down to the insignificant sum represented by certain valuable presents she had received from the Count, and which his relatives could not deprive her of. Many different notifications bearing upon the features of the case were found amongst the Count's papers; but since such statements, that a will was in existence, could not take the place of the will itself, they proved not to be of the slightest advantage to the Countess. She had consulted many learned lawyers about her unfortunate situation, and had finally come to Bamberg to have recourse to old Eichheimer; but he had directed her to young Engelbrecht, who, being less busy and equipped with excellent intellectual acuteness and great love for his profession, would perhaps be able to get a clue to the unfortunate will or furnish some other circumstantial proof of its actual existence.

The young advocate set to work by requesting permission of the competent authorities to submit the Count's papers in the castle to another searching investigation. He himself went thither along with the Countess; and in the presence of the officials of the court he found in a cupboard of nut-wood, that had hitherto escaped observation, an old portfolio, in which, though they did not find the Count's document of receipt relating to the deposition of the will, they yet discovered a paper which could not fail to be of the utmost importance for the young advocate's purpose. For this paper contained an accurate description of all the circumstances, even the minutest details, under which the Count had made a will in favour of his wife and deposited it in the keeping of a court. The Count's diplomatic journey from Paris to Petersburg had brought him to Königsberg in Prussia. Here he chanced to come across some East Prussian noblemen, whom he had previously met with whilst on a visit to Italy. In spite of the express rate at which the Count was travelling, he nevertheless suffered himself to be persuaded to make a short excursion into East Prussia, particularly as the big hunts had begun, and the Count was a passionate sportsman. He named the towns Wehlau, Allenburg, Friedland, &c., as places where he had been. Then he set out to go straight forwards directly to the Russian frontier, without returning to Königsberg.

In a little town, whose wretched appearance the Count could hardly find words to describe, he was suddenly prostrated by a nervous disorder, which for several days quite deprived him of consciousness. Fortunately there was a young and right clever doctor in the place, who opposed a stout resistance to the disease, so that the Count not only recovered consciousness but also his health, so far that after a few days he was in a position to continue his journey. But his heart was oppressed with the fear that a second attack on the road might kill him, and so plunge his wife in a condition of the most straitened poverty. Not a little to his astonishment he learned from the doctor that the place, in spite of its small size and wretched appearance, was the seat of a Prussian provincial court, and that he could there have his will registered with all due formality, as soon as he could succeed in establishing his identity. This, however, was a most formidable difficulty, for who knew the Count in this district? But wonderful are the doings of Accident! Just as the Count got out of his carriage in front of the inn of the little town, there stood in the doorway a grey-haired old invalid, almost eighty years old, who dwelt in a neighbouring village and earned a living by plaiting willow baskets, and who only seldom came into the town. In his youth he had served in the Austrian army, and for fifteen successive years had been groom to the Count's father. At the first glance he remembered his master's son; and he and his wife acted as fully legitimated vouchers of the Count's identity, and not to their detriment, as may well be conceived.

The young advocate at once saw that all depended upon the locality and its exact correspondence with the Count's statements, if he wanted to glean further details and find a clue to the place where the Count had been ill and made his testament. He set off with the Countess for East Prussia. There by examination of the post-books he was desirous of making out, if possible, the route of travel pursued by the Count. But after a good deal of wasted effort, he only managed to discover that the Count had taken post-horses from Eylau to Allenburg. Beyond Allenburg every trace was lost; nevertheless he satisfied himself that the Count had certainly travelled through Prussian Lithuania, and of this he was still further convinced on finding registered at Tilsit that the Count had arrived there and departed thence by extra post. Beyond this point again all traces were lost. Accordingly it seemed to the young advocate that they must seek for the solution of the difficulty in the short stretch of country between Allenburg and Tilsit.

Quite dispirited and full of anxious care he arrived one rainy evening at the small country town of Insterburg, accompanied by the Countess. On entering the wretched apartments in the inn, he became conscious that a strange kind of expectant feeling was taking possession of him. He felt so like being at home in them, as if he had even been there before, or as if the place had been most accurately described to him. The Countess withdrew to her apartments. The young advocate tossed restlessly on his bed. When the morning sun shone in brightly through the window, his eyes fell upon the paper in one corner of the room. He noticed that a large patch of the blue colour with which the room was but lightly washed had fallen off, showing the disagreeable glaring yellow that formed the ground colour, and upon it he observed that all kinds of hideous faces in the New Zealand style had been painted to serve as pleasing arabesques. Perfectly beside himself with joy and delight, the young lawyer sprang out of bed. He was in the room in which Count Z---- had made the all-important will. The description agreed too exactly; there could not be any doubt about the matter.

But why now weary the reader with all the minor details of the things that now took place one after the other? Suffice it to say that Insterburg was then, as it still is, the seat of a Prussian superior tribunal, at that time called an Imperial Court. The young advocate at once waited upon the president with the Countess. By means of the papers which she had brought with her, and which were drawn up in due authenticated form, the Countess established her own identity in the most satisfactory manner; and the will was publicly declared to be perfectly genuine. Hence the Countess, who had left her own country in great distress and poverty, now returned in the full possession of all the rights of which a hostile destiny had attempted to deprive her.

In Nanni's eyes the advocate appeared like a hero from heaven, who had victoriously protected deserted innocence against the wickedness of the world. Leberfink also poured out all his great admiration of the young lawyer's acuteness and energy in exaggerated encomiums. Master Wacht, too, praised Jonathan's industry, and this trait he emphasised; and yet the boy had really done nothing but what it was his duty to do; still he somehow fancied that things might have been managed in a much shorter way. "This event I regard," said Jonathan, "as a star of real good fortune, which has risen upon the path of my career almost before I have started upon it The case has created a great deal of sensation. All the Hungarian magnates are excited about it. My name has become known. And what is a long way the best of all, the Countess was so liberal as to honour me with ten thousand Brabant thalers."

During the course of the young advocate's narration, the muscles of Master Wacht's face began to move in a remarkable way, till at last his countenance wore an expression of the greatest indignation. "What!" he at length shouted in a lion-like voice, whilst his eyes flashed fire-- "What! did I not tell you? You have made a sale of justice. The Countess, in order to get her lawful inheritance out of the hands of her rascally relations, has had to pay money, to sacrifice to Mammon. Faugh! faugh! be ashamed of yourself." All the sensible protestations of the young advocate, as well as of the rest of the persons who happened to be present, were not of the slightest avail. For a second it seemed as if their representations would gain a hearing, when it was stated that no one had ever given a present with more willing pleasure than the Countess had done on the sudden conclusion of her case, and that, as good Leberfink very well knew, the young advocate had only himself to blame that his honorarium had not turned out to be more in amount as well as more on a level with the magnitude of the lady's gain; nevertheless Master Wacht stuck to his own opinion, and they heard from him in his own obstinate fashion the familiar words, "So soon as you begin to talk about justice, you and everybody else in the world ought to hold your tongues about money. It is true," he went on more calmly after a pause, "there are several circumstances connected with this history which might very well excuse you, and yet at the same time lead you astray into base selfishness; but have the kindness to hold your tongue about the Countess, and the will, and the ten thousand thalers, if you please. I should indeed be fancying many a time that you didn't altogether belong to your place at my table there."

"You are very hard--very unjust towards me, father," said the young advocate, his voice trembling with sadness. Nanni's tears flowed quietly; Leberfink, like an experienced man of the world, hastened to turn the conversation upon the new gildings in St. Gangolph's.

It may readily be conceived in what strained relations the members of Wacht's family now lived. Where was their unconstrained conversation, their bright good spirits, where their cheerfulness? A deadly vexation was slowly gnawing at Wacht's heart, and it stood plainly written upon his countenance.

Meanwhile they received not the least scrap of intelligence from Sebastian Engelbrecht, and so the last feeble ray of hope that Master Wacht had seen glimmering appeared about to fade. Master Wacht's foreman, Andreas by name, was a plain, honest, faithful fellow, who clung to his master with an affection that could not be matched anywhere. "Master," said he one morning as they were measuring beams together--"Master, I can't bear it any longer; it breaks my heart to see you suffer so. Fräulein Nanni--poor Herr Jonathan!" Quickly throwing away the measuring lines, Master Wacht stepped up to him and took him by the breast, saying, "Man, if you are able to tear out of this heart the convictions as to what is true and right which have been engraven upon it by the Eternal Power in letters of fire, then what you are thinking about may come to pass." Andreas, who was not the man to enter upon a dispute with his master upon these sort of terms, scratched himself behind his ear, and replied with an embarrassed smirk, "Then if a certain distinguished gentleman were to pay a morning visit to the workshop, I suppose it would produce no particular effect?" Master Wacht perceived in a moment that a storm was brewing against him, and that it was in all probability being directed by Count von Kösel.

Just as the clock struck nine Nanni appeared in the workshop, followed by old Barbara with the breakfast. The Master was not well pleased to see his daughter, since it was out of rule; and he saw the programme of the concerted attack already peeping out. Nor was it long before the minor canon really made his appearance, as smart and prim and proper as a pet doll. Close at his heels followed Monsieur Pickard Leberfink, decorator and gilder, clad in all sorts of gay colours, so that he looked not unlike a spring-chafer. Wacht pretended to be highly delighted with the visit, the cause of which he at once insinuated to be that the minor canon very likely wanted to see his newest models. The truth is, Master Wacht felt very shy at the possibility of having to listen to the canon's long-winded sermons, which he would deliver himself of uselessly if he attempted to shake his (Wacht's) resolution with respect to Nanni and Jonathan. Accident came to his rescue; for just as the canon, the young lawyer, and the varnisher were standing together, and the first-named was beginning to approach the most intimate relations of life in the most elegantly turned phrases, fat Hans shouted out "Wood here!" and big Peter on the other side pushed the wood across to him so roughly that it caught the canon a violent blow on the shoulder and sent him reeling against Monsieur Pickard; he in his turn stumbled against the young advocate, and in a trice the whole three had disappeared. For just behind them was a huge piled-up heap of chips and saw-dust and so on. The unfortunates were buried under this heap, so that all that could be seen of them were four black legs and two buff-coloured ones; the latter were the gala stockings of Herr Pickard Leberfink, decorator and gilder. It couldn't possibly be helped; the journeymen and apprentices burst out into a ringing peal of laughter, notwithstanding that Master Wacht bade them be still and look grave.

Of them all the canon cut the worst figure, since the saw-dust had got into the folds of his robe and even into the elegant curls which adorned his head. He fled as if upon the wings of the wind, covered with shame, and the young advocate hard after him. Monsieur Pickard Leberfink was the only one who preserved his good humour and took the thing in merry part, notwithstanding that it might be regarded as certain he would never be able to wear the buff-coloured stockings again, since the saw-dust had proved especially injurious to them and had quite destroyed the "clock." Thus the storm which was to have been adventured against Wacht was baffled by a ridiculous incident. But the Master did not dream what terrible thing was to happen to him before the day was over.

Master Wacht had finished dinner and was just going downstairs in order to betake himself to his workyard, when he heard a loud, rough voice shouting in front of the house, "Hi, there! This is where that knavish old rascal, Carpenter Wacht, lives, isn't it?" A voice in the street made answer, "There is no knavish old rascal living here; this is the house of our respected fellow-citizen Herr Johannes Wacht, the carpenter." In the same moment the street-door was forced open with a violent bang, and a big strong fellow of wild appearance stood before the master. His black hair stuck up like bristles through his ragged soldier's cap, and in scores of places his tattered tunic was unable to conceal his loathsome skin, browned with filth and exposure to rough weather. The fellow wore soldier's shoes on his feet, and the blue weals on his ankles showed the traces of the chains he had been fettered with. "Ho, ho!" cried the fellow, "I bet you don't know me. You don't know Sebastian Engelbrecht, whom you've cheated out of his property--not you." With all the imposing dignity of his majestic form, Master Wacht took a step towards the man, mechanically advancing the cane he held in his hand. Then the wild fellow seemed to be almost thunderstruck; he recoiled a few paces, and then raised his doubled fists shouting, "Ho, ho! I know where my property is, and I'll go and help myself to it, in spite of you, you old sinner." And he ran off down the Kaulberg like an arrow from a bow, followed by the crowd.

Master Wacht stood in the passage like a statue for several seconds. But when Nanni cried in alarm, "Good heavens! father, that was Sebastian," he went into the room, more reeling than walking, and sank down exhausted in an arm-chair; then, holding both hands before his face, he cried in a heart-rending voice, "By the eternal mercy of God, that is Sebastian Engelbrecht."

There arose a tumult in the street, the crowd poured down the Kaulberg, and voices in the far distance could be heard shouting "Murder! murder!" A prey to the most terrible apprehensions, the Master, ran down to Jonathan's dwelling, situated immediately at the foot of the Kaulberg. A dense mass of people were pushing and crowding together in front of him; in their midst he perceived Sebastian struggling like a wild animal against the watch, who had just thrown him upon the ground, where they overpowered him and bound him hand and foot, and led him away. "O God! O God! Sebastian has slain his brother," lamented the people, who came crowding out of the house. Master Wacht forced his way through and found poor Jonathan in the hands of the doctors, who were exerting themselves to call him back to life. As he had received three powerful blows upon the head, dealt with all the strength of a strong man, the worst was to be feared.

As generally happens under such circumstances, Nanni learnt immediately the whole history of the affair from her kind-hearted friends, and at once rushed off to her lover's dwelling, where she arrived just as the young lawyer, thanks to the lavish use of naphtha, opened his eyes again, and the doctors were talking about trepanning. What further took place may be conceived. Nanni was inconsolable; Rettel, notwithstanding her betrothal, was sunk in grief; and Monsieur Pickard Leberfink exclaimed, whilst tears of sorrow ran down his cheeks, "God be merciful to the man upon whose pate a carpenter's fist falls." The loss of young Herr Jonathan would be irreparable. At any rate the varnish on his coffin should be of unsurpassed brightness and blackness; and the silvering of the skulls and other nice ornaments should baffle all comparison.

It appeared that Sebastian had escaped out of the hands of a troop of Bavarian soldiers, whilst they were conducting a band of vagabonds through the district of Bamberg, and he had found his way into the town in order to carry out a mad project which he had for a long time been brooding over in his mind. His career was not that of an abandoned, vicious criminal; it afforded rather an example of those supremely frivolous-minded men, who, despite the very admirable qualities with which Nature has endowed them, give way to every temptation to evil, and finally sinking to the lowest depths of vice, perish in shame and misery. In Saxony he had fallen into the hands of a petti-fogging lawyer, who had made him believe that Master Wacht, when sending him his patrimonial inheritance, had paid him very much short, and kept back the remainder for the benefit of his brother Jonathan, to whom he had promised to give his favourite daughter Nanni to wife. Very likely the old deceiver had concocted this story out of various utterances of Sebastian himself. The kindly reader already knows by what violent means Sebastian set to work to secure his own rights. Immediately after leaving Master Wacht he had burst into Jonathan's room, where the latter happened to be sitting at his study table, ordering some accounts and counting the piles of money which lay heaped up before him. His clerk sat in the other corner of the room. "Ah! you villain!" screamed Sebastian in a fury, "there you are sitting over your mammon. Are you counting what you have robbed me of? Give me here what yon old rascal has stolen from me and bestowed upon you. You poor, weak thing! You greedy clutching devil--you!" And when Sebastian strode close up to him, Jonathan instinctively stretched out both hands to ward him off, crying aloud, "Brother! for God's sake, brother!" But Sebastian replied by dealing him several stunning blows on the head with his double fist, so that Jonathan sank down fainting. Sebastian hastily seized upon some of the rolls of gold and was making off with them--in which naturally enough he did not succeed.

Fortunately it turned out that none of Jonathan's wounds, which outwardly wore the appearance of large bumps, had occasioned any serious concussion of the brain, and hence none of them could be esteemed as likely to prove dangerous. After a lapse of two months, when Sebastian was taken away to the convict prison, where he was to atone for his attempt at murder by a heavy punishment, the young lawyer felt himself quite well again.

This terrible occurrence exerted such a shattering effect upon Master Wacht that a consuming surly peevishness was the consequence of it. This time the stout strong oak was shaken from its topmost branch to its deepest root. Often when his mind was thought to be busy with quite different matters, he was heard to murmur in a low tone,

"Sebastian--a fratricide! That's how you reward me?" and then he seemed to come to himself like one awakening out of a nasty dream. The only thing that kept him from breaking down was the hardest and most assiduous labour. But who can fathom the unsearchable depths in which the secret links of feeling are so strangely forged together as they were in Master Wacht's soul? His abhorrence of Sebastian and his wicked deed faded out of his mind, whilst the picture of his own life, ruined by Jonathan's love for Nanni, deepened in colour and vividness as the days went by. This frame of mind Master Wacht betrayed in many short exclamations--"So then your brother is condemned to hard labour and to work in chains!--That's where he has been brought by his attempted crime against you--It's a fine thing for a brother to be the cause of making his own brother a convict--shouldn't like to be in the first brother's place--but lawyers think differently; they want justice, that is, they want to play with a lay figure and dress it up and give it whatever name they please."

Such like bitter, and even incomprehensible reproaches, the young advocate was obliged to hear from Master Wacht, and to hear them only too often. Any attempt at rebutting these charges would have been fruitless. Accordingly Jonathan made no reply; only often when his heart was almost distracted by the old man's fatal delusion, which was ruining all his happiness, he broke out in his exceeding great pain, "Father, father, you are unjust towards me, exasperatingly unjust."

One day when the family were assembled at the decorator Leberfink's, and Jonathan also was present, Master Wacht began to tell how somebody had been saying that Sebastian Engelbrecht, although apprehended as a criminal, could yet make good by action at law his claim against Master Wacht, who had been his guardian. Then, smiling venomously and turning to Jonathan, he went on, "That would be a pretty case for a young advocate. I thought you might take up the suit; you might play a part in it yourself; perhaps I have cheated you as well?" This made the young lawyer start to his feet; his eyes flashed, his bosom heaved; he seemed all of a sudden to be quite a different man; stretching his hand towards Heaven he cried, "No, you shall no longer be my father; you must be insane to sacrifice without scruple the peace and happiness of the most loving of children to a ridiculous prejudice. You will never see me again; I will go and at once accept the offer which the American consul made to me to-day; I will go to America." "Yes," replied Wacht filled with rage and anger, "ay, away out of my eyes, brother of the fratricide, who've sold your soul to Satan." Casting upon Nanni, who was half fainting, a look full of hopeless love and anguish and despair, the young advocate hurriedly left the garden.

It was remarked earlier in the course of this story when the young lawyer threatened to shoot himself *à la* Werther, what a good thing it was that the indispensable pistol was in very many cases not within reach. And here it will be just as useful to remark that the young advocate was not able, to his own good be it said, to embark there and then on the Regnitz and sail straight away to Philadelphia. Hence it was that his threat to leave Bamberg and his darling Nanni for ever remained still unfulfilled, even when at last, after two years more had elapsed, the wedding-day of Herr Leberfink, decorator and gilder, was come. Leberfink would have been inconsolable at this unjust postponement of his happiness, although the delay was almost a matter of necessity after the terrible events which had fallen blow after blow in Wacht's house, had it not afforded him an opportunity to decorate over again in deep red and appropriate gold the ornamental work in his parlour, which had before been gay with nice light-blue and silver, for he had picked up from Rettelchen that a red table, red chairs, and so on, would be more in accordance with her taste.

When the happy decorator insisted upon seeing the young lawyer at his wedding. Master Wacht had not offered a moment's opposition; and the young lawyer--he was pleased to come. It may be imagined with what feelings the two young people saw each other again, for since that terrible moment when Jonathan had left the garden they had literally not set eyes upon each other. The assembly was large; but not a single person with whom they were on a friendly footing fathomed their pain.

Just as they were on the point of setting out for church. Master Wacht received a thick letter; he had read no more than a few lines when he became violently agitated and rushed off out of the room, not a little to the consternation of the rest, who at once suspected some fresh misfortune. Shortly afterwards Master Wacht called the young advocate out. When they were alone together in the Master's own room, the latter, vainly endeavouring to conceal his excessive agitation, began, "I've got the most extraordinary news of your brother; here is a letter from the governor of the prison relating fully all the circumstances of what has taken place. As you cannot know them all, I must begin at the beginning and tell you everything right to the end so as to make credible to you what is incredible; but time presses." So saying, Master Wacht fixed a keen glance upon the advocate's face, so that he blushed and cast down his eyes in confusion. "Yes, yes," went on Master Wacht, raising his voice, "you don't know how great a remorse took possession of your brother a very few hours after he was put in prison; there is hardly anybody whose heart has been more torn by it. You don't know how his attempt at murder and theft has prostrated him. You don't know how that in mad despair he prayed Heaven day and night either to kill him or to save him that he might henceforth by the exercise of the strictest virtue wash himself pure from bloodguiltiness. You don't know how that on the occasion of building a large wing to the prison, in which the convicts were employed as labourers, your brother so distinguished himself as a clever and well-instructed carpenter that he soon filled the post of foreman of the workmen, without anybody's noticing how it came about so. You don't know how his quiet good behaviour, and his modesty, combined with the decision of his regenerate mind, made everybody his friend. All this you do not know, and so I am telling it you. But to go on. The Prince-bishop has pardoned your brother; he has become a master. But how could all this be done without a supply of money?" "I know," said the young advocate in a low voice, "I know that you, my good father, have sent money to the prison authorities every month, in order that they might keep my brother separate from the other prisoners and find him better accommodation and better food. Later on you sent him materials for his trade"---- Then Master Wacht stepped close up to the young advocate, took him by both arms, and said in a voice that vacillated in a way that cannot be described between delight, sadness, and pain, "But would that alone have helped Sebastian to honour again, to freedom, and his civil rights, and to property, however strongly his fundamental virtuous qualities had sprung up again? An unknown philanthropist, who must take an especially warm interest in Sebastian's fate, has deposited ten thousand 'large' thalers with the court, to"---- Master Wacht could not speak any further owing to his violent emotion; he drew the young advocate impetuously to his heart, crying, though he could only get out his words with difficulty, "Advocate, help me to penetrate to the deep import of law such as lives in your breast, and that I may stand before the Eternal Bar of justice as you will one day stand before it.--And yet," he continued after a pause of some seconds, releasing the young lawyer, "and yet, my dear Jonathan, if Sebastian now comes back as a good and industrious citizen and reminds me of my pledged word, and Nanni"---- "Then I will bear my trouble till it kills me," said the young advocate; "I will flee to America." "Stay here," cried Master Wacht in an enthusiastic burst of joy and delight, "stay here, son of my heart! Sebastian is going to marry a girl whom he formerly deceived and deserted. Nanni is yours."

Once more the Master threw his arms around Jonathan's neck, saying, "My lad, I feel like a schoolboy before you, and should like to beg your pardon for all the blame I have put upon you, and all the injustice I have done you. But let us say no more; other people are waiting for us." Therewith Master Wacht took hold of the young lawyer and pulled him along into the room where the wedding guests were assembled; there he placed himself and Jonathan in the midst of the company, and said, raising his voice and speaking in a solemn tone, "Before we proceed to celebrate the sacred rite I invite you all, my honest friends, ladies and gentlemen, and you too, my virtuous maidens and young men, six weeks hence to a similar festival in my house; for here I introduce to you Herr Jonathan Engelbrecht, the advocate, to whom I herewith solemnly betroth my youngest daughter, Nanni." The lovers sank into each other's arms. A breath of the profoundest astonishment passed over the whole assembly; but good old Andreas, holding his little three- cornered carpenter's cap before his breast, said softly, "A man's heart is a wonderful thing; but true, honest faith overcomes the base and even sinful resoluteness of a hardened spirit; and all things turn out at last for the best, just as the good God wishes them to do."

Printed in Great Britain
by Amazon.co.uk, Ltd.,
Marston Gate.